VAMPIRE HUNTER D

OMNIBUS BOOK ONE

VAMPIRE HUNTER D

VOLUME I

Written by

HIDEYUKI KIKUCHI

Illustrations by

YOSHITAKA AMANO

English translation by

KEVIN LEAHY

Dark Horse Books

Milwaukie

VAMPIRE HUNTER D

Accursed Bride

The setting sun was staining the far reaches of the plain, its hue closer to blood than vermilion. The wind snarled like a beast across the barren sky. On the narrow road that cut through a sea of grass, high enough to hide all below the man's ankles, the lone horse and rider ceased their advance as if forestalled by the wall of wind gusting straight at them.

The road rose a bit some sixty feet ahead. Once they'd surmounted the rise they would be able to survey the rows of houses and greenbelts of farmland that comprised Ransylva, just another hamlet in this Frontier sector.

At the foot of that gentle slope stood a girl.

The horse had likely been startled by her appearance and stopped. She was a beautiful young woman, with large eyes that seemed alight. Somewhat tanned, she had her black tresses tied back. An untamed aura, unique to all things living in the wild, emanated from every inch of her. Any man who laid eyes on her, with those gorgeous features like sunlight in summer, would undoubtedly draw his attention to the curves of her physique. Yet below the threadbare blue scarf swathing her neck she was concealed to the ankles by the ash-gray material of a waterproof cape. Except perhaps for her snug leather sandals and what seemed to be a coiled black whip in her right hand, she wore no necklaces or torques, or any other accouterments that would have lent her a feminine feel.

An old-fashioned cyborg horse lingered at the girl's side. Until a few minutes earlier, the girl had been lying at its feet. Woman of the wild or not, the fact that she noticed a horse and rider, not running but approaching silently amidst the kind of howling wind that would leave others covering their ears, and that she stood her ground meant the girl probably wasn't some farmer's wife or the daughter of a pioneer.

Having stopped briefly, the horse soon began walking forward. Perhaps realizing the girl wasn't going to get out of the road, it stopped once again about three feet shy of her.

For a while there was nothing but the sound of the wind racing along the ground. In due time the girl opened her mouth to speak. "I take it you're a drifter. You a Hunter?" Her tone was defiant and full of daring, and yet also a touch worn.

The rider sat on his horse but made no answer. She couldn't see his face very well because he had a wide-brimmed traveler's hat low over his eyes and was covered from the nose down by a scarf. Judging from his powerful frame and the combat utility belt, half revealed from his faded black long coat, it was safe to say he was no seasonal laborer or merchant dealing with scattered villages. A blue pendant hanging just below his scarf reflected the girl's pensive expression. Her large eyes fixed on the longsword strapped to his back. Limning an elegant arc quite different from the straight blades cherished by so many other Hunters, it spoke of the vast expanses of time and space its owner had traveled. Disconcerted, perhaps, by the lack of response, the girl shouted, "That sword purely for show? If so, I'll take it off you to sell down at the next open market. Set 'er down!"

As if to say that if that didn't get an answer out of him then the time for talking is done, the girl took one step back with her right leg and crouched in preparation. The hand with the whip slowly rose to her side.

The rider responded for the first time. "What do you want?"

The girl's expression was one of amazement. Though the voice of her opponent was low, and she could barely pick it out over the snarling of the wind, it sounded like the voice of a seventeen- or eighteen-year-old youth.

"What the hell—you're just a kid! Well, I'm still not gonna show you any mercy. Show me what you've got."

"So, you're a bandit then? You're awfully forthcoming for one."

"You dolt! If I was looking for money, you think I'd go after a lousy drifter like you? I wanna see how good you are!" The wind shot with a sharp snap. The girl cracked her whip. It didn't look like she was doing any more than playing it out lightly with her wrist, but the whip twisted time and again like an ominous black serpent in the light of the setting sun. "Here I come! If you fancy some good eatin' in the village of Ransylva, you'll have to go through me first."

The youth remained motionless atop his mount. He didn't reach for his sword or for his combat belt. What's more, when the girl saw how nonchalant he remained when challenged to battle by a good-looking young lady who gave no reasons but showered him with a murderous gaze, a tinge of consternation rushed into her expression. Letting out a rasp of breath, the girl struck with her whip. The weapon was made from intertwined werewolf bristles painstakingly tanned over three long months with applications of animal fat. A direct hit from it would sunder flesh.

"What the?…"

The girl leapt back, her expression changed. Her whip was supposed to strike the youth's left shoulder but for some reason, just at the instant she saw it hit him, the whip changed direction and shot instead for her own left shoulder. The youth had reversed the vectors of the whip without the slightest injury to himself and turned the attack back upon its source. To grasp the speed and angle of that black snake striking so fast it escaped the naked eye,

and have the reflexes to do something about it, was something that defied description.

"Damn it! You're good!"

Worked by her right hand, the whip did not strike her shoulder but danced back through thin air, yet the girl stood rooted to the spot and made no attempt at a second attack. She realized his fighting skills were as high above hers as the heavens were over the earth.

"Out of my way, please," the youth said, as if nothing whatsoever had transpired.

The girl complied.

The youth and his horse passed by her side, but when they'd gone a few steps more, the girl once again stepped into the road and shouted, "Hey, look at me!"

The instant the youth turned around, the girl grabbed her cape with her left hand and whipped it off in a single motion.

For a moment, the venomous glow of twilight seemed to lose its blood-red hue.

Clad in not a single stitch, a naked form so celestial none save the goddess Venus herself could have fashioned it glittered in the breeze. At the same time, the girl extended her other hand and undid her ponytail. Her luxurious raven mane splayed in the wind. Her nakedness alone had been beautiful, but this was truly enchanting. The wind twisted around, bearing nothing but the scent of a woman in the full of her bloom.

"Let's try that again!"

Once more her whip cracked.

Through some masterful handling, the single tip whistling toward the youth split into eight parts just as it was about to strike. Each tip had a separate target, coiling around his neck, shoulders, arms, and chest with slightly different timing, making a hit much more difficult to avoid than if all struck simultaneously.

"You sure fell for that one," the girl laughed. "That's what you get for letting a little nudity distract you." She hollered the words, conceding nothing to the snarling wind. And then, almost disappointed, she suddenly added, "You're the ninth. Looks like I'm out of luck after all. How do you wanna play this? You drop the weapon you've got on your back and the ones around your waist and I'll have you undone in no time."

The reply she received was totally unexpected. "And if I said I wouldn't?"

The girl became indignant. "Then you get your choice of how I knock you out. Either I strangle you or I drag you to the ground. So, which of those suits your fancy?"

"Neither appeals to me."

With his words as her signal to start, the girl concentrated all her might into her right hand. Her power coursed down the whip to the tips, trying to send the youth sailing through the air. But it didn't! In fact, all eight loops passed right through the youth's body without losing their circular form!

"What the—?"

Not merely surprised but dumbfounded, the girl stood rooted and dazed. After all, here was an opponent who had beaten an attack that incorporated every bit of skill she possessed without so much as lifting a hand...

The youth's mount started to walk away calmly.

Though she remained in her absentminded stupor for a bit, the girl wrapped her fallen cape around herself and scrambled after the youth with a speed that was hard to believe from such slender legs. "Hold up. I apologize for that craziness just now. I'd like you to hear me out. I just knew you were a Hunter. Better yet, you're a Vampire Hunter, aren't you?"

The youth finally turned his eyes to the girl.

"I'm right, aren't I? I wanna hire you!"

The horse stopped.

"That's nothing to joke about," the youth said softly.

"I know. I know Vampire Hunters are the most skilled of all Hunters. And I'm well aware what fearsome opponents vampires are. Even though only one Hunter in a thousand is good enough to make the grade, your chances of fighting a vampire and winning are still only fifty-fifty, right? I know all that. My father was a Hunter, too."

A tinge of emotion stirred in the youth's eyes. With one hand he pushed back the brim of his hat. Long and thin and cold, his dark eyes were quite clear.

"What kind?"

"A Werewolf Hunter."

"I see, so that's where you get that trick with the whip," the youth murmured. "I'd heard all the vampires in these parts were wiped out during the Third Cleansing War. Of course, the war was a good thirty years back, so I suppose we can't put much stock in that. So, you want to hire me? I take it someone in your family or one of your friends has been attacked. How many times have they been preyed upon?"

"Just the once, so far."

"Are there marks from two fangs, or just one?"

The girl hesitated for an instant, then laid her hand to the scarf around her neck. "See for yourself."

The wind-borne cries of wild beasts streamed like banners across the darkening sky.

On the left side of her neck in the vicinity of the main artery, a pair of festering wounds the color of fresh meat swelled from the sun-bronzed flesh.

"It's the Kiss of the Nobility," the girl said in a low voice, feeling all the while the eyes of the youth bearing down on her from horseback.

The youth tugged down the scarf shielding his face. "Judging by that wound, it was a vampire of some rank. It's surprising you can even move." His last remark was a compliment to the girl. The reactions of people who had been preyed on by vampires varied with the level of their attacker, but in most cases the victims became doll-like imbeciles, with the very soul sucked out of them. Their skin lost its tone and became like paraffin, and the victim would lie in the shade day after day with a vacant gaze, waiting for a visit from the vampire and a fresh kiss. To escape that fate, one needed extraordinary strength of body and spirit. And this girl was clearly one such exception.

However, at the moment the girl wore the dreamlike expression of the average victim.

She had lost herself in the beauty of the unmasked youth, with his thick, masculine eyebrows, smooth bridge of a nose, and tightly drawn lips that manifested the iron strength of his will. Set amid stern features shared only by those who had come through the numerous battles of a grief-ridden world, his eyes harbored sorrow even as they sparkled. That final touch made this crystallized beauty the image of youth incarnate, chiseled, as it were, by nature itself, perfect and complete. Nevertheless, the girl was shaken back to her senses by something vaguely ominous lurking in the depths of his gaze. It sent a chill creeping up her spine. Giving her head a shake, the girl asked, "So, how about it? Will you come with me?"

"You said you were knowledgeable about Vampire Hunters. Are you also aware of the fees they require?"

Scarlet tinged the girl's cheeks. "Uh, yeah..."

"Your offer being?"

The more powerful the supernatural beasts and monsters a Hunter specialized in, the more expensive their fees. In the case of Vampire Hunters, they got five thousand dalas a day minimum. Incidentally, a three-meal pack of condensed rations for travelers was about a hundred dalas. "Three meals a day," the girl said, as if she'd just settled on it.

The youth said nothing.

"Plus..."

"Plus what?"

"Me. To do with as you please."

A faint smile played across the youth's lips, as if mocking her.

"The Kiss of the Nobility is probably preferable to being bedded by the likes of me."

"The hell it is!" Suddenly tears glittered in the girl's eyes. "If it comes down to that or becoming a vampire, I have no problem with someone havin' his way with me. That doesn't have anything to do with a person's worth anyway. But if you must know, I'm ... no, forget that, it doesn't matter. So, how about it? Will you come with me?"

Watching the girl's face for a while as anger and sorrow churned together, the youth quietly nodded. "Very well then. But in return, I want to be clear on one thing."

"What? Just name it."

"I'm a dhampir."

The girl's face froze. This gorgeous man couldn't be ... But come to think of it, he was *too* gorgeous ...

"Is that okay? If you wait a while longer, another Hunter may come by. You don't have to do this."

Swallowing the sour spit that filled her mouth, the girl offered a hand to the youth. She attempted a smile, but it came out stiff.

"Glad to have you. I'm Doris Lang."

The youth didn't shake her hand. Just as expressionless and emotionless as when he first appeared, he said, "Call me 'D.'"

Doris' home was at the base of a hill about thirty minutes at a gallop from where the pair happened to meet. The two of them rode at a feverish pace and arrived there in less than twenty minutes. The second she wrapped up her discussion with D, Doris put the spurs to her horse, as if pushed by the encroaching twilight. Not only vampires, but also all the most dangerous monsters and supernatural beasts waited until complete darkness fell before they became active. There wasn't cause to be in such a hurry, but D remained silent and followed his attractive employer.

Her home was a farm surrounded by verdant prairies that were most likely rendered permanently fertile by the Great Earth Restoration Project three millennia earlier. At the center was the main house. Constructed of wood and tensile plastics, the house was surrounded by scattered stables, animal pens, and protein-synthesizing vegetation in orchards consisting mainly of thermo-regulators fastened to reinforced sheets of waterproof material. The orchards alone covered five acres, and second-hand robots were responsible for harvesting the protein produced there. Hauling it away was a job for the humans.

When Doris had tethered her horse to the long hitching post in front of the main house, the reason for her hasty return threw the door open and bounded out.

"Welcome home," a rosy-cheeked boy of seven or eight called down from the rather lofty porch. He hugged an antiquated laser rifle to his chest.

"This is my little brother Dan," Doris said to D by way of introduction, and then in a gentle voice she asked, "Nothing out of the ordinary while I was gone, was there? Those mist devils didn't come back now, did they?"

"Not at all," the boy replied, throwing out his chest triumphantly. "Don't forget, I blasted four of the buggers just the other day. They're so scared they wouldn't dare come back again. But just supposing they do, I'll fry 'em to a crisp with this baby here." That said, his expression suddenly grew sullen. "Oh, I almost forgot … That jerk Greco came by again. Carrying some bunch of flowers he says he had sent all the way from the Capital. He left 'em here and asked me to pass them along to my 'lovely sister when she gets home.'"

"So what happened to the flowers?" Doris asked with obvious interest.

The boy's mouth twisted into a delighted grin.

"Chopped 'em up in the disposal unit, mixed in some compost, and fed it to the cows!"

Doris gave a deep, satisfied nod. "Good job. Today's a big day. We've got company, too."

The boy, who'd been sneaking peeks at D even as he spoke with his sister, now smiled knowingly at her. "Say, he's a looker, ain't he? So, this is how you like 'em, eh, Sis? You said the robots were in such lousy shape you were going out to look for someone to replace them, but it looks to me like you went out hunting for a man."

Doris flushed bright red.

"Oh, don't be ridiculous. Don't talk that foolishness. This is Mr. D. He'll be helping us out around the farm for a while. And don't you be getting in his way now."

"There's nothing to be bashful about," the boy chuckled. "I know, I know. One eyeful of him, and old Greco don't look much better than a man-eating frog. I like him a heck of a lot better, too. Pleased to meet you, D."

"The pleasure's mine, Dan."

Showing no signs of being bothered by the emotionless tone D used even when addressing a child, the boy disappeared into the main house. The pair followed him inside.

"I'm sorry, he must have really gotten on your nerves," Doris said in an apologetic tone when dinner was finished and she'd finally managed to drive Dan off to his bedroom, ignoring the boy's protests that he wasn't sleepy yet.

D passed the sword he normally wore on his back from his right hand to his left as he stood at the window gazing at the darkness beyond. Thanks to the clear weather that had persisted the past four or five days, the solar batteries on the roof were well charged and glittering light showered generously on every corner of the room from lighting panels set in the ceiling.

Apparently there was something about the inhospitable stranger the boy liked, and he'd planted himself by the man's side and wouldn't leave, imploring him to talk about the Capital, or to tell him about any monsters or supernatural creatures he might have slain in his travels. Then, to top it all off, he created quite a commotion when he said his sister was being a pest and grabbed D by the arm to try and bring him back to his room where they could talk man-to-man all night long.

"You see, he gets like that because travelers are so rare. And we don't usually have much to do with the folks in town, either."

"It doesn't bother me. I take no offense at being admired."

As he spoke, he made no attempt to look at Doris sitting on the sofa, wearing the shirt and jeans she'd changed into earlier. His tone was as cold as ever. Closing his eyes lightly, he said, "It's now nine twenty-six Night, Frontier Standard Time. Since it has already fed once on the person it's after, I don't imagine it'll be in that much of a hurry, so I suppose after midnight will be the time to watch. In the meantime, could you tell me everything you know about the enemy? Don't worry; your brother is already asleep. I can tell by his steady breathing."

Doris' eyes went wide. "You can hear something like that through the door and everything?"

"And the voice of the wind across the wilderness, and the vengeful song of the spirits wandering the forest shade," D murmured, then he came to stand at Doris' side with the smooth strides of a dancer.

When she felt that cold and righteous visage peering down at the nape of her neck, Doris shouted, "Stop!" and pulled away without thinking.

Though the abhorrence was quite evident in her voice, D's expression didn't change in the least. "I'm just going to have a look at your wounds. To get a general idea of how powerful a foe I'm up against."

"I'm sorry. Go ahead, take a look," she said, turning her face away and exposing her neck. Even if the slight trembling of her lips was a remnant of her reaction seconds earlier, the redness of her cheeks was caused, no doubt, by the embarrassment of a virgin having her flesh scrutinized by a wholly unfamiliar young man. After all, in her seventeen years, she hadn't so much as held hands with a boy before.

Seconds later, D's expression had a distant air to it. "When did you run into *him?*"

Doris breathed a sigh of relief at the sound of his voice, which was entirely without cadence. But why was her foolish heart pounding so? Unaffected by her racing pulse, and gazing raptly at D's face all the while, she began to recount the tale of that terrible night in the most composed tone she could muster.

"It was five nights ago. I was chasing a lesser dragon that'd slipped onto the farm while we were fixing the electromagnetic barrier and killed one of our cows, and when I finally thought I'd finished it off, it was already pitch-black out. To make matters worse, it was near *his* castle. I was all set to hightail it home when what should happen but the dying beast suddenly spits fire and burns the back half of my horse to a cinder. I'm thirty miles from home, and the only weapons I've got to speak of are the spear I use to kill lesser dragons and a dagger. I ran as fast as I could. I must've run for a good thirty minutes when I noticed something, like there was someone running along right behind me!"

Doris suddenly fell silent, not only because the memory of that terror had become fresh again, but also because a fiendish howl had just pierced the darkness from somewhere very close. The breath was knocked out of her as she turned her beautiful face in that direction, but soon enough she realized it was only the sound of some wild animal. Her expression became one of relief. Though rather dated, an electromagnetic barrier that had cost them a pretty penny sealed the perimeter of the farm, and within it they had a variety of missile weapons set up.

She resumed the account of her horrid experience. "At first I thought it was a werewolf or a poison moth man. But there was no sound of footsteps or wings flapping, and I couldn't even hear it breathing. Yet I just knew there was someone right behind me, no more than a foot away, and moving at exactly the same speed I was. I finally couldn't take it any more and I whipped around—and there was nothing there! Well, there was for a fraction of a second, but then it circled around behind me again."

Memory was sowing terror across the girl's face. She gnawed her lip and tried to force her trembling voice out. D said nothing, but remained listening.

"That's when I started shouting. I told whoever it was to stop hiding behind me and come out that instant. And when I'd said that, out he came, dressed in a black cape just like I'd always heard. When I saw the pair of fangs poking over his mean, red lips, I knew what he had to be. After that, it's the same old story. I got my spear ready, but then my eyes met his and all the strength just drained right out of me. Not that it mattered much, because when that pasty face of his got closer and I felt breath as cold as moonlight on the base of my neck, my mind just went blank. The next thing I knew it was daybreak and I was lying out on the prairie with a pair of fang marks on my throat. That's why I've been down at the base of that hill each and every day, morning till night, looking for someone like you." Her emotional tale over at last, Doris slumped back onto the sofa exhausted.

"And he hasn't fed on you again since?"

"That's right. Though I do wait up for him every night with a spear ready."

D's eyes narrowed at her attempt at levity. "If we were merely dealing with a blood-starved Noble, he'd be coming every night. But, you see, the greater the interest they take in their victim, the longer the interval between attacks so they can prolong the pleasure of feeding. But the fact that it's been five days is incredible. It seems he's extremely taken with you."

"Spare me the damn compliments!" Doris cried. No trace of the spitfire who had challenged D to battle at twilight remained now. She sat there, a lovely seventeen-year-old girl trembling in fear.

As D surveyed her coolly, he added words that only made the hair on her neck stand higher. "The average interval between attacks is three to four days. More than five is extremely rare. He'll come tonight without a doubt. From what I can tell from your wounds, he's quite powerful, as Frontier Nobility go. You said something about 'his castle.' His identity is clear to you, is it?"

Doris gave a little nod. "He's been lord over this region since long before there was any village of Ransylva. His name is Count Lee. I've heard some say he's a hundred years old, while others say he's ten thousand."

"Ten thousand years old, eh? The powers of a Noble grow with the passing years. He could prove a troubling adversary," D said, though his tone didn't sound particularly troubled.

"The powers of a Noble? You mean things like the power to whip up a gale with a wave of the arm, or being able to turn into a fire dragon?"

Ignoring Doris' query, D said, "There's one last thing I need to ask you. How does your village handle those who've been bitten by vampires?"

The girl's face paled in an instant.

In many cases those who'd felt the baleful fangs of a vampire were isolated in their respective village or town while arrangements were made to destroy the culprit, but if they were simply unable to defeat the vampire, the victim would be driven from town or, in the worst cases, disposed of. This was the custom because a night fiend, crazed with rage at not being able to feed on the one it wanted, would attack anyone it could get its hands on. More towns and villages than anyone could count had been wiped out for just that reason. Ransylva had similar policies in effect. That was the reason Doris hadn't asked anyone else for help, but had privately sought a Vampire Hunter. Her failure to confide in her brother was for fear that his conduct might tip off the villagers if they happened to go into town. Had she no younger brother to consider, she'd surely have gone after the vampire on her own, or done away with herself.

Vampires dealt with their victims in one of two ways. Either they drained all the blood from their prey in one feeding and left them a mere corpse or, through repeated feedings, they turned the individual into a companion. The key point in the latter was not the number of times the vampire fed but rather something D had touched on earlier: whether or not the vampire took a liking to its victim. Sometimes a person joined their ranks after a single bite, while other times they might share the kiss of blood for months only to die in the end. And it went without saying that those transformed into vampires had to bear their destiny as detestable demons, wandering each night in search of warm human blood, living in darkness eternal. For Doris, and for every other person in this world, that was the true terror.

"Everywhere it's the same, isn't it," D muttered. "Accursed demons, ghouls from the darkness, blood-crazed devils. Bitten once and you're one of them. Well, let them say what they will. Stand up, please," he said to Doris, who was caught off-guard by the one remark meant for her. "It looks like the guest we were expecting has come. Let me see the remote control for your electromagnetic barrier."

"What, he's here already? You just said he'd be here after midnight."

"I'm surprised, too."

But he didn't look it in the least.

Doris came back from her bedroom with the remote control and handed it to D.

In order to keep all kinds of strange visitors from sneaking onto the farm while both Lang children were away, they had to have some way to erect the force field from the outside. Acquired secondhand off a black market in the Capital shortly after their father's death four years ago, the barrier was their greatest treasure except, of course, for the rare occasions when it broke down. Their losses to the wraiths and rabid beasts that wandered the night were far less than those of other homes on the periphery; to be more exact, their losses were practically nonexistent. But the purchase came with a price. After they bought it, they were left with less than a third of their father's life savings.

"How are you gonna fight him?" Doris inquired. It was a question that sprung from the Hunter blood flowing in her veins. The fighting techniques of Vampire Hunters, who were rare even out on the Frontier, were rumored to be gruesome and magnificent, but almost no one had ever witnessed them firsthand. Doris herself had only heard of them in tales. And the youth before her now was completely different from the rustic Hunter image conjured up by those stories.

"You should see for yourself, and I wish I could let you, but I need you to go to sleep."

"What—?"

The youth's right hand touched Doris' right shoulder, which was taut with swells of muscle while still retaining some delicacy. Whatever the technique or power he now employed, as soon as Doris noticed the frightening cold charge coursing through her body from her shoulder she lost consciousness. But just before she did, she glimpsed something eerie in the palm of D's left hand, or at least she believed she did. She thought she saw something small, of a color and shape she couldn't discern, but whatever it was it clearly had eyes and a nose and a mouth, like some sort of grotesque face.

Apparently confident in the efficacy of his actions, D didn't even bother to check if Doris was actually unconscious before leaving the room with his sword over his shoulder. The reason he'd put her to sleep was to prevent her from interfering in the battle that was about to begin. No matter how firm their resolve, anyone who'd felt the vampire's kiss once could not help but heed the demon's commands. Many were the Hunters who had been shot from behind or had their hearts pierced by the very women they sought to save from cursed fangs. To guard against that, veterans would give the victims a sedative or confine them in portable iron cages. But the extraordinary skill D had just displayed with his left hand would have been viewed by even the most veteran of Hunters as impossible in all but dreams cast by the Fair Folk.

Once out in the hall, D opened the door to Dan's room. The boy snored away peacefully, oblivious to the deadly duel about to ensue. Quietly shutting the door, D slipped through the front hall and down the porch steps onto the pitch-black earth. No trace of the midday heat remained now. The green grass swayed in a chilled and pleasant night breeze.

It was around September. It was to the great credit of the Revolutionary Army that they hadn't destroyed the dozen weather controllers buried beneath the seven continents. If not by day then at least by night the most comfortable levels of heat and humidity for both the Nobility and humans were maintained all year round. There were, however, still the occasional violent thunderstorms or blizzards, written into the controller's programs by some uniformity-hating Nobles to recreate the unpredictable seasons of yore.

With a graceful stride that was a dance with the breeze, D passed through a gate in the fence and went another ten feet before coming to a stop. Before long there came from the depths of the darkness, from the far reaches of the plain, the sound of horse hooves and wagon wheels approaching. Could it be that D had heard them even as he talked with the young lady in that distant room?

A team of four horses and a carriage so black it seemed lacquered with midnight appeared in the moonlight and halted about fifteen feet ahead of D. The beautifully groomed black beasts drawing it were most likely cyborg horses.

A man in a black inverness cape was seated in the coachman's perch, scrutinizing D with glittering eyes. The black lacquered whip in his right hand reflected the moonlight. By the light of the moon alone D could make out a touch of beast in his face and the terribly bushy backs of his hands.

The man quickly alighted from the driver's seat. His whole body was like a coiled spring; he even moved like a beast. Before he could reach for the passenger door, the silver handle turned and the door opened from the inside. A deep chill and the stench of blood suddenly shrouded the refreshing breeze. As D caught a glimpse of the figure stepping down from the carriage the slightest hue of emotion stirred in his eyes. "A woman?"

Her dazzling golden hair looked like it would creep along the ground behind her. If Doris was the embodiment of a sunflower, then this woman could only be likened to a moonflower. Her snow-white dress of medieval styling was bound tight at her waist, spreading in bountiful curves reaching to the ground. The dress was certainly lovely, but it was the pale beauty unique to the Nobility that made the young lady seem an unearthly illusion, sparkling as she did like a dream in a shower of moonlight. But the illusion reeked of blood. The flames of a nightmare crackled in her lapis-lazuli eyes, and her beckoning lips were red as blood as they glistened damply in D's night-sight, calling to mind a hunger that would not be sated in all eternity. The hunger of a vampire.

Gazing at D, the young lady laughed like a silver bell. "Be you some manner of bodyguard? Hiring a knave like you for protection is just the sort of thing a lowly human wretch would do. Having heard from Father that the girl who lives here is not only of a beauty unrivaled by the humans in these parts, but that her blood is equally delectable, I came to see her for myself. But as I expected all along, there is no great difference between these foolish, annoying little pests."

Ghastliness rushed into the girl's face. The pearly fangs that appeared without warning at the corners of her lips didn't escape D's notice.

"First I shall make a bloody spatter of you, and then I'll drain the humble blood from her till not a drop remains. As you may well know, Father is inclined to make her part of our family, but I will not stand by while the blood of the Lee line is imparted to a good-for-nothing that would stoop to a trick of this sort. I shall strike her from the face of the earth into the waiting arms of the black gods of hell. And you shall accompany her."

As she spoke, the young lady made a sweep of her slender hand. Her driver stepped forward. Murderous intent and malevolence radiated from every inch of him like flames licking at D's face.

You lowly worms have forgotten your station, his mien seemed to say. *Turncoat scum you are, forgetting the debt you owe your former masters, rebelling against them with your devious little minds and weapons. Here's where you learn the error of your ways.*

The transformation had begun. The molecular arrangement of his cells changed, and his nervous system became that of a wild beast born to race across the ground at great speeds. The four limbs clutching at the earth began to assume a shape more befitting a lower animal. A prognathous jaw formed, and revealed rows of razor-sharp teeth jutting from a crescent-moon mouth that split his face from ear to ear. Jet-black fur sprouted over every inch of him.

The driver was a werewolf, one of the monsters of the night resurrected from the dark depths of medieval legend along with the vampires. D could tell just by watching the transformation, which some might even term graceful, that the driver was not one of the genetically engineered and cybernetically enhanced fakes the vampires had spread across the world.

A throaty howl blazing with the glee of slaughter split the wordless void. With both eyes glittering wildly, the inverness-wearing wolf lurched up onto his hind feet. This was exactly what made the werewolf a lycanthrope among lycanthropes, for despite its four-footed form, a werewolf's speed and destructive power were greater when it stood erect.

Perhaps taking the fact that the youth had stood stock still and not moved a muscle since their arrival to mean he was paralyzed with fright, the black beast crouched ever so slightly. Trusting its entire weight to the powerful springs of its lower body, it leapt over fifteen feet in a single bound.

Two flashes more brilliant than the moonlight split the darkness.

D didn't move. The werewolf, dropping down on D from above with every intention of sinking its iron-shredding claws into his skull, changed course in midair. It sailed over D's head as if poised to make another jump, and landed in the bushes a few yards behind the Hunter.

Staged completely in midair, a jump like that was a miraculous maneuver only possible by coordinating the power of the lungs, the spine, and extremely tenacious musculature for a split second, and it was something werewolves alone could do. Even groups of seasoned Werewolf Hunters occasionally fell victim to attacks like this because the attack was far more terrible than any rumors the Hunters might have heard, and they weren't prepared to counter the real thing. These demonic creatures could strike at their prey from angles and directions that were patently impossible as far as three-dimensional dynamics were concerned and the attack was entirely silent.

However, moans of pain spilled from the beast's throat as it huddled low in the brush. Bright blood welled from between the fingers pressed against its right flank, soaking the grass. Its eyes, bloodshot with malice and agony, caught the blade glittering with reflected moonlight in D's right hand as the Hunter stood facing it silently. Just as the werewolf was ready to drive its claws home, D had drawn the sword over his shoulder with ungodly speed and driven it into his opponent's flank.

"Impressive," one of them said. Strangely, that someone was D, who'd been under the impression that he had cleanly bisected the werewolf's torso. "Until now, I'd never seen what a true werewolf was capable of."

His low voice sowed the seeds of a new variety of fear in the heart of the demonic beast where it lay in the bushes. The beast's legs could generate bursts of speed of three hundred and seventy miles per hour—almost half the speed of sound. There had been less than a fiftieth of a second between the time it jumped and its attack on D, which meant the youth had been able to swing his sword and split its belly open even more quickly. Worse yet, the werewolf's wound wouldn't close! That wouldn't be so unusual when it was human, but once it assumed the beastly form, the cells of a werewolf's flesh were like single-cell organisms, giving it the regenerative power of a hydra. Cells created more cells, closing wounds instantly. But the blade the werewolf had just tasted made regeneration impossible, though it was probably not due to the blade but rather the skill of the youth who wielded it. Skin and muscle tissue that could reject bullets weren't showing any signs of regenerating!

"What's wrong with you, Garou?" the young lady shouted. "In wolf form, you should be unstoppable! Do not make a game of this. I demand you tear this human apart immediately!"

Though he heard his mistress scolding him, the werewolf Garou didn't move, partly because of the wound but also because of the youth's divine skill with a sword. What really tapped the wellspring of horror was the lurid will to kill that gushed from every pore of the youth just before the werewolf could unleash its deadly attack. That hadn't come from anything human!

Is he one of those? A dhampir?

Garou realized he'd finally run into a real opponent.

"Your guard is wounded," D said softly, turning to the young lady. "If he doesn't come at me again, he might live to a ripe old age. You might, too. Go home and tell your father a dangerous obstacle has cropped up. And that he'd be a fool to attack this farm again."

"Silence!" the young lady screamed, her gorgeous visage becoming that of a banshee. "I am Larmica, daughter of Count Magnus Lee, the ruler of the entire Ransylva district of the Frontier. Do you think I can be bested by the likes of you and your sword?"

Before she'd finished speaking, a streak of white light shot toward her breast from D's left hand. In fact, it was a foot-long needle he'd taken out at some point and thrown faster than the naked eye could follow. It was made of wood. As it traveled at that unfathomable speed, the needle burned from the friction of the air, and the white light was from those flames.

But something odd had happened.

The flames had come to a stop in front of D's chest. Not that the needle he'd thrown had simply stopped there. The instant it was about to sink into Larmica's breast, it had turned around and come back, and D had stopped it with his bare hand. Or to be more accurate, Larmica had caught the needle with superhuman speed and thrown it back just as quickly. The average person wouldn't even have seen her hand move.

"If the servant is no more than a servant, still the master is a master. Well done," D murmured, heedless of the flaming needle in his hand or the way it steadily scorched his naked flesh. "For that display of skill you get my name. I'm the Vampire Hunter D. Remember that, should you live." As he spoke, D sprinted for the young lady without making a sound.

Terror stole into Larmica's expression. In a twinkling, the distance between them closed to where she was within sword's length of him, and then—

"Awooooooooooh!"

A ferocious howl shook the night air, and an indigo flash of light shot from the coachman's perch on the carriage. D dove to the side to dodge it, only able to escape the beam because his superhuman hearing had discerned the sound of the laser cannon on the perch swiveling to bear on him. The beam pierced the hem of his overcoat, igniting it in pale blue flames. Presumably, the cannon was equipped with voice recognition circuits and an electronic targeting system that responded to Garou's howls. Avoiding the flashes of blue that flew with unerring accuracy to wherever he'd gone to dodge the last, D had no choice but to keep twisting through the air.

"Milady, this way!"

He heard Garou's voice up in the driver's seat. There was the sound of a door closing. As D attempted to give chase, another blast from the laser cannon checked his advance, and the carriage swung around and was swallowed by the darkness.

"I'll settle with you another day, wretch, mark my words!"

"You'll not soon forget the wrath of Nobility!"

Whether he was pleased at having staved off the enemy or perturbed he hadn't managed to put an end to the vampiress, D wore no emotion on his face as he rose expressionless from the bushes, the malice-choked parting words of the pair circling him endlessly.

People on the Frontier

CHAPTER 2

The year is A.D. 12,090.

The human race dwells in a world of darkness.

Or perhaps it might be more accurate to call it a dark age propped up by science. All seven continents are crisscrossed by a web of super-speed highways, and at the center of the system sits a fully automated "cyber-city" known as the Capital, the product of cutting-edge scientific technology. The dozen weather controllers manipulate the climate freely. Interstellar travel is no longer a far-fetched dream. In vast spaceports, hulking matter-conversion rockets and ships propelled by galactic energy stare up at the empyrean vault, and exploration parties have actually left their footprints on a number of planets outside our solar system—Altair and Spica, to name just two.

However, all of that is a dream now.

Take a peek at the grand Capital. A fine dust coats the walls of buildings and minarets constructed from translucent metal crystal; in places you'll find recent craters large and small from explosives and ultraheat rays. The majority of automated roads and maglev highways are in shambles, and not a single car remains to zip from place to place like a shooting star.

There are people. Tremendous mobs of them. Flooding down the streets in endless numbers. Laughing, shouting, weeping, paying their respects to the Capital, the melting pot of existence, with a vitality that borders on complete chaos. But their garb isn't what you'd expect for the masters of a once-proud metropolis. Men don shabby trousers and tunics redolent of the distant Middle Ages, and threadbare cassocks like a member of a religious order might wear. Women dress in dim shades and wear fabric rough to the touch, completely devoid of flamboyance.

Through the milling crowd of men armed with longswords or bows and arrows comes a gasoline-powered car most likely taken from some museum. Trailing black smoke and popping with the firecrackers of backfires the vehicle carries along a group of laser-gun toting lawmen.

A dreadful scream rises from one of the buildings and a woman staggers out. From her inhuman cry people instinctively know the cause of her terror, and call out for the sheriff and his men. Before long, they race to the scene, ask the wailing woman where the terror is located, and enter the building in question with faces paler than the bloodless countenance of the witness herself. They ride an independently powered elevator down five hundred stories.

In one of the subterranean passageways—all of which had supposedly been destroyed ages ago—there's a concealed door, and beyond it a vast graveyard where the Nobility, blood-craving creatures of the night, slumber as in days gone by in wooden coffins filled with damp soil.

The sheriff and his men soon go into action. Fortunately, it seems there are no curses or vicious beasts here, no defense system of lasers or electronic cannons. These Nobles were probably resigned to their fate. The lawmen hold rough wooden stakes and gleaming metal hammers in their hands. Their expressions are a pallid blend of fear and sinfulness. The mob of black silhouettes encircles a coffin, someone's arm rises toward the heavens then knifes back down. There's a dull thud. A horrifying scream and the stench of blood fill the graveyard.

The anguished cry grows thinner and dies out, and the group moves on to the next coffin.

When the lawmen leave the graveyard not long after that, their faces are adorned with crimson beads of blood and a shade of sinfulness much deeper than the one they wore before this mission.

Though the Nobility was nearly extinct, the feelings of pride brought on by the awe humanity held toward them had seeped into their very blood over the course of ten long millennia and would not be shaken off so easily. Because they had indeed reigned supreme over the human race. And because the automated city—now populated by people who couldn't fathom its machinery or receive the tiniest fraction of the benefits it might provide—and everything else in the world that could be called civilization was something they had left behind. They—the vampires.

This strict stratification of vampires and humanity came about when one day in 1999 mankind's history as lords of the earth came to an abrupt end. Someone pushed the button and launched the full-scale nuclear war that the human race had been warned about for so long. Thousands of ICBMs and MIRVs flew in disarray, reducing one major city after another to a white-hot inferno, but the immediate fatalities were far outstripped by the wholesale death dealt by radiation more potent than tens of thousands of x-rays.

The theory of a limited nuclear war, where sensible battles would be fought so the winners might later rebuild and rule, was obliterated in a split second by a million degrees of heat and flame.

The survivors barely made it. Their numbers totally insignificant, they shunned the surface world and its toxic atmosphere and were left with no choice but to live in underground shelters for the next few years.

When they finally returned to the surface, their mechanized civilization was in ruins. With no way of contacting survivors in other countries, any thoughts these isolated pockets of humanity might have had of things returning to the way they'd been before the destruction, or even of rebuilding to the point where it could be called a civilization, were flights of fantasy, and nothing more.

The regression began.

With generation after generation striving merely to survive, memories of the past grew dim. The population increased somewhat after a thousand years, but civilization itself plunged back to the level of the Middle Ages. Dreading the mutant creatures spawned by radiation and cosmic rays, the humans formed small groups and moved into plains and forests that over the years had gradually returned to verdure. In their struggles with the cruel environment, at times they had to kill their newborn babies to keep what little food they had. Other times the infants went toward filling their parents' empty bellies.

That was the time. In that pitch-black, superstitious world they appeared. How they—the vampires—kept themselves hidden from the eyes of man and lived on in the luxuriant shadows was unclear. However, their life form was almost exactly as described in legend and they seemed the best suited to fill the role of the new masters of history.

Ageless and undying so long as they partook of the blood of other creatures, the vampires remembered a civilization the human race could not, and they knew exactly how to rebuild it. Before the nuclear war, the vampires had contacted others of their kind who lurked in dark places around the globe. They had a hidden super-power source that they'd secretly developed in fallout shelters of their own design, along with the absolute minimum machinery required to reconstruct civilization after the absolute worst came to pass.

But that's not to say they were the ones who caused the nuclear war. Through cryptesthesia, the black arts, and psychic abilities mankind never guessed they'd cultivated, the vampires simply knew when the human race would destroy itself and how they, the vampires, could restore order to the world.

Civilization was rebuilt and the tables were turned for vampires and humans.

How much friction and discord that course created between the two sides was soon apparent. Within two thousand years of stepping onto history's great stage, the vampires gave the world a sprawling civilization driven by super-science and sorcery, dubbed themselves the "Nobility," and subjugated humanity. The automated city with its electronic brain and ghostly will, interstellar spaceships, weather controllers, methods of creating endless quantities of materials through matter-conversion—all this came into being through the thoughts and deeds of them and them alone.

However, who could have imagined that within five short millennia of this golden age they would be treading the road to extinction? History didn't belong to them after all.

As a species, the vampires possessed an underlying spark to live that was far less tenacious than that of humans. Or perhaps it would be better to say that their life held an element that ensured their future destruction. From the end of the fourth millennia A.D., the vampire civilization as a whole started to show a phenomenal decline in energy, and that brought on the start of mankind's great rebellion. Though they had an expertise in the physiology of the human brain, and had developed the science of psychology to such extremes they could manipulate the human mind in any way they chose, in the end they found it impossible to eradicate the innate urge to rebel that lurked in the depths of the human soul.

Weakened by one great uprising after another, the Nobility entered dozens of armistices with the humans, each of which maintained the peace for short periods. But before long the Nobles faded away, like gallant nihilists who realized their destiny.

Some took their own lives, while others entered a sleep that would last until the end of time. Some even headed off into the depths of space, but their numbers were extremely few; in general the vampires had no wish to establish themselves in extraterrestrial environs.

At any rate, their overall numbers were on the decline; ultimately they scattered before mankind's pursuit. By the time A.D. 12,090 arrived, the vampires served no purpose beyond terrorizing the humans on the Frontier. Yet, precisely because this was their sole purpose, the humans felt a special terror of them that shook their very souls.

To be honest, it was miraculous that mankind was able to plan and execute a rebellion no matter how utterly desperate they might have been.

The horror all felt for vampires—who slept by day and awoke at night to suck the lifeblood from humans and ensure their own eternal life—became part of the vampire mythology, right along with the ancient legends of transformations into bats and wolves, and their power to control the elements. As a result of clever psychological manipulation that continued throughout this mechanized age, the horror laid roots down into the deepest layers of the human psyche.

It is said that the first time the humans signed an armistice with the vampires—their rulers—all the representatives on the human side save one were shaking so badly their teeth chattered. Even though vampires could no longer be found in the Capital, it had still taken the humans nearly three hundred years to check every street and building.

Given how much strength the vampires had in their favor, why hadn't they set about exterminating the human race? That is the eternal question. It couldn't be that they were simply afraid of destroying their source of the blood, since they had mastered a method of perfectly synthesizing human blood in the first stage of their civilization. As far as manual labor went, they had more than enough robots to bear the load by the time the revolution broke out. In fact, the reason why they allowed humans to continue to exist in the first place, even in their role as subordinates, is a mystery. Most likely it was due to some sort of superiority complex, or out of pity.

Vampires were rarely seen by humans any more, but the fear remained. On very rare occasions, they appeared from the depths of the darkness and left their vile bite on the pale throats of their victims; sometimes a person would seek them out with wooden stake in hand like a man possessed, while at other times the humans would drive the victim out from their midst, earnestly praying they wouldn't receive another visit from the vampires.

The Hunters were a product of the people's fear.

Being nearly indestructible themselves, the vampires weren't so eager to exterminate the mutant creatures humanity feared so much in the years just after the war. Quite the contrary, the vampires loved the vicious beasts, nurtured them, and even created others like them with their own hands.

Thanks to their unparalleled knowledge of biology and genetic engineering, the vampires unleashed one legendary monster after another into the world of man: werewolves, were-tigers, serpent men, golems, fairies, mer-creatures, goblins, raksas, ghouls, zombies, banshees, fire dragons, salamanders resistant to flames, griffins, krakens, and more. Though their creators neared extinction, the creatures still ran rampant on the plains and in the mountains.

Working the land with the scant machinery the Nobility allowed them, defending themselves with replicas of old-fashioned gunpowder weapons or homemade swords and spears, the humans studied the nature of these artificial monstrosities for generations, learning their powers and their weaknesses. In time, some people came to work exclusively on weapons and ways to kill these things.

Of those people, some specialized in producing more effective weaponry, while those of surpassing strength and agility trained themselves to use those weapons. These exceptional warriors were the first Hunters.

As time went by, Hunters became more narrowly focused, and specialists like the Were-tiger Hunter and Fairy Hunter were born. Of them all, Vampire Hunters were universally recognized as possessing strength and intellect beyond the rest, as well as an ironclad will impervious to the fear their former rulers inspired in others.

The next morning, Doris was awakened by the shrill whinny of a horse. White light speared in through her window, telling her it was a fresh day. She was lying on the bed dressed just as she was when D knocked her out. Actually, D had carried her to the bed when his first skirmish was over. Her nerves had been frayed with worry after her vampire attack, and she was incredibly tense from her search for a Hunter, but when the power of D's left hand put her to sleep she was totally at peace and had slept soundly till morning.

Instinctively reaching for her throat, Doris recalled what had happened the night before.

What happened while I was asleep? He said we had company, and that had to be him. I wonder how D made out? As she sprung out of bed in a panic, her expression suddenly grew brighter. She was still a little lethargic, but physically nothing else seemed out of the norm. D had kept her safe. Remembering that she hadn't even shown him where his room was, she pawed at her sleep-disheveled locks and hurried out of her bedroom.

The heavy shades in the living room were fully drawn; at one end of the murky room sat a sofa with a pair of boots hanging off the end.

"D, you really did it, didn't you? I knew hiring you was the right thing to do!"

From beneath the traveler's hat that covered his face came the usual low voice.

"Just doing my job. Sorry, it seems I forgot to put the barrier back up."

"Don't you worry about that," Doris said animatedly, checking the clock on the mantle. "It's only five past seven in the morning. Get some more sleep. I'll have your breakfast ready in no time. And I'll make it the best I can."

Outside a horse whinnied loudly again. Doris was reminded she had a visitor.

"Who the hell would be making such a racket at this hour?" She went over to the window and was about to raise the shade when a sharp "Don't!" stayed her hand.

When Doris turned to D with a gasp, her face was twisted by the same terror that had contorted it the night before when she tried to escape his approach. She remembered what the gorgeous Hunter really was. And yet she reclaimed her smile soon enough; not only was she stouthearted, but she also had a naturally fair disposition. "Sorry about that. I'll fix you up a room later. At any rate, get some rest." As soon as she'd said that she went ahead and grabbed a corner of the shade anyway, but the moment she lifted it and took a look outside, her endearing face quickly became a mass of pure hatred. Returning to her bedroom for her prized whip, she stepped outside indignantly.

Astride a bay in front of the porch was a hulking man of twenty-four or twenty-five. The explosive-firing, ten-banger pistol he was so proud of hung from the leather gun-belt that girt his waist. Below a mop of red hair, his sly eyes crept across every inch of Doris' frame.

"What's your business, Greco? I thought I told you not to come around here no more." Her tone just as commanding as it had been in her search for the Hunter, Doris glared at the man.

For a brief instant, anger and confusion surfaced in his cloudy eyes, but a lewd smile soon spread across the man's face and he said, "Aw, don't say that. I come out here all worried about you and this is the thanks I get? Seems you been looking for a Hunter now, haven't you? Couldn't be you've gone and got attacked by our old lord, could it?"

In a heartbeat, vermilion spread across Doris' face, the result of the anger and embarrassment she felt at Greco hitting it right on the mark. "Grow up! If you and your trashy friends in town go around spreading wild stories about me just because I won't have nothing to do with you, I'll teach you a thing or two!"

"Come on, don't get so worked up," Greco said, shrugging his shoulders. Then his gaze became probing as he said, "It's just, the night before last there was this drifter in the saloon blubbering on about how he got himself challenged to a test of skill out at the hill on the edge of town by a right powerful girl, then got his ass handed to him before he could even draw his sword. So I buy him a drink to hear all the details and it turns out looks-wise and build-wise, the girl sounds like the spitting image of you. The frosting on the cake was he said she's damn handy with a weird kind of whip, and there ain't no one in these parts that could be besides you, missy." Greco's eyes were trained on the whip Doris had in her right hand.

"Sure, I was out looking for someone. Someone good. You should know as well as anyone how much damage mutants have been causing around town lately. Well, things are no different out here. It's more than I can take care of all by my lonesome."

On hearing Doris' reply, Greco smiled faintly. "In that case, all you'd have had to do was go ask Pops Cushing in town, seeing how he's in charge of scouting new talent. You know, five days back, one of the hands at our place seen you chasing a lesser dragon toward the lord's castle right around dusk. Now, on top of that, you've got this need for hired help you don't want anyone in town to know about." Greco's tone of voice changed entirely. He threateningly suggested, "Let's see you take that scarf off your neck."

Doris didn't move.

"Can't do it, can you," he laughed. "I figured as much. I think I'll go into town and have a few words with ... well, I don't think I have to tell you the rest. So, what do you say? Just be sensible and give me your okay for what I've been asking you to do all along. If we got hitched, you'd be the mayor's daughter-in-law. Then no one in town could lay a stinkin' finger on you or—"

Before his vile words were done, a snap rang through the air and the bay reared up with a whinny of pain. Doris' whip had stung the horse's flank with lightning speed. In a heartbeat, Greco's massive frame was thrown out of the saddle and crashed to the ground. Hand pressed to his tail, he groaned in pain. The bay's hoofbeats echoed loudly as it fled the farm, heartlessly leaving its master behind.

"Serves you right! That's for all the filthy things you've gotten away with by hiding behind your father's power," Doris laughed. "I never cared too much for your father or anyone in cahoots with him. And if you got a problem with that, you bring your daddy and your buddies out here any time. I won't run or hide. Of course, the next time you show that ugly, pockmarked mug of yours around here, you'd better be ready to have me flay the skin right off it!"

Color rose in the big man's face as words so rough you had to wonder where a beautiful young lady kept them shot at him like flames.

"Bitch, you fucked up real good ..." As he spoke, his right hand went for his ten-banger. Once again, a surge of black split the sunlight-soaked air, and the pistol he'd tried to draw was thrown into the bushes behind him. And he could draw in less than half a second.

"Next time I'll send your nose or one of your ears flying."

The man knew there was more to her words than empty threats. With no parting quip, Greco scurried off the farm, rubbing his backside and right wrist by turns.

"That scumbag's nothing without his daddy behind him." After she spat the words, Doris turned and froze on the spot.

Dan stood in the doorway, still dressed in his pajamas and armed with a laser rifle. His big, round eyes were brimming with tears.

"Dan, you … you heard everything then?"

The boy nodded mechanically. Greco had been facing toward the house and he hadn't said anything about Dan, so the boy must've stayed behind the door. "Sis … were you really bit by a Noble?" The boy lived in the wilds of the Frontier. He was well aware of the fate of those with the devil's kiss on their throat.

The young beauty who had just sent a brute twice her size packing with a crack of her whip was now rooted to the spot, unable to speak.

"No, it can't be!" The boy suddenly ran over and threw his arms around her. The sorrow and concern he'd been wrestling with surged out in a tidal wave, soaking Doris' slacks with a flood of hot tears. "You can't be, you just can't! I'd be all alone then … You can't be!" Though he didn't want it to be true, he had no idea what he could do about it, and his sorrow sprung from his helplessness.

"It's okay," Doris said, patting her brother's tiny shoulder as she fought back tears of her own. "No lousy Noble's put the bite on me. These are bug bites I've got on my neck. I only hid them because I didn't want you getting all worried."

A ray of light streamed into his tear-streaked face. "Really? Really truly?"

"Yep."

Surely the boy had a heart that could shift from low gear to high on the fly if that was all it took to calm him down. "But what'll we do if the folks in town believe all Greco's fibbing and come busting in here?"

"You know how good I am in a fight. Plus, I've got you here—"

"And we've got D, too!"

At the boy's exuberant words, the girl's face clouded. That was the difference between someone who knew the way Hunters worked and someone who didn't. In fact, the boy hadn't been told D was a Hunter.

"I'm gonna go ask him!"

"Dan—"

Before she could stop him, the boy disappeared into the living room. She hurried after him, but was too late.

In a completely trusting tone, Dan addressed the youth on the sofa. "A guy just came out here trying to get my sister to marry him, and he says he gonna spread the worst kind of lies about her. He'll be back with a bunch of folks from town, I just know it. And then they'll take my sister away. Please save her, D."

Imagining his answer, Doris unconsciously closed her eyes. The problem wasn't the reply itself, but the effect it would have. A cold, adamant rejection would leave a wound on the boy's fragile heart that might never heal.

But this is how the Vampire Hunter replied: "Leave it to me. I won't let anyone lay a finger on your sister."

"Okay!"

The boy's face shone like a sunny morning.

From behind him, Doris said, "Well, breakfast will be ready soon. Before we eat, go have a look at the thermo-regulators out in the orchards."

The boy galloped off like the spirit of life itself. Doris turned to the still prone D and said, "Thank you. I know it's the iron law of Hunters that they won't lift a finger for anything but dealing with their prey. I'd be in no position to complain no matter how you turned him down. You did it without hurting him ... and he loves you like a big brother."

"But I do refuse."

"I know. Aside from your job itself, I won't ask any more of you—what you said to him just now will do fine. I'll handle my own problems. And the sooner you get your work finished the better."

"Fine."

Not surprisingly, D's voice was emotionless and bitterly cold.

As expected, "company" came as the three of them were just finishing a somewhat peculiar breakfast. What made it peculiar was that D only ate half as much as young Dan. The menu consisted of ham and eggs on a colossal scale—mutant-chicken eggs a foot across on an inch-thick slab of light, homemade ham—along with preservative-free black bread hot out of the oven, and juice from massive Gargantua grapes cultivated right on their own farm. Of course, the juice was freshly squeezed and the three large glasses were filled from a single grape. And those were just the main dishes; there was a gigantic bowl of salad and fragrant floral tea, too. Only a farm like the Langs' could offer a rich menu like this, and the freshness of the ingredients alone should have been enough to make a good-sized man take seconds or thirds on the ham and eggs. The refreshing morning sunlight and giant lavender blossoms that adorned the table were in essence part of a sacred ritual to give all those gathered around it the strength to fight the cruel Frontier for another day.

And yet, D quickly set down his fork and knife and withdrew to the room in the back Doris had just given him.

"That's weird. I wonder if he ain't feeling too good?"

"Yes, I'm sure it's something like that." Though she pretended nothing was wrong, Doris pictured D back in his room now taking his own kind of breakfast, and started to feel ill.

"Not you too, Sis! What's the matter? I know you like him and all, but don't get sick just because he does."

Doris was about to lay into Dan for his teasing remarks when tension suddenly flooded her face.

Outside, a thunder of hoofbeats drew closer. Lots of hoofbeats.

"Damn it, here they come," Dan shouted, dashing over to where a laser rifle hung on the wall.

He started to call out for D, but Doris' quick hand silenced him.

"But why not? It's gotta be Greco and his thugs," he said with disgust.

"Let's see if the two of us can't handle it first. If that doesn't work, maybe then ..." But she was perfectly aware that no matter what was going to happen to the two of them, D wouldn't do anything.

Armed with a whip and a rifle, the pair stepped out onto the porch. She let her little eight-year-old brother join her because the law of the Frontier was that if you and your family didn't defend your own lives and property, no one else would. If you always relied on others, you wouldn't last long against the fire dragons and golems.

In no time, a dozen men on horseback formed up in front of them.

"Dear me, the cream of local society is out in force. A no-account little farm like this don't deserve such distinguished guests." As Doris greeted them in a calm tone, her eyes were cautiously trained on the men in the second and third ranks. In the foremost rank were prominent villagers like Sheriff Luke Dalton, Dr. Sam Ferringo, and Mayor Rohman—this last was Greco's father, whose face was unusually oily for a man nearing sixty. There was no reason to worry about any of those three suddenly trying anything funny, but behind them was a mob of brutal hooligans just itching to make a statement with the Magnum guns and battered heat-rays they wore on their hips should the opportunity arise. They were all hired hands from Mayor Rohman's ranch. Doris glared at each of them in turn without a trace of fear until she came across a familiar face at the very tail of the mob, and her gaze became one of pure contempt. When it looked like trouble was brewing, it was just like Greco to shut his big mouth, find the safest possible place, and try to look like he didn't have the faintest idea what was going on.

"So, what's your business?"

Apparently by mutual consent, Mayor Rohman spoke first.

"As if you don't know. We're out here on account of the marks you've got under that scarf. You show them to Doc Ferringo now, and if they're nothing then fine. But if they're ... well then, unfortunately we'll have to put you in the asylum."

Doris snorted in derision. "So you believe the nonsense that damn fool son of yours been talking? He's been out here five time asking me to marry him and I've turned him down every time, so he's stuck with some pretty damn sour grapes. That's why he's spreading these stories when they ain't true. You keep spouting that filth and you won't like what happens, mayor or not."

The bluff rolled from her so fluently the mayor couldn't get a word in edgewise. His bovine countenance flushed with rage.

"That's right! My sister ain't been bit by no vampire! So hit the road, you old pervert," Dan shouted from his sister's side, pushing the mayor over the edge.

"What do you mean by calling me an old pervert? Why, you ... you little bastard! To say something like that about the mayor even in jest ... A pervert of all things! I'll have you know ... "

The old man had lost all control. He might hold all the real power in town, but he was still just the mayor of one tiny village. Simply touch on one of his sore spots, and his emotional restraints would burst. In that, he wasn't so different from the thugs behind him.

From the back, Greco bellowed, "They're making fools of us! C'mon boys, don't pay them no nevermind. Let's grab them and burn the damn house down!"

Cries of "Hell yeah!" and "Damn straight!" resounded from the rowdies.

"Hold everything! You pull any of that crap and you'll answer to me!"

The rebukes flew from Sheriff Dalton. For a moment, Doris' expression was placid. Though still under thirty, the sincere and capable sheriff was someone she was willing to trust. The hoodlums stopped moving, too.

"Are you with them, Sheriff?" Doris asked in a low voice.

"I need you to understand something, Doris. I've got a job to uphold as sheriff in this here village. And checking out your neck is part of it. I don't want things getting out of hand. If it's nothing, then one peek will do. Take your scarf off and let Doc have a look."

"He's right," Dr. Ferringo said, rising in his saddle. He was about the same age as the mayor, but thanks to his studies of medicine in the Capital, he had the intelligent look of a distinguished old gentleman. Because Doris and Dan's father had been a student of his at the education center, this good-natured man worried about their welfare on a daily basis. Before him alone, Doris couldn't hold her head up. "No matter what the result may be, we won't do wrong by you. You leave it to me and the sheriff."

"No way, she goes to the asylum!" Greco's spiteful words came from the back. "In this village, we got a rule that anyone that gets bit by a Noble goes to the asylum, no matter who they are. And when we can't get rid of the Noble ... heh heh ... then we chuck them out as monster bait!"

The sheriff whipped around and roared, "Shut up, you damn fool!"

Greco was shocked into an embarrassed silence, but he drew power from the fact that he was surrounded by his hired hands. "Well, put a badge on you and you get pretty damn tough. Before you give me any more back talk, check out the bitch's neck. After all, that's what we're paying you for, isn't it?"

"What'd you say, boy?" The sheriff's eyes had a look that could kill. At that same moment, the hoods were going for their backs and waists with their gunhands. An ugly situation was developing.

"Stop it," the mayor barked bitterly at the entire company. "What'll we prove by fighting among ourselves? All we have to do is take a look at the girl's neck and we'll be done here."

The sheriff and the hoods had no choice but to begrudgingly go along with that. "Doris," the sheriff called out to her in a gruffer tone than before, "you'd best take that scarf off."

Doris tightened her grip on the whip.

"And if I say I don't wanna?"

The sheriff fell silent.

"Get her!"

With Greco's cry, the mounted thugs raced right and left. Doris' whip uncoiled for action.

"Stop!" the sheriff shouted, but it looked like his commands would no longer do the trick, and just when the battle was about to be joined—

The toughs all stopped moving at once. Or to be more accurate, their mounts had jerked to a halt.

"What's gotten into you? Move it!"

Even a kick from spurred heels couldn't make the horses budge. If the men could've looked into their horses' eyes, they might have glimpsed a trace of ineffable horror. A trace of overwhelming terror that wouldn't permit the horses to be coerced any further, or even to flee. And then the eyes of every man focused on the gorgeous youth in black who stood blocking the front door, though no one had any idea when he'd appeared. Even the sunlight seemed to grow sluggish. Suddenly, a gust of wind brushed across the fields and the men turned away, exchanging uneasy looks.

"Who the hell are you?" The mayor tried his level best to sound intimidating, but there was no hiding the quiver in his voice. The youth had about him an air that churned the calm waters of the human soul.

Doris turned around and was amazed, while Dan's face shined with delight.

Without a word, D stopped Doris from saying whatever she was about to say and stepped in front of the Langs as if to shield them. His right hand held a longsword. "I'm D. I've hired on with these people."

He looked not at the mayor, but at the sheriff as he spoke.

The sheriff gave a little nod. He could tell at a glance what the youth before them really was. "I'm Sheriff Dalton. This here's Mayor Rohman, and Dr. Ferringo. The rest back there don't count for much." After that reasonable introduction, he added, "You're a Hunter, aren't you? I see it in your eyes, the way you carry yourself. I seem to recall hearing there was a man of unbelievable skill traveling across the Frontier, and that his name was D. They say his sword is faster than a laser beam or some such thing." Those words could be taken as fearful or praising, but D was silent.

The sheriff continued in a hard voice. "Only, they say that man's a Hunter, and he specializes in vampires. And that he's a dhampir himself."

There were gasps. The village notables and hoods all froze. As did Dan.

"Oh, Doris! Then you really have been ..."

Dr. Ferringo barely squeezed the hopeless words from his throat.

"Yes, the girl's been bitten by a vampire. And I've been hired to destroy him."

"At any rate, the mere fact that she's been bitten by a vampire is reason enough not to let her remain at large. She goes to the asylum," the mayor declared.

"Nothing doing," Doris shot back flatly. "I'm not going anywhere and leaving Dan and the farm unattended. If you're hellbent on doing it, you'll have to take me away by force."

"Okay then," Greco groaned. The girl's manner and speech, defiant to the bitter end, reawakened his rancor at being spurned.

He gave a toss of the chin to his thugs, whose eyes burned with the same shadowy fire as a serpent's.

The rowdies were about to dismount in unison, but at that moment their horses reared up simultaneously. There was nothing they could do. Each gave their own cry of "Oof" or "Ow," and every last one of them was thrown to the ground. The sunny air was filled with moans of pain and the whinnying of horses.

D returned his gaze to the sheriff. Whether or not the sheriff comprehended that a single glare from the Hunter had put the horses on end was unclear.

An indescribable tension and fear flowed between the two of them.

"I have a proposal." At D's words, the sheriff nodded his assent like he was sleepwalking. "Hold off on doing anything about the girl until I've finished my work. If we come out of it okay, that's fine. If we don't ..."

"You can rest assured I'll take care of myself. If he's beaten by the lord, I'll drive a stake through my own heart." Doris gave a satisfied nod.

"Don't let her fool you! This jerk's in league with the Nobility. You shouldn't be making deals with him—he's out to turn every last person in Ransylva into a vampire, I'm sure of it!" Having been thrown to the ground for the second time that day, Greco was still down on all fours, screaming. "Let's do away with the bitch. No, better yet, give her to the lord. That way, he won't go after any of the other women."

With a *pffft!* a four-inch-wide pillar of flame erupted from the ground right in front of Greco's face. The earth boiled from a blast of more than twenty thousand degrees, and the flames leapt to Greco's greasy face, searing his upper lip. He tumbled backwards with a beastly howl of agony.

"Say anything else bad about my sister and your head'll be next," Dan threatened, perfectly aligning the barrel of his laser rifle with Greco's face. Though it's true the weapon had no kick, it was still unheard of for a child a good deal shorter than the weapon's length to be skilled enough to hit a target dead-on.

Far from angry, the sheriff wore a grin that said, "You done good, kid."

D addressed the sheriff softly.

"As you can see, we have a fierce bodyguard on our side. You could try and plow through us, but a lot of people will probably get hurt unnecessarily. Just wait."

"Well, some of them could do with a little hurting if you ask me," said the sheriff, glancing briefly at the hoodlums moaning behind him. "What do you make of this, Doc?"

"Why don't you ask me?!" the mayor screamed, veins bulging. "You think we can trust this drifter? We should send her to the asylum, just like my boy says! Sheriff, bring her in right this moment!"

"The evaluation of vampire victims falls to me," Dr. Ferringo said calmly, and then he produced a cigar from one of his inner pockets and put it in his mouth. It wasn't a cheap one like the local knock-off artists hand rolled with eighty percent garbage. This was a high-class cigar in a cellophane wrapper that bore the stamp of the Capital's Tobacco Monopoly. These were Dr. Ferringo's treasure. He gave a little nod to Doris.

Her whip shot out with a wa-pish!

"Oof!" The mayor gave an utterly hysterical cry and grabbed his nose. With one slight twist of Doris' wrist, her whip had taken the cigar from the doctor's mouth and crammed it up one of the mayor's nostrils.

Ignoring the mayor, whose entire face was flushed with rage, the doctor declared loudly, "Very well, I find Doris Lang's infection of vampirism to be of the lowest possible degree. My orders are rest at home for her. Sheriff Dalton and Mayor Rohman, do you concur?"

"Yessir," the sheriff replied with a nod of satisfaction, but suddenly he looked straight at D with the intimidating expression of a man sworn to uphold the law. "Under the following conditions. I'll take the word of a damn-good Hunter and hold off on any further discussion. But let me make one thing crystal clear—I don't want to have to stake you folks through the heart. I don't want to, but if that time should come, I won't give it a second thought." And then, throwing the Lang children a look of pathos, he bid them farewell. "I'm looking forward to the day I can enjoy the juice of those Gargantua-breed grapes of yours. All right, you dirty dogs, mount up and make it snappy! And I'm warning you, any of you so much as make a peep about this back in town, I'll throw you in the electric pokey, mark my words!"

The crowd disappeared over the hill, glancing back now and then with looks of hatred, compassion, and, from some, encouragement. D was about to go into the house when Doris asked him to wait. He turned to her coolly, and then she said, "You sure are strange for a Hunter. You might've taken on some work you didn't have to, and I can't pay you for it."

"It's not about work. It's about a promise."

"A promise? To who?"

"To your little bodyguard over there," he said with a toss of his chin. Then, noticing Dan's stiff expression, he asked, "What's wrong? You hate me because I'm supposedly 'in league with the Nobility'?"

"Nope."

As he shook his head, the boy's face suddenly crumpled in on itself and he started to cry.

The young hero who'd put Greco in his place minutes earlier now returned to being an eight-year-old boy. He blubbered away as he threw his arms around D's waist. This child had rarely cried since the death of his father three years earlier. As he watched his sister struggling along as a woman on her own, the boy had secretly nurtured his own stores of pride and determination in his little heart. Naturally, life on the Frontier was hard and lonely for him too. When his youthful heart felt he might be robbed of his only blood relative, he forgot himself and latched onto not his sister, but rather to the man who'd only arrived the day before.

"Dan ..."

Doris reached for her brother's shoulder with one hand, but D gently brushed it away. Before long, the boy's cries started to taper off, and D quietly planted one knee on the wooden floor of the front porch, looking the boy square in his tear-streaked face.

"Listen to me," he said in a low but distinct voice. Noticing the unmistakable ring of encouragement in his voice, Doris opened her eyes in astonishment.

"I promise you and your sister I'll kill the Noble. I always keep my word. Now you have to promise me something."

"Sure." Dan nodded repeatedly.

"From here on out, if you want to scream and cry, that's your prerogative. Do whatever you like. But whatever you do, don't make your sister cry. If you think your crying will set her off too, then hold it in. If you're being selfish and your sister starts to cry, make her smile again. You're a man, after all. Okay?"

"Sure!" The boy's face was radiant. It glowed with an aura of pride.

"Okay, then do your big brother a favor and feed his horse. I'll be heading out on business soon."

The boy raced off, and D went into the house without another word.

"D, I ..." Doris sounded like something was weighing greatly on her.

The Vampire Hunter ignored her words, and said simply, "Come inside. Before I head out, I want to put a little protective charm on you." And then he vanished down the dark and desolate hall.

The Vampire Count Lee

From the farm he rode hard north by northwest for two hours, until he came to a spot where a massive ashen citadel towering quietly atop a hillock loomed menacingly overhead. This was the castle of the local lord—the home of Count Magnus Lee.

Even the shower of midday sunlight changed color here, and a nauseating miasma seemed to come from the morbid expanse of land surrounding the castle. The grass was green as far as the eye could see, and the trees were laden with succulent fruit, but not a single bird could be heard. Still, as one would expect around noon on a sunny day, there were no signs of life in the vampire's castle. Constructed to mimic the castles of the distant middle ages, the walls were dotted with countless loopholes. The dungeon and courtyards were surrounded by broad, stone stairways that linked them together, but there was no sign of android sentries on any of them. The castle was, to all appearances, deserted.

But D had already sensed the castle's bloodied nocturnal form, and the hundreds of electronic eyes and vicious weapons that lay in wait for their next victim.

The surveillance satellite in geo-stationary orbit 22,240 miles above the castle—as well as the uncounted security cameras disguised as fruit or spiders—sent the castle's mother-computer images so detailed that an observer could count the pores of the intruder's skin. The photon cannons secreted in the loopholes had their safety locks switched off, and they were drawing a bead on several hundred points all over the intruder's body.

As the Nobility was fated to live by night alone, electronic protection during the day was an absolute necessity. No matter how much mystic-might the vampires might wield by night, in the light of day they were feeble creatures, easily destroyed by a single thrust of a stake. It was for precisely this reason that the vampires had used all their knowledge of psychology and cerebral biology in their attempts to plant fear in the human mind throughout the six or seven millennia of their reign. The results of this tactic were clear: even after the vampire civilization had long since crumbled—it was rare to catch even a glimpse of one about—they could take residence in the midst of their human "foes" and, like a feudal lord, hold complete mastery over the region.

According to what Doris told D before he set out, the villagers in Ransylva had taken up sword and spear a number of times in the past, endeavoring to drive their lord off their lands. However, as soon as they set foot within the castle grounds, black clouds began swirling in the sky above, the earth was rent wide, lightning raged, and not surprisingly, they were ultimately routed before they even reached the moat.

Not giving in so easily, a group of villagers made a direct appeal to the Capital and succeeded in getting the government's precious Anti-Gravity Air Corps to execute a bombing mission. Because the government was afraid of depleting its stores of energy or explosives, however, it wouldn't authorize more than a single bombing run. The defense shields around the castle prevented that single attack from accomplishing much before it was forced to return home. The following day, villagers were found butchered with positively unearthly brutality, and, by the time the villagers had seen the vampires' vengeance play out, the flames of resistance were utterly snuffed.

Home to the feudal lord who would taste D's blade, the castle the Hunter approached was the sort of demonic citadel that kept the world in fear of the now largely legendary vampires.

Perhaps that was what brought a haggard touch to D's visage. No, as a Vampire Hunter he should've been quite familiar with the fortifications of the vampires' castle. As proof, he rode his horse without the slightest trace of trepidation to where the drawbridge was raised. But against the lord and his iron-walled castle, crammed with most advanced electronics, what chance of victory did a lone youth with a sword have?

Blazing-white light could have burnt through his chest at any moment, but a tepid breeze merely stroked his ample black hair, and soon he arrived at the edge of a moat brimming with dark blue water. The moat must have been nearly twenty feet wide. His eyes raced across the walls as he pondered his next move, but when he put his hand to his pendant the drawbridge barring the castle gate amazingly began to descend with a heavy, grating noise. With earth-shaking force, the bridge was laid.

"It is a great pleasure to receive you," a metallic voice called out from nowhere in particular. It was computer-synthesized speech—the ultimate in personality simulation. "Please proceed into the castle proper. Directions shall be transmitted to the brain of milord's mount. Please pardon the fact no one was here to greet you."

D said nothing as he urged his horse on.

Once he'd crossed the bridge, he entered a large courtyard. Behind him came the sounds of the drawbridge being raised again, but he advanced down the cobblestone way toward the palace without a backward glance.

The orderly rows of trees, the marble sculptures glittering in the sunlight, stairways and corridors leading to places that couldn't be guessed—all gave the feeling of scrupulous upkeep by machines. Though no one could say how many millennia ago they'd been planted or sculpted, they looked as fresh and new as if they'd been placed there only yesterday. But there were no signs that life went on here. The machines alone lived, and their mechanical eyes and fiery arrows were trained on D.

When his horse halted before the palace gates, D quickly slipped out of the saddle. The thick doors dotted with countless hobnails were already open wide.

"Enter, please." The same synthesized voice reverberated from the dark corridor.

A hazy darkness bound the interior. Not that the windowpanes were dampening the sunlight—this effect was a result of the artificial lighting. In fact, the windows in the vampire's palace were no more than ornamentation, impervious to the slightest ray of light.

As he walked down the corridors guided by the voice, D noticed that each and every window was set in a niche in the wall. It would take two or three steps up the scaffolding to climb to the window from the hallway: one couldn't walk over to the window, but would rather pop up in front of it. The design had been copied from German castles in the middle ages.

The predominant element of vampire civilization was their love of medieval styles. Even in their superiorly advanced, tech-filled Capital, the designs of many of the buildings closely resembled those of medieval Europe. Perhaps something in their DNA cried out for a return to the golden age that lived on in their genetic memory, a time when superstition and legend and all manner of weird creatures prevailed. Maybe that explained why so many detestable monsters and spirits had been resurrected by their super-science.

The voice led D to a splendid door of massive proportions. At the bottom of the door there was an opening large enough for a cat to come and go as it pleased. This door opened without a sound as well, and D set foot into a world of even deeper darkness. His haggard air was gone in an instant. His nerves, his muscles, his circulation—every part of him told him the time he had known had suddenly changed. The instant he smelled the thick perfume wafting throughout the room—which appeared to be a hall—D knew the cause. *Time-Bewitching Incense. I've heard rumors about this stuff.* When he sighted the pair of silhouettes hazily sketched by wispy flames at the far end of the vast hall, his suspicion became conviction.

The silhouettes gave off a ghastly aura that made even D's peerless features stiffen with tension. Beside a slender form—which he knew at a glance to be female—stood a figure of remarkable grandeur dressed in black. "We've been waiting for you. You are the first human to ever make it this far in one piece." From the corners of the vermilion lips that loosed this solemn voice poked a pair of white fangs. "As our guest, you deserve an introduction. I am the lord of this castle and administrator of the Tenth Frontier Sector, Count Magnus Lee."

Time-Bewitching Incense could be called the ultimate chemical compound born of the vampires' physiological needs.

For the most part, the information and rumors people passed along about the physiology of these fiends—the various stories told since time immemorial—were essentially true. Outlandish tales about transforming into bats, turning themselves into fog and billowing away, and so on—stories that there were vampires who could do such things and others who couldn't were taken as fact. Just as in human society ability varied according to an individual's disposition, so too among the vampires there were some demons who freely controlled the weather, while other fiends had mastery over lower animals.

Many aspects of the vampire's fantastic physiology, however, remained shrouded in mystery.

For example, the reason why they slept by day but awoke at night remained unclear. Even enveloped by darkness in a secret chamber that blocked out all possible light, a vampire's body grew rigid with the coming of that unseen dawn, their heart alone continuing to beat as they fell into death's breathless slumber.

Despite a concerted effort at explanation spanning thousands of years and investing the essence of every possible field of science—ecology, biology, cerebral physiology, psychology, and even super-psychology—the damned couldn't shed a bit of light on the true cause of their sleep. As if to say, those who dwelt in the darkness were denied even the rays of hope.

Born of the vampires' desperate research, Time-Bewitching Incense was one means of overcoming their limitations.

Wherever its scent hung, the time would become night. Or rather, appear to be night. In a manner of speaking, normal temporal effects were so altered by this chemical compound, the incense made time itself seem hypnotized. In the glistening sunlight of early afternoon, the night-blooming moonlight grass would open its gorgeous white flowers, people would doze off and remain asleep indefinitely, and the eyes of vampires would shine with a piercing light. Due to the extreme difficulty of finding and combining the components, the incense was very hard to come by, but rumors spread to every corner of the Frontier about Hunters who forced their way into a vampire resting place when the sun was high only to be brutally ambushed by Nobles who just happened to have some on hand.

There, in the false night, D faced the dark liege lord.

"Did you come here expecting to find us asleep, foolish one? As you managed to stop my daughter, I believed you to be a more stalwart opponent than the usual insects, and I allowed you this meeting. But, where you sauntered into the blackest hell without even suspecting the danger awaiting you, I may have erred gravely in my assessment."

"No," said a voice he'd heard before. The figure at the Count's side was Larmica. "This man doesn't exhibit the least trace of fear. He's a thoroughly exasperating and deliciously impudent fellow. Judging by the skill he demonstrated this past evening when dealing Garou a grievous wound, he could be nothing save a dhampir."

"Human or dhampir, he remains a traitor. A bastard spawned by one of our kind and a mere human. Tell me, bastard, are you a man or a vampire?"

To this scornful query, D gave a different answer. "I'm a Vampire Hunter. I came here because the walls opened up for me. Are you the fiend that attacked the girl from the farm? If so, I'll slay you here and now."

For a moment, the Count was left speechless by the gleaming eyes that bored through the darkness at him, but an instant later he seemed indignant. He laughed loudly. "Slay me? You forget your place. Do you not realize the sole reason I allowed you to come this far is because my daughter said it would be a shame to kill a man such as yourself, that we should persuade you to join us in the castle and make you one of our kind? I have no idea which of your parents was of our kind, but judging by the speech and conduct of their son, it was obviously a buffoon without an inkling of their own low station. This is a waste of time. Dhampir, shame of our race, prepare to meet your maker." Having roared these words, the Count raised his right hand to strike, but was stopped by Larmica's voice.

"Please wait, Father. Allow me to speak to him."

Fluttering the train of a deep blue dress quite unlike the one she wore the previous night, Larmica stepped between the Count and D.

"You spring from the same noble blood as our family. Regardless of what Father said, no son of a humble-born vampire could ever possess such skill. When I caught the missile you hurled at me, I thought my blood would freeze."

D said nothing.

"What say you? Will you not apologize to Father for your boastful speech and join us here in the castle? What reasons have you to dog us? Is being a Hunter a job worth wandering the untamed plains in such shabby apparel? And what of the human wretches you've protected—what manner of treatment have you received from the humans who should be grateful to you? Have they accepted you as their fellow man?"

In the unknowably deep twilight of the hall, the voice of the beautiful young woman flowed without hesitation. Her haughty and domineering mien was unchanged from the night before, but one had to wonder if D noticed the faint shadows of entreaty and desire that clung to her.

Dhampir—a child born of the union between a vampire and a human. There could be no existence more lonely or hateful than that. Normally, dhampirs were no different from humans, relatively free to work by the light of day. When angered, however, they lashed out with the unholy power of a vampire, killing and maiming at will. Most detestable of all were the vampire urges they inherited from one of their parents.

Based on their innate and intimate knowledge of vampires' strengths and weaknesses, many chose to become Vampire Hunters in order to make a living in human society. The fact was, they demonstrated a level of ability head and shoulders above merely human Hunters, but outside of hunting, they were nearly completely ostracized by humanity and kept their distance. Occasionally, their vampire nature would awaken so powerfully they themselves couldn't suppress it, causing them to crave the blood of the very people that depended on them.

As soon as a dhampir finished a job, the people who barely tolerated him while he went about his mission would chase him off with stones, their gaze full of malice and contempt. With both the cruelly aristocratic blood of the Nobility and the brutally vulgar blood of the humans, dhampirs were tormented by the dual destinies of darkness and light; one side called them traitors while the other labeled them devils. Truly, the dhampirs—like the Flying Dutchman cursed to wander the seven seas for all eternity—led an abominable existence.

And yet, Larmica was saying all she could to get him to join them. Still she spoke.

"You can't possibly have a single pleasant reminiscence from your life as a Hunter. Of late, the insects in the village have been rather boisterous. At some point they will no doubt send in an assassin like yourself. If Father and I were to have a stalwart individual like you acting as a sort of guard when they do, we would feel most secure. What say you? If you are so inclined, we may even make you truly one of us."

The Count was ready to explode with rage at the words his daughter—gazing with sleepy, painfully lustful eyes at motionless D—had said. But before he could, he heard a low voice.

"What do you plan to do with the girl?"

Larmica laughed charmingly. "Do not overreach your bounds. The woman shall soon belong to Father, soul and all." And then, staring fixedly at her father with a cutting and highly ironic gaze, she said, "I believe Father wishes to make her one of his concubines, but I cannot allow it. I shall drain her of her very last drop of blood, then leave her for the human worms to rip apart and put to the torch."

Her words suddenly stopped. The Count's eyes gave off blood light. The fearsome night-stalking father and daughter surmised through their supernaturally attuned senses that the trivial opponent before them—the youth who was trapped like the proverbial rat—was rapidly transforming. That he was becoming the same thing they were!

"Still you fail to comprehend this," Larmica scolded. "What can come of this obligation you have toward the human worms? Those menials spared no pains in exterminating each and every living creature on the face of the earth besides themselves, and managed to nearly wipe themselves out through their own carelessness. They only continued living through the charity of our kind, yet the first time our power waned, the insurgents were all too happy to fly the flags of revolt. They, not we, are the creatures that should be expunged from this planet and from all of space."

At that moment, the Count thought he'd heard a certain phrase, and his brow knit. The muttered words had clearly come from the young man before him, but he promptly dredged the same phrase from the depths of distant, half-forgotten memories. Reason denied the possibility of such a thing.

Impossible, he thought. *Those are the very words I heard from his highness. From the great one, the Sacred Ancestor of our species. That filthy whelp couldn't possibly know such things.*

He heard D's voice. "Is that all you have to say?"

"Fool!"

The screams of both father and daughter resounded through the vast chamber. Negotiations had fallen through. The Count's lips warped into a cold-blooded and confident grin. He gave a crisp snap of the fingers on his right hand, but a rush of consternation came into his pale visage a few seconds later when he realized the countless electronic weapons mounted throughout the hall weren't operating.

The pendant on D's chest emitted a blue light.

"I don't know what you have up your sleeve, but the weapons of the Nobility don't work against me." Leaving only his words there, D kicked off the ground. Lightning fast, there would be no escaping him. Drawing his sword in midair, he pulled it to his right side. Just as he landed, his deadly thrust became a flash of silver that sank into the Count's chest.

There was the sound of flesh striking flesh.

"Eh?!"

For the first time, a look of surprise surfaced in D's handsome but normally expressionless countenance. His longsword was stopped dead, caught between the Count's palms about eight inches from the tip. Moreover, from their respective stances, D was in a far better position to exert more force upon the sword, but though he put all his might behind it, the blade wouldn't budge an inch, just as if it was wedged in a wall.

The Count bared his fangs and laughed. "What do you make of that, traitor? Unlike your vulgar swordplay, this is a skill worthy

of a true Noble. When you get to hell, tell them how surprised you were!" As he said that, the figure in black made a bold move to the right. Perhaps it was some secret trick the Count employed in the timing, or the way he put his strength into the move, but for whatever reason, D was unable to take his hand off the hilt. He was thrown along with the sword into the center of the hall.

However …

The Count quite unexpectedly found his breath taken away. There were no crunching bones to be heard; the youth somersaulted in midair like a cat about to land feetfirst on the floor with the hem of his coat billowing out around him. Or rather, he was ready to land there. With no floor beneath his feet, D kept right on going, falling into the pitch-black maw that opened suddenly beneath him.

As he heard the creaking of trapdoors to either side of the massive thirty by thirty-foot pit swinging back up into place, the Count turned his gaze to the darkness behind him. Larmica appeared from it. "It's a primitive trap, but it was fortunate for us we had it put there, was it not, Father? When all your vaunted atomic armaments were useless, a pitfall of cogs and springs rid us of that nuisance."

At her charming laughter, the Count made a sullen face. He had reluctantly allowed this trap to be installed due to Larmica's entreaties. *There's no way she could have foreseen this day's events*, the Count thought, *but this girl, daughter of mine though she may be, seems on occasion to be a creature beyond imagining.*

Shaking off his grimace, he said, "At the same instant I hurled him, you pulled the cord on the trapdoor—who but my daughter would be capable of as much? But is this for the best?"

"Is what for the best?"

"Last night, when you returned from the farm and spoke of the stripling we just disposed of, the tone of your voice, the manner of your complaints—even I, your own father, cannot recall ever hearing you so indignant, yet your indignation held a feverish sentiment that was equally new. Could it be you're smitten with the scoundrel?"

Unanticipated though her father's words were, Larmica donned a smile that positively defied description. Not only that, she licked her lips as well.

"Do you believe I could let a man I loved drop *down there*? Father, as its architect you know far better than anyone what a living hell that subterranean region is. Dhampir or not, no one could come out of that benighted pit alive. But …"

"But what?"

Here Larmica once again made a ghastly smile that even caused Count Lee, her own father, to flinch.

"If he can escape from there with naught but a sword and the power of his own limbs, I shall devote myself to him body and soul. By the eternal life and ten thousand bloody years of the history of the Nobility, I swear I love him—I love the Vampire Hunter D."

Now it was the Count's turn to smile bitterly. "It is hell for those you despise, and a worse hell for those you desire. Though I don't believe there is anything in this world that can face *the three sisters* and live to tell the tale."

"Of course not, Father."

"However," the Count continued, "should he survive and you meet him again, what will you do should he spurn your affections?"

Larmica responded in a heartbeat. Flames of joy rose from her body. Her eyes glittered wildly but were moist with hot tears, her crimson lips parted slightly, and her slick tongue licked along her lips as if it possessed a will of its own. "In that case, I will deal the deathblow to him without fail. I shall rip out his heart and lop off his head. And then he shall truly be mine. And I shall be his. I will taste the sweet blood as it seeps from his wounds, and after I have kissed his pale and withered lips, I shall tear open my own breast and let the hot blood of the Nobility course down his gaping throat."

When Larmica had taken her leave, following her incredibly gruesome yet fervent declaration of love, the Count's expression was a mixture of anger and apprehension, and he turned his gaze to the pit. He pressed one hand against the left side of his chest through his cape. The fabric was soaking wet. With blood. Though he seemed to have masterfully caught D's blade, more than an inch at the tip had sunken into his immortal flesh. Some trick with the sword may have been involved, for, unlike any wound he'd heretofore taken in battle, the gash still hadn't closed, and the warm blood that was the fount of his life was flowing out. *Now there is a man to be feared. He might even have ...*

The Count erased from his mind all thoughts of what might happen should he face the youth again in a battle to the death. Considering the *things* that awaited the whelp in the subterranean world, D didn't have one chance in a million of returning to the surface.

Turning his back to the hall, the Count was about to walk back to his dark demesne when the words the youth had whispered flitted through his brain. Words the Count had heard from *that august personage*. A phrase that could render the faces of every Noble, extinct or still living on, melancholy every time it was recalled. How could that stripling know those words?

Transient guests are we.

The Demons' Weakness

"**S**is, you sure we don't need more fertilizer than this?" Dan's apprehensive tone as he took the last plastic case and set it down in the bed of their wagon stabbed into Doris' breast. This was right about the time D was passing through the gates of the vampires' castle.

The pair had gone into Ransylva to do their shopping for the month. However, the results were something pitiful. Old Man Whatley, proprietor of a local store, had always been kind enough to bring things out from the storeroom that he didn't have displayed, but today he coldly refused as he'd never done before. As Doris named off necessities, he replied with apparent regret that they were either sold out or on back order. And yet, behind the counter and in the corner Doris saw he had stacks of them. When asked, however, he fumbled to say that the merchandise was already spoken for.

Doris caught on quickly enough. There was only one person low enough to cause her such grief.

Still, she didn't have time to waste arguing with Whatley, so she choked back her rage, swung by the home of an acquaintance, and somehow managed to get what she needed for the time being. At present, every minute from sunrise to sunset was as precious as a jewel to Doris. At night, her ghastly life-or-death battle with the demon awaited. No matter what happened, she had to get home before nightfall—that was the message D had drilled into her before he set out. Well, she knew that, but ... Once she'd loaded the last package of dried beef into the wagon bed, Doris gnawed her lip. The uncharacteristically forlorn expression Dan wore back there in the wagon became a smile the second his face turned toward her. The boy was doing all he could to keep her from worrying on his account. Because she understood that, Doris' heart was filled with a concern, a sorrow, and an anger that would not be checked. One of her hands reached over and unconsciously tightened around the handle of the whip she had tucked in her belt. There was only one place to direct her rage.

"Darn it, I forgot to swing by Doc Ferringo's place," she said with feigned agitation. "You wait here. It wouldn't do to have our goods get swiped, so don't you leave the wagon."

"Sis ..."

Her brother's word seemed to cling to her, as if he sensed something, but Doris replied, "Hey, a big boy like you should be ashamed to make a face like that. D would laugh if he could see how down in the mouth you look. Stop your worrying. As long as I'm around, everything'll be fine. Ain't that the way it's always been?" Speaking gently but firmly, and giving him no chance to disagree, she quickly set off down the street, thinking, *At this hour, I figure those scumbags'll be in the Black Lagoon or Pandora's Hotel. I'll learn them a thing or two!*

Her supposition proved correct. The second she opened the batwing doors of the saloon, Greco and his gang smirked and stood up from their table in the back. Quickly counting their number at seven, Doris narrowed her eyes suddenly when she saw what Greco was wearing.

His whole body was sparkling. From the top of his head to the tips of his feet Greco was covered by metallic clothing—actually, a kind of weapon called a combat suit. Doris had never seen one before, but her amazement soon faded, and with a scornful expression that said, *looks like that frivolous fool has jumped a new fashion bandwagon*, she laid into him. "You were all hot under the collar about what happened this morning, so you went and leaned on Old Man Whatley so he wouldn't sell us nothing, didn't you? And you call yourself a man? You're the lowest of the low!"

"What the hell are you yammering about?" Greco smiled mockingly. "I don't have to take that off no one who's about to be some vampire's fun toy. You should thank your lucky stars we didn't let that little tidbit out. You'd better get it into your head that it's gonna be the same thing next month and the month after. Looks like you probably managed to scrape something together today, but how long'll that pitiful amount keep your orchards going and your cows fed? Maybe two weeks, if you're lucky. Of course, that's supposing you're still walking around and throwing a shadow that long. Well, you'll be okay because pretty soon you won't have to eat anything to survive, but what'd you have planned for your poor little brother?"

Before his snide comments had ended, the whip streaked from Doris' hand. It wrapped around the helmet portion of his combat suit and she channeled her power into toppling him. But her recklessness was born of her ignorance. Greco—or rather, his combat suit—didn't budge an inch. He pulled the end of the whip with his right hand, and with one little tug, the whip flew into his hands.

"How many times did you think I was gonna fall for that, bitch?"

Shocked though she was, Doris was indeed the daughter of a Hunter, and she leapt back almost six feet. As she jumped, eyes that sparkled vulgarly with the light of hatred, lust, and superiority followed her.

"Don't forget it's my daddy that runs the show in town. There's nothing to keep us from seeing to it you and your stupid little brother starve to death."

Doris was a bit shaken, and it showed on her face—she knew the truth of what he'd just said.

A committee generally governed village operations, but the ultimate authority in town was the mayor. Under the harsh conditions of the Frontier lands, time-consuming and half-hearted operating procedures like parliaments and majority rule would bring death down on the villagers in no time. Monsters, mutants, bandits—the hungry eyes of outside forces were focused relentlessly on Ransylva. And naturally, village operations included the buying and selling of goods. It would be a piece of cake to come up with some reason to suspend a shop from doing business. When it came to the life or death of his business, Old Man Whatley had no choice but bow under duress. For Doris, a hard two-day ride to go shopping in Pedros, the nearest neighboring village, was out of the question under the present conditions. Anyway, it was clear Greco and his cronies would try to stop her.

"You have a lot of nerve, saying a despicable thing like that. I don't care if you are the mayor's son ..." Doris' voice trembled with rage.

Ignoring that, Greco said, "But if you'd be my wife, all that'd be different. We've got it all set up so when my daddy retires, the folks with pull in this town will see to it I'm the next mayor. So, what do you say? Won't you reconsider? Instead of busting your ass on that rundown farm, you could have all the fancy duds you could ever wear and all you could eat of the classiest fixin's. Dan would love it, too. And we could run off that creepy punk because I'd protect you from the vampire. If we put the money out there, you'd be surprised how many Hunters'll show up. What do you say?"

In lieu of an answer, Doris drew closer. *Well, look at that—no matter how tough she tries to act, she's still a woman after all,* Greco thought for a split second before a mass of liquid spattered against the helmet's smoked visor. Doris had spat on him.

"You—you crazy bitch! I try and treat you nice, and you pull this shit!" Greco wasn't accustomed to using the suit, and his right hand clanked roughly as it mopped his faceplate clean. But then he grabbed at Doris with incredible speed. He had hold of her torso before she had a chance to leap away. He pulled her into him. Purchased mere hours earlier from a wandering merchant, the combat suit was second-hand and of the lowest grade, but the construction—an ultra-tensile, steel armor built on a base of reinforced, organic, pseudo-skin over an electronic nervous system—increased the wearer's speed three-fold and gave him ten times his normal strength. Now that Greco had Doris, there was no way she could get away.

"What are you doing? Let go of me," she screamed, but she only succeeded in hurting her own hand when she slapped him.

Greco had no trouble whatsoever restraining both of Doris' hands with one of his own, and he hoisted her a foot off the ground. The helmet split down the middle with a metallic rasp. The face peering out at her was that of bald-faced, fiendish lust. A thread of drool stretched from the corner of his lips, which held a little smirk. Doris glared at him indignantly, but he said, "You're always putting on the airs. Well right here, right now, I'm gonna make you mine. Hey, dumbass, don't do anything funny and just stay the hell out of this!" With that last remark—roared at the middle-aged bartender who had left the counter to try and break things up—the bartender returned to his post. After all, he was up against the mayor's son. Eyes bloodshot with lust, Greco's filthy lips drew close to the immobilized young beauty. Doris turned her face away.

"Let me go! I'll call the sheriff!"

"That ain't gonna do much good," he laughed. "Hell, if it came right down to it, he likes his neck a little too much to stick it out. Hey, the bar is closed now! Someone stand guard so no one comes in."

"You got it." One of Greco's lackeys headed for the door, but then halted abruptly. Suddenly, there was a wall of black in front of him, blocking his path. "What the hell do you—"

His shout was truncated almost immediately, and a split second later, the lackey flew through tables and chairs, crashed into two of his cohorts, and smacked headfirst into the wall. Not that he was thrown at it. The black wall had merely given the man a light push backwards. But his strength must have been inhuman: both the lackey that had gone flying and also the two others he'd hit were all laid out cold on the floor, and some of the plaster had been knocked out of the wall.

"You bastard! What the hell do you think you're doing?" As the thugs grew pale and reached for the weapons at their waists, the black wall looked at them and shrugged casually.

Easily over six-and-a-half-feet tall, he was a bald giant. Arms, knotted like the roots of a tree, protruded from his leather vest. He must have weighed three hundred and fifty pounds if he weighed an ounce. Judging from the well-worn, massive machete hanging from his belt, the thugs realized their foe had more than just size on his side, and their expressions grew more prudent.

"Please forgive us. My friend here is wholly unfamiliar with the concept of restraint."

Wriggling in Greco's embrace, Doris forgot her struggles for a moment and turned toward the newcomers only to have her eyes open wide with surprise. The voice had been beautiful, but the man himself positively sparkled.

His age must have been around twenty. He had gorgeous black hair that spilled down to his shoulders, and deep brown eyes that seemed ready to swallow the world, leaving all who beheld them feeling gloriously drunk. The youth was an Asian Apollo. He, along with the giant and two other companions, seated himself at a table.

The only other people in the Black Lagoon aside from Greco and his gang, the newcomers began to amuse themselves with a game of cards. If the keen glint in their eyes was any indication, they had to be traveling Hunters of some confidence.

"What the hell are you fools supposed to be," Greco asked, still holding Doris.

"I am Rei-Ginsei, the Serene Silver Star. My friend here is Golem the Tortureless. We're Behemoth Hunters."

"The hell you are," Greco bellowed, as he looked the four of them over. "You're telling me you hunt those big ol' behemoths with so few people? A baby behemoth can't even be killed without ten or twenty guys." He laughed scornfully. "Granted, you've got that big bastard, but that still leaves you with a sissy boy, a pinhead, and a fucking hunchback. So please help me out here—how exactly does a bunch of rejects like you hunt anyway?"

"We shall show you—here and now," Rei-Ginsei said with his sun-god smile. "But before we do, kindly release the young lady. If she were ugly, it might be another matter, but to treat a beautiful woman in such a manner is a grave breach of etiquette."

"Then why don't you make me stop, you big, bad Hunters?"

The vermilion lips that framed his pearly white teeth bowed with sorrow. "So that's how it's to be then? Very well ..."

"Okay, come on then!"

Greco was used to getting into fights, but the reason he forgot the power of his combat suit and threw Doris aside with all his might may have been because he had some inkling of how the coming battle was going to end.

Unable to prepare for her fall, Doris struck her head on the edge of a table. When she regained consciousness she was held in a pair of powerful arms, and matters had already been settled. "Ow, that hurts," she said, rubbing her forehead.

Rei-Ginsei gave her a gentle smile and swept her up off the floor. "We dealt with those ruffians. I'm not completely clear on the situation here, but I think leaving before the sheriff is summoned might avoid complications."

"Um, yeah, you're right." Due to her throbbing headache her answer was muddled, but Doris noticed the sharp squeak of wood-on-wood behind her and turned around in time to be utterly astonished. Every last one of Greco's hoodlums was laid out on the floor. Despite the pain in her head, Doris was still sharp enough to notice something strange about them almost instantly.

The arms and legs of the two sprawled closest to her on the floor had been bent back against the elbow and knee joints and were twisted into horrific objets d'art. Most likely, the hoodlums had fallen victim to Golem's monstrous strength, but what caught Doris' eye were the remnants of a longsword and a machete lying near them. She wasn't sure about the machete, but the longsword was definitely a high-frequency saber with a built-in sonic frequency wave generator, able to cut through iron plate. Both weapons were shattered down to the hilt as if they'd tried to chop through a block of steel.

Just behind one of the round tables squirmed Greco's right-hand man, O'Reilly. He was known for his skill with a revolver; once, Doris saw him knock a bee out of the air from fifty yards with his quick draw. When she'd seen him last, he was already going for his gun. When one of the four came at him, the barrel of his weapon should have spit flame in less than three-tenths of a second. Yet here he was, sprawled face-down on the floor with his hand still locked around the pistol grip. But what truly made Doris shudder was the location of the wound that felled him. The back of his head was split open. One of the four—well, perhaps not Golem but one of the other three—had got behind him and dealt the blow without giving him the three-tenths of a second he needed to work his quick draw.

Diagonally across from O'Reilly someone else raised his head. Doris felt as if all the blood had drained from her body. The first three thugs who'd been slammed into the wall were still unconscious, and they could be considered lucky for that. The remaining man's face looked like it'd been stung by vicious killer bees—his skin was swollen with dark red pustules that dripped a steady stream of discharge onto the floor. Though Doris didn't notice it at first, at that very moment a black insect crawling across the floor stopped at her feet, scurried a little closer, and then walked right past her as if someone was calling it back. It was a tiny spider. It went from the leather sandals of the hunchback to his leg, then climbed farther up his back to a massive hump, covered by a leather vest. Both the vest and the hump split right down the middle, and the spider disappeared into the fissure. The fissure closed promptly.

"Surprised? I fear it may be too much of a shock for a beautiful young woman like yourself ..."

Doris heard Rei-Ginsei's voice as if from a distance, like the pealing of a bell, for her soul had been stolen when she saw the most frightening outcome of the whole unearthly battle: she saw Greco, the only one unharmed, still seated in his chair with his hands locked around the armrests and the expression of a dead man on his face. The squeak of wood-on-wood she had heard was the sound of his trembling body rattling the legs of the chair against the floor. Whatever he'd witnessed from the safety of his combat suit, it had thrown his eyes wide open, and they reflected nothing but paling terror.

"What'd you guys do?" Doris asked in a firm voice when she finally looked back at Rei-Ginsei and slipped from his arms.

"Not a thing." Rei-Ginsei made a mortified expression. "We simply finished what they started—in our own inimitable style, of course."

"Thank you," Doris said gratefully. "I truly appreciate your help. If you're going to be in town a while, I'd like to do something to thank you later."

"Don't trouble yourself about it. There is nothing in this world more profane than the ugly making the beautiful submit by force. They merely got a taste of heaven's wrath."

"You flatter me, but would you have done the same for another girl if she was being treated the same way?"

"Of course I'd come to her aid. Provided she was beautiful."

Doris averted her eyes from the calmly smiling face of the gorgeous man. "Well, thank you again. Now if you'll excuse me."

"Yes, allow us to take care of this mess. We're well accustomed to it." As Rei-Ginsei nodded jovially, something black gushed into his gaze. "I'm quite sure we'll meet again."

A few minutes later, Doris had the wagon racing back toward the farm.

"Did something happen back there, Sis?"

Her distant expression didn't change at the concerned query from Dan, who rode shotgun. The anxieties running amuck in her mind wouldn't allow her a smile.

She could only expect that Greco would make things even harder for her now, and on top of that she had no guarantee D would be back tonight. She just knew she should've stopped D when he told her he was going into the lord's castle during the day to take advantage of the dhampirs' ability to operate in daylight. If he didn't make it back, they would be left helpless and alone before the Count's next onslaught. She had no proof the Count would come tonight, but she was pretty sure of it. Doris shook her head unconsciously. No, that would mean D was dead.

I know he's coming back, she thought.

Her right hand brushed the nape of her neck. Moments before he'd set out, D had put what he said was a charm on the fang marks there. The charm was disappointingly simple, consisting merely of a light press of the palm of his left hand to the wound; he hadn't even explained what effect it was supposed to have, but it was all Doris had to rely on now.

Another face formed in her mind. That dashing young man in the saloon could also be considered her savior in a way, but Doris felt an ominous shadow fall across her heart. When he'd lifted her from the floor and she saw his handsome visage up close, she had in truth swooned. But her virgin instinct had caught the sickly sweet smell of rotting fruit that lingered around his gorgeous face.

No, most likely it wasn't her instinct that caught it, but rather the work of something firmly etched in a deeper part of her: the visage of a young man more beautiful and more noble than Rei-Ginsei. Doris had a foreboding that the handsome new arrival would prove a greater danger to her than Greco had. That was another of her concerns.

Come back. I don't care if you can't beat the Count, just come back to me.

That these thoughts had nothing to do with her safety was something the seventeen-year-old had not yet noticed.

For the past few minutes, the tepid, waist-deep water had been growing warmer, and the mist licking its way up the stony walls had become denser. He had been walking for thirty minutes now. The drop from the great hall must have been around seventy feet. A vast subterranean aqueduct brimming with water had awaited D. As the water only came up to his chest, it didn't matter much that he'd fallen feet first—what had saved D from a brutal impact was his inhuman skill, and the indisputably superhuman anatomy all dhampirs possessed.

Vampire anatomy—primarily their bones, muscles, and nerves—allowed them to absorb impact and recover from damage hundreds of times better than humans could. While it naturally varied from individual to individual, dhampirs inherited at least fifty percent of those abilities. From a height of seventy feet, a dhampir could probably hit solid ground and survive. It would be nigh impossible to keep from breaking every bone in their body and rupturing some internal organs, but even then some of the faster dhampirs would be able to heal completely in about seventy-two hours.

At any rate, D hadn't been hurt in the least, and he stood chest-deep in the black water surveying his surroundings. This was most likely a pre-existing subterranean cavern that had been buttressed through later construction. Places here and there on the black, rock walls to either side showed signs of being repaired with reinforced concrete. The water throughout was lukewarm, and a pale, white mist lent the air an oppressive humidity. The aqueduct itself was roughly fifteen feet wide. It seemed to be a natural formation, and an odor peculiar to mineral springs had reached D's nostrils even as he was falling into the pit. All around him stretched a world of complete darkness. Only his dhampir eyesight allowed him to distinguish how wide the aqueduct was. He turned his gaze upward, but, not surprisingly, he was unable to discern the trapdoor seventy feet above. As the doors had long since been reset, it was only natural he couldn't see them. And of course there was no means of egress to be seen on the rock walls that boasted mass beyond reckoning.

"What to do, what to do ...," D muttered this rare comment in a deep voice, yet started walking purposefully in the direction from which the water all around him flowed, though the flow was soundless and so gentle as to be imperceptible. Hard and even, the bottom of the aqueduct seemed to be the work of some external force. That wasn't to say that he had merely to walk long enough and far enough for an exit to present itself. He was unaware of *the three sisters* the Count had mentioned so ominously in the chamber far above.

Something was waiting for him.

D was cognizant of that much. And he knew that his thrust had dealt a wound to the Count. There was no way the vampire lord would let such a fearsome opponent just drop into the subterranean waterway and then sit idly by. D was positive some sort of attack was coming. And yet, as he walked along, there was no hesitation in the legs that carried him across the firm bottom of the aqueduct, and no hint of tension or fretfulness in the shining, handsome face that seemed to make the darkness retreat. And then he halted.

About twenty-five feet ahead, the aqueduct grew wider and a number of eerily shaped stones jutted from the water's surface. There alone the mist was oddly thick—or rather, it hung so heavily it seemed to rise from the very waters, twisting the stones into far more outrageous and disturbing shapes and sealing off the waterway. The air bore a foul stench of decay. D's eyes saw a film of oily scum covering the water and white things concealed in the recesses of the stones. Bleached bones. Deep in the mist there was a sharp splash, like a fish flicking its tail up out of the water.

There was something here. Its lair was beyond the eldritch stones.

Still, D showed no sign of turning back, and he continued walking calmly into the mist at the center of the stones. Once inside, the space between the stones looked like a sort of pool or a fishpond. The stones formed rows to either side that completely enclosed the waterway. The water sat stagnant there, blacker than ever, and the white mist eddied savagely. It seemed the source of the mineral springs wasn't too far off. The more he advanced, the greater the number of eldritch stones, and, as the number of bones multiplied, the stench grew ever more overpowering. Most of the bones were from cattle and other livestock, but human remains were also evident. There was a skeleton that, judging from the quiver on his back, looked to be a huntsman, a woman's skull resting in the tattered remnants of a long dress, and the diminutive bones of a child. Many of them hadn't had time to be denuded; dark red meat and entrails hung from their bones, rife with maggots. In this vile, disturbing scene—a scene that would make the average person go mad or stop, paralyzed with fear—D noticed the spines and ribs of all the stark skeletons had been pulverized. This was not the

result of being gnawed by tenacious fangs and jaws. They'd been crushed. Like something had squeezed them tight and twisted them ways they were never meant to go.

Once again, D halted.

There was another splash, this time much closer. The whine of a blade leaving its sheath rose from D's back. At the same time, ripples formed on the surface a few yards ahead of him, and a white mass bobbed to the surface. And just after that, another one bobbed to the right. Then one to the left. Unearthly white in the darkness—they were the heads of carnal, alluring women.

Perhaps D had lost his nerve, because he stood stock-still instead of holding his sword at the ready. The women gazed at him intently. Their facial features were distinct, but all were equally beautiful, and the red lips of the three women twisted into broad grins. Far behind them there was another sharp splash. Perhaps these three swam this way to escape whatever was chasing them? If that was the case, the way they kept all but their heads submerged after meeting D was quite out of the ordinary. And the grins they wore were so evil, so enticing. He looked at them and they at him for a few seconds. With the sound of a torrent of drops, the three women rose in unison. Their heads came up to the height of D's. And then above his—far above.

Who in the human world could imagine such an amazing sight? Three disembodied but beautiful heads smiling down charmingly at him from a height of ten feet. These women had to be the three sisters the Count had mentioned.

At that point, D said softly, "I've heard rumors about you. So you're the Midwich Medusas I take it?"

"Oh, you know of us, do you?" The head in the middle, which would be the eldest sister, wiped the smile from her face. Her voice was like the pealing of a bell, but it also dripped with venom. However, it wasn't the fact that the dashing young man before them seemed to recognized them for what they truly were that gave her voice a ring of surprise, but rather because there wasn't a whit of fear in his words, so far as she could detect.

The Midwich Medusas. These three women—or these three creatures—were supernatural beasts of unrivaled evil that fed on the lust of young men and women. They had devoured hundreds of villagers in a part of the Frontier known as Midwich. Years earlier, they'd supposedly been destroyed by the prayers of an eminently virtuous monk passing through the region, but, unknown to all, they had escaped. After a chance encounter with Count Lee, they agreed to take up residence far below his castle on the condition they received three cows per day. Unlike the faux monsters the Nobility engineered, nothing could be more difficult to destroy than a true demon like this one. The Medusas had survived tens of thousands of years and had even outlived their own legend. Like the hydra of ancient myth, the three heads of the Medusas, which appeared to be separate, were in fact joined a few yards down in a massive pillar of a torso clad with scales of silvery gray that remained sunken in the water. The splashing sounds to their rear came from the end of the torso—a tail that thrashed in delight at finding prey.

But D could only see the women's heads. The reason he knew what they really were was because he'd recognized the heads of three beautiful women as the objects of one of the many bizarre rumors out on the Frontier. But the real question was, why did they melt into the darkness below the neck?

"He's a fine specimen, sisters." The whispers from the head on the right sounded deeply impressed, and she licked her lips. Her red flame of a tongue was slim, and the tip was forked. "At long last, we have a man worthy of our pleasuring. And not just a pretty face, either—look at how muscular he is."

"Sisters, you can't have him first," the third head—the one on the left—declared. "Just five days ago, the two of you fed on the huntsman who wandered in here while I was asleep. This time I shall be first. First to take him to the heights of rapture, and first to taste his blood when he hits that peak."

"The nerve of you! We are your elders," the head on the right—and apparently the second-in-command—bellowed.

"Stop your sibling quarrels," the middle head scolded them, turning to the head on the left. "You may be the first to drink of his blood. However, the three of us shall pleasure him together."

"Yes."

"I'm amenable to that."

Without another word the three heads nodded in agreement. Little flame tongues flicking in and out and the women fondled every inch of D with smitten eyes.

"But be on guard," the oldest sister said quite plainly. "This man does not fear us."

"Rubbish! Could anyone know what we are and not tremble? When we grew angry at our meager repasts and bared our fangs, did not the Count himself beat a hasty retreat, never to return to our realm again?" asked the second sister.

"Even supposing that he is not afraid, what could he do? Manling, can you move?"

D remained silent. In truth, he couldn't move. From the first moment he laid eyes on the women's heads, his whole body had been gripped by countless hands.

"Do you comprehend, manling," the second sister went on. "That's our hair at work."

Exactly. The reason why the necks and torso of the Midwich Medusas melded with the darkness was because everything below their jaws was hidden by black hair that fell in a cascade of tens of thousands of strands, shrouding the rest completely. However, this was no ordinary hair. Once on the water's surface, the strands spread out like tentacles, drifted about, and when they felt the movement of something in the lair, in accordance with the will of the three sisters, they would lure the prey into the center. Then, when the appropriate time came, they could wrap around the victim's limbs in a split second and rob the victim of his freedom with the strength of piano wire.

And that wasn't all. The truth was, it wasn't water that was in the three sisters' stone-bordered den. The eldritch stones diverted the aqueduct and sent the water flowing around either side, while their lair was actually filled with a secretion from the hair itself. The liquid flowed subtly to complement the gently swaying movements of the hair, swirling it around, and even D—with a sense of touch far more sensitive than that of humans—hadn't been alerted to the presence of the strands. Unbeknownst to D, the hair had crept up from his waist and wrapped itself around his wrists and upper arms, as well as his shoulders and neck, completely restraining his limbs.

Even more disturbing, the rest of those countless hands—nay, tentacles—had started slipping in through the cuffs and seams of his clothes, creeping across him, rubbing against his naked flesh, teasing him, plotting to make D a slave of inflamed desire. No matter how resolute their will, a person's reason would dissolve after a few seconds of these delicate movements, reducing them to lust-driven mindlessness—this was the Midwich Medusas' obscene torture, and no one could resist it.

"Well, have you come to crave us?" the oldest sister asked. "Ordinarily, we would take your life at this point. Like so." With her words as their signal, the three heads twisted through the air to part their locks. The black cataract changed its course, and three lengthy necks striped with black and blue, as well as the massive torso that supported them, came into view. The torso was so thick, two grown men would have trouble reaching around it. The long necks swooped down at D, wrapping around and around the powerfully built man held captive by the bonds of their black hair. For its part, the hair continued its tiny wriggling movements below D's clothes.

"We can break your bones whenever it suits us," the oldest sister said, her red eyes ablaze as she stared at D's face. The fire in her eyes was an inferno of lust. "But you're such a gorgeous man. Such a well-proportioned man." Her tongue licked D's cheek.

"Verily. Lo these past three centuries we've not seen one so beautiful." The moist lips of the second sister toyed with D's earlobe from behind. Her hot, rank breath blew into his ear.

"But we won't kill you. The three of us will see to it you taste more than your share of unearthly rapture, and then drain you to the marrow." The youngest sister fairly moaned the words.

The source of the Midwich Medusas' life was not only the energy they derived from the consumption of living organisms. With bizarre abilities only demons possessed, they reduced strapping men and lovely women in the bloom of youth to wanton creatures aching with desire, then imbibed the aura of pure rapture the victims' radiated at their peak—this was the secret of the three sisters' immortality, and this was how they had lived on since before the vampires, since the ancient times when humans ruled.

Of course, that wasn't to say they would feed on just anyone. The sisters were gourmands in their own way. Though the Count had sent hundreds of people into the subterranean world, and still others had wandered in from various entrances, the sisters hadn't tasted pleasure like this for centuries, and had devoured their victims' flesh greedily but joylessly year after year. Now the time had come for pleasure to burn through their shared body once again. A heady blush tinged the three beautiful faces, their eyes danced with flames, and the hot breath spilling from their vermilion lips threatened to melt D's frostily gorgeous visage.

"Well now," the oldest sister fairly moaned. Three sets of damp, bewitching lips closed in on the firm iron gate that was D's mouth.

The instant their lips met his, the sisters saw it. They saw the crimson blood-light glinting from D's eyes. It dealt a mysterious blow to their wicked minds. In that instant, the three sisters felt a sweet thrill racing through their body, the likes of which they'd never experienced before.

"Oh, those lips," the oldest sister said in a husky voice.

"Show me your throats," a low, rusty voice commanded.

Without time to comprehend it was D's voice they heard, the sisters raised their necks as one and brought the slick white base of their throats to D's lips. Something told them there was no other way to snuff the feverish excitement gnawing its way through their bodies. The Midwich Medusas' wits were no longer functioning properly.

"Undo your hair."

D's limbs were immediately set free. His right hand returned his sword to its sheath while his left scooped up a fistful of hair.

"A trap baited with pleasure—but who caught whom?" Before his muttered words had faded, D dropped the strands he held and pulled the three lengthy necks to himself with both arms. "I don't like doing this, but it's the only way to find a way out of here. Someone's waiting for me." As he spoke, his eyebrows suddenly rose and his eyes rolled back. His lips spread wide, exposing a pair of fangs. Brutal and evil, his visage was that of a vampire.

There in the darkness, what happened in the moments that followed?

The cries of the women melded with the repeated splash of their tail beating the water's surface, suggesting unearthly delights had just taken mastery of them. It was the sisters who had blundered into the pleasure-baited trap. Before long, there was the sound of something heavy dropping into the water three times in succession, and then D quickly gave the command: "Arise."

Twisting their torso and serpentine necks, the three sisters rose again. A hollow shadow clung to their countenances, and their bloodshot eyes were as damp as the mist, as desire choked the vitality from them. And it was truly eerie how their glistening, greasy faces were completely bloodless, with a luster like paraffin.

At the base of each of the three necks a pair of deep red dots could be seen. Fang marks.

Who could have known the demonic blood slumbering within D would awaken at the last possible second? He wiped his mouth with the back of his hand. Now, as his gorgeous countenance returned to the cool mountain spring it always was, he commanded the three sisters to lead him to an exit in a voice that resembled a moan of pain.

The three heads bobbed wordlessly in midair, then moved off into the darkness. As D followed them and vanished into the darkness also, a taunting voice could be heard from around his waist. "No matter how you hate it, you can't fight your blood. That's your destiny—and you know it deep in your bones."

In a split second came the response. "Silence! I don't remember telling you to come out! Get back in there!"

The angry shouts clearly belonged to D. So, who had been speaking before ? What could D have meant by those strange expressions? And most of all, why had his ice-cold exterior shattered, even if only for a moment?

While the edge of the plains swallowed the last bit of afterglow from the sunset, and Doris continued waiting for D, Dr. Ferringo's buggy pulled up to her house. Doris was somewhat embarrassed, and tried to get the doctor to leave. Doctors were far too precious on the Frontier for her to put one in such danger. After all, this fight was hers and hers alone. She'd mixed a sedative in with Dan's dinner and he was already fast asleep. That was probably the best thing to do with him, since a Noble stalking their prey wouldn't even spare a glance at anyone who wasn't in their way.

"Um, Doc, I'm a little busy today with stuff here on the farm," Doris called preemptively from the porch.

But the doctor responded, "That's quite all right, I don't mind. I was just out on a house call—could I trouble you for a glass of water?" Dispelling her objections with a wave of his hands, he went ahead and opened the door, trotted into the living room, and installed himself on the sofa.

He'd been a friend of her late father, he'd brought Doris and Dan into the world with his own two hands, and since the death of their parents to this very day, he'd helped them in countless ways. Because of this, Doris couldn't very well toss him out on his ear. To make matters worse, for some reason he began to recount his youthful adventures battling supernatural creatures—or "the damned things," as he liked to call them—and Doris had no recourse but to sit and listen attentively. He must've been aware the Noble would most likely be coming for her, so she had to wonder why he seemed so dead set on hanging around.

Night rolled closer with each passing minute, and D wasn't back yet. The moment the sun set, Doris resolved to fight alone. All the armaments and traps spread across the farm had been double-checked, but she only grew more afraid. And now she had not only herself but the physician to worry about as well.

No matter what happens to me, I've got to protect Doc at all costs. Please, don't let him strike till after Doc has gone. As she made this wish, another concern annoyingly crept up on her.

No matter what happens, I can't let myself think about that. If he makes me one of them, what'll happen to Dan? He can't live the rest of his life knowing his only blood relative is one of the Nobility—that's just too big a burden to carry. Nothing doing, Doris. Get your arms and legs ripped off trying if you have to, but fight that bastard off. The bravery she mustered only lasted a heartbeat before sinking into the shadow of her fears. Coupled with centuries of psychological conditioning, the horror of actually falling victim to the pernicious fangs of the Nobility had more than enough dark power to daunt a young girl of seventeen, no matter how distinguished a fighter she may have been.

When the hands on the clock indicated nine thirty Night, Doris finally came out with it. "Well, Doc, I think I'm gonna turn in now." *So please hurry up and go home*—this much Doris implied, but Dr. Ferringo showed no signs of rising. Instead, he said something that shocked her senseless.

"You'll have a dangerous customer paying you a call real soon."

"That's right, Doc, so you'd best be on your way—"

"My, but you are a sweetie," the elderly physician said, showering her with a gaze of boundless affection. "But there's a time and a place for restraint. You don't have to be that way with me. Seventeen years ago, I brought you into this world with my own two hands, and you've always been like a daughter to me, haven't you? Now this old fool ain't the sort to just stand by while a young lady does battle with a demon straight from hell." As Doris stood at the door to the living room watching the old man, her eyes glistened softly with tears. "Don't look so down in the mouth," the old man said jovially. "I may not look it, but it was yours truly that taught your father the tricks of the Werewolf Hunting trade."

"I know that. It's just—"

"If you know it, then why don't you stop your blubbering? Of course, it is interesting to see a little spitfire like you squirt a few tears from time to time. Anyway, where's that young fellow? You hired him for protection, but when night started coming on, he probably took to his heels, I suppose. He was a spooky character, that one, but he turned out to be a worthless drifter, did he?"

"No, he didn't!" Up to that point Doris stood silently, touched by his words and nodding in agreement, but this sudden about-face, and her exclamation, made the elderly physician jump in his seat. "That's not the sort of man ... uh, I mean, he's not the kind to do that. No, sir. The reason he's not here tonight is because he went into the Count's castle alone. And he hasn't come back yet. I just ... Something's happened to him, I just know it ..."

An ineffable light sparked in Dr. Ferringo's eyes. "So you were kind of ... Now I see ... I didn't know you felt that way about him."

Doris regained her composure and hastily wiped at her tears. "What do you mean by that? It's not like I ... I mean ..."

The physician grinned at the young girl as a rosy blush suffused her face. Then he made a gentle wave of his hands. "Okay, okay. My mistake. If you think that much of him, then we needn't worry about him. I'm sure he'll be back soon. Until he does, what do you say to working up the nerve to capture the Count?"

"Sure," Doris said with a cheery nod, then suddenly, with great apprehension, she asked, "How are we gonna do that?"

There was no precedent for a human capturing a member of the Nobility—a vampire. Battles between the two species were normally a matter of kill or be killed. It went without saying that one side ended up dead more often than not. Particularly when doing battle at night, in the Nobility's element, the respective weapons and abilities of the combatants made the outcome painfully obvious.

"With this." The elderly physician produced a small glass bottle from his faithful medical bag. It was filled to its corked neck with yellowish granules.

"What in the world is that?" Doris' tone was a jumble of expectation and misgivings.

Dr. Ferringo didn't answer, but rather pulled a battered envelope from the same bag and unfolded the letter it contained. He held it out to Doris.

The second she laid eyes on the characters scrawled in sap-based ink on the yellowed paper, Doris turned to the physician with a perplexed expression. "This handwriting ... My father wrote this ..."

His hoary head bobbed in agreement. "Your dear father used to send me these while he was out on the road honing his fighting skills, back before your brother and you were born. But this was the last of them. If you read it, you'll see that it relates an encounter between your father and a vampire."

"My father and a vampire?" Doris forgot everything else and began poring over the letter. The first sentence or two informed the reader he'd arrived at his lodging. Then, the very characters themselves became jumbled with excitement and fear.

I've found it. The bastard's weakness is a t ...

That was all there was. After the last character, the rest of the sheet was just a lonely expanse of rough, yellowed paper. Doris fixed a confused gaze on the elderly physician. "Why didn't my father finish what he was writing? Was there anything in any of his other letters?"

The physician shook his head. "While your father was writing that letter in his lodgings, he was attacked by a vampire, but he fended it off. There can be no doubt your father somehow discovered some weakness of theirs. That much he stated plainly in another letter. The point is, he fought off the fiend, put his mind to order, and had just taken up a pen to record his discovery when he realized he'd completely forgotten what that discovery was."

"Are you serious? How could that happen?"

"I'll address that later. At any rate, less than five minutes after the danger had passed, your father found himself standing like a zombie with a pen in his hand. Like a man possessed, he sifted through his memories, wracked his brain, and eventually even tried to reenact his own half of the engagement, but all his efforts were for naught. The vampire appeared and they scuffled. Then, when all hope seemed lost, he narrowly managed to make his foe take flight—that much he could clearly recall, but the form of that decisive attack and manner in which he'd learned it were completely expunged from his memory."

"But why? How did that happen?"

Ignoring the same question from Doris a second time, the physician went on. "We had that last little 't' as a hint, but your father never did figure out what that was supposed to stand for. He wrote again about how the situation developed in another letter and sent it along to me, entrusting me to make something out of it. Unfortunately, I failed to live up to his expectations ..."

"Well if that's the case," Doris said, completely forgetting the danger creeping steadily closer and whipping herself into a frenzy, "all we have to do is solve the mystery of the little 't' to find out what the Nobility's weakness is, right?" Her voice trembled with expectation, but it quickly withered. She recognized that the shadow clinging to the face of the elderly physician said that the situation was not merely grave, but close to hopeless.

In the past, attempts to learn a definitive way to protect themselves from vampires had been tried time and again, but all of them had proved fruitless. Though humans must have had ample opportunity to learn that secret in the countless conflicts that raged ever since their species lost the right to rule the world, not one such method had been passed down to posterity. Now, ages had passed since anyone had even tried to discover them.

"The Nobility is going to beat us after all, aren't they? I mean, if they don't have any weaknesses ... "

As Dr. Ferringo heard Doris' words crawling across the floor like a beaten dog, he shook his head and stated firmly, "No. If that were the case, we wouldn't have these rumors being passed down all these years that there are things that can hurt them. Didn't your own father state he managed to drive a vampire off in some manner or other? Your father wouldn't have lied to save his own life. I've heard tell of knights and travelers who've had experiences similar to his, and I've even spoken to a few in person."

"And did you find out anything?"

"No, all of them had the same thing happen that your father did. They escaped the loathsome fangs of the fiend by some means ... or rather, they forced the fiend to escape. And yet, despite that, not one of them could recall anything at all about what they'd done."

Doris was speechless.

"More recently, I've been tempted to view these rumors of a weakness in the Nobility as legends born of wishful thinking, but I plowed through a mountain of records, and based on the actual cases I could assemble, I'm positive that a weakness does in fact exist. People simply can't remember what it is. In my view, it's a kind of manipulation of our memories."

"Manipulation of our memories?" Doris knit her brow.

"To be more precise, perhaps we could call it a selective and automatic editing of our memories. To wit, our minds have been programmed to automatically erase all memories of a certain kind."

"You mean, memories of their weaknesses? Of weapons that can drive them off?" Unconsciously, Doris was trying to peek inside the old man's head. Was that what the powder in the bottle really was?

Watched by eyes that were a battlefield between hope and uncertainty, the physician went on undeterred. "Remember, we're talking about the bastards who ruled the world for ten thousand years. I'm sure it would be mere child's play for them to alter human DNA and reprogram our minds to selectively weed out any memories of those sorts. That's a theory that's been around for quite some time, and based on my own research, I've taken up with that camp. I'm not usually the type to go along with theories when I don't know the folks behind them, but what's right is right. That being the case, the rest is simple."

"The rest being?"

"All we have to do is bring those memories back."

Doris gasped. "Can you really do that?"

The physician looked very pleased with himself as he rolled the bottle in question in the palm of his hand. "Here we have the fruit of that very endeavor. I hypnotized a dozen of the men and women I interviewed, and tried to regress them with the help of reenactment-stimulating drugs I procured from the Capital. What I have here is something two of them mentioned. You see, even with all their science, the creatures of the night couldn't completely erase our memories."

Doris noticed that the physician seemed to hesitate at the last sentence, but couldn't fathom why. She pursued a different matter instead. "But if what you say is true, Doc, won't the two of us lose all memory of that powder soon?"

"No, I've been fine so far. Again, this is purely a hypothesis, but the loss of memory only occurs when the subconscious mind has actual proof that we've discovered a weakness of the damned Nobility. In our heart of hearts, neither you nor I completely believe in the efficacy of this powder. As a result, the enemies' programming hasn't gone into action, either."

"Then why don't we just write it down somewhere?"

"That wouldn't do any good. On reading it, even the person who wrote it would take it as the deluded ravings of a madman."

A somewhat deflated Doris changed her tack. "So is that powder the same little 't' thing that was in my father's letter?"

Once again the physician shook his head. "I'm afraid not. I've given the matter much consideration, but I simply can't connect the powder with that initial. Some might say your father, overwhelmed by the excitement of this great discovery, miswrote it, but I don't believe that's the case. The reason I don't is because most of the other interviewees failed to mention the powder as well. I think it's safe to assume the letter 't' refers to something else entirely."

"But if some of them could remember the powder, why didn't they remember the other thing?"

Dr. Ferringo faltered. And then he began to speak in the gravest tone Doris had ever heard. "I've always felt there was something somewhat ironic about human/Nobility relations—in the Nobility's view of humanity, to be specific. In your present circumstances, I can't expect you to appreciate this, but they may well feel a kind of affection toward us."

"What the hell! The Nobles think they're our friends? That's ridiculous!"

Rougher than her tone was the way Doris' hand tugged at the scarf around her neck. For the first time in her life, she glared at the elderly physician. "I don't care who you are, Doc, that's ... I just don't have the words ... "

"Don't pull such a face." The physician waved his hands in an attempt at placating her. "By no means is that to say all of the Nobility feel that way. Any examination of the historical facts will show that, in the preponderance of cases, they don't demonstrate affection, but rather act as if human beings were lower than machines. Emotionally speaking—if we assume for a moment that they indeed have emotions—as much as ninety-nine percent of them are no different from the lord who attacked you. But it's very difficult to discount the possibility that the other one percent exists. I'll have to relate all the facts I've unearthed to you another day ..."

Am I gonna see another day? Doris wondered. Beyond the window, something evil was on its way, tearing through the pleasantly sweet air of the spring-like evening.

Dr. Ferringo wasn't looking at Doris any longer. His eyes seemed nailed to a spot on the floor as he continued to expound on long-held suspicions. "For example, why would they make distinctions between their weaknesses and the weapons that exploit them? Why did some memory of this powder remain when it could've been erased as completely as whatever the 't' stands for? My guess is that compared to this 't' thing, the powder is a minor hindrance, at best. Could it be the bastards are just teasing us? Is this our masters saying, 'Let them have a minor weakness like this,' as they throw us a bone? If that's the case, then why not make it common knowledge from the start?" Here

Dr. Ferringo's words trailed off. Pausing a beat, he added, "This is the conclusion I've come to after a humble little investigation that's occupied half this old fool's sixty years—I take this as a challenge from a race that reached the pinnacle and now slides toward extinction. It's a challenge being offered to us humans, a race that can't even begin to be measured against them. But we may eventually rise to their level, or perhaps even surpass them. And I believe this is what they say: 'If you humans want to inherit our throne, then try to beat us into submission by your own power. If you have the powder, then try to solve the mystery of the 't' thing. And when you've solved it, try to prevent it from being shrouded again in the mists of forgetfulness.'"

"That's impossible ..." To Doris, the words spilling from her own lips sounded a million miles away. "That'd make them just like an instructor breaking in a Hunter trainee ..."

Though he gave a slight nod, it was unclear if the elderly physician truly fathomed Doris' words. His gaze didn't deviate in the least as he said, "This isn't something the Lesser Nobility would be capable of. It may well be ..."

"It may well be what?"

"Him. All the true Nobility in the world were united under the thousand Greater Nobility, the seven Kings, and the legendary dark lord who ruled them all—the great vampire, the king of kings, Dra—"

At that moment, a wave of tension swept into Doris' countenance. "Doc!" she shouted, but it sounded more like a cry for help than a warning. Snapping back to reality, the physician turned his head to follow Doris as she made for the living room window.

The light of the moon on the cool plains showed no signs of anything on the move, but the ears of both caught the sounds of wagon wheels and hooves pounding distant terrain.

"Looks like he's coming."

"I've got a hell of a welcome party set up for him." Though she'd reclaimed the stalwart mien of an Amazon, in her heart of hearts the girl let a plaintive cry escape.

You didn't make it back in time after all, D.

The black cyborgs seemed to run on unearthly clouds, and, when their hoofbeats echoed so close that it was impossible Doris was mistaken, she went to the other side of the living room and twisted one of the silver ceremonial masks adorning the wall to the right.

With a dim sound, part of the floor and wall rotated and pulled out of sight. In a matter of seconds, a wooden control-console and armchair appeared. Though the control console itself was wood, the switch- and lever-dotted top was iron, with a riot of colored lamps and gauges adding to the confusion. This was a combat control center—Doris' father had summoned a craftsman all the way from the Capital to install it. Every weapon on the farm could be controlled from here. As far as being prepared for the attacks by the creatures that ran rampant in the wild, this was about as good as money could buy. A full-field prismatic scope lowered from the ceiling.

"Ha! Back in those days, I asked your father what kind of work he was having done, and he told me he was having a new solar converter put in. Your father was a sly one to even keep this from me."

There wasn't time to respond to the recollections of the still-easygoing physician. The prismatic lens of the view scope showed a black carriage drawn by a team of four horses coming down the road to the farm at full speed. Doris' hand reached for one of the levers. The view scope doubled as a targeting system.

"Steady," Dr. Ferringo told her as he peered out the window, the little bottle in his hand. "You've still got the electromagnetic barrier." Before he had finished speaking, the triple-barred, wooden gate opened without a whisper. As the black carriage was about to sprint through the gate with a gust of wind, it was enveloped by a blinding flash of light.

Powerful enough to char a lesser dragon through tough scales otherwise impervious to blades, the electromagnetic barrier set off a shower of sparks that turned blackest night to brightest day for a fleeting moment. Bursting through a giant, white-hot blossom of fire, the ball of white light forced its way onto the farm. The horse, the driver, the wagon wheels—white flames clung to them all. It was an outlandish sight, like a carriage from hell that had suddenly appeared on earth.

"They're through. What in the world?..." Doris' puzzled exclamation came as she watched the cyborg horses—as soon as they'd broken through the barrier, she'd expected the four of them to tear right into her front yard like a veritable hurricane, but not a single hoof was out of step as they executed a brilliant stop right on the spot.

The magnetic flames swirling around them quickly dispersed. The enemy was protected by a more powerful barrier.

"Not yet. Look! He's getting out!" Once again, her hand was checked by the physician's hopeful command, but in his voice Doris caught a ring of both tension and fear that outweighed the former emotion by far. Embodiment of courage and intellect that the elderly physician was, the damage of scores of centuries of brainwashing by the Nobility had seeped well into his subconscious.

The black door opened, and a massive figure garbed in sable trod down steps that automatically projected onto the ground.

"He must be some kind of idiot—look at him, jumping out like he doesn't have a care in the world."

Ostensibly encouraged, Doris' voice still lacked strength. Her foe knew that any defenses she might be ready to spring on him would pose no threat. When the villain that had left his filthy mark on her neck bared his pearly fangs in a grin and started toward the house alone, Doris pulled the lever.

All over the farm there was the sound of one spring releasing after another. Black chunks flew through the air toward the Count, only to bounce back inches shy of him. What fell to the ground were boulders a good four feet in diameter. Fired in rapid succession, all of the rocky missiles were robbed of their kinetic energy by an invisible barrier, falling around the calmly advancing Count.

"Just as I thought—he's no pushover." Doris pulled a second lever. This time it was steel javelins the launchers disgorged. All of the first ten bounced off him, but the eleventh and final javelin pierced the Count's abdomen.

"I got him!" Doris exclaimed, squeezing the lever so hard she threatened to break it. What froze her smile was the way the temporarily motionless Count gave a horrible grin before he resumed his deliberate stride, the steel javelin still protruding from his stomach and back.

The bastard's trying to tell me he doesn't even need his force field to stop my attacks!

It felt like an icy paw of fear was stirring her brains as Doris suddenly realized that there was no need for a vampire to "go get" a former victim. For those who'd felt the kiss of blood on their neck but once, a single word from a fiend outside their door would suffice to call them out into the waiting arms of Death. That was precisely the sort of thing D was guarding against when he rendered her unconscious the first time she had unwanted guests.

"He's toying with me!" Doris pushed and pulled levers like a woman possessed. So long as nothing pierced its heart, a vampire would not die. Though undoubtedly aware of this immutable fact, seeing the fearsome power in action with her own two eyes had completely robbed the girl of the cool judgment the daughter of a skilled Hunter should possess. She was robbed of her reason by the same fear that slumbered in all mortals, the fear of unknowable darkness.

Machine guns concealed in the shrubbery spat fire, and explosive-tipped arrows set aflame by a lens on the solar storage unit fell like rain.

Through the oily smoke, the fiery explosions, and the deafening roar that surrounded him, the Count grinned. It was clear this was the stiffest resistance humanity could currently offer. Their kind remained on earth, tough as cockroaches, while his species slid silently and inevitably toward extinction, dwindling like the light of the setting sun.

Suddenly, his anger flared, consuming all the admiration he'd felt for the resistance his prey offered. His eyes became flame. As he gnashed his naked fangs together, the Count dashed to the porch, took the stairs in a single leap, yanked the javelin from his abdomen, and heaved the weapon at the door. The door burst off its hinges and toppled into the house. Beyond the door hung a black, iron netting. The instant he heedlessly thrust the steel javelin into it to sweep it out of his way, there was a flash at the point of contact, and the Count felt a violent burning sensation flowing into his body through the hand he had around the weapon. For the first time, the flesh beneath his black raiment shuddered in agony, and his hair stood on end. The vampire's accursed regenerative abilities did their best to counteract the vicious electric shock, and then set to adjusting the molecular arrangement of the cells that needed to be removed. The shock he received came from a transformer that converted energy collected in the solar panels on the roof by day into a high-tension load of fifty-thousand volts. Even as he felt his cells charred and nerves destroyed by the precipitous electrical shock, the Count swung the javelin. With a parting gift of fresh agony and a shower of sparks, the conductive net of interlaced wire tore and fell to the floor.

"Well done for a lone woman," the Count muttered with admiration, his eyes bloodshot. "She's every bit the fighter I thought she'd be. Child, I must have your blood at all costs. Wait for me."

Doris knew she had exhausted all means at her disposal. As the monitor was switched to the interior of the house, the visage of a thirsting demon filled the screen. Suddenly the living room door was knocked back into the room. Doris leapt up from the control console and stood in front of Dr. Ferringo to shield him.

"Child," the figure in the doorway said, "while you fight admirably for a woman, the battle is done. You must favor me with a taste of your hot blood."

The snap of a whip split the air.

"Come," the Count commanded in a penetrating voice.

The tip of her whip lost its impetus in midair, and the weapon fell to the floor in coils. Doris began walking with the shaky steps of a marionette, but the elderly physician grabbed her shoulder. His right hand covered her nostrils, and the young woman slumped to the floor without a sound. The physician had kept a chloroform-soaked cloth concealed in his hand all along.

"So you intend to interfere with me, old fool?" the Count asked in a stark, white voice devoid of all emotion.

"Well, I can't stand back and do nothing," the old man responded, stepping forward with his left hand clenched. "Here's something you hate—garlic powder."

A wave of unrest passed across the Count's face, but he soon gave a broad grin. "You should be complimented on your discovery—but you truly are foolish. True enough, I am powerless against that scent. You may slip through my grasp this night. But the instant you confirm how effective it is against me, that confirmation shall cost you all memory of the very thing you hold in your hand. And tomorrow evening I shall come again."

"I'm not gonna let you do that."

"Oh, and what shall you do?"

"This old fool had a life once, too. Thirty years back, Sam Ferringo was known as something of an Arachni-man Hunter. And I know a thing or two as well about how to do battle with your kind."

"I see." There was a glint in the Count's eyes.

The elderly physician gave a wave of his hand. Powder and a strange odor swirled through the air.

Gagging, the vampire reeled back with his cape over his nose and mouth. He was struck with a horrible urge to vomit. He felt utterly enervated, as if his brains were melting and life itself was draining from his body. The cells in his sinus cavity—the olfactory nerves that make the sense of smell possible—were dealt a devastating blow by the allicin that gives garlic its distinctive aroma.

"Your kinds' days are over. Back to the world of darkness and destruction with you!" At some point, Dr. Ferringo had pulled out a foot-long stake. With the rough wooden weapon in his right hand, the physician advanced. Right before his eyes, a black bird snapped its wings open. It was the Count's cape. Like a sentient being, it wrapped around the elderly physician's wrists, then swept around wildly to hurl the man clear across the room—all without the Count appearing to lift a finger. This was one of the secret tricks of the Nobility. The Count had learned it from no less than the Sacred Ancestor of his race.

Scrambling desperately to rise from the floor, the elderly physician was horrified to see the still wildly coughing Count climbing onto Doris.

"Wait!"

The Count's face eclipsed part of the girl's throat.

What the physician saw astonished him.

The Count fell backward, his face pale. Perhaps no one had ever seen a Noble wear such an expression of stark terror as the elderly physician now witnessed. Ignoring the awestruck physician, the figure in black disappeared through the door, his cape fluttering behind him.

When the elderly physician finally got to his feet, rubbing his hip all the while, he could hear the echo of wagon wheels fading into the distance. *Somehow or other, it looks like we're out of the woods for now.* Just as this tremendous feeling of relief welled up inside him, Dr. Ferringo suddenly got the feeling he'd forgotten something important and cocked his head to one side. *What in the blazes is that smell? And why did that bastard take to his heels?*

Soaring Shrike-Blades of Death

A s soon as the sun was up the next morning, Doris entrusted the still slumbering Dan to the elderly physician and left the farm. "Are you dead set on going? Even supposing he's still alive, you've got no idea whether or not you'll find him." Doc was referring to D, of course. Doris kept her silence and smiled. It wasn't a disheartened smile. She'd save him all right, even if it killed her. That was the conviction that bolstered her smile.

"Don't worry, we'll be back for sure. Take care of Dan for me." And with that, she wheeled her horse around toward the vampires' castle.

She was scared. She'd already felt the vampire's baleful fangs once, and had nearly been attacked again scant hours earlier. And she'd already lost all memory of the effectiveness of garlic. Having heard from Dr. Ferringo that the Count had run off for some unknown reason, Doris assured herself the powder really had worked. As soon as she came to believe it, however, every memory of the powder was purged from her brain. In its place, Doris remembered how the previous night, the fearsome Noble dealt with every attack she threw at him like it was mere child's play. The memory of it was etched vividly in her mind.

She couldn't beat him. There was no way to stop him.

While she raced across the plains with a display of equestrian skill that would put any man to shame, her heart was poised to drop into a pit of the darkest despair until the innocent face of her brother Dan caught her and pulled her back. *Don't worry, your big sister ain't about to let that bastard get the best of her. I'll bring D back, and then we'll get rid of the lot of them,* she thought.

Beyond Dan's face, another face flickered. Colder than that of the Count, a visage so exquisite it gave her goose bumps.

Be alive. I don't care how bad you're hurt, just please still be alive.

E ven after the weather controller's "comfort-control time" was over, the chill-laden morn on the prairie was so beautiful and charged with vitality that the green of the landscape took on a deeper hue. A dozen men on horseback, looking like they'd ridden hard all night, kicked up a cloud of dust as they came to an abrupt halt on a road traversed only by a pleasant morning breeze. The road ran on into the village of Ransylva, stitching its way between prairies of waist-high grass. Seventy feet ahead, four figures had sprung from the undergrowth and now stood in the middle of the road, blocking the traveler's way.

"What the hell are you trying to prove?!"

"We're the Frontier Defense Force, dispatched on orders from the Capital. Out of our way!" The eyes of the second man to shout narrowed cautiously. The outlandish appearance of this foursome touched on remembered dangers.

"A girlish little punk, a big freaking bastard, a bag of bones with a pointed head, and a hunchback—you pricks wouldn't happen to be the Fiend Corps would you?"

"An excellent deduction," Rei-Ginsei said with a grin wholly befitting the lush, green morning. With that gem of a smile, it was hard to imagine this dashing youth as the head of the brutal bandit gang that had terrorized the northern part of the Frontier. "We came down here to make a little money after our faces got a wee bit too well known up north, but before we can even get started, it comes to our attention you boys are going from village to village posting warrants for us, so we decided to wait for you out here. Kindly refrain from doing anything untoward."

To the man, the members of the FDF were enraged by his insolent tone. The solemn-faced man who was apparently their commander barked, "Shut your damn flap! We made double-time to Pedros after we got word you pricks had been seen in town there, but we just barely missed you, much to our regret. I can't believe our luck. You clowns just jumped into our laps. We're busting you right here. I don't care if you're the meanest bandits to ever walk the earth, you've all gotta be soft in the head. You know, we're the fucking Frontier Defense Force, dumbass!" His self-confidence wasn't a bluff. Dispatched by the Capital at regular intervals to police the entire Frontier, the FDF had been trained to combat all manner of beasts and creatures. They were equipped with serious firepower, and in a fight, each and every one of them was worth a platoon of normal men.

Heavy metallic clinks echoed from the saddles of the squad members serried behind him. That was the sound of shells being automatically fed into the recoilless bazookas each man was issued. The squad members already had Rei-Ginsei and his group in the unswerving sights of their laser rifles. No matter how the bandits' battle in the saloon the previous day had defied imagining, it seemed unlikely that mortal men like themselves could weather the FDF's assault.

"How does this strike you—since you went to all the trouble of turning yourselves in, we'll let you throw down your weapons, okay? That way you'll at least get to go on living till they get you up on the hangman's scaffold," said the commander.

"I don't fancy that."

"Why, you little punk!"

"By all means, shoot me if it'll make you feel any better. But before you do, there's one thing you seem to be forgetting."

The commander knit his brow in consternation. "The Fiend Corps is not a quartet," Rei-Ginsei said in an exquisite voice.

"What?!"

A stir ran through the FDF members. At some point, the foursome had taken their eyes off the FDF and turned them straight to the side.

"We have a guardian angel the rest of the world knows nothing about." Still looking off to the side, Rei-Ginsei pulled the corner of his lips up sharply. His was the devil's own smile. "Oh, here it comes now!" When an unremitting source of terror to the human body and soul appeared right in front of them, the degree of shock each of the victims felt seemed to be directly dependent on their proximity to it.

The instant *the thing* materialized from thin air, hovering over the commander's horse, the leader died of shock, and the five FDF members within ten feet of him went insane. And that wasn't all. Apparently even animals could see the thing, or perhaps they could sense its troubling presence; the lead horses forgot all about running away, but instead dropped to a spasming heap on the ground, frothing from the nose and mouth. The rest of the steeds reared up.

Most likely, the FDF members who fell from their mounts as a result didn't cry out because part of their psyches had already been shattered. Some of them had their heads staved by the hooves of the rampaging horses, while others seemed frozen as they watched it coming closer and closer.

The thing leisurely made its way from one survivor to the next, touching each of the members in turn.

The Capital's greatest fighting men quietly died of madness, powerless to stop it.

"Well, what do you think? The fifth member of the Fiend Corps is quite the looker, isn't it?"

The last member of the FDF was crawling across the ground, but as he listened to Rei-Ginsei's sardonic laughter *the thing* suddenly vanished without a trace.

"What the—?!"

As the startled Rei-Ginsei looked over his shoulder, the sole surviving FDF member trained his laser rifle on the bandit's forehead. Thanks to a Spartan training regime, he could still muster murderous intent toward the enemy despite his insanity.

"Boss!"

Before Golem could move, a beam of red light pierced Rei-Ginsei's brow.

However, it was the FDF member who jerked backwards. Incredibly, the laser beam that hit Rei-Ginsei right between the eyes burst out of the back of the other man's head. A stench of seared flesh and brains hung in the otherwise refreshing air.

"Are you okay, boss?" the man with the pointed head asked as he cast a loathsome gaze on the soldiers littering the ground. Not merely his head, but the man's entire frame was streamlined like a shooting-star class rocket. He was called Gimlet.

"I believe I'll survive," Rei-Ginsei laughed, rubbing his forehead. There was a black circle about a quarter inch in diameter scorched right between his eyebrows.

While the others inquired no further after his condition, the four fiends looked at each other with concern over another suspicious occurrence.

"Something must've happened to Witch," said the hunchbacked man.

"Chullah's right," Rei-Ginsei chimed in. "The only reason I made such a blunder is because I never in a million years imagined that *thing* just disappearing in the middle of an operation." He certainly had a strange way of covering his blunders. Turning back to the expanse of prairie to his left, he muttered, "If one of her spells should break at her age, she'll be walking the cold, dark road to hell ..."

"Would you like me to go check it out?" asked Gimlet.

He shook his fine head from side to side. "No, I shall look into this. The rest of you kindly dispose of these unsightly remains. Burn them or eat them, whichever suits your fancy," he said, smiling at his disturbing orders.

And this is what was happening while the gruesome battle neared its conclusion, or rather, to be precise, just before the sudden disappearance of *the thing* that had materialized from thin air.

Racing across the plains, Doris was just about to turn her steed in a new direction when she discovered something unexpected in someplace unimaginable and jerked her horse's reins in the opposite direction instead. The spot was less than a mile and a quarter from Count Lee's castle. Bypassing the more circuitous roads, she'd galloped straight through a hilly region, but from here on out, she'd have to take a somewhat less direct route.

Her father had brought her here just once when she was little and she'd seen it from a distance then, but she'd never seen the place from this close before. Half of her frightened, the other half deadly serious, she took in the mysterious scenery stretching out in the morning light. The villagers called this place The Devil's Quarry. In this part of the endless expanse of prairie, there were countless statues standing like stone forests, or laying on the ground and looking to the heavens. No two had the same face or form, and there wasn't a single statue that didn't have the aspect of some bizarre monstrosity. A sculpture of a baldheaded man with incredibly large eyes, a bust of a creature with dozens of arms baring its fangs, a full-length statue with thousands of beastly bristles each individually carved—all these pieces of incomparably detailed craftsmanship were covered with moss, as were the remnants of stone walls and columns that called to mind the ruins of some ancient citadel. Together, they seemed to form a completely alien dimension. Even the morning sunlight, that should've breathed life into every hill and valley in the world, lent the faces of the sculptures weirder shadows than it might have, as the particles of light were swallowed by the moss and the desolate atmosphere, or sank with leaden weight. Even the air was dank. People said this was the place where the Nobility had once held their wretched ceremonies, or a quarry used in the construction of the castle, but the latter theory was easily dismissed. After all, there wasn't any stone in this whole region to be quarried. At any rate, this was a forbidden area, and no one from the village ever entered.

What had caught Doris' eye was an old woman seated in a deep, bowl-shaped depression near the center of the Devil's Quarry doing the same baffling gestures over and over. Her age was unclear. Judging by her gray hair and the wrinkles creasing her yellowed skin, both of which were obvious even at this distance, she looked to be nearly a hundred, and yet her body seemed strangely imbued with vitality.

What is this? Some old lady lost in her travels, taking a breather?

Even if Doris couldn't bring her all the way into town, she could at least give the woman directions back to the main road. But as Doris was just about to give her mount a flick of the reins, she stayed her hand and quietly slipped down to the ground instead.

Wrapped in a dull gray overcoat, the crone's torso was bent forward at an extreme angle, and there was something about the sight of her—with eyes fixed on her own fingertips as they clutched at nothing—that just felt evil. Of course, Doris was completely unaware that at that very moment on the road a few miles distant, a strange entity that appeared out of thin air was busy delivering death by insanity to the members of the FDF.

Muffling her own footfalls as she led her horse, Doris made her way into the Devil's Quarry, tethered her mount to a nearby pillar, and came up behind the crone. Apparently the old woman didn't notice, as she didn't move at all. As Doris drew closer, she felt goose bumps spread across her flesh.

A poisonous miasma was rising from the crone's vicinity. Clearly she was using some arcane skill toward foul ends. The sound of a low voice chanting a spell reached Doris' ears.

"Stop that!" she shouted despite herself as she took a few steps forward. At that instant, something whizzed out of the bushes and glanced off her cheek. Doris dropped to the ground with lightning speed. Holding her breath and remaining alert, she touched her left hand to her cheek. Warm blood clung to her fingertips.

A spirit beast, eh? Looks like she's got her warded zone set up right around here, Doris thought.

To her left, Doris felt a keen presence. She made a quick combat roll to one side and let fly with the whip in her right hand. Unfortunately, her deadly strike only kicked grass into the air, but she sensed her opponent changing direction to fall back a good distance.

When conjurers and sorcerers worked their art, they established an area around themselves with a radius of ten or so feet in order to have the best chances of success. This was known as their warded zone. Since their concentration might be disturbed, and, in extreme cases, their spell might even lose its efficacy if someone were to step into this zone while they were working, sorcerers conjured up creatures and set them as watch dogs outside the warded zone, ready to attack intruders. The task often fell to massive hounds, poisonous toads, and serpents suckled on pure malice, but this crone used a transparent creature formed of her own force of will—a spirit beast. And a particularly nasty one at that.

Doris was well aware the only thing that had saved her was the superb reflex of a trained Hunter. The average person would've had their throat torn open a few seconds ago. In her heart, she whispered thanks to her father. "It's forty feet to the old lady. Guess this calls for a bit of trickery," Doris muttered to herself. This dangerous gamble was her only choice. She had no idea what kind of misery her opponent could be causing with her spell.

Once again, her whip mowed through open air right toward the crone.

Slashing through the air, the spirit beast attacked Doris. At that moment, her whip snapped back. An instant later, she could feel something in the air rip in half. The air was suddenly flooded with a choking malevolence, but it dispersed quickly enough.

"Waagh!"

The scream that escaped the crone as she doubled over made Doris leap to her feet in the brush. Doris had drawn the spirit beast out by appearing to attack the crone, then used a flick of her wrist to turn the blow on the beast at the last possible second. Of course, if her timing had been off by a split second, Doris would have been the one to die.

Her suicidal gamble had paid off, but it had also had an unforeseen side effect. Because the crone had created the spirit beast with her own sorcery, the destruction of the beast meant a disturbance to her other spell as well. She invested the whole of her life force in performing that spell, and when it was broken, the crone's black heart beat its last. It was at just that moment the outlandish creature bearing down on the last remaining FDF member vanished.

"Hey, lady! C'mon, snap out of it!" Doris raced over and took her in her arms, but the crone's eyes showed dead white, foam spilled from her mouth, and the mortified look on her wrinkled features defied description. There was a pentagram branded on her forehead, the mark of a sorceress. "Oh, crap! This isn't quite what I had in mind ... " Though this was an evil sorceress, and her own actions had clearly been in self defense, the thought that she'd brought about the death of an old woman weighed heavily on Doris' heart.

"I'm sorry, but you'll have to wait here until I can come back. I've got serious business to attend to."

Doris laid the corpse out on the ground, and was about to head back to her horse when she hesitated. She'd already decided that finding out whether or not D was okay was more important than bringing this corpse back to town. She'd come out here aware of all the risks that entailed.

Still, the dark body of the crone looked so terribly sad and forlorn stretched out on the ground. The wind tugged at the sleeves of her overcoat. And a corpse abandoned in the wilds was a tempting target for monsters. It would be bad enough to have them feasting on her, but if one of them *got inside her* that would be yet another threat to humanity. Even in broad daylight, there were probably some creatures around that might risk turning into a ball of flame to slink out and take possession of a corpse that hadn't been disposed of properly.

Doris didn't have any of the gear she'd need to take care of the body. She didn't see a horse or wagon for the crone. On inspection, the inner pocket of the crone's overcoat contained nothing aside from a few suspicious-looking trinkets.

Doris went back to the body and lifted it gently. "I don't really think there are any critters to *take you over* out here, but I'm gonna bring you with me anyway. Of course, I can't offer any guarantees we'll make it back in one piece, either."

Loading the corpse onto the horse behind the saddle, Doris used rawhide lacing to secure its arms and legs around the steed. That was to keep it from falling off, and just to be safe in the event something did possess it. Leave it to the daughter of a Hunter to be accustomed to this sort of work—she had the whole thing done in less than three minutes. Doris got in the saddle. *At any rate, I'll make for the main road.*

When her horse had gone but a few steps, Doris suddenly spun around. At the same moment, she heard a thunk as something heavy buzzed by at neck level. The decapitated head painted a gory parabola as it sailed through the air, and just before it hit the ground, its eyes snapped open. It bared its teeth. They were the eyes of a demon, and the foul fangs of one as well. It flew toward the person responsible for separating it from its body. Black lightning streaked from a mounted figure topping a hill quite some distance off. Split in two from forehead to chin, the crone's head fell to the ground and moved no more.

Doris realized she'd had a very close call.

Right behind her was the decapitated corpse of the crone, frozen in place with its claws a heartbeat away from tearing into the girl's throat. The snapped binding dangled from its wrists. An evil spirit had possessed the corpse before Doris had even touched it. The instant it snapped its bonds to attack Doris from behind, the figure on the distant hill had lopped the head off with consummate skill and speed.

Her horse gave a shake, and the headless corpse dropped to the ground. Doris finally turned to face her savior. "Oh, D, I was … " An elated hue lit up her face, but it was gone all too soon.

While the figure coming down off the hill fresh from his graceful display of skill certainly had beauty on par with D, he was clearly someone else. "I can't believe you picked up on that." As he pulled up along side her on his horse, Rei-Ginsei smiled blindingly. He was referring to how she had sensed a strange presence, and turned around a split second before the possessed corpse attacked.

"That was nothing. It looks like I'm in your debt again. What kind of weapon did you use?"

Rei-Ginsei took a playfully surprised expression at her less than ladylike inquiry. "If you'll forgive my saying so, judging by your clothing and that whip, you appear to be a Hunter."

"My father was. I just sorta play at it," Doris said without embarrassment or modesty, and then she smiled. She wasn't entirely sure why, but her smile felt strangely forced.

Realizing that even after they'd exchanged civilities Doris' eyes were not focused on his face but rather on his weapon-girt waist, the dashing youth smiled grimly.

"What brings you here of all places at this hour of the morning, sir? You been out on the road?"

"Yes, that's it exactly."

"In that case, you suppose you could bring this old lady's body back into town for me? Normally I'd have to go and explain what happened to the sheriff, but the truth is, I'm kind of in a hurry." Doris stopped her horse and proceeded to recount the entire incident.

Listening silently until the end, Rei-Ginsei then muttered, "I see now. So that's what happened to it ... I can take care of the corpse for you. I shall see to it both are disposed of properly."

"Both?" Doris knit her brow, but as the dashing youth's carefree smile struck her, she reflected a smile of her own. "Okay, then. Thanks."

As she was reining her horse around, her arm was grabbed from the side, drawing the lovely young woman into an embrace on horseback. The sweet aroma that lingered around his mouth wasn't what she'd expect from any man.

"What the hell ..."

"I have saved your life, even though it meant slaying one of my four companions. Of course, you're also quite beautiful. And then there's the matter of your rescue yesterday. I hardly think anyone would blame me for taking a little compensation."

"You'd better leave me alone, or else—"

"You've also seen something you shouldn't have. We really can't have you going into town and telling everyone about that. So you'll have to die out here. Why don't we just say I'm avenging my fallen comrade? Don't put up such a fight. You'll live a while longer. Until I've taken my pleasure, at least." The dashing youth's mouth locked over the virgin's lips.

There was a gasp, and Rei-Ginsei quickly pulled back. He pressed his hand to his mouth, and blood spread across the back of it. A bite from Doris had torn his lips open.

"Don't fuck with me! I've got someone I care about. I wouldn't let a creep like you touch me!"

Her tone was awe inspiring. She thought Rei-Ginsei's countenance would flush with anger, but he simply smiled. Only it wasn't the charming smile that people couldn't help but return. It was the satanic grin he'd worn on the main road.

Giving a shudder, Doris lashed her whip at the center of his face. Less than a foot and a half lay between them. It was really too close to swing the whip. And yet the swirl of black from the girl's fist leapt right up at the youth's dashing face. It was about to land there when it disappeared into the black streak of lightning shooting up from her foe's waist. Rei-Ginsei's skill in drawing his bizarre, v-shaped weapon—and slashing off the end of her whip in the blink of an eye—was truly miraculous. And yet, his face had none of the tension of a battle about to be joined, but rather held the same smile as before.

"Hyah!"

Realizing in a heartbeat she didn't stand a chance of victory, Doris reined her horse toward the ruins and took off at full speed.

In her haste to take flight, she forgot the might of her foe's weapon, and the way it had taken off the crone's head from a hilltop over sixty feet away. Rei-Ginsei didn't throw his weapon immediately. As Doris' mount neared the heart of the ruins, he finally let the weapon fly with an underhanded throw. Whirring as it chased down the rapidly dwindling speck of Doris and her steed, it mercilessly slashed through the horse's right-rear leg and right-front leg, turned a graceful loop, and came right back at

them, severing both legs on the left side. As the loss of one leg would've sufficed to prevent the girl's escape, this was a display of sheer brutality. A bloody mist went out as the horse fell.

"Oh! Just beautiful!" As he felt the weight of his weapon returning to his outstretched palm, Rei-Ginsei admired the scene before him.

As the horse toppled over, a lithe body leapt into the air, somersaulted, and landed on the ground with only the slightest break in form.

But Doris' face was deathly pale.

She hadn't forgotten her foe's weapon, or his unholy skill with it. With those very things in mind, she'd had her horse galloping along a zigzagging course. The black weapon seemed to take their movements into consideration nonetheless as it cleanly severed the first two legs. The falling beast threw them into the air as Rei-Ginsei came back and visited a similar fate on the remaining pair.

Doris realized she'd run into a foe that in some ways was even more fearsome than the Nobility. There was a javelin and a longsword strapped to her saddle, but she had the whip in her right hand. Still, the weapon felt strangely light and ineffectual in her grasp.

Rei-Ginsei leisurely rode into the ruins. "After seeing that last display of agility, I find myself even less inclined to kill you soon. Will you not lay with me before you depart this mortal coil?"

"Who'd be low enough to do that? I'd sooner have my head bashed open on one of these rocks than lie down with a self-important snake like you," Doris replied, quickly slipping behind the closest of the massive sculptures. Almost twenty feet high, the statue of a figure with a pair of bared fangs tilted slightly forward, set off balance by the long years and the shifting of the ground. Rei-Ginsei's intimidating, ranged weapon couldn't be expected to do much through this stony shield, but with no way to strike back, Doris remained in the same predicament.

"The stronger the prey, the greater the huntsman's thrill. Even more so when it's such an exquisite beast. Oh, I'm sorry— you're supposed to be a Hunter as well, aren't you?" Rei-Ginsei ended the question with scornful laughter. The second he looked down from that hill, and spotted Doris with Witch's body loaded on her horse, he had decided to kill her. If the connection were made between the disappearance of the FDF squad and the corpse of an old woman who'd been working some sort of sorcery, it would only be a question of time before the name of his gang came up.

Witch had been like a reserve unit no one knew about. Operating independently, her job was to summon a creature more ghastly than the human mind could bear. Her creations left the bandits' foes psychologically devastated. When Rei-Ginsei lopped off the head of the demonically possessed Witch and saved Doris, part of the reason was because of the natural sexual attraction he felt toward the beautiful girl. On the other hand, he'd also intended to get rid of the burdensome old sorceress eventually. Now he had the girl cornered like an animal, she was largely unscathed, and her eyes blazed with animosity as she glared at him from behind the monolith.

"It would be so easy for me to send you into the hereafter, but I fear dispatching you so quickly would leave you ill-equipped to testify to my infamy in the afterlife." The weapon in his right hand glistened in the sunlight. "I believe I shall have to make your frail heart quake a bit more in fear of me. Ah, yes, I recall one of the cardinal rules of the Hunter—first you must flush the elusive prey from its hiding place."

Something howled through the air, and there was an incredible noise from the base of the monolith sheltering Doris. Giving a cry of astonishment, Doris wisely leapt out of the way. Stuck in the ground at an angle, the several tons of sculpted stone didn't look likely to budge an inch, even under a sizable impact, but suddenly its balance seemed to upset, and it started to tilt in her direction.

The weapon that had done this was already back in Rei-Ginsei's hand. It resembled the boomerang the ancient natives of Australia used so effectively. Unlike the boomerang, however, Rei-Ginsei's weapon was razor sharp on both the inner and outer edges. What's more, it was made of iron. Most non-Aborigines had trouble throwing a plain wooden boomerang effectively, yet this handsome youth, as limber as a sapling swaying in the breeze, could throw the iron blades any way he pleased with just one flick of the wrist. His unholy skill lent blades of mere metal the kind of cutting power reserved for magic swords, pushing them through a human body, or the trunk of a tree, or even through stone.

Furthermore, they didn't just strike in a straight line. They could come at the target from the right or the left, from above, even from the feet—there seemed to be nowhere they couldn't go. And while it was impossible to defend oneself from even one of these blades, it seemed unlikely there was anyone in the world that could fend off two or three successive attacks, let alone multiple blades thrown at the same time. The iron blades were liable to slice through any shield as easily as they went through their usual prey. Such were Rei-Ginsei's "shrike-blades."

The ground shook and verdant moss flew everywhere as the monolith fell.

Doris stood at the bottom of a lush green bowl of a depression, stock still with amazement. It was ten feet to the nearest stone wall.

Swaying like a flower in the morning breeze, Rei-Ginsei laughed. "What's wrong? I thought the nature of the beast was to flee when hunted—"

Suddenly, he swallowed his words.

Doris' expression filled with hope, because two things had suddenly changed.

A heavy white mist from nowhere in particular had begun to fill the ruins. It clung to Rei-Ginsei's hand as he held his weapon, and to Doris' cheeks, forming tepid beads. And far off, a horse was whinnying.

Doris made a mad dash for the stone wall. While the fog might protect her from an attack, she didn't think it would blind her foe long enough for her to get away. She would try to get close enough to whoever was riding the horse she'd just heard to call out, and would try to borrow some weapons, though she might lose an arm or a leg in the process. Of course, she didn't think that would be enough to beat him anyway.

Nothing came knifing through the air after her. Leaping over the wall headfirst, she held her breath and tried to judge the distance to the next bit of cover.

The voice that echoed across the distance rendered her determined gaze as lifeless as that of a corpse.

"Boss, I'm gonna help myself to your playmate."

In a dimly lit world, where a dripping, white veil hid the blue of the sky, the shadow of death crept ever closer to the one, lone girl. Rei-Ginsei and his three henchmen—any one of them was more than a match for her.

"What happened to Witch, boss?" another voice inquired.

"She got put down. Lost her head to a pretty little bird."

A low, rumbling stir went through the fog. The voices she heard were choked with blackest rage.

"I'll gouge her eyes out."

"I'm gonna twist the arms and legs off her."

"I'll tear her head off."

Then Rei-Ginsei was heard to say, "And I shall take my pleasure from what remains of her body."

Doris hadn't spoken. She couldn't even be heard to breathe. The men had simply sensed the presence of a girl paralyzed by imminent death. The milky fog reduced everything to vague silhouettes.

Rei-Ginsei held a shrike-blade ready in his right hand. Without a single word of prompting, at that same moment elsewhere in the fog, Golem drew his machete, a bowie knife gleamed in Gimlet's hand, and Chullah's hump split in half.

"Well, now…"

Just as they were about to unleash their murderous assault, Rei-Ginsei suddenly froze.

There's something out there!

Yes, out in the eddying mist, out in the sticky, unsettling fog that steadily gnawed away at their psyches, which soaked through their skin to threaten the flame of life, Rei-Ginsei clearly sensed the presence of something other than his group and their helpless prey. Not only was there something out there, but it was enough to stop a man like him in his tracks. Rei-Ginsei couldn't physically see it, but he felt the presence near the monolith he'd toppled with his lightning-fast throw.

He'd hadn't known anything about this. How could he have guessed the monolith had stood there since time immemorial, blocking an entrance to the subterranean world? The fog around them was one that had risen from the bowels of the earth.

"So, this is the outside world?"

The query came in just the sort of unsettling voice one would expect from a demon of the mists. It had such an inhuman ring to it that Rei-Ginsei and his three brutal henchmen found themselves swallowing nervously. Stranger yet, it was a woman's voice.

"It's so chilly … I like it so much better down below," said another woman.

A third said, "We really must find something to fill our bellies—oh, well, isn't there something right over there? One, two, three, four—five in all."

Rei-Ginsei shuddered, realizing that the three speakers could see perfectly well in the fog that left all others blind. Due to the weirdness of the presence he sensed out there, he'd forgotten all about lowering the shrike-blade he'd raised earlier. He felt there were two things out there. And yet, he couldn't help thinking that one of those was split into three!

"Your guide duties have been fulfilled. Get below again," a rusty but much more human voice commanded. No doubt that was the other presence he felt. But while the voice was more human, the presence itself was far more daunting than the source of the disturbing female voices.

"Oh, you can't ... Look at how handsome he is ... He looks absolutely delicious ..."

Quickly surmising that these plaintive cries referred to himself, Rei-Ginsei got chills.

"No, I forbid it."

He felt extremely thankful for this second command.

"Let us go, my sisters. We have our orders."

"It's such a waste, but I suppose we must."

"But, well ... when shall you visit us again? When will you come to our abode far below, oh beloved one?"

The last voice was entreating.

There was no response, and before long, the strange thing with three voices and one presence moved reluctantly through the fog and disappeared back underground.

The source of the remaining presence spoke.

"I'm not interested in fighting anyone but the Nobility, but if you're hellbent on starting something, then step right up"

He's challenging us! Even with this realization, the quartet found that their will to fight remained weak.

"D ... I know it's you, isn't it?"

Doris sounded on the verge of tears.

"Come to me. Relax. There's no need to hurry."

Out in the fog, there was the sound of teeth grinding together. He said there was no need to hurry because he was sure the quartet wouldn't do a thing to stop him. The gnashing teeth testified to the gang's resentment of his scathing insult.

But the fact of the matter was the unearthly aura radiating from somewhere out in the fog bound the villains tight, preventing them from so much as lifting a finger.

The little bird that had almost been in hand walked over to the source of the voice. Shortly after that, the bandits felt the two of them moving far away.

"Wait ... wait just a minute." At long last, Rei-Ginsei succeeded in forcing words from his mouth. "At least tell me your name ..." Forgetting his customary eloquence, he shouted into the fog, "So, is that your name, asshole? D?"

There was no response, and he felt the pair getting further and further away.

The spell over him was broken.

With a scream, Rei-Ginsei hurled his weapon. Extraordinary in its power, speed, and timing, nothing could stop it; with complete confidence in that fact, he let the shrike-blade fly.

Out in the fog, there was the sound of blade meeting blade. After that there was no sound at all, and silence settled over the white world. All trace of the pair was gone.

"Boss?" Golem inquired dejectedly a few minutes later, but the beautiful spawn of hell-sent supplications just stayed there with his right hand stretched out for a shrike-blade that never returned, his countenance paler than the fog as he sat frozen in the saddle.

A sculpture of a gargoyle with folded wings trained its mocking gaze on the room from its lofty perch. The room was one of many in Count Lee's castle. Completely windowless and far from spacious, it was simple in design, but the robot sentries lined up along one wall, the chair on a dais a step up from the stone floor, the person in black scowling from a colossal portrait that covered much of the wall behind the chair, and the general air of religious solemnity that hung about the room suggested it was a place of judgment—a courtroom of sorts.

The defendant had already been questioned about their crimes, and as the ultimate judge, Count Lee raised his eyebrows in rage.

"I will now pronounce the sentence. Look at me," the Count commanded. He spoke with the dignity of a feudal lord, in a low voice from his place on the dais as he desperately fought back the flames ready to leap from his throat. The defendant didn't move. Brought to the room earlier by the robot sentries, the defendant remained sprawled on the cold stone floor. *Three pairs* of vacant eyes wandered about the room, across the floor, into space, and then up to reciprocate the gaze of the gargoyles near the ceiling. The black hair that reached to the end of the defendant's massive tail made the floor a sea of silky black. It was the three sisters from the subterranean aqueduct—the Midwich Medusas.

"You have forgotten the debt you owe me for sheltering you three long millennia in the waters of the underworld, safe from the eyes of man, and fed to the point of bursting. Not only did you fail to dispatch the worm I sent you, but you even aided his escape. This sort of betrayal is not easily forgiven. And so I condemn you here and now!"

The three heads didn't seem to be shaken in the least by the Count's barrage of abuse as they drifted through space and their eyes seemed to be covered by a milky membrane. Then, all at once, they let out a deep sigh and murmured, "Oh, the divine one ..."

"Kill them!" Before his indignant shout was done—a cry that some might even call crazed—the robot sentries unleashed crimson heat-rays from their eyes, vaporizing the trio of heads. Without so much as a glance at the corpse still smoking and wriggling on the floor, the Count curtly ordered, "Get rid of it," then looked sharply to one side.

He hadn't noticed her entrance, but Larmica stood beside the dais. Even garbed in a snow-white dress, the girl had an air of darkness about her. Returning her father's bloodshot gaze with eyes full of icy mockery, she said, "Father, why have you done away with them?"

"They were traitors," the Count spat. "Of course, there were extenuating circumstances. The stripling drank their blood and made them his slave, and they led him back to the surface. You see, when I awoke, the computers informed me that one of the entrances to the subterranean world had been opened early this morning. My first thought was to have them dragged from their lair for questioning, and they confessed everything. Not that it was difficult—they seem to have been robbed of their souls. They were only too happy to answer my questions."

"And what of the entrance?"

"The robots have already sealed it."

"Then you mean to tell me he made good his escape?"

Averting his gaze from his daughter's face as her expression became ever more fascinated, the Count nodded.

"He got away. But the fact that he beat the three sisters ... not by killing them, but that he bit their throats like one of us and made them do his bidding ... I get the feeling he is no ordinary dhampir ..."

Dhampirs with less self-control fed on human blood from time to time, but there had never been a case where the person they fed on became the same sort of marionette Nobles made of their victims. Being only half-vampire, dhampirs' powers didn't extend that far. Stranger yet, this victim hadn't been a human, but rather a true monster among monsters—the Midwich Medusas.

Larmica's eyes began to sparkle with an ineffable light. "I see. You let him get away from you ... Just like the girl."

Not surprisingly, the Count's visage twisted in rage, and he glared at Larmica.

The girl, of course, was Doris. Larmica referred with sarcasm to how he'd set out flush with confidence to claim his prize, but had been forced to flee after meeting brutal resistance. Even more filled with the pride of the Nobility than her father, Larmica sternly opposed elevating any human to the ranks of her kind, no matter how much her father might be attracted to his prey.

With feigned innocence, she asked, "Will you be sneaking off again this evening to see her? Will you pay another call to that beastly smelling excuse for a farm?"

"No," the Count replied, his voice once again composed. "I believe I'll refrain from that for a while. Now that the stripling is back with her, it might prove difficult to have my way."

"Then you have abandoned your plans for the human girl?"

Now it was the Count's turn to grin slyly. "Again, no. I must pay a call on someone else. Before I had the Medusas executed, the eldest of the sisters made mention of some curious characters."

"Characters? You mean humans, don't you?"

"Yes. Using them, I shall see to it the whelp is destroyed— though you shall have my condolences." There was nothing whatsoever of a consoling nature in his tone.

In a low voice Larmica asked, "Then you will have the girl, come what may?"

"Yes. Such exquisite features, such a fine, pale throat, and such mettle. These last few millennia, I've not seen such a precious female." Here the Count's tone changed. "Seeing the grueling battle she gave me the other night, never giving an inch, has only increased my ardor. Ten thousand years ago, was there not the case of our Sacred Ancestor failing to attain a human maiden of his heart's desire?" As he said this, he gazed with reverence, equal to what any of the Greater Nobility would show, at the colossal painting occupying the wall behind him. "I have heard that the woman our Sacred Ancestor desired was named Mina the Fair, and she lived in the ancient Land of Angles. And it seems our Sacred Ancestor found the blood coursing beneath her nigh translucent skin sweeter and more delectable than any to ever wash across his tongue, though he had already drunk from the life founts of thousands of beauties."

"Because of that woman, our Sacred Ancestor was reduced to dust," Larmica added coldly, giving her father a plaintive look that wasn't at all like her. "Then you won't reconsider this under any circumstances, Father? The proud Lee family has occupied this region of the Frontier for five long millennia, and no human should ever be allowed to join it. All you have ever preyed upon have been drained of blood and left to die, and never have you suggested bringing any of them into the family. So why this one girl? I am certain I'm not alone in questioning this. I have no doubt my late mother would ask exactly the same thing."

The Count gave a pained smile. He nodded, as if acknowledging the inevitable.

"That's the point. I have been meaning to bring this up for some time now, but I intend to take the girl as my wife."

Larmica looked as if a stake had just been pounded through her heart. Nothing shy of that could have delivered the same shock to this proud young woman. After a while, her characteristically pale skin became the color of paper, and she said, "I understand. If you have considered that far ahead, then I will no longer be unreasonable. Do as you wish. However, I believe I shall take my leave of this castle and set off on a long journey."

"A journey, you say? Very well."

For all the distress in the Count's voice, there was also a faint ring of relief. He knew in the very marrow of his bones that his beloved but temperamental daughter would never be able to coexist with the human girl, no matter how he might try to persuade them both.

"So, Father," Larmica asked, her face as charming as if the problem had completely been forgotten, "how exactly do you intend to destroy the young upstart and claim the girl?"

By the time Doris got back to the farm with D, the sun was already high in the sky. Having heard an account of the previous night from his babysitter, Dr. Ferringo, Dan's little heart was steeped in anxiety as he awaited his sister's return. When he saw the two of them return safely he was overjoyed, though his eyes nearly leapt out of his head at the same time.

"What the heck happened to you, Sis? You fall off your horse and bust your behind or something?"

"Oh, you hush up! It's nothing, really. I'm just making D do this to make up for all the worrying he put us through," Doris shouted from her place on D's back. D was carrying her piggyback.

Her nerves had borne her through heated battles with two equally fiendish adversaries—the Count last night and Rei-Ginsei this morning—but the instant she stepped out of the foggy world and heard D tell her, "You're all right now," her nerves had just snapped. The next thing she knew, she was on his broad back and he was treading the road home. "Hey, that's not funny. Put me down," she had cried, her face flushing bright red. D quickly complied, but Doris, seemingly overcome with relief, couldn't muster any strength in her legs. They wobbled under her when they touched the ground, forcing her to sit on the spot. And so he had carried her the rest of the way to the farm.

D carried Doris right on into her room and put her to bed. The second she felt the spring of the mattress beneath her, she dropped off to sleep, but at that moment she got the distinct impression she heard a vulgar voice laugh and say, "She had a nice big butt on her. Sometimes this job has its perks."

When the sun was getting ready to set, Doris awoke. Dr. Ferringo had long since returned to town, and D and Dan were busy repairing the door and hallway damaged in the previous night's conflict. "Don't bother with that, D, we can take care of it ourselves. You've got to be worn out enough as it is."

On the way back to the farm from the ruins, D hadn't really told her the circumstances that had prevented him from returning the night before. He'd simply said, "I blew it."

She understood that he meant he'd failed to destroy the Count. But beyond that, he didn't say anything like, "Sorry I was gone so long," or ask, "Did anything happen last night?" Quite peeved by that, Doris subjected him to a somewhat exaggerated account of the evening's events. She didn't even think it particularly odd that things she'd normally be too terrified to speak of now rolled right off her tongue, simply because D was with her.

Once she'd finished, D said, "Good thing you are all right," and that was the end of it. It seemed a cold and insolent thing to say, but it left Doris thoroughly satisfied nonetheless, and if she was a fool for that, then so be it.

At any rate, she somehow knew D had done battle with the Count, and that, in addition, he'd had some other far from ordinary experience. That was why she said he must be worn out.

"Aw, that's okay," Dan countered. "My big brother D here is great at this stuff. Sis, you and I couldn't have handled all this in a month. Take a gander outside. He took care of everything—he refilled the weed-killers, fixed the fence, and even swapped out the solar panels."

"My goodness," Doris exclaimed in amazement.

Earning premium pay, a Hunter might keep up his own home, but she'd never heard of one helping his employer with repairs. Especially in D's case, where his reward was only... Doris' train of thought got that far before she flushed red. She remembered what she'd promised him before she brought him there to work. "Anyway, sit down over there and have a rest. I'll get dinner going straight away."

"We'll be done soon," D said, screwing the door hinges back into place. "It's been a while since I did this, and it's tougher than I thought."

"Yeah, but you're great at it," Dan interjected. "You tie the knot with him, Sis, and you're set for life."

"Dan!" Her voice nearly a shriek, she tried to smack the boy, but the little figure ducked her hand and scampered out the open door. Only the gorgeous youth and the girl of seventeen remained. The sun stained the edge of the prairie crimson, and the last rays of light spearing through the doorway gave the pair a rosy hue.

"D ..." Doris sounded obsessed as she said his name. "Uh, I was wondering, what were you planning on doing once your work here is done? If you're not in such a hurry, I was thinking ..."

"I'm not in a hurry, but we don't know if my work here will get finished or not."

Doris' heart sank. In her frailty, the girl instinctively reached out for support and piece of mind, only to run into this sledgehammer. There was no guarantee her foe would be destroyed. She'd been lucky to weather two assaults so far, but the battle still raged on.

"D," Doris said once again, the same word sounding like it came from a completely different person this time. "Once you finish up with that, come on back to the living room. I'd like to discuss what kind of strategy we should take from here on out."

"Understood."

The voice that came over his shoulder sounded satisfied.

Their enemy was extraordinarily quick about making his "visit." That evening, Greco was out carousing with his hoodlum friends, trying to work off some of the rage they still felt from the beating they'd taken at the hands of Rei-Ginsei's gang. He was headed down a deserted street for home when he happened to see a strange carriage stop in front of the inn, and he quickly concealed himself in the shadows.

Stranger than strange, from the time the black carriage appeared out of the darkness till the time it came to a halt, it never made a single sound. The horses' hooves beat the earth clearly enough, and the wagon wheels spun, but not even the sound of the scattering gravel reached Greco's ears.

That there's a Noble's carriage...

This much Greco grasped. His drunken stupor dissipated instantly.

So, this is the prick that's after Doris? Curiosity—and feelings of jealousy toward this rival suitor—held Greco in place. The door opened and a single figure garbed in black stepped down to the ground. By the light of a lamp dangling from the eaves of the inn, the pallid countenance of a man with a supernatural air to him came into view. *I take it that's the lord of the manner then.*

Greco knew this intuitively. Though he'd never seen the man before, he matched the reliable descriptions of the fiend that'd been hammered into his head by village elders when he was still a child. Soon the carriage raced off, and the Count disappeared into the inn. *What the hell brings him into town?* Clouded as they were by low-grade alcohol, his brain cells weren't up to neatly fitting the Count, the inn, and Doris together, but they did manage to give him a push in the right direction and tell him, *Follow him, stupid.*

On entering the inn, Greco found the clerk standing frozen behind the counter. The clerk seemed to be under some sort of spell; his eyes were open wide and his pupils didn't track Greco's hand as he waved it up and down. Greco opened the register. There were ten rooms. All of them were on the second floor. And there was only one guest staying there. The register put him in room #207.

Name: Charles E. Chan. Occupation: Artist.

Careful not to make a sound, Greco padded lightly up the stairs and made his way down to the door of the room in question. Light spilled out through crevasses around the door. *The guest is a guy, so I don't suppose the vampire is here to drink his blood. Maybe he's one of the Count's cronies? I wonder if this clown had to call in help to try and make Doris his own.* Greco pulled out what looked like a stethoscope made of thin copper wire. Hunters swore by this sort of listening device. Quite a while back, Greco had won it in a rigged card game. The gossamer fairy wing, set in a tiny hole in the bell, could catch the voices of creatures otherwise inaudible to human ears, and those sounds were conveyed up the copper wire and into the listener's ears. Ordinarily, the device would be used when searching for the hiding places of supernatural creatures too dangerous to approach, or to listen in on their private conversations, but Greco had made an art out of putting it to the windows of all the young ladies in town. Securing its bell to the door with a suction cup, he put the ear tips in and began to listen. An eerie voice that was not of this world reverberated from the other side of the door. Greco put his eye to the keyhole for good measure.

Rei-Ginsei was astonished when the supposedly bolted door opened without a sound and a figure in black leisurely strolled in. Quickly realizing the intruder was a Noble, he puzzled over the meaning of the visit even as he reached for the shrike-blades on the desk.

The intruder gazed at him with glittering eyes as he made a truly preposterous proposal. "I know all about you and your cohorts," the figure in black said. "That you wiped out a Frontier Defense Force patrol, and that you tried, and failed, to kill a certain young lady. I have business with that particular girl. However, someone remains in my way. That was the person you encountered out in the fog, the one you were powerless to stop."

"What on earth could you be referring to?" Rei-Ginsei asked, with feigned innocence. "I am but a simple traveling artisan. The mere mention of such sordid goings-on is enough to chill my blood."

The black-garbed intruder laughed coldly and tossed a silver badge onto the bed. It had belonged to an FDF patrolman. "I know you believe all the horses and corpses were eaten or burned, and their ashes scattered to the four winds, but unfortunately such is not the case," the voice said coolly. "Monitoring devices in my castle are linked to a spy satellite stationed overhead, and when I awake, it keeps me minutely informed of movements on the Frontier. That badge was reconstructed from molecules of ash recovered at the site, and I also have images of you and yours taken during the attack, and beamed down from the satellite. I needn't tell you what would happen should this information be sent to not only this village, but also every place the lowly human race calls home."

Having heard that much, Rei-Ginsei hurled a shrike-blade. It struck an invisible barrier in front of the fearsome blackmailer's heart and imbedded itself in the floor. In truth, it was then that Rei-Ginsei gave up.

"There is the girl who eludes me to consider as well, " the voice continued. "I shouldn't be surprised if she were to pay a call on the sheriff tomorrow, and I assure you she would tell him all about you and your cohorts. I suppose the reason you've taken up lodging here in town alone is to kill the girl before she can do so, but as long as she has that man by her side, you'll not have an easy time of it. After all, your foe is a dhampir—he has the blood of my kind in him. No matter which course you choose, naught save doom awaits your group."

"Then why would you tell me this? What would you have us do?"

The reason Rei-Ginsei's tone was surprisingly calm was because the intruder had been right on all points but one, and he'd decided that putting up any more of a struggle would be futile.

"I thought I might lend you some assistance," the voice said—a remark that was quite unexpected. "So long as the stripling that's frustrating my efforts is slain, and the girl comes into my possession, I have no interest in what happens in the lowly world of mankind."

"But how?"

A vicious, vulgar light shone in Rei-Ginsei's eyes. He realized he might have a chance now to slay the young punk—his opponent back in the fog. That was the one point on which the

Count had been mistaken. He hadn't left his three henchmen camped in the woods and come into town alone to keep the girl from talking. Well, that had been part of the plan, but his true aim was much more personal. He'd had the little bird where he could rip her wings off, tear her legs off, and wring her dainty neck, and his foe had taken her right out from under his nose. Worse yet, he'd known the humiliation of being paralyzed by a ghastly aura that kept him from lifting a finger against his foe, and he'd had the invincible shrike-blade he prided himself on knocked from the air with a single blow. He'd gone into town to see to it his foe paid for all these things. It was malice. Just as full of hatred and longing for vengeance as he was, his henchmen agreed to his plan. He returned to town alone to be less conspicuous as he looked for the girl and his mysterious foe.

However, wait as he might at the entrance to town, there was no sign of his prey. In asking around, he only managed to learn what the girl's name was and where she lived. Normally he would've gone right out there and attacked her, but the proven strength of this other enemy—who no one in town had been able to identify—was enough to throw cold water on the wildfire that was his malice. He'd left town again briefly to meet with his cohorts and order them to keep an eye on Doris' farm. Then he went back into the village to gather as much information as possible on his enemy for his own murderous purposes. And, while he hadn't exactly gathered any information, he now had a more powerful ally than he ever could've imagined standing right before him.

"How shall we do it?" Rei-Ginsei asked once again.

"This is what you should do."

Discussions between the demon in black and the gorgeous fiend went on for some time.

Presently, the visitor in black dropped something long, thin, and candle-like on the bed.

"That's Time-Bewitching Incense. It's a tool for turning day to night, or night to day. This is an especially potent version. Light it when you're near him, then quickly extinguish it again. That should throw his defenses off. That's when you kill him. However, just to keep you from getting any ideas about other uses you might put this to, it can only be used twice. You have only to give it a good shake and it should light."

"Please, wait a moment," Rei-Ginsei cried out, hoping to stop the departing figure. "I have one additional favor to ask of you."

"A favor?" The shadowy figure sounded both puzzled and angered.

"Yes, sir." With a nod and a smile, Rei-Ginsei made his outlandish request. "I ask that you make me one of the Nobility. Oh, you needn't be so angry about it. Please, simply hear me out. I have to wonder why you bothered selecting me as your partner in this. If this incense alone is enough to do the trick, there must be any number of humans you could have entrusted this to. We live in times where parents will kill their own child for a gold coin and a new spear. And yet, the very fact that you went to all the trouble of coming to see me is proof enough that you need someone of my skill in order to kill the dhampir. I know a thing or two about dhampirs myself. I know they tend to be the very worst sort of enemy you could ever make. And there's something so powerful, so terrifying about the one we're dealing with now, it cuts me to the quick. That is no ordinary dhampir. With all due respect, it's not enough to merely have you overlook my group's misdeeds. I do not ask the same favor for all four of my party—I alone would like to rise to the hallowed ranks of the Nobility."

The shadowy figure fell silent.

Anyone with a heart who heard Rei-Ginsei's overture would've wanted to scream "Traitor!"—to say nothing about what his three henchmen might have done—but then the world has never lacked for turncoats. Even as they hated and feared them like demons from hell, deep in their heart of hearts people looked at the dreaded vampires with a covetous gaze. Power and immortality had such an alluring scent.

"What say you?" Rei-Ginsei asked, pressuring his visitor for a response.

The shadowy figure gave a nod, and Rei-Ginsei nodded in return.

"Then thy will be done."

"See to it."

The shadowy figure left the room. He still had another visit to pay before he returned to his castle. By the guttering lamplight, he failed to notice the other person in the hallway.

The Bloody Battle—
Fifteen Seconds Each

CHAPTER 6

I t was early the next morning that Dan's disappearance came to light.

Weary as she was from her deadly battle the previous night and from staying up almost all night preparing for the Count's attack, Doris failed to notice her younger brother racing out to the prairie at the crack of dawn.

Having told D the details of her run-in with Rei-Ginsei and his gang, Doris had decided to go see the sheriff today to inform him. Though Dan had been told not to leave the farm until they were ready to go into town, the boy was just bursting at the seams with energy. Apparently he'd switched off the barrier and gone out alone with a laser rifle to hunt some mist devils.

Fog-like monsters that slipped in with the morning mist, the creatures were a nuisance on the Frontier mainly because they had a propensity for dissolving their way through crops and the hides of farm animals. They didn't fare well against heat, however, and a blast from a laser beam was enough to destroy them. Being rather sluggish, they posed little threat to an armed boy used to dealing with them.

Hunting mist devils was really Dan's specialty.

Soon after she awoke, Doris realized her brother wasn't on the farm. She raced frantically to the weapon storeroom and saw that he'd taken his rifle, which let her relax for a moment. But when she ran outside to call him back in, she froze in her tracks at the entrance to the farm.

His laser rifle had been left as a paperweight on a single sheet of paper that was lying on the ground, right in front of the gate. The following words were written on the page in elegant lettering:

Your brother is coming with us. The Hunter D is to come alone at six o'clock Evening to the region of ruins where we met the other day. Our goal is simply to ascertain which Hunter has the superior skills, and nothing more. We have no need of observers, not even you, Doris. Until this test of skill has been decided, you are to mention this to no one.

If you deviate from the above conditions in the least, a sweet little eight-year-old will burn in the fires of hell.

—Rei-Ginsei.

Doris felt every ounce of strength drain from her body as she returned to the house. She was still trying to decide whether or not she should show the letter to D when D noticed all was not right with her. Trapped in the gaze of his lustrous eyes, Doris finally showed him the letter.

"Well, half of it is true, at least," D said, as if the matter didn't concern him in the least, though it was quite clear he was being challenged to a duel.

"Half of it?"

"If he just wanted to face off against me, all he had to do was come here and say so. Since he took Dan, he must have another aim—to separate the two of us. The Count is behind this."

"But why would he have gone to all that trouble? It'd be a lot faster and easier if he'd said I was the one who had to come alone ..."

144 | H I D E Y U K I   K I K U C H I

"One reason is because the author of this letter wants to settle a score with me. The other—"

"What would that be?"

"Using a child to get you would reflect poorly on the honor of the Nobility."

Doris' eyes blazed with fury. "But he really is using Dan to—"

"Most likely his abduction is the only part of the plan Rei-Ginsei and his gang came up with."

"The honor of the Nobility—don't make me laugh! Even if it wasn't his idea, if he approves of it it's the same damned thing. Nobility my ass—they're nothing but blood-sucking monsters!" After she spat the words like a gout of flame, Doris was shocked at herself. "I'm sorry, you're not like that at all. That was a rotten thing for me to say."

Tears quickly welled in her eyes, and Doris broke down crying on the spot. The recoil from putting all her violent emotions into words had just hit her. Her situation was grim, with one misfortune after another piling onto her as if she was possessed by some evil spirit that drew all these calamities to her. In reality, it was amazing she hadn't surrendered to tears long before now.

As weeping shook her pale shoulders, a cool hand came to rest on them. "We can't have you forgetting you hired a bodyguard."

Even with the present state of affairs, D's voice remained soft. But within the coolly composed ring of his words, the ears of Doris' heart clearly heard another voice propped up by unshakable assurance. And this is what it seemed to say: *I promised to protect you and Dan, and you can be certain I will.*

Doris raised her face.

Right before her eyes was the face of an elegant, valiant young man gazing quietly at her.

It felt as something hot fell onto her full bosom.

"Hold me," she sobbed, throwing herself against D's chest. "I don't care what happens. Just hold me tight. Don't let me go!"

Gently resting his hands on the sob-wracked shoulders of the seventeen-year-old girl, D gazed out the window at the blue expanse of sky and the prairie filling with morning's life.

What was he thinking about? The safety of the boy, his four foes, the Count, or something else? The emotional hue that filled his eyes remained a single shade of cold, clear black. Before long, Doris pulled back from him. With a spent, sublime expression she said, "I'm sorry. That wasn't exactly in character for me. It's just … I suddenly got the feeling you might stay here with me forever. But that's not right. When your job's done, you'll be moving on, won't you?"

D said nothing.

"This is almost over. Something tells me that. But what are we gonna do about Dan?"

"I'll go, of course. I have to."

"Can you take them?"

"I'll bring Dan back, safe and sound."

"Please, see that you do. I feel awful making you look out for him, but I think I'm gonna head into town to hole up. I'll have Doc Ferringo put me up at his place. You know, he saved me the night before last. I'm sure I'll be fine this time, too."

Doris still didn't know that the real reason the Count had run off was the protective charm D had placed on her neck. And most likely the reason D said nothing when the girl told him she was going to the physician's home was because he knew he couldn't guarantee that the charm would ward off someone with the Count's power forever.

When the angle of the sunlight spearing through the window became sharp, the two of them got on their horses and left the farm. Regardless of what D had said, Doris' expression remained dark.

If anyone can bring back Dan, he can—she had no trouble making herself believe this. But she remembered how powerful his enemies were. She could still hear the shrike-blade screaming up behind her in the ruins; the horrid sight of her horse falling over with all four legs cut off was burned deep into her eyelids. Now there were four such fiends out there. A dark spot of despair remained in Doris' heart.

What's more, even if D made it back alive, if the Count were to strike while D was gone, there was no way she could escape him this time. She'd said nothing about it to D, but she still wasn't entirely sure going to Dr. Ferringo's was the right thing to do.

On entering town, countless eyes focused on the pair as they rode down the main street. The looks were colored more by fear than by hate. For people on the Frontier, who lived surrounded by dark forests and monsters, a girl who'd been preyed on by a vampire and a young man with vampire blood in his veins were beyond the normal level of revulsion. Thanks to Greco, everyone had heard what had happened.

A little girl who seemed to recognize Doris said, "Oh, hi," and started to approach, but her mother wasted no time in pulling her back.

Among the men, there were some whose faces showed the urge to kill, and they reached for swords or guns the second they saw D. Not because they'd been told what he was, but rather because of the eerie aura that hung about him. All the women, however, looked like they would swoon as they watched him go by, and given how beautiful he was, that came as little surprise.

And yet, the pair made their way down the street without a single hot-head running out to stop them, and finally they arrived at a house with the sign "Dr. Ferringo" hanging from the eaves.

Doris got down off her horse and rang the bell, and presently the woman from next door, who acted as a nurse and watched the place while Doc was out, answered. Apparently ignorant of Doris' situation, she smiled and stated, "Doc's been out since this morning. It seems there was someone out at Harker Lane's house that needed urgent care and he went off to see to 'em. He left a note saying he'd be back around noon, but where he's still not back yet, he may be dealing with something serious. You know, the lady of the house out there is apt to put anything in season into her mouth, even if it's a numbleberry or a topsy-turvy toadstool." Lane was a huntsman, and his home was out in the middle of the woods, two hours of hard riding from town. "I hate it when this happens. On my own I can't do much besides treat scrapes and hand out sedatives, but since everyone always says that's good enough I've been running myself ragged all morning. Why don't you come in and wait. I'm sure Doc will be back soon, and if you're willing, I could sure use the help."

Uncertain about what to do, Doris looked to D. Sitting on his horse, he gave her the slightest nod.

She decided. Giving a bow to the housewife—who was watching D with starry eyes—Doris said, "It looks like I'll be in your hair until Doc gets back then." She sounded a little tense, but that was unavoidable. While she thought D would come with her, as soon as he saw she'd made up her mind, he started to ride off slowly.

"Dear me, isn't he with you?" the woman asked Doris excitedly. She didn't even try to hide her disappointment. At that point, before Doris could get angry at the thought of a woman of the nurse's age getting all worked up about D, she was sharing the woman's confusion.

"Hold on. Where are you headed?"

"Just taking a look around the perimeter."

"It's still midday. There's not going to be anything out. Stay with me."

"I'll be back soon."

D let his horse go on without once looking back.

After they'd gone a ways he took a left turn. In a needling tone, a voice asked, "Why don't you stick close to her? You mean to tell me you're so worried about that little tike you can't sit still? Or is just that you can't stand to see the suffering on his sister's face? Dhampir or not, seems you're still a little wet behind the ears. Heh heh heh. Or could it be you're in love with the girl?"

"Is that what you think?"

Just whom was D talking to?

The road ahead was a dusty path that continued on between walls of earth and stone. Aside from the lethargic, vexing rays of the sun as it moved past noon, there was no sign of anyone around. And yet, there was still that voice.

"No chance. You're not that kind of softy. After all, you've got *his* blood in your veins. It's perfect, the way you told them to call you D."

"Silence!"

Judging by the way the man in question had roared in reaction to his name, it seemed the voice had touched on a rather sensitive point.

An instant later his tone became soft once again. "You've been full of complaints lately. Would you like to split with me?"

"Oh no!" the voice exclaimed, sounding a touch threatened. But then, as if to avoid showing any weakness, it replied, "It's not like I'm with you because I like it. Well, you know how it goes— give-and-take makes the world go round. Not to change the subject, but why didn't you tell the girl about the mark you put on her neck? Out of loyalty to *your father?* Just a word from you would've put her at ease, I bet. It must be tough having the blood of the Nobility in you."

The voice sounded sincere enough, but the fact that its heart held an entirely different sentiment was made apparent by a burst of derisive laughter.

Still, one couldn't help but wonder if the young man had completely lost his mind to continue a dialogue with an imaginary companion as he sat there on his horse. But because the tone, quality, and everything else about the two voices were completely different, the weird scene only seemed possible through some truly ingenious ventriloquism.

D's eyes sparkled brilliantly, but soon reclaimed their usual, quiet darkness, and the conversation came to an end. Shortly thereafter he took a left at the next corner, came to a similar corner, and once again turned the same way. Eventually, he returned to the front of the physician's home.

"Any strange characters out there?" the voice once again echoed from nowhere in particular.

"None."

Given the way he'd answered, it seemed he had in fact gone off to check the surrounding area for any hint of anything out of the ordinary.

However, he showed no sign of dismounting as he lifted his beautiful visage and grimaced at the sun listing westward from the center of the sky.

"Is that all I can do?" he muttered. Perhaps some vision of the grisly battle to come flitted through his mind; for an instant, a certain expression rose on his oh-so-proper countenance, and then it was gone.

A few horses hitched up across the street suddenly grew agitated, and people walking by shielded their eyes from the dust kicked up by an unpleasantly warm wind blowing by without warning.

The momentary expression on D's face was the same one the Midwich Medusas had seen in the subterranean waterway— the face of a blood-crazed vampire.

Gazing for a brief moment at the closed door to the doctor's home, D reined his horse around and headed out of town. The ruins were two hours away.

"Here he comes. You should see him on top of the hill any minute," Gimlet said, returning with the wind in his wake. When Rei-Ginsei heard this news he pulled himself up off the stone sculpture he'd been leaning against. Gimlet was their lookout.

"Alone, I take it?"

"Yessir. Just like you told him."

Rei-Ginsei nodded, then addressed the other two henchmen who'd been standing there for some time like guardian demons at a temple gate, with their eyes running out across the prairie.

"Everyone is set, I see. Engage him just as we've planned."

"Yessir."

Nodding as Golem and Chullah bowed in unison, Rei-Ginsei walked to the horse hitched up behind him. The place the four of them had chosen for this showdown was the same bowl-like depression where Witch had been killed. Challenging D to a grudge match in the same location where D's aura had battered them and kept them paralyzed was just the sort of thing this vindictive ruffian would do, but consideration had also been given to how useful this location would be for restricting their opponent's movements when they fought him four against one.

Rei-Ginsei squatted next to Dan, who lay behind a rock, gagged and bound hand and foot, and pulled down the cloth covering the boy's mouth. Called a gag rag, the cloth was a favorite of criminals. The fabric was woven from special fibers that could absorb all sound, and its usefulness to kidnappers made it worth its weight in gold.

Still, there was no call for the cruelty displayed by keeping a boy barely eight years old gagged ever since the morning.

"Look, your savior is coming. I put this plan together yesterday after hearing about you and your sister, and I must confess it seems to be going beautifully."

Just as Rei-Ginsei finished speaking, the furious gaze that had been concentrated on him was colored by relief and confidence. Dan looked toward the hills.

Twisting his lips a bit, Rei-Ginsei sneered, "How sad. Neither of you is fated to leave here alive."

"Ha, you guys are the one who won't make it out of here alive." Worried and hungry and looking gaunt, Dan still managed to fling the reply with all his might. He hadn't been given so much as a drop of water since he'd been captured. "You have no idea how tough ol' D is!"

His words were strong, but they were also a childish bluff. He'd never even seen D fight.

Dan thought Rei-Ginsei might fly into a rage, but, to the contrary, Rei-Ginsei only smirked and turned his gaze to his three henchmen standing in the center of the depression. "You may be right. That would certainly mean less work for me."

Dan's eyes opened wide, as if he must have heard that wrong.

But it was true. This gorgeous fiend fully intended to bury his three underlings here along with D. At first he'd only intended to take care of D and Doris, who'd seen his face, but after receiving the Count's oath to turn him into one of the Nobility, Rei-Ginsei's plans had taken a complete turn. The power and immortality of a Noble would be his—he would no longer be a filthy brigand wandering the wilderness.

So, in accordance with the Count's plan, he left Doris for the Noble to handle, while he decided to add three more people to the pair the Count wanted him to kill. In his estimation, if he allowed his henchmen to live, he would come to regret it later.

If D should dispatch them all here, so much the better. But if luck is not with me and some survive, I shall kill them myself.

A solitary rider popped up over the hilltop. He didn't reduce his speed, but galloped toward them at full tilt.

"Well, time to make yourself useful." Grabbing hold of the leather straps that hung around the boy's back, Rei-Ginsei carried Dan over to his horse with one hand, like he was a piece of baggage. The shrike-blades on his hip rubbed together, making a harsh, grating noise. Groping in his saddlebag with his free hand, he pulled out the Time-Bewitching Incense. "That's strange," he said, tilting his head to the side.

"Boss!"

At Chullah's tense cry, Rei-Ginsei whirled around, still gripping the candle.

"D," Dan called out, his shout flying off on the wind.

Rei-Ginsei's sworn enemy had already dismounted and now stood at the bottom of the earthen depression with an elegantly curved longsword across his back.

"Dear Lord ..."

The beauty of his foe left Rei-Ginsei shocked ... and envious.

"I wish I could tell you what an honor it is to have one of my blades knocked down by a man of your kind, but I won't. The fact that you're a miserable cross between a human and a Noble takes the charm out of it."

To Rei-Ginsei's frigid smile and scornful greeting, D softly replied, "And you must be the bastard son of the Devil and a hellhound."

Rei-Ginsei's entire face grew dark. As if his blood had turned to poison.

"Let the boy go."

In lieu of a reply, Rei-Ginsei gave Dan's leather bonds a twist with one hand. An agonized cry split the boy's young lips.

"Ow! D, it really hurts!"

Though they looked like ordinary leather straps, they must have been tied with some fiendish skill, because they started pressing deep into Dan's shoulders and arms.

"These bonds are rather special," Rei-Ginsei said, twisting his lips into a grin and making a small circle with his thumb and forefinger. "Apply force from the right direction and they pull up tight like this. I figure for a child of eight, it should take twenty minutes or so for them to sink far enough into his flesh to choke the life out of him. If you haven't finished us all off by then, this boy will be cursing you from the hereafter. Does that light a little fire under you?"

"D ..."

What an utterly heartless tactic. The bonds had already begun working their way through his clothes. As the boy writhed in agony, D gave him a few powerful words of encouragement.

"This'll just take a minute."

Meaning he would take care of them in fifteen seconds each?

"O ... okay."

Unlike the bravely smiling Dan, the four men were livid.

The ring formed by Rei-Ginsei's three henchmen began to tighten like a noose. All of them were painted by the vermilion rays of the setting sun, but the palpable lust for blood rising from each seemed to rob the light of its color.

"Now, let's show him what you can do one by one. Golem, you go first."

As his boss gave him the command, not only Golem but all three henchmen began to look dubious. After all, the initial plan had been for all four of them to attack at once and kill him. But a moment later, Golem's massive brown body raced toward D with the silent footfalls of a cat. The broad blade of his machete glittered in the red light. There was a loud clang! His machete was big enough to chop a horse's head off, but just as it was about to hack into the Hunter's torso, D drew his blade with lightning speed, bringing the tip of it down through Golem's left shoulder. Or rather, it looked like it was going to go right through his shoulder, but it bounced off him.

Golem the Tortureless—a man with muscles of bronze. His body had even proved itself impervious to high-frequency wave sabers.

Once again, Golem's machete howled through the air, and D skillfully dodged it with a leap that carried him yards away in an instant. And once again, the giant went after him, closing on the Hunter.

"What's wrong? You said fifteen seconds each!"

Like a cry to battle borne on the wind, D's angry roar shook the grass and filled the mortar-shaped depression in the earth.

Doris awoke from her nap as someone gently shook her shoulder. A warm, familiar face was smiling down at her.

"Doc! I must've dozed off while I was waiting for you."

"Don't worry about it. I'm sure you're exhausted. It took quite some time to take care of my patient at Harker's, and I've just gotten back here myself. I swung by your place and no one was there, so I hustled back with the sneaking suspicion I might find you here. Did something happen? Where's Dan and that young fellow?"

All her memories and concerns flooding back to her, Doris looked around. After D left, she'd helped the nurse deal with the patients, then she'd stretched out on a sofa in the examination room and fallen asleep.

There was no sign of the nurse, who'd apparently gone home, and the rows of houses and trees beyond the windowpanes were all steeped in red. The curtain was set to rise on her time for terror.

"Well ... the two of them are hiding out in Pedros. I figured I'd join 'em there once I'd paid my respects to you ..."

As she attempted to rise, a cool hand came to rest on her shoulder. Pedros was the name of a nearly deserted village the better part of a day's and a night's ride from Ransylva. Even at that, it was still their closest neighbor.

"Even though you'll have to get through at least one night before you arrive?"

"Uh, yeah."

As he peered at her face with an uncharacteristically hard gaze, Doris unconsciously looked down at the floor.

Giving a little nod, the elderly physician said, "Very well then, I'll press the matter no further. But if you're really going to go somewhere, there's a much better place for you." At these surprising words, Doris looked up at the old man's face. "I found it on my way back from Harker's place when I decided to go through the north woods."

Dr. Ferringo pulled a map out of his jacket pocket and unfolded it. The passing years had dulled his memory, so he often used this map of Ransylva and its surroundings anytime he had to travel far to treat a patient. It had a red mark on it in part of the north woods. It was a huge forest, the thickest in the area, and not a single soul in the village knew their way around the whole of it.

"Part of a stone wall caught my eye, and when I hacked away the bushes and vines covering it I found this place—ancient ruins. It appeared to be the remains of some sort of place of worship. It's pretty large, and I only examined a small portion of it, but I guess you could say luck was with us, because that stone wall was inscribed with an explanation of the site. It seems it was constructed to keep vampires at bay."

This left Doris completely speechless.

Now that he mentioned it, she could recall her father and his Hunter friends gathered around the hearth sharing stories about this place when she was a child. They said that far in the distant past, long before the Nobility rose to power in the world, people who'd been preyed on by vampires were locked up in a holy place and treated with incantations and electronics. Perhaps what Dr. Ferringo had discovered was one such facility.

"Then you mean to tell me if I'm in there, he can't get at me?"

"In all likelihood," Dr. Ferringo replied, smiling broadly. "At any rate, I imagine it's better than trying to reach Pedros now, or holing up here in my house. Shall we go out and give it a try?"

"Yes, sir!"

Less than five minutes later, the two of them were jolting along in Dr. Ferringo's buggy as it hastened down the dusky road to the north woods. They must have rode for nearly an hour. Ahead, tiny walls of trees blacker than the darkness came into view. This was the entrance to the forest.

"Woah!"

Once they were in the buggy, the elderly physician hadn't answered her no matter how she tried to get him to talk, but suddenly he'd given a cry and pulled back on the reins.

A small figure stood at the entrance to the forest. The face was unfamiliar to Doris, but with paraffin-pale skin and ivory fangs poking from the corners of her mouth—it had to be Larmica.

Doris grabbed the doctor by the arm as he prepared to lash the horses again. "Doc! That's the Count's daughter. What in the name of hell is she doing out here? We've got to get out of here, and fast!"

"That's odd," Dr. Ferringo muttered in an uncertain tone. "She shouldn't be here."

"Doc, hurry up and get this thing turned around!"

Seemingly frozen, the doctor didn't move at her desperate cries, while the woman in the white dress standing up ahead came toward them, smoothly gliding through the grass without appearing to move her legs in the least. Doris had already pulled her whip out and was on her feet.

She felt a powerful pull at her hands, and before she knew it her whip had been taken from her. Taken by Dr. Ferringo!

"Doc?!

"So I was known until yesterday," Dr. Ferringo said, fangs sprouting in his mouth.

Come to think of it, the hand he'd placed on Doris' shoulder back at his hospital had been cold. And he was wearing a turtleneck shirt, which wasn't like him at all! The instant hopelessness and fear were about to wrack her body, a fist sank into the pit of her stomach, and Doris collapsed into the shotgun seat.

"Well done," said the lovely vampire, now hovering beside the buggy.

"Larmica, I presume. You honor me with your praise." With bloodshot eyes and a hunger-twisted mouth, Dr. Ferringo's smiling countenance was now that of a Noble. The previous night, he'd been attacked by the Count and made into a vampire.

The call on Harker's home, and the ancient vampire-proof ruins, were complete fabrications, of course. Taking his orders from the Count, he'd concealed himself in the basement by day, appeared in the evening at a time when D would already have left, and played his part in luring Doris out of town. If separated from D, Doris would surely turn to the doctor—the Count's assessment had been right on the mark.

"You're to bring the girl to my father, are you not? I believe I shall accompany you." Even though she was a fellow vampire, Dr. Ferringo donned a wary expression at Larmica's formal speech and the frigid gaze she turned on him.

He'd been commanded to bring Doris into the heart of the forest and to the waiting Count, but he hadn't heard that Larmica would be coming. And yet she suddenly appeared at the entrance to the forest and said she would go with him. Why wasn't she with her father? But the doctor had only just become the Count's servant, and it would be unpardonable for him to question his master's daughter. Opening the door to the buggy's backseat, he bowed and said, "Be my guest."

Larmica moved into the vehicle like a mystic wind.

The buggy took off.

"Rather fetching for a human, isn't she," Larmica mumbled, peering at the face of the unconscious Doris.

"That she is. When I was human, she was like a daughter to me, and I never had occasion to view her in any other light. But when I look at her now, she's so beautiful it's a wonder I never tried anything with her. To be quite frank, I intend to ask a favor of my lord the Count and see if he won't allow me to partake of a drop or two of her sweet, red blood in return for all my hard work—although I would not be so bold as to seek it from her throat."

These were the words of the kind and faithful old physician? Now he was lost in fantasies of slowly sucking the blood from the very girl who two days earlier he'd risked his life to protect. His teeth ground together greedily.

He heard Larmica's cheery voice behind him. "For the time being, allow me to give you my reward." Without even allowing him time to turn, she took the steel arrow she'd kept concealed and thrust it through the elderly physician's heart, killing him instantly. Tossing his body to the ground, Larmica sailed gracefully through the air, landed in the driver's seat, and quickly brought the horses to a halt. Taking a furtive glance at the woods, she said, "I dare say Father will be furious, but I simply cannot allow a lowly human worm to be made a member of the glorious Lee family—and I most certainly won't welcome one as his bride." When she turned her eyes on the still-sleeping Doris, they had the most lurid light to them. A wolf could be heard howling out on the distant plains.

"Human, I shall show you your place now—as I rip you limb from limb before delivering you to Father." She reached for Doris' throat with both hands. Her nails shone like razors.

In the middle of the wilderness, with no one to protect her, hemmed in by the darkness, the girl remained in her stupor, oblivious to the very real danger she was in.

That was the moment.

A weird sensation shot through every inch of Larmica's body. All her nerves were being pulled out and burned off, each and every cell was decaying with incredible speed. Black ichor squirted out through holes in her melting flesh, and she felt her intestines twist with the urge to vomit, as if the entire contents of her stomach had started to flow in reverse. That's what the sensation felt like.

It was almost as if the night that had just begun had suddenly become midday. A familiar scent struck Larmica's nose.

She had no idea how long it had been there, but a tiny speck of light burned in the darkness to her back. Apparently someone had heard Larmica's anguished cries, and there was the sound of cautious footsteps coming closer through the grass. In its hand, the figure held Time-Bewitching Incense.

Having dodged a third horizontal slash of the machete, D once again took to the air.

To anyone watching, it would have looked like the act of a beaten man. Every time D went on the offensive, the bronze giant kept his eyes—clearly his only weakness—well covered with his massive club of a forearm.

"Give 'em hell, D!"

Golem dismissed Dan's feverish support with a laugh. "Look, you're making the little baby cry—" The sentence went no further.

The four pairs of eyes on the two combatants bulged in their sockets. None of the spectators had any idea what had happened.

D had his right leg out behind him for balance, and his sword ready and pointing down at the ground. The way his blade moved was like a jump cut in a film. The part where it slashed through the air was missing, and it skipped straight to where it went into Golem's mouth, wide with laughter.

Though this freak could control the density of his musculature on the surface, an inch below, his body remained as soft as any other living creature's. D's sword slipped in through the only real opening in his defense aside from his eyes, and drove up to the top of his skull in one smooth thrust.

D must've been aiming for that ever since he discovered the giant's flesh couldn't be cut, but the way he found an opening at the end of the giant's chatter, and made the thrust literally faster than the eye could follow, was nothing short of miraculous.

"Gaaah—"

It was actually rather humorous the way the scream didn't escape the impaled giant until several seconds later. As his massive form dropped backwards, its toughness fading rapidly, D stepped closer and split the giant's skull with one emotionless slash of his sword. This time the giant didn't make a sound. The sight of their staunch friend falling—sending up a bloody mist a shade more crimson than the setting sun—snapped his spellbound compatriots back to their senses.

"Looks like you did it, punk. I'm up next," Chullah said in a voice that sounded crushed to death, but as he stepped forward he was checked by a human awl—Gimlet.

"What speed. Kid, I'm willing to put my life on the line to see which is faster—my legs or that freaking sword of yours." He was in front of D in a flash, like he'd ridden the wind over there, and he had a world-beating grin on his lips. Was it due to self-confidence, or was it the thrill in his bandit blood at meeting his worthiest opponent ever?

D held his sword at chest level, pointed straight at Gimlet's heart.

In an instant, his opponent vanished.

Dan gasped.

Looking in the brush to D's left, at the feet of a statue diagonally behind him, right behind his back—there was now a circle of countless Gimlets fifteen feet from him in any direction.

Gimlet—the man was as streamlined as the tool he was named for. As a result of a mutation, he was capable of superhuman bursts of speed in the vicinity of three hundred miles per hour. His body didn't sport a single hair, and his face was relatively free from sharp features; it was nature's way of reducing wind resistance during his superhuman sprints.

However, moving at super speed wasn't his only talent. He would run a few yards, pause for an instant, and then run some more. By doing this over and over, he could leave afterimages of himself hanging in midair.

The foe right before you would multiply and be to your left one second, to your right the next—what warrior wouldn't be distracted by that? Show him an opening for even an instant, and all the Gimlets to the front and to the rear, to the left and to the right, would brandish their bowie knives and move in for the kill.

Taking on Gimlet was the same as engaging dozens of opponents at the same time.

It came then as little surprise that quick-draw master O'Reilly hadn't even freed his precious pistol before he was dropped from behind.

D's gonna get himself killed! Tears glistened in Dan's eyes. Not so much tears of fear as of parting.

As he raced around doing his special technique, it was actually Gimlet who was horrified. *It's not that this bastard can't move, it's just that he won't let himself be moved!*

That's right. Eyes half closed, D stood without making the slightest movement. Gimlet knew better than anyone that D's tactic was the only way to negate his disorienting movement.

His powers could be used to their best advantage when his countless other selves made his enemy change their stance, forcing them to leave themselves open. Nevertheless, the gorgeous young man before him didn't look at him or change his stance. Gimlet was little more than a clown prancing around in circles.

"What, aren't you coming for me? Only three seconds left."

When that icy voice pushed him over the brink, was it despair or impatience that launched Gimlet at D's back? His murderous dash at three hundred miles per hour was met by the blade of Vampire Hunter D—who'd taken down a werewolf running at half the speed of sound. A flash of steel shot out, cutting Gimlet from the collarbone on his left side to the thoracic vertebrae on the right. Sending bloody blossoms of crimson into the air, the streamlined body of the runner hit the ground with incredible force.

The next battle was truly decided in a heartbeat.

"Look out behind you!"

D turned even faster than Dan could shout the words, and found a black cloud eclipsing his field of view. A massive swarm of minute poisonous spiders was pouring out of Chullah's back, riding the wind to attack him. No matter how ungodly his skill, D's sword couldn't possibly stop this.

However, Dan saw something as the wind roared.

D's left hand rose high above his head, and the black cloud that covered half the depression became a single line that was sucked into the palm of his hand. The roar was not the sound of a wind blowing out, but rather of air being sucked back in.

The cloud was gone like *that*.

D raced like a gale-force wind.

His head split by a silvery flash of light, Chullah fell backwards—but from the moment his beloved spiders had been lost, he'd been nothing more than an empty husk with the shape of a man.

"Forty-three seconds all told—nicely done." Rei-Ginsei watched D with fascination as the Hunter walked toward him, holding his bloody sword and not even breathing hard. Taking a shrike-blade from his belt, for some reason Rei-Ginsei slashed through the bonds that held Dan.

"D!"

Dan ran over to D without even bothering to rub his bruised arms and legs, and the Hunter gently put the boy behind a statue for safety's sake before squaring off against the last of his foes.

"I'm in a hurry. Let's do this!" Moving faster than his words, D's longsword made a horizontal slash that reflected the red sunset.

Barely leaping out of the way, Rei-Ginsei stood at the bottom of the depression that until now had served as an arena.

"Please, wait—" he said, unable to conceal the quavering of his voice. His shirt had a straight cut running from the right side of his chest to the left, the result of D's attack. D was ready to pounce on him.

"Wait—Miss Lang's life hangs in the balance!"

Those words left Dan paler than D. Satisfied at the hint of unrest showing in D's eyes, Rei-Ginsei felt his cheeks rise at last with his trademark angelic smile.

"What are you talking about?" Surprisingly, D's tone was as calm as ever.

"Miss Lang is with Dr. Ferringo, is she not?"

"So what if she is?" D said.

"Right about now, the girl is being delivered to the Count. The poor thing had no way of knowing the good doctor she trusts more than anyone became a servant of the Count last night."

"What?!"

Rei-Ginsei was shocked to see the look of naked surprise and remorse that came over D. He didn't know that D had personally escorted Doris to the doctor's house. "Come now. Relax, relax. I shall tell you exactly where they're to meet the Count. That is, if you agree to what I propose."

"And what proposition would that be?"

"That the two of us replace the Nobles," Rei-Ginsei said, his voice brimming with confidence. "I have an arrangement with Count Lee. If he can take possession of the girl as a result of me slaying you, I shall be made one of the Nobility. To be perfectly honest, if I decided to kill you, there's still a very good chance I would succeed. However, having seen you in action for myself, I've had a change of heart. Even if I were to be made a Noble, as the good doctor was, I'm certain that, as a former human, I would be treated as a servant. I would prefer to become the Count instead." Having rattled all that off in a single breath, Rei-Ginsei paused. Tinged with a hint of blue, the glow of sunset left delicate shadows on his beautiful profile. The shadows made his visage so indescribably weird that Dan trembled in the safety of the statue.

"In the world today, what keeps the Count in that position, aside from his immortality as a vampire? It's his castle, and the fear that's been fostered in the hearts and minds of the populace since ancient times. It's that and that alone. They had their time once. But now they lie shrouded in the afterglow of destruction, vanishing into the depths of legend. If you and I should join forces, we could do so much—kill the Count and all his followers, claim their fortune and their throne as the new Nobility. We might even bring the majesty of true Nobles into the world with no destruction."

D watched Rei-Ginsei's face. Rei-Ginsei watched D's.

"You are already a dhampir—half Nobility. Let me pretend I have killed you and have the Count drink my blood. And then ..." Rei-Ginsei laughed, "Surely there has never been such an exquisite couple in the entire history of the Nobility."

Rei-Ginsei's laughter was cut short by what D said next. "You like to kill, don't you?"

"Huh?"

"It's only fitting the Nobility be destroyed."

In a flash, Rei-Ginsei was leaping away for the second time. In midair he shouted, "You fool!"

Count Lee's daughter had called D exactly the same thing once.

Three flashes of black shot from his right hip. One flew over D's head, arced, and came at him from the rear. One zipped right along the ground, clipping every blade of grass it touched until it turned up at his feet and shot toward his armpit. And one came straight at the Hunter as a distraction. Each was a shrike-blade unleashed on a different course with breathtaking speed.

However ...

All of Rei-Ginsei's murderous implements were knocked out of the air with a beautiful sound.

A pained cry of "Ah" could be heard from the bushes, as Rei-Ginsei's left hand was severed at the elbow. It flew through the air, a candle still held tight in its fist. D, who'd rushed to where Rei-Ginsei had landed the moment he'd fended off the three attacks, had chopped it off.

As blood spilled from Rei-Ginsei—just as it had from his three companions—his expression said less about his pain than it did of his disbelief. At the same time he was hurling his shrike-blades, he shook the Time-Bewitching Incense, but it hadn't given off its beguiling scent. In fact, the candle hadn't even lit. It's a fake! *But when was it switched, and who could've done it?!*

As agony and suspicion churned together in his gorgeous face, a naked blade was thrust under his nose.

"Where is Miss Lang?"

"How foolish," Rei-Ginsei groaned as he pressed down on his bloody, dripping wound. "Out of some duty you feel for no more than a human girl, you would cut me down—me, a human who told you of my contempt for the Noble, and that I would take his life. Accursed one, thy name is dhampir ... You share the Noble's world by night and the mortal's by day, but are accepted by neither. You shall spend all the days of your life a resident of the land of twilight."

"I'm a Vampire Hunter," D said softly. "Where is Miss Lang? That face you're so fond of will be the next thing I carve."

There was something about his words that wasn't a mere threat. The ghastly aura that had stopped Rei-Ginsei in his tracks that time in the fog now hit him with several times its previous power. Rei-Ginsei heard his words come out of his mouth of their own volition, due to a terror beyond human ken. "The forest ... Go straight in at the entrance to the north woods ... "

"Fine." D's ghastly aura died down instantly.

Rei-Ginsei's body shot up like a spring, and was pierced by a flash of silver.

And yet it was D that fell to one knee with a low moan.

"What?! That's impossible ... " It was only right that Dan exclaimed this as he peeked around the statue.

As Rei-Ginsei was leaping into the air, D's sword slid into his belly in the blink of an eye. Half the blade's length had clearly gone into his opponent. And yet the tip of the blade had emerged from D's own abdomen!

"Damn!" Rei-Ginsei spat, leaping away. And as he did, something even stranger happened—naturally the sword in D's hand came out of Rei-Ginsei's belly, but at exactly the same rate the blade jutting from D's stomach pulled back *into the Hunter's body*!

Dan watched in astonishment.

"I see now. I'd heard there were mutants like you," D muttered. Not surprisingly, he was still down on one knee, and wincing ever so slightly. A deep red stain was spreading across the bottom of his shirt. "You're a dimension-twister, aren't you, you son of a bitch? That was close."

Having leapt ten feet away, Rei-Ginsei's eyes sparkled, and a loathsome groan escaped his throat. "I can't believe you changed your target at the last second ... "

Here's what they meant by "that was close" and "you changed your target."

Rei-Ginsei hadn't beat back the pain of his severed arm and leapt up to launch an attack of his own. He expected to have his own heart pierced by D's sword. At that instant, the sword was indeed headed straight for his chest, but at the last second it pulled back and pierced his stomach.

That was why he shouted, "Damn"—Rei-Ginsei realized D had noticed the way he'd adjusted the speed of his leap so his chest would be right where the Hunter could stab it. After all, a single thrust through the same vital spot as vampires could kill dhampirs too. Still, why had he resorted to such an outrageous tactic—allowing himself to be stabbed to kill his opponent?

Rei-Ginsei was a dimension-twister; through his own willpower, he could make a four-dimensional passageway in any part of his body but his arms and legs and link it with the body of his foe. In other words, when his foe attacked him, the bullets and blades that broke his skin would all travel through extra-dimensional space into the body of his assailant, where they would become real again. A bullet that was supposed to go through his heart would explode from the chest of the person that fired it;

bringing a vicious blade down on his shoulder would only split your own. What attack could be more efficient than that?

After all, he simply had to stand there, let his attackers do as they pleased, and his foes would die by their own hands.

But Rei-Ginsei leapt away. A belly wound wasn't life threatening for a dhampir, and he was badly wounded himself.

"I'll see to it you pay for my left hand another time!" he could be heard to say from somewhere in the bushes, and then he was gone without a trace.

"D, it's all right now—oh, you're bleeding!"

Ignoring Dan's cries as the boy ran over to him, D used his sword like a cane and got right up.

"I don't have time to chase after him. Dan, where's the north woods?"

"I'll show you the way. But it'll take three hours to ride there from here." The boy's voice was filled with boundless respect and concern. The sun was already poised to dip beneath the edge of the prairie. The world would be embraced by darkness in less than thirty minutes.

"Any shortcuts?"

"Yep. There is one, but it cuts right through some mighty tough country. There are fissures, and a huge swamp…"

D gazed steadily at the boy's face. "What do you say we give it a shot?"

"Sure!"

Death of a Vampire Hunter

I t was Greco who'd used the Time-Bewitching Incense to save Doris. The morning after he eavesdropped on the conversation between Rei-Ginsei and the Count, Greco had one of the thugs who usually watched out for him pose as a visitor and call Rei-Ginsei down from his hotel room to the lobby. The thug was gone before Rei-Ginsei got there, however, and by the time Rei-Ginsei returned to his room, the Time-Bewitching Incense had been replaced with an ordinary candle that looked just like it. With the incense in his possession, Greco had kept watch on Dr. Ferringo's house, and when the vampire-physician left with Doris, he'd followed after them but kept far enough back so they wouldn't notice.

He intended to rescue Doris and bind her fast with the shackles known as obligation. And, if the fates were kind, he would also slay their feudal lord, the Count. In one fell swoop, he would become a big man in town, and he had ambitions of heading to the Capital. The fact that he had single-handedly dispatched a Noble would clearly be his greatest selling point to the Revolutionary Government, and his best chance to win advancement into their leadership.

However, the situation had changed somewhat. The buggy was supposed to go straight to the Count, but it had stopped when a girl in white suddenly appeared, and on top of that, the very same girl staked Dr. Ferringo. No longer sure exactly what was going on, Greco was convinced that something had gone wrong. He got closer to the wagon. Seeing the vampiress and her lurid expression as she prepared to sink her claws into Doris' throat, he'd given the Time-Bewitching Incense a desperate shake.

Timid at first, when he saw Larmica writhing in agony and he approached the buggy with his head held high. The incense was in his left hand. In his right hand, he was gripping a foot-long stake of rough wood so fiercely that it pressed into his fingers. Stakes were everyday items on the Frontier. The ten-banger pistol holstered at his waist with the safety off, and the large-bore heat-rifle stuck through the saddle of the horse he'd tethered in the trees, were for dealing with the Nobility's underlings. His beloved combat suit was in the shop for repairs, just like most of his flunkies' gear.

"Oh," Doris groaned as she got up. In her writhing, Larmica must've struck some part of Doris' body and brought her around. Her eyes were torpid for a brief moment, but they opened wide as soon as she noticed Larmica. Then she looked at Dr. Ferringo's body, lying on the ground not far from the buggy, and at Greco and said, "Doc ... why in the world?...What are you doing way out here?"

"So that's the thanks I get," Greco said, clambering up into the backseat of the buggy. You know, I kept that bitch from making chunky splatter out of you. I followed you out here from town in the dark of night. You'd think that'd win a little favor from you."

"Did you kill Doc, too?"

Doris' voice shook with sorrow and rage.

"What, are you kidding? The bitch did it. Although, it did making rescuing your ass a little easier."

Being careful not to let the tiny flame go out, Greco moved Larmica into the backseat with his other hand. The young lady in white curled up under the seat without offering the slightest resistance. Not only was she deathly still, but she also seemed to have stopped breathing.

"That's the Count's daughter. Was she responsible for turning Doc into a vampire, too?"

"No, that was the Count. See, he attacked him last night so he could use him to lure you out here." Greco quickly shut his mouth, but it was too late.

Doris stared at him with fire in her eyes. "And just how the hell do you know all this? You knew he was gonna be attacked and you didn't even tell him, did you? You dirty bastard! What do you mean you saved me? You're only looking out for yourself!"

"Shut your damn mouth, you!" Turning away from her burning gaze, Greco reasserted himself. "How dare you go talkin' to me that way after I saved your life. We can hash that out later. Right now, we've got to decide what to do about her."

"Do about her?" Doris knit her brow.

"Sure. As in, do we kill her or use her as a bargaining chip to negotiate with the Count."

"What!? Are you serious?"

"Dead serious. And don't act like this don't concern you. I'm doing all this for you."

Doris was in a daze as she watched the young tough make one preposterous statement after another. Then her nose twitched ever so slightly. She'd caught the scent of the Time-Bewitching Incense.

Come to think of it, the moonlit night felt strangely like a brilliant, sunny day. Greco said with pride, "The perfume in this candle is to thank. The Nobility has them, and apparently they can change day into night and vice versa. As long as it's lit, the bitch can't move a muscle and the Nobility can't come near us—which is what got me thinking. It'd be so easy to kill her, but considering how she's the Count's daughter, there'd be hell to pay later. So, we take her hostage to set up a trade, then take the Count's life, too, if all goes well."

"Could you ... could you really do that?" Her plaintive voice made Greco's lips twist lewdly, and when Doris averted her gaze she saw the pale face of Larmica as she lay beneath the backseat breathing feebly.

Larmica was lovely, and didn't look very far in age from herself. Doris felt ashamed for having considered for even a moment using the young lady as a bargaining chip.

"Noble or not, there ain't a parent out there who don't love their own daughter. That's how we can trip him up good. We'll say we want to trade her for some treasure. Then when he comes out all confident, bang, we use the incense to nab him and drive this here stake through his heart. Rumor has it their bodies turn into dust and disappear, but if someone like my father or the sheriff is there to see it, they'd make a first-class witness when I give the government in the Capital my account."

"The Capital?"

"Er, forget I mentioned it." In his heart, Greco thumbed his nose at her. "At any rate, if we kill 'em, the two of us will get the Noble's stuff—their fortune, weapons, ammo, everything! All for the huge service to humanity we'll be doing."

"But this woman ... she hasn't done anything to anyone in the village," Doris said vehemently, sifting through everything she could remember hearing since childhood.

"Open your eyes. A Noble's a Noble. They're all bloodsucking freaks preying on the human race."

Doris was dumbstruck. This coarse thug had just hurled the same curse on them that she had once said to D! *I was just like him then. That's not right. Even if they are Nobles, I can't use someone's helpless daughter to lure them to their death.* Just as Doris was about to voice her objections, a voice dark as the shadows held her tongue.

"Kill me ... here ... and now ..."

Larmica.

"What's that?" Greco sneered down at her in his overbearing manner, but her expression was so utterly ghastly it took his breath away. Even as she was subjected to the agony of her body burning in the midday sun, she showed incredible willpower.

"Father ... is not so foolish he would exchange his life for my own. And I will not be a pawn in your trade ... Kill me ... If you don't ... I shall kill you both someday ..."

"You bitch!" Greco's face seemed to boil with anger and fear, and then he raised his stake. As a rule, he hadn't had much self-restraint to start with.

"Stop it! You can't do that to a defenseless person!" As she spoke, Doris grabbed his arm.

The two of them struggled in the buggy. Strength was in Greco's favor, but Doris had fighting skills imparted to her by her father. Suddenly letting go of his arm, she planted her left foot firmly and put the full force of her body behind a roundhouse kick that exploded against Greco's breastbone.

"Oof!"

The cramped buggy, with its unsteady footing, was too much for him. Greco reeled back, caught his leg on the door, and fell out of the vehicle.

Not even looking at where the dull thud came from, Doris got out of her seat and tried to talk to Larmica. "Don't worry. I'm not gonna let that jerk do anything to you. But I can't very well just send you on your merry way, either. You know who I am, right? You'll have to come back to my house with me. We'll figure out what to do about you there."

A low chuckle that seemed to rise from the bowels of the earth cut off all further comment from Doris. "You are free to try what you will, but I won't be going anywhere." Doris thought her spine had turned to ice when she saw the beautiful visage look up at her, paler than moonlight and filled now by an evil grin of confidence. She didn't know what had just happened. When Greco had fallen from the buggy, the Time-Bewitching Incense had gone out!

Larmica caught hold of Doris' hand with a grip as cold as ice. In the darkness, Doris' eyes made out pearly fangs poking over the lips of the child of night as she got to her feet.

Doris was pulled closer with such brute strength Greco couldn't even begin to compare. She couldn't move at all. Larmica's breath had the scent of flowers. Flowers nourished with blood. Two silhouettes, two faces overlapped into one.

"Aaaagh!" A scream stirred the darkness, and then was gone. Trembling, Larmica shielded her face.

There in the dark she'd seen it. No, she'd felt it. Felt the pain of the same holy mark of the cross her father had seen on the girl's neck two days earlier! It would make its sudden appearance only when the breath of a vampire fell on it.

The vampires themselves didn't know why they feared it. All that was certain was that even without seeing it their skin could feel its presence. In that instant some nameless force bound them. This was the mark they couldn't allow humans to know about, something that had supposedly sunk into the watery depths of forgetfulness thanks to ages of ingenious psychological manipulation—so how could this girl have the holy mark on her neck?

Though Doris didn't understand why Larmica—who'd enjoyed an overwhelming advantage until a second earlier—had suddenly lost her mind, she surmised that she'd been saved. Now she had to run!

"Greco, you all right?"

"Oooh, kind of." The dubious response that came from the ground beside her suggested he might have hit his head.

"Hurry up and get in! If you don't get your ass in gear I'll leave you out here!"

And with that threat she took the reins in hand and gave them a crack. She intended to throw Larmica off with a sudden jolt forward. But the horses didn't move.

Doris finally noticed a man wearing an inverness standing in front of the horses and holding them by their bridles. For some time now, a number of figures had been standing at the edge of the woods.

"As the doctor was late, I thought something might be amiss, and my suspicions proved correct," one of the silhouettes said in a voice of barely suppressed rage. It was the Count. Though her heart was sinking into hopelessness, Doris was still the same warrior woman who'd bitterly resisted the Count all along. Seeing that the whip Doc had taken from her earlier was lying on the seat beside her, Doris snatched it up and swung it at the man in the inverness.

"Huh?" Doris cried, and the man—Garou—grinned broadly. She was sure she'd split the side of his face open, but he bobbed his head out of the way and caught the end of the whip between his teeth. Grrrrr! With a bestial growl he—it—started chewing up Doris' whip, a weapon that had stood up to swords without a problem.

"You're a werewolf," Doris shouted in surprise.

"That's correct," the Count responded. "He serves me, but unlike me he is rather hot-blooded. Another thing you may wish to consider—I told him that, should you give us any trouble, he had my permission to hurt you. It might be amusing to see a bride missing some fingers and toes."

Suddenly a boom rang out. Still flat on his ass on the ground, Greco had fired off his ten-banger. High-power powder—the type that could easily punch a hole through the armor of larger creatures—enveloped the Count and those near him in flames. The Count didn't even glance at Greco, and the flames were promptly swallowed by the darkness. Such was the power of the Count's force field.

"Raaarrrrrr!" The werewolf snarled at Greco. Halfway through its transformation, it glared at Greco with blood-red eyes. Greco gave a squeal and froze. White steam rose from the crotch of his pants. Fear had gotten the better of his bladder, but who could blame him?

Doris' shoulders sank. The last bit of will she possessed was thoroughly uprooted.

"Father … "

Larmica drifted down to the ground like a breeze. With glittering eyes, the Count gave her a hard look and said, "I have an excellent idea of what you were trying to do. Daughter or not, this time I'll not let you get away with it. You shall be punished on our return to the castle. Now stand back!" Ignoring Larmica as she headed silently to the rear, the Count extended a hand to Doris.

"Well, now, you had best come with me."

Doris bit her lip. "Don't be so pleased with yourself! No matter what happens to me, D is gonna send you all to the hereafter."

"Is he really?" The Count forced a smile. "Right about now the stripling and your younger brother are both being taken care of by our mutual acquaintances. In a fair fight, he might have prevailed, but I gave his foes a secret weapon."

"Father … " From the tree line to the Count's rear, Larmica pointed to where Greco crouched on the ground. "That man had Time-Bewitching Incense."

"What!" Even through the darkness the sudden contortion of the Count's face was clear. "That cannot be. I gave it to Rei-Ginsei." Here he paused for a beat, and after closely scrutinizing his daughter's face said, "I can see that you speak the truth—which means the stripling is—"

"Correct."

A low voice made all who stood there shrink in fear. The Count looked over his shoulder again, and Doris' eyes darted in the same direction—toward Larmica. Or rather, toward something looming from the trees to her back. A figure of unearthly beauty.

"I'm right here."

A groan that fell short of speech spilled from the Count's throat.

Never did I imagine this rogue might come back alive ...

If Time-Bewitching Incense hadn't played its pivotal role in the duel, the Hunter's survival was far from impossible. But unless he had an aircraft of some sort, it should've taken D another hour by horse to cover the distance from the site of his duel with Rei-Ginsei.

And yet D was here. He had been one with the darkness, and neither the Count's night-piercing gaze nor the three-dimensional radar of the robot sentries had detected him.

The robot sentries turned in D's direction, but an attack was impossible, of course.

"Don't try anything funny—I'll show her no mercy." Garou was just about to pounce on Doris when a low but not particularly rough voice stopped him in his tracks.

"Doris, you and what's-your-name—bring the wagon over here. Be quick about it!"

"Ye—yessir!" Doris answered dreamily, not just because of the relief she felt in being rescued, but because D had called her by name for the first time ever.

"Garou, grab the girl," the Count commanded sharply.

As the black figure prepared once again to leap up into the buggy, it was buffeted with another castrating voice—Doris'. "You come near me and I'll bite my tongue off!"

The werewolf snarled loudly and stopped. So many irritations. Greco flopped into the buggy.

"I'm prepared to die before I'd ever become one of your kind. If it's gotta be here and now, that won't bother me." The threats of an insignificant human—a mere girl of seventeen—silenced the Count. To all appearances, D and Doris had won this *outré* encounter. The Count was obsessed with Doris, and would have her at any price. Conversely, if Doris were to die, that would be the end of everything.

"We shall settle this another time."

The buggy stirred the night air as it sped to D's side, and the Count put his arm around Larmica's shoulder for the first time. The next instant, the two figures nimbly made their way up into the buggy.

What was astonishing about this whole encounter was that D never even touched the sword on his back. Even when he'd taken Larmica hostage, he hadn't threatened her with his blade. Larmica had moved to the back as her father ordered, and the second she sensed D's presence behind her, she found she couldn't move a muscle. She was paralyzed by the overwhelming aura that radiated from him—one that the superhuman senses of vampires alone could fully appreciate. The same aura had prevented the Count and Garou from raising a hand against him.

"What do you intend to do with my daughter?" the Count called out to D, who kept a steady gaze trained on him and his party from the backseat of the buggy.

There was no reply

"The little imbecile has crossed me at every turn and cost me the chance of a lifetime—I no longer consider her my daughter. Let her lie in the sun till decay takes her to the marrow of her bones!"

His words were unthinkably harsh for a father, but then, on the whole, the vampire race had extremely dilute notions of love and consideration, compared to human beings. Quite possibly it was this trait that had both led them to the heights of prosperity and guided them to their eventual downfall. When her father's words reached her ears, Larmica didn't even raise an eyebrow.

"Doc, we'll come back for you later!" Following Doris' sorrowful cry, the buggy took off.

After they'd gone a short way across the plains, they could hear a horse whinnying up ahead. Apparently, whoever was out there had noticed them.

"Who's that? Is that you, Sis?!"

"Dan! You're all right, are you?!" Doris asked, her voice nearly weeping as she drove the buggy over to her brother. He was on horseback. And he held the reins to a second horse. That one had been Rei-Ginsei's, and they'd brought it for Doris. They'd planned on having her ride home with them, but unfortunately they'd picked up some unwanted baggage. The whole reason D had taken Doris and Greco out in the buggy was to solve their transportation problems.

"I'm going to lighten our load. You two get on the horse. Dan, you come over here with me."

By "you two" he meant Doris and Greco. Because so many of the things that'd been happening were beyond his comprehension, Greco felt like his brains were half scrambled, so he followed orders without the slightest protest. The transfers were effected in a matter of seconds.

"Are you sure you can still handle the buggy if you've got her riding with you?" Doris asked from her seat in the saddle. The real question was: how many present noticed the jealousy in her voice? D made no answer, but silently lashed the horses with Doris' whip.

The wind howled in the girl's ears as the forest and fiends were left further and further behind.

"Dan, you weren't hurt, were you?"

Doris barely squeezed the question out as she rode alongside them. They were going full speed to keep the Count from catching up, and the wheels of the buggy spun wildly.

"Not a bit. I was gonna ask you the same thing—hey, of course you're fine. D's on the job. He wouldn't let anyone harm a hair on your head."

"No, I suppose he wouldn't," Doris concurred, her eyes full of joy.

"I wish you could've seen it," Dan said loudly. "It took him less than fifteen seconds each to get rid of them freaks. It's too bad the last one got away, but that couldn't be helped with D being hurt and all."

"Huh? Was he really?"

It was understandable that Doris grew pale, but why Larmica suddenly looked over at D from her seat was unclear.

"Hunters are really great, though. He got stabbed through the gut and it didn't even bother him—good ol' D rode through the roughest country with me on the back and pulling another horse behind us. You should've seen it. When D had the reins, them darned horses would jump right over the biggest crevice or a swamp full of giant leeches without batting an eye. Oh yeah, and they wouldn't stop no matter how steep the grade got—I'm gonna have him teach me all that horse and sword stuff later!"

"Oh, that's great. You pay good attention when he does now..." Doris' words were exuberant, but the power petered out of them and they were shredded by the wind. Perhaps her maiden instincts had given her some hint of how their story was going to end.

Deathly still and watching the darkness ahead, Larmica suddenly muttered, "Traitor."

"What did you say?!" Doris was the picture of rage. She realized the vampiress was referring to D. Larmica didn't even look at the girl, but bloody flames fairly shot from her eyes as she stared at D's frigid profile.

"You have skill and power enough to intimidate Father and myself, but you have forgotten your proud Noble blood. You feel some duty to the humans—worse yet, you are foolish enough to serve them by hunting us. I feel polluted simply speaking to you. Father wouldn't bother to follow you this far. Slay me here!"

"Shut up! We don't take orders from prisoners," Doris roared. "What have you high-ranking Noble types done to us? Just because you wanna feed, because you want hot human blood, you bite into the throats of folks who never did you any harm and make them vampires. They just turn around and attack the family that loved them—in the end, their family has to drive a stake through their heart. Demons is what you are. You're the Devil. Do you have any idea how many people die every year, parents and children crying out to their loved ones as they're killed in tidal waves and earthquakes caused by the weather controllers your kind runs?" Doris spat the accusations at her like a gob of blood, but Larmica just smiled coolly.

"We are the Nobility—the ruling class. The rulers are entitled to take such measures to ensure the rebellious feelings of the lower class are kept in check. You should consider yourself lucky we even allowed your race to continue." And then, with a long gaze at Greco as he brooded and raced along on his horse, she said, "Indeed, we will attack your kind to drink but a single drop of sweet blood. But what has that man done? I heard. For wanting you, he did nothing to warn that decrepit old man, even when he knew he was to be attacked, did he not?"

Doris couldn't find a thing to say.

Larmica's voice continued to dominate the night. "But I do not condemn him for that," she laughed. "To the contrary, the man is to be lauded. Is it not appropriate to sacrifice others to satisfy our own desires? The strong rule the weak, and the superior leave the inferior in the dust—that is the great principle that governs the cosmos. There are many among you who seem to share our point of view."

"Ha ha ha," Doris suddenly laughed back mockingly. "Don't make me laugh. If you're such great rulers then what do you want with me?" Now it was Larmica's turn to be silenced. "I heard something, too. It made me sick to hear it, but it seems your father wants to make me his bride. Every night he comes sniffing around my place like a dog in heat, and I turn him down—you'd think he'd be tired of it by now. The Nobility must be hard-pressed for women. Or is it something else? Could it be your father's just weirder than the rest?"

The killing lust in Larmica's eyes was like a heat ray that flew at Doris' face. Not to be outdone, Doris met it with a shower of sparks from her own hatred. It was as if there was a titanic spray of invisible embers between the galloping horse and racing buggy when their eyes locked.

Suddenly, D pulled back on the reins.

"Oh!" Doris gasped as she hastened to stop her horse as well. Greco alone was at a loss as to what to do, but then he decided staying with them any longer would only make matters worse, and he rushed away into the darkness.

Though no one was quite sure what he was doing, all of them followed D's lead, dismounting when he climbed down from the buggy. Larmica quickly turned to face the other three.

"What do you intend to do?" Larmica asked.

"As you yourself said, we've gone far enough the Count won't give chase. Now all we have to do is deal with you," D said softly. A tense hue raced into Larmica's face, and then into those of Doris and Dan. "I've been hired to keep her safe. Therefore, I'll have to slay your father. But anything else is another matter—meaning I now need my employer to decide what to do about you. Well?"

His final "Well?" had been directed at Doris. She was perplexed. They'd just been arguing a few seconds earlier. She'd thought she hated the vampiress enough to kill her, but the girl she saw looked like a beautiful, defenseless young lady about her own age.

This daughter of the detestable Nobility. *If not for her family, me and Dan would be living in peace now—I wanna kill her. I've got it. I can give her my whip and have her fight D. That'd be fair. If we gave her a chance like that, there'd be nothing to be ashamed about.*

"What do you want to do?" D asked.

"Slay me," Larmica said with eyes ablaze.

And then Doris shook her head.

"Let her go. I don't have it in me to murder. I couldn't do that to her, even if she's a Noble ..."

D turned to Dan. "What about you?"

"It's plain as day, ain't it? I couldn't do nothing as low as cutting down a woman in cold blood—and you couldn't either, could you?"

Then the Langs saw a smile spread across D's face. For years after, even for decades after, the two of them would remember D's expression, and take pride in the fact they were responsible for it. It was just such a smile.

"Well, there you have it. You'd best go now."

And with that D turned his back to Larmica, but she flung abuse at him anyway.

"The stupidity of the lot of you amazes me. Do not delude yourselves that I am in any way grateful. I will make you rue your decision to set me free! Had I been in your position, I would have had you slaughtered like a sow. And your brother as well."

The other three didn't turn to look at her again, but went back to the buggy.

"Take this horse."

Doris dropped the reins in front of Larmica.

"Even children know the cosmic principle, it seems," D said calmly from the driver's seat.

"What?"

"Survival of the fittest, might makes right—that's not what your Sacred Ancestor used to say."

Larmica's eyes bulged, but a moment later she laughed out loud. "Not only are you sickeningly soft-hearted, but it appears you're given to delusions as well. Did you mention the Sacred Ancestor? There's no chance a lowly creature like you would know someone of his greatness. He who made our civilization, our whole world, and the laws by which we ruled. Every one of us faithfully followed his words."

"Every one of you? Then why was the poor old bastard always so troubled ..."

"The poor old bastard? You mean ... No, you couldn't ..." Larmica's voice carried a hint of fear. She recalled a certain plausible rumor that had been whispered at a grand ball at the castle when she was just a child.

"Such skill, and such power ... Might it be that you are ... "

The whip cracked.

When the buggy had dashed off leaving only the tortured squeal of its tires in its wake, the daughter of the Nobility forgot all about gathering the reins of the horse before her as she stood stock still in the moonlight.

"Milord, might it be ..."

The next day, Dan and D accompanied Doris when she went out to claim Dr. Ferringo's body. They then paid a call on the sheriff and entrusted him with the remains before bringing all of Rei-Ginsei and Greco's misdeeds to light.

Having received a communiqué from the village of Pedros about the Frontier Defense Force, the sheriff had been out to the ruins himself and discovered the trio of lurid corpses there. Based on Doris' testimony, he concluded Rei-Ginsei's gang was connected to the disappearance of the FDF patrol. In an attempt to ascertain the whereabouts of that patrol, special deputies rushed off to the neighboring villages.

"Well, Rei-Ginsei won't be at large for long now. Of course, there's also a good chance he made like the wind last night right after you lopped off his cabbage-collector."

On the way back to the farm, Doris' expression was sunny— she had at least one of her problems taken care of. But D told her simply, "If he becomes a Noble, he could lose all his limbs and still be a threat."

Rei-Ginsei had ambitions of joining the Nobility. Given his skill and scheming nature, to say nothing of a vindictiveness that put a serpent to shame, it was unthinkable that he would run off with his tail between his legs, or quit before he'd achieved his ends. He may have fled, but it was clear he'd hidden himself somewhere and would be vigilantly watching what they did. He might still carry out the Count's orders.

A daylight foe—because of him, D's movements were greatly restricted. Up until now, he'd only had to worry about taking up his blade by night. But now, it would be patently impossible to go attack the Count in his castle and leave Doris and Dan under the scrutiny of an appreciable foe who possessed both weird weapons and even stranger skill.

"Still, it's too bad they didn't lock that bastard Greco up," Dan muttered.

The sheriff was wrapped up in the Rei-Ginsei case, but couldn't get to the bottom of Greco's activities. The three of them had accompanied the lawman to the mayor's house to question him, but the thoroughly disgusted mayor appeared and informed them that Greco had returned quite agitated the previous night, grabbed all the money in the house as well as the combat suit that'd just come back from the repair shop, and took off on his horse. The sheriff had Doris and the others wait in his office while he checked with some of Greco's partners-in-crime, but they all said they didn't know where he was.

Rei-Ginsei and Greco—with the whereabouts of both of them unknown there was little the sheriff could do. He informally sent Greco's description to the other villages and requested that if the man was found, he was to be detained for having important information about the murder of Dr. Ferringo.

"But we can't charge him in this case," the sheriff told a visibly dissatisfied Doris. "From what you tell me, it seems Doc was killed by this Noble girl. And as for the matter of being turned into a vampire in the first place—well, even now it's not clear if a person suffers any harm when that happens. I wish to hell the Capital would give us a clear ruling on that ..."

Doris nodded reluctantly.

It was unclear whether or not turning someone into a vampire could be considered murder. From one perspective, the change merely caused a shift in personality, not an absolute loss of life. The question dogged mankind throughout history, remaining undecided to this very day. Consequently, Greco couldn't be charged with a crime, even though he didn't inform the sheriff when he knew the Count was going to "kill" Dr. Ferringo.

"Quite the contrary, in the eyes of the law Greco might be considered a hero for rescuing you." Seeing Doris' slender eyebrows rise in wrath, the sheriff hurriedly added, "And while I don't have any authority to get caught up in personal squabbles ..." The rest was implied—*when I find the weasel, I'm gonna belt him good.* Doris and Dan looked at each other and grinned.

Doris found herself in the first peaceful lull since the Count had attacked her.

There was a mountain of work to be done. Synthesized protein harvested by the robots had to be put into packages, stacked at the edge of the garden, and covered with a water-repellent tent until the traveling merchant made his monthly call. The Langs didn't sell it, but rather traded it for daily necessities. The protein Doris and Dan grew was well known for its density, and the merchant always gave them an exceptional rate in trade for it.

The milking and general care of the cows had been neglected as well. Of course, the village of Ransylva was where most of that was traded; even though she'd been shut out of all the shops, she couldn't let the cows go any longer. Doris' battle with the Count didn't put food on the table.

With Dan and a battered robot to help her, the job would've taken three whole days, but D did it in half a day. He skillfully poured huge bowls of milky protein extract into plastic packages, and then carried them from the processing area to the garden when he had a pile of a certain size. The boxes weighed a good seventy pounds each, and he carried three of them at a time. When he first saw it, Dan bugged out his eyes and exclaimed, "Wow!" but after three straight hours of this superhuman toting, his jaw dropped and he was left speechless.

The speed with which D milked the cows was almost miraculous. In the time it took Doris to do one cow, he did three. And that was only using his left hand. His right hand was left empty to go for the sword by his side at any time. That was the way Hunters were.

I wonder what kind of family he comes from?

It wasn't the first time this question had occurred to her, but it hadn't been answered in the days they'd been fighting, and even then Doris hadn't had the time ask anyway. Actually, it was the code of the Frontier that you didn't go poking into the background of travelers, and D's bearing in particular didn't invite questions.

Doris watched D's profile with a distant look in her eyes as he silently worked one hand on the cow, the white fluid collecting in an aluminum-plated can.

The scene seemed so familiar; maybe it was the girl's feverish, young heart that made her feel like it would go on this way forever. While it wasn't that long ago that Doris had lost her father—and her battle to protect her brother and the farm began—she suddenly realized how exhausted she was.

"Done. Aren't you finished yet?"

At D's query, Doris returned from her fantasies. "Er, no, I'm done here."

As she stood up and pulled the can out from under the cow, she felt as if she was naked before him.

"Your face is flushed. You coming down with a cold or something?"

"No, it's not. It must just be the sunset."

The interior of the barn was stained red.

"I see. The Count will probably come here again. You'd best eat early and get Dan to bed."

"I suppose you're right."

Doris grabbed the handle of the can with both hands and carried it to one side of barn. For some reason she had no strength.

"Leave it. I'll carry it," D said, having seen how wobbly her legs were.

"I'll be fine!"

Her tone was so rough she surprised herself. Tears rolled out with the words. Dropping the can to the ground, she ran out sobbing.

As D went after her—though his casual pace hardly made it seem like pursuit—Dan trained an apprehensive gaze on him from the porch.

"Sis ran around back crying. You two have a fight or something?"

D shook his head. "No. Your sister's just worried about you."

"You know, someone told me a man shouldn't make women cry."

D smiled wryly. "You're right. I'll go apologize."

Taking a few steps, D then turned to Dan again.

"You still remember that promise you made, do you?"

"Yep."

"You're eight now. In another five years, you'll be stronger than your sister. Don't forget."

Dan nodded. When he raised his face, it was shining with tears.

"Are you gonna go away, D? Once you've killed the Count, I mean."

D disappeared around back without giving an answer.

Doris was leaning against the fence. Her shoulders were quaking.

D's footsteps didn't make a sound as he went and stood behind her.

A cool breeze played through the grassy sea beyond the fence and through Doris' black tresses.

"You should go back to the house."

Doris didn't reply, but after a bit she mumbled, "I should've looked for someone else. Once you're gone, I won't be able to live like I did before. That milking can just now—I used to be able to carry two at a time. I won't be able set Dan straight when he needs it, or have the strength to fend off any fellahs who come out here courting me. But you're gonna go just the same."

"That was the deal. That will end your sorrow. That or my death."

"No!" Doris suddenly buried her face in his muscular chest. "No, no, no."

She didn't know what she was protesting. Nor did she know why she cried. Neither the young woman weeping—as if weeping could keep a phantom from vanishing—nor the young man with the melancholy air supporting her moved for the longest time. And then, after a little while …

Doris lifted her face suddenly. Just above her head, D had started to growl softly. Doris was about to ask, "What is it?" when her head was forced back against his chest by his formidable strength. A few seconds more passed.

The two silhouettes were fused in the red glow, but from between the two of them came the words, "I'm okay now," in a feverish voice.

Nothing else was said, and soon D gently pushed Doris away and quickly walked back toward the house.

As he rounded the corner of the barn, a voice said teasingly, "Why didn't you drink her blood?" It originated around his waist.

"Shut up." For once D's voice bore undisguised emotion.

"The girl knew. She knew what you wanted. Oh, now don't you make that face with me. You can fight it all you like, but you've got the blood of the Nobility in the marrow of your bones. The fact that when you fancy a woman you're more interested in latching onto her pale neck instead of getting her in the sack is proof of that."

It was true. When Doris had bared her soul to him, and he felt her warm body sobbing against his chest, D's expression became the same lurid vampire visage he'd worn when he drank the blood of the Midwich Medusas in the darkness of the subterranean aqueduct. But somehow, with his truly impressive willpower, he'd managed to fight the urge this time.

As D kept walking, the voice said to him, "The girl saw your other face. Not just that, but I bet she smelled your breath as it brushed her neck. Smelled the scent of your cursed blood. And still she said she didn't mind. Go easy on the nice guy routine. You fight your own desire and deny the wishes of the girl—is that any way for a grown dhampir to act? You're always on the run—from your blood, and from the people who want you. When you tell them you were fated to part, that's just dressing it up in a pretty excuse. Listen to me. Your father—"

"Shut up." The words D said were the same as a moment earlier, but the eerie aura behind them made it plain this was far more than just a threat. The voice fell silent. Climbing the stairs to the porch, D turned a thoughtful gaze to the prairie and muttered, "Still, I've got to go—go and find *him*."

"Oh, shit!" As D's hard gaze filled the lenses' field of view, a shadowy figure hurriedly ducked, afraid that D would see him. But he forgot he was now on a hill a good thousand feet away. It was none other than the mayor's hell-raising son Greco, who most believed to have long since fled the village. He was wearing his combat suit.

"That son of a bitch gets to have all the fun," Greco said, slamming his electronic binoculars against the ground. The previous night, after deciding discretion was the better part of valor, he'd come up to the top of this hill and kept an eye on the farm. Lying flat on his belly, he reached over to his saddlebags and pulled the Time-Bewitching Incense out from among the food and provisions packed in there.

"Heh, you'll get yours once the sun's down. I'll use this baby to get you down crawling on the ground, then nail you with a stake. Then yours truly will take Doris by the hand and kiss this godforsaken shithole goodbye," he said spitefully, turning his eyes toward the farm again. The previous night he'd been so scared by the Count and his werewolf that he'd abandoned all thought of killing them and decided to abduct Doris instead. And clearly, the person he talked about dispatching with a stake was D.

"I wonder if it'll go as smoothly as all that?" The words rained down on Greco in a cool voice.

"What the—?!"

Looking up, Greco saw a handsome young man sitting on a branch directly overhead. He wore an innocent smile, but his left arm was missing below the elbow, and its stump was wrapped in a bloody white cloth. He needed no introduction. And yet, less than twenty-four hours after losing one arm he'd climbed up into a tree and scared the daylights out of Greco while looking no worse for wear, aside from a little darkness around his eyes. What strength he had, both physically and mentally!

Rei-Ginsei got back down to the ground without making a sound.

"Wh ... what the hell do you want?"

"Don't play the innocent. I'm the rightful owner of that candle. Thanks to you, I lost my arm. I came out to the farm in the hopes of encountering the Count, but lo and behold, I've run across someone else of interest to me. So, are the three of them still hale and hearty?"

His speech was refined, but Greco felt a crushing coercion in it that left him bobbing his head in agreement.

"I suspected as much. In which case, I shall have to score some quick points here if I'm to be made one of them." After that enigmatic statement, the handsome young man addressed Greco with familiarity. "What do you say to joining forces with me?"

"Work with you?"

"From what I observed up in the tree, you seem obsessed with the young lady on the farm. Yet her bodyguard remains an obstacle. I have another reason for wanting him out of the way. What say you?"

Greco hesitated.

Rei-Ginsei chided him. "Are you certain you can finish him, even with the candle and your combat suit? With your skill?"

Greco was at a loss for an answer. That was exactly why he hadn't gone down and abducted Doris yet. Thanks to the effect it had on the Count's daughter, he'd been able to verify that Time-Bewitching Incense was highly effective against pure vampires, but when it came to a half-human dhampir, he didn't have much confidence. He'd donned the combat suit, but since it was just back from the repair shop he wasn't used to wearing it or using it, and if he had to call upon its power, it was doubtful he could use it to its full potential. "You mean to say, if I hook up with you, we might be able to do this?" His words were proof enough he'd fallen under Rei-Ginsei's spell.

Killing his smile, the handsome young man nodded. "Indeed. Once the sun has set I shall fight him, so watch for the right moment to light the candle, if you please. Should he leave himself open for even an instant, well, that's where my blades come in," he said, pointing to the shrike-blades on his hip.

Greco made up his mind. "Sure ... but what happens after that?"

"After that?"

"I know you're planning on handing the girl over to the Count, but that's exactly what I've been busting my hump to keep from happening."

"In that case, take her and flee," Rei-Ginsei said casually. Seeing the now-stupefied Greco, he added, "I merely promised him I would slay the dhampir. I don't care a whit whose property the girl becomes. That matter is between yourself and the Count, is it not? But you being a fellow human and all, if you like I shall tell my compatriots scattered across the Frontier to aid you in your flight from the Count."

"Would you really?" Greco's tone had become an appeal. The question of how he could shake the pursuing Noble if he managed to make good his escape with Doris was a point of concern for him. But why on earth would Rei-Ginsei say such a thing to him? Because he wasn't sure that just getting the Time-Bewitching Incense would be enough to beat D.

The indescribable swordplay the Hunter displayed as he made good his promise to dispatch three of the superhuman gang leader's valued henchmen in less than fifteen seconds each, and the invincibility he demonstrated in getting to his feet again despite the sword sticking out of his belly—the mere thought of these things was enough to give Rei-Ginsei gooseflesh. Just to be prepared for any eventuality, he decided to use the stupid little hood he'd found. Once D had been slain, Greco would have outlived his usefulness, and he would be crushed like an insect. "Well, I believe we have a bargain then." Rei-Ginsei flashed a smile so beautiful it would put a flower to shame, and held out his remaining hand.

"Um, okay." Greco hesitated to take his hand. "But I don't completely trust you yet. Just so we're clear, if you try anything funny I'll wreck the candle on the spot."

"Fair enough."

"Then that's just great."

They shared a firm handshake.

The round moon rose. Strangely large and white, the unsettling lunar disc sent wild waves of anxiety across the hearts of all who looked up at it. An old farmer named Morris snapped awake when he felt a chill. Sitting up in bed, the old man looked to the bedroom window and felt his hair rising on end. The window he was certain he'd locked was open now.

But that wasn't what terrified the old man.

His granddaughter Lucy, whom he'd looked after since she'd lost her parents in an accident, stood by the window in her little nightgown, staring at her grandfather with vacant eyes. Her face was paler than the moonlight spilling in through the window.

"Lucy, what's the matter?"

When he noticed the twin streaks of red coursing down his granddaughter's throat, the old man froze in his bed.

"I am ... Count Lee," Lucy mumbled. In a man's voice! "Give me Doris Lang ... If you do not ... tonight, tomorrow night ... every night the ranks of the living-dead shall swell ... "

And then his granddaughter collapsed on the floor.

After dinner, Dan had been inseparable from D, but even he couldn't resist the sandman indefinitely, and he had to retire to his room. Doris disappeared into her own bedroom, leaving D alone in the living room, which was lit only by stark moonlight. He'd been sleeping there since the first night, since he said the room to the back of the house was too cramped. He lay on the sofa, his eyes cold and clear as ice. The hour was nearing eleven Night.

A white light flickered.

The bedroom door opened, and Doris stepped out. A threadbare bath towel covered her from her breasts to her thighs. Crossing the living room without a sound, she stood before the sofa. Her ample bosom was heaving. Taking two deep breaths, Doris let the towel fall.

Unmoving, unblinking, D fixed his eyes on the girl's naked form. Her well-proportioned and slightly muscled body wasn't yet endowed with all a woman's sensuality, but it had more than enough of the pale virgin charm that always took men's breath away.

"D ..." Doris' voice caught in her throat.

"I haven't finished my work here."

"I'll pay you in advance. Take it ..."

Before he could even speak, her warm flesh was on top of him and her sweet breath was tickling his nose.

"Hey, I'm ..."

"The Count's gonna come again," Doris panted. "And this time it's gonna get settled—at least, that's the feeling I get. I probably won't get a chance to give you your reward—so take me, suck my blood, do whatever you like to me."

D's hand brushed the girl's lengthy tresses aside, exposing the face they'd hidden to the night air. Their lips met.

For a few seconds they remained together—and then D sat up quickly. His eyes raced to the window. That way lay the main gate.

"What is it? The Count?" Doris' voice was taut.

"No. I sense two groups. The first is a pair, and the second—there's a lot of them. Fifty, no, close to a hundred strong."

"A hundred people?!"

"Go wake up Dan."

Doris disappeared into her bedroom.

Near the gate to the farm, a pair of silhouettes suddenly halted their horses and looked back across the prairie. Countless points of light swayed closer, coming from the direction of town. As the pair strained their ears, they could hear a rumble of voices that bordered on rage, mixed with the beating of numberless hooves.

"What could that be?" mumbled Rei-Ginsei.

"Folks from town. Something must've happened," Greco said, watching the points of light nervously. Those were flaming torches.

"At any rate, we'd do well to conceal ourselves and see what transpires."

The two of them quickly melted into the shadows of the farm's fence.

They didn't have long to wait; the procession of villagers assembled before the entrance to the farm shortly after they'd hidden themselves. Greco's brow furrowed. Leading the pack was his father, Mayor Rohman. Steam was rising from his bald pate. Around him were his family's hired hands, all armed to the teeth with crossbows and laser rifles; the villagers carried spears and rifles as well.

More than half of them looked like they'd just been dragged out of bed, dressed in pajamas and slippers. Humorous as it appeared, it testified to exactly how serious the situation had become. The shadows of hatred and fear fell heavily on every face.

This was a mob. There was no sign of the sheriff.

"Doris! Doris Lang! Turn this barrier off," the mayor roared in front of the gate.

A light went on in one window of the house.

Soon after, a pair of figures loomed on the front porch.

"What in the blazes is your business at this hour of the night! You bring the whole damn town out here to rob the place or something?" That was Doris' voice.

"Just turn the barrier off already! Then we'll discuss it," the mayor bellowed back.

"It's already off, you moron. You gonna stay out there all night?"

A number of fiery streaks shot out from around the mayor, melting the chain off the gate.

The crowd spilled into her front yard.

"Hold it right there! Come any closer and I'll shoot you dead!" More than Doris' threat, more than the laser rifle propped against her shoulder, it was the sight of D standing there behind her that checked the crazed mob and stopped them ten feet shy of the porch.

To cow a group, you had to take aim at a person at the center of their rampage and carefully cut them off from the others. Just as her father had taught her, Doris aligned the barrel of her laser rifle perfectly with the mayor's breastbone, letting the promise that she wouldn't give an inch flood through her entire being.

"Okay, I want some answers. What's your business? And where the heck's the sheriff? I'm warning you right now, if he's not here I don't owe you a good answer no matter what kind of complaint you got. Dan and I both pay our taxes."

"That pain in the ass got slapped around a little and thrown in his own jail. We'll let him out again once we've taken care of the lot of you," the mayor said with disgust. And then, still glaring at Doris, he gave a wave of one hand. "Come on, show her."

The crowd parted and a hoary-headed old man stepped to the fore. In his arms he held a little girl with braids in her hair.

"Mr. Morris, is Lucy..." Doris began, but swallowed the rest of her words. Two repugnant streaks of blood marked the girl's paraffin-pale throat.

"There are more."

With the mayor's words as their cue, two pathetic couples came forward.

The miller Fu Lanchu and his wife Kim, the huntsman Machen and his spouse—both couples were in their thirties, though the wives of both men were still renowned in the village for their beauty. The sight of the women—now held up by their husbands as their vacant eyes pointed to the heavens and fresh blood dripped down their throats—told Doris everything.

"The Count did this, the ruthless bastard ..."

"That's right," Machen said with a nod. "The wife and I were tuckered out from a hard day's work, and headed off to bed early. Not long after that, I woke up feeling chilled and found my wife not by my side where she should be but standing over next to a wide-open window, glaring at me with these burning eyes. And when I jumped out of bed to see what the hell was going on—"

The miller Lanchu picked up where Machen left off. "All of a sudden my wife said in a man's voice, 'Give me Doris Lang. If you don't, your wife will remain like this forever, neither alive nor dead.' He said those exact words."

"The moment she stopped speaking, she just keeled over, and she hasn't moved or spoken since!" Machen's voice was a veritable scream. "I rushed to take her pulse, but there wasn't a trace of one. She's not breathing either. And yet, her heart's still beating."

"Now, I didn't believe any of what Greco was saying," said Mr. Morris. "Knowing you, I figured if some vampire had bit you, you'd have done away with yourself. Why, if it was true, I thought I'd lend what aid an old fool could and help you destroy our lord. But why did my granddaughter Lucy have to suffer in your place ... She's only five!"

The old man's teary, grief-stricken appeal gradually brought down the barrel of Doris' weapon. Her voice now stripped of its willfulness, Doris asked, "So what are you saying we should do?"

The mayor turned his dagger-filled gaze at D. Stroking his bald head, he said, "First, chase the punk behind you off your farm. Next, you're going into the asylum. I'm not saying we're going to grab you and give you to the Count as tribute or anything as heartless as all that. But you've got to follow the law of the village. In the meantime, we'll take care of the Count."

Doris vacillated. What the mayor proposed had its merits. Since she'd been bitten by a vampire, the only thing that kept her out of the asylum was the aid of Dr. Ferringo and the sheriff. Now the elderly physician was dead, and the sheriff wasn't here. But there were three people here who'd been made living-dead in her stead, and lots of villagers with hate-filled eyes. Her rifle drooped limply to the floor.

"Take her away," the mayor commanded triumphantly.

And at that moment, D said, "How will you take care of *him*?"

The buzz of the mob, which had gone on incessantly during Doris' discussion with the mayor, came to an immediate halt. Hatred, horror, menace—as they gazed upon him with every emotion they felt toward the unknown, Vampire Hunter D slowly made his way down the porch stairs with his sword over his shoulder. The mob shrank back without a word. All except for the mayor. The instant D's eyes caught him, he became utterly paralyzed. "How will you take care of him?" D asked again, stopping a few paces away from the mayor.

"Well, um ... actually ..."

D reached out his *left hand* and stuck the *palm* of it against the mayor's octopus-like face. For a moment the man's voice broke off, and then he went on again.

"Throw her ... in the freaking asylum ... and then negotiate. Tell him ... he's not to harm anyone in town any more ... If he does, we'll kill the love of his life ..."

The mayor's face twisted and beads of sweat formed chains across his brow, almost as if he was battling some titanic force within himself.

"After we talked to him ... we'd tell Doris we'd destroyed the Count or something ... let her out ... After that, he could do what he liked—make her one of his kind, bleed her to death, whatever ... You're the devil ... you little punk. If you give Doris any more help ... "

"Aren't you the cooperative one?"

D took his hand away. The mayor took a few steps back, his face looking like whatever demon had possessed him had just left. Beads of sweat streamed down his face.

"This young lady hired me," D said darkly. "And as I haven't finished what I was hired to do, I can't very well leave now. Especially not after hearing your detailed confession."

Suddenly, his tone became commanding. "The Nobility won't die out if you stand around and do nothing. How many times will you give in, and how many people are you willing to sacrifice to those who have nothing but extinction ahead of them? If that's the human mentality, then there's absolutely no chance I'll let you have the girl. An old man who can only weep for the child taken from him, and husbands who would have another girl take the place of their own defiled wives—the flames of hell can take you, and everyone else in this village as well. I'll take on humans and Nobles alike. I will defend this family even if I have to leave a mountain of corpses and a river of blood the likes of which you can't begin to imagine— any objections?"

The people saw the crimson gleam of his eyes through the darkness—the eyes of a vampire! D took a step forward, and the silenced mob was pushed back by a wave of primal fear.

"I object."

Everyone stopped at what was a beautiful voice for such a loud shout.

"Who's that?"

"Let him through!"

One voice after another arose from the back of the pack, and as the crowd split down the middle, a young man who was almost blindingly handsome stepped forward. While the beauty of his countenance was great, it was the unusual state of both his left and right arms that drew the people's attention. His right arm was sheathed all the way to the shoulder in what looked like the metallic sleeve of a combat suit, and his left arm was missing from the elbow down. Proffering the stump of his arm, Rei-Ginsei said, "I came to thank you for doing this yesterday." His tone made it seemed like an amiable greeting.

"You? Everyone, this is the bastard who attacked the FDF patrol!" The mayor and the rest of the mob started murmuring when they heard Doris shout that.

Rei-Ginsei calmly replied, "And I suppose you have some proof of that, do you? Did you find some trace of the patrol—

their horses' corpses, anything? True, there has been some unpleasantness between us in the past, but I can't have you heaping any further aspersions on my good name."

Doris ground her teeth. Rei-Ginsei definitely had her at a disadvantage where the FDF case was concerned. Without victims, he couldn't be charged with a crime. Though if the sheriff was there, there's little doubt he'd have promptly taken Rei-Ginsei into custody as a material witness.

"Mister Mayor, may I be so bold as to make a suggestion?"

Greeted by a flash of pearly teeth, the mayor smiled back nervously. Like all who'd been enslaved by Rei-Ginsei's grin, he did not notice the devil that hid behind it. "And what would that be?" the mayor asked.

"Please allow me to do battle with our friend, here and now. Should he win, you will leave this family alone, and should I win, the girl shall go to the asylum. How does that suit you?"

"Well, I don't know ..." The mayor vacillated. His position really wouldn't allow him to entrust a matter of this magnitude to a man he didn't know in the least—particularly someone as shrouded in suspicion as Rei-Ginsei was.

"Can the lot of you do something then? Come tomorrow evening, there shall be more victims."

The mayor made up his mind. All the villagers were held at bay by D's energy. He had to see what the man could do. "Very well."

"One more thing," Rei-Ginsei said, extending a single finger of the combat suit. Of course it was Greco's. To keep Doris from realizing as much, he'd only donned the one sleeve. If his connection to Greco came to light, they would realize where the Time-Bewitching Incense was now. "Dispatch someone to the neighboring villages and have the warrants out on me withdrawn."

"Okay—understood," the mayor said, the words coming out like a moan. With no one but this dashing young man to rely on, he had no resort but to concede to his every demand.

Rei-Ginsei turned to Doris and asked, "And is that fine with you, too?"

"Sure. You'll just wind up getting your other hand lopped off," Doris replied.

D asked, "Where do you want to do this?" He made no mention of the fact that his opponent was trying to curry favor with the Nobility, or that he'd attempted to strangle a helpless young boy.

"Right here. Our duel will soon be over."

Only the moon watched the moving people.

In front of the porch the two of them squared off, ten feet apart.

The villagers filling the front yard, and Doris and Dan up on the porch, were on pins and needles. When they all let out a deep breath seemingly on cue, three shrike-blades flew from Rei-Ginsei's right hip. The combat suit's muscular enhancement system made them all faster than ever, faster than the human eye could follow, and yet all of them were knocked from the sky just in front of D by a silvery flash.

In the blink of an eye, D was in the air over Rei-Ginsei's head. Sword raised for the kill, the moment the crowd gasped at their premonition of the blade cleaving Rei-Ginsei's head, the victorious Hunter wobbled in midair.

Who could miss that chance? Once again Rei-Ginsei's right hand went into action, sending out a stream of white light. That was Greco's wooden stake, which he'd kept tucked through the back of his belt. With Rei-Ginsei's normal skill, D most likely would have dodged it despite his throes of agony, but now it had the added speed of the combat suit. Longsword still raised above his head, with the stake stuck through his heart and sticking out his back, D sent out a faint mist of blood as he thudded to the ground.

"Nailed him!"

The jubilant cry came from neither Rei-Ginsei nor the villagers. The crowd was more confused by the strange feeling that night had become day than they were by the duel's gruesome finale.

"Greco! Oh, so you were in cahoots with this jerk!"

With that shout, Doris took aim with her rifle at the figure who'd popped up in front of the fence holding a candle in one hand, but a sudden massive blow to the barrel of the weapon knocked it back, striking its owner in the forehead.

"Now's our chance! Grab her!"

Giving a faint smile to the villagers as they charged Dan and the unconscious sister Dan clung to, Rei-Ginsei fastened the last returning shrike-blade to his belt and stripped off the combat suit sleeve.

The limp Doris was thrown on a horse, as was her bellowing and far-from-cooperative brother, and the villagers went back out through the gate.

"What are you up to?" Greco grimaced, about to go get the horse he'd hidden at the rear of the farm.

Rei-Ginsei was stooping down over the body of the already deceased D. Raising the left hand, he eyed the palm and back of it suspiciously. "I simply don't understand," he groaned. "This is the same hand that swallowed Chullah's spiders and made the mayor spill his secrets …There must be some secret to it." As he said that, he took a shrike-blade from his hip and slashed the left hand off at the elbow, which made Greco's eyes bug in his head. He then discarded the hand in the nearby bushes. "I couldn't rest easy if I didn't do that. Also, I believe that makes us even," he said coolly.

Rei-Ginsei walked toward the gate without so much as a glancing back, but Greco called out in an overly familiar tone, "Hey, wait up. Why don't we have a drink in town or something? Together, me and you could do big things."

Stopping dead in his tracks, Rei-Ginsei turned around. The look in his eyes riveted Greco. "The next time we meet, consider your life over."

And then he left.

"Sheesh, you're pretty damn full of yourself," Greco muttered with all the venom he could muster, and then he too headed for the exit. His legs froze. He turned around, looking scared out of his wits. "I must be imagining things," he mumbled, and then he wasted little time getting back out through the gate.

He thought he'd heard what sounded like chuckling. And it hadn't come from D's corpse, but from the dark bushes where his severed left hand had been discarded ...

"Ha ha ha ... Everything has gone exactly as planned. It's unfortunate I had to wait an additional day, but I suppose that has only increased my ardor all the more."

Standing on the same hilltop where Greco had encountered Rei-Ginsei by day, the figure took the electronic binoculars from his eyes and laughed softly. With white fangs spilling over his red lips, it was none other than Count Magnus Lee.

A carriage was parked by a tree, and the moonlight illuminated the werewolf Garou standing beside it in his inverness. Naturally, he had his human face and form at the moment.

He asked, "So, what shall we do next?"

"That should go without saying. We force our way into that miserable little hamlet and take the girl. That damned mayor of theirs undoubtedly plans on locking her in the asylum while he negotiates with me, but I shall have none of that. For all the inconveniences they've caused me thus far, I shall create more living-dead in their village tomorrow night, and still more the night after that. Their children and their children's children shall have a tale to tell of the horror of the Nobility. Consider it a gift to commemorate my nuptials. Upon our return, order the robots to commence preparations for the ceremony immediately."

"Yessir."

Giving a magnanimous nod to his deeply bowing servitor, the Count was about to get into his carriage when he turned and asked, "How is Larmica?"

"As you instructed, sire, she was punished with Time-Bewitching Incense, and she appeared to be in severe pain as she was still lying on the floor of her room when I took my leave."

"Is that so? Very well then. If this serves to keep her from harboring any further thoughts of disobeying her father then everything will once again be as it should. I merely wanted to take the human girl as my wife. To live forever, sucking the blood as it gushes from her pale-as-wax throat night after night. Transient guest? The words of our Sacred Ancestor do not apply to me, I dare say. The rest of my kind may face extinction, but the girl and I shall stay here forever and hold the humans down with power and fear. Just you watch!"

Once again Garou gave a deep nod.

The Count shut the carriage door firmly from the inside.

"Go! The dawn is nigh. Of course, I don't believe there shall be any need to burn it, but I have Time-Bewitching Incense ready just in case."

Neither the Count nor Garou had noticed that, soon after D had been felled by Rei-Ginsei's stake, a carriage had come from the woods on the opposite side of the farm and headed toward town.

For some time after Greco left, only a refreshing breeze and the light of the moon held sway at the farm. The cattle were sleeping peacefully, but an unsettling chuckle suddenly arose in the otherwise silent, solemn darkness.

"Heh heh heh ... It's been a while since I got to take center stage. Eating spiders and making baldy spill his guts is all well and good, but I want a little more time in the limelight—of course, he and I might both be happier if I left things the way they stand now, but there's still things that need doing in this life. And I kinda like that firecracker and her squirt of a brother. I'm loathe to do this, but I guess I can bail him out once again."

By "him" it meant D.

The voice came from within the bushes. At the same time, something seemed to be moving around in there. Oh, it was the hand. The fingers. As if it possessed a mind of its own, the left hand Rei-Ginsei had hacked from D and thrown away was now moving all five of its fingers.

The hand had its back to the ground and its palm pointed to the sky. The surface of the palm rippled, like a lump of muscle was being pushed to the surface from the inside. But the truly startling part was still to come. A few creases shot across the surface of the lump, depressions formed in the flesh in some places while other parts swelled up—forming at last a human face!

Two tiny nostrils opened on the slightly crooked, aquiline nose, and when the lips twisted in a sarcastic smile they exposed teeth like tiny grains of rice. The disturbing tumor with a face took a breath, and then its hitherto closed eyelids snapped open.

"Well, time to get started I suppose."

With those words as a cue, the arm started to move. Though the nerves and tendons had been severed, the weird countenanced carbuncle had the ability to reanimate the arm portion and make it do its bidding. The fingers of the prone hand swam in the air and grabbed hold of a branch of the shrubbery directly overhead. Clinging to the branch and pulling itself up, the hand flopped back to the ground palm down. "Okay, time to take a little trip." The five fingers curled like spider legs and the wrist arched into the air. Dragging the heavy forearm behind it, it cleverly wound its way through the bushes and inched toward D. When it came to the stump of his left arm, the fingers once again scurried around busily, turning to the right and matching both sides of the cut together perfectly.

D had fallen on his back, so the palm of his hand naturally faced the sky. The countenanced carbuncle's bizarre visage was left naked in the moonlight. And this is when it—the hand—began to act truly strange. It inhaled for a long time, like it was taking a deep breath. Given the relatively small size of D's palm, it seemed to have an incredible lung capacity. The wind whistled and howled as it coursed into the tiny mouth. After this amazing display of suctioning skill had gone on for a good ten seconds, it paused for a breath and repeated the same behavior three more times. And then the countenanced carbuncle did something even more wondrous.

Cleverly flipping over from the elbow so that the palm faced down, the fingers sank into the ground and began tearing up the soil.

Thanks most likely to D's steely fingertips, they scooped up the hard ground like it was mud, and before long there was a sizable mound of dirt into which the palm proceeded to shove its own face. In the hush, an eerie munching sound could be heard. The tumor was eating the dirt! By the light of the moon this unearthly repast continued, and several minutes later the mound of dirt had vanished completely. Where had it gone? Right into the countenanced carbuncle's maw. But where in the world could it put all that dirt? The shape of the arm hadn't changed in the least. And yet, the severed hand had consumed both the air and the earth. But toward what end?

The down-turned palm let out a small burp.

"Without water and fire this may take a while, but there's not much we can do about that," it said to itself, and then the whole arm abruptly reached for D's chest.

It couldn't be! The two sides of the slice along D's arm were together again, even though reattaching the arm after both sides had bled dry should've been impossible. But the arm rose nonetheless.

Then the countenanced carbuncle said simply, "This should be a lot faster than using my fingers."

With that it opened its mouth wide and bit down on the end of the stake jutting from D's chest.

"Oof!"

With a weird grunt it pulled the stake right out.

Disposing of the wooden implement with a flick of the wrist, the palm once again turned to the sky.

The air howled. Once more it was being savagely sucked in, though it was now clear it was being consumed just as the earth had been. Pale blue flames could be seen flickering deep in the cheeks of the countenanced carbuncle every time it inhaled. With its third such breath, flames spouted from its mouth and nose. Earth, wind, fire, and water were commonly known as the four elements. Having consumed only two of them—earth and wind—the countenanced carbuncle had turned them into heat within itself, and then into life force, and now it was pumping life itself back into D's body.

This gorgeous youth—the great Vampire Hunter D—had a life-force generator living in the palm of his hand!

At some point the wind died down, and the tranquil farm was made all the more serene by the moon, but in one part of the farm the disturbing miracle continued. And the wound the stake had left in D's heart—a wound that was certain death for all descendants of vampires—gradually closed.

Flashing Steel Cuts the Ceremony Short

CHAPTER 8

"Let us out of here, damn you! Let us out!"

"If you don't let my brother out, I swear I'm gonna come looking for you every night once the Nobility make me one of their own!"

Wham!

Slamming the door shut with all his might and cutting off further bluster from the Langs, the man returned to his cramped office. Moments earlier, the mayor and other important members of the community had headed home. Here in the asylum, with no furniture save a battered desk and chair, their buzz still seemed to hang in the air.

"Those freaking kids. I figured at least one of 'em would be crying and pleading, but both of 'em go and threaten a grown man."

As he grumbled to himself, the man pulled out the wooden chair and took his post in front of the steel door that separated the office from the lock-up area otherwise known as the cages. There were ten individual cells in the cages, each surrounded by bars of super-high-density steel. They'd been built to be a comfortable size, and Doris and Dan had been locked up together. Originally, a family had kindly volunteered to look after

Dan while Doris was confined, since the boy wasn't involved in this, but Dan had fought like a tiger and said he'd die without his sister. There was also a very good chance that, if left to his own devices, he'd have tried to spring Doris, which is how the current arrangement had been reached.

Victims of the Nobility were confined here regardless of the degree of their affliction; if the Noble responsible was destroyed then the curse on them would be lifted and all would be well. If not, the standard operating procedure was to release the victim after a given period and chase them out of town.

That "given period" was the number of days until the frustrated Noble attacked someone else, but this varied from village to village. In Ransylva it was approximately three weeks. The reason it was so long was because, based on past experience, it took an average of three attacks before the Count was done draining his victim, and there was usually an interval of three to five days between attacks.

Of course, because every village could expect their asylum to be stormed by the Nobility during the victim's confinement, for the most part the asylums were guarded by well-armed men confident in their fighting abilities. Because they'd have the Nobility to contend with, no village ever skimped on buying armaments for the asylum. In fact, in addition to the five fully automated, steel-spear launchers and the ten remote-controlled catapults surrounding this thirty-foot-long, half-cylinder building, there were also three laser cannons to neutralize the vehicles of the Nobility, and a pair of flame-throwers from the Capital. The villagers wanted an electromagnetic barrier as well, but the Capital's stores were running low, and they were hard to come by even for those willing to pay black-market prices.

The man guarding the cages was a member of the mob that stormed Doris' farm. The reason the mayor left only one man on watch was because he'd decided that, after sucking the blood from three people tonight already, the Count wouldn't be in quite such a hurry to attack Doris. But if it came to that, the guard could wake up the whole village with a single siren, and the weapons outside could be operated from the control panel on his desk. Most importantly, in four more hours the eastern sky would be growing light. The man wasn't concerned.

Just as he was starting to doze off, there was a rap at the door. The man raced over to the video panel and struck a single key. Greco's face showed on a small video monitor inside the asylum. "What do you want?" the man said to the intercom operating through the wall.

"Be a pal and open up. I came to see Doris."

"No way. Your father told me specifically not to let you in."

"Come on, don't be a jerk. You must know how crazy I am about Doris, right? This is just between you and me, but when day breaks they're gonna bring her up to old fang-face's place on orders from my father. Meaning tonight's my last chance to see the woman I love. And, as you can see, you stand to get a little something for your trouble." Greco pulled a few gold coins out of his pocket and waved them in front of the camera. They weren't the new dalas currency the revolutionary government started issuing five years ago. These were the "aristocrat coins" the Nobility had used. When the revolutionaries finally managed to take power, they destroyed vast quantities of these coins in order to get their new government's economic policies off to a good start. One of them was worth at least a thousand dalas on the black market. That was enough to live off for half a year out on the Frontier.

After staring at the shiny gold for quite some time, the man hit a button without a word. The electronic lock on the door was disengaged, the handle spun around, and in sauntered Greco.

"Thanks, buddy. Here you go!"

Three gold coins clattered down on the desk. Forgetting to shut the door, the man snatched up one of the coins and busily bounced his gaze back and forth between it and Greco's face before eventually nodding with satisfaction. As he dropped all three into his shirt pocket he said, "I suppose it'll be all right— but you've only got three minutes to see her."

"C'mon, make it five."

"Four."

"Okay—you drive a hard bargain."

The man shrugged his shoulders, and then turned toward the door to the cages and reached for the key ring on his belt. The keys jingled together as he chose one and fit it into the lock. It wouldn't do to have this door opening automatically.

"Say—" As the man turned around again, his eye caught Greco's strangely bloodless countenance, and a flash of white light headed right for his own chest.

Killed instantly by a stab to the heart, the man's body was laid out at one side of the room, and then Greco turned the key still jammed in the lock, opened the door, and went into the cages. His knife was already back in the case on his belt.

"Greco!"

There were cages to either side of the narrow corridor, and Doris' cry came from the first one on the left. "You bastard, you come here to get your block knocked off or something?"

"Shut up."

Doris fell silent. She got a bad feeling from Greco's expression, which was more foreboding then she'd ever seen it. *What the hell's he up to?*

"I'll get you right out of there. You're gonna run away with me."

Beyond the iron bars, the Lang children looked at each other. In a low voice, Doris said, "Don't tell me you ... you didn't seriously kill Price ..."

"Oh, I killed him all right. And he's not the only one. My father got his, too. That's what he gets for trying to whip the shit out of me when I came home. The old bastard. I help make his job easier, and that's how the ingrate repays me. But that don't matter now. At any rate, I've got to get out of town tonight. Are you with me?" His eyes had an animalistic gleam to them, but his voice was like molasses.

The propriety of his actions aside, some might even go so far as to say the devotion he showed to the woman he loved was admirable, but Doris said flatly, "Sorry. I'd rather go up to the Count's castle than run off with you."

"What the hell do you mean? ..."

Tears sparkled in the girl's eyes. Tears of hatred. "You teamed up with that butcher and ... and killed him of all people ... Just you wait. I don't care what happens to me, I'm personally gonna see to it you get sent to hell."

She'd always been strong willed, but seeing in those beautiful eyes of hers a fundamentally different and desolate light, Greco abandoned all his schemes and dreams. "So that's how it is? You're saying you'd prefer the Nobility to me?"

When he looked up, all emotion had drained from his face, but the gleam in his eyes was unusually strong.

"If that's the way it's got to be, I guess when you've got to go, you've got to go—and you're about to go join that punk in the hereafter." Taking a step back, he drew the ten-banger from his hip.

Dan shouted, "Sis!" and grabbed onto Doris' neck for dear life while she tried to hide the boy behind her back.

"You're out of your mind, Greco!"

"Say what you like. But I'd rather do this than have any other man take you—vampire or otherwise. You and that smart-mouthed little squirt get to check out of this life together."

"Stop!"

That Doris' cry had been to beg for her own life was the last coherent thought to go through Greco's mind. Someone behind him grabbed the hand with the ten-banger by the wrist. Though whoever it was was just barely touching him, his finger lost the strength to finish pulling the trigger. An unearthly chill spread from his wrist to the rest of his body. Breath with the sweet scent of death tickled his nose, and frosty, dark words struck his earlobe.

"Better you had killed me when you had the chance." Larmica's pale face eclipsed the nape of Greco's swarthy neck. Frozen in horror, Doris and Dan watched as Greco's face grew paler and paler, like he was disappearing into a fog. Seconds later, the young lady in the black dress pulled away from the man and approached their cage. With a thread of blood running from the pale corner of her mouth, this beauty that seemed to sparkle in the darkness could be likened to nothing save a vengeful wraith. Perhaps her thirst wasn't sated yet, for a glance from her bright red eyes shook Doris and Dan to the bottom of their souls.

An expression of unfathomable terror plastered on its face, Greco's body fell to the floor, an empty husk drained of the very last drop of blood.

"What do you—"

The tremble in Doris voice was apparent, but Larmica simply urged, "Go." The hue of madness had left her eyes and, quite to the contrary, her expression now seemed tinged with sorrow.

"Huh?"

"Make good your escape. Father will be coming soon. And when he does, I shan't be able to do any more."

"But ... we can't get out of here. Get us the keys, please," Dan said, grabbing the bars. His flexible, eight-year-old mind had already adjusted to this vampiress being their ally.

She seized the steel bars with dainty hands that looked like they'd break in a strong wind. What strength the vampires possessed! With one good pull, the bars of super-high-density steel tore free of the ceiling and floor, sending screws shooting in all directions.

"Unbelievable ... "

Still trying to keep the wide-eyed Dan behind her, Doris asked Larmica, "You're serious—you really want us to get away, don't you? But why are you helping us?"

A shade of sorrow colored Larmica's moonflower of a face when she turned around.

"*He* died ... but he defended you right to the very end. It would sadden him to see you fall into Father's hands. I have no desire to cause the dead any more sorrow ... "

As Dan took her hand and tugged her out to the corridor, Doris realized this fearsome young woman harbored the same feeling as herself.

"You ... you felt something for him ... "

"Go—make haste."

The three went into the office.

A figure in black stood in the center of the room.

"Father!" Larmica cried out in terror.

"What the hell, still nothing?!" the countenanced carbuncle spat in disgust, its face pressed to D's chest. "A sword or spear wound wouldn't have been so bad, but after taking a wooden stake, his little ticker ain't listening to me. Beat. Just give me one good thump—c'mon and beat already."

Making a fist of the hand it occupied, it rose to strike D's chest as hard as it could, but stopped in midair.

Something was coagulating in the night sky.

A host of white, semi-transparent membranes swirled above the house, then started to come together to form a single mass. Once it had drawn itself together, the glowing cloud swooped down toward the farm, oddly shaped organs becoming visible through its partially transparent body. This was another of the artificial monstrosities spawned by the Nobility—a night cloud. A life-form able to reform itself from single cell organisms, by day the cloud remained in the freezing extremes of the stratosphere, and at night it came back down to earth in scattered form to hunt for prey.

Frighteningly enough, these damned things were dangerous carnivores that would form a single mass when they found a victim, enveloping their prey from all sides to digest and absorb it. They posed a major threat to lost children and inexperienced travelers, and, along with dimension-ripping beasts, they caused a great many people to go inexplicably missing. The electromagnetic barrier had been a godsend in that it alone kept them from wreaking havoc on Doris' farm.

At one point the cloud came down about fifteen feet above D's head, but it seemed to catch wind of something and drifted off to one side, toward the barn where the animals were stabled. Only pausing before the doors for a heartbeat, it spread itself flat as a sheet and easily slipped through a gap between the wall and the doors. The shrill cries of cattle reverberated, the walls shook two or three times, and all too soon it was silent again.

"Those things eat like pigs. It'll be back soon. So get busy beating already, you lousy, good-for-nothing heart!" The complaining fist beat wildly against D's chest and sucked in air. The body didn't move in the slightest. "C'mon, you bastard!"

If there'd been anyone there to see the bizarre but desperate one-man show that went on for a few minutes more, they most likely would've laughed out loud.

And then …

The barn doors bowed out from the inside and splintered, flying everywhere. A second later, an unspeakably grotesque thing appeared in the moonlight. Within the semi-translucent cloud mass was a cow, writhing in agony as it dissolved! Its hide split, red meat melted, and the exposed bone slowly wasted away like popping soap bubbles. As flesh and blood mixed in a narrow tube that seemed to be an esophagus of sorts, the liquid swirled around and the cloud began glowing brighter than ever. It was feeding. For a few seconds the corpulent mass wriggled at the entrance to the barn and then, perhaps sensing other prey, it began to drag itself toward D. Thanks to the weight of the half-devoured cow, it was moving in slow motion.

"Look how close it is already. C'mon and start already!" The fist gave D another smack.

The cloud had closed within ten feet of D. Close enough to hear the tortured cow within it.

Three feet away. The cloud rose into the air and flew straight for D.

A flash of light raced through its translucent mass.

The blade seemed to pass right through it without meeting any resistance, but when the bisected cloud fell to the ground in two chunks, it lost its color before it had a chance to split into smaller pieces. It gave off a whitish steam and soaked into the earth. Only the remains of the cow were left behind.

D got to his feet, scattering moonbeams.

"Nice going. You know, you had me scared out of my wits, as usual."

As if this somewhat inappropriate greeting for someone just risen from the dead hadn't reached his ears, D asked, "Where are the two of them?"

"In the asylum, I'd imagine. Every village seems to put it on the edge of town."

With that, all conversation ceased, and D leapt to his feet and headed for the stables.

The tall trees spread their branches like monsters, fending off the invading moonlight. The only light to speak of was the phosphorescent glow of guidepost mushrooms here and there among the roots of the trees, though that didn't amount to much before the mass and density of the crushing darkness. Even a traveler with some source of light would have a hard time traversing this forest late at night without getting lost in the process.

This was the Ransylva Forest—where night was said to live even at midday. And through it, Dan ran desperately. He wasn't alone. From the darkness less than thirty feet behind him came the growl and footsteps of a carnivore. Its identity was clear. The Count's servant—Garou—pursued him.

Caught by the Count just as they were about to flee the asylum, his sister and Larmica had been put into the carriage, while Dan had been left there alone. Promptly deciding to rescue Doris, he'd headed back to the farm to arm himself. Despite his youth, it was clear to him it would be futile to seek assistance in rescuing his sister from anyone in town. And there wasn't a moment to lose. The shortest possible route would be to cut right through the Ransylva Forest instead of taking the road. With only his sister in mind, he did it without a moment's hesitation. However, less than a minute after he'd entered the forest he heard the snarling of the werewolf behind him.

The deadly marathon had begun.

His father and sister had brought him here before in the relative safety of day, and he could even recall playing in the forest alone. Tapping all the knowledge he had, Dan raced down the most serpentine paths he could find, snuck into hollow trees, and hid in the brush in an attempt to confuse his unsettling pursuer.

But whenever he stopped, it stopped. If he ran again, it took off as well. No matter what he tried, the distance between them neither grew nor shrank.

Dan finally figured out it was toying with him. The moment this occurred to him, his admirable sense collapsed and pure, black terror became the sole occupant of his heart. He ran for all he was worth. And yet, the pursuer to his back remained the same thirty feet behind him as always.

His heart was about to explode and his lungs gasped for more air. He could taste his own salty tears on his tongue. And just when he thought he could take no more, he saw a spot of light in the darkness. The way out!

Hope pumped him full of energy. His feet beat the ground in powerful strides until something suddenly grabbed hold of them.

"Waaugh!" Falling face forward, he tried to get up again but was caught by a pair of hands. "Deadman's hand!"

The scant moonlight barely spilling through the interwoven trees showed him what it was. A pale corpse's hand reached from the ground, its five fingers wriggling in a disgusting way. No, not fingers but rather five flowers. Dan was being held to the ground by a pale blossom that looked just like a corpse's hand. As the various botanical horrors sown by the Nobility went, these were rather bizarre but innocuous plants—and the fact that Dan had known where they grew and had still ended up jumping right into the middle of this patch said volumes about how the terror behind him had wiped everything else from his mind. But who could blame a boy of eight for that?

Using all his might, Dan got to his feet again. The deadman's hand still hung from his wrist, pulled-up roots and all.

Just as he was about to start running again—

"Awoooooooooh!"

A terrific howl assailed him from behind, rooting his feet. Seeing the exit so close at hand, this was the battle cry Garou gave when it decided the time had come to put an end to their horrifying chase. It'd been pursuing Dan because the Count was allowing it to dine on a living person for the first time in ages.

All the strength drained from the boy. Sorry, Sis. Looks like I won't be able to save you. Tears of regret rolled down his cheeks.

And then, the howling abruptly halted. In its place, Dan could sense trembling.

At that same moment, Dan heard something. He caught the echo of hoofbeats out beyond the exit, distant but drawing closer with a vengeance. He couldn't hear a voice or see a shape. But Dan knew in a second who it was. "D!" His hopeful cry speared through the darkness.

Once again a howl rang out behind him, and a black whirlwind raced by his side.

"D, watch out!"

He ran a few steps, kicking the tenacious deadman's hand blossoms out of his way. An incredibly bestial roar rose beyond the exit, and was suddenly silenced.

Fairly tumbling headlong out of the forest, Dan saw a rider on a hillock ahead, bathed in moonlight. At his feet lay the fallen werewolf. D galloped over. Getting down off a horse Dan recognized, he asked, "What are you doing out here? Where's your sister?"

Dan was overcome with emotion. "I just knew you were still alive, D. I ... I knew there was no way you'd die on us ... " He couldn't say anything more. When Dan finally settled down and explained the situation, D picked him up without a word and set him on the horse. He didn't tell the boy to go home or offer to bring him back to the farm.

Looking out across the prairie at the Count's castle with a steely gaze, D asked, "Are you coming with me?" It was the same question he'd asked the boy in the ruins a night earlier.

"Sure!"

There was no reason to expect any other reply from the boy.

There was one particular characteristic of the castles of the Nobility that suited their vampire lords. While there were gorgeous sleeping chambers ready for guests and other visitors, there were none for the lord and his family.

They slumbered in a place most befitting their rank, an exalted place that was the stuff of legend: in coffins beneath the earth.

In vast subterranean chambers filled with tiny organisms, where the stench of dankness mixed with the sweet perfume of ancient soil, here alone the true past slept, free of computer controls. The smell of long-unused torches hung in the air of this special place. A stone wall that looked to be perhaps thirty feet tall was covered by a colossal portrait of the Sacred Ancestor. On the crimson dais before it stood the Count in his black raiment and Doris, garbed in a gown of snow white. The girl's eyes were lifeless. She was hypnotized.

To the left of the dais was Larmica, but her eyes looked just as dazed as they wandered through space, avoiding her father and his bride-to-be. This had less to do with the reprimand she'd been given by her father for trying to help Doris escape and more to do with something the beautiful vampiress' heart had lost.

The dark nuptials were about to begin.

"Look. There you shall make your bed from this night forth."

The Count gestured to a pair of black, lacquered coffins positioned on a stone slab in front of the dais. Below where the falcon-and-flames coat of arms was carved, the coffin on the right had a plate with the name "Lee," while the one on the left had already been inscribed "Doris."

"They contain dirt. The same proud soil the Lee family castle is built upon. I am quite sure it shall give you dreams of sweet blood each and every night. Now, then."

The Count took Doris' chin in hand and tilted her head back, exposing more of her pale throat. "Before we exchange the vows of man and wife, I must rid you of that loathsome mark." He pulled out a small signet from the folds of his cape. Its square face was carved with the same coat of arms that decorated the lids of the coffins.

"First the right." White smoke arose from her pale throat as he pressed the signet down into the flesh, and Doris trembled. Performing the same act again, only a little lower, the Count said, "Now the left." Once finished, he brought his abhorrent mouth closer to his bride's throat. Though white smoke still hung in the air, now there wasn't a mark on her virgin neck, aside from the pair of bite marks the Count left the first time he fed on her. Breath that reeked of blood crept along her throat. The mark of the cross that had kept the girl safe didn't reappear.

"Very well. Now I need fear nothing when I give her my kiss."

Grinning broadly as he returned the signet to his cape, the Count turned to his beloved daughter—in a stupor by his side—and said, "You shall have a new mother. Will you not recite some words of congratulation for us?"

Her vacant gaze focused on her father. Larmica's mouth moved sluggishly. "I …" she began. "I, Larmica Lee, your three thousand seven hundred and twenty-seven-year-old daughter, congratulate my three thousand seven hundred and fifty-seven-year-old father Magnus Lee and my seventeen-year-old mother Doris Lang on the occasion of their marriage." Her voice was vapid, but the Count nodded and pricked up his ears.

What at first had seemed to be Larmica's voice bouncing off the stone floor and ceiling became a unified chant that reverberated through the dim subterranean chamber, like the cries of the writhing dead rising from the earth. "We give Count Magnus Lee our most heartfelt congratulations on the creation of this new union."

The voices came from the occupants of countless coffins stuck in the walls and beneath the floor. A number of them shook and rattled a bit, causing the Count to narrow his gaze.

"Now it's time—" Saying that, as he brought his lips to Doris' still-upturned throat, the transmitter in his jacket pocket emitted a siren. "Oh, you infernal machine," the Count said irritably and pulled it out. "Whatever is it?"

The metallic voice of what must have been a computer responded. "A pair of humans and a horse have just arrived at the main gate. One of the humans is male, approximately eight years of age, the other is a male estimated to be between the ages of seventeen and eighteen."

"What?" The Count's eyes glowed with blood light.

Larmica turned in amazement.

"They must not be allowed to enter. Do not lower the drawbridge. Open fire on them immediately."

"Actually ... " the computer hesitated. "The bridge went down as soon as they drew near. We are unable to fire the weapons. It is my belief that the animal or one of the humans possesses a device that interferes with my commands. At present, all of the castle's electronic armaments are inoperable."

"You wretch ... " the Count groaned with hatred. "So the stripling still lives, does he? But, how on earth did he come back? Even I know of no way to return from a wooden stake through the heart."

"For one such as he ... " Larmica muttered.

"*One such as he?* Larmica, could it be you have some idea as to his identity?"

Larmica said nothing.

"Very well. That question may wait until later. For the time being, I must first slay him. When something interferes like this in the middle of a ceremony, it is customary to postpone the festivities until the nuisance has been dealt with."

"Understood, Father. But how exactly do you intend to deal with him?"

"I know of someone who would like very much to make amends for a blunder."

As a pale blue finally tinged the eastern sky, in the castle's courtyard D and Dan once again faced Rei-Ginsei.

"I haven't been given any more Time-Bewitching Incense," Rei-Ginsei said with a beautiful, devilish smile. On his way from Doris' farm to the castle, Rei-Ginsei had encountered the Count's carriage as it raced back from town at perilous speed, and had accompanied the carriage the rest of the way. "I can understand why the Count was so upset. However, if I dispatch you to the next life once again, I'm quite certain his anger will be appeased. Kindly dismount."

They were ten feet apart, just as they'd been at the Lang farm. Dan took cover along with the horse behind a stone sculpture and waited for the battle to be decided.

But basically it was an absurd challenge. So long as he had no Time-Bewitching Incense, Rei-Ginsei had no way to overcome D. On the other hand, any critical wounds D might deal would be turned back on the Hunter through the extra-dimensional passageway in Rei-Ginsei's body. And yet, each one apparently thought they stood a good chance of prevailing and both of them went into action at once.

"Ugh ... "

D doubled over, and then fell to his knees. A flame danced atop the stick of Time-Bewitching Incense in Rei-Ginsei's right hand. He'd deceived D. In the blink of an eye, a shrike blade was whizzing through the air.

But the reason he'd defeated D back at the farm was because he had the muscle-amplifying components of the combat suit aiding him. His face twisted with agony, D knocked the shrike-blade out of the air and leapt.

It was like a complete reenactment of their duel at the ruins. What was different was that Rei-Ginsei didn't dodge, but left his head wide open for the silvery flash. He imagined D would be aiming for his limbs. However, the instant he realized that the blade coming down at him was unmistakably aimed at his head, he let the extra-dimensional gateway within his body open and didn't try to run.

D's forehead split, but it was just a thin layer of skin. An instant later, bright red blood gushed from Rei-Ginsei's abdomen. The dashing young man's expression was one of stupefaction as he gazed at the blade protruding from his belly...the same blade that was supposed to split D's head in two. The Vampire Hunter had swung his sword overhead and only cut the outermost layer of skin on Rei-Ginsei's brow, then changed his grip on his sword in midair, and drove it right through his own stomach. Already linked by the extra-dimensional passageway, when the blade went into D's body it materialized in Rei-Ginsei's belly instead. Aside from his ability to twist and link points in space, Rei-Ginsei was otherwise a normal human who couldn't survive that sort of punishment. This was the sort of absurd method of killing only a dhampir like D would be capable of.

"Dan, put that candle out for me."

As he listened to the boy dash into action, Rei-Ginsei thudded to the ground. The incense left his hand, and his bright blood stained the earth.

"Hey, don't you keel over yet. Do at least one good thing before your miserable life ends," Dan said, stomping the incense out. A chill came over him as he watched the blade poking from the abdomen of the fallen Rei-Ginsei slide smoothly back into his body. D was pulling his own sword out of himself.

"And what is that ... one good thing?" asked Rei-Ginsei.

"Tell me where my sister's at."

"I don't know ... Search to your heart's contentment ... By now, the Count has made her his bride ... " A clot of blood spilled from his mouth, and the last spasms of impending death twisted his gorgeous countenance. "If only I had been made one of the Nobility ... " And then his head dropped to one side.

"He bit it, the damn jerk," Dan said with sorrow. "If he'd actually acted good instead of just looking good he might've lived a nice, long time ... "

"That's right," D said, breathing heavily. The effects of the Time-Bewitching Incense were gone the instant it was extinguished. The reason he looked to be in such pain was the wound to his stomach.

"Where do you think they've got my sister? This place is so huge, I don't even know where to begin to look." Dan was on the verge of tears, but D tapped him on the shoulder.

"You're forgetting that I'm a Vampire Hunter. Come with me."

The two of them went straight down to the subterranean chamber. Dan watched in wonder as shut doors flew open as soon as D approached. Nothing could stop them. From time to time, they passed expressionless people who seemed to be servants and ladies-in-waiting, but none of them so much as attempted to look at them before disappearing into the darkness.

"Robots, I guess," Dan said.

"Leaders of a false life—this castle flickers in the light of destruction now. As the Nobility themselves have for a long, long time."

Descending a narrow staircase for two stories, they came to a massive wooden door. Studded with hobnails from top to bottom, it testified to the import of the dark ceremony taking place beyond it.

"This is it, right?" Dan was tense.

D took off his blue pendant and put it around the boy's neck. "This will repel the robots. You stay here."

The door had neither lock nor bolt. It looked to weigh tons, but when D's finger brushed it, the hinges creaked and the doors opened to either side. Wide stone stairs worn low in the center flowed down into the darkness. Somewhere far below there was a barely perceptible light. On descending the staircase, D came to the subterranean chamber. Far off to his right flames danced.

Coffins caked with dust, some with skeletal hands and feet protruding through gaps in the half-decayed boards, others with wedges of wood driven right through their lids—this was what greeted D in the darkness. Weaving his way through the final resting place of rows upon rows of the dead, D arrived at last at the blood-hued dais, where he came face to face with the Count.

"I am impressed by the way you managed to come back to life. And to come here." The Count's tone went beyond awe. D turned his eyes to Doris, standing stock still on the dais. A cool smile nudged his cheeks for an instant.

"It seems I'm just in time."

At some point Larmica had vanished.

"There shall be plenty of time for that when you are dead," the Count replied. "However, as Larmica herself has said, it is truly a shame to slay you. You came back to life after taking a stake through your chest—now there is a secret I myself should very much like to know. What say you? Will you not reconsider this one last time? Have you no wish to take Larmica as your wife and live here in the castle? She has lost her soul to you."

"The Nobility died out long ago," said D. For some reason, his voice seemed to have a sorrowful ring to it. "The Nobility and this castle are no more than phantoms forgotten by time. Return to where you belong."

"Silence, stripling!" the Count moaned, gnashing his teeth in rage. "Born of Noble blood as you are, surely you must know what immortality means. Life given until the end of time—it is our duty to do just that, crushing the human worms underfoot all the while."

As he finished speaking, the Count knit his brow. He had just noticed that D was not looking up at himself, but rather at the portrait behind him.

If it had been that alone, he wouldn't have paid it much heed. What triggered this surprise—which was actually closer to horror—was that he saw that the face of the youth in the flickering torchlight was the same as the visage in the portrait holding his gaze.

At the same time, the Count realized words he'd heard twice before were ringing in the depths of his ears. Unconsciously, he let them slip from his mouth.

"Transient guests ... "

In all the proud, glorious history of the Nobility, this one pronouncement of their godlike Sacred Ancestor alone had met suspicion and denial from all Nobles. The Nobility's Academy of Sciences had developed a method of mathematically analyzing fate, and, after they cross-referenced these figures with the historical import of all known civilizations they canceled all presentations on the findings of their research. When they came under fire for this decision, it was the Sacred Ancestor who came to face the critics, appearing in public for the first time in a millennium to control the situation. And those words were the ones he'd let slip out then.

The great, eternally flowing river that was history had a civilization temporarily resting on its placid surface—the Sacred Ancestor referred to those propping up the civilization as transient guests. The question was, did he refer to the Nobility or humans?

The tangled skein of the Count's thoughts grew more knotted, and then a single thread suddenly pulled free. A bizarre rumor that had circulated briefly among the highest-ranking Nobility whispered into life in his ear once more. *Our Sacred Ancestor, it seems, swore to a human maid—they would make children and he would slay them, but even after slaying them he would still have her bear more. Impossible!* The Count's brain was driven to the limits of panic and confusion. *He couldn't possibly be … Could the Sacred Ancestor have planned the joining of human and Noble blood all along?*

Not knowing what was truth or lies, the Count stepped forward, chilled by his own thoughts. "Stripling, I shall see to it you feel the full might of the Nobility before you die."

As he finished talking, his cape fluttered. The lining was red and glistening. The air howled around the chamber and every flame danced a step shy of being snuffed. Astonishingly, the cape spread like a drop of ink dissolving in water and tried to wrap around D.

D drew his sword and slashed at the edge of it in one fluid motion. His blade stuck to the lining. This was the same blade D had used to destroy the bronze monstrosity Golem and slay a werewolf running at half the speed of sound!

The lining twined around and around his sword, tearing it from D's grasp a second later. But actually, D himself had released it. Had he resisted, his own hand might have been wrapped up and crushed in the process.

"And now you stand naked," the Count laughed snidely, taking D's sword in his right hand. His cape returned to its normal dimensions. Making another grand sweep of it, the Count said, "This was stitched together from the skin of women who'd slaked my thirst, and it was lacquered with their blood. Thanks to secret techniques passed down through my clan, it's five times as strong as the hardest steel and twenty times more flexible than a spider's webbing. And you have just witnessed its adhesive power for yourself."

Several flashes of light scorched through the air. The cape spread. All the wooden needles D had hurled dropped to the floor in front of the Count.

"Enough of your foolish resistance." The cape opened like the wings of a dark, mystic bird and the Count threw it and himself forward.

D leapt out of the way. The sleeve of his coat sported a fresh tear. That was thanks to the trenchant blade the cape had become.

"Oh, whatever is the trouble, my good Hunter? Could it be you're powerless now?" His snide laughter came over the top of the attacking cape. The speed with which he swept it around was incredible. Unable to close the gap between the Count and himself, D moved like the wind to evade the assaults.

At some point the two of them had changed positions, so that D now stood in front of Doris, shielding her.

The Count's eyes glowed. His cape howled through the air.

As D was about to leap away once more, something wrapped around him from behind. Doris' arms!

A heartbeat later D's body was entwined in the cape. In this battle that demanded the utmost concentration, even he'd forgotten for a moment that Doris was in the Count's thrall.

D's bones creaked from the enormous pressure. His gorgeous countenance twisted. And yet, who else would've been skilled enough to push Doris out of harm's way a split second before the cape engulfed him? D's sword glittered in the Count's hands.

"Your destruction will come on your own blade."

The Count intended to lop off his head. D's body was wrapped in a cape his blade hadn't been able to pierce, and the sword mowed through the air with all the Count's might behind it, until it suddenly it stopped.

At the same time the cape crumpled and D leapt clear of the bizarre fabric restraints. The instant the Count's concentration had been broken, the spell over his cape had faltered as well. He landed right before the Count. And what did the Count make of that?

"Ha!"

With a premonition of his firmly skewered foe bringing a smile to his face, the Count thrust the blade. The sword was caught and stopped dead right in front of D's chest. Caught between the palms of the Hunter's hands. Their roles had been completely reversed from their first encounter!

Without letting up in the slightest on the unspeakable pressure he brought to bear four inches from the weapon's tip, D twisted both hands to one side. The Count didn't go sailing through the air, but the end of the blade snapped off. The broken tip still between his hands, D leapt back ten feet.

"Why, that's the very same trick ... "

It was truly grand the way the Count sent out his cape even as he shouted this, but the difference between being the one doing the trick and the one on the receiving end in this case became the difference between life and death. The tip of the sword flew from D's folded hands in a silvery flash that neatly knifed through the heart beneath that black raiment.

For a few seconds the Count stood stock still. Then the flesh on his face began to melt away, and his eyes dropped to the floor, trailing optic nerves behind them.

Mere moments after he hit the floor, his rotting tongue and vocal chords forced out his final words.

"I ... I had to beg our Sacred Ancestor to teach me that very same trick ... Could it be ... *Milord, are you truly his ...* "

D quickly made his way over to Doris, who lay on the floor. Something strange was happening to the castle. The faint ringing of the warning bell from the Count's chest was proof of that. The Count's deadly attack had faltered because the bell had caught his ear—turning him from the path of certain victory to a plunge into the abyss of death. The floor shook ever so slightly.

A light tap to her cheek was enough to wake Doris. There was no trace of the fang marks on her neck any longer.

"D—what in the world is going on?! You're alive?"

"My work is done. The wounds on your throat have vanished." D pointed to the far end of chamber and the way he'd come. "If you go up that staircase you'll find Dan. The two of you should go back to the farm."

"But you—you've got to go with us."

"My work is finished, but I still have business here. Hurry up and go. And please be sure to tell Dan not to forget the promise he made his big brother."

Tears sparkled in Doris' eyes.

"Go."

Turning time and again, Doris finally disappeared into the darkness. A salutation rang from D's left hand, though it probably never reached her ears.

"So long, you tough, sweet kids. Godspeed to you."

D turned around. To one side of the chamber stood Larmica. "Was that your doing?"

Larmica nodded and said, "I reversed all the computer's safety circuits. In the next five minutes the castle shall be destroyed—please, flee while you may."

"Why not live here in your castle until the end of time, with the darkness as your companion?"

"There's no longer time for that. And the Lee family died out long ago. It died when my father chose a pointless, eternal life of nothing save drinking human blood."

The trembling grew stronger, and the whole chamber began to groan. The white detritus falling from the ceiling wasn't common dust, but rather finely powdered stone. The molecular bonds of the entire castle were breaking down!

"So, you'll stay here then?"

Larmica didn't answer the question, but said instead, "Kindly allow me to ask one thing—your name. D … Is that D, as in Dracula?

D's lips moved.

The two of them stood motionless, with white powder raining down. His reply went unheard.

Appropriately enough, the vampire's castle turned to dust like its lord and was gone. Their field of view rendered pure white by the clouds of powdered rubble, Doris and Dan couldn't stop coughing from all the dust.

They were atop a hill less than a hundred yards from the castle.

Wiping at her tearing eyes, when Doris finally raised her face again another sort of tears began to flow.

"It's gone … everything. And he's not coming back either … "

Putting a hand on his distracted sister's shoulder, Dan said cheerily, "Let's go home, Sis. We got a heap of work to do."

Doris shook her head.

"It's no use … I just can't do it anymore … Can't use a whip like I used to, can't look after you or do my work around the farm … And all because I found someone I could depend on … "

"You just leave it to me." The boy of eight threw out his chest. His little hand gripped D's pendant. "We've just gotta hold on for five more years. Then I'll be able to do everything. I'll even find you a husband, Sis. We got a long road ahead of us—so buck up."

He knew that he was no longer just an eight-year-old child.

Doris turned to her brother, looked at him like he was someone she'd never seen before, and nodded. Five years from now, he'd still be a boy. But in ten years, he'd be able to rebuild the house and hunt down fire dragons. It would take a long while, but time had a way of passing.

"Let's go, Dan."

Finally reclaiming her smile, Doris walked toward their horse.

"Sure thing!" Dan shot back, and, though his heart was nearly shattered with sorrow, he smiled to hide it.

With the two of them on its back, the horse galloped off to the east, where blue light filled the sky and their farm awaited them.

D had kept his promise.

Now it was the boy's turn.

Postscript

O r actually, an explanation of the dedication.

Most fans of *outré* cinema should be familiar with the film *Horror of Dracula*, produced in Britain by Hammer Films in 1958. Along with the previous year's *The Curse of Frankenstein*, this classic helped fire a worldwide boom in horror films, and, in addition, served as the first inspiration for this humble horror novelist. I've seen quite a few horror and suspense movies, but no film before or since accomplished what this one did—to send me racing out of the theater in the middle of the show. Though most will find this information superfluous, Terence Fisher directed it, Jimmy Sangster wrote the script, and Bernard Robinson was the production designer. Surely the film's stars, Christopher Lee and Peter Cushing, require no introduction. The whole incredible showdown between Count Dracula and Professor Van Helsing—from the fiend's appearance in silhouette at the top of the castle's staircase, to the finale where sunlight and the cross reduce him to dust—is something horror movie fans will be talking about until the end of time. I hope it's made available on video as soon as possible.

At present, Kazuo Umezu could be regarded as the leading man of horror manga in Japan, but so far as I know, the only male manga artist in the past with such a distinct horror style

(I don't know about female manga artists) would be Osamu Kishimoto. But rather than aiming to produce more of the same Japanese-style horror that had preceded him, this man created a gothic mood in the Western tradition. Whether it was a weird western-style mansion standing right in the middle of the city, with coffins resting in its stone-walled basement and a horde of creepy inhabitants, or the logic of the conflict that runs through all his stories (such as the cross against vampires or the power of Buddhism against kappas), the way he succeeded in bringing his creatures to life in a field like Japanese horror manga, where they were so sorely lacking, was, in a word, refreshing.

It would be most unfair if someday someone were to write a history of horror manga in Japan and dismiss Osamu Kishimoto as merely one more author of sci-fi and adventure manga. Even now I get goose bumps as I recall the short tale about the kappa that turned itself into a beautiful woman when runoff from a factory polluted its lake, and later took up residence in a brother and sister's house, as well as many other tales. Lately I haven't seen much work by him, but I sincerely hope to see him in better health and producing new stories in the future.

Hideyuki Kikuchi
December 6, 1982, watching *Dracula* ('79)

VAMPIRE HUNTER D

OMNIBUS BOOK ONE

VAMPIRE HUNTER D

VOLUME 2
RAISER OF GALES

Written by
HIDEYUKI KIKUCHI

Illustrations by
YOSHITAKA AMANO

English translation by
KEVIN LEAHY

Dark Horse Books
Milwaukie

VAMPIRE HUNTER D

A Village in Winter

Wintry sunlight fell from high in the hollow sky to the valley below. Bright enough to trick a smile out of you and cold enough to empty your lungs in a cloudy white chain of coughs, the rays bound for the narrow and more or less straight trail were also quite refreshing. Perhaps that was because spring wasn't so far off.

Not far from there, the road through the valley came to a modest plain surrounded by black woods and ushered travelers into a tiny Frontier hamlet.

Including the ranches and solar farms scattered about the area, there were still probably less than two hundred homes. The roofs of wooden and tensile-plastic houses were crusted white with remnants of snow, as were alleys that never saw the light of day. And the people in the hamlet, so bundled in heavy furs they might easily be mistaken for beasts, wore stern expressions. Even for the littlest of children, the single-minded determination to live made a hard mask of their features.

A narrow stream ran through the center of town from east to west. The surface of its clear waters reflected a sturdy bridge, and at this moment a silent procession of people crossed the bridge with a grave gait.

Ten men and two women were in the group. Sobs spilled from one woman's lips as she hid her face with the well-worn sleeve of an insulated overcoat. Graying hair reached her shoulders. The other woman—also in her forties, by the look of her—stood by her side, with an arm around her back for support. No doubt they were neighbors. Although this pair set the tone for the whole party, their grief hadn't yet elicited a sympathetic response from the men.

The old man at the fore wore a robe heavily adorned with magical formulae and all manner of strange symbols, and his face was wrought with terror. The other men were plastered with almost identical expressions, though six of them were also plainly in physical pain caused by the abominable burden digging down into their shoulders.

An oak coffin.

However, more disquieting by far was the heavy chain wrapped around the coffin. It almost seemed like a concerted effort had been made to keep whatever rested within the coffin from getting back out, and the way the chain rattled dully in the wintry light echoed the desperate fear of those who bore the oak box.

The party came to a halt at the center of the bridge. That was where the structure jutted out an extra yard on either side, forming a small gathering place over the river.

The old man who led them pointed to one side.

With much shuffling of their feet, the men bearing the coffin hustled over to the railing.

Giving a shudder, the sturdy man by the elder's side reached for the weapons girding his waist—steel stakes a good foot and a half long. The man had at least half a dozen of them in a pouch on his belt. His other hand pulled out the hammer he wore on the opposite side of his belt. The old-fashioned gunpowder revolver he had holstered there didn't even merit a glance.

Loosing an anguished scream, one of the women scrambled toward the coffin, but her neighbor and the rest of the men managed to restrain her.

"You simmer down," the old man shouted at her reproachfully.

The woman hid her face in her hands. If not for those supporting her, she'd undoubtedly have collapsed on the spot.

Casting an emotionless glance at the slender coffin, the elder raised his right hand to his shoulder and began to intone the words befitting such a ceremony.

"I am here today, my heart like unto a mournful abyss beyond description. Gina Bolan, beloved daughter of Seka Bolan and resident #8009 of the village of Tepes, Western Frontier Sector Seven, fell victim to the despised Nobility and passed away last night . . ."

At this, the faces of the pallbearers grew visibly paler, but the elder may not have noticed.

Six pairs of eyes restlessly shifted about, their collective gaze turning imploringly to the calm surface of the river.

There was nothing to see there. Nothing whatsoever out of the ordinary.

Within the coffin, something stirred. Not someone. Some*thing*. The men's faces inched closer to the coffin, as if caught in its gravity.

Clank clank, went the chains.

The men's faces grew white as a sheet.

The mayor shouted the name of the man with the stakes.

"Down! Put it down now!" the armed man said in a terror-cramped tone as he stepped closer. The other men didn't comply with his command. Brains and nerves and even muscles stiffened as fear stampeded through their bodies. This was by no means the first such ceremony they'd been involved in. However, the phenomenon now taking place in that box on their shoulders was patently impossible. For pity's sake, it was *daytime*!

Seeing the condition of the others, the man with the hammer and stake clanged his weapons together, shouting tersely, "Set 'er down on the railing!" The result was evident enough.

Whatever spell had held the men waned, and the coffin, which was a heartbeat shy of being thrown over the side, came to rest on the thick handrail. Three of the men still supported the other side of it.

It was a weird frenzy of activity on the bridge that fine, prevernal day.

The well-armed man dashed over and set the sharpened steel tip of a stake against the lid of the coffin.

His granite-tough face was deeply streaked by fear and impatience. The timing of this flew in the face of his vast personal experience and undermined the confidence he drew from long years on the job.

Sounds continued to issue from the coffin. From the way it shook and the sounds it made, it seemed that whatever it contained had awakened and was fumbling around without any idea of its present predicament.

The man raised his hammer high.

Suddenly, the sounds coming from the coffin changed. Powerful blows struck the lid from the inside, shaking not only the coffin with a powerful pummeling but also the men carrying it.

The elder cried something.

With a low growl, the hammer tore through the air. Shouting and the sounds of destruction melded into one.

The stake pierced the coffin at almost exactly the same second a pale hand smashed through the heavy planks and clawed at the air. The hand of a mere child!

Wildly twitching, the hand clutched at the air again and again. In a split second, the hand flew to the throat of the man who stood there, hammer still in hand and utterly dumbfounded.

". . . Coffin . . . drop . . . the damn coffin!"

Blood gushed from the man's throat along with those words.

This ghastly tableau did more than his orders to rouse the men's consciousness. Shoulder muscles bulging, they tilted the coffin high on the railing. It fell with the other man still pinned to the lid, sending up a splash that flowered in countless droplets across the surface of the river.

Surely the coffin must have been weighted, for it rapidly sank and merged with the ash-gray bottom. Amid the remaining ripples, crimson liquid bubbled up from one of those who sank with it, but in the world above the tranquil light of winter blanketed all creation. Only a woman's sobs remained to testify to the gruesome tragedy that had just played out.

†

Blades of grass that had long borne the weight of the snow took advantage of the reverberations from the heavy footfalls to throw off their burden. After all, their day would be here soon enough.

The footsteps came from a number of people, each and every one of them looking as tough as a boulder and as beefy as a Martian steer. Even through their heavy fur coats the bulging of their well-developed muscles was plain. All were in their twenties. Not even their apparent leader, a man a bit taller than the rest, had hit thirty yet. They belonged to the village's Youth Brigade.

The reason they were breathing so heavily was because they'd already been climbing this slope for nearly nine hours. But it was clear from their expressions and the look in their eyes that they weren't here for a picnic. Faces hardened by brooding, frustration, and rage, they seemed on the verge of tears. From the look of it, they were trying in vain to hold back the pitch-black terror welling inside them. The pair bringing up the rear was especially short of breath, partly because each had a wooden crate full of weapons strapped to his back, but mainly because of the gently rolling hill they were trying to climb.

It was a weird piece of geography.

A mile and a quarter in diameter at the base and roughly sixty feet high, it looked like an ordinary hill from both the ground and the air. Those who set foot on its slopes, however, found that it took several hours to reach the summit no matter how great they were at hiking.

Black ruins rose from the summit of the hill.

That was where the men were headed. However, that simple goal, glowering down at the surrounding landscape from a scant altitude of sixty feet, was not unlike the mirages that were said to occur in the Frontier's desert regions—it taunted these men as they tried to reach it, and would do the same to anyone else who accepted the challenge.

The distance never decreased.

Their feet clearly tread the slope, and their bodies told them they were indeed steadily gaining elevation. And yet, the further reaches of the incline and the ruins they sought never got any closer.

Taking into account the reports of all who had experienced this phenomenon, it was estimated that a man in prime condition took thirty minutes to climb three feet. Ten hours to the top—even on level ground, that much walking would leave a man exhausted. Climbing the hill, it only got worse, as the slope grew steeper and the trek became ever more fatiguing. It really came as little surprise that no one had even tried to climb it in the last three years.

The man at the forefront of the group—Haig, their leader—took no notice of his companions as he scanned the western horizon. The sun would be going down in two hours, falling behind the forest and the silvery chain of peaks far beyond them. That made it roughly three o'clock Afternoon, Frontier Standard Time.

If they didn't reach the top, accomplish their aim, and take their leave in the one hundred and twenty remaining minutes, Haig knew as well as anyone what fate awaited them when darkness fell.

To make matters worse, once they eventually made it to the summit, the fact of the matter was they didn't have the faintest idea where in the ruins the thing they sought would be slumbering. Although a roughly sketched map was stuffed in the leader's breast pocket, it had been drawn decades earlier by someone who had since passed away, so they weren't entirely sure whether they could rely on it or not.

And then there was their exhausted state to consider. Though this group had been selected from the proudest and strongest of the Youth Brigade, the taxing climb was actually far more fatiguing mentally than it was physically. While no amount of struggling would bring them any closer to their goal, sheer impatience could physically destroy them. This psychological test was said to be a particularly effective defense against intruders from the world below. Once the members of the Youth Brigade set foot in the ruins, there was some question as to whether or not they would have sufficient strength remaining to search out *its* resting place.

The only thing they had working in their favor was the fact that on the way down, at least, the hill lost its mystic hold over climbers. If they ran all the way, they could be down to the foot of the hill in less than two minutes.

Suddenly, Haig's sweat-stained countenance was suffused with joy.

He knew the distance between the summit ahead and him was "real" now. Less than thirty feet remained. Ignoring the panting of his air-starved lungs, he shouted, "We're there!" From behind him, satisfied grunts rose in response.

A few minutes later, the whole group was resting in the courtyard of the ruins. The shadow of fatigue fell heavily on each and every face, rendering them almost laughable.

"Just about time to get down to it. Break out the weapons," ordered Haig. He alone remained standing, surveying their surroundings.

The group huddled around the two wooden crates.

Off came the lids. Inside were five hammers, ten wooden stakes honed to trenchant points, and twenty Molotov cocktails that had been fashioned from wine bottles filled with tractor fuel and corked with rags. In addition, they had five bundles of powerful mining explosives with individual timers. Each of the men also had a bowie knife, sword, or machete stuck through the belt around his waist.

Everyone took a weapon.

"You all know the plan, right?" Haig said, just to be sure. "I don't know if we can put a whole lot of stock in this copy of the map or not, but right about now we ain't got any other options. If you think you're in trouble, give a whistle. You find out where *it* is, give two."

Bloodshot eyes bobbed up and down as the men nodded and got to their feet. Their grand scheme was going into action.

A wholly unexpected voice stopped them in their tracks.

"Just a second. Where the blazes are you boys off to all charged up like that?"

Every one of them moved like they'd been jerked back on a leash, turning toward the voice even as they went for their weapons.

From a shadowy entrance in the sole remaining wall of the stony ruins—a cavernous opening that faced the courtyard—a lone girl stepped casually into the afternoon light. Raven hair hung down to the shoulders of her winter coat, and what showed of her thighs looked cold but inviting.

"Well if it ain't Lina! What brings you up—," one of the men started to ask, swallowing the rest of the question. The eyes of all took on a tinge of terror, as well as the scornful hue of someone whose suspicions have proved correct. They'd known the answer to that question for quite some time.

"What the hell do you boys think you're doing? You'd better not go and do anything stupid," the girl said, as she looked Haig square in the eye. Although her visage was still so innocent it couldn't look stern if she tried, her face shone with the sagacity and the allure of a mature woman. She was at that awkward stage, a neat little bud waiting for spring, a heartbeat away from bursting open into a glorious blossom.

"Suppose you tell me what the hell brings you up here," said Haig, his words dripping out like molasses. His gaze had fallen to Lina's bare feet. "It ain't like you don't know the shit that's going on in town. The whole place's been turned inside out and we still didn't find *it*. Meaning this is the only place left for it to hide, wouldn't you say?"

"Well, that doesn't mean you have to haul a load of bombs up here, does it? Stakes and Molotov cocktails should do the job."

"That's nothing that concerns you," Haig said scornfully. "Now answer the damn question. Why the hell are you up here?

We sure as shit didn't see you on our way up here. Just how long you been up here, anyway?"

"I just got here. And for your information, I came up the other side. So of course you didn't see me."

As the men looked at each other they had a strange glint in their eyes.

"Well in that case, I guess the hill *can't fool you* none—looks like we had it figured right all along. Unless I miss my guess, you're the one responsible for what's happening in town."

"Spare me your conjecture. You know I've been at home every time anything happened."

"You don't say. Hell, the whole bunch of you have been screwy since *that* happened. We got no way of knowing what kind of powers you been using behind our backs."

Haig suddenly had nothing more to say. He gave his cohorts a toss of his chin. All of them smiled lasciviously as they started to close in on Lina.

"We're gonna have to check you out now. Gonna peel you down buck-ass naked."

"You stop this foolishness right now. Do you have any idea how much trouble you'll get in if you even try it?"

"Ha! That supposed to be a threat?" one of them jeered. "Everybody in town knows full well what's going on between you and the mayor, missy. If we can prove you're a plain ol' woman now, the old geezer'll be happier than a pig in shit."

"And that ain't the half of it," another added. "After all of us have had a turn with you, you'll be feeling so damn good you'll lose your tongue for ratting us out."

Haig licked his lips. These young men were known to be rough customers—that was precisely the reason they were perfect for protecting the village from brutal groups of roving bandits or vicious beasts. But now, their exhaustion and the fear of the work to come churned together into a slimy mess that suffocated what little sense they'd been born with.

Lina made no attempt to escape. Haig grabbed her by the arms and pulled her close. His greasy lips savagely latched onto her fine mouth. Pulling her coat up with one hand, he groped at her thighs, while his tongue tried to force its way between her perfect teeth.

Suddenly, there was a dull smack and his massive frame doubled over at the waist. With lightning speed, Lina had slammed her knee into Haig's privates, leaving him speechless and on his knees. She didn't even spare him a backward glance as she disappeared into an entrance of the ruins.

"You little bitch!" shouted one of the three men who went after her.

Because it was still daytime, only anger and lust managed to beat back the thugs' fear of entering the ruins.

Weird machinery and furniture seemed to float in the chill darkness, but they ignored these objects as they ran. Twisting and turning down one sculpture- and painting-adorned corridor after another, they eventually caught up to Lina in a vast room, a hall of some sort.

Stripping off her coat when they caught her by the shoulder, she stumbled and fell face first, but the three of them tackled her and rolled her onto her back.

Lina cried, "Quit it!"

"Stop your squirming. We're gonna do you real good. All three of us at once!"

Just as the men were pinning her pallid and desperately thrashing hands and closing on her sweet lips . . .

They were struck by the creepiest sensation. Even Lina forgot her struggles and donned a hue of terror. From that strange knot of humanity, four pairs of eyes focused on the same spot in the darkness simultaneously.

Out of the unplumbed depths of the blackness, a single shadowy figure emerged. A figure that seemed to them darker by far than the blackness shrouding this whole universe.

"One civilization met its end here," said a soft voice flecked with rust, the words drifting through the darkness. "While it's impossible to halt the progress of time, you would do well to show some respect for what's been lost."

Lina scrambled up and took cover behind the figure, but the men didn't so much as twitch. They couldn't even speak. Animal instincts honed by more than two decades of doing battle with the forces of nature told them just what this person was. It was something far surpassing what they'd expected to find here.

Footsteps rang out at the entrance to the hall, but soon halted. Haig and the rest of the men had burst into the room with enraged expressions, but then froze in their tracks.

"Wha— what the hell are you?"

Not surprisingly, it was the leader of the suicide squad who finally managed to speak, but just barely. His tremulous voice and the chattering of his teeth told volumes about how he, too, had been laid low by this ghastly aura beyond human ken. At that moment, the only thoughts running through the minds of Haig's men concerned getting down off the hill as fast as humanly possible.

"Leave. This is no place for you."

At the stranger's bidding, the men got to their feet and started to back away. The reason they remained facing forward was not so much due to the old adage about never letting your foe see your back as it was due to their terror at not knowing what might happen to them if they turned around. *Some things are worse than dying*, the men all muttered in their heart of hearts.

Once they'd fallen back to the hall's entrance, the men regained some of their spirit. The roof of the windowless corridor was laced with cracks that let the sunlight pour in.

Haig pulled out a Molotov cocktail and another man produced some matches. Striking the match on his pants, he put the flame to the rags. Haig heaved the firebomb with such an exaggerated throw he seemed to be trying to blast his own fears away. No consideration at all was given to Lina's safety.

The blazing bottle limned a smooth arc across the room and landed at the pair's feet. But no two-thousand-degree lake of flames spread from it. The bottle simply stood upright on the intricately mosaicked floor. There was a tinkling *clink* as the neck of the bottle and the flaming rag it contained dropped to the floor.

The men probably hadn't even seen the silvery flash that had split the air.

Panic ensued.

Loosing an audacious chorus of screams, the men scrambled over each other in an effort to flee down the hallway. And they didn't look back. The fear of the supernatural world bubbled from a gaping wound where their reason had just been severed, and that fear threatened now to take shape. The men drove their legs with all their desperate might to avoid having to see what shape it took.

Once she was sure their footsteps had died away, Lina finally stepped away from the stranger's back. Sticking out her cute little tongue, she turned to the exit and made the rudest gesture she knew. She must've been amazingly sedate by nature, because she no longer seemed in the least bit troubled as her eyes gazed first at the truncated bottle and the guttering flame, then up at the muscular stranger with admiration.

"You're really incredible, you . . ." she began to say, but her voice gave out on her.

Now her eyes had become accustomed to the darkness, and they'd taken in the face of her savior. An exquisite face, like a silent winter night preserved for all time.

"What is it?"

Shaken back to her senses by the sound of his voice, Lina said the first thing that popped into her mind. She was a rather straightforward girl.

"You sure are handsome. Took my breath away, you did."

"You'd best go home. This is no place for you," the owner of that gorgeous countenance said once more, his words not so much cold as emotionless.

Lina had already reclaimed enough of her senses to shamelessly eye the man from head to toe.

He couldn't have been a day over twenty. His wide-brimmed traveler's hat and the elegant longsword he wore across the back of his black longcoat made it clear he was no tourist. A blue pendant dangled on his chest. The deep, soul-swallowing shade of blue seemed to fit the youth perfectly.

Like hell I'm leaving. I'll go wherever I damn well please, Lina wanted to say, but the words she hastily uttered were the exact opposite of what she actually felt.

"If you insist, the very least you could do is walk me out."

At this unexpected request, the youth headed toward the exit without making a sound.

"Hey, wait just a second, you. Aren't we the hasty one!" Flustered, Lina hurried after him. She thought about latching onto the hem of his coat or maybe his arm, but didn't actually go through with it. This young man had an intensity about him that completely locked him off from the rest of the world.

Mutely trailing after him, the girl stepped out into the courtyard.

To Lina's utter amazement, the youth quickly turned around and headed back toward the entrance. She jumped up again.

"For goodness sake, would you just wait a minute? You didn't even give me a chance to say thank you, you big dolt!"

"Go home before the sun sets. The way down is normal enough."

The shadowy figure didn't turn to face her as he spoke, but his words made Lina's eyes go wide.

"And just how would you know that? Come to think of it, when did you get here, anyway? It couldn't be you can walk up here *like normal,* could it?!"

Just shy of the entrance, the young man halted. Without facing her, he said, "So, you can climb the hill normally, too, I take it?"

"That's right. My circumstances are kind of special," Lina said, sounding strangely resolved for once. "Wanna hear about it?

Of course you do. After all, you came all the way up here to see these ruins—the remnants of a Noble's castle."

The youth started to walk away again.

"Oh, curse you," Lina cried, stomping her feet in anger. "At least give me your name. If you don't, I'm not heading home—come sunset or not. If I get attacked and maimed by monsters, it'll be on your conscience for the rest of your days. I'm Lina Sween, by the way."

Apparently her badgering paid off, for a low voice drifted from the silhouette as it melded with the darkness filling the doorway. He said but a single word.

"D."

†

Later that night, a Vampire Hunter paid a call on the home of the village's mayor.

"Well I'll be . . ."

Having pulled a dressing gown over his pajamas and come downstairs, the sleepy-eyed mayor forgot what he was about to say when he saw the beauty of the Hunter standing at the other end of the living room with his back to the wall.

"I see now why our maid's walking around like something sucked the soul out of her. Well, I can't very well put you up here in my house. I've got a daughter for one thing, and the women's groups are always coming and going through here."

"I've already put my horse and my gear in the barn," D said softly. "I'd like to hear your proposition."

"Before we start, why don't you set yourself down. You must be coming off a long ride, I'd wager."

D didn't move. Nonchalantly drawing back the hand he'd used to indicate a seat, the mayor gave a nod. The valet, who'd just thrown a load of kindling and condensed fuel into the fireplace and was awaiting further instruction, was ordered out.

"Never show the enemy your back, eh? Indeed, I suppose you've got no proof I'm on your side."

"I was under the impression you hired Geslin before me," D suggested. It almost appeared he hadn't been listening to a word the mayor had to say.

By the look of him, the mayor was a pushy man, but he didn't let the slightest hint of displeasure show on his face. In part, this was because he'd heard rumors about the skill of the super Grade A Hunter he was dealing with. But more than that, it was because just having the Hunter standing beside him made the mayor feel in his flesh and bones that the Hunter was a being from a whole other world. Though he had exquisite features far more beautiful than any human, the ghastly aura emanating from the Hunter shook to the fore something mankind usually kept buried in the deepest depths of its psyche—the fear of the unknown darkness.

"Geslin's dead," the mayor spat. "He was a top-notch Grade A Hunter, but he couldn't find us our *vampire*, and he went and got himself killed by an eight-year-old girl to boot. Got his throat ripped clean open, so we don't have to worry about him *coming back*, but we paid him a hundred thousand dalas in advance— what a fiasco!"

"I understand the circumstances were somewhat unusual."

The mayor pursed his lips in surprise. "You know about that, do you? Well, that's a dhampir for you! Seems there might be something after all to them rumors that you can hear the winds blowing out of Hell."

D said nothing.

The mayor gave a brief account of the disaster that had occurred on the bridge roughly two weeks earlier, saying in conclusion, "And all of this happened in broad daylight. By the look of you, I'd wager you've seen more than I have in my seventy years on this earth. But I don't suppose that'd happen to include victims of vampires who can walk in the light of day, now would it?"

D remained silent. That in and of itself was his answer.

It just wasn't possible. The Nobility and those whose lives they'd claimed were permitted their travesty of life by night alone. The world of daylight had been ceded to humanity.

"I think you have a pretty good notion why I've called you here. Think about it. If those damnable Nobles and their retinue were free to move not just by night but by light of day as well, do you have any idea what would become of the world?"

The darkness and chill of the room seemed to increase exponentially. To save wear on their generators, it was commonplace to use lamps fueled with animal fat for lighting at night on the Frontier. The old man's eyes seemed to smolder as he stared at the hands he held out to warm. D didn't move a muscle, as if he'd become a statue.

Really set my hooks into him that time, the mayor snickered in his heart of hearts. His words had been chosen for maximum effect on the psyche of his guest, and surely they would've dealt a severe blow to the beautiful half-breed Hunter. *Oh, yes—come tomorrow, things are bound to be a bit more manageable around here.*

However, all did not go quite as expected.

"Could you elaborate on what's happened in this case so far?"

D's voice carried no fear or uneasiness, and, for a moment, the mayor was left dumbstruck. So, the horrifying thought of bloodthirsty vampires running amuck in the world by day had no impact on this dhampir? Wrestling down his surprise a split second before it could rise to his face, the mayor began to speak in a tone more subdued than was necessary.

It all started with the ruins and four children.

Even now, no one knew for sure just how long the ruins had stood on that hill. When the village founders had first set foot in this territory nearly two centuries earlier, the ruins were already choked with vines. Several times the hill had been scaled by suicide squads who produced roughly sketched maps and studied its ancient history, but while they were doing so a number of strange phenomena had occurred. Fifty years ago a group of investigators had come from the Capital to see it, and they were the last—after that, there were very few with any interest in surmounting the hill.

It was about ten years earlier that four children from the village had gone missing.

One winter's day, four children vanished from the village—farmer Zarkoff Belan's daughter (eight at the time), fellow farmer Hans Jorshtern's son (aged eight also), teacher Nicholas Meyer's son (aged ten), and general-store proprietor Hariyamada Schmika's son (aged eight). There was some furor over the possibility that it might be the work of a dimension-ripping beast that had been terrorizing the area at the time, but then there were villagers who had seen the four children playing partway up the hill on the day they went missing. Their disappearance forced the community to eye the ruins with suspicion.

For the first time in fifty years, a suicide squad was formed, but, despite a rather extensive search of the ruins, no clue to the children's whereabouts could be found. Rather, toward the end of a week of searching, members of the suicide squad started disappearing in rapid succession, and the search had to be called off before all the passageways and benighted subterranean chambers that comprised the vast complex of ruins could be investigated.

The grief-stricken parents were told that their children had probably been taken by slave-traders passing by the village, or had been lost to the dimension-ripping beast. Whatever fate awaited the children in either of those scenarios, it was a far more comforting hypothesis than the thought of them disappearing into the remains of a vampire's mansion.

One evening, about two weeks after the whole incident had started, the tragedy came to its grand—if somewhat tentative—finale. The miller's wife was out in the nearby woods picking lunar mushrooms when she noticed a couple of people trudging down the hill, and she let out a shout fit to knock half the town off its feet.

The children had returned.

That was to be both a cause for rejoicing and a source of new fears.

"For starters, only three of the kids came back." The elderly mayor's voice was so thin, it was fairly lost to the popping of the logs in the fireplace. "You see, Tajeel—that would be Schmika's boy, from the general store—never did come back. To this day we still don't know whatever became of him. Can't say it came as any great surprise when his father and mother both passed away from all their grieving. I'm not saying we weren't glad to get the rest of them back, but maybe if he hadn't been the only one that didn't make it—"

"Did you *examine* the children?" D asked as he turned his gaze toward the door, on guard, no doubt, against any foe who might burst into the room. It was said that even among Hunters, there was an incredible amount of animosity, with hostility often aimed at the more famous and capable. D's eyes were half-closed. The mayor was suddenly struck with the thought that the gorgeous young man was conversing with the night winds through the wall.

"Of course we did," the mayor said. "Hypnosis, mind-probing drugs, the psycho-witness method—we tried everything we could think of. Unfortunately, we used some of the old ways, too. I tell you, even now the screams of those kids plague my dreams. But it was just no use. Their minds were a blank, completely bare of memories for the exact span of time they'd been missing. Maybe they'd been left that way by external forces, or then again maybe it was something the kids' own subconscious minds had pulled to keep them all from going insane. Though if it was the latter, I suppose you'd have to say that as far as Jorshtern's boy went, the results weren't quite what you'd hope for—to this day, Cuore's still crazy as a bedbug.

"The upshot of this is, exactly what happened in the ruined castle and what they might've seen there remains shrouded in mystery. I suppose the only saving grace was that none of them came away with the kiss of the Nobility. Cuore's case was unfortunate, but the other two grew up quite nicely, becoming one of our schoolteachers and the village's brightest pupil, respectively."

Having progressed this far in his story, the mayor seemed to be finally at ease. He walked over to a sideboard against the wall, got a bottle of the local vintage and a pair of goblets, and returned.

"Care for a drink?"

As he proffered a goblet, his hand stopped halfway. He'd just remembered what dhampirs usually consumed.

As if to confirm this, D replied softly, "I never touch the stuff." The Hunter's gaze then flew to the pristine darkness beyond the window panes. "How many victims have there been, and under what conditions did the attacks occur?"

"Four so far. All close to town. Time-wise, it's always at night. The victims have all been disposed of."

Just then the mayor's voice gave out on him. Surely the ghastly task of their disposal had come back to haunt his memory, for his hand and the drink it held trembled. After all, not every victim had been given a chance to turn into a vampire before they met their end.

"Finding missing kids and *putting 'em down*—this is a nasty bit of business to go through, with spring so close and all."

With a strident *clang*, the mayor slammed the steel goblet down on his desk. The contents splashed up, soaking his palm and the sleeve of his gown.

"It's by no means certain that Schmika's boy Tajeel had a hand in this. There's a very good chance one of the remaining Nobility has slipped in here, or a vampire victim run out of another village is prowling the area. I'd like you to explore those possibilities."

"Do you think there are Nobles who can walk with their victims in the light of day?"

At this softly spoken query, the mayor clamped his lips shut. It was the very question he'd posed to D earlier. Suddenly, the mayor donned a perplexed expression and turned his eyes toward

264 | HIDEYUKI KIKUCHI

D's waist. Though the sound was faint, he could've sworn he'd heard a strange voice laughing.

"Sometime tomorrow, I need all the information you have on how the victims were attacked, their condition following it, and how they were handled," D said without particular concern. His voice was callous, completely devoid of any emotion concerning the work he was about to undertake. Apparently, this Vampire Hunter knew no fear, even when confronted with a foe the likes of which the world had never known—demons who could walk in the light of day. With an entirely different kind of terror than he felt toward the Nobility, the mayor focused his gaze on the young man's stunningly beautiful visage. "Also, I'd like to pay a visit to the three surviving abductees. If it's any great distance, I'll need a map to their homes."

"You won't need a map," a feminine voice cooed.

The door swung open, and a smiling face like a veritable blossom drew the eyes of both men.

Eyes that shone with curiosity returned D's gaze, and she said, "Not the least bit surprised, are you? You knew I was standing out there listening in the whole time, I'm sure. I'll tell you all you need to know. Lukas Meyer will be at the school. After classes I can take you to where Cuore lives. And you needn't look far for the third. So, we meet again, D."

Farmer Belan's daughter, now the mayor's adopted child, made a slight curtsy to D.

†

"Say, are you sure this is okay?" Lina asked the next morning, gripping the reins to the two-horse buggy she drove toward the school.

"Sure *what's* okay?"

"Going out like this first thing in the morning and all. Dhampirs don't like the daytime, right, on account of having part Noble blood in them."

"Just full of weird tidbits, aren't you?" D muttered, looking over the backs of the six-legged mutant equines. If a telepath had been there, they might've caught a whisper of a grin deep in the recesses of his coldly shuttered but human consciousness.

Inheriting characteristics of both their human and vampire parents, dhampirs were physiologically influenced by both parents in different respects.

Humans slept by night and were awake by day, while the opposite was true for the Nobility. When the genes of the respective races came into conflict, it was generally the physiological traits of the Noble half—the vampire parent—that proved dominant. A dhampir's body craved sleep by day, and wanted to be awake at night.

However, just as a left-handed person could learn through practice to use either hand equally well, it was entirely possible for dhampirs to follow the tendencies of their human genes and live just as mortals did. And, while they might have nearly half the strength, sight, hearing, and other physical advantages of a true vampire, it was that adaptability that was their greatest asset. With that fifty percent, they had a measure of power within them no human being could hope to attain, allowing them to cross swords with the Nobility by day or night.

Still, while it was true they could resist their fundamental biological urges, it was also undeniable that operating in daylight severely degraded a dhampir's condition. Their biorhythms fell off sharply after midnight, reaching their nadir at noon. Direct sunlight could burn their skin to the point where even the gentlest breeze was pure agony, like needles being driven into each and every cell in their body. In some cases, their skin might even blister like a third-degree burn.

Ebbing biorhythms brought fatigue, nausea, thirst, and numbing exhaustion. Fewer than one in ten dhampirs could withstand the onslaught of midday without experiencing those tortures.

"Still, it looks like you don't have any problems at all. That's no fun." Lina pursed her lips, then quickly hauled back on the reins. The horses whinnied, and the braking board hanging from the bottom of the buggy gouged into the earth.

"What's wrong?" D asked, not sounding the least bit surprised.

Lina pointed straight ahead. "It's those jerks again. And Cuore's with them. Yesterday was bad enough, but now what the hell are they up to?"

Some thirty feet ahead, a group of seven men walked past a crumbling stone wall and turned the corner. Three of them, most notably Haig, Lina and D had met in the ruins the day before.

A young man of seventeen or eighteen dressed in tattered rags walked ahead of the group as the others pushed and shoved him along. He was huge—over six feet tall and weighing more than two hundred pounds. His gaze completely vacant, he continued down the little path, pushed along by a man who barely came up to his shoulder.

"Perfect timing. We were just going to see him. What's down that way anyway?"

"The remains of a pixie breeding facility. It hasn't been used in ages, but rumor has it there's still some dangerous things in there," Lina said. "You don't think those bastards would bring Cuore in there?"

"Get to school."

By the time the last word reached Lina's ears, D was headed for the narrow path, the hem of his coat fluttering out around him.

As soon as he rounded the corner of the stone wall, the breeding facility buildings came into view. Although "buildings" wasn't really the word for them. It appeared the owner had removed all the usable lumber and plastic joists, leaving nothing more than a few desperately listing, hole-riddled wooden shacks that were on the edge of collapse. The winter sun glinted whitely on this barren lot, which was surrounded by naked trees frosted with the last crusts of snow.

The men slipped into one of the straighter structures. They seemed fairly confident that few people passed this way, as they never even looked back the way they'd come.

Perhaps thirty seconds ticked by.

Shouting exploded from within the building. There were screams. Lots of screams. And not simply the kinds of sounds you make when you encounter something that scares you. Startled, perhaps, by the ghastly cries, the branches of a tree that grew beside the building threw down their snowy covering. There was the cacophony of something enormous shattering to pieces.

Just seconds after the reverberations died away, D entered the building.

The screaming had ceased.

D's eyes took on the faintest tinge of red. The thick smell of blood had found its way to his nostrils.

Every last man was laid out on the stone floor, convulsing in a puddle of his own blood. Aside from a few steel cages along one wall that evoked the building's past as a pixie breeding facility, the vast interior was filled only with the stink of blood and cries of agony. For something that had been accomplished in the half minute the men had been inside with Cuore, the job was entirely too thorough. There could be no doubt that some sort of otherworldly force had completely run amuck.

Two things caught D's eye.

One was Cuore's massive frame, sprawled now in front of the cages. The other was a gaping hole in the stone wall. Six feet or more in diameter, the jagged opening let the morning sunlight fall on the dark floor. Whatever had left the eight strapping men soaking in a sea of blood had gone out that way.

Without sparing a glance to the other young men, D walked over to Cuore. Crouching gracefully, the Hunter said, "They call me D. What happened?"

Muddy blue eyes were painfully slow to focus on D. His madness was no act. The boy's right hand rose slowly and pointed to the fresh hole in the wall. His parched lips disgorged a tiny knot of words.

"The blood . . . "

"What?"

" . . . The blood . . . Not me . . . "

Perhaps he was trying to lay the blame for this massive bloodshed.

D's *left* hand touched the young man's sweaty brow.

Cuore's eyelids drooped closed.

"What did you see in the castle?" D's voice sounded totally unaffected by the carnage surrounding them. He didn't even ask who was responsible for this bloodbath.

However, could even his left hand pull the truth from the mind of a madman?

A certain amount of "will" seemed to sprout up in Cuore's disjointed expression.

The boy's Adam's apple bobbed up and down, preparing to spill a few words.

"What did you see?" D asked once again. As he posed the question, he reached over his shoulder with his right hand and turned.

The half-dead men were rising to their feet from the floor.

"Possessed, eh?" D's gaze skimmed along the men's feet. The gangly shadows stretching from their boots weren't those of any human. The silhouette of the body was oddly reminiscent of a caterpillar, while the wiry, thin arms and legs were a grotesque mismatch for the torso. Those were pixie shadows!

A single evil pixie who'd been kept here must have escaped and remained hidden somewhere in the factory all this time. Unlike the vast majority of the artificially created beasts the Nobility had sown across the earth, most varieties of pixies were exceptionally amiable. But other varieties, based on goblins, pookas, and imps from ancient pre-holocaust Ireland, kept the people of the Frontier terrified with their sheer savagery. The redcap variety of pookas lopped off travelers' heads with the ax they were born holding, then used their victims' blood to dye the headgear that gave them their name. Few of these creatures possessed the ability to manipulate half-dead humans, but with proper handling they could help make otherwise untamable unicorns clear vast tracts of land, or they could boost the uranium pellet production of Grimm hens from one lump every three days to three lumps a day. In light of this, some of the more impoverished villages on the Frontier were willing to assume the risks of breeding these sorts of creatures. The blood-spattered and still unconscious men were being animated by an individual of the most atrocious species.

The shadow held an ax in its hands.

Smoothly, the weapon rose.

The men each raised a pair of *empty* hands over their heads.

As the nonexistent axes whirred through the space D's head had occupied, the Hunter leapt to the side of the room with Cuore cradled in his arms.

With mechanical steps, the shadow's marionettes went after him.

Unseen blades sank into the wall and dented the roof of an iron cage. Cutting only thin air, one of the men fell face first and set off a shower of sparks a yard ahead of him.

This was a battle for control of the shadows.

A stream of silvery light splashed up from D's back, then mowed straight ahead at the invisible ax one of the unconscious men raised against him.

There was no jarring contact, but a breeze skimmed by D's cheek and something imbedded in the wall.

These weapons weren't just invisible, they were nonexistent. But deadly nonetheless.

Three howling swings closed on the Hunter, all from different directions. The blades clashed together, but D and Cuore flew above the shower of sparks that resulted.

Twin streaks of white light coursed toward the floor.

The men went rigid and clutched their wrists. Thud after thud rang out in what sounded like one great weight after another hitting the floor. Actually, it was the men *dropping* their weapons.

Having sheathed his longsword, D headed over to one of the men who'd collapsed in a spray of blood.

Going down on one knee by the man's side, he asked, "Can you hear me?"

As the man's feeble gaze filled with the sight of D, his eyes snapped wide open. The fallen man was none other than Haig.

"Dirty bastard . . . How the hell did you . . . ?"

His pitiful voice, which hardly matched his rough face, ground to a halt when he noticed something on the floor.

Now pinned to the stone floor by two stark needles, the unearthly shadow stretching from Haig's feet was rapidly fading from view. Stranger still, it wasn't just the twice-pierced shadow that was affected. The shadows of the other men contorted and writhed in the throes of intense pain. And yet the movements of all remained perfectly synchronized!

It must've taken incredible skill to hurl those needles from midair and nail the shadow precisely through the wrist and heart, but it seemed doubtful someone like Haig could ever truly grasp the amount of focus D needed to perfect such a technique.

Because, amazingly, the needles stuck in the stone were made of wood.

Soon enough, the disquieting shadows vanished and those of the men returned.

"I'm hurting . . . Damn, it hurts! Hurry up, call the doctor . . . please . . . "

"When you've answered my question." D's tone conjured images of ice. Not surprising, as he was dealing with the same guys who'd already tried to gang-rape an innocent girl. "What happened after you got Cuore in here?"

"I don't know . . . We was thinking one of them's to blame . . . so we planned on taking 'em one by one, smacking 'em around a little to see if we was right . . . and then . . . "

The light in Haig's eyes rapidly dimmed.

"And then what?"

"How the hell should I know . . . ? Get me a doctor . . . quick . . . As soon as we got in here and had 'im surrounded . . . all I could see was blood red . . . *like something was hiding in there* . . . "

The last word out of Haig's mouth became a leaden rasp of breath that rolled across the ground. He wasn't dead. Just unconscious, as the rest of them were as well. Though thin trails of fresh blood leaked from their ears, noses, and mouths, their condition was quite bizarre, given they showed no signs of external injuries.

D turned around.

Cuore stood groggily in the doorway, but much further outside there was the sound of numerous footsteps getting closer. Either Lina or one of the villagers who had seen the Youth Brigade with Cuore must have summoned the law. Apparently the bullying these young men did was far from appreciated in these parts.

D glanced at Cuore, then quickly spun to face the hole blown through the wall.

"What's wrong? Aren't you gonna keep grilling him? You'll never get to the bottom of this mess if you're afraid of stepping on the sheriff's toes," chided a voice from nowhere in particular.

The voice didn't faze D in the least. He and his black coat melted into the morning sun.

The One Who Gets to Leave

CHAPTER 2

"Lina, you have something on your mind?"

Sensing the ring of suspicion underlying his mild tone, Lina hurriedly turned her attention to the teacher before her. His youthful, gentle face wore a smile. Who would have believed a boy that disappeared into the ruins of a Noble's castle for a fortnight would grow up to be such a man?

"I called you into the teachers' room because you've been staring off into space all day long, and then you go and pull the same thing in here—what the heck's going on? We haven't got the official word yet, but the exam board from the Capital will be here in less than a week."

Along with Lina, he was one of the three children who'd returned safely after the four of them had disappeared—Lukas Meyer. Following in his father's footsteps, he worked as a teacher for the Department of Higher Education in the village. He was Lina's homeroom teacher, though there was actually only one class in the department of higher education and less than fifty students in that.

"It's, uh, nothing . . . really." Lina pawed at her hair and worked at concealing the blood rising in her face. Wild horses couldn't drag out of her the fact she'd taken a fancy to a certain man.

"I certainly hope so," Mr. Meyer said with a nod as he held his hands over the decrepit atomic heater whining before them.

Suddenly, both his tone and the look in his eyes became grave. "You mustn't forget the responsibility you bear," he said.

His earnest pitch left Lina in reverent silence.

"You're the hope of the village. When winter's over, you've got to take your chance to leave. We're all pulling for you, you know."

"Yes, sir."

"So, the test itself shouldn't be a problem, but have you decided what it is you'll study at the academy in the Capital?" Mr. Meyer's tone had changed. He knew the answer, and though it was a field he'd helped choose, he asked as if not wanting to know.

Lina made no reply.

"Mathematics, wasn't it?" He uttered the words like an admonishment.

"Yes, sir."

"That's fine. You can't allow yourself to be distracted before the day of the exam. Better you just focus on the future," the teacher said cheerily. Lina smiled as well. There was a knock at the door. Her classmate, Harna, came in.

"What is it?"

The girl's face was flushed crimson, and her eyes were glazed with dreams. Mr. Meyer rose instinctively from his chair of hardwood and hides. For some reason, Lina snapped to attention.

"There's someone here to see you. Someone . . . Well, he's very good-looking . . . "

That meant nothing to the teacher. Knitting his brow for a moment, Mr. Meyer told Harna to send the visitor in. Looking at Lina, he said, "Well then, be careful on your way home. What, is there something else?"

"Not really. It's just the weather's so nice today." Standing by the windows, which had been specially treated to block the blinding glare from the snow, the girl tried to think of some ploy to remain in the room.

"No more so than usual."

"This room's filthy. I could start tidying it up for you today."

When Mr. Meyer's expression became one of deepest concern, Lina thought, *Damn!* A tall figure came through the low doorway, though in doing so he was nearly forced to stoop.

Lina gave a gasp of wonder and caught an involuntary round of introductions while they were still deep in her throat. Watching her, the reason for her suspicious behavior and her scheme to linger became apparent to Mr. Meyer. Sending off Harna, who stood absentmindedly in the doorway, Mr. Meyer inquired if their guest was an acquaintance of Lina's.

"I'm enjoying the hospitality of her home," D said, as he stood by the wall. He was exactly the sort of visitor unwelcome by an educator entrusted with coeds. "I'm D. A Vampire Hunter. And I suppose you can guess from that what brings me here."

Not surprisingly, Meyer's warm, intellectual countenance stiffened. As he invited D to have a seat, the look in his eyes was one he might give to any envoy dispatched to lay bare the dark secret he'd long concealed in his heart.

"No thanks," D said tersely, declining to take a seat. His manner was curt but not entirely disagreeable.

"Lina," the teacher said urgently. What was set to begin was not a tale for a young girl to hear. Lina glanced imploringly at D, then, with a slightly sullen look, she left the room, displeased by D's indifference.

As soon as the door shut, Mr. Meyer looked gravely at D. There was nobody else in the room.

"If you're staying at Lina's, then I guess you've heard all the particulars from the mayor. To be honest, there are a few things I'd like to know myself. Personally, if there's some sort of connection between these recent events and what happened to us in the darkness-shrouded days of our youth, I want to be there when you find out who or what's behind it all. That's just the way I feel."

Somehow D managed to parry his earnest tone.

"If you have any memory of what happened ten years ago, I'd like to hear it. I only know what the mayor told me."

That he nodded without hesitation testified to the fact that Mr. Meyer's hard expression was in fact without substance.

"I'm sorry to say it, but what you heard from the mayor is probably all there is to tell. One day ten years back we were all playing at the bottom of the hill. Lina said she wanted to pick flowers and make some garlands, and I remember Tajeel—that would be the boy who still hasn't been found—being against the idea, saying it was no fun. In the end we boys had to give in—even at that age women just have this strength—and we set to our irksome task. Even I got a bunch and handed them to Lina, and then . . . "

"What then?"

"I wandered off someplace else, picked a bunch more, and then turned around. That's it. Next thing I knew it was two weeks later and we were halfway down the hill and headed for the bottom. You're aware that every conceivable technique was used to try to restore that portion of our memories, aren't you?"

"There's something I'd like you to have a look at," D said, changing his location for the first time. Approaching a sturdy-looking desk made of thick logs, he took a harpy-quill pen from a penholder fashioned out of a greater dragon's fang. He also tore a page from the block of recycled notepaper.

"What is it?"

"Just something I have trouble with, too." D's expression didn't change as he made two swift strokes with the pen, then thrust the stiff recycled sheet before the teacher's eyes.

"What . . . what exactly is it?" Mr. Meyer turned to give D a dubious look.

"It's nothing. Sorry about that." D balled up the memo page on which he'd scribed a huge cross and tossed it in the trash. The barrel was also of greater dragon bone. A beast like that was sixty or more feet of unrivaled ferocity, but not a bit of bone or a single tendon went to waste when they fell into human hands. In a small village like this, the greater dragons were seen more as a way for the villagers to earn their daily bread than as a threat to their lives.

"Have you been up the hill since?"

"No, not me. Nor have I discussed the incident with Lina."

"One more thing. Cuore Jorshtern went mad. Is there anything unusual about you?"

Mr. Meyer forced a smile. "Perhaps my students could give you a more credible response to that. I believe myself to be an ordinary person, but, to be perfectly frank, I can't prove I wasn't at the scene of these recent crimes. I live alone, and it's possible I've been slipping out at night without knowing it. Once the deed was done, I could've destroyed all evidence of my crime, then returned to being an average schoolteacher asleep in his bed till morning. I can't say for sure that's not the case. If Nobility who can walk in daylight really do exist, the victims of such a Noble would have the same physiological characteristics as the assailant—isn't that so?"

D nodded.

When a human fell to the vampire's baleful fangs and was transformed into a demon of the night, common sense dictated that by and large the victim would inherit the characteristic abilities of that Noble when they rose again. The victim of a Noble with the power to assume lupine form would likewise be able to take that feral quadruped shape at will; the Noble who could command certain savage beasts would gain a new servitor with a mastery of animals.

However, just as a newborn baby isn't a carbon copy of one of its parents, there were certain obvious differences in the genetically linked powers. A victim couldn't remain transformed for as long a duration as their master. In addition, while in that altered form physical attributes such as speed, strength, and regenerative ability would all be several ranks lower. These newly made vampires weren't true Nobility, but rather they were little more than pale imitations.

As far as the people of the world were concerned, the most important thing about these pseudo-Nobles was that, whenever one was captured, they could be used to discern the full strength of the true threat—the real Noble. A hundred and fifty years earlier, an official named Summers Montague investigated several hundred cases while traveling across the Frontier. During his investigation, Montague divided the victims of the Nobility into different classes, and also left behind precise statistics relating to the powers of their masters. Another tome on the subject, *Methods of Discerning Nobility Levels Via Victims and Defensive Countermeasures* by Nobility scholar T. Fisher, was widely read and handed down by the Frontier people, despite the fact the Capital's Revolutionary Government had banned the book.

However, the threat of the Nobility now assailing this small village would add an astonishing new page to humanity's shared knowledge; or, rather, the threat was so grave, it would shake the most basic beliefs people held about the Nobility, undermining the sense of security that allowed people to go about their daily lives. Nobles who walked by day!

"I'm aware that Vampire Hunters have their own special techniques of identifying and classifying the Nobility. I'll spare no effort to assist you. Ask what you like, or try what you will. You see, I still want to know what happened up there on the hill, just as much as you do."

There seemed no cause to suspect the sincerity of the young schoolteacher.

D's left hand moved.

The teacher pulled away reflexively as the hand moved toward his brow. The movement was stopped when a knock sounded and a girl with golden tresses came in without waiting for a response. The tray the girl carried was simply a cross-sectional slice of a tree trunk. A pair of metal cups sat on it.

"What's all this? If you've finished cleaning up, go home."

As if the dubious words from Mr. Meyer had flown right past her ears, the girl set the cups on the table, saying, "Here you go." The profile she showed D was flushed carmine.

"I'd say your behavior as hostess leaves something to be desired," Mr. Meyer said in a slightly discontented tone. "Why the blazes is there such a huge difference in what you poured us? I'll have you know the money for the brew we have here at school comes out of my own pocket."

D's cup held more than three times as much drink as the teacher's.

In this village where single-digit temperatures were commonplace in winter, there were no taboos about consuming alcohol during class.

"Umm, well, this was all there was," the coed said, absorbing D in a series of fluttering glances of infatuation. "You're a pretty heavy boozer, Mr. Meyer, and you've drunk our share on the side. And besides, we don't hardly ever get visitors, so we all put our heads together to come up with a plan and I won the draw . . . What a handsome young man."

"That's enough of your rubbish." Mr. Meyer rose with a look of disgust and herded the young lady toward the exit. Just as he pulled the door open, an avalanche of girls thumped to the floor, and the teacher's eyes nearly shot out of his head.

"What's the meaning of this? Your rudeness amazes me. The lot of you'd better get out right this minute. And tomorrow, it's thirty strokes with the strap for the leader of this little ring!"

"Make it forty for all we care," said one. "Please let us talk with him, too. We want to hear about the world outside, about the Capital."

"No fair, Mr. Meyer," another protested. "You being in here all alone with this gorgeous hunk of man—there's something awful suspicious about that."

"He—hey, don't talk crazy!" Not surprisingly, the normally calm and composed Mr. Meyer lost his head. After all, he was still young. Ordering them to get out, the teacher shut the door in the face of the far-from-cooperative coeds, who were still clamoring as politely as they could for an autograph from D, at the very least.

The teacher mopped his brow and returned to his seat, but his eyes were calmly chuckling despite everything. "I'm sorry you had to see that ugly bit of business. I hope you don't take offense."

Strangely, D gave a shake of his head. The Hunter's mind was something rarely made manifest. Not only that, but even the eerie aura of a dhampir that usually emanated from every inch of him seemed to have waned.

Mr. Meyer was apparently sensitive enough to detect this change, and his tone became infused with familiarity. "You see, it's pretty rare that a traveler calls on our village. Apparently there's something wrong with the weather controller in this sector; spring and summer are fine, but as soon as fall comes the snow flies. And on account of that I don't suppose there's been a visitor—well, a trader or other traveler—that's stayed more than a couple days any given winter. For girls getting to that age, this village is really a pretty harsh place."

"Not just here," D said softly, even as he admired the azure sky beyond the window panes. "It's like that in every little village. But spring will be here soon."

"Yes, spring will come, but they won't leave."

For the first time, D noticed what a gravely dark gaze the young teacher had.

Frontier villages were tiny and poor. Even the smallest shift in population could be disastrous. The life of wringing crops from the nearly depleted soil, and fending off monstrosities that lay in wait with hungry eyes fixed on human prey, required the strength of every available person, right down to the last reasoning child. The Revolutionary Government in the Capital made reclamation of the Frontier a major item on its agenda; prohibiting any movements of population pending word from the government was an appropriate measure. So, in addition to the snow, another barrier, invisible to all eyes, shut off the wintry village.

"Here's an idea," the teacher said, watching D with new resolve. "If you have some free time while you're in town— "

"I've got other work." The Hunter's reply was icy cold. "I'll finish this as quickly as possible, and leave the village as soon as I'm done. That's all there is to it."

Mr. Meyer said simply, "I see," then drained the contents of his cup. He didn't appear in the least bit resentful. Because teachers were very rarely permitted to move, many of them gave themselves up to alcohol and hallucinogens to escape the despair of the future and the coldness of the present. But, even with the difficulties of the profession, Mr. Meyer was a truly grand individual. "I was asking too much, I know. But before you investigate me, there's one thing I'd like to ask of you."

"What's that?"

"Could you please just leave Lina out of this?"

"She's one of the children who came back, too."

"She's going places."

D's brow crinkled ever so slightly. This, too, was rather uncommon. As if to draw him in further, the teacher went on. "I'm sure you're probably aware of the system whereby once a year the government singles out the most promising child from a given village in that Frontier sector for instruction in the Capital's educational system. This year our village has been selected. I dare say it may never happen again. The whole place was in such a state you'd think the carnival had come to town. After months of skill tests, Lina was the unanimous choice."

"I see."

"We're just a poor little village struggling to survive, but she's a shining star rising for the Capital. Rumor has it the government might even be planning to launch one of those galactic energy propulsion ships to another planet. If she's picked for something like that, she might well become a star in every sense of the word.

Imagine . . . a girl from a village locked in long, dark winter for half the year and graced by the sun for a scant spring and summer might travel to the stars. Can you understand how proud that would make us, what a boost it would be?"

"If the selected child makes such a contribution, the village is due remuneration of some sort. That much I understand." Saying this, D fixed his eyes on Mr. Meyer's face. "Do you think you serve the best interest of the village, too?"

As Mr. Meyer's proper countenance hardened at this unanticipated query, a ghastly aura gushed from every inch of D.

"Huh?!" Frozen by what seemed a brutal assault on his deepest psyche, the teacher followed D's gaze, caught by the sight of a pupil rushing for the gate to the school, which was visible from the window. Beads of sweat clung to the boy's face. His hands were stained scarlet.

The teacher understood in an instant.

When he rose to follow D, who had already slipped through the doorway, he heard a bizarre, hoarse voice say, "Put on hold again? It's just one interruption after another today."

†

A dozen minutes later, Mr. Meyer was scampering through the woods. There was neither sight nor sound of D, who'd gone before him.

The well-drained road was dry and bare but for the occasional chunk of remaining snow, so the Hunter's running was unhindered and his speed was superhuman. Entrusting the blood-smeared youth to one of the elementary schoolteachers who'd joined him out on the school grounds, Mr. Meyer had gone after D. Having left the building ahead of the teacher, the Hunter had raced off after exchanging a few words with the boy. At that point he'd been less than ten feet away. *Even the wind itself is afraid to stand in the way of this gorgeous youth*, the teacher thought.

Here and there, bloodstains dotted the black road. These had dripped from the hands of the boy. He was the son of a huntsman who lived in the woods not far from the edge of town. Fooling with a homemade crossbow on his way home from school, he'd accidentally shot a quarrel into a thicket. He found it soon enough, and with it something else. The next thing he knew he was at the gates of the school, he said. He didn't know when he'd managed to get blood all over his hands. He was just a boy of nine.

Mr. Meyer could see the thicket ahead. Crimson snow sat on the boughs. Finding a narrow break, Mr. Meyer forced his way through.

His legs froze.

Before he knew it, his whole being was being hammered by an aura lurid to the extreme, awakening a primeval fear in each and every one of his cells. Though his mind demanded he move forward, his body rebelled. Man was not an animal of unified spirit and flesh.

Roughly ten feet ahead of him stood D.

And another six feet beyond the Hunter lay a corpse, face down and clad in red fur. He couldn't see the face, but from the long, ponytailed hair he knew it was a woman. There was nothing else, and no one else, to be seen.

Despite that, the teacher got the distinct impression that the body itself emanated the unnerving sense of evil that was crushing him like a vise. He wondered if D, too, had fallen victim to it. But no . . .

D had already unsheathed his longsword. The pose he took, with the tip of his blade low enough to prick the end of his right foot, was so unnatural it could hardly be called a fighting stance. But by extension, it suggested that whatever tack he took next was going to be positively unearthly.

And then the teacher noticed something that made joy buoy up in his withered heart. While the malicious aura was eddying all about D, it hadn't so much as touched the Hunter.

He wasn't the least bit afraid of it!

The evil aura over the girl moved. It pounced!

D flew through the air, too. He was the veritable image of a graceful hawk, chiseled in all its majesty in the chill air.

The teacher saw only a silver flash.

Space and time twisted—at least that was the way it felt.

Something slipped by the teacher's side, burst through part of the thicket, and vanished. Mr. Meyer ran toward D, who had landed by the girl's side. The spell was now broken, and only an air of cold tranquility spread through the area. They could even hear the chirping of birds again.

Going down on one knee beside the girl, D took her pulse. His expressionless face didn't so much as glance off to where the thing, whatever it was, had fled. And his sword was in its scabbard. The teacher felt like he was looking at an entirely different form of life. Though the youth was gorgeous enough to make even another man like Meyer swoon, the Hunter seemed even more fearfully unsettling than the thing with its aura of malevolence had been.

Dropping the girl's hand, D rose. He pressed the palm of his left hand to his right arm. When the teacher asked him if he'd been injured, he shook his head. "Seems we got here just in time," the Hunter said.

Relief spread through the teacher's chest. "You think *that thing* was what you're looking for?" he asked hopefully, but consternation quickly knit his brow.

"No," D said. "Judging by the temperature of the body and her drying blood, she was attacked this morning. What's more, that nasty just now left no teeth marks on her throat. It seems I ran across it almost as soon as it found the woman."

"What the blazes was that thing anyway?"

"I don't know. But this is the second time I've run into it."

"What?"

"Never mind that—this woman, would you happen to know her?"

At last Mr. Meyer could be of some small use. He rolled the woman, who had two threads of vermilion trailing from the nape of her neck, onto her back. Seeing the small basket lying nearby, he nodded.

"She's married to a farmer by the name of Kaiser. Must've been out picking aluminon blossoms for salves when she was attacked."

"And where were you this morning? You don't have to answer that. We'll know who the culprit is soon enough."

"We will?"

"Based on her wounds, whoever attacked her is the sort that gets very attached to its prey. It'll probably go after her again tonight. I'll keep watch. If it doesn't come . . . "

Feeling that he should be terrified by the sentence D left unfinished, the young teacher said in a hollow voice, "If it doesn't come *what*?"

"Then it would have to be someone who knows I'm here. Those students who saw me earlier were unaware of my profession, so that just leaves the mayor, Cuore, Lina, . . . and you."

Even though the season was so near to spring, Mr. Meyer's face had all the color of someone who'd died of exposure.

†

Before long, the sheriff and mayor hurried to the scene and carried Kaiser's wife off after a purely perfunctory investigation. The sheriff stared at D with suspicion, but he said nothing. For his part, D made no mention of the invisible entity.

D alone remained at the scene. When all the others had taken their leave, he said to the palm of his left hand, "What kind of shape are you in?"

"Not too good, as you might expect," came an exhausted voice in reply. "That was a hell of a lot of psychic juice to get hit with at once. I won't be back up to snuff for four, maybe five days. As for me getting down deep into those three returnees, that's completely out of the question. I couldn't get an order through to their subconscious, or even to the uppermost layer of their consciousness for that matter."

"That's a problem."

"If it is, it's your own fault for always driving me like a slave. Sometime today or tomorrow you'll need to feed me *the big four*."

"How about now? Is that why you're still hanging around?"

"Hmm . . . think I'll take a little nap first."

"Fine."

The bizarre dialogue concluded and D left the scene of the tragedy. The winter sun was still high. D chose the shade as he walked. That there wasn't even a tinge of weariness marring his beauty was truly astounding.

Irrespective of the weather, during the daylight hours those of vampire lineage craved rest at a basic physiological level. If it were merely a matter of remaining conscious, they could do so for up to eight hours if they confined themselves to a place where the sun virtually never shone. But if they engaged in any walking or standing around in sunlight, after four hours they'd lapse into a near-death state. Super Grade A Vampire Hunters could barely manage five to six hours of full activity. Their exhaustion was entirely different from that felt by a human working all night long, and it was solely because of this major weakness in the Hunters that the human wish to have all the Nobility exterminated remained unfulfilled.

Nearing the edge of the forest, D's steps came to a sudden halt. There was Lina, waiting for him in a wagon. D silently took a seat riding shotgun and the wagon sped off.

After a while D said, "If you're headed home, you're going the wrong way."

"Not a problem. See, we're headed for the happiest spot in the whole village."

Presently the wagon left the far end of the village and came to the highway, where it halted before a tiny shack facing the road.

A sturdy-looking but rough wooden bench had been crammed into the space, and snow had drifted into the lampless interior.

"The bus stop," Lina said brightly. "It's the only station leading out of town. The winters are impassable, but in another five days the electric bus will be by. And that morning, I'll be on the first one out of here."

"Seems you're bound for the Capital."

"Aren't you happy for me?!"

As the glint in the black pupils trained directly on him, D made a slightly awkward expression. "You certainly are an odd girl. Why would you say that?"

"How should I know?"

D looked puzzled.

"Just kidding," Lina said, after the fashion of a sister explaining the workings of a sleight-of-hand to her bewildered kid brother.

D was silent. The warrior who evoked shudders from the bloodsucking Nobility was completely at the mercy of a girl barely seventeen years of age. There was nothing he could do. If Mr. Meyer or the mayor of the village could have seen him then and noticed how the terrific unearthliness which was rightfully his had faded, their eyes would have popped right out of their heads.

"Hey, how come you don't smile? Do you think it'd kill you to laugh?"

At this coquettish query, D once again was at a loss for a reply. This young lady was a severe challenge.

"But you do cry, don't you? There must be a lot of hard times, aren't there. I just know there are."

With some difficulty he managed to say simply, "Yeah."

Lina suddenly became very serious. "You've got some sort of connection to the Nobility, don't you? You don't have to say anything; I just know. The mayor wouldn't tell me anything, but not so much as a bird goes near you. And look! Even though you walk normally, the tracks you leave in the snow aren't a third as deep as mine. Then there's the ruins . . . "

Lina faltered.

"What about the ruins?"

Watched by icily gleaming eyes, Lina realized that her cheeks had suddenly become hot. As if she was just now noticing that the youth before her was a man of such beauty it made her hair stand on end.

"I hid behind you, remember?" Even her tone of voice had a blush to it. "The first time I saw you I was really scared, but as soon as I heard what you said I shook it right off. 'While it's impossible to halt the progress of time, you would do well to show some respect for what's been lost'—when you said that, you seemed so sad."

This young lady must have heard the echoes of another world, echoes that no one else could hear.

"You've got good ears and an excellent memory," D said in his usual tone, looking to the highway. "The sun will be down in a little while, so we'd best be on our way. It's about time for the fiend to make another move on the woman from this morning."

"Hey," Lina rasped in a tone entirely inappropriate to the situation, poking meaningfully at D with her elbow. "Could you get your work done in the next five days and leave the village with me? I've got an awful bright future ahead of me."

"Maybe. Better get in now."

The pair clambered into the wagon and D took the reins in hand. Stealing glances at his profile, Lina sported a mischievous grin. "You really don't want to lose that scowl, do you, you big worrywart? I'm going to make a prediction for you."

"A prediction?"

Perhaps knowing how D's eyes glinted and perhaps not, Lina ceremoniously shut her lids and twitched her nose as if tasting the air. "That's right. See, mine are almost always right on the money. Let's see . . . okay, I got it."

Then, gazing upon the beautiful profile beside her as if entranced, she said, "You'll definitely be wearing a smile when you leave this place."

†

Eight faces surrounded a single cot.

There was the sheriff and mayor, Mr. Meyer and Lina, three strapping members of the Vigilance Committee, and standing all alone with his back to the wall was D.

"Haven't you caught that Cuore yet?" the mayor asked the sheriff in very ill humor, and the sheriff looked in turn to the powerfully built individual who seemed to lead the local vigilantes. His name was Fern.

"Well, he's not holed up in his usual rat's nest," Fern stated. "But we got the Vigilance Committee and Youth Brigade out in full force, and I expect we'll have him in no time."

"If we have him here and a vampire shows up, it should clear up any doubts about the three of them. Get it done," the mayor added, hurling an arrogant look at Lina and Mr. Meyer. Fern nodded deeply in agreement and looked over at D. Glaring hatred eddied like a whirlpool. He must've heard about the two minor altercations with Haig and his Youth Brigade.

"Visiting hours are about to begin. You'll all have to step into the next room."

While the others rose at D's bidding, all three vigilantes turned their sullen faces away. His gelid gaze focused on them, and, though their eyes never met his, the way they suddenly left their seats suggested their backs had turned to ice.

"You can count on us to keep an eye on these other two. But are you sure you'll be okay on your own?" The sheriff's words sprang from the fear that if by some chance D was defeated, the curse of the undead wouldn't just claim the woman, but that more victims would follow as well.

It really didn't matter what happened to the woman. The treatment of vampire victims varied from village to village, but here they were promptly driven out of town and left to their fate. Her husband had gone off to a neighboring village, but he was bound by the same laws they all were, so the sheriff didn't have to worry about any censure.

However, this new Vampire Hunter planned to use the woman as bait to draw the demon. What's more, the Hunter didn't want the trio still under suspicion in the same room, but rather asked that they all wait together close by.

If not for the support of the mayor, the sheriff surely would have railed against this. There had been more than a few cases in the past when similar plans had failed, and those lying in wait hadn't been the only ones to fall to the baleful fangs—whole villages had gone vampire. But, above all else, there was the salary the sheriff drew from the Capital to consider, a sum nearly five times what the average villager earned. It wasn't the sort of job he'd just hand to someone else.

"Trust me, Sheriff," the mayor said, clapping him on the shoulder. "After all, I called in just the man for the job."

In his mind, he muttered, *You called in the last Hunter, too.* But, without wasting another word, the sheriff led the whole group into an adjacent room.

As soon as the click of the lock died, D curled his right hand into a loose fist, put it to his mouth, and aimed the scant opening at the lamp on the side table. With a puff of his breath, the flame burning within the glass of the hurricane lamp was extinguished. The room fell to the mastery of the dark.

Lowering clouds obscured the moon this eerie night, as wintry gales incomprehensible so near to spring rattled the window frames.

The woman lying in the cot was the same one who had been attacked earlier. Though she'd been unconscious since they'd found her, with the deepening of night her skin had lost its rosy hue; her face was now strangely imbued with the luster of paraffin. In that darkness unmarred by any spark of light, D could discern even the paling blood vessels lacing the woman's cheeks.

Suddenly he spun toward the window.

There was naught but the rattle of the wind's incessant blows to be heard, but D's ears must have caught some other sound.

At the same time, his gaze returned to the bed.

From the nape of the woman's neck—and the wound known as the Kiss of the Nobility—two vermilion rivulets began a trickling flow.

The tension was like a line snapped taut.

Something jet black pressed against the window pane. A face with both nose and mouth mashed flat was peering into the room, vested with a grin that was not of this world.

With a dull flutter, something thick flew through the air. A blanket.

D's gaze was drawn to the door that was the boundary between this room and the next. That was where the nightshirt-clad woman was headed. Eyes as red as blood shone on D. The call had come from her master.

A vampire could beckon to its prey without actually going to see them, moving their victim by sheer will alone. It was a commonly used ploy. However, normally the victim would leave by a window. The vampire certainly wouldn't send the victim all the way to the front door, where they'd most likely run into other people. What's more, there had been a lurid figure outside the window. Was that a diversion?

The woman took a step back and made ready to ram her way through the door. D sprinted. With a piercing shriek, the window panes flew outward in shards and a sudden gust of wind rushed in.

Screams arose in the next room.

D could discern each and every individual noise. Even before the woman could smash herself against the door, something in the next room made the door buckle out from the inside. Screws shot from the hinges. A concussive blast erupted, and splintery chunks of the door ripped into the wooden floor, blowing shards of the broken windows outward. All without a sound.

The woman was now in a corner of the room. A guttural cry had been heard, but it had died in the shadows of a black coat. Just as the door splintered, D had taken the woman under his

arm and leapt to safety. And it had taken less than a second for the buckling door to fly to pieces. His speed was ungodly.

It seemed that *it* had appeared for a third encounter with D.

The room swam with intense psychic power as the thing sought out its opponent with a raging, unvoiced howl. Strangely enough, D could even make out the thing's body.

The head faced D and the woman.

Coagulated malevolence. Raising itself on all four limbs, it charged forward menacingly.

Looking askance at the woman rendered senseless by the ramming, D drew his longsword. What followed was an unanticipated ending.

With a scream that thundered outside the window, the malevolence was utterly dispelled. The growls of the night wind reverberated, but D just stood there confused in the normal winter air.

This just wasn't right. It was impossible for such a fierce aura to disperse, to just disappear. Fragments of it—the remaining energy alone—should've hung in the air like gaseous clots. But there wasn't the faintest trace of anything like that left in the room. The best course of action, at this point, would be to believe the thing hadn't existed in the first place.

Instead of mulling this over, D sprung to work. Running his eyes over the devastated door and fallen woman, he hurled himself out the window.

The source of the cries was lying on the ground just below the window ledge. The Hunter rolled him over, revealing Cuore's pale countenance. His chest rose and fell faintly under his bedraggled garments. Though there was no bleeding or wounds, his colossal frame looked withered from head to toe. His cheeks sank haggardly, starkly tracing the bones beneath. It looked as if the very essence of life had been torn out of him.

D was just about to scoop the man up when the Hunter's body flew instead through the air and back into the room.

An ash-gray figure clung to the woman. An outlandish individual who seemed entirely bound in dark fabric. A scarf of rough cloth shrouded the figure's face, and, from the core of that countenance, eyes the color of blood stared back at D. The woman didn't move in the slightest. An expression of rapture at the taste of otherworldly pleasure suffused her waxen visage, and her ample and now naked breasts were mashed against the chest of the shadowy figure. Yes, even her supple thighs had been bared and were now twined around the figure's legs. The ravager and the ravaged painted an image of secret lasciviousness.

The instant D spied the pair of fangs jutting from the corners of the creature's detestable lips—the only part of the figure clearly visible as he nosily lapped at the blood bubbling from the wounds on the woman's throat—the Hunter's right hand unleashed a volley of white light.

As the sound of five wooden needles sinking into the planks of the wall was heard, those bloody lips formed a grin. Not a single change had occurred in the figure's twisting embrace of the woman. Without moving a muscle, the creature had avoided the needles D had hurled.

D bounded from the floor.

The wan body of the woman flew up, and averting it introduced a delay of a mere hundredth of a second in his attack. A flash of silver slashed the sleeve of the ashen cloak, and D and the figure swapped positions.

An air of desolation filled the room.

At long last he'd met a worthy opponent. In any battle, the most important factors were, primarily, speed and, secondarily, strength. In terms of speed, at least, the shadowy figure was D's equal.

However . . .

From the throat of that figure, a moan which could never be mistaken for human came as if borne on the wintry wind itself.

A splash of black seemed to make a smooth streak from the upper edge of the figure's scarf down to the chin. The rent fabric fell away to either side, draping over the shadowy figure's shoulders. It was the work of D's blade, which in truth should have split his opponent's body in half. Not losing a second, the figure shielded his face with his hand and leapt out the window.

D ran as well.

The distance between the two remained unchanged.

A shooting star in silver!

With one of the most exquisite sounds in the world, D's blade was parried by the longsword the figure wielded. Like the scattering sparks, the two faces grew fainter and farther apart.

At the same time they landed, a series of noises echoed in the space between them. Iron caltrops the figure had launched in midair as he gripped his sword in his teeth had intercepted the needles thrown by D.

Each caltrops was a mass of iron spikes radiating out in all directions. Though traditionally spread across the ground by ordinary huntsmen or Hunters specializing in land-bound beasts, with practice they might be used as missiles. An expert could hurl three in a single second and pack them in a two-inch-wide bull's-eye from a distance of some thirty feet. When coupled with the horrendous strength unique to the Nobility, caltrops could achieve the stopping power of a magnum gun—a weapon renowned for its ability to pierce the armor of greater dragons.

A streak of crimson coursed down D's left cheek.

But the shadowy figure who'd dealt the wound slammed on the brakes as well. He backed off. Perhaps the moon finally peeping through the bank of clouds had revealed to the figure the fact the left hand he held over his face had lost its thumb clear down to the base.

The opponents held their longswords at eye level, in the tradition of Asian fencers. Preparing for battle, neither moved.

Borne on a wind that howled of winter's imminent demise, no one could say how long this battle to the death between a superhuman and a demonic fiend would go on.

A deafening report called a sudden close to the duel.

D's upper body jolted ever so slightly. The tension was broken. About to make a thrust, the figure halted. An instant later, the figure leapt through the air, cleared a stone wall, and melted into the darkness with a speed that shamed the wind itself.

Not that the figure feared the gunfire which had just put two rounds into D's body. Rather, the figure had seen D take the massive slugs through the side of his chest without letting the point of his sword quaver in the least bit.

The especially strong wind scattered all trace of the enemy, so D limned a fluid arc of silver that returned his longsword to its sheath. On the right flank of his coat the material was rent wide, marking the spot where a magnum gun had scored a pair of direct hits, but there was no trace of emotion whatsoever in his exquisite face.

A tangle of angry shouts came from the direction of the window. The voices of Lina and the mayor churned against vehement protests from the sheriff that it had been an accident that his shots had gone wide.

D approached Cuore's weakened body and lifted the boy effortlessly. Though the most distinguished Hunters were renowned for never using their sword arm unless it was absolutely necessary, D coolly disregarded that convention.

"No use giving chase," he said to keep the sheriff from clambering out through the window. "What about the woman?"

"She's still alive," Lina replied from her place at the bedside of the sleeping woman.

D climbed back into the room without a sound.

"Get this boy to bed."

"Weren't you hit?" the sheriff asked as he alternated his stares between the weapon in his hands and D. Without responding, the Hunter passed Cuore into Lina's arms.

"D, you're bleeding!"

"It'll heal soon enough. What happened?"

"I don't know." Shaking her head, Lina looked at the sheriff.

He seemed unharmed. There was a large lump rising on the mayor's forehead. "Something happened, that's for sure—all of a sudden we're floating in midair, then the next thing I know we're dropping to the floor headfirst. Believe you me, I'd like to know what the hell that was all about!"

"What about Mr. Meyer?"

"Over here . . . " The speaker was slumped by the threshold of the shattered door, breathing heavily. There were a number of scratches on his cheeks. Judging by the way he held the back of his head, that was the severest of his injuries. "At least this should get rid of any lingering doubts about me and Lina," he muttered, then his eyes went wide as he saw Cuore.

The trio of vigilantes tottered toward them, and, in the wild confusion of the room, D could be heard murmuring as if nothing at all had occurred. "So we've finally flushed it out, have we?"

Those Who Desire Darkness

CHAPTER 3

T he pale rays of the sun had melted most of the light snow on the slope. Young sprouts raised their heads from the ground, diligently drawing to themselves the energy they would need to send out shoots in the season to come.

Like a pastoral painting, green already covered the gently rolling terrain, and off in the distance a young Adonis stood in stark relief against the blue sky, walking as the wind fluttered the hem of his coat.

One only had to draw a step closer, however, to be struck by the ineffable eldritch aura swelling from that tall, black-clad form to realize he was an otherworldly entity thoroughly in keeping with that perfectly preserved beauty.

Vampire Hunter D—in spring, in summer, his emotionless eyes reflected a demon-haunted darkness.

Halfway up the slope D stopped.

A wagon was approaching from town. It was Lina, with her black manelike hair streaming out behind her. Realizing that D had caught sight of her, a smile suffused her face and she waved.

While he didn't wave back, it was still unlike the youth to wait while Lina halted the wagon, gathered up her long, blue skirt, and climbed up the hill to him. It seemed not just humans, but all living creatures had difficulty traversing the hill.

"What brings you out here?" he asked with a dour look.

"Oh, aren't you Mister Personality. It just so happens I was going to ask you the very same thing. But the least I can do is keep you company. After all, you were kind enough to wait for me and all."

Though her breath was ragged, an untroubled grin rose on Lina's lips.

It wasn't just that the young man was so gorgeous he gave her gooseflesh, but also that she found standing by his side fun—or if "fun" wasn't exactly the right term, standing by him was certainly intriguing. Lina had no way of knowing what a mighty Hunter he was, or how the roughest characters on the Frontier cringed at the mere mention of his name. She was seventeen—girls at that stage tended to view boys their own age as punk kids, which is probably how Lina saw D. But, appearances to the contrary, who could really say just how old the Hunter was, springing as he did from the ageless and undying blood of the Nobility?

"I wasn't exactly waiting for you," D said frostily. "I was going to tell you to turn around. You should go home."

"Not a chance," Lina pouted. "I'm a lot safer with you than I'd be back in town."

That was certainly true.

"Have it your way."

D turned without another word. Though his leisurely yet deliberate pace remained unchanged, no matter how Lina scrambled she could not close the gap between them. On reaching the summit of the hill she collapsed in the shade of the ramparts. Cruel as it may seem, D immediately slipped into the ruins without so much as a backward glance, and was gone.

"I don't believe this! Of all the cold-blooded—" Lina was shouting and stomping her feet when something white fell from her breast. Hurriedly snatching it up, she brushed it off gently and slipped it into the front of her blouse. And then, with a cry of, "Wait for me, you cold-hearted ninny," she slipped through a breach into the ruins.

Humans remained afraid to enter the castles of the Nobility. Their owners having disappeared for reasons unknown, the homes and the untended grounds were usually overrun by weeds and rats. In some cases automated maintenance devices had broken down, in others the Nobility had disconnected them before they vanished. Such actions seemed to state that these were still places no human hand should ever touch. Seeing these ruins with that in mind was enough to send chills climbing the viewer's spine.

Ramparts notwithstanding, the main gate and chapel, which had once been the principal edifices here, were all blown from their foundations. Even the pitiful figure of the belfry, top half now lost, glared at the blue empyrean vault. Stony heaps of rubble and the remains of buildings formed from mysterious materials were scattered throughout the snow-covered central courtyard. The courtyard also barely retained its original shape, though it did an excellent job now of slowing Lina's pace.

Of course, Lina didn't know when the castle had been reduced to this state, or by whose hand. All that was shrouded by the dark veil of history, and, aside from the tentacles of unknown terror it sent out, this place had no relation to the humans' existence.

Even within, the history of these ruins remained elusive. Every part of it was a mystery.

A great many castles had been built by the Nobility in the Frontier region, all of them for the express purpose of providing a base from which they could rule over the mortals. The Nobility usually chose a spot on high ground to build their castles, so they might look down and see the humans toiling at their feet. Consequently, descriptions of those castles, and tales of their tenants, became part of the oral tradition of the humans who worked below. The stories were inevitably passed down through the ages, but nothing like that had happened in the village of Tepes.

How the Nobility had lived, and what work they had undertaken in this valley locked in by snow and darkness, were questions the villagers did not want to consider.

D was in the darkness of the same hall where Lina first met him. At the sight of him silently studying something on the wall, Lina got the distinct impression the pale blue stream of time had ceased to flow.

"One of those pictures strike your fancy?" she called out as she approached. D, who hadn't answered no matter how she'd shouted, turned toward her. At last she could relax a bit.

"Oh, yes, I have to remember you can climb up here normally. You come here often, do you?"

"Uh-huh," she said with an affirming nod. "When it comes to the castle here, I'd have to say I'm the best-informed person in town. You know, I'm not sure what you came here for, but why don't we look at some of these together?"

For the briefest instant, D scanned the face of the innocuously grinning girl, then nodded.

The two of them played their gaze across one piece after another in the prodigious collection of paintings set in the walls.

As she looked at these paintings, all made sufficiently mysterious by the mere fact they'd been left behind, Lina felt the same profound emotion as the first time she'd seen them. Her breast flooded with heat as she looked at them anew.

Lovers, wrapped in the gossamer wings of some flying machine, gliding through the pale shadows of a moonlit grove.

A wan Noblewoman laughing as she chases a glowing, moonlike orb through the thick fog of a lakeshore.

A black-clad Noble goading the unearthly beast that draws his hover-carriage, while flashes of lightning from the eddying pitch-dark sky bathe them both.

Moonlight glinting off the horn of a unicorn, prismatic dancing girls scattering flower petals, the land is transformed to a garden of luminescent grasses in those paintings, which showed shadow and light, symphonies of light and shadow . . .

"Nobles painted all of these?"

Lina did not address this question to anyone in particular, but it felt like a song ringing from her mouth.

"The setting is always darkness and blackness, night and moonlight and mist—so why do they look so gorgeous? How could they paint that world so softly, so surreal, when we can't set foot outside the village without getting so scared we collapse in a heap? Is the Nobility's night somehow different from ours?"

D watched the girl silently. Her eyes were big and bright and sparkling with an abounding curiosity that stripped away the veil of innocuousness—this girl of seventeen who would learn about the future in the Capital.

"From the time we're little kids we all grow up hearing about how fierce the Nobility are, how frightening," Lina continued, forgetting that D stood by her side. "Civilization doesn't produce anything that isn't fit to serve it. That's why the evil Nobility have died off, they say. And yet, when I look at these paintings, my heart races. The first time I saw them I even thought, 'If this is what they can paint, then make me a Noble any day.' After that, I studied up on them on the sly. Mr. Meyer, who was missing with me way back when, well, he's interested in the Nobility, too, and since he's collected all sorts of literature he's loaned me a couple of books—though lately he's been telling me to just buckle down on the math and he won't let me have any more. For the most part, they're all things humans have recorded about Nobility and pretty much all of them were from the same point of view the grownups in town have, but there was this one volume, a book about the history of the Nobility. Oh, what was it called now . . . "

"*Dawn of the Nobility*, by J. Sangster. It was banned as soon as it saw print, and the author was exiled to the Frontier."

"I'm impressed. That's exactly the one I meant!"

Lina snapped her fingers sharply, not so much surprised that a drifting Hunter would know such an arcane tidbit as she was delighted to find a thread for conversation.

"As I recall, it analyzed art the Nobility had left behind—paintings and holographic images and three-dimensional music of some sort—and brought some of their civilization's finer points to light. I read it and reread it till it was falling apart. I wanted to learn about the other world, the night civilization, and the Nobility of course. About the knowledge they had and their beauty. And I . . . "

At this point the girl's words died as if she were returning to her senses, and she turned again to face D.

"It's already been decided I'm to study mathematics in the Capital. But what I'd really like to get into is the history of the Nobility."

†

For a while, the pair stood studying each other's faces as they felt the crush of the darkness.

"Just kidding," Lina laughed suddenly, like the gust that snuffs a candle. "Oh, it's true I want to study their history, but as a candidate I have to get up in front of a panel from the Capital and state for the record just what I intend to major in. Math, physics, music, art—hell, I could even choose gymnastics and they'd be fine with it. But if I ever said anything about the history of the Nobility . . . "

Lina didn't have to say that it would mean the end of her hopes for the future. History had been penned in the blood of those crushed by an unbearable weight of fear, and the oppressed would never forgive that.

"Well," D began, "I hear policies in the Capital are gradually changing. It seems the director of the Ministry of Education is a man with some appreciation of the Nobility's heritage."

"Not a chance," Lina laughed mischievously, flitting behind D like a butterfly. "I'm not about to lose my only ticket out of this town. The final decision rests on the feelings of the panel, you know. I'm going to tell them 'mathematics,' and that's that."

D said nothing in reply, but turned to face a painting several yards distant.

It was a picture Lina herself had always wondered about. Of all the paintings left behind, only this one had had its entire ten-foot-high, six-and-a-half-foot-wide surface painted over pitch-black. It seemed to radiate the most sinister intent.

"I recall seeing this sort of thing a couple of times in my travels. Out of tens of thousands of paintings, hundreds of thousands of pieces of art, I've found an oddity like this mixed in from time to time. Some have been completely destroyed, some have been burned. Of them all, only one had ever been restored again."

Though Lina was unaware that having this youth relate his personal experiences was not only unparalleled but bordered on the miraculous, her eyes sparkled nonetheless.

"Don't keep me in suspense. What's the painting of?"

"Nobles rising from their coffins, their hands reaching for the sun."

The most fruitless of dreams.

Who could've painted it, Lina wondered.

Who painted it, who ruined it, who restored it? Could this painting here be another? Did the Nobility really want to be like us?

There were no answers.

Unbeknownst to her, the hem of her skirt had begun to flutter. There was a breeze coming in from somewhere.

"Why did you tell me that, D?" Lina inquired softly. "You say I'm strange, but if so I guess that makes you plain *loony*. No matter what I ask you, I know you won't give me an answer, but there's one thing I'd like to know just the same. When I first met you, mister big bad Vampire Hunter, you were here looking at the paintings, weren't you? Are you sure you *really* hate the Nobility?"

D looked back into the darkness.

"I've wasted more time than I intended. Time for me to get back to work, so wait outside."

"Not on your life. Not after coming this far. I'm going with you—it's as simple as that."

"You're on your own if anything happens. I won't bail you out."

"No, you'll save my bacon sure enough. I'm your valued assistant, after all."

"Hey, don't fool yourself," D shot back with agitation. Lina was something of an expert at causing miracles.

"For the time being, kindly tell me what brings you to these ruins, Boss," she said with a grave face. D heaved a sigh. Once again, it looked like a mere slip of a girl had him right where she wanted him.

"To find out just what happened here ten years ago."

"Knew it," Lina said with a heavy-hearted nod. "No matter how you look at it, there's something strange about us. There's no way Nobles are walking around in broad daylight. And then there's the shape Cuore's in."

While the boy had regained consciousness that morning, his physical strength was depleted to a phenomenal degree, and he hadn't responded to questioning by the mayor and sheriff.

It was extremely difficult to believe he'd just happened to be in the wrong place at the wrong time during that incident the night before. Even if he'd heard about the attack on the woman, which was unlikely—everyone involved in the case had been urged to keep silent—he'd still been the object of a manhunt by the entire Youth Brigade. Well, it went without saying they'd thoroughly searched the area surrounding the house. And, the creature that for lack of a better name could be called a "spirit-beast," had appeared on one other occasion when Cuore was also present.

"Even now everyone still suspects us. It's common knowledge me and Cuore can climb the hill *normally*, and I bet Mr. Meyer wouldn't have any trouble, either. And you know, all three of us have been attacked by goons from the local Youth Brigade, just because they think we might be the Nobles who walk by daylight."

"You're lucky you haven't been hurt."

"That's on account of the mayor. He's the big wheel in this town, no doubt about it. He's good at getting resources from the Capital, and he gives a lot of thought to keeping us protected from monsters. If it weren't for him, the village would've been wiped out a long, long time ago—though I think that would've been for the best."

Perhaps realizing the harshness of her words, Lina cast her eyes down. The mayor was her adopted father, after all.

"Even he couldn't prove we're not connected to these attacks. You see, there hasn't been anyone around us during past incidents."

That fact, along with the list the mayor had handed him a night earlier, had been duly filed in D's memory.

Mr. Meyer was single and living on his own, Cuore of course lived alone in an otherwise deserted house in town, and Lina was in the habit of holing up in her room just after sundown.

All strong-arm tactics by the mayor aside, the real reason the trio had been unharmed thus far was that nearly a decade had passed since their disappearance.

"You've climbed the hill before. Has anything else out of the ordinary happened?" D asked as he held his right hand up by his face.

As she wondered at this curious gesture, this apparent testing of the wind flow, Lina shook her head. It was an honest response.

D gave a nod and muttered, "Over here, I'd say." It was unclear whether the nod was related to Lina's response or not.

They angled swiftly through the darkness. An elaborately carved door appeared before the pair soon enough. While she knew of its existence, Lina had never been beyond it. She wasn't quite to the age where curiosity could get the better of her fear.

Though the girl was prepared to be told once more to go home, D promptly pushed his way through the doorway and melted into an even greater darkness. Following frantically, Lina was amazed when she brushed past the door. It was a four-inch-thick slab of a renowned supersteel alloy. Twenty strapping men would probably have a hard time budging it. For the first time, Lina sensed what an uncanny individual the youth who'd gone before her into the darkness was.

She took a step forward, even as the terror of being swallowed by the blackness of an unimaginable world sank ice into the nape of her neck.

†

The woods brimmed with life. Light subdued the aura given off by the leaf-bare trees, spreading from Bess Fern's lungs to her whole body and adding a cheery spring to her step.

Leaving the path, she found that the air had abruptly assumed a certain dampness. Though it was still winter, this corner of the woods was strangely warm. On the trunks of trees clung mosses and fungi in every shade from blue, green, and purple down to tones that were patently nauseating.

Bess made her way in, taking care not to slip, and at last she dropped to her knees at the roots of a colossal trunk.

Word from the sheriff's office that no one should be out wandering around alone for the next day or two hadn't reached her house until after she'd left.

A smile spread across her plump, boyish face.

Just as anticipated, the edible moss that had supposedly been plucked clean three days earlier tightly packed the space between the snaking roots. She hadn't slept for fear someone might've harvested it already, but she'd been right to come check.

In the villages and hamlets of the Frontier, this moss was a valuable food substitute, used in practically any kind of cooking, from steaks to soups and jams. When sun dried, the moss was good for six months to a year. What's more, the essence of the moss could be extracted using a centrifugal separator. Wounds plastered with this salve closed up almost instantly, and its usefulness in counteracting the venom of poisonous moth men made it an indispensable item for travelers and others afield.

Bess planned on swapping the moss she harvested with the trader, due to come to the village in the first of spring, for some fashionable apparel from the Capital. The teen's eyes swam with images of herself in her new finery.

Cautiously slipping a shovel in where moss met soil, she put the green spoils in her basket in such a way as not to crumble the friable surface. After ten minutes, the basket was filled to the brim.

There was still a fair patch left. And she was pretty sure those things her father kept must have a sweet tooth for moss, too.

Maybe she'd take just a little bit more—but the hands she extended with that intent stopped halfway to the mark. A cloud had moved across the sun. No, it was no cloud—the inky blackness blanketing Bess was clearly the shadow of something humanoid.

The scream she unleashed was her last act of defiance before losing her life of seventeen years.

Cyrus Fern immediately recognized the cry rising to echo in the treetops as his daughter's. On hearing the sheriff's broadcast, and realizing his daughter had gone out alone, he'd set out after her with a strong hunch she'd be in the mossy woods she talked about so much. His whole body quivered with anger and despair.

Calling his daughter's name as he dashed onward, he laid his hands to the lids of the fair-sized baskets he had hitched on either hip and unlatched them. The *things* inside grew ever more restless, and, from the opening of the basket on the right, a base, brutal growl escaped.

Suddenly, violet sparks shot from the mouth of the basket on the left, and Fern wasted no time in pulling his hand away. You'd think he'd be used to it, but these *things* were always tough to handle. The fingertips of the nonconductive glove he had on his left hand were scorched, and bluish smoke wafted skyward.

The instant he sprinted into the place he sought, Fern's eyes went wide with outrage.

Cradled in the arms of a figure in ash-colored cloth, Bess vapidly stared into the heavens, as twin streams of lifeblood coursed down her throat. Her skin faded to paraffin. Despair became a torrent of rage that flooded every fiber of Cyrus Fern's being. He forgot any chance of saving his daughter and he flung open the basket lids.

The ashen figure turned in his direction.

With the thud of Bess' body falling to the mossy carpet, monstrous things in Fern's baskets came to rest on the ground.

There was a pair of them, and yet they were hardly a matched pair.

Checked by their master's monumental anger, a titanic spider, whose octet of firmly planted legs were easily ten feet in length, and a cloud of scintillant purple both glowered at the ashen figure.

Anyone who knew Fern's line of work would sorely regret ever laying a hand on his daughter. Those who did a lot of traveling needed something to defend themselves against merciless bandits and Nobility-spawned demons, and more often than not it made sense to purchase a supernatural creature of like power—a guard beast. And it so happened Fern, the head of the Vigilance Committee, trained and sold them.

Though the guard beasts descended from the original demons and magical monstrosities propagated by the Nobility, as generations passed, numerous mutations and new species had been born. About two thousand years earlier, some extreme rarities, able to be domesticated by the humans, appeared. As far as the beasts' training went, they were taught from birth to be strictly inactive until some sort of sonic wave or magic formula was used to trigger them—something no one else would understand.

And what monsters Fern had.

If it seemed incomprehensible that the massive arachnid had been shut up in a basket the size of a bird cage, the adjacent purple cloud presented an even stranger sight. The smoky mass boiling up from the heart of the cloud formed a perimeter more than a foot and a half wide, and, every time a light of some sort pulsed in the central portion, violet-hued sparks flew from all over the cloud.

It was one of the most bizarre forms of life on earth—an electricity beast.

Fern let fly an arcane and indecipherable cry—a harsh command to attack.

With speed belying its size, the spider advanced. The coruscating cloud rose in the air.

The ashen figure crouched just a bit.

Silver flashed, and then violet sparks fanned out like touch-me-nots, blending darkness and light in a corner of the woods.

An arachnid leg, severed at the second joint, sailed through the air.

As the figure sheared off the leg of the approaching spider with a single flourish of his longsword, he had also parried an electrical assault by the cloud with one of his sleeves.

Amazement suffused the face of ever-watchful Fern. The cloud's sparks carried more than half a million volts.

The longsword whirled, fending off the electricity beast's next two attacks and driving for the beast's body. The figure's sleeve was ablaze.

The sword tip came to an abrupt halt.

Though the shadowy figure put all his strength behind it, the blade didn't quiver in the least, as if it was imbedded in solid stone.

Abandoning his weapon, the figure bounded from the ground in a great leap. Above its head, something like flimsy white threads drifted down to earth, fixing the figure in midair.

Just above the figure's wildly craning head was the supposedly earthbound spider. But in light of how the thread was expelled from between the massive mandibles rather than from the abdomen, it seemed likely that the monster was actually a mutant that merely resembled a spider. By a single thread—thinner than a true spider's and of fiercely adhesive mucus—the pseudo-arachnid hung itself from a huge branch on an equally cyclopean trunk. The strength of that silken line was evident; the spider easily dangled the massive form of the figure beneath it, steadily drawing its prey up toward its fearsome giant mandibles.

Perhaps the shadowy figure had already given up, for his motionless body was struck by a number of violet lightning bolts and flames. Black smoke rose from the outline of the form.

"Take that, you freaky son of a bitch. Piece of shit born-again bloodsucker. Either them blasts will burn you to a crisp or my spider'll crush the life out of you with his big old pincers." A hatred-filled laugh echoed up from Fern. "But before they do, I'll have me a look at your face, you little bastard. Who the hell are you? Cuore? Lina? That schoolmarm Meyer? Or are you—"

Another thread fastened itself to the mask hiding the features of the shadowy figure and deftly stripped it off.

"But you're—?!"

What was it that made his cry of shock die half-uttered? Was it the sight of the burning vermilion shafts of light blazing from the middle of that bared face? Perhaps it was caused by the gentle laying of hands as cold as ice to both his shoulders.

"Oh, Papa . . . "

The lilting words of his daughter crept across the nape of his neck just ahead of her fangs.

†

From the cover of a titanic tree a short distance away, someone saw the denouement. Having slipped out of bed, Cuore stood with his normally leaden eyes gleaming in his wasted, haggard face, straining with all his might to suppress a scream.

†

When her eyes became accustomed to the dark, Lina found that she and D were descending a wide passageway. The walls and ceiling were stonework, though the corridor was strangely bereft of the usual sense of crushing claustrophobia felt in tight tunnels. To the contrary, Lina got the feeling there were great, spacious chambers just beyond the walls they passed.

At various points on the walls and ceiling, the gleams of what seemed to be intruder sensors and radiation-containing devices could be seen.

"You know, it's pretty hard to believe there are still underground chambers so big. We must be, like, a hundred yards underground by now," Lina said in disgust to D, who walked a few paces ahead. They had been walking for about a half an hour, and she was no longer amused by the adventure.

"We haven't even gone down ten."

"You've got to be joking!"

"You can relax. We'll reach the end of the line in a minute."

Just as he said, less than sixty seconds later the pair came to a shutter made out of what seemed to be steel.

D pointed the pendant from his chest at the computerized identification device.

The shutter vanished instantly and the pair went in.

Silence like the blue embrace of dusk awaited them.

Lina's jaw dropped.

It looked like an enormous laboratory, but there could never be another place of research to match this.

Like the corridor, the walls were stonework, boulder-fashioned ramparts rising to a height of thirty feet. The desks, laid in rows across the floor, were made of sturdy hardwood and adorned with flasks, beakers, and vials of unsettling, colored liquids—it looked for all the world like the lab of a medieval alchemist. Here and there, ghastly things appropriate to such a place jutted up, mixing with the bluish light to create a mood that beggared description. But positioned perfectly among that old-fashioned apparatus was what could only be a positron brain, an electro-analyzer, a matter-converter—the very embodiment of superscientific technology. Here was a perfect example of the ambivalence that epitomized the world of the Nobility.

"I can't believe this place is still intact," Lina said, scanning the surroundings. "Looks like it was some sort of research center, doesn't it? Can you tell what they were working on, D?"

Receiving no answer, she looked back over to D, who stood before a bench, intently scrutinizing the flasks and bizarre globes that were heaped atop it. He stepped up to a nearby control panel and his hands began to glide across the myriad keys.

"Don't tell me you do computers, too . . . "

Before Lina had finished saying the words, the air began to hum, and all about the room machines began springing to life.

The strangest imaginable designs, unintelligible symbols, and numerical expressions—none in the least bit familiar to Lina—shot in a riotous race across the computer's screen. D stared at the screen for no more than a second or two before he quickly toggled off the switch and started across the spacious chamber without so much as glancing at the girl.

"Hey, wait for me. You're being such a jerk. Can't very well leave your assistant behind, can you?!"

But, just as she was about to scamper after him, her foot slipped and, squealing and clutching a rack of half-filled beakers, she tumbled to the floor with an impressive noise and no small amount of breakage.

"That hurt . . . "

Luckily, she hadn't bashed her head open, but, as she kneaded her sharply throbbing backside, she glared at the unavoidably returning D with the deepest loathing.

Her eyes suddenly narrowed.

There. Where the tendril-like splashes of liquid intermingled, wasn't a wall of mysterious color forming? Wasn't it rising from the floor in what was neither fog nor smoke? Yes, and it seemed that something was wriggling within the vapor. Struggling. As if bitter and cursing.

As something round and fat suddenly slashed out of the smoke and caught hold of her ankle, Lina screamed.

Crisscrossed with dark red tendons and blood vessels, drenched in some unknown slime, it was the gigantic arm of a baby. But it had only three fingers.

Lina tore herself loose with wild abandon, and the fingers vainly clutched at the air before curling powerlessly on the floor.

As she watched in a daze as the arm liquefied to a goo, D caught hold of her and effortlessly hoisted her to her feet.

"That's a homunculus," he said. "An artificial life-form spawned by lightning and congealed ether."

"Yeah? Well, what's one doing here? What the hell was this place?"

"Better come with me. If that's all it takes to scare you, you really should go home, but I suppose it's too late for that."

"You seriously think there's any chance of getting me to go home?"

Unruffled, D scanned the laboratory. Without warning he said, "I hear there was another kid lost with you who didn't come back. Do you recall if anything happened to you here?"

"No. And I've tried to remember hundreds of times before. I've tried, Mr. Meyer's tried, even Cuore has."

"Even Cuore?"

Lina looked up at D. He stood a head taller than she did. Her expression was so disturbed, it made one wonder where it could've lurked so long in this young woman.

"Right after we got back, you see, they took us away from our parents and put us in an asylum. For a full week the sheriff and Vigilance Committee examined us. When they realized the drugs and hypnotism weren't working, they stripped us naked and stuck us with needles. See, that's a method of finding Nobles unique to our very own village. They put silver needles in your nipples and backside and depending on how the blood comes out they divine whether you're one of the Nobility or not."

D said nothing.

"In the case of a girl, ordinarily the wife of someone on the Vigilance Committee will do it, but no one but men examined me. They were taking turns, trading off—when they stuck me they'd change people. Old Man Gaston from the mill was there, and the boys from the slaughterhouse, and the mayor. I suppose he must've taken me in to make amends for that."

Suddenly Lina smiled brightly and took aim at D's face with her forefinger.

"Goodness, don't make such a puss. I'm the kind to forgive and forget, after all. When I look at your face, I don't think back on old grudges. So why don't you try smiling for a change?"

"I was born like this."

"Wow! That's the first time you've said anything about yourself." She giggled. "Do you feel sympathy for me? That's not like you at all."

"Don't trouble yourself about it."

When D said this, the bluish light filling the room was extinguished abruptly.

Without even time to think that somebody had done that on purpose, Lina was grabbed from behind with great force and dragged toward the wall.

"D!"

Something like a strangely sticky, cold palm stopped her shout-widened mouth, but the instant she saw a silvery flash race through her field of vision, a thunk like the sound of bone being severed resounded and she was set free.

A wail arose that made her want to slap her hands over her ears, and every time D's longsword sheared through the air there was the sound of something being cleaved and falling to the ground—a sound that was to be heard over and over again.

At last it dawned on Lina that she was encircled by unknown creatures.

A dusky conjecture choked her heart. What she'd just felt touching her was beyond doubt a human hand. And that would mean, it had to be—Tajeel. But there was certainly more than one of them out there in the dark.

Dreamily, Lina sifted her memory for some recollection of Tajeel as he had been in his boyhood. She remembered the look of his swarthy face trying to appear sullen, as he handed her flower necklaces he crafted more skillfully than she could, though he still griped about how boring it was picking flowers. And it was Tajeel who had come running with nails in one hand and an arc welder in the other when the roof of her house blew off in a gale, then worked half the day to fix it. It was only natural that the thought of him doing these things out of love for her made her hold both pride and conceit in her little seven-year-old heart. More than even his own parents, it was Lina who had grieved over the loss of him.

"Stop it, D! Stop it!"

As if waiting for just that shout, a blue light threw Lina's shadow onto the stone floor.

A few paces ahead, D was putting his longsword away. In place of the grotesque figures she expected to see, there was a profusion of deep red fluid spreading across the stones of the floor. Blood. When she strained her eyes, a number of the thin, red streams ran to a rock wall to one side of the chamber. Instinctively racing closer, she asked, "What is it, D? You must've got a good look at it."

D didn't answer, but as he locked his gaze on the rock wall in question he muttered, "Strange, it wasn't alone."

"What do you mean by that?"

"The answers lie behind the stones of that wall. We could press forward, but now that we know something's down here, I'd say for today our best bet is to go home. When *these things* get a hand chopped off they leave, carrying everything but the blood."

"But what the blazes—it couldn't be Tajeel . . . "

She received no reply, but, looking askance at D as he turned his ever-frosty form toward the shutter, Lina was struck by a deep emotion more puzzling than dread. She continued to keep her eye on the rocky wall.

†

Without so much as exchanging a word, the pair made their way back down to the base of the hill.

The Hunter's beautiful profile betrayed not a hint of a tremble at the eerie monstrosities they'd so recently encountered. Lina stole glimpses of D's face, terrified by his implacable silence.

There were a million things she wanted to ask him: the reason why it had been so easy to find the subterranean laboratory; what he had noticed there; what those monsters really were; where Tajeel was; and, more than anything, what had been done to her and the others down there a decade ago.

As she gazed at the young Vampire Hunter's profile—one some might call melancholy—her curiosity about all those things dwindled away and something warm covered her heart.

Was she really tagging along with D in an attempt to shed some light on the shadows of a decade earlier? She had her doubts.

"I'm going to take a ride around the village," D said suddenly. Lina noticed they were standing by her wagon. Not far away, D's horse was nibbling the grass, paying them no heed.

"Well then, I'll go with you . . . " Lina said reflexively, but disappointment slapped her heart.

"We part company here. And in the future, I'll thank you not to interfere with my work."

Neither his expression nor his tone differed in the least from the usual, but Lina felt the biting cold like a sudden frost. Out of habit, she started to refute him, only to have her voice vanish down her throat.

"Go to school or head home, but don't make any stops along the way. And don't let your guard down even with those you know," D said from astride his mount.

Yeah, right. Meanie. What do you care how anyone else feels?

Suddenly trying to look sullen, her cheeks stiffened. She tried to say something back, but no words came. Making matters worse, the corners of her eyes grew hot. No, she couldn't start bawling this early in the day.

At this point the air abruptly grew tense. It was due to the lurid aura D emanated. She could feel every inch of her skin rising in gooseflesh.

The sensation was so eerie Lina couldn't even ask what was the matter, but could only turn her face in the direction D was now gazing.

A lone cyborg horse was coming down the trail from town. With its familiar chestnut hue and type ten energy tank slung from its abdomen, Lina saw it was the sheriff's mount. Coming on at a full gallop, horse and rider came to a halt with a small shower of earthen clods.

"Thought I'd find you here. You'd better come with me." The sheriff's face and voice were tinged with impatience.

"How did you know where we were?" D asked softly.

"A farmer saw Lina's wagon headed for the hill. Cuore's run off."

"I thought someone had been put in charge of watching him."

"One of the guys from the Vigilance Committee dozed off while the kid was still asleep. Can't help that. We're only flesh and blood."

"Maybe if you tell that to the next Noble to attack you they'll just make their apologies and be on their merry way."

The sheriff didn't respond to the Hunter's bitter sarcasm.

"Where did he go?" D asked.

"Don't know. But I'm afraid if we don't find him fast we'll have a lynching on our hands. See, since Cuore was at the scene last night, the whole Vigilance Committee's got the idea that he's not the culprit but he's still in cahoots with it. We've been keeping an eye on where Cuore lives, but it looks like he hasn't been back there. Which would leave the forests. I'll check in the north woods. I want you to take the south."

Without giving a reply, D wheeled his mount around. All he knew of the local geography he'd learned in a single glance at a map the mayor had given him a day earlier.

"Hurry on home," he said to the motionless Lina, just as he was about to gallop off. "You've got a date with the Capital."

By the time the girl had raised her face in consternation, D was racing like a scythe through the wind.

The sheriff hastened after him.

As he gave pursuit, the lawman watched with disbelieving eyes. Despite his own speed, the gap between them rapidly grew. It wasn't on account of D's horse. Due to his line of work, one of the first things the sheriff noticed about any outsider was their mount. He'd found that if he had some idea what sort of beast everyone was riding, it made it that much easier to come up with some strategy in the event he had to chase them down. D's horse was just the standard, run-of-the-mill type that could be picked up in any village. Even tuned up, it shouldn't be able to match the sheriff's custom grade steed, two miles per hour faster and twenty percent more durable than the average. It shouldn't have, but it did.

What the blazes . . . Does this guy use magic or something? I thought I heard something about him being a dhampir . . .

Finally, some idea of the uncanny power of the Vampire Hunter—abilities he had only heard rumors of—began to seep into the lawman's understanding.

Pulling far ahead of the sheriff, D entered the south woods. Halting his horse, he shut his eyes. A moment later, he pointed his mount at a grove of trees to his right. Had he heard the words of the wind, or caught some presence tingeing the air?

Before another minute had passed, he met some vigilantes with odd expressions running deeper into the forest.

"Watch it!" cried one.

"Whoa there!" shouted another.

The flinching, scattering men watched D's rein-handling as he sharply halted his hitherto galloping steed.

"Where's Cuore?" At the sound of the Hunter's voice, which could rightly be called soft, nearly a dozen roughnecks froze as if stitched in place. D trained his gaze on the man heading the pack, their apparent leader—the one who had been at the site of the disturbance the night before.

"He . . . uh, he's alright. We ain't done nothing. Yeah, we was gonna knock him around a little bit I suppose, but when we found him Mr. Fern come by."

"Fern? Was he out looking for Cuore, too?"

The man shook his head with uncomfortable haste.

They'd set out on a search for Cuore that Fern had no part in, and had found the former standing stupefied in the middle of the forest. Determined to make him spill his guts, they'd surrounded him and were just starting in on their threats when Fern showed up. A brute of a man who ordinarily would've been the first one in line to lay into Cuore with a whip, Fern had been like a changed man, sticking up for Cuore and leading him away to stay at his own house. Or so this man said. That certainly helped account for the bewilderment gracing the faces of the men.

"Did Fern have anyone else with him?"

"Nope."

"How long ago did they leave? And where did you find Cuore?"

The man pointed back behind them.

"Go straight and you'll know it when you get there. The spot's got moss all over the place and there should be plenty of footprints. It couldn't have been ten minutes ago."

The ring of iron horseshoes mixed with the man's words.

D first headed in the direction of Fern's home. In less than five minutes his eyes lighted on a structure which looked like split logs set in the ground—the guard beast kennel. A wooden palisade rimmed the perimeter, and a pair of people—Cuore and Fern—stood before the oddly shaped gate.

"What's your business?" Fern asked, even as his expression registered surprise at D's sudden stop.

"What did you go into the woods for?" asked D from the back of his horse.

Fern grinned devilishly and put his hands to the baskets at either hip. "I take it you don't know what line I'm in. Fact is, I went out to get some of the moss and bugs I feed my guard beasts. I don't know what you're trying to get at asking a question like that, but I've two of them right here. You wanna see if I'm telling the truth or not?"

Just then, Fern got the impression that an instantaneous white light flashed between him and D. Fern blinked his eyes.

D ignored the provocation. "I want the boy back."

"Oh, you sure have a funny way of putting things. Here you are talking to me like I'm some sort of sneak thief. Well, he's a lot better off here at my house than with some half-assed attempt at a Hunter from who-the-blazes-knows-where. There's a woman's touch here, and I don't think it would hurt him none to learn how civilized folks live."

"Suddenly overcome with love for your fellow man?" D inquired, an eldritch aura condensing about him. In a low tone trenchant as the finest blade he asked, "What happened in the forest?"

Fern was silent. His face was solemn, brimming with murderous intent, and his bony fingers crept to the lids of the baskets. D didn't move. But one had to wonder how he hoped to fend off a pair of beasts from atop his mount, restricted as his movements would be.

A large figure suddenly interrupted the ghastly flow of bloodlust between the men.

Cuore stood before D, blocking his way. Eyes pleading, he shook his head and pointed to the gate. Was he trying to say he wanted him to go?

Shortly thereafter, D wheeled his horse about.

"Heading home already? Next time you show up here, you'd better have that pig-sticker of yours drawn. See, I've got all kinds of 'goods' here of the scary-bad kind. Like these!"

Fern's confidence-stoked voice faltered. The lids hadn't come off his baskets.

The face he raised, now paled by the knowledge that tapered needles of unfinished wood skewered the lids and baskets, was pounded by the hearty laughter of hoofbeats.

†

Racing all the way back to the forest, D dismounted in the malice-shrouded bog. Just as the man from the Vigilance Committee said, there was a confusion of tracks. This was where they'd encountered Cuore, yes, and the place where just previous to that Fern and his daughter had met with the vampire's baleful fangs.

It is debatable whether this youth, too, was apprehensive of the unpleasant heat, but D set foot into the kaleidoscopic world without so much as a knitted brow.

From D's lightly clasped left hand a malicious, drifting voice suggested, "Things are starting to get interesting."

"How so?"

"That Fern character—there's something funny about the way he's acting. Then there's the kid, who must be seriously wet behind the ears. Why on earth would he want to go with that guy? Ol' basket-pants is in charge of the guys who beat the stuffing out of him, ain't he? So what's the story? You seem like you're on to something already."

"That boy wanted to go with him more than anything." A rare teasing tone had entered D's voice. "Try to read my mind about the rest. Which reminds me—if you've got your strength back, I need your help with something."

"Still far from recovered. Can't you spare me another two or three days to recuperate at my own pace? When the time comes, I'll have a hell of an interesting tale for your ears."

"I can hardly wait." Halting his stride, D terminated the conversation. Strangely, it was at just the spot where the ashen figure had attacked Fern's daughter.

D looked to the ground before his feet.

A multicolored carpet already concealed all signs of the struggle. The growth rate of these fungi was remarkably swift.

His intently scanning eyes gradually gave off a red brilliance. The miasma around him eddied suspiciously, and his gorgeous visage became that of a vampire.

His vermilion gaze halted on a certain piece of ground. Drawing a translucent cylinder the size of his little finger from a pouch on his belt, D knelt on the ground.

What could he be searching for that would necessitate becoming a vampire? Putting what appeared to be a piece of ground into the tube, D slowly surveyed his surroundings. As if beckoned by that ominous gaze, a black cloud surged from the distant sky.

Nightmares on a Rainy Night

CHAPTER 4

As the last period was finishing, droplets began to hammer the window panes, and, by the time the teacher left school, it had really started coming down. The sound of rain rebounding off his hooded slicker was nearly deafening.

Put just a mite too much grease on this one, Mr. Meyer ruminated as he walked the muddy path. The thicker the were-tiger fat they treated the heavy moose hides with, the faster it dried, and, in the fierce squalls particular to the region, the stiffened coat made a sound like cheeks being slapped.

Not five minutes after passing through the school's front gate, the noise became all the more intense, and the teacher began to regret his haste to return home. He couldn't see fifteen feet in front of him.

Be that as it may, to villagers menaced by the bloodsucking Nobility, rain was one of the most welcome sounds. As one would expect from legends of vampires' inability to cross running water, statistically speaking the incidence of attack on rainy days was, for all purposes, nil. Though they might be grimacing, these Frontier people were gleeful as they hustled homeward.

"What on earth . . . ?" Spying a shape moving with inhuman speed through the sheets of falling droplets, the teacher came to a stop. It definitely looked very much like a man, but its bizarre gait, somehow different from that of an ordinary person, cast a foreboding pall over his heart.

All the water demons and vicious river sprites that loved to come out on rainy days had been exterminated years ago, and the talismans mounted at strategic points around the village should have kept the area safe from more of their kind until the end of time. But if that was true, what could the figure be . . . ?

Recalling that there was a lone farm off in the direction the figure had vanished, Mr. Meyer turned back toward the school. He hoped to get help. But it wasn't much more than a quarter mile to the farmhouse. More than enough distance for the fear in his heart to become reality.

Hesitating momentarily, Mr. Meyer went after the shadowy figure.

A narrow footpath ran between fields planted with gargantuan produce. The soft topsoil was gouged by the driving rain, sending up an uninterrupted spray of yellow. Here and there, the sharp crack of vegetable leaves snapping from their respective stems could be heard.

The figure had long since left his range of vision. Without a doubt, it was headed for the farmhouse. Mr. Meyer picked up the pace.

His fears had been well founded.

When the silhouette of the farmhouse floated into the rain-soaked world, a scream split through the roar of the rain. There was the sound of something breaking, then it was lost beneath a bellow that couldn't be attributed to man or beast.

The teacher sprinted, stripping off his coat. He fished in his blazer pocket as he ran and clumsily pulled out a buckshot-firing tube intended for self-defense.

He stood rooted before the farmhouse door. The door itself was undisturbed, but in the mud wall beside it a huge hole gaped like a blackened maw. It was large enough for a full-grown man to pass through with ease. The teacher's legs turned weak at the thought of the brute strength needed to make that hole.

Another scream. This time it was a child's voice. Fear was banished in an instant by a powerful sense of professional duty, and Mr. Meyer flew in through the entrance. The teacher couldn't have imagined the scene he would glimpse in that first heartbeat, a sight that replaced his sense of mission with a kind of numbness.

†

His field of vision was filled by a broad room and the body of a woman prone on its dirt floor. On top of the Rubenesque form of what was apparently the farmer's wife squirmed a *thing* with disheveled locks. The thing, whatever it was, was roughly the size of a child seven or eight years old.

An ample breast spilled from the woman's shredded clothing, and across the breast crept a scarlet tongue. There was the sound of licking, but it wasn't the sort of sound that came from the loving play men and women engaged in. The thing was lapping at the redness that coursed down the woman's bosom, running from the base of her throat.

The ebony head moved over the woman's breast and her body twitched. It raised its visage gingerly to face the teacher. Weirdly jutting cheeks it had, and sunken eyes. Not a sliver of humanity was to be found in its bloodshot orbs, and its lips, uncommon only in their size, warped in an evil smirk at the appearance of fresh prey. With a wet thud, it spat something out on the earthen floor. One didn't need to see the thing's bloodstained teeth to know that what it spat was the well-gnawed tip of a breast.

The side door creaked open. In Mr. Meyer's eyes, what came out of the back room looked like a werewolf with the body of a child in its jaws.

He still had the buckshot tube in his hands, but he didn't bring it to bear on either of the creatures. Not only was he a teacher, but he was a Frontier person as well. Demons and monstrosities dwelt all around them, and he knew ways to deal with them. On two previous occasions he had fended off attacks with the weapon in his hands—by a harpy in one case and a man-serpent another time. But this time he didn't move.

Realizing where his mind was starting to lead him, the teacher trembled violently.

The one that had been gnawing at the woman's corpse rose, while the creature crawling about on all fours dropped the child's body. The monsters closed in . . .

"Hold it. Don't come near me." The words barely escaped his throat. Side to side the buckshot tube wavered without fixing on a target.

Two creatures, the teacher tried to impress upon himself. *Two things. Not people.*

Eyes crazed solely with murder burned like flames, and blood-smeared lips hauled back to expose rows of teeth. Teeth that were average and human.

These things are just like me, the teacher mused.

From the front and flank dark shapes pounced.

Stop it!

A deafening report and thirty balls of shot stifled the teacher's cry. Outside, the squall grew stronger.

†

While that small but fearsome battle was taking place at one end of the village, Lina was already back at her home. After what had happened in the ruins it was no surprise she couldn't focus in class, but the cause of her singular depression was what D had said.

Don't follow me around anymore—that's what she'd been told. In light of how she had fancied herself the young Vampire Hunter's assistant, D's order was a grievous wound to her pride.

Can't allow myself to fly off the handle. Gotta get him to take that back.

Keeping these two sentiments in mind, Lina dropped her book bag in her room, then burst into D's abode—the barn. D's horse was tied up in one of the stalls. *Goody*, she thought. *He's in.*

"Now I've seen everything," she exclaimed, her amazement at this unforeseen tableau forming the words of its own accord.

She had heard from the mayor that D was a dhampir. And she had some knowledge about their nature. Though she had been certain that he would either be sleeping or feeding, D had in fact found a wooden desk and chair that had been moved out to the barn years ago. He was at them now, shaking what looked like a little flask.

Approaching dumbstruck, Lina saw the instruments laid out on the desktop. Her eyes went wide again, and this time wider than before. Not only were there a number of silvery cylinders and medicine bottles filled with draughts of unsettling shades, there was also a rack of flasks with pale vapors rising from the flasks' openings. Unless her eyes deceived her, beside the rack a microcomputer hummed dully and gave off flashes of cyanic light. "Wow! Can all Vampire Hunters do chemical analysis?"

Though he'd probably long since noticed his visitor, D made no move to face her. But there wasn't necessarily any enmity in that.

"Hey," she called out, firming her shoulders for a struggle.

"I thought I'd dismissed my assistant."

"Yippee!" Lina snapped her fingers. A smile spilled from her. "What are you so happy about?"

"It looks like I get to be your assistant again. Oh, now don't try and talk your way out of it. I see some hope for me yet in the way you phrased that. See, I'm a mind reader, too. I know full well where your mind's headed."

Really just yours and no one else's, Lina thought.

D turned to Lina and said, "If I say it some other way will you get out?"

Her body trembling with chill at something carried in that soft tone, Lina shook her head as gaily as possible. "Not on your vampire-hunting life."

She wondered what she'd do if her words offended him, but D returned to his desk expressionless.

She wasted no time going over to him. Shifting her eyes to the computer, she said, "An estimated 14.3 grams per 100 cubic centimeters, 4.5 million in a cubic millimeter—that's the amount of hemoglobin and blood count for a woman you've got displayed there. Has someone else been attacked?!"

D turned to her and said, "Good call." He wasn't referring to the disturbing incident, but rather to her take on the numerical data displayed on his computer.

"What do you expect from a prodigy?" Lina chuckled, puffing her already ample chest. A second later, she slipped her cheek in by D's face. "Your assistant would like to know something, Boss. Whose blood is this?"

D met the mischievous girl's look with his sparkling eyes, then turned the other way.

Humph, that was an unexpected move. Does he think I'll call it quits so easily? "Fine," said Lina. "Don't tell me. I guess I'll just have to tag along and do my own thing. Wherever you go, I'll be there on my own little agenda. So try not to get bent out of shape when I trample all over your precious evidence."

"Do what you like." End of discussion.

Of course, throwing a sulking fit wouldn't sway D. And it would be galling to go now with things the way they stood. Lina wound up hovering over the computer.

Once, several years back, she'd seen a computer that a traveling merchant had brought to town. A legacy of the Nobility's vanished scientific culture, computers were few in number, and rarer still were people who could use them. Clearly this must be one of the most powerful models, with a built-in ability to draw inferences in addition to the usual data-analyzing functions. Still, it was hard to believe a Vampire Hunter was used to using such a device.

D's fingers gently brushed the magnetic ball and the display changed.

"That's sixteen grams of hemoglobin, blood count of five million—that one's a man's. D, you don't suppose—"

"There were drops of the woman's blood in the middle of the woods where Cuore was found. Thanks to the high humidity, it hadn't dried completely. It still had its scent, too. I've added some blood from the woman last night to it."

Just as Lina was about to jump for joy at finally receiving a civil reply, the computer began to display something other than numerical data. Top and bottom, left and right, the pale spark dragged its tail.

"Oh, I get it. From saliva mixed with the blood of its victim you can deduce who the Noble really is. Sensational!" Lina trained a gaze of fear and curiosity on the display.

Where the randomly flowing flashes made contact, a cluster of luminous points formed and shifted locations in a manner that was momentarily dizzying. In no time, a single face had been rendered on the dark-green display.

Lina swallowed her spittle.

"Recognize this?" D inquired.

Lina shook her head. The screen was filled with a three-dimensional image of a man she'd never seen. D's hand moved and the perspective of the "face" changed several times, but Lina couldn't recall seeing it. "It's no one from the village. Not Tajeel, either. That's a relief . . . "

That seemed to dispel some of her doubts. The sound of falling rain came clearly to her ears.

"Why are you crying?" D asked, switching off the computer. The sample of blood he'd collected in the forest had since dried, making it impossible now to deduce the identity of the woman who had been bitten there.

"Hmph," Lina snorted, turning the other way and dabbing at her eyes. "Rainy days are supposed to make you sentimental, you know. What kind of girl would I be if they didn't?"

She hoped D would pick up the conversation, but instead he looked out of the entrance, commenting on how it was really pouring down.

"Why is it the Nobility have problems with the rain?" Lina had wondered about this for years. When she was little, it seemed any time there were rumors of Nobles appearing in some distant village she'd only been allowed outdoors on rainy days.

As he replied, "I don't know, either," D's face became mysteriously pale. He was questioning why he bothered answering each and every question the girl posed. "From a biological standpoint, a number of mysteries remain about how their metabolisms work. The question of why they can only move by night, or how their bodies can heal wounds from bullets, or why they can be destroyed with a single wooden stake. The same can be said for their inability to cross running water, or the way rainy days prevent them from venturing outdoors. It's rather ironic that so many defects remain when they've attained what's believed to be the pinnacle of biological evolution—true immortality."

"Looks like the all-revealing light of science isn't perfect after all," said Lina, eyes alight with inquisitiveness. "I wonder if the Nobility themselves ever solved those mysteries."

"So far as I know?" D shook his head. "Biological weaknesses are linked to some defect of the species. If they had seized on some clue, some explanation, I doubt the day when men ruled the earth would have ever come. The Nobles vanished from history without even knowing why they were doomed. All told, I suppose they were rather good sports about it."

"A fundamental defect of the species," Lina muttered, deeply moved by what D had said. "The Nobility died off, while mankind remained. But even now we're terrified of some vision of those who've gone. Doesn't that seem sort of pitiful for the supposed rulers of the earth?"

D kept his silence as he moved to the entrance, then put his hand out into the cascade pouring down from the eaves. As he did so, his eyes fixed on a spot outside. Lina tilted her head in consternation and followed after him.

Beyond the blurring gray membrane they could see the profile of the hill and a number of human silhouettes. People swinging hoes up and down. They could hear the whine of atomic tractors, too. If you didn't mind getting a little wet, this was the finest weather one could ask for to put in some extra hours in the fields without the threat of the dreaded Nobility.

"If I were to go out now, my body temperature would drop nearly four degrees," D said, watching the droplets smashing against his outstretched hand. "My running speed would fall by thirty percent, you see, as my whole metabolism slowed down. On the other hand, your kind . . . "

Reading the faraway look in D's eye, Lina felt pained by the destiny the gorgeous youth bore. What was it like to spring from Noble and mortal blood? When stalking one of the two, what went through his heart?

Lina took D's soaked arm.

"What the . . . ?"

Clasping everything from the wrist up with both hands, she pressed it to her cheek without saying a word. *His hand's so cold, but maybe I can warm it up just a bit. Maybe it'll make me his temperature.* Lina shut her eyes and heard only the sound of the rain.

Suddenly the eeriest sensation struck her countenance. Goosebumps rising all over her body, Lina let go of his hand. D's gaze hadn't moved in the least; his profile still pointed in the same direction. But what stood before the girl wasn't the same young man, gorgeous, solitary, and proud.

"Don't leave this spot." His parting words vested with an authority that made them impossible to disobey, the Vampire Hunter stalked out into the falling droplets. It took a minute before Lina realized he also carried his longsword in his left hand.

D's speed didn't appear to have dropped the least bit below normal. A hundred yards took him less than six seconds. He didn't even close his eyelids against the wind-whipped rain lashing his face.

Easily clearing the fence, he entered a field. This didn't cause even the slightest delay. Not even the mire would think of catching the youth's feet or making him slip.

He arrived at his destination some fifty yards distant in another three seconds flat.

The farmers had formed a ring, but they whirled about as the ghastly aura struck them. Their faces were fearful as they cleared a path.

D planted his knee by the side of the *thing* lying on the ground.

The creature had a diminutive body and was crowned with a head of lengthy hair. Its flesh was as pale and blue as a drowning victim, but something red leaked from it. Apparently there was still some life in it.

D had no difficulty flipping the body over. A murmur ran through the assembled farmers. The chest and flank of the creature bore a number of entry wounds. Probably left by buckshot, judging from the spread.

"Which way did it come?" D asked without turning.

"Over yonder . . . from the direction of the school," a tremulous voice answered.

"Relax. It won't be moving anymore," D said, pointing at the creature. "Carry it back to the mayor's barn. Or if you don't feel like touching it, summon the sheriff."

"You . . . you do it. Ain't that your job?" someone on the other side of the group protested. "If we touch that there abomination, our hands will rot and drop off. Hell, I say one monster should clean up after another." The boldly blurted words became a shriek and the farmer dropped on the spot. Nothing had happened, aside from D standing up again. But as the wind and rain unexpectedly grew wilder, the men saw something blazing with a brilliant red light.

D's eyes.

"I said carry it." His tone hadn't changed at all—if anything, it was calmer—but the men seemed to sense something in it and they jostled to be the first to the corpse of the creature. Without sparing them another glance, D returned to the barn with the same speed he'd come.

Lina and the mayor stood in the doorway.

"What the blazes is going on?" the old man asked. His wrinkle-rimmed eyes had a glint approaching madness.

Replying simply, "I don't know," D swiftly moved inside and made the necessary preparations. He donned his coat and traveler's hat. Around him and only him the flow of time seemed different. From where the mayor and Lina stood, the clothing seemed to move to D's body as if magnetically attracted. Less than ten seconds after returning, D passed the pair again on his way back out.

A considerable while after the thunder of shod hooves faded into the far reaches of the rain, the farmers came into the barn carrying the remains of the thing.

†

Going on for a mile and a quarter, D halted his horse. Mortal eyes would have seen nothing but rain, but D could discern the black shape of the schoolhouse wavering some five hundred yards ahead.

"Lost the scent. Your turn," he said to his left hand. His palm puffed and swelled into a masculine face that needed no introduction—the ghastly countenanced carbuncle.

In a tone of undisguised displeasure it said, "Sheesh, and right in the middle of a good dream. Oh, raining, is it?" No sooner had he said this than he opened his tiny mouth to greedily gulp down a share of the torrential downpour.

"What about the scent?" D pressed him. There was a frigid anger in his voice.

"Keep your drawers on. Just because I've been asleep don't mean I haven't worked up an appetite. East of here. Four hundred yards, give or take a smidge."

It seemed both of them—D and his companion in his palm—were able to catch the bloody scent of the beast that'd disappeared in the heavy rain. In less than a minute, D was making his way through the entrance to a lone farmhouse—the same home where a mere hour earlier Mr. Meyer had encountered tragedy.

The thick stench of blood assailed his nose.

On the room's earthen floor lay the bodies of the farmer's wife and child. Confirming that both had expired, D knelt by the entrance to the room.

Lifeblood was spilled across the packed earth, and the stains crept outside like a serpent. Probably blood from the monstrosity. Just as he had in the forest, D sealed some bloodstained soil in a glass vial from a pouch on his combat utility belt, then retrieved another object with his right hand.

The buckshot cylinder. It was the one Mr. Meyer had used, but D didn't know that. Holding the muzzle to his left hand, he asked, "How about it?"

"Fired an hour ago, more or less."

"From the look of those corpses, this wasn't the work of a Noble. There were two of them. One being was the thing in the field, I take it. So whose blood is this—the weapon's owner or whatever the owner shot?"

"Can't say. But there's no one here anymore."

D stood up again and went outside. Once more the wind and rain covered his dashing profile. "No need to involve myself with anything aside from vampires, but those things . . . " D muttered as he was about to place his foot in the stirrup. Suddenly, his body tensed.

There was nothing anywhere near him. Nothing and no one.

Despite that, D didn't move a muscle. Perhaps he couldn't move; then again, maybe he wouldn't be moved.

Somewhere behind him, neither near nor far, a certain presence had gushed into being.

D, it called. Not with a voice, but the presence itself. *I thought you'd come.*

"You were here, weren't you?" D's voice was almost mechanical. From the way he phrased it, he seemed to be acquainted with whoever the presence behind him belonged to. "I've been looking for you for a long time."

Most likely failed, the presence muttered gravely. *Best you come once again to the computation center. I'm always there.*

D's right hand moved. A lethal swipe mowed through the air. *Most likely failed.*

Rain spattered against the naked longsword as D whirled around. *I'm in the computation center.*

As if blown to the four winds by the silently speeding needle of wood, the presence was swallowed by the darkness.

D stared at the empty point in space while the rain, rebounding off every inch of his body, sounded like derisive laughter.

†

T he mayor's home was being battered by stormy waves of the supernatural. Nobles that walked by day were more than enough to send shivers through the entire village; now a new type of monster had appeared and attacked a farm. The disappearance of another villager only added to the mayor's woes.

After hearing D's account, the sheriff and a party from the Vigilance Committee visited the scene. Based on the other corpses and the vast quantity of blood spilled on the dirt floor, the consensus was Mr. Meyer had most likely been slain. His identity had been established when a member of the Vigilance Committee verified that the buckshot cylinder D brought back belonged to the teacher.

The corpse of the monstrosity was carted to the village physician for dissection, but the news from this hadn't been particularly bright either.

It wasn't a creature but rather a human being, though it differed from them in terms of its skeletal structure, musculature, and intestinal regions; all told, nearly two hundred distinct disparities had been noted. No incision had been made in the head, but from the shape of the skull the doctor concluded that its brain was exceedingly small. Its intelligence would be reduced proportionally. As for why the head hadn't been opened, the government stipulated that, when new forms of life were discovered, the brain was to be properly refrigerated and shipped to the Capital, skull and all.

At that point, D, who happened to be present, made a surprising request. He wanted them to loan him the corpse and viscera for the evening.

"What the blazes for?!" the mayor shouted, knitting his brow. Like the physician, he was highly skeptical.

"I'd like to examine them with my own instruments. No disrespect intended."

Perhaps the infamous eldritch aura gently brushed the nape of their necks, for the physician paled and held his tongue while the mayor nodded reluctantly. After all, he'd summoned D to their village, and, though the results so far could hardly be called favorable, after witnessing the nightmarish might of the vampire the previous night he knew in the marrow of his bones that this gorgeous youth alone could slay it, whatever it turned out to be.

"Have it your way. But just for the day. Tomorrow it goes off to the Capital. But I'm more interested in what you plan on doing with the woman."

The woman in question was Kaiser's wife, who'd been attacked by a vampire twice and now lay in bed dangling between life and death. A young man from the Vigilance Committee stood watch over her night and day with stake in hand. Her husband still hadn't returned.

"No problem there. Bring her to the barn along with the cadaver."

And so it came to be that D was going to spend the night with a pair of corpses.

With all that had happened—monstrous new creatures appearing, then encountering that presence in the downpour and seeing his lethal blow slashing through empty air—D's nerves must have been extraordinary for him not to display any tinge of either excitement or concern.

When he got the news from the sheriff that the exhaustive search of the town had turned up nothing, D was composed, perhaps, because he hadn't expected anything from the start. And when they told him Mr. Meyer hadn't returned home, D didn't so much as raise an eyebrow.

Left alone in the barn, D stood by the bench that bore the monstrosity. By its side were a number of jars with its organs in formaldehyde, the glass glinting harshly with light from a mercury lamp on the ceiling. Both the body and the jars had been brought from the physician's home. Outside, the rain made a considerable din.

"You there?" he asked in a low voice.

"Yup," his palm responded. The face was already surfacing.

D held his left hand over the cadaver. The eviscerated abdominal cavity sagged pitifully. And, on the neatly sutured incision on the flank, the stitches of cauterizing thread on the flesh were unusually grotesque.

From the clawed tips of the thing's swollen toes the left hand crept slowly to the twisted ankles, then to the badly bowed thighs. Naturally, D had his eyes trained in that direction, too, but, as he held his hand close to the cadaver, the way the countenanced carbuncle in his palm continued to survey the unmoving patient with the gravest of expressions was more comic than spooky.

Moving his left hand over the flanks, chest, and face, then finally lightly touching the hair flowing from the crown of its head, D said, "Well?"

"Hmm, just as you expected. But at the moment it remains dead."

D nodded. What exactly did it mean by "at the moment it remains dead"?

"When will it awaken?"

"Don't ask stupid questions. From ancient times the demons have always gathered at three Morning. On another note, while I was dozing I overheard talk about some teacher named Meyer gone missing. Think this one's playmate got him?"

Apparently the countenanced carbuncle could still see and hear what went on in the outside world while deep in the palm of D's hand.

"Probably," D said. "But there's still one thing about this case I can't figure."

"Hmph," the other voice snorted derisively. "No doubt the key would be in them ruins. You could always go up there alone and check it all out. Bringing the girlie along would be safe enough, too, I suppose. That is, so long as *you-know-who* is up there."

The chiding voice died abruptly. D had clenched his left hand in a tight fist. He did it with such strength his flawless young flesh shook, and, along with the hoarse groan of agony, a trickle of bright blood spilled from between his curled fingers.

"*Him*," D muttered, sending his gaze to the wide-open doors. "It all started with him. All the dreams, and all the tragedies."

A fierce wind gusted in through the doorway, setting the ceiling lamp swaying. In that light D's face became a devilish one.

†

"Stop it . . . "

Fishy lips sucked up the girl's entreaty as the mayor pressed his face against hers.

When the impassioned breath and tongue invaded her ear, Lina let out an involuntary moan. Beneath her pajama top a wrinkled hand kneaded her breast.

"Please . . . just stop . . . I don't want this."

"Why is that?" Enjoying Lina's refusal, the mayor pinned her white arms against the sheets. "Because that Hunter's here?" he asked, letting a faint smile rise to his lips. "Can't say as I blame you. I'm a man, and I have to confess his looks make even my heart beat faster. Well, that's fine and dandy. Once in a while, it's nice to get a piece of tail from someone with a little fight in 'em."

His lips attached themselves to her breast. Lina twisted her body, but there was nothing she could do. Tears spilled from the corners of her eyes, dampening the white sheets.

After a bit, the old man took his lips away and said, "You're mine. It was me that saved you from becoming the village plaything, who adopted you, who kept them from doing anything against you. Soon you'll be leaving town. Afraid there's not much we can do about that. But until you do—hell, even after you're in the Capital, I won't let any other man have you. And I won't have you falling for anyone, either."

His voice was charged with obsession. Lina averted her face.

"I'll see to it you don't forget about me. I'll hammer my memory into your body. Like so."

The old man's face sank below her waist, and Lina bit her lip to keep from voicing the fruit of that torment. A bony hand crept along the exposed whiteness of her thigh.

She looked to her pillow in desperation. Under the pillow she spied a single white bloom. It pulled the passion from her frame in an unbelievable way. Thoughts of the face of someone she'd never seen came to Lina.

Noticing a slight change in the way the girl's body was responding, the old man increased the pace of his tongue, and yet the expression Lina wore was mysteriously serene.

The face conjured in her heart of hearts bore a striking resemblance to the Vampire Hunter.

†

Winds joined the torrential downpour, and the level of the river continued to rise. Although the flow had been intense to begin with, it couldn't keep pace with the cresting waves whipped up by the wind. At the angry tone of the muddy tributary, now surpassing even the piercing sound of the rain, the residents along the riverbanks exchanged anxious looks.

Two figures moved at the foot of the bridge. Both were men from the Vigilance Committee. In their black raincoats, they were reminiscent of the creatures of the night they so feared.

"Looks like trouble. Could be she's gonna give way."

Hearing the opinion of the bigger man, the smaller one stood on the incline shaking his head. "Nah, it rained just as hard last year. The bridge's girders have been reinforced, and they even built up these embankments. Nothing to worry about. Of course, I don't know what'll happen if it keeps up like this for another day or two more. And how many times have I got to tell you not to grab hold of my legs like I was your own personal ladder?"

A silence fell between the pair. Actually, the bigger man was *above* the little man on the embankment.

It took a long time for the little man to summon the nerve to look down at his ankles.

The arm wrapped around them belonged to a man whose upper body jutted from the black water.

"You, you're . . . " The little man recalled the face of the Vampire Hunter who'd fallen off this very bridge, coffin and all, not so many days earlier. Pale face expressionless, the Hunter drew a stake from his belt and drove it through the little man's heart. Death spasms wracked his short frame. Lifeless, he tumbled into the water and was quickly washed away.

Climbing the embankment coolly, the reanimated Hunter came to stand before the petrified giant.

Just before the pale figure's upraised stake stabbed into the big man's chest, he saw the dark shapes of men and women creeping one after another from the black surface of the water and up the slope. Something long and round stuck in the heart of each. They were all the victims of the Nobility who had been disposed of at the river.

So this is how I die, the big man thought. *With a stake through the heart from this freak.* The stake sank into his chest. He saw a bloody spray billow out with a poof.

An unexpected wind blew against the gigantic body that rolled halfway down the embankment, ruthlessly tearing off his coat. There was no bloodstain to be seen. What's more, neither the chest of the big man nor the heart of the little man had been pierced by a stake. And there wasn't a trace of the horde of corpses that had risen from the watery depths.

†

At two fifty-nine Morning, D rose from his bed of hay and turned the light controls on, keeping the solar lamp dimmed as much as possible. A faint darkness ruled the barn. Strange things, creatures and phenomena alike, had a strong aversion to light.

Returning to his resting place, he stared at the corpse on its hastily improvised bed and at the woman who was neither living nor dead.

The matter of the woman herself didn't seem so urgent. If it wanted to, the vampire that had gorged itself the previous night could hold off for an interval of several days. What's more, because the vampire knew what D was capable of, the vampire wasn't likely to make a casual call on his victim. Despite the slim chances of attack, D had taken custody of her because he'd surmised what would happen if she were to be summoned.

Victims who fell under a vampire's spell came under a kind of long-range hypnosis and could unleash brutal attacks even on the people who were trying to protect them.

The most fearsome thing about this hypnotic state was the way it could surpass the subconscious limits humans imposed on their own flesh. Trying to hold down a victim thrashing about with the full power inherent in the human body—roughly seven times their normal strength—was a difficult task for a team of five men of like physiques. A graceful maiden shattering the shinbone of a professional combatant wouldn't even be considered news on the Frontier. Before it came to such a struggle, those attending to the victim would do their best to make merciless use of a stake. Those who should be protecting them became their murderers—was that a tragedy or a comedy?

But if that was the case, toward what end had D appropriated the creature's corpse? And what was the meaning of his weird conversation with the countenanced carbuncle?

The change came at exactly three Morning.

D's eyes shone mysteriously.

Without any extraneous action, the cadaver slowly raised its torso.

The dead body got up now and slipped off the table, its face alone remaining set in the blank mask of death. But, for something with all its internal organs extracted and a great subsidence in its abdomen, it possessed a tenacious, even mysterious, vitality.

"Just as I thought," D muttered.

The living corpse went to the jars and began a hair-raising activity. Skillfully removing the spring-loaded cap from one and plunging its hand in, it extracted the dripping entrails, ripped open its sealed wound, and lovingly pushed inwards, shoving its intestines back into their rightful place.

This activity, the sight of which might have driven anyone but D to madness, continued for some time. Having reclaimed its heart, lungs, stomach, and other parts, and naturally heedless of the great lump of viscera that had collected in its abdomen, the cadaver ran its muddy pupils over the surroundings. It began to move toward the entrance with an awkward gait.

D got up, too. The sheath of the longsword on the back of his coat shone dimly. Not a single bit of hay stirred. With muted footsteps he followed after the reanimated monstrosity.

The small silhouette went out through the entrance.

D stopped, and seemed to consider following it. He had no fear of the lashing rain, of course, but all of his dhampir senses detected a mass of powerful mental energy thronging to the back of the barn. Whatever it was, he couldn't yet see it.

From D's back rose the sound of his blade unsheathing. After that, there was no movement at all.

The presences—a horde of soaking corpses—surrounded him, young ladies and lads with stake-pierced hearts, their burial vestments vividly dyed with their own blood. They were the corpses of all who had fallen under the pernicious fangs of the Nobility and been thrown into the rushing waters since this village was first incorporated.

However . . .

"A psychological attack? They're using rather advanced abilities." D had already noticed that the rows of corpses cast no shadow.

"Long time no see, D. Never thought I'd find you here." The bloated corpse of a drowning victim, the only one that had been spared a staking, stepped forward. It was the Vampire Hunter Geslin. Could the enemy be trying to use some memory of this man as a *way in*, to project their illusions into D's mind?

"How about it, D? Can you cut us down?" Geslin's right hand moved, and white lightning brushed D's cheek. Raindrops spattered the running blood. "You can't cut us with that sword of yours. But we can stick you with our stakes."

Wedges of wood glistened in the bloodied hands of the dead.

The needles of plain wood flying from D's right hand passed through the bodies of the dead and stuck in the barn wall behind them. Geslin chortled. "What do you make of that, D? Is this the best you can do? Just try it. Can't you cut us down?"

"I can cut you."

"What?!"

D's eyes gave off a fierce red glare. Parrying all the nonexistent stakes roaring toward him with a graceful movement, D charged into the very center of the besieging horde of dead.

Geslin's head was split in two, the expression of shock still plastered to his face. The head flew off a youth who had a stake held high and was ready to strike. Naked steel penetrated the bosom of a woman who was retreating in screams. A pair of fangs jutted from D's mouth. Who could have stood to look directly at that ghastly visage? This was no less than the slaughter of the dead by a demon of a man.

Rain splashed off the silver blade.

Amidst the wind and rain and darkness stood the lonely figure of D.

There was no one there. Just as it always was.

Even the cut on his cheek had disappeared. The whole battle had taken place in his mind.

"That's a relief. No matter how many times I see it, it's always an intense show," came the thoroughly disgusted voice from D's left hand. The Hunter had already regained his paraffin beauty and was scanning the area. "Can't fight your blood, I say. At any rate, that threw quite a monkey wrench into your scheme to see where that beastie was going to hook up with his cohorts. The question is, was it a coincidence or not?"

"If it was a coincidence, then that creature and the attacker yesterday are unrelated. If it was intentional, then all our mysteries are coming together around a single point," D said, brushing the raindrops from his shoulders at the door to the barn. Raven hair clung to his nigh translucent skin, and a desolate unearthliness hung over him, but still his beauty was beyond description. Surely even the most dazzling of women would pale before this youth.

Why, even the voice of the left hand seemed rapt as it said, "Heh, it's hard to believe you've gone all this time and never once turned your fangs on all the women and men who pursue you. I bet the most gorgeous princess on earth would offer you her smooth white throat if you just said the word. I have to give you credit for the strength of your will, if nothing else. So, what do you plan on doing?"

"Concerned about me?" D asked softly.

"Don't be ridiculous. I was just asking if you were going up to those castle ruins. I've got a vague inkling of what went on there. Might even be that creature came from—"

"I know." D's words cut the grating voice short.

Exactly. Ever since he'd laid eyes on the creature lying in the field, D knew it was just like the things that had attacked Lina and him in the dark depths of the castle.

"Guess we've got to go then. Since his highness is up there, too." Down on D's palm, the countenanced carbuncle bared its teeth in an eerie laugh.

In the middle of a dim room, several shadowy figures gathered. The room was filled with such a sense of the unearthly, it made the snarls of a multitude of beasts coming from very close at hand seem stripped of energy.

"I failed," one of the shadows moaned. But, despite the import of its words, it didn't seem perturbed. The voice was all the weirder for its serenity. "If that Hunter can parry a psychological attack, he's a man to be feared. A dhampir, no doubt. And no average half-breed, either. What do you think?"

The shadow it addressed was silent.

"Forget I asked then," said the first shadow, fairly spitting the words.

Surprisingly, the voice was still young. Judging by the way he spoke, this was the leader of the group—the ashen figure in gray. And, if that were the case, might the remaining two be his victim Fern and the boy Cuore? Even that young man wouldn't have been safe for long in a den of vampires.

"Whatever the case, we can't allow him to remain in the village any longer. Or to find out who we are." The shadow's arm extended, and he pointed to the third shadow. "Tomorrow, collapse the entrance way. Let me say this now to be perfectly clear—I will not allow him to interfere again. Next time, it'll be *you* that gets taken care of, *regardless of what you are*."

The shadow he'd indicated shook as if frightened, but it said nothing.

Something small moved over by the wall. All eyes focused on the entrance, catching the diminutive creature that entered to the creaking of the heavy door. From its strangely protruding abdomen up to its clavicle there ran a raw black surgical incision.

"Is this the only one to come back?" the shadow leader asked. "It would've been better to catch them right away when they got loose, but that was beyond our control. With the scent of fresh blood and meat everywhere, it doesn't matter that they don't have to eat or drink—they're going to want to run wild. Oh, well, soon enough this village, no, the whole Frontier will be in our hands. It all happens tomorrow."

The shadow's foreboding laughter was full of confidence. Pregnant with horror and mystery, darkness alone covered the downpour-drenched village.

Genes of Light & Darkness

D awoke when cold light filled the barn to the eaves. He'd slept perhaps all of three hours. To a dhampir like him, it didn't matter whether he worked by night or day, but even his body demanded the occasional respite and sleep. Perhaps the shadow clinging to his exquisite countenance was due to the strain of having to work solely by day of late.

A fog had moved in, it seemed, and the whiteness slipped into the barn through the entrance and cracks around the windows, but it was not so thick as to hinder action. All the more so because in D's eyes this was no different from midday in fine weather.

Making his preparations with characteristic superhuman speed, he exited the barn.

His stride was smooth. More like a shadow than a cat. If stealth was an innate characteristic of the Nobles, they could hope for no greater silence than D possessed.

Entering a stable a short distance away, D stopped cold. Seven or eight yards ahead of him, the stone walls of the main house reflected the morning sunlight. Dressed in a white nightgown, Lina opened one of the windows and leaned out into the street. Right below the sill there hung a small window box. Stretching out her hand, Lina snatched up something white that lay in it.

D saw it quite clearly. It was a single white blossom. Though he didn't know what it was called, this tiny expression of life was a common enough sight along the roads of the Frontier. Who could've left it?

Pressing it to her breast, Lina looked down the road with an expression bordering on tears. The girl gazed for an eternity down the white road, hazy with fog.

Before long, the window shut quietly. D went into the stable, came out with his mount, and pointed it toward the ruins. Oh so quietly, as if trying not to make a sound, as if trying not to shatter a young girl's dream.

As soon as D was off the mayor's property, he started to gallop at full speed. The horse tore through the mist. The crusted remains of snow flew in all directions. Mist devils out to ravage crops were startled by this early morning rider and drifted down to see what he was all about, but they were crushed before they could even touch him, and were left swirling in his wake.

Racing through the village, in less than twenty minutes he had climbed the hill and arrived at the entrance to the ruins. Hitching his horse to the edge of a shattered stone wall, the Hunter entered the courtyard.

Fog permeated the ruins.

Passing from the corridor to the hall, D was going to make straight for the entrance to the laboratory, but he came to a stop almost in the center of the hall.

He looked back at a picture on the wall. It was the same painting that put a sparkle in a young girl's eye as she stood before it, saying she wanted to study history.

The instant he turned back around and began walking deeper into the ruins, the ceiling and the wall around the door cracked. A red flash of light and savage gaseous energy came from the crack, headed for D. The time it took D to see this and make a conscious choice of how to avoid it would be the difference between life and death.

The impact swept D's feet out from under him and slammed him into the wall to his rear. Thick chunks of stone went flying, and the roar echoed through the hall.

Now a mountain of rubble lay in front of the entrance. It would be impossible to get into the rooms beyond without bringing in motorized equipment.

D was on the floor, his upper body resting against the base of the wall. The flap of his longcoat was caked white from the dust that rose from the impact. There was no way he could move. He had taken a blast of energy that destroyed hundreds of tons of rock in the walls and ceiling, and he had been smashed headfirst into a stone wall. Of course, an ordinary person would've been killed instantly by internal injuries alone.

To say the least, it was an unhappy coincidence that D happened to be passing through the place when the project to block the entrance the figure in gray had mentioned the night before was underway.

†

A lone traveler advanced on horseback through a forest road a few miles from the village. Bristles covered his rocklike chin, and the atrocious gaze he wore complimented his face perfectly. His look, and the rivet gun at his waist, gave clear testimony to the nature of this man. He was one of the outlaws that roamed the Frontier.

When there was even a little money to be made, this man would stoop to blackmail or extortion, and he had no qualms about murder, either. The skin beneath his thick, electrically heated coat was carved by countless wounds from bullets and blades, and his right earlobe was missing, though horrible traces remained where it had been ripped off. While he was strangling a young lady in some village way up north, she'd torn it off in her death throes.

These last few days, he'd been hard pressed to find either good grub or a woman. Chances were he was imagining the pleasures that awaited in the next village, because a vulgar smile surfaced on his filthy lips.

"What the—?"

Before he pulled back on the reins, the man found himself doubting his own eyes. Fifteen feet or so ahead, a young lady stepped out from behind some trees and onto the road. That was enticing enough. But her curvaceous figure burned into the man's retinas.

The girl was stark naked.

What's this . . . a Frontier whore? Pro or not, I can't figure why she'd be out running around like that . . . Maybe she's wacko?

Although his mind had plodded along that far, the crass thug's reason melted away in an instant, and his brain became occupied solely by deeds that might be done with the girl. Still, he waited a moment, scanning the surroundings with a caution he'd learned through his numerous bloody encounters.

No one around? If so, this honey's a nut job all right. I can have her every which way, and kill her when I'm done. Way out here I won't have to worry about anyone finding her till she's nothing but bones.

His plan, however, didn't prove quite so easy.

When the man dismounted with a disarming grin, the girl looked back over her shoulder and, giving him a seductive glance, dashed off into the forest. The curves of her backside drove him crazy—round and firm as a succulent fruit ready to explode, as only a young lady's could be. Hitching his horse to a nearby tree, he took off after her into the woods, into a world of darkness from which there would be no return.

He gave chase for perhaps all of five minutes, the breath rasping loudly from his nostrils.

Plunging through the same luxuriant foliage that had swallowed the naked form, the man suddenly jolted to a halt.

The girl was lying in the meadow right in front of him. His gaze was riveted to her breasts, turning up to remarkable rosy knobs, and her damply glistening thighs. The girl moaned and twisted her lower half. There was precious little chance he'd realize her intent was to show more of her ass than was really necessary. Her pale skin was strangely bloodless, and yet her lips alone were weirdly crimson, but the thug did not notice.

He fell on that white body like a black hunk of stone. Sucking and twisting her lips, he forced his tongue into her mouth. And the girl responded.

This is fantastic!

Raising his eyes in delight, he glimpsed the face of the girl.

She was laughing with the face of a devil.

As he tried to jump off, one frail arm held his body down, and the fingers of the other sank into his right hand as he made a grab for his rivet gun.

When the lips that curled back to reveal fangs closed on him, the man finally screamed. And long though it lasted, the deep woods drank it all.

†

When they were informed that Mr. Meyer was absent from school, Lina felt the eyes of the whole class boring into her. The village had learned of the incident the night before.

A monster of hitherto unknown type had broken into a farmhouse near the school, killing and eating a mother, child, and someone who was just passing by. To top it all off, one of the Vigilance Committee members who'd gone missing after he went to check the water level was found dead this morning under the bridge, and the confirmation that the body had been completely free of wounds caused quite a uproar.

That much might have been excusable, but when the mayor learned of this and headed straight for the barn, there was no sign of either D or the corpse of the monster there, just the woman sleeping as soundly as ever, but with a mark like a "t" on her forehead. Lina still wasn't sure if it had been drawn in blood or something else.

Of course the mayor was outraged, and he lambasted the Vigilance Committee for their negligence. On one hand he'd told them to ascertain D's current whereabouts, but he'd also admonished them to keep this information secret. But it was a very small village. By the time Lina and the others headed off to school, a sketchy version of the events had made the rounds to almost every home in the area. The fact that Mr. Meyer was the one who had apparently been carried off by the monster was probably leaked by one of the Committee members who had visited the teacher's house the night before.

Even though the secondary school instructor who came to inform them of their teacher's absence pretended the absence was due to a cold, there was no chance of that shaking the dark conviction that flowed between the students.

Oh, not again. I hate this, thought Lina, sighing with grief.

School wasn't always a warm, nurturing place, partly because of the incident that occurred a decade earlier. Abducted by the Nobility, the children had returned after some horrible things had been done to them; in a Frontier village, that alone was sufficient cause for exile. The humiliation of the examination Lina underwent over the next few weeks opened dark wounds on her soul that still lurked, somewhere, even now. The strain had killed both her parents in rapid succession, and, even after the mayor adopted her, she hadn't been allowed to go near the other children for another two years. During that time, no matter where she went or what she did, the gleaming, probing gaze of the mayor or Vigilance Committee was locked on her every move.

They all know what's going on between the mayor and me, I bet.

Lina wanted to blubber like a baby.

Most likely they didn't know how he had forced himself on her on her seventeenth birthday, but knowledge of their immoral relationship had spread throughout the entire village.

Some rather iniquitous relationships were commonly permitted in Frontier communities. Villages that could be cut off from the outside world by rain or snow needed a guaranteed labor force—that was their greatest concern. If it weren't purely in the pursuit of pleasure, then any relations—be it between a man and someone else's wife, a mother and her own son, or a father and his daughter—could be termed valuable insofar as it might sow the seeds of new life.

In this era, mental defects and other problems traditionally caused by inbreeding no longer existed. For some reason, the Nobility had chosen to share the fruit of their genetic engineering expertise with the human race. Hereditary diseases were a thing of the past. Even the names of the diseases were no longer remembered by humanity.

No doubt it was the shadow from ten years earlier that made Lina's spirit sink like lead.

Cuore had never recovered from his dementia, and that fact alone was enough to terrify the villagers. And then, at the opposite extreme, examinations had determined that both Lina's and Mr. Meyer's intelligence had risen to a startling degree. That was the reason the mayor had adopted Lina; it was also the reason why all her classmates abhorred her relationship with him.

A woman made clever at the hands of the Nobility.

And yet, Lina wasn't openly teased or shunned, thanks to the brightness of her disposition, her splendid bearing, and the efforts of Mr. Meyer, who'd endured the cold shoulder from the villagers and did an excellent job of passing the circuit committee's test to become a teacher. It was impossible to say how much strength Lina drew from seeing him—a weakling and a crybaby in their childhood—standing up to the bullies and protecting her now.

Even Cuore, who started aimlessly wandering about the village after his parents' premature death, had saved Lina from harm. His decline in intelligence had done nothing to change his innately courteous and gentle character. Lina could still clearly remember how reliably his hulking form had shielded her from the stones other children had thrown.

And now she no longer had either of them to protect her. Although Cuore was in Fern's care, Mr. Meyer's disappearance was more than sufficient to earn Lina the evil, suspicious glances of the whole class.

"Well, Lina, we finally know the real reason you were chosen to go to the Capital," her worst enemy, Viska, said, loudly enough for everyone to hear. "I don't know what went on up in that castle, but you didn't have to keep all the rest of us living in terror for the past ten years. As soon as you're gone, things should be pretty peaceful around here again."

"Yeah, but there'll be hell in the Capital!" a member of Viska's clique said sarcastically, laughing shrilly.

Oh, that does it. I might have to smack someone now, Lina thought, about to arm herself with one of her leather slippers. But she restrained herself because she knew the remarks reflected what everyone in the class felt. The others just didn't say anything because they still counted her as one of their own.

That being said, it was undeniable that the whole class had become exceedingly distant since it had been decided Lina would go to the Capital. When one considers the import of getting to leave the Frontier, there were those who would never understand why the person representing the village was someone with a connection to the Nobility.

Well, let 'em say what they will.

Just as Viska was about to say something else to Lina, who was now in a fresh and easier state of mind, the substitute teacher from the secondary school came in and the morning's tribulations were at an end.

Advancing vapidly through math and physics, the school day was just about to enter third period when an unexpected siren resounded.

"Hey, what's that all about?"

"Three successive blasts—it means to assemble in the square!"

"Maybe they captured a Noble alive?"

"Don't be stupid!"

"Quiet," the teacher ordered. "I have to go out. Your class representative will have to accompany me. The rest of you will have a free study period." But he knew the students had ignored him.

When he'd gone, and taken Callis, the class rep, with him, everyone else busily prepared to leave—this was just what they'd been waiting for. There were some who rattled around in the lockers full of weapons kept in case monsters attacked, and others who raced to get their lunch boxes to bring home; in no time, the sound of the activity grew to quite an uproar, and a second later the students had all vanished, leaving the windows and doors still shaking.

Seeing how even the eyes of Marco, the shyest boy in class, gleamed with anticipation, Lina wanted to laugh. On the diversion-starved Frontier, children were more inclined to be excited rather than frightened when fearsome beasts ran amuck, so long as they didn't directly harm the village. Aside from the giant behemoth or roc or other colossal monsters of legend, arrangements had been made to defend against most everyday creatures.

Plenty of adults were bustling down the street, but they said nothing when they saw Lina with her schoolmates.

The square was just about in the center of the village. Even if every one of the village's nearly one thousand inhabitants were to assemble there, from 120-year-old Gramps Shakra down to the baby born some four months earlier, the square still boasted more than enough space to accommodate them all. Whether it was a festival or an exhibition of merchandise by traveling vendors, this was just the place for large-scale events of any kind.

When the students arrived with mud flying from their feet, some sort of bizarre show was just about to begin up on the wooden stage that'd been dragged into the square.

There, beside Vigilance Committee leader Fern and his haughtily puffed chest, was a type-three electrified cage—an iron enclosure that could contain supernatural beasts or savage, human-sized birds with high-voltage current. This in and of itself was not in the least bit unusual, but on seeing the prey it contained, the eyes of one and all went wide.

It was a human. However, what plunged every last one of them into the deepest depths of horror wasn't the threatening physique or countenance of this apparent outlaw, but the pair of fangs jutting from his greasy lips.

A vampire that walked by day.

Is this their leader? This thought screamed in the minds of all of them. The rain had abated near dawn, and the gray clouds that had masked the sky had finally broken. Waves of tranquil light tinted everything a pearly hue, but this square alone was congested with dark, night-evoking fear. Jostling through the elders who were settled before the stage, the mayor climbed a set of folding stairs to stand by Fern's side. He made a great show of ignoring the man in the cage gazing out at him with malicious eyes.

"Good people of Tepes . . . " he started to say in a voice much louder than necessary, then paused as he took up the wireless mike he'd just noticed on the floor. Not a snicker escaped from his listeners. Whether it was a Noble or one of their victims, they were looking at a nightmare creature that couldn't possibly exist—a vampire that could act without restraint in the sunlight. The gravity of the situation deeply shook them all.

"Good people of Tepes . . . " the voice of the mayor finally echoed to their stupefied ears through the ultracompact speakers set about the square. "As you know, in our recent trouble with the Nobility four from our village have died, and I've burdened our meager finances by hiring not one but two Vampire Hunters. But in the end, that was for naught—happily, it seems they are no longer needed. To be more precise, early this morning Fern here caught this thing on the northern road. The leader of our very own Vigilance Committee has good reason to brag—taking a vampire alive is something few out on the Frontier have done."

Seemingly frozen by the sight of this vampire scanning his surroundings with blood-soaked eyes, the villagers were finally returned to their senses by the mayor's somewhat coercive compliments. The audience mustered a smattering of applause. Of course, none of them could see the sardonic humor in the situation.

Fern took the mike in turn and told how, when the search perimeter had extended beyond the village, he'd run into a man in the woods who attacked him before he could say a word. With the help of his guard beasts he'd managed to take the attacker alive.

Everyone knew far too well the power of guard beasts, but still those creatures wouldn't do much good against a Noble, or even against one of their victims. Yet those normally inclined to doubt had proof positive right before their eyes; as the leader of the Vigilance Committee finished his war story, a tumultuous applause broke out.

"That's great, Lina. Now you're in the clear."

Turning toward the encouraging voice, Lina was taken aback. The class rep Callis was smiling at her. A born leader and first-rate organizer, he was clear-headed and quite handsome. But Lina despised the coolness that lurked like a shadow behind his bright, smiling face, and she'd rarely spoken with him. For his part, he was used to the other girls in the village making a big fuss over him, which made approaching Lina a waste of time.

"What do you mean? Were you worried for me?"

"Of course. After all, we're classmates, aren't we?"

At his honeyed words, Lina retched in the cockles of her heart. *How stupid can this jerk be? Here he comes, sidling up a little bit closer.*

"Hey, the mayor's getting ready to slather another address on us," Lina said, as she pinched the palm that'd stealthily been placed on her hand.

"It's almost certain the fiend in this very cage is the cause of all our recent troubles. That being the case, I propose we slaughter it now and pray that this offering will give us peace. What do you say to that?"

By this point, convinced that the true source of their terror had been captured, the villagers put their hands together as one, and the square was buried in vocal approval. In Frontier villages, it was not uncommon for animals to be sacrificed when praying for a bountiful harvest or safety in the coming year.

"That's horrible!" Without noticing the meaning of the words that spilled from her own lips, Lina felt her heart stop when Callis' shocked expression turned toward her. It was the first time she was ever aware of feeling that way.

Do I pity a vampire?!

Suddenly, purple sparks flew from the iron bars of the cage, and the man within shrank back with a scream.

"Okay, Fern, finish him off."

With a bow to the triumphantly nodding mayor, Fern stepped forward. The long wooden stakes he held in either hand were more like spears. The other members of the Vigilance Committee moved in and surrounded the stage.

The vampire in the cage seemed frightened and backed away, only to receive a massive electric shock. Discerning unrest and fear in that atrocious face, the people loosed mocking laughter and catcalls.

"You like that? Go on, try and run away again!"

"Ha ha, I think it's gonna start bawling. Some Noble you are!"

"Fern, don't kill 'im with one shot. Do it slow, real slow!"

As if to acknowledge the cheering, the Vigilance Committee leader waved to the crowd. Intoxicated with pleasure by this murderous show, the villagers couldn't see that his lips were redder than normal and that something eerie lingered in his smile. Nobody questioned his assertion that this vampire was indeed a Noble, and that the vampire was the cause for the village's woes.

The spear lunged forward.

The vampire twisted out of the way. Sparks leapt from his right hand, and his exposed back was pierced by a quick thrust of the tip into his right shoulder.

Cheers rocked the square.

With a faint smile rising on his lips, Fern poised his spear again.

Lina pushed forward from the very back of the crowd.

Sending mud flying everywhere, she shouted, "Stop!" Shoving people out of the way as she ran, she finally got to the stage.

"What the hell you think you're doing, Lina? Keep out of this!"

The girl didn't flinch at the mayor's words. Beautiful face and softly curved body trembling with rage, she opposed everything that was happening here.

"You're the one who should keep out of this, mister Mayor. I can't believe you'd do something so cruel. You're dealing with a human being."

"It's not 'mister Mayor,'" the old man bellowed. His gray hair fluttered more from anger than from the wind. "I'm your father. Why can't you call me that? Keep out of this, you little idiot! I'll whip the tar out of you later!"

"I said no, and I mean no," Lina replied, and mentally she tossed her head in defiance. *I couldn't even stand by and watch an animal slaughtered now. Why have these feelings come over me?* As if to push those thoughts back into their hiding place, she said, "Don't you think this is awful? If you were human, you'd be ashamed of yourself for torturing an unarmed person to death, and one locked in a cage no less!"

Restraining the mayor, who was about to explode with rage, Fern leaned down off the stage. Thrusting the bloodied point of the spear right under Lina's nose, he said, "Oh, I see. Then what you're saying is, it'd be better if we gave it a weapon before we do it, right? Fine by me. Why don't we let you do the honors, little chatterbox? You've had some training with swords and spears, haven't you?"

On the Frontier, where life and death existed side by side, it was customary for women to learn how to use weapons. Although it wasn't necessary to master gunpowder firearms, crossbows, and laser guns like it was for men, all of them could wield a short spear, a lighter version of a longsword, or a whip.

When the head of the spear was thrust before her, Lina grabbed it without hesitation. The wrath she felt toward the mayor and Fern and the villagers—for the entire human race for that matter—wouldn't allow this girl of seventeen to be cowed.

The mayor went pale, and a clamor ran through the inhabitants of the village.

At that moment . . .

A beautiful, rusted voice raced across the ground, leaving the wind twisting in its wake. "That's my job."

†

E very face—even that of the vampire in the cage, who seemed to forget the pain of his wounds—turned to the young man in black astride his horse. Each face took on an expression of wonder. With the sunlight spilling through gaps in the clouds for his backdrop, this youth of a beauty rarely seen in the world glared down at them from his mount.

The instant they set eyes on his beauty, the men burned with envy, and the women became slaves of desire. However, in the next instant, those higher emotions were effortlessly blown away, and an ineffable terror took hold of the dark recesses of their psyches. It was a terror instilled by the unearthly aura of the Nobility.

The crowd parted, and D arrived at the stage without meeting so much as a second's delay.

Easily taking the spear from Fern and Lina, who'd both retained a steady grip on it, he asked, "So, what do we do?"

"Oh," Fern responded, his bonds of paralysis finally melted by D's voice. "I don't know where the hell you've been up till now, but it sure is nice to see that at least you didn't run off with your tail between your legs. This is just perfect. No matter how you slice it, you were gonna be out of a job anyway. If you're a Hunter, then act like one and give us a show before you're on your way. Right, Mayor?"

The mayor hemmed and hawed. D's steadfast gaze bored through him. The pressure Fern put on him couldn't begin to compare to the unearthly aura radiating from that youth.

"It, err . . . Well, it was me that called him here . . . And his work's not quite finished yet . . . "

"That's right."

The next instant, D leapt easily from the saddle and onto the stage. He exhibited remarkable recuperative powers for someone who'd met with an intense explosion mere hours earlier, but his stamina was probably due, at least in part, to the thing that lived in his left hand.

Seemingly heedless of Lina's infatuated gaze, he went over by Fern and clicked off the power for the electrified cage, having already removed the electronic lock.

"Hold it," came the cry from what sounded like the sheriff, but, seeing the door to the cage swing open smoothly, the hitherto paralyzed crowd gave a scream and retreated.

The loud thud reverberating behind D was the sound of the fleeing mayor tumbling down the stairs.

D tossed the rough wooden spear to the vampire sluggishly slipping out of the cage.

"It's strange meeting like this, but this is our destiny, hunter and hunted. Come on." As he said this, he didn't reach for the longsword over his shoulder.

The vampire started to move slowly to the right. Unable to use his right hand, he held the spear with a single finger of his left, his whole body boiling with flames of murderous rage.

Without a single telltale movement, the spear became a streaking blur in flight. Seeing it pierce D's chest, which was exactly where it had been aimed, Lina had the breath knocked out of her. The vampire leapt at Fern, grabbing the rivet gun at his waist. The muzzle, as thick as a man's thumb, pointed skyward with a speed that escaped the naked eye.

D was in midair. What Lina had witnessed was an afterimage left when he flew up with superspeed.

Along with a roar, high-energy gunpowder sent a stream of iron tacks racing at D's heart.

With one of the most glorious sounds in the world, the iron tacks were deflected.

Before he even realized they'd been parried by the drawn longsword, the vampire's gun-wielding hand was chopped off at the wrist by the naked steel slashing down from above. A backward thrust of the blade penetrated the deepest reaches of his heart.

Not sparing so much as a glance at the massive form as it fell in a bloody mist, D started to walk toward where Fern had frozen in his tracks.

Noticing that it was his left hand that held the bloody blade now pointed at Fern's throat, Lina knit her brow. The girl didn't understand that because of his opponent's injured right shoulder, D had fought with only his left hand.

"You got what you wanted. Next time, you'll be the one doing what I say."

His voice was low, but would brook no resistance. Fern's pale face bobbed negligibly up and down. D thrust his left hand right in front of it.

Seeing the red cross limned in the middle of that powerful palm, Fern's eyes shot wide open. For a few seconds, a wind pregnant with bloodlust cut across the square.

D's hand came down, and Fern let out a sigh of relief. There was nothing, it seemed, out of the ordinary.

The crowd stirred again.

"So, what are you going to do?" D called down from the stage to the mayor, cleaning the blood from his longsword with one shake and gracefully returning it to its sheath. He must have meant what were they going to do about him.

Pale faced and still holding down the lump on his forehead, the mayor said, "I know what I said a moment ago . . . But, well, I believe we've pretty much accomplished what we set out to do. Needless to say, you'll be paid the amount we agreed on. Good work."

"Fine," said D, nodding impassively. "But I can't leave the village just yet."

"What?!"

"There's something I still have to look into. Or is there some reason you'd want me gone?"

This time it was the sheriff's turn to shudder as that gorgeous countenance turned his way. "At the moment . . . no," he said with great difficulty. "But if your being here causes us any inconvenience whatsoever, we'll have to run you out of town."

"Agreed. I'll tell you one thing—if this man was responsible for your difficulties, then the female victim we have should be regaining consciousness right about now. We should check on that."

When the mayor and his group arrived at the barn, however, the woman they'd left there had a rough wooden stake hammered deep into her breast, and the dirt floor practically seemed to drink the lifeblood dribbling from the sleeves of her formerly white clothing, now soaked with red.

"Who could've done such a thing?" the mayor moaned, looking to the heavens.

"Don't know who it was, but someone in the village must've gone off half-cocked. I don't care if having her around gave people the creeps, there was no need to put her down like this." Saying this, Fern turned his eyes up at D. "How do we know it wasn't you? If that other guy wasn't behind all this, you still stand to make some more money . . . "

Fern's tough talk vanished in the back of his throat. Shifting his gaze from Fern back to the depths of the barn, D moved away from the group and started to put a saddle and saddlebags over his shoulder.

"Hey, wait. Where do you think you're going?" the mayor asked, running over to him in a fluster.

"You're a suspect in this murder. We can't just let you leave town whenever you please. After all, you were here with the woman until this morning." There was a tone of fretfulness in the sheriff's voice.

Silently, D pointed in a certain direction.

The mayor and sheriff followed his finger with their eyes, then turned back to him. "So that's where you're headed?" said the lawman. "The abandoned waterwheel mill out there on the edge of the village?"

"If you want me, that's where I'll be. I'll be back later for my pay."

The men just watched in a daze as D galloped off.

When Lina's classes had finished and she was getting into her wagon, Callis was waiting near the gate to the schoolyard. This was a rare occurrence, perhaps even a first.

When she rode past oblivious to him, he ran after her in a state.

"Please, wait up, Lina. I thought maybe we could go home together."

"What's gotten into you? You suddenly feel all friendly toward me? Tina and Miria and all the rest of your little friends will be none too happy with you."

"Spare me. They just have this one-sided thing for me!"

Presumptuous as it was, he got his foot up on the step of the wagon, and, after quickly taking a seat, this optimistic Romeo even went so far as to try to take the reins. Lina slapped his hand and made a disapproving face. "Don't try anything funny. Why don't you just climb back down."

"Oh, you're a cold one. I was waiting because I wanted to talk to you. Say, wanna go into the woods?"

"And what, pray tell, would we do in the woods? Earlier, you grabbed my hand in front of everybody. I can't imagine what you'd try if you were alone with me. If you so much as lay a finger on me, I'll knock you flat."

Facing him squarely to lay down the law, Lina swallowed her words. Something resting in Callis' breast pocket glittered in her eye.

A single white blossom.

The one at my window this morning . . . It couldn't be.

"Oh, this? I picked it just for you. Here." The sharp-eyed playboy had read Lina's reaction like a book and made his opening move.

She didn't say a word.

This courageous girl was too kind to call him a liar. The flower passed into her pale hand.

"We'll do the woods some other time," Callis said, nearly in a whisper.

A dozen minutes later, as the boy watched the wagon disappear through the gate to the mayor's home there arose in his eyes a look of cunning and self-confidence not at all appropriate for his age.

†

The wrath of the mayor awaited Lina at home.

As soon as she'd closed the door to her room, it was thrown open again. Lina's cheek rang with a slap as she whirled around, and the girl fell to the floor.

"What do you think you're doing? That hurts, you know." Knowing what she'd expected had come, she still put up some spirited resistance.

The mayor was furious. "You . . . you stupid little girl. Embarrassing me like that in front of everybody. Standing up for a Noble . . . a damn vampire. You little . . . "

Lina stuck her red tongue out at the old man as his ugly face congested with rage.

"Nobility or not, what's wrong with trying to stop someone alone in a cage from being killed like a wild beast? Did you have some kind of proof he was even a Noble? He was probably just a plain old victim. If so, he wasn't that way because he wanted to be. If the Nobility made me one of their kind, I sure as hell wouldn't want to go out that way. And since I wouldn't want it done to me, I couldn't let you do it to anyone else. You gonna lock me in a cage and have Fern stab me to death, too?"

The mayor's eyes were bulging in fury. Though his Adam's apple was moving, no words came out.

However, even though she'd gotten off her little rant, Lina questioned her own position. *Really, what's wrong with locking a Noble in a cage and torturing them to death?*

Before Lina was born, a group of Nobles had assailed the village and claimed nearly twenty victims before they were done. The tragic tableau ended with fathers driving stakes through their daughters' hearts, or husbands through their wives'. What the children later heard was a tale of tragedy between loved ones told with tears of blood, and they learned a deep hatred for the Nobility. In the hearts of these people, the Nobility were vicious beasts to be slaughtered—a feeling that the severe Frontier life helped foster. If by chance one were to be taken alive, anyone would think it perfectly natural that it would face the same fate as the vampire in the cage.

"You bitch, you. So you side with the Nobility, eh? You lousy little ingrate. You won't get away with this. Hell, no!" The mayor had the look of a madman.

"What makes me an ingrate?" Lina shot back. "The whole reason you adopted me was because you knew what kind of mind I had and wanted to send me off to the Capital, wasn't it? You were looking forward to the reward the village would get. And that's not all. You had your way with me when I didn't know anything. Who is it that comes sneaking into my room every night even now?! Even the Nobility don't act like such filthy beasts. Even your touch makes my skin crawl."

Silence descended. Lina watched somewhat unnerved as the mayor's face swiftly paled.

"Is that so? Can't even stand my touch? Good enough. I'll touch you with this then!"

A black whip glistened in the mayor's right hand. Threads of drool hung from the corners of his mouth, and his eyes were laughing. The change was extraordinary, as if some darkness lurking within him had suddenly gushed to the surface.

Before Lina could turn and make a break for the window, the mayor's hand caught the collar of her shirt, tearing it open with a loud rip.

"Stop it. Have you lost your mind, you old fool?!"

A sharp crack turned her angry protests into screams. Lina fell, and in seconds, black and blue welts were rising on her back, their number growing with each snap.

Pushing the howls that had risen to the top of her throat back down with all her might, Lina endured the beating. She'd decided she didn't want to let the likes of this man get the better of her.

She tried to think about the white flower. Her expression became calm.

The mayor discarded his whip and climbed on her from behind. His dark red tongue licked at her wounded flesh.

"Quit it," Lina protested, writhing.

"Not a chance," said the mayor, getting her struggling hands out of the way while he kneaded her shapely breasts. "Does it hurt? I bet it does. But I'll make it better now. I'll make you feel good all over with this tongue of mine."

A clammy, lukewarm sensation crept over the nape of her neck, and Lina's whole body squirmed wildly. The mayor continued speaking, even as he took pleasure from the young body struggling in his arms. His voice was like coagulated obsession.

"I could keep at this and screw you to death now if I wanted to. Getting you run out of town would be child's play, too. But I can't do that. After all, you're going to the Capital for the sake of our little village. Mr. Meyer's vanished, and Fern's taken custody of Cuore. No doubt he'll spend the rest of his days as no more than a dim-witted errand boy. But you're special. I can't get rid of you. On the other hand, I can't let you get away, either. And I'm gonna keep having my fun with you till the day you have to leave town."

The mayor's mouth clamped onto the nape of Lina's neck. A forbidden act. Unable to stand it, Lina let out a scream. Because kiss marks on the nape of the neck were far too reminiscent of the marks left by the Nobility, it was taboo for even married couples to do this. The cruelty in the heart of this old man rivaled that of the very Nobility.

"No, don't, stop! Please . . . D!" she screamed with all her might.

The old man's lips pulled away from her. With evident bitterness he said, "Oh. So that's how it is, eh? That punk's caught your eye? Well, he's not around. I sacked him. Right about now he's setting up house all by his lonesome in the old mill. That's the perfect place for a drifter with the blood of the Nobility."

When Lina's head sank forward, the old man tried to push the girl down on the floor, and, for an instant, the strength went out of his arms. She swung her head right back up, smashing into the old man's nose with a terrific whack.

He fell over, squealing. Vivid blood gushed from between his cupped fingers. "Bitch! Now you've gone and done it!"

Lina grabbed the vase off the table and smashed it over the mayor's head as he attempted to rise. Fashioned from the ribs of a fire dragon, the container was light, but it had sharp protrusions jutting from all sides. Quite a few fragments lodged in his head, and the old man's face was stained with blood. Giving a cry, he collapsed again.

Lina's blood boiled. Now their situations were reversed. And, to Lina, it was a pleasant change. She pulled back her foot to kick him where it counts, but, true to form, she thought better of it and stopped.

As she gave the door an energetic slam, her litany of curses carried right through it. "Screw you. I won't be coming back here any time soon. I hope your head wounds get infected and you die."

†

Lina headed off to the mill in her wagon. The past few days these streets had seen little pedestrian traffic, but apparently everyone felt safer since that vampire had been killed, and a number of faces now watched with astonishment as the wagon raced by.

She was there in about twenty minutes, but, taking measure of the old, dilapidated mill, she saw and heard nothing but the squeal of the waterwheel and the bass growls of its hydroelectric motor. D's things weren't even there.

Maybe he'd already left town?

Anxiety quickly withered Lina's spirit. A chill that she hadn't felt in the least when she left her house now seeped into her through her pores. Looking up, she saw the sky was still dark.

The world was rife with fear.

Lina left the shack.

The wind whistled over her head. Though the wind should have borne some foreshadowing of spring, it was colder than she ever could have imagined. It invaded her leather coat through the collar and sleeves, stabbing at her exposed back.

"Damn. Of all the lousy luck. Wonder if I should go back home? But then, I don't much fancy another beating. What to do, what to do . . . "

Deciding to wander around a bit while she mulled it over, Lina went back to the wagon and took a sliver gun out of the storage compartment for self-protection before setting off on foot down the path.

It seemed that even Lina was comforted by the death of the vampire this afternoon. She was as yet unaware that the female victim had been killed, so the possibility that the vampire in the cage had been guilty still had a strong base to work from.

When she'd gone so far the outline of the mill was no longer visible, the wind called her name.

She turned, but could sense no one around her.

The new grass fluttered in the wind.

Tightening her grip on her weapon, she started walking again. Before she'd gone ten steps, she heard it.

Lina.

This time there was absolutely no mistaking the sound.

"Who is it, and where are you?" she turned around and shouted, and the wind responded.

Lina, Lina, Lina.

"Come on, where are you already? Seriously, I'll shoot." Heedless of the contradiction in that, the girl was overtaken by fear.

Awaken, Lina, the wind said.

It was a voice she'd heard before. Lina sifted through her memories intently.

Still don't understand, do you, Lina? Awaken. You must awaken.

The voice danced all around her. It laughed beneath her feet, whispered at her ear, bellowed above her head. *Lina, Lina, Lina.*

"You're starting to piss me off, mystery pest!"

When she raised the sliver gun, still lacking a target, a particularly powerful gust of wind smacked her between the eyes. Her balance was gone in a flash. The hand she was certain she'd set on the embankment beside her swept right through the air without meeting the slightest resistance. Lina fell headfirst to the bottom of a benighted pit. Judging from the impact, the drop couldn't have been that great.

Looking back the way she'd fallen, she saw a circular opening about seven feet above her. The soil banked up toward it, forming an incline. Surmising that she'd be able to climb out somehow or other, Lina gave a sign of relief.

Lina, the voice cried out. Without a doubt it was a man's voice, and this time it was very close.

Fixing her gaze before her, Lina was enveloped by surprise.

Ahead of her lay an unsettlingly spacious area—a subterranean chamber. The depths were shrouded in darkness, but in the light stabbing down through the hole above her she could see it was quite vast.

On the boundary between darkness and light stood a gray figure—the source of the voice.

"Damn, that hurt . . . " Starting to rise, Lina pressed her hand to her hip. Desperately garbing herself in an air of calmness, she wrung the words from her throat. "You're that character from the night before last. I just knew the guy they caught this morning was someone else. So, is it supposed to be my turn now? If you come near me, I'll shoot!"

She aimed the sliver gun at him, but the shadowy figure didn't seem in the least bit perturbed. In a leaden, low voice he asked, "Don't you understand? Seeing this place, don't you recall anything?"

"What is with you?! You just keep saying the same damn things over and over," Lina said angrily. "This is the first time I've ever fallen into this blasted hole. No reason why I should remember anything. So stop your yammering and reach for the sky. I'll shoot!"

The figure raised one arm. Just as she was admiring this docile display, he swung it in a wide arc.

"Take a good look. At this place. At this *lab*. Remember. Remember what happened ten years ago."

Finally Lina noticed that the scene before her was the interior of some sort of room. It was apparent at a glance that destruction had ravaged this place, leaving a mountain of rubble on the stone-paved floor, but the toppled tables and the shapes of what seemed to be colossal machines looming motionless in the depths of the darkness testified that the gray man spoke the truth.

However, there was something strange about the scene.

Although the place where Lina stood was a dirt floor in a hole in the ground, the boundary between that and the room was terribly indistinct.

The room looked so close she could reach out and touch it, but it was in fact preposterously far away—at least that was the impression she got.

However, it was something else entirely that shocked Lina now. The shadowy gray figure whose face D's computer had revealed—someone she was sure she had never seen before—knew about what'd happened a decade earlier!

"Don't you remember, Lina? Very well then, how about this?" Disregarding Lina's astonishment, the shadow made a sweep of his hand.

Ripples ran through the depths of the darkness, eerie things defying any attempt at metaphor.

"Well, Lina, how's that?"

"I . . . I don't know. What are these things? Keep . . . keep away from me . . . " Her voice cut out. As if a white scalpel had sliced open her brain, fragmented memories blazed to life.

That's right, this is where . . . And where they . . .

The vision faded away abruptly.

"I don't understand. Don't come near me!" Anxiety and relief hung in her cries, and her finger worked of its own volition.

Fired off with a sigh-like snap unique to highly pressurized gas, a tiny tungsten needle pierced the heart of the shadowy figure. The figure smiled silently.

The eerie things continued forward.

Lina's pupils opened wide, like one who has peered into the abyss at things no one was meant to see.

They—the eerie things approaching—had called her name. *Lina*, they said.

There was a flash. And another. Light knifed in through the incisions in her clouded mind. *All these people are . . .*

Suddenly, the shadowy figure looked upward.

The *things* raised a commotion. And yet, she couldn't hear their voices.

A problem has cropped up. We'll meet again, Lina, the dwindling shadow said.

A fear completely different from what she felt before now assailed Lina. Dropping the sliver gun, she started to scale the incline without so much as a backward glance. She had the feeling that as soon as her hands reached the lip of the hole some seven feet away the vision would vanish.

The forest awaited her.

What Lina crawled out of was a small hole in the ground just over a foot and a half in diameter. The grass grew thick and wild around it, and even the most concentrated gaze would be hard pressed to discover the opening.

Lina swiftly brushed the dirt off herself.

Taking a deep breath, she set off back down the road. After she'd walked forty or fifty yards, she heard the echo of hoofbeats closing on her from the rear.

Was *this* the problem the gray man had been talking about? If so, that shadowy figure must have been able to discern this sound several hundred yards away, and through the ground no less.

Having stepped to the side of the road, when Lina turned around her face was quickly suffused with joy.

"D!"

Unsettlingly beautiful, he gazed down at Lina from his horse. "What are you doing? What brings you out here?"

Lina paused for a moment, then made a quick answer. "Well . . . actually, I was out looking for you. Would you be so good as to put me up this evening?"

An inquiring glance from D.

Lina told him she'd left after a falling out with the mayor. Without asking the reason or any of the petty details, D silently offered his hand, then pulled her up on the back of his mount. Before the horse had taken a step, she stammered, "Er . . . umm . . . "

"What is it?"

"Is it okay if I put my arms around your waist?"

"You'd fall off if you didn't, wouldn't you?"

"Yep." Her cheek pressed against his back. Hard and wide, the firmness of the skin beneath came right through his coat. She'd heard that the bodies of dhampirs were much colder than those of humans, but that didn't seem to be the case with D. He was warm.

Before she knew it, tears spread across her cheeks.

"Are you crying?" D asked. He inquired in the same way one might ask for directions on the street.

"So what if I am? Everyone gets the blues from time to time. Don't keep badgering me about it."

Lina didn't know that it bordered on miraculous when this youth asked anyone anything about themselves.

D fell silent.

"Say, D . . . the ruins are off the way you were coming. Were you up there again?"

"That's right. Looking for another entrance."

"Another one? What about the usual one?"

"It's been sealed. No one can get in that way now." Giving a little shake of his head, he said, "You can forget about all that stuff. Shouldn't you be studying or something?"

"Killjoy," Lina replied, butting D's shoulder with her head. "With a brain like mine, it's not like I need to do any more studying at this late date."

"Oh, that's right. You're the girl genius."

"That's me all right."

The horse arrived at the mill, and the pair crossed a bridge over the fairly swollen brook before going into the shack. Perhaps due to the evening almost upon them, the wind bore a chill, but it was a far cry from the harshness of the white season.

As Lina watched him from behind with a mystified expression, D asked the girl, "Is it so strange that I crossed running water?"

"Er . . . yeah. After all, you're a dhampir, right? Oh, I probably shouldn't have mentioned that."

"To be sure, water poses a problem for me. Nobles have been known to drown in water less than waist deep."

"I wonder why that is? The biology of the Nobility is so mysterious." Her questions seemed completely at odds with her innocent voice and naive countenance. For some reason, Lina had an intense curiosity about the Nobility.

Giving no answer, D went to the corner of the dusty shack and set down the saddle and bags he'd brought from the horse, then pulled out a blackish palm-sized package. With a tug on the protruding cord, the package rapidly expanded into a very comfortable-looking sleeping bag.

"You'd better sleep in this. It has a built-in heater. You should get through the night without catching a cold."

"But what about you?"

"I'll be resting outside. Being down against the earth suits my nature more. Don't give it another thought . . . I've never even used that before."

"But . . . " She was about to say more, but she noticed D concentrating his senses on something outside.

"It seems they've come for you," the Hunter said.

"No way. I refuse to go back there."

Before long, nearly a dozen men on horseback had arrived at the far side of the brook. Both the mayor and the sheriff were there, and the rest were members of the Vigilance Committee led by Fern. Each and every one wore a strangely stiff expression. What they had to do—and the thought of who might stand in their way—made them look tense. Their opposition was standing in front of the shack.

The blue glint of the pendant on his chest made the men uneasy. Perhaps the horses sensed something, too, for there was no end to their whinnying. Atop their mounts, the men shook ever so slightly.

"State your business," D said softly. His was a tone well suited to the tranquil afternoon light, but the horses halted at once. Did their riders realize they were frozen with fear?

"As if you didn't know already," sneered the mayor, who now sported a black hat, and he jabbed out one arm to point to one of the shack's windows. "We're here to take Lina home. No use trying to hide her. If you don't hand her right over, we'll make you wish you had."

"It doesn't matter to me either way, but I don't know what she'll have to say about it."

Suddenly the wooden shutters of the window swung open, and Lina poked her head out. Well prepared, she had her tongue sticking out already.

"Screw you. Who'd be stupid enough to go back there? I'll be staying here a while. I'm practicing up on surviving in the wilderness. Kindly keep out of the way, Daddy. Oh, did you know your face looks kind of swollen?"

The special spitefulness she saved for the last bit was delicious. The distended purple face of the mayor donned a look five times more crimson than his wounds. With a glance to his side, he said, "What the hell are you doing, Sheriff? What we got here is a case of a father trying to get his daughter back. We'll take her back by force if necessary, right?"

"Well . . . " the sheriff began hesitantly. The rest of the men looked the other way. Every one of them had witnessed D's swordplay in the village square. "Well, if she says she doesn't want to go, there's nothing we can do. And I believe your parental authority over Lina ran out the year before last, to boot."

Parental authority expired—in other words, an individual became responsible for his or her own actions at the age of fifteen in most communities on the Frontier. Their environment demanded independence.

"Oh, you worthless sack of dung. You'd just stand by and let this half-breed drifter ruin my daughter? Your ass is fired. When we get back to town, the first thing I'm going to do is convene a council meeting."

The sheriff shrugged.

"Okay, now will somebody . . . "

"Leave it to me," Fern said to the mayor, his voice brimming with self-confidence as he leisurely dismounted.

Resting both hands on the baskets on his hips, he had a steady stride as he headed over to square off with D.

"Knew it'd come down to this sooner or later." He sounded like his position was well covered. "It's too late, so don't even think about saying we can have her now."

D didn't make a move. He had the air of a young poet listening to the song of the wind.

It seemed as if even the voice of the brook had been silenced.

"Watch yourself, D. He's got guard beasts in those baskets." Lina's words injected tension into a situation that wasted no time in exploding.

Pale flashes shot from D's right hand, and the baskets still attached to Fern's waist fell to pieces. Two creatures fell to the ground—a weird spider and a lightning-discharging cloud. As the legs of the spider were free from injury, either it'd regenerated already or this was a new beast.

Fern egged them on with eerie syllables.

A jolt of purple shot through the spot where D had stood, spraying the wall of the shack with sparks; the needles launched by the airborne D stopped halfway between him and the monsters. The instant he realized billowing white threads were twisting around him, D mowed through the wind with the longsword in his right hand.

"Oh," Fern exclaimed. He'd just watched the adhesive liquid that'd held not only behemoths but the figure in gray cut to shreds like so much cotton thread.

However, D's body veered appreciably as he tried to leap the brook in a single bound. In the next instant, he landed waist-deep in the current with a splash.

Who, if anyone, had actually seen the tentacle that'd shot from the water and wrapped around his ankle like a whip?

And there wasn't just one—the second D hit, a number of identical tentacles flew up and wrapped around both his wrists as tightly as possible. Something with what looked like a striped carapace broke the current ahead of D.

"I thought as much—not quite as sharp in the water, now are you?" Fern laughed, showing a lot of teeth. "See, when I heard we'd be going up against you, I went back to my house and picked up one of my aquatic guard beasts. From what I hear, dhampirs are as weak in the water as the Nobility. Okay, so now you get your pick—stay where you are and drown, or let the sparks from my electric cloud shock you to death."

"Stop it. I'll go back!" As Lina screamed these words, the cloud and spider approached the water's edge.

"Don't do it, Fern!"

"Never mind that, kill him!"

The conflicting shouts of the sheriff and mayor were effaced by an awe-inspiring sight.

The purple bolt aimed at the immobilized D bounced off the oval carapace bursting through the water's surface.

All of the spectators felt their eyes bulge from their sockets. Who could have believed that the gorgeous youth was rising from the water along with the beast that held him? The one who'd been dragged down was doing the dragging.

All of them had just witnessed the monstrous power of the Nobility, what many said was the strength of fifty men, and now, before their watchful eyes, D's left hand flashed out. Extending his five fingers and making a slashing motion, every tentacle his hand touched was severed. Free from his bonds, D sailed through the air like a mystic bird.

A silvery light deflected the flash of purple, then bisected the body of the cloud, swinging back with a speed the eye couldn't follow to sever the head from the giant spider, as well as the web of threads it dropped on him.

The sound of the brook returned to the ears of the onlookers.

Throwing the gore from his blade with an elegant flick, D turned his back as if nothing had happened.

"Too much for you, boys? See how tough my bodyguard is?" Lina jeered in a voice bursting with joy. The men had lost even the will to say anything as D walked away.

†

After the aborted battle, their rude visitors had gone on their way. The dark of night seeped between the trees, and the pale moon came out.

Lina heated some synthetic coffee over a small electronic traveling lamp. She'd brought the beverage from her wagon. The lamp belonged to D. A silver cylinder six inches high and two inches in diameter, the lamp could also serve as a thermostat and heater, or as a refrigeration unit. And, obviously, you could cook on it, too. Travelers couldn't be bothered carrying around a lot of bulky items.

Deftly lowering the heat-absorbent silicon pot, she poured the contents into two cups made of the same material, then called out to D.

"It's ready."

"I thought I told you I didn't want any."

"Oh, no you don't. Drink it. It'll warm you up. Oh, what a beautiful moon." Going to D's side, she forced him to take hold of the cup. "I'll cut us some jerky, too."

"I don't want any."

"And what are you supposed to do if you don't eat?" But even as she said this, Lina withdrew the offer. "Well, fine then. I don't have much appetite either, today."

"Is your stomach bothering you?" D asked without turning around.

"Let me think. I'm not always like this—anyway, dhampirs are really awesome."

Nothing from D.

"A little while ago, I took a look at the corpse of that guard beast out in the middle of the river. The marks on its tentacles almost made it look like they'd been bitten off. Surprised the heck out of me."

D was silent. Lina closed her eyes softly and drank in the perfume of the moonbeam grass wafting in through the window. The wind was singing in the trees. Maybe D was listening to it.

"D . . . that's an odd name. What's the D for? Devil, death, danger? Any of them would fit you to a T."

"Tomorrow, you go home," D said in a subdued tone.

"No way."

"Surely you know what I am by now. If anyone tells the exam board about this, it'll probably spell the end for your dreams of the Capital."

"I don't care," Lina giggled, taking D's left arm. "If that happens, I'll go off with you. The wife of a Hunter . . . now wouldn't that be a life of thrills galore?"

When D turned his rightfully dumbfounded face to her, she added, "Just kidding, that was a joke. Just say I can go with you, and that'll be fine."

"Quit your nonsense and go to bed. I have to leave early tomorrow morning."

"I'll have lunch waiting for you," Lina joined her thumb and forefinger in the okay sign. She even winked at him. "Give 'em hell . . . hubby."

D heaved a sigh. It was a long sigh, the kind that hadn't once escaped as he battled monsters or the Nobility. It seemed even this youth, who was like clockwork crafted from ice, was subject to the occasional malfunction.

"Tell me, D, where do you come from?" Lina asked with a sober expression. "Where did you come from, and where are you going? Or the Nobility? Or even mankind?"

D turned and gazed at Lina. Perhaps he had caught a certain minute anxiety in the words of the girl. "Tough questions."

"Don't you know? Even someone like you, who knows both worlds, even you don't have the answer? What is it to live by both day and night, what is it to be human, what is it to be a Noble . . . don't you know?"

"Why do you ask?"

"I really want to know. Tell me."

The aroma of moonbeam grass wafted around the two of them.

D moved to the door without a word, then leaned his body against one wall. Lina took a seat on a piece of framework hanging a foot off the ground.

The world of the night lay before their eyes.

"To be a Noble, most likely, is to live by night," D began softly, with his longsword in his right hand and a cup of steaming coffee in his left. "The potential power inherent in the darkness of night and the shadowy influence it has on the Nobility down at the very molecular level are mysteries today—even during the Nobility's golden age of science, they couldn't begin to unravel them. The question of why the flesh of the Nobility is invincible, the secret of how they can live eternally, ageless and immortal so long as they're spared from sunlight or a blow from a stake, or the riddle of why that blow has no effect whatsoever unless taken through the heart. It's nothing if not ironic that they, the first creatures in the history of the world to reach a measure of longevity that could never be surpassed, were anguished as no others by trying to discover the secret of their powers."

"I wonder if the field of genetic engineering could've offered some clues? Although I did hear the information from every possible gene was collated in the Nobility's computers."

"The process of decoding the information contained in every single gene was completed more than five thousand years ago. But that's not where the problem lies. Once they'd discovered the gene that prevented aging, they must have asked themselves why such a gene had come into existence."

"Where do we come from, where are we going? I guess that remains the eternal question for all of us. Noble and human alike. But what did the power of darkness you just mentioned have to do with any of this?"

D nodded and brought the cup to his mouth. Noticing how Lina smiled, he scowled and took a drink.

"Is it any good?" Lina asked in a buoyant tone.

"Yep."

"I'm glad."

Clearing his throat, D began to speak again. "It's common knowledge that the vital functions of the Nobility all center around darkness itself. This gave rise to a certain hypothesis. It suggested that the darkness of night might hold the primary cause of the powers of the Nobility, or the gene responsible, if you will. That is to say, perhaps the Nobility absorbed some ghostly information belonging to the very darkness in the form of this gene, or so the theory went."

Lina's eyes were sparkling, shining with the expectation and anxiety held solely by those who wrenched open the heavy door of the unknown and beheld the light of truth spearing freely forth. Sparkling relentlessly.

"That's the gene of darkness, isn't it?"

"That's right."

"If only we could understand the structure of it, the riddles of the Nobility would be solved. 'Where do we come from, where are we going?' And the answers would apply to mankind, too. D, didn't they ever form this hypothesis—that humans are furnished with the gene of light?"

The moonlight caused their neat profiles to stand out stronger and whiter. The song of the wind, the aroma of grass.

"That's right," D said. "To be human is to live in the light. When you consider the length of their respective life spans, humans don't amount to much when compared to the Nobility. From a physiological standpoint, they're terribly frail as well. But when you take the potential energy of the race as a whole—"

"Light surpasses darkness," Lina muttered softly.

That was one sort of destiny.

"But the Nobles we've been seeing now . . . " Lina was about to say more, but hemmed and hawed.

In the cockles of her heart, someone was crying out to her. *Don't say it*, they said. She got the feeling the dark voice was somehow connected to her fate.

"Nobility who walk in the daylight . . . "

D brought the cup to his mouth again, and gazed at Lina. Shaking her head as if to reassure herself, she said, "There couldn't be any such thing."

Something shiny rose in Lina's eye. Before it could spill over the rim, Lina threw herself around D's waist. Sobs rocked her shoulders.

She didn't understand what made her so sad. She didn't know what she was afraid of, either.

She felt helpless, like she was alone at night walking down the road. And that night would see no dawn, for all eternity.

D set his cup on the floor and stroked her hair softly.

I just want to get out of this village, Lina wished with all her heart. *I want to go to the Capital with him. Just the two of us, together forever.*

The song of the wind could be heard. The pair didn't move for the longest time.

Unexpectedly, tension raced through D's body.

Lina fell to the floor, still posed as when she'd clung to him.

D stood by the babbling brook.

There was no change to the surroundings.

Perhaps D's sense of them alone had changed.

Why haven't you come yet? It was the same presence from the rainy night. *I'm waiting for you. Waiting there.*

Where is "there"? What's the significance of those ruins? D asked this without uttering a word, without even thinking.

That was the only rule in this conversation.

I may have failed, the presence said. *If so, I must dispose of them all. There isn't much time. I'm waiting.*

Waiting for what, or for whom? D asked. *What do you mean by waiting?*

There was no answer to those questions.

Come quickly. I must go. This has gone on for such a long time, but it'll go on so much longer. Much longer . . . So much longer . . .

Somewhere within D, the presence suddenly vanished.

So, it's the ruins after all then? D looked back at the shack. Lina was standing in the doorway. D's eyes narrowed.

An expression that was not quite fear nor wholly anger occupied Lina's face.

"What's wrong?" he asked as he approached her.

Lina shook her head. "It's nothing . . . really. You took off so fast . . . I was just a little scared, that's all."

Pausing a bit, D then nodded. "You should get some rest."

"I suppose you're right."

Lina wasted no time in returning to the hut and getting into the sleeping bag. It was so warm, thanks to the thermal sensors that read the external air temperature and body temperature and maintained the level of warmth most conducive to sleep.

D's presence faded away. *I bet he'll sleep with the darkness and the song of the wind for companions, his ear to the ground,* Lina thought. *Or does he have trouble sleeping at night? What are the dhampirs anyway?*

Behind her closed lids, an ash-gray figure floated, and it spoke in a weird voice. *Remember what happened ten years ago.*

Lina shook her head ever so slightly.

Another voice. *I must dispose of them all.*

Lina had heard the voice of the presence, too.

People of the Twilight

CHAPTER 6

H er surroundings were awash with crimson.

What stained them was a mixture of hunger and thirst. It made noises and beckoned to her will.

Her will tried to resist. It had accumulated much thus far—love, hope, kindness, dreams, grief, and, finally, rage. This will developed as she had lived her life, and some called it her "personality." The answer it always gave to the invitation was no.

But the time was drawing near.

The crimson surroundings busily besieged her will, diligently trying to pacify the tough walls of reason with the caress of instinct.

Gradually, the walls were crumbling.

The falling fragments were instantly assimilated by the hunger and thirst. Her will felt something sweet, as its senses were stripped away. The feeling was something akin to the joy of discovering the world where she really belonged.

And yet the core of her will resisted.

Swelling with spitefulness, the crimson lurched forward, ready to swallow the will whole.

The gruesome battle raged on.

I'm melting. Being absorbed. Changing. Becoming a . . .

†

When Lina opened her eyes, D was just about to leave the shack. The light slipping through the window and cracks in the walls was a hazy blue. It was near dawn.

"You heading off already?" she asked, rubbing her eyes. D stopped in his tracks and turned.

"It's still early. Go back to sleep. And when you get up again, go home."

"No way! I wish you'd get that through your head." As she spoke, Lina crawled from the sleeping bag.

"Aren't you cold?"

At this remark from D, Lina realized she was wearing nothing but a blouse.

Now that he mentioned it, though the wind was quite cold, she didn't feel the chill.

"It's kind of warm today, isn't it? I always have been warm-blooded."

Whether her answer satisfied him or not, D went outside without seeming to take much notice. Stretching, Lina followed.

"The ruins again? There's nothing there, I'm sure."

D was silent as he put the saddle on.

"Wait up, I'm going, too."

"You can't. Go home. And then go to school. Shouldn't the exam board be here by now?"

Doing some quick figuring, Lina extended two fingers and waved them at him. "Not yet. I've still got two days." She remembered that soon a great load would be off her chest. In two short days, she could bid farewell to this village.

But, Lina thought, *all my tomorrows will be here in two days. I wonder if tomorrow coming is a good thing or not?* "Please, D," she said. " I won't get in your way. If I do, you can send me right home. Take me with you. I'm afraid to be left alone."

"Do what you like," D said with a nod, though she'd been certain he'd refuse. "But if you come, it's because you want to. I won't even spare you a thought."

"Fine by me. Leave me behind whenever you like."

Lina gleefully strode toward the wagon.

"You forgot something." D gave a toss of his chin toward the entrance to the shack.

"Huh?"

"Seems someone came and left this while I was sleeping. It's not for me. Must be a sophisticated guy."

The dubious face of the girl shone like the morning sun when she caught sight of something, a small white shape, left by the entrance.

A single bloom.

Gently taking it in hand, she slipped it into the breast pocket of her blouse. It seemed the mysterious delivery boy was always watching over Lina.

"Looks like you're not all alone after all." Even D's voice, as emotionless as ever, sounded like it was showering her with blessings. "If anything were to happen, someone would grieve for you."

Perhaps D knew something already.

Lina's thoughts were a thousand muddled pieces. "When school's over, is it okay if I come back here?" she asked.

"Do as you like. Of course, there's no guarantee I'll make it back in one piece."

Lina fell silent. Behind his soft words lay a world of carnage a young girl couldn't possibly begin to imagine.

Lina shook her head. She shook it over and over, desperately. "Not to worry. I'm sure you'll be back," she said, trying to convince herself. "I'll wait as long as it takes."

D reined his horse around silently. He kicked the heels of his boots into its flanks, and his mount galloped away without a moment's hesitation.

After the thunder of hooves had faded into the depths of the forest, Lina climbed up into her wagon and took a peek at the sundial in the storage compartment.

It was much too early to head off to school. However, she didn't think she could handle her anxiety if left alone with it for long.

Why didn't I tell D about what happened yesterday? she thought. *About that mysterious hole, and the shadowy figure and bizarre creatures I ran into down there? Or about those words?*

The shadow of the abominable events of a decade earlier grew all the heavier in the silence, and now it was poised to clamber onto her shoulders at any opportunity.

Lina suddenly remembered Cuore. Maybe the shadows of the past were giving instructions to him, too.

Guess I'll go see him, she thought. She'd heard where he was from the mayor.

Lina gave the horses a lash.

On a narrow road, D suddenly stopped his horse and scanned his surroundings.

It was a perfectly normal track through the forest. Here and there, the last white traces of snow punctuated what grass remained, and the brown strip of road ran on forever. Nor was there anything out of the ordinary about the morning breeze blowing against him. Nevertheless, D's senses, the supernatural perception possessed by dhampirs alone, told him he wasn't going where he wanted to go.

How was this any different from the road he'd taken the day before?

Pausing a bit, D once again clomped down the road. After riding for a minute or so, he stopped. The scene that greeted his eyes differed not one iota from the last one. The brown strip, the grass, the trees.

"Stop running around in circles," his left hand suggested.

"So, we've been sealed off in another dimension then, as I thought," D muttered. "We could keep going down the road like this until the end of time and not get anywhere."

Take two points in space and fuse them together at both ends, and whatever lies between is trapped forever, only able to keep moving within the confines of the closed dimension. The real question was, when had his enemy learned this little trick?

"So, what do we do now?" the voice asked with delight.

"We've got no choice but to get out."

"Oh. And how would we do that? If we were on the outside it'd be a different story, but in the whole history of the Nobility there's never been a case of anyone busting a containment dimension from the *inside*."

"There was a magnetic containment field in the lab up in the ruins," D said, getting off his horse. "As you could tell by watching the way the hill works, it was made to deal with normal human beings. It's not *half* enough to contain me."

The voice was silent, but it was a silence pregnant with agitation and fear. "You're the boss," it finally replied, "but I don't know where on earth you get these crazy ideas. I don't want to be anywhere near you when you break through."

"As you like. But until then, I need you to do your job."

Tethering his horse to a nearby tree, D entered the woods. Gathering dead branches as he walked, he snapped off the twigs before piling them on his shoulder. When he returned to the road some ten minutes later, both shoulders were loaded with as much as would possibly fit.

Piling the heap of wood on the ground like kindling for a fire, D began digging up the soil. He didn't use his sword, a stake, or anything else. With all five fingers lying flat, he artlessly thrust his left hand into the ground, scooping out clods of dirt like his hand was a shovel, and piling the dirt in a mound beside the kindling.

But this was no plain soil. The earth was black and hard, packed solid by countless passing loads. What indescribable strength that hand must've possessed, to slide wrist-deep into the earth with such consummate ease. In no time, he'd dug a hole big enough for one person to lie in comfortably, and had accumulated a corresponding volume of dirt.

"We're all set," he said, smacking the soil from his hands.

"Not quite," the left hand protested. "Earth, water, fire, wind—we're still short water. Bringing you back to life is one thing, but we can't hope to succeed in breaking out of a sealed dimension if we're short even one of them."

"No cause for alarm."

Standing before the mound of dirt, D rolled back his coat and shirt sleeves, exposing his left forearm to the wind. He brought his right index finger to bear just above the wrist, at a point where the artery was. Both finger and nail were gracefully in keeping with their owner. Just what sort of trick he'd employed was unclear, but merely running the finger across the white flesh left a thick vermilion line, and bright blood gushed from the wound, pouring down on the lumpy black earth like a warm waterfall.

With evening so far off, this was a weird piece of work to see on a sunny little trail through the woods.

After making sure his lifeblood had sufficiently soaked the clods of earth, D wiped the same finger across the gash. The bleeding stopped, and there wasn't even a trace of the wound.

Not surprisingly, his complexion was a bit paler, but it was disturbing to see how deftly he put the fingertip dripping with his own blood in his mouth, taking that little bit of sustenance.

Did he plan on using these arcane materials against a physics-based phenomenon like this sealed dimension?

"Taking from life to give life, eh?" the left hand fairly moaned. "A miserable bit of business to be sure. But really, it's scary how coolly you can do it. Guess it should come as no surprise, since you're . . . "

"Enough."

With that one word from D—his look pale, cold, and unearthly, changed by the single drop of blood he had tasted—the voice was silenced.

Taking two branches from the pile of kindling and holding one in each hand, D put the end of one against the side of the other and rubbed them together vigorously. He didn't appear to put much strength into it, but both branches burst into flame, and, when they were tossed back onto the mound of dead wood, heavy black smoke and fierce flames instantly sprung skyward.

Earth, water, fire, wind—all four elements had been assembled.

"Now it's your turn," he said.

His left hand reached for the flames. Then into the flames.

The wind howled, and, perhaps guessing something, even the horse whinnied.

There. The blazing pillar of flame became a thin line that was sucked, like smoke, into D's palm!

"That makes fire and wind, right? Earth and water are next," he muttered in a beautiful voice, as his pale skin regained a luster that could rightly be termed bewitching.

†

L ina stopped the wagon a short distance from Fern's house. She didn't think relying on common courtesy would see her through this visit safely. She'd probably be sent back to the mayor before she'd even had a chance to see Cuore.

So she decided to do it by less legitimate means.

Walking until she could see the walls of Fern's compound, she ducked the woods. Following the wall, thirty feet down she found what she wanted. There was an opening at the bottom of the wall just about big enough for Lina to fit through. It was a little-used bolt hole she remembered hearing Fern's daughter mention. The precocious Bess had used this to escape the watchful eye of her nagging father and meet with boys.

A little more, just a little more now, Lina mentally chanted as she squeezed through, eventually coming out behind a plastic structure that appeared to be some sort of breeding coop. Not far ahead she could see the main house, and behind that the roof of the barn. The property was eerily quiet, perhaps because it was still early morning, but she knew from the growls and howls spilling from various small structures spread about the place that the guard beasts were already awake.

I'm in trouble if any of these critters has a sharp nose and a loud bark, Lina thought. *But I suppose I'll be fine so long as none of them sinks their teeth into me.* Checking that there was no one around, Lina made a quick dash for the barn.

Maddening as it was, there was truth in what the mayor had said—there was no way a man like Fern would give Cuore a room in the main house.

The barn was quite a bit larger than the one at the mayor's residence. The door wasn't barred. That was proof someone was inside. When she pushed open the door, the reason was immediately clear.

The heavy stench of the beasts assailed her nostrils.

The barn doubled as a breeding place for guard beasts. Given that Fern had lost his wife early, and that he only had Bess to help him take care of the creatures, there was an extraordinary number of them. Lina cocked her head.

The shack was sectioned off by panels—partitions fashioned from metallic alloys, glass, plastic, and various other materials that had to withstand the acid, flames, and whatever else the guard beasts could spew. The sight of a giant spider like the one she'd seen a day earlier, a monstrous snail-like creature some seven feet long, a mammoth quadruped going berserk behind a semi-translucent barrier, and countless other strange beasts made Lina nauseous. With a sudden whoosh, a gout of flame shot into the air down at the far end of the barn.

"I've had quite enough of this. What kind of sicko would keep these creepy things?" she cursed in a low voice, though she continued bravely on. Once past the monsters' pens, she entered an area hemmed in by farm implements and piles of feed containers. The stink of the savage beasts was thinner, but the air had become strangely chilly.

"Cuore?" she called out in a low voice. "Cuore, it's me, Lina. Are you in here?"

"Too bad."

Why did that cheery voice make her whip around with a scream?

"Bess! For goodness sake—don't scare me like that!"

As Lina took a breath of relief, her classmate approached her in a pure white robe with the collar turned up.

"If you're looking for Cuore, he's not here. He's staying somewhere else."

"Somewhere else? But your father took him in."

Bess laughed. She drew closer. For no particular reason, Lina backed away. Before she knew it, she was in the corner of the room. She felt boxed in. Her foot brushed something hard.

Turning to look, Lina's face grew stiff. It was a coffin. Apparently, it had been exhumed from a graveyard, as dried mud still clung to it. She hadn't seen it before, hidden there behind the bales of hay.

"Bess, what's this for? Did someone pass away?" Even as she was saying it, Lina half-realized the truth. "Aaaaaah!"

Something cold caught hold of her ankle just as she was about to step away. She screamed, and the lid of the coffin slipped ever so slightly, revealing a pale hand.

Desperately, she wrenched her way free, but Bess blocked her escape. "Relax and stay a while, Lina," she said. The bloodshot eyes gazing fixedly at Lina nailed her to the spot.

Behind her, there was the sound of something hard hitting the ground. She spun around.

Fern was standing in front of the coffin. His insulated vest and somewhat filthy pants—these clothes she'd seen so many times before—served to fuel the fear bearing down on Lina's reason.

"That's a hell of place to be taking a nap." Her voice quavered pitifully as she said it half in jest, and Fern's mouth twisted into a grin.

"I was gonna go out and get you, but I'm glad you came to us. I'm sure everyone will be plenty happy."

"Hold on there. Who exactly is this '*everyone*'? I came here to see Cuore. Where is he?" Lina asked, estimating how long it would take to run to the door.

"He's with *everyone else*. I'll bring you to meet them all soon enough." Fern laughed again.

Seeing the fangs peeking from either corner of his lips, Lina cried out to Bess in desperation.

While the girl in the white robe bared her fangs, she was also unbuttoning her clothes. "I've been so lonesome, Lina," she cooed. "I couldn't go out to see anyone, and I've been so hungry. After all, ever since I drank Papa's blood, I haven't had anything to feed on but the guard beasts. And on top of that, Papa . . . "

Her pale-as-paraffin hand made a motion, and the white garment fell to the ground.

For the first time, Lina realized there were some things so terrible you couldn't scream, no matter how badly you wanted to.

From the neck down, her classmate's body wasn't that of a living human being. Her flesh was black-and-blue and shriveled dry, and beneath the painfully prominent ribs only the lump that must have been her heart continued grotesquely hammering away, beating out the pulse of something without life.

"Papa's been drinking my blood." Bess smiled enigmatically. "Every day now, every single day, he kisses me on the neck and drinks his fill, you know. He says he's wanted me for a long time. And after all that, he won't even let me drink a little bit of his."

"This is . . . this is just too . . . "

New fears shattering the old. When Lina bolted for the door like a scared rabbit, one of the withered branches that were Bess' arms caught her and held her close.

She felt cold breath like moonlight on the nape of her neck.

"You know, I wanted you. I always used to think about you at school. I wanted to kiss you at least once. And now I will."

"Stop it!" Struggle as she might, the arm pressing against her body had the strength of steel.

"It's okay, isn't it, Papa?" The hunger and passion was now laid bare in Bess' voice.

Fern considered for a bit, then nodded. "The others will probably have a fit, but a mouthful or two should be okay. After all, even if we leave her be, you know what'll happen sooner or later."

These weighty words hammered Lina with a strong primal fear. *What* would happen to her sooner or later?

When those raw, warm lips brushed the nape of her neck, Lina's reason utterly collapsed. Madness battered its way through the wall of fear, and something burning hot gushed out all at once.

Bess was thrown against the far wall, screaming awfully, her body spinning like a dervish. Regardless of how Fern felt at the sound of those thick boards snapping, not even a trace remained of the faint smile of a vampire watching his prey.

"Well, now . . . we should've expected no less," he groaned. Lina began to run. He pursed his lips, and eerie syllables flowed throughout the barn, calling to his guard beasts.

Lina slowly returned toward Fern, walking backwards now.

A few yards ahead of her, grotesque figures began filing through the door one after another—a giant spider, a colossal snail, a mucus-dripping creature shaped like a sea anemone, a mass of writhing purple tentacles. There was an army of guard beasts.

The mob of shapes closed around Lina as she backed away, her color completely fading.

"We won't let you get away again," Bess laughed, as she leisurely got to her feet. "So, come to me. At any rate, you're already . . . "

Lina covered her ears, her whole being recoiling against whatever Bess was about to say.

The ring of foul-smelling beasts squeezed tight around her.

†

"Okay, all set," came the voice from D's left hand. D nodded.

With the exception of a smattering of bloody mud and a fistful of ashes giving off a thin wisp of smoke, the outlandish materials had disappeared. Who would've believed all of that could be consumed by a little mouth no bigger than the tip of a pinky finger?

Without a sound, D sailed up onto his mount.

Giving his cyborg horse a pained glance for just the merest instant, he lashed it hard.

But, in this eternally sealed dimension, what was the point of this dash on horseback?

"Where's it been fused?" he asked, training his piercing gaze straight ahead. The wind rang in his ears.

"Three hundred yards from here. It'll start warping back around any time now, so you'd better watch yourself," the left fist said teasingly.

And what did it mean by that? The dimension was onto them.

Watch. See how the stands of trees lining the road, the bushes, even the sky and the road itself twist like a veritable mirage, dissolving like paints in water and surging after D as he gallops by?

It was a wondrous sight, as the gale raised by this gorgeous youth melted the world and pulled it after him.

"One hundred and fifty to go," the voice said with pleasure. "One twenty . . . One hundred . . . Almost there."

D's pupils reflected only the landscape before him. No fear, no anger, no sorrow there. It seemed he was always that way. Increasing his speed even more, the moans of the wind became a maddened scream.

"Fifty . . . Thirty . . . Ten . . . Now!"

With this word, the whole melted and the crumbled universe touched D's back and reversed direction. It was as if the dimension had been turned inside out.

The next instant, however, up in the laboratory in the ruins, fire spouted from a small device.

A millisecond later, the auto-repair circuits went into operation, but the speed of the destruction wreaked by the extreme energy force that had broken through the sealed dimension far exceeded that of the countermeasures.

Destruction pitted against reconstruction.

Losing the ability to make proper assessments, the repair circuits adjusted the programs to draw on all the energy in the ruins. The rip in the sealed dimension overlapped with dimensions in other completely different locations.

D's body flew through the air, sailing up into a space that held nothing. From the corner of his eye, he glimpsed his cyborg horse being broken back down to its constituent atoms.

1945. It was unfortunate, to say the least, that five Avenger torpedo bombers happened to be flying over the seas around Bermuda when the sealed dimension made contact with the area.

1872 and 1888. The crew of the ocean liner *Marie Celeste*, sailing the Atlantic bound for Genoa, Italy, and Jack the Ripper, out prowling the East End slums of foggy London, were *simultaneously* sucked into the sealed dimension, vanishing from the pages of history. The repair circuits should probably be praised for the part they played in the latter of those disappearances.

3046. An alpha-class black hole moving at 1250 miles per second, with a perigee 170 million miles from the solar system suddenly disappeared an instant after swallowing Pluto. Because of this incident, scientists among the Nobility, who were in the process of constructing interstellar rockets to escape to other planets, were subjected to great criticism, and the senior staff on the project, from the director down, were reassigned.

The overlap took zero real time to occur.

1901. Visiting the Palace of Versailles in Paris, Anne Moberly and Eleanor Jourdain both ran into one Marie Antoinette as she was sketching in an arbor in the garden. Under pseudonyms, they penned a faithful account of their experiences, publishing it in 1911 under the title *An Adventure*. Needless to say, that Marie Antoinette was none other than the French queen who, along with her husband Louis XVI, was dispatched into the mists of time by the revolution's guillotine in 1793.

4018. While eating dinner in his home, the *human* artist Vernon Berry witnessed a certain *Noble* attacking a beautiful woman in her bedroom in London, 1878. Though it took Berry three months, he managed to complete a portrait of the attacker. And thus the painting that for nearly six thousand years stood as the crowning masterpiece of all the images of the Sacred Ancestor came into being.

All the shortest effective distances between two points had overlapped.

An intense gale knocked Lina and the others to the ground, and, as she tried desperately to get up, Lina saw the most gorgeous figure in the world standing between her and Fern, as if to shield her.

"D!"

Comprehending the situation at a glance, the Vampire Hunter advanced without a sound. In this terrific gale that made it hard to even raise one's face, this daring figure actually looked like he was enjoying it. The monstrous beasts retreated with groans.

"So, it was you after all," D said softly, gazing at Fern and his daughter. "Tell me something before you meet your end. Where's your master, the figure in gray? How do you get in?"

Even crushed as he was by the otherwordly aura emanating from the Hunter's physique—beautiful as darkness crystallized—Fern bared his fangs. "They're all in the ruins. But there's no way to get to them anymore. Anyway, you're gonna die right here."

D was in motion before he heard the arcane call to arms, moving of his own volition right into the heart of the pack of savage beasts that surged forward.

His naked blade snarled. A head with compound eyes flew off, tentacles like those of a cephalopod rained down. Fresh blood gushed out, and the flames issuing from one of the monsters were truncated by a flash of silvery light.

It was battle beyond compare, and a quiet one.

There was neither whoosh of slashing blade nor scream of severed bone. The wind even blasted away each and every cry from the monstrous beasts. Finally, the guard beasts lay at D's feet, without having scored a single hit with their pernicious claws or beaks or fangs.

A flash of light flew.

About to pounce on Lina, Fern tumbled to the floor with wooden needles piercing both knees. Making a desperate grab for the compressor-powered gun on his hip, his hand was nailed to the ground. Bess had her back up off the ground, but couldn't move any further. The gaze she trained on D was strangely feverish.

The bare blade was shoved in front of Fern's face.

"Answer me—where's the way into the ruins?"

His soft words, devoid of threats or coercion, froze the blood of a fearless vampire. For the first time, it dawned on Fern that the dashing youth before him was no ordinary dhampir.

"What . . . what the hell are you?" he asked in the midst of a crushing fear that made him oblivious to the pain in his shattered knees and his now two-fingered right hand. "Someone who's been made one of the Nobility ought to be more than a match for a human half-breed bastard. And yet, you're . . ."

The naked blade swished through the air, and one of Fern's ears went flying.

"I'm a Vampire Hunter. Now answer me." His tone was as just as soft as before, but with an underlying force that was overwhelming.

"I . . . I know," Bess fairly moaned. Slowly, she approached the site of her father's bloody battle with the youth.

"Don't you dare tell him—arrrgh!"

Fern's threat was cut off together with his other ear, which went sailing through the air.

"I'll tell you . . . Just let me taste your blood, O gorgeous one . . ." Bess' voice quivered with longing and delight.

Clutching the arms she extended to him like withered branches in his left hand, D asked just one thing. "Where?"

"It's . . . "

"Watch out, D!"

With Lina's cry, D made a backward leap of some ten feet. While still in midair, a mass of energy that defied imagination struck his beautiful face.

The air rang twice, with a bang like an air-filled paper bag suddenly popped.

Bess and Fern's bodies had swollen from the inside, then blown apart in an explosion of blood and chunks of flesh. With gory spray and scraps of meat raining down on her, Lina let out a scream.

The wind, which had just died down, rattled the barn on a completely different scale. Beams of heavy steel alloy bent, and screws shot loose.

D realized that the energy mass that had annihilated the bodies of Fern and Bess was the same life-form that he'd encountered three times before. The laws of physics stated that two things couldn't occupy the same place at the same time.

So, I was right—this is a foe after all, he thought. *But someone's consciousness summoned this thing. And, whoever that is, even they can't completely control it.*

He had an idea who that *someone* was.

The invisible being raised its voice.

Lina covered her ears.

It was then that the fragments of red and pink started moving toward the energy mass. The blood and bits of flesh that had once been Fern and his daughter were sucked toward the thing, briefly coming to rest against its indiscernible form, before being almost instantly absorbed.

It wasn't that this manifestation of mental energy desired them. Rather, it used them as sustenance for its creator.

Someone or something was just beyond the door.

Leaping, D was struck once again by a massive invisible fist of energy. He fell back to earth. He shook his stinging head lightly and put his left hand to the ground to support his body. This concentration of energy surpassed imagination.

There were many supernatural powers that could create something from nothing. The spirit beasts spawned by conjuration were one example. However, the energy beings were subject to the same laws of nature as everything else, so naturally there were limits to their power. It would have been a different matter if they were nothing but raw energy, but these energy forms also had intelligence.

In light of that, the energy mass that hindered D's actions must have been created by a being of unearthly power. D had only survived the first hit because of his own powers, and because some of the energy from shattering the sealed dimension remained with him. But he might not be able to stand another hit.

The energy form turned and headed for D. The wall creaked, then snapped with an awful sound.

"D!"

D's face, which had been turned toward the floor, looked up now.

Did the death bearing down on him catch a glimpse of the eyes radiating beams of crimson light, or the pair of jutting fangs? The left hand resting on the ground gripped the hilt of his sword.

As she watched, Lina got the impression she could clearly see the arc as D swung his blade and the "shape" of the hulking thing as it relentlessly advanced.

When the two met, sparks devoid of color or sound flew throughout the barn. Lina's brain burned.

The energy vanished.

D dropped to one knee in exhaustion.

Rubbing her head all the while, Lina ran to him. "D, are you okay?"

"Nothing to worry about. But could you take a look outside the door for me? See if there isn't someone lying out there."

"I'll be back in a flash."

Lina went to the door, looked around a bit, then returned. "There's no one out there. You think maybe they got away?"

D thought for a moment, then laid back on the ground.

"Are you okay? Should I go get a doctor?"

"You needn't be concerned. I'll heal soon enough. What I'd like to know is, what brings you here?"

"I came out looking for Cuore. Just a sec, I'll go get you some water."

Before D could stop her, the girl had disappeared through the doorway.

When she returned a short while later, tin cup in hand, D had already gotten up. Even when he'd been on the floor, his expression hadn't shown that anything was wrong with him, or that he was even in pain. Lina was half-tempted to wonder if he'd just been teasing her.

"Sorry. I had the darnedest time finding the well. Here you go."

D was silent as he took the cup she proffered, then drank a mouthful. Not that his body desired it. He was merely responding to Lina's hospitality. When this girl was around him, D did things that those who knew him would never imagine. Perhaps realizing as much, Lina was beaming, but soon her brow clouded and she asked, "So, what the heck was that thing? Is it the same thing that showed up that night we found Cuore?"

"Probably. It's a mass of superdense energy. When they found out they'd not only failed to keep me sealed away but that I'd also broken through here, they probably came by to keep Fern and his daughter from talking."

When Lina asked him about it, D briefly recounted the incident with the sealed dimension. While she was only a girl of seventeen, he recognized she was intelligent enough to comprehend his story.

"Wow. I guess you can do some pretty amazing stuff," Lina said, her eyes wide with wonder, as they walked away from the barn.

When all signs of the living had left the barn, two things remained: a deep depression in the ground right where D's left hand had been until the instant he'd met the energy form with his blade, and something lying in one of the guard beasts' cages near the doorway. Not only was the latter hidden by a metal partition, but it was also in a state that bordered on catalepsy, so it wasn't all that surprising that D had taken no notice of it.

It was Cuore Jorshtern.

†

"**A**nother failure, it seems . . . "

At last, the low voice was colored by impatience. In a room in the ruins illuminated weakly by a single lamp, two silhouettes deeper than the darkness were conversing quietly, as if crushed by the density of the Stygian blackness.

"If they're not back by now . . . ," another voice said, trailing off glumly.

If one of the voices belonged to the shadowy figure in gray, who could the other be?

"My, but that Hunter's a tough one," the first shadow said. "I never would've thought he could break out of that dimension."

"My sentiments exactly."

"Oh, well, I've already thought of a way to beat him. Rest assured. I'm more concerned about Lina. Hasn't she *remembered* yet?"

"I did try to persuade her." The second shadow paused thoughtfully. "Her time just hasn't come. Remember, each of us awakened separately, didn't we?"

The first voice, gravely weighing the situation, didn't immediately respond. "Only two days until the exam board arrives," it said at last. "This has to be settled today or tomorrow. We're left little choice. We should bring Lina out here instead of waiting for her."

"But that's . . . " The second voice was clearly shaken. "It's by no means certain the amplifier would yield favorable results. Lina's mental processes, in particular, are delicately complex. If it were to go poorly, the damage could be irreparable. Just look at Cuore."

This time it was the first voice's turn to groan. "Hmmm . . . But in return, he gained the power to produce *that thing*. Very well. We'll wait just one more day then, shall we? In the meantime, we can take care of that interloper. Good enough?"

Saying nothing, the other shadow seemed to nod.

After a short silence, one of the shadowy figures began to mumble, "And yet . . . " It wasn't clear which of them spoke. "Can't you feel it? That there's someone here besides us . . . "

"Impossible."

"Someone is watching us. Someone is laughing. Watching our actions and laughing at them . . . from somewhere in the long distant past."

"Stop talking like that."

The voice was silenced and the pair of shadows moved off through the murk. In their wake, only the darkness remained, almost as if to say darkness alone suited them.

†

Lina stopped the wagon at a fork in the road. If she continued straight ahead she would go back to town, while the path stretching to the left led to the hill with the ruins.

"Nothing else will bother you now," D said from horseback. The mount had been commandeered from Fern's place. "I'm going to the ruins. And you—"

"I'm going home. I know that part by heart by now." Lina shrugged her shoulders and stuck out her tongue.

"Good. Come tomorrow, this will all be over."

Feeling the gentleness in D's voice, Lina bugged her eyes a little. She thought she should say something, but, by the time her lips moved, the beautiful silhouette was already dwindling against the sun that filtered through a sieve of overlapping trees.

For a long time, Lina didn't move from the spot. When she did move, however, it wasn't to go straight ahead, but to the side.

The wagon turned a hundred and eighty degrees, thanks to some surprisingly masterful handling by the young lady, and sped back the way it had just come, wheels creaking in the tire ruts all the while.

Lina lashed with the whip. The wind ruthlessly buffeted her brooding countenance.

In about twenty minutes she was back at Fern's house.

Riding as far as the courtyard, she leapt down from the driver's seat, a canteen from the storage compartment in hand. Racing to the barn as if she'd forgotten all of her earlier fears, she pulled Cuore from the guard beast's cage.

Lina had deceived D. Cuore had been lying out on the path, and she'd hidden him in the cage when she said she was going to fetch some water. Even she didn't know for sure why she'd done such a thing. Was it that she didn't want D to find out something she needed Cuore to tell her? She wasn't sure.

Propping his head—which reeked of grease and dandruff—on her knee, she forced Cuore to drink some water, and he opened his eyes, coughing and sputtering.

Spying Lina, sense took residence in his muddy pupils.

Though she gave a sigh of relief, Lina found her heart wrung by how horribly emaciated his face looked as he tried, with little success, to form a smile.

He looked like a skeleton draped with skin. He was so terribly thin, like everything in his powerful frame had been ripped right out of him; he looked like he might be on the brink of death.

His body felt unusually light to Lina, as she lifted him up, and, while carrying him, she couldn't keep a few tears from coming to her eyes.

Why now, now that a good ten years had passed had all the gears started running in reverse? Didn't Cuore's wasted form presage her own fate and that of Mr. Meyer? Her tears sprung from that thought.

When she'd finally slid Cuore up onto the driver's bench, Lina heard hoofbeats approaching quickly from the direction of the gate.

Lina bit her lip. Who should discover them but the very last people she wanted to see right now—the men of the Vigilance Committee.

"Well, now, look who we have here," said the second-in-command, Corma, as he stood up in the stirrups. Noticing Cuore's condition, his eyes glittered cruelly. He had a pole of shiny black iron slung across his back. His real trade was clubbing lesser dragons and bears to death for meat and hides that he could sell. "Seems like something ain't quite right here. What's up with Fern? Ain't he around?"

"How should I know?" Lina replied, glaring back at the gawking men. "Go ahead and look for him. I just came out to talk with Cuore. He looks so bad off, I was just taking him to the doctor's. If you don't have any further business with us, kindly get out of the way."

"That's awful serious, now, ain't it? Well, I wish I could just tell you to be on your way, but something just ain't right about how thin he's got. You'll have to hold your horses a minute."

At a signal from Corma, a few of his men went into the barn and the main house, then came right back. One came out of the barn with an agitated expression and reported that the guard beasts had been massacred.

In a threatening tone, Corma said, "Looks like we've got business with you now. So, are you gonna come along with us?"

†

Having thoroughly combed the interior of the ruins, D returned to the courtyard. The passageway to the subterranean lab was sealed by several tons of rubble, and there was no sign of another entrance.

Why was D still so obsessed with the ruins? His contract as a Vampire Hunter had been terminated, but he knew his work wasn't yet done. Could it have been professional pride that kept him in the village? Well, that was part of it. But that gelid beauty of his—a sublimation of anger, sorrow, joy, and all other human emotions—was lent a hue akin to vindictiveness by the outcome of the activities that had continued for centuries in the depths of this laboratory. Still, even if those feelings were the reason, did D himself even notice?

"Can't find it at all, eh?" his left hand laughed scornfully. "But even if you did find it, what'd you intend to do? What happens when you know for sure the results of those experiments a decade ago? It'll just make for that many more dark nights. The fate of those four kids was decided ten years back. No one can change that. Or could it be . . . "

"Could it be what?"

"That you're doing this to meet *him?*"

D's expression stiffened for a moment, but calm quickly returned. "You may be right."

"Oh ho! Grown a human side, have you? Then it looks like this interminable wandering hasn't been a complete waste."

Suddenly, the sky clouded darkly. Even the sound of the wind died sharply.

D's right hand stretched for the sword on his back.

The courtyard was no longer the courtyard.

With every inch of his body, D felt *it* rising into being.

His immediate vicinity was pitch-black. Allowing not even light itself to pass, its density was comparable to that of a black hole. But as incredible as the density of the darkness was, it was several orders of magnitude lower than the presence that stood before D, blocking his path.

D sent all that density right back at the presence.

I should have expected as much. You did well to resist it, a disembodied voice said disinterestedly. It wasn't praise. This was something the meaning of which was beyond words. *Anyone else would have been crippled by this point, their psyche physically crushed. You certainly are a success.*

"Silence," D said. He didn't have to speak the words, nor even think them. This was a conversation of an altogether different kind. "What did you do here? What were the results of your experiments ten years ago?"

You mean the genes of darkness and light? Simply remarkable. How well you've done to fathom that much, the presence said, as it circled around D. *How cruel it is—that the genes of one person, even one solitary gene, can prove the deciding factor for its entire species. Crueler still when their race knew glories unrivaled by any other creature, yet gallantly accepted their fate in time. In that sense, couldn't one say that the Nobility are truly superb?*

"So they've all quietly accepted their demise then?" D laughed scornfully. "If that was the case, there'd be no need for Vampire Hunters."

It's not the Nobility that needs them. It's the humans. Why don't you give us as much time as we need to die off?

"I've grown tired of listening to your quibbling. What were you doing here, tell me that."

In place of an answer, a certain image appeared.

Light didn't suddenly spring into being in the blackness. The image wasn't projected into D's mind or his brain. Nonetheless, there was that one image.

It was the naked body of a woman.

Not just one. There were countless bodies, pale and nude, existing simultaneously in one simple image.

A black shadow bent over her. The shape of that silhouette alone blackly eclipsed parts of the woman's body. It looked like finger-shaped holds opened on her breasts, and the shadow's thick legs seemed to lop off her slick, writhing thighs.

The woman was reaching her peak. Her climax seemed to stretch on forever. Plunging her nails into the figure's back, she bit the flesh of its shoulder. The rapture on her face as she turned away became a voice spilling from her gleaming, wet lips.

However, an eternal climax might also mean eternal anguish.

A number of the faces were etched by death and faded away from the image. And more, so many more. D counted tens of millions.

The presence inquired, *Have you no memory of this? You of all people should remember it. It was the instant you came into this world. You were my only success.*

"You bastard—you were doing the same thing all over again here, weren't you?" D asked, resorting to normal words—words ablaze with white-hot rage—for the first time.

Exactly. You see, this was once a computational center for such things. Over the course of three and a half millennia, I conducted countless experiments and all ended in failure. All the by-products were erased.

The scene changed.

D was surrounded by strange-looking creatures. Though clearly reminiscent of human beings, they were such weird creatures. Craniums swollen, limbs twisted, eyes glittering like those of a cat. Their whole bodies were mantled in fur. Infants cried feebly.

D realized each of them possessed an unimaginable strength. He saw their power. Every last one of them could operate night and day, without sleep. They could breathe in a vacuum, too. They could swim freely underwater, and their cells could regenerate from even fatal blows.

They were the pinnacle of biological evolution. However, a sole drawback brought death upon them.

The accursed deed—the need to drink blood.

That was the reason they were erased. Hundreds of thousands of them, still infants and unable to offer any protest, were buried in the darkness for all time.

"Why did you do all these things?" The strictly serene query bore an infinite weight of grief.

In the pursuit of possibility. There were more ten years ago. But it all ended in failure.

"And do you intend to erase them, as you did all those young lives?"

It's not my habit to leave failures around, the presence said in conclusion. His final word on the matter was spoken with silence, but was all the more frightening for its import. *I shall dispose of all the genes of darkness. You can watch to make sure, if you wish. You've seen a great many things. A few more shouldn't pain you.*

While he listened to the presence, D half-closed his eyes. He was changing this being that possessed the density of infinitely compacted darkness into a form like his own.

That was his only chance of victory.

Of course, this was totally unrelated to the actual physical form of his opponent. D would only cut down the form made manifest to him—that was the extent of it. Somewhere within D, a gigantic, powerful figure was moving toward completion. An image of the Sacred Ancestor, wrapped in a black cape, a pair of fangs jutting from the vermilion lips chiseled into his pale skin.

The instant it was complete, D focused all of his physical and mental energy into the sword racing from its sheath.

Light cut the darkness.

With the sunlight of midday showering down on him, D thrust his blade into the ground and clung to it almost like a crutch as he got to his feet. The heavy shadow of fatigue clung to his beautiful countenance.

"Looks like he's taken off," he said, even his breath ragged. He was answered by a quavering voice.

"You scare the hell out of me. That you could wound *him* . . . your own . . . "

Without replying, D started to walk over to the gate where he'd tethered his horse.

"Where are we headed?"

"I don't know what the four of them have planned, but now at least I know their fate."

"Then let's get out of town. Wash your hands of it, D. You've got no connection to these people."

"Tomorrow, it's going to be decided whether or not one of them goes to the Capital. For that reason alone she made it through the winter. Through a winter that's lasted a decade."

"So what you're trying to say is you'd like to watch over her so that she doesn't know the truth right up till the very end? What a sentimental softy you are."

D didn't say a word as he lashed his horse.

†

The whip rebounded off her white back.

Sobs escaping through her grit teeth, Lina opened her eyes and fought off the sudden urge to faint.

Though her face and her fully exposed torso were both soaked with sweat, her body was quite cold.

When she opened her eyes, she saw before her a bunch of jeering men. A bloodstained Cuore lay on the stone floor.

Lina's wrists were bound together by a rough rope, and she hung from a pulley in the ceiling. There were a great many welts across her back. The men laughed and told her they were still going easy on her. Though there'd been a few pauses along the way, she'd been whipped for nearly twenty minutes so far. This wasn't about getting a confession out of her. This was all about Lina's pain— about them enjoying the agony their whip wrung from the girl's flesh.

The men had no questions of any sort for her. Before they brought Lina and Cuore to the interrogation chamber, located in one of the outbuildings at Fern's place, they'd asked things like where Fern and Bess were or what their connection was to the vampire attacks. But when Lina steadfastly maintained she didn't know, the men looked at each other, smiled, and started to torture the already half-dead Cuore. Perhaps trying to protect Lina as much as he could, Cuore held on through more than an hour of electric shocks and dunkings before he passed out.

"Hey, call the sheriff!"

Aware in her hazy, dim state of consciousness that this entreaty hadn't come from her, Lina let a smile rise on her lips. *What, is that the best they can do? Aside from the physical pain, this is nothing compared to what I've been through the last ten years.*

One of the men approached her. Judging by the unkempt beard, it had to be Corma. A powerful grip on her chin spun her around to face him.

"Oh, still got some fight in you, do you? We don't have to call no freaking sheriff, boys. We can handle this just fine. First of all, you ain't told us nothing yet."

"And I don't have anything to tell you, you fuzz-faced sadist! Don't touch me!"

While his grimy hands stroked her white breasts, Corma brought his vulgar lips close to Lina's face.

"Oh, you got a million things to spill. Like where's Fern at? And how the hell are you tied in to the Noble that's been running wild in town lately? Well? If you ain't inclined to tell, we'll just have to get the answers from your body then."

A warm tongue traced the nape of her neck.

She tried to pull her face away from him, but he held her tightly by the chin.

"Hey, stop that! Let me go!"

"Getting a little feisty, are you?" Corma turned to the others "Hey! Give me a hand with her."

With nods and grunts of agreement, three or four more men gathered around her.

Hands and tongues wriggled against her back, across her belly, between her tightly shut legs.

"Stop it, just leave me alone!"

But as she squirmed, something was about to change deep inside Lina. She felt an anger unlike any emotion she'd known, a white blaze, directed more at the boundless depravity of human nature than at the outrages against her own body.

These bastards—these damned humans!

Her pale body flew up. It was a fierce snap. The men, on her like a pack of hyenas ravaging a corpse, were smashed against the walls and floor.

The blaze raced into the blood vessels in her wrist. With the exertion of just a modicum of power, the coarse ropes burst and Lina fell to the ground.

"You . . . bitch!" Corma exclaimed, jumping back up from the floor.

He grabbed the iron club leaning against the wall. It was a vicious weapon, with sharp conical knobs protruding from all sides. In Corma's hands, it could knock through a stone wall, and, used against prey at close range, it hit harder than a slug from a high-caliber rifle.

The other men got up and surrounded Lina.

"No more mercy for you. Tear them bottom duds off, too, and then we'll fuck her to death."

"Heh heh. We'll stick it to her from the front and the rear!"

Vulgar promises and violent threats spewed from every mouth. They were just about to pound across the floor to her when—

The door opened with a dull creak.

All eyes turned that way, and while five pairs looked dubious, one pair widened in surprise and delight.

"Mr. Meyer!" Picking her clothes off the floor, Lina took cover behind the young teacher.

Not surprisingly, the men were trembling. They looked embarrassed, averting their gaze. Corma alone challenged the teacher, and just barely at that. "What are you here for? Why all the way out here? I could've swore you was among the missing."

"I went on a rather long journey," the teacher said, as if wholly unsurprised by the strange circumstances. "I've just now gotten back to town. I merely dropped by with the intention of asking Fern what new developments there'd been in our local problem."

"Fern ain't here," Corma spat, jabbing a finger at Lina. "Now he's the one missing instead of you. The girl knows where he's gone. So we was just interrogating her."

"You don't say?" Mr. Meyer said with a nod. Looking straight at Corma, he said, "Well, from the look of things, it doesn't seem to have gone very well. Leave this to me. Let me try discussing this leisurely with her at my home. That's fine with you, isn't it?"

For some reason, Corma swallowed the "no" that was just about to leave his throat.

"Well then—begging your pardon." With a simple bow, Mr. Meyer pushed Lina along and disappeared through the door.

Between the men who exchanged idiotic looks, spirits that contained equal amounts of relief and fear were rising.

†

Once the wagon had gone out through the gate, Mr. Meyer looked at Lina's wrist and said, "Got a little rope burn, I see. That was just horrible of them. How did you get out of your bonds, anyway?"

"Uh, well . . . when I was fighting back, they came undone on their own."

"You don't say."

The teacher asked nothing more, but gazed straight ahead. Growing somewhat anxious, Lina inquired, "Um . . . where are we going?"

"Where do you want to go? I'll take you wherever you like. I've got today off, too."

D's face and the shack out by the waterwheel drifted into her mind, then Lina shook her head. Such precious memories. The girl knew there'd never be another day like that one.

"I want to go to school."

"Good enough. But before that, Cuore needs some looking after, wouldn't you say? Let's take him to the doctor's."

He sounds kind of dejected, Lina thought. *Something troubling must've happened to him while he was gone.*

The wagon headed toward town.

†

When the members of the Vigilance Committee had gathered in the center of the compound, the horse bearing D galloped in.

With an impressive display of skill, the Hunter executed a dead stop about a yard shy of the men, who wore doltish expressions of astonishment. Not wasting any time, D said, "The girl must have been here. Where is she?"

"How the hell should we know?" Corma said, stepping to the fore. His voice brimmed with hostility. He'd just been thinking how they needed a little diversion. And now the perfect target had fallen right in their lap. "We was showing her a little bit of a good time," he continued, "and she was sobbing and carrying on, but when we was done with her she sprouted wings and just flew right out the damn window. I reckon she's at the school now."

"The wagon tracks lead back here," D said, in a strangely soft voice. Icy fingers of dread stroked up and down the spines of the ruffians. "How exactly were you showing her a good time?"

The gorgeous youth was standing in front of the men now, having dismounted without making a sound. A white sensation they couldn't meet head-on buffeted their incipient faces. It was his eerie aura.

"What did you do to the girl? Answer me."

Knowing D would not accept silence, Corma tried to bluff. "Heh. She just happened to be here when we came by. We tried to ask her a couple of questions about how she tied in to the Nobility, but the bitch wouldn't play along. So then we took her inside and showed her a good time, naturally. Man, when we spread her legs and stuffed it in her, she was sobbing with joy. After that, we whipped her, and then all of us cleaned her wounds. Oh yeah, we cleaned them with our tongues!"

"Really?" D said with a nod, his voice not really soft but just low. Then, without another word, he turned his back and began to walk away.

"You freak!"

Carving a path through the air, the iron club swung in a downward arc aimed for D's head.

The men's gasp of surprise could be heard at the same time as the ring of iron meeting steel. At the base of D's neck—or just a little bit above it—the iron club had halted, imbedded on the blade he'd partially unsheathed.

The men's eyes bulged. More than the timing necessary to evade the skull-splitting attack of the club, more than anything, the men were shocked to see that D's thin blade withstood the hundreds of pounds of pressure from the iron club.

But the real shock was yet to come.

Little by little, but without pause, D pulled the sword from its sheath. One-handed, of course. Behind him, the giant, who couldn't have been less than two hundred and twenty-five pounds, gripped his hundred-pound iron club with both hands, trying with every ounce of might in his body to stop the unsheathing of the blade.

For those unaccustomed to seeing such a display, it had to be the most frightening sight in the world.

When he'd finished pulling his sword free, D slowly turned around. Unwilling to let go, Corma slid one hand down to the far end of the club—now the man was poised with both arms bracing the club up over his head. Locked together, neither the sword nor the club trembled in the slightest.

Though they could see no twinge of movement in D's emotionless visage or the muscles of his beautiful, powerful hand, the men perceived the sinking of Corma's hulking frame, and they were paralyzed with fear and awe.

The sweat pouring from Corma soaked his beard. His knotty muscles shook, and he couldn't help sinking to his knees. His hulking form was forced down by a sword wielded single-handedly.

Without use of his trunklike legs, Corma had to rely on the strength of his two arms. When he turned his fearful eyes up at the foe standing over him, the boundless pressure was suddenly gone. *Okay*, he thought, *I was just getting warmed up, you dirty vamp bastard.*

However, in the next instant Corma lost himself in true horror.

D's blade was coming down now!

Realizing that the steel was slowly slicing through his iron club, Corma was an instant away from total panic when he heard D's voice.

"Where's the girl?" the gorgeous god of death inquired.

Despite his present situation, Corma found himself intoxicated by the voice and the beauty of the one who gazed at him. "Meyer came . . . took her away in the wagon. Took Cuore with them, too . . . "

D nodded, and then, with one slash, he split the iron club in half and Corma from skull to crotch.

Without so much as a glance at the body—sending out a bloody spray when it fell onto its back and split in two—D mounted his horse.

It wasn't until the pounding of iron-shod hooves striking the plain had faded into the distance that the men, standing vacant-eyed as if in a daydream, could finally breathe again.

†

At the point where it could slip out of the forest and be at the entrance to town, the wagon made a sudden stop. Lina, who'd been in the back assiduously tending to Cuore, leaned over into the front seat and cried out in surprise, "Mr. Meyer, what in the—?!"

Standing in the road about five yards ahead of them was the dreaded figure in gray.

"We've got to get out of here, Mr. Meyer!"

"It's no use. The horses won't budge."

"No problem. There's a stake gun in the storage compartment!" As she spoke, Lina returned to the bed and armed herself with a long, slim weapon she pulled out of the box. With propellant smeared on the butt of the stakes surrounding the two-inch-thick stock, and a small motorized lighter for rapid firing, the weapon's effectiveness tended to diminish over long distances. At close range, however, it demonstrated tremendous power.

"Stand back! This is nothing like the sliver gun I had last time!" Lina shouted, standing as tall and fierce as the temple guardians of yore.

The shadowy figure approached without a sound.

"Stay back! I don't want to have to shoot you!"

"Shoot it, Lina!"

The sound of Mr. Meyer's voice ever so slightly upset the power she put into her finger, which was already squeezing the trigger.

Leaving only a kick and a resounding bang in its wake, the stake pierced the shadowy figure's heart.

Turning its body ever so slightly, the figure reached its right hand around to its back. Lina shuddered as she watched the butt end of the stack sucked through the figure's body. Holding the bloody stake in his right hand, the figure leapt into the air.

He swung the stake down at Lina in the bed of the wagon. Rough wood slashed through the air.

Lina found herself standing in the road.

Without even giving her time to wonder how she had gotten from the wagon to the ground, the shadowy figure hurled the stake at her. Before she could scream, the wind-ripping growl abruptly stopped in front of her chest.

Lina gazed absentmindedly at the stake she'd caught as it flew through the air. Somehow it seemed like she'd become an altogether different creature.

"Don't you understand yet?" the shadowy figure asked her from the bed of the wagon. "Your movements, your speed—you're not the same old Lina any more."

"You dolt, if you're gonna start talking in your sleep, save it for nap time!" Effortlessly stopping the stake Lina threw back at him, the figure raised his right hand.

"D?!"

Seeing the gorgeous youth standing quietly off to the side, Lina was shocked.

"What's wrong?" the figure asked. "Don't you desire this man?"

As she heard the distant voice of the shadowy figure, Lina felt a sudden, hot, rapacious desire burning in her flesh.

I want D. I want those exquisite arms to hold me.

"That image is your very heart made manifest. It'd certainly never deny you what you wish. Love him any way you please."

The low voice was pregnant with expectation. While she was aware this was a psychological attack, Lina touched her hand to D's powerful, hard chest. His lovely lips panted.

D's breath was sweetly fragrant.

I want to suck . . . Lina's heart mumbled. *I want to suck . . .*

"I can't!"

As soon as she'd desperately wrenched herself away, D became Mr. Meyer.

An enigmatic aroma wafted to her nose from the glass receptacle he cupped with both hands.

While averting her face from its color and scent, Lina heard another voice call out to her.

Drink. You must drink. It will set you free. Come back to me.

The container was proffered.

When it reached her mouth and the crimson liquid surged forward, Lina struck wildly at the cup with both hands. The glass shattered, and her field of view was stained deep red.

There was no one by her side. Her hands hadn't been injured, either.

Lina started to run. She worked her legs without looking back. If she stopped, the shadowy figure would catch up to her. Worse yet, she'd be completely changed. That was her greatest fear.

The next thing she knew, she was at the edge of the forest.

She glimpsed the familiar school building. Though she got the feeling she shouldn't go there, she had nowhere else to go.

"Lina," the figure in gray called out, stopping the girl just as she was about to walk on.

She whirled around with a scream of terror, but, at the sight of a familiar face, her fear gave way to relief. Even if it was the most disagreeable of people, in her present state Lina was simply glad it was one of her classmates.

"What are you doing out here?" Callis, who was evidently on his way to school, asked. A flirtatious smile arose on his smooth, handsome face.

"Nothing really. Run along to school now."

"That's some greeting. And after how long I waited to catch up to you."

"How long you waited?"

"Ever since the last time I saw you, you're all I've been thinking about. Look, I picked these for you yesterday."

A white bouquet was thrust before her.

The understated single flowers had been delivered on summer days and winter days, but this bouquet was one huge bunch, ripped up roots and all.

Lina remembered her window sill in the morning—the slight fluttering of her heart as she opened the window, thinking maybe today he hadn't come. The white flower she hugged gently to herself, knowing that someone was looking out for her. All these things were a million miles away.

Taking the bouquet, she heard a voice that was not her own say, "Uh, Callis, I have a favor to ask."

"What is it?"

"As I recall, your family processes beast carcasses, right? Don't you have a warehouse around here somewhere?"

"That's right." Even as he knit his brow in suspicion, the lustful laughter that arose in his thin eyes didn't escape Lina's notice. Not that it mattered.

"Take me there. I want you to hide me for a while. On account of my father's always doing these gross things to me."

"Wow, I had no idea." The young rake swallowed loudly, affected by Lina's physical presence. She seemed like a completely different person from the one he'd seen two days earlier. "Sure thing. It's not like they use it at all during the winter anyway. You wanna go right now, or after school?"

Lina turned toward the schoolhouse. Several students looked at them before disappearing through the gates. She got the feeling Viska and Marco were among them. Someone waved to her, and Lina lifted her hand a little in a half-hearted response. Almost as if to say goodbye.

Then, her decision made, she took Callis' hand.

Lips that seemed visibly redder said, "Okay, let's go."

†

About the same time the girl and the bewitched boy disappeared into the depths of the forest, D arrived at the school. The wagon tracks that he had followed all the way from Fern's place through the forest had come to a sudden end. Finding some signs of a struggle on the ground, he'd rushed to the schoolyard.

He entered the sole academic building. The high school classroom was the one closest to the gate.

Without knocking, he opened the rickety door. Instantly, countless eyes focused on him.

"Well, do come in. I haven't seen you for a while." Chalk in one hand, Mr. Meyer bowed a greeting.

At someone's command of "stand for our guest," the students rose in unison. "Bow." Each head dropped simultaneously, without the slightest flaw in timing, then came back up again. Every one of them had Lina's face.

No one told them to take their seats again.

D's pupils emitted a weird and beautiful light.

A psychological attack. And I walked right into it.

Reprimanding himself lightly, D tried to focus his senses on the source of the force field covering the area, but couldn't find it. Perhaps having learned a lesson from the failure of the attack on the rainy night, the enemy was concealing its position by using diversions on a multitude of levels.

It's not that the field couldn't be penetrated by a concerted mental effort, but the effort itself would consume a great deal of time and psychic energy.

"Are you here to observe the class?" asked the Lina holding the chalk.

A forced smile skimmed D's lips. Somewhere in that gelid psyche, capable of freezing all thought, there might have been a trace of the innocent lass after all.

Linas beyond number approached him. In their right hands, each held a rough wooden stake. Surrounding D, they swung their stakes in unison. D tried to leap away, but his feet were stuck to the floor, and a number of stakes drove into his chest, spraying blood everywhere.

In extreme pain, but without changing expression in the slightest, D leapt to the corner of the classroom. Since he'd weathered that first attack, much of the efficacy of his opponent's spell had been lost.

That's not to say there were really stakes stuck in D's body. This whole battle was taking place within D's mind. If his body—which was equivalent to his will—were to surrender, the real D could die without a single physical wound. Conversely, if he could hold out, the result would be a trenchant blade to turn against his assailant. It was a quiet battle.

Lina, Lina, and Lina hurled their stakes. Two were deflected, but the last one stuck in his shoulder.

With especially long pickets clutched at their waists, Lina and Lina rushed in. D drew his longsword and hacked through both of their necks.

The blade met no resistance, and the two pickets sank into his abdomen. Letting go of the pickets, Lina and Lina laughed sweetly.

D gazed at the blade of his sword. It was just an ordinary tree branch. Even if on the surface his consciousness was ordering him to butcher her, his subconscious was trying to save "Lina."

Swiftly growing ever more enervated by massive blood loss and scorching heat, D grinned bitterly.

Lina leapt, swinging a stake down at him from over her head. His left hand caught her by the wrist, and he threw her back into the midst of the net of attackers closing on him. Though his pain had increased, mobility was returning to his body. His opponent was growing weaker as well.

Suddenly, there was a change in the world.

D stood on a section of ice field crossed only by the howling wind.

He didn't have a mark on him. The sword in his right hand had returned to being his peerless weapon.

D shut the door more firmly than ever on the cage of his psyche.

His foe was gambling his victory on this image. They'd make every lethal effort to leave a beautiful corpse lying there, exposed to the wind on the fields of ice.

Shooting stars flew across the pitch-black sky.

D, someone called out to him. The voice twisted in the wind, became a desolate scream, and raced off across the icy plains. Again it cried, *D*.

Ahead of him at a distance that was impossible to judge—it might as easily have been a yard as a thousand miles—there stood a lone woman.

The long garment of pure white she wore wasn't a dress, but rather a shroud. He couldn't see her face, hidden as it was by her black hair. Much like D, she had nearly translucent skin.

D.

It seemed to be both a voice issuing from the woman, as well as the song of the wind.

D stood completely still, as if frozen solid.

From what part of D did his opponent pull such an image? Truly, the vastly spreading plains of nothingness were a world befitting this youth. On the other hand, the woman . . .

D, we meet at long last. The voice was like the wind sweeping the fields of ice. *How I've waited . . . with just one thing I've been wanting to ask.*

D's whole body tensed.

Whatever question she asked, to grant that request would mean death for his psyche. His enemy's trap was perfect.

I want to know the name of your father.

And so the question came. The question to which this woman knew the answer better than anyone else.

For the first time, a dark shadow resided in D's serene beauty. The wind became even more insistent, and, as D grew ever colder, the icy plains dyed his shadow even darker.

Please answer me, D. What's your father's name? What is it? What is his name?

D's lips parted ever so slightly. The tiny tremble in his cheek testified to the intensity of the battle of wills he was now engaged in.

What's his name? What's your father's name?

The wind frayed the edges of his exceedingly grave words.

"His name . . . is . . . Dra—"

The fields of ice were buried by white light.

†

D had just opened the door to the classroom.

With chalk in hand, the middle-aged teacher turned a dumbfounded expression to him, and all the students were left breathless.

He had triumphed over the psychological attack.

"Is there something we can do for you?" the teacher, the substitute for Mr. Meyer, inquired.

"You haven't seen Lina, have you?" D asked, moving his eyes from the teacher to the students. The fields of ice, the woman, and her question were already far behind him. He was a Hunter, after all.

There was no answer. Unable to turn away, the girls trained their gazes on D's countenance, and even the cheeks of the boys stained with bashfulness. They had to wonder if such beauty could actually exist.

"The girl's in serious danger. Not just her life, but her soul is in peril. If anyone knows anything, please tell me."

A scrawny figure—the boy Marco—stood up over by the windows and told him where to go. D raced from the room.

By the time D reached Callis' processing plant, however, only the boy's body was there, lying on the floor with its throat torn out. Yet, not a drop of blood remained anywhere, and Lina was gone without a trace.

†

The dozen riders climbing the hill on horseback turned at the sound of hoofbeats coming up behind them. The riders were the mayor and the sheriff, accompanied by the members of the Vigilance Committee.

"Where are you headed?" D asked, leaving about fifteen feet between himself and them.

The sheriff came forward. He pointed to the silver cylinder strapped to the back of his horse. A proton bomb. "We're gonna take care of those ruins. That way, the sight of them won't upset the folks from the exam board. We found out from some kids who were picking flowers out here that anyone can climb it normally now."

"Perfect timing," the mayor shrieked, his mouth spreading across the better part of his face. "When we were done with this, we'd planned on coming around to arrest you. On suspicion of murdering Corma. Then we were going to grill you about where Lina is."

When D's gaze fell upon them, several of those who'd been there when Corma was cut in two grew pale.

"I hate to tell you this, but that doesn't constitute a crime," the sheriff said, turning to the mayor. "According to the others' testimony, Corma attacked him from behind. That being the case, no matter how he got killed, he brought it on himself. We've got nothing to ask this Hunter except for information about Lina."

The mayor bit his lip. Looking at D with a cheerful expression, the sheriff continued, "They told me the truth even after they saw one of their own killed right before their very eyes. It looks to me like they're really, truly scared of you. Honestly, the thought of it leaves me speechless. Fact of the matter is, I'd love it if you could show me the technique you used."

Noticing how strange the atmosphere had become, the mayor shrieked, "What are you doing shooting the shit with him? At the very least, he must know where Lina is. Take him in before he gets away."

"If he was gonna run, I reckon he'd have left town when you fired him," the sheriff said in a forceful tone. "But he stayed. I don't know why. And he risked his life to protect Lina when she jumped into that mess half-cocked. Tell me, mister Mayor—you think any of us would feel like fighting for a girl who was a complete stranger with a couple of them guard beasts coming at him? A man like that won't run or hide, even in the face of certain death. There's no need to take him in."

The mayor fell silent, his face flushed vermilion.

"I know it might sound overly cautious, but it'd be wise not to meddle with the ruins," D said softly. "Since the way up the hill has returned to normal, it's only proper to assume there's some other kind of defenses now. That castle did belong to the Nobility."

"We're not leaving anything to chance." Shading his eyes with his right hand, the sheriff turned his gaze to the rear of the hill.

D had already perceived the low rumbling sound.

He saw a black gun barrel spearing the sky.

Sunbeams scattered off its gigantic metallic body, displaying an overwhelming mass. The flat body of the vehicle was treated with a special coating resistant to lasers and other light-beam weaponry. Only the radar dish and caterpillar treads were vestiges of ancient times.

"It's a M-8026 CT—a computerized tank," the sheriff said in a hearty tone. "We dug it out a couple of years back after someone found it buried in the ground on the edge of town. Called a mechanic in all the way from the Capital to give it a tune-up. Thanks to this baby, our losses to bandits and colossal beasts in the three years since have been nil, but the village is still as poor as ever. This model is over two thousand years old, but it still had the manual, and it gets the job done. Seems to have been abandoned for some reason or other. Anyway, you can see we got backup in spades."

D didn't say a word as he turned his horse toward the foot of the hill. Not mentioning that the shadowy gray figure might be lurking deep within the ruins, or that there was a definite possibility it had made off with Lina, he went down the hill silently.

"Once we've taken care of business here, we'll be paying a visit to your little hut out by the waterwheel," the sheriff yelled after him. He and the other inhabitants of the village continued to believe that the Noble was dead. "I'd appreciate it if you could manage to find out where Lina's at by then."

What the sheriff must have meant was that if the Hunter handed her over instead of hiding her, things could be settled peacefully.

D didn't turn around again.

"All right, move out," the mayor commanded. "Okay, Sheriff, let's give it a blast, just to set the mood!"

The sheriff smiled wryly and gave the command to fire.

Raising the 150-millimeter barrel of the laser cannon, the tank took aim at the outline of the ruins without a single wasted motion. There wasn't even the sound of gears grinding together.

The thick beam of light caused a white-hot globe of light to erupt on the castle wall. That scorching sphere of some ten million degrees made the stone wall evaporate nearly instantaneously, and it glittered like a rainbow as the sunlight rained down on it.

The men gave a cheer.

"Now, move in!" the mayor cried.

The hill responded.

Abruptly, the tank turned. Taking a blast from a weapon mounted on the howling ceramic turret, some of the men and mounts had their heads pulverized like ripe persimmons.

"Fall back! Retreat to the base of the hill!" The sheriff's voice was blotted out by shock.

Meanwhile, the enormous form of the tank was being sucked into the ground. It was like the sinking of a gigantic ship bound in a whirlpool of earth and green, a vision beyond imagining.

The creak of grinding metal rose from the earth, and when the barrel alone was left poking skyward, a terrific shock rocked the hill. The energy of the ultracompact atomic reactor became lotus-red as flames spouted into the sky, staining the world crimson.

"The hill swallowed it then?" D muttered softly, watching from a distance as the group of men and horses scurried down the hill, rolling and stumbling. Now that way into the ruins had been cut off, too.

D returned to the shack by the waterwheel.

Watering his horse at the brook, he retrieved a silver cup and a bottle full of tiny capsules from his bags. He scooped up some crystal-clear water and dropped in a capsule.

In a matter of seconds, the water became the color of blood. Downing it in one gulp, he drew an easy breath.

The capsules, filled with dried blood, plasma, and nutrients, were food for dhampirs. Ordinary dhampirs took them three times a day. However, this was the first D had taken since coming to the village. His stamina far exceeded the bounds of the average dhampir.

The sky started to turn a darker blue.

Would dawn come again for a certain girl?

D set his cup down by the window and headed over to his horse. Even if his efforts were in vain, he still couldn't give up.

Why did he go through it time and again, all the deaths and wasted effort? Straddling his horse, he started once more retracing the path to the ruins. He galloped for a few minutes, then, suddenly, he stopped.

A lone youth stood by the side of the road. It was Cuore.

In an instant, he'd vanished.

Dismounting and moving closer, D spied the small hole concealed in the thicket. It was the same hole where Lina had her encounter with the ash-gray shadow.

It was probably a trap. Without the slightest pause, D threw himself in.

A strange sensation prickled his body. That could only mean one thing—a spatial distortion. Two points were connected, warping the space and distance between them. Those two points were probably the hole . . . and the ruins.

There was dirt beneath his feet. Less than a foot away was someplace with an expansive floor paved in stone. This was probably one of the ruins' emergency exits. Either all the circuits blown when D broke free from the sealed dimension had been repaired, or power had been restored to this area alone.

D picked up a pebble by his foot and pitched it forward. At the boundary line between the dirt floor and the paving stones, the pebble gave off a pale flash of light and fell on the other side. The shape was exactly the same, but the pebble's substance was different.

"So it's *dead*? Looks like I'll have to pass a compatibility test."

There was a powerful guard on duty here. Anyone or anything failing to match the predefined physical criteria of the spatial rift would meet a silent material death.

Perhaps D would be transformed into diamond?

Without taking time to think, he stepped silently forward.

Every one of his cells emitted the sparkle of jewels, and dreamy flames colored his countenance.

As soon as he set foot on the stone floor, the glow flickered and faded away.

With just a light toss of his head, D ventured into the depths of the darkness.

A foul stench and presences condensed around him. D's eyes could clearly discern the vastness of this area, and the form of those who dwelled here—twisted, transfigured, *former* human beings.

The wind whistled, and two of them that'd leapt at him fell to the ground decapitated. An evil, malicious intent poured unbridled from the bloodshot eyes at D, making the darkness seethe. These creatures delighted in slaughter and hatred. What could they possibly have been granted in return?

A few more lost their lives, too, and then the strange things receded into the depths of the darkness. The iron door set in the far wall started to shut, swallowing their footfalls.

D became a black wind, slipping through the thin opening.

He came into a shining corridor. Some sort of luminescent material must have been mixed into the silicon steel of the walls and ceiling. The floor, which hadn't deteriorated over the millennia, hazily reflected his form.

Following the sounds of the twisted creatures, D proceeded down a long corridor. In the distance, the groan of machinery was audible.

These were the remnants of a dream. But whose, and what had they dreamt of?

The scenery changed, and D's way was obstructed by a wall of cyclopean rocks. Crumbling stone steps stretched into the darkness above. Once he'd climbed them all, a steel door came into view.

The blue pendant on D's chest grew more brilliant, and the door opened without a sound.

The vast chamber was filled by an almost twilight illumination. It was a laboratory reminiscent of the one he'd explored with Lina. But this one looked several times larger. The memory of any number of castles he'd seen before came and went in D's mind. Indeed, they'd been filled with blue light, too. Perhaps that was the color of extinction?

On the stone floor, two naked bodies were intertwined.

With every movement of the gray shadow lying on the pale female body, a low pant escaped. Her white hands raked fingernails down the ash-gray cloth, and her thighs tightened around his waist. The face of that beautiful woman, who looked like she was being violated by a mummy of antiquity, was the face of Lina.

Unexpectedly opening the eyelids that rapture had nailed shut, her eyes met D's. Her expression faded.

The gray shadow leapt up without even stirring the air. The blade of his sword drank in the blue light.

Simultaneously, there rose the whine of sword leaving sheath from D's back.

"I see . . . Cuore's to blame, isn't he?" Making a voice of his anger, the shadow squeezed out the words. "It was unwise of me to leave him unattended like that, even if all his psychic energy was spent and he was more dead than alive. But you're too late, Hunter. My wish has been fulfilled. Do you have it in you to cut down Lina?"

Narrowing his gaze to take in just the ash-gray shadow, who was brimming with murderous intent, and Lina, who had lethargically raised her sweaty torso, D analyzed the situation. "So this is the birth of a new Nobility? What would you do if I could cut her down?"

The shadowy figure slowly lowered his blade until it scraped along the floor. "Could you do it? Could you really cut down a friend?"

Flashes of white light crossed.

The shadow closed on him with unbelievable speed, slashing his demonic blade from ground to sky, but D's longsword deflected the blow and split the suddenly unbalanced figure's shoulder.

The deep red wound yawned wide, and vivid blood flew—but the gash closed quickly.

A look of admiration raced through D's pupils. No matter how powerful their vaunted recuperative abilities may be, none among the Nobility had taken a hit from D and been unaffected.

As the shadow backed away, he brushed the lab table beside him. Made of oak, the table looked to be about ten feet long. Moving his left hand slightly, the shadow sent the table flying at D. It roared with the force behind it.

The instant it appeared to impact on D's body, the table changed direction, went over his head, and fell to the floor behind him.

Realizing that D had flipped it with the tip of his longsword, the shadow was rooted to the spot.

This was a showdown between things that had the shape of men, but weren't men.

D leapt into the air.

The shadow seemed to have forgotten to move, and his heart was pierced by a naked blade that poked clear through his back.

Lina gasped with astonishment.

The moment the two figures had overlapped, one of them had leapt backwards—with a sword still stuck through his body. Behind his mask, a sneering grin rose in his bloodshot eyes.

A vampire invincible to even D's sword through the heart! Yes, surely this must be proof that the demon who could walk in the light of day didn't have to resign himself to the destiny of the night.

There was a silvery flash of light right in front of the now empty-handed D, and the Hunter soared through the air like the shadow had. As he closed in after him, the ash-gray shadow swung his left hand.

A metal cylinder struck the floor, sending pillars of flame up toward D.

Fending off the flames born of the ultracompact atomic grenade with the hem of his coat, D came to a halt. Behind him was a stone wall.

He could see the shadowy figure smiling through his mask.

What froze his grin was that the arm that had shielded D's chest seconds before had halted his deadly sword thrust with its palm.

As the terror-struck shadow watched, the face that arose in D's palm laughed heartily. The tip of his sword was held in that wicked little mouth. Clearly someone had bitten off more than they could chew.

Perhaps the ashen figure's shock was too great, or perhaps he couldn't match the strength of that uncanny mouth, but, for whatever reason, the shadow let go of his longsword and jumped out of the way. He was trying to extract the sword that was still stuck through his chest when the crunch of severed vertebrae came from around his neck.

This time, blood spouted out like a fountain, and, without even watching the decapitated torso drop, D approached the ash-gray head rolling around on the floor.

The impact after its flight through the air had knocked the mask off, and the face of what was still a young man glared at the heavens. The right half of the face looked like it had been caught in a press, with both the eye and the ear shrunken to half their normal size. Ugly and grotesque, the face was completely covered with wrinkles.

"Such is the price of receiving powers none of the Nobility have ever known!" Lina said from beside D. It was unclear where she'd got it from, but she now wore a white death shroud—raiment that until a day earlier would have been the furthest thing from appropriate attire for her. "In return for the amplification of his psychic energy, Cuore's cognitive powers degenerated. I see it all now. That was Tajeel Schmika."

"Is Mr. Meyer okay?" D asked, attentive to his surroundings but without taking up his sword. Perhaps he was getting ready for the other one, the unrecognized vampire rendered on the computer screen.

Lina happened to smile then. "You'll see him soon enough. Do you want to know the whole truth? I think you already know most of it anyway."

D gazed at Lina, at the girl of seventeen whose whole body brimmed with energy, who perhaps wanted to stun the Hunter with a sight of her supple thighs peeking through the slit of her death shroud.

"Then all this is the result of experiments a decade ago? And now all of it's coming to light."

Lina nodded at his serene tone. Casting a sympathetic glance at the creatures in the corner of the room, their eyes glittering, she said, "They were children taken from other villages about the same time we were. In their present form, they've gone a decade without food or drink—yes, they could live that way forever. I wonder if we could say they benefited in some way? What do you think? I guess you could say that compared to them, we were lucky. The experiments left us with no external abnormalities, so at least we got to live the last ten years as normal human beings. Without even realizing we'd died a decade earlier . . . "

With a brief glance at Tajeel's head and body, which gave off a purplish smoke as they dissolved, D moved his eyes to the enormous electronic apparatus hemming the laboratory.

Remnants of the abominable experiments that had once been performed here, gene-altering equipment, automated surgical units, clusters of ultralarge-scale integrated circuits—all these listened without a word as the tragic truth reached them.

"Why was Tajeel left here?"

"He was a failure, after all. Right from the very end of the experiments he was wild, with an excessive lust for blood. That's why only the three of us were released. Given a grace period of ten years. It seems we were the best of the guinea pigs."

Ten years—a long, long time until the results of the experiments would become clear. During that time, the modifications made to their cells caused the cells to change one by one, mixing a different hue into the blood flowing through their veins, and making their genes long for the darkness . . .

"I suppose you could say the experiments, including the ones to increase my intelligence, succeeded for the most part. Now I can see perfectly well in the dark, and the cells of my body produce energy even if I don't eat anything. Though I haven't tried it, I suppose I could even survive in a vacuum or underwater. D, can you do all that?"

Without waiting for an answer, Lina took the sword D had discarded from atop Tajeel's remains. Thrusting it deep into her own heart, she let him watch as she pulled it out again.

"So long as we don't get our heads cut off, we're immortal. Tajeel knew that, so he brought me into the fold, and I fulfilled his desire. As I'm sure you could see. I wonder if my child will be a good one?"

"Why did he wait until now to make you his? He must've had countless opportunities."

"Because, as the only one who had awakened, there was nothing he could do until our genes of darkness were perfected. All he had to do was wait. I would automatically learn the truth about everything and gladly let him have his way with me. So that we might increase our numbers."

So, was that the real purpose of the ruins?

"But it seems the experiment failed after all. The same urge that Tajeel had dwells in me, as well."

Within her slightly opened mouth, D saw a pair of fangs.

The girl frolicking on a road crusted with remnants of snow because she was going to the Capital.

The girl at the windowsill, a white blossom at her breast, gazing for an eternity at the road that had carried her mysterious suitor away.

"I don't know if you found him or not, but before I came here I killed one of my classmates. Once we were alone, he suddenly grabbed hold of me, pushed me down, and demanded that I transfer my right to go to the Capital to him. He said that was the only reason he'd ever pretended to be interested in a Noble victim like me. At that point, something inside me changed forever. I wonder if that makes his murder justified?"

D was silent, just listening. There was nothing else he had to do. What had he fought for in this village anyway?

"And do you have the same urge, too?" Oh, but the Hunter's voice was as cold and clear as ever when he sent the question back over his shoulder.

"Yes." Cuore stood paralyzed in the blue light. He had an intelligent, rational expression that seemed to belong to someone else entirely—and he had pearly white fangs.

"He tried to protect me right up to the very end. Even knowing the fate in store for him, he did his very best, asked them not to bring me into the fold. Though he was the one who found the entrance in the forest and set Tajeel free in the first place, the night Tajeel attacked Kaiser's wife for the second time, he was sneaking around after him trying to stop him. Unfortunately, he hadn't mastered the use of his psychic energy, and he let it all out at our place."

Letting a chagrined smile arise, Cuore came over and stood by Lina's side. Twining her pale arms around his neck, Lina smiled lasciviously.

"I intend to let him have his way with me, too. What'll you do, D—try to cut me down? Aren't you supposed to be a Hunter?"

"I don't work without compensation. Besides, my business here is done." That was his farewell to the girl who'd listened to the song of wind and the brook with him.

D spun on his heel in the blue light. He made it as far as the door before a voice filled with positively unearthly malice drifted from a dark corner.

"Why . . . are you letting him leave?"

D saw the ash-gray shadow walking closer with a laser gun in his right hand. The last one—the man the computer had rendered.

"Stop it," Lina said in a strident tone. "Killing him will accomplish nothing. We can live anywhere at all. Given time, we can probably discover some way to get by without lusting for blood."

The shadowy figure shook his head. It was an oddly sluggish movement. "We haven't been *given time* . . . Take a good look."

One of his hands tore off the mask.

There were gasps of surprise.

What made Lina and Cuore's eyes bulge wasn't the fact that the face belonged to Mr. Meyer, of course, but rather that the face itself was warped and melting like a waxwork. One eye drooped all the way to his chin, trailing red tendons behind it.

D's memory replayed a certain phrase. *I must dispose of the failures.*

"You don't . . . seem surprised," Mr. Meyer said. "You knew after all, didn't you?"

D nodded. "When that farmhouse was attacked by a couple of creatures that escaped from here, there wasn't enough blood to account for you. There could only be one reason. Because you were one of them." His voice seemed pained. The man who'd let a light shine on the future of a girl. These, too, were words of farewell. "Apparently your vampire nature seems to have awakened without you being aware of it. Are you the one who attacked Fern and his daughter? That'd explain why, when the two blood samples from two different attackers were mixed together and analyzed, an unrecognizable face was displayed."

A sapphire beam converted the floor by D's feet to steam and ions. D didn't so much as flinch.

"Why are you the only one who's fine? Weren't we . . . humans made in the same fashion? How come we're the only ones . . . who must die? . . . "

There was a sound like something shattering, and the teacher collapsed on the floor.

"Mr. Meyer!"

"Keep away from me . . . " Checking Lina before she could run over to him, the teacher tried to stand again.

Blue light speared through the twilight, burning through the walls and floor in succession.

The barrel of the weapon dropped.

A voice saddled with infinite anger and protest crept across the ground. "Lina . . . You mustn't . . . study . . . the history of the Nobility . . . "

Watching the putrid ichor and clothing fall to a heap on the floor, Lina asked D, "Is that our fate?"

D was silent. He heard a voice. *You were my only success.*

"I envy you."

How must Lina's words have sounded to D?

"I'm so jealous of you, I could hate you. When will we end up like that, do you know?"

"No, I don't."

Absentmindedly, Lina wound her arm around the neck of the frozen Cuore and said, "I'd planned on just dropping out of the picture, but I'm going to go before the exam board tomorrow. You'll come, too, won't you? True to Mr. Meyer's dying wish, I've got to tell them how much I loathe the Nobility. To say there's no tomorrow for them, and no history—just like the four of us."

Suddenly, Cuore stepped away from Lina.

Speechless with surprise, Lina was ready to go right after him, but D caught her by the arm.

"He doesn't want you to see him."

Tottering, the youth disappeared into the reaches of the darkness. The time had come for him, too.

In the blue light that would most likely fill this place for all eternity, the beautiful Hunter and the girl trained their eyes on the depths of the darkness as they both, individually, bore witness to the cruelty of fate.

†

The next day, the trio of examiners who arrived in the village early in the afternoon received a strange proposal from the mayor, who looked somewhat pale. He said that the town wanted to conduct the exam in the ruins that'd once belonged to the Nobility.

The selection of a human being who would help build the future would take place in the ruins of those that had ruled the past. Wouldn't that be thrilling?

The proposal was accepted. That evening saw many in attendance in a subterranean hall filled with chairs.

Although the members of the exam board furrowed their brows as Lina stood in her white dress in front of mysterious devices, after a captivating smile from her they took their seats without complaint. The villagers lined up behind them.

Only one person, the mayor, wore an expression of discontent, and that was because D and Lina had coerced him into using this location. If his relationship with his adopted daughter was made public before the exam board, he'd have been run out of town, regardless of the power that he held. But, more than that, more than anything, it was the eerie aura from D as the Hunter stared at him that made the mayor tremble.

D stood quietly behind Lina, hidden in the depths of the darkness.

When everyone had gone to their seats, Lina bowed quietly, and the mayor stood up. "This year's representative of the village of Tepes: Lina Belan. Her score on the selection tests—twelve hundred out of a possible twelve hundred points. Her excellent work has earned her a place before this exam board."

Though they tried their level best to preserve their stern demeanor, the expressions of the examiners softened. Despite the fact that the results had been communicated ahead of time, Lina's performance still had the power to inspire awe.

"Very well. Now, there's just one question I must ask before the final decision is made. What studies do you intend to pursue in the Capital?"

A wave of tension passed through the assembly.

Many of her classmates knew of the girl's desire. However, to say it aloud would be to throw away all her tomorrows. But they didn't know that for Lina there was no tomorrow.

As D stood there, he had a fleeting shade of sorrow in his eyes.

"Before I answer, there's something I'd like to show you."

The assembly stirred at Lina's comment. Such a proposal was out of the norm. This examination, which could have been concluded with a brief answer, was becoming a long, drawn-out affair.

"Once, this castle was referred to as the Nobility's Frontier Center for Calculation," Lina began. "Constructed about five thousand years ago—well, five thousand, one hundred and twenty-seven years ago, to be exact—certain top-secret experiments were conducted here. Five thousand years—isn't there something familiar about that number? From the historical point of view, it's generally said that the decline of the Nobility as a race began in this era."

The blue light stirred. What was the girl trying to tell them?

Lina raised her right hand.

Between the girl and the audience, an image formed. While it was completely two-dimensional, it had depth and color. Realizing that the image was of the same subterranean hall they were now in, the people looked at one another.

Machinery ensconced in the darkness glittered, shadowy people dashed about, flasks spouted gouts of prismatic smoke. Children were sealed in medical casings on what looked to be lab tables, and men in black garb studied data rendered in strangely glowing points of light.

"This is a recording of the experiments," Lina explained. "Experiments by the Nobility that were no less than an attempt to halt the decline of their species. However, their science had already come to the conclusion that their decline was inevitable. To them, this unavoidable decline also meant eventual extinction. How the few who reached that conclusion must have cursed their fate, perhaps even wallowed in the deepest despair, I can well imagine."

Here, Lina smiled broadly.

"Gives you a warm, fuzzy feeling, doesn't it?"

The assembly stirred a bit, the tension broken. The examiners exchanged glances and laughed. Still beaming her smile, Lina continued. "The way they chose to combat their despair was through these experiments. If the inevitability of their ruin was written in their genes like letters carved into a milestone, then they had only to make those genes into something else. Turn night into day, darkness into light. Become a creature with a far greater will to survive as a race—a higher potential energy. In this way, they began trying to genetically combine humans with the Nobility."

It took a few seconds before all assembled there could catch the import of Lina's words.

This time, shock waves ran through the assembly. The mayor and one of the examiners rose to their feet.

"How—how do you know that? What are you?"

As if to answer the examiner's question, the image hanging in space changed.

Warped children were born one after another, men and women transformed into something no longer human. A part of the ruins was suddenly consumed by flames, crumbling.

"These experiments were carried out secretly in one area of the Frontier, far from the Capital, and you can easily imagine what the results would have meant to many of the Nobility. Just as we find it repulsive to even consider such a thing, they, too, detested the thought of mixing with humans. Let's say that the destruction by the opposing faction you just witnessed was one answer. Those privy to the secret fled from the ruins, and silence reigned here for five thousand years."

About to say something, the examiner saw a look rising in the girl's eyes. He held his tongue. Such a mysterious look it was. When hatred and sorrow are mixed together, could they produce a picture of supreme bliss?

"Ten years ago, the ruins came back to life. A being of tremendous importance, one whom even I find difficult to comprehend, took four children from our village and performed the same procedures on us. Why at this late date? And why were those children chosen? That I don't know. Perhaps the decline of their race had highs and lows, like a biorhythm, and there was an optimal time for starting up again. At any rate, the children underwent the treatment, and were then returned to the village. All memories erased, unaware that the results would manifest in their bodies a decade later. And now the results are in. Taking this shape . . . "

The eyes of people focused on Lina—on the pair of fangs poking from the corners of her lips.

There was no more stirring of the crowd. A deathly silence fell over them, and the mayor covered his face with both hands.

Erasing the image with a slight wave of her right hand, Lina continued softly. "Yes, but now it's all over. The four children, in accordance with fate, will leave the village. Even if that fate was forced on them by someone else."

At this point, Lina turned her back to the audience, as if to let someone standing in the darkness hear her last malediction. "There's no need to mourn for them any longer," the girl said, "because now they finally understand. What was hoped for them. What's waiting for them where they must go. And though in the long run they themselves didn't quite get to the top, they were one step in what will continue to be a very, very long climb.

"The Nobility perished, and the human race remains," Lina continued. "However, couldn't we say the biological disposition of human beings—in both their physiology and psychology—is superior to that of the Nobility? Who could claim that the worth of a creature is based on the height of the biorhythm for its species? Brutality and cruelty on par with the Nobility, an urge to destroy anything more beautiful than yourself—these things have been all too familiar to me."

Transfixed by those freezing cold pupils, the mayor grew pale.

Once again, an image hove into view.

The people saw stars glittering in a pitch-black ocean. In the distance, a hundred billion more stars sparkled, a vast spiraling nebula nurturing a multitude of life-forms, the sea of hydrogen atoms giving birth to existence itself.

"The four children were supposed to go there."

Lina's voice sounded as if it had crossed a great distance when it rang in the ears of those assembled in the rows.

"Free from the black destiny hanging over the humans and Nobility, they were to go out and join the universal consciousness as a perfect form of 'intelligent' life. Now even that dream is gone, but because of that, I suppose they don't mourn for themselves."

Suddenly, the image changed.

The darkness faded rapidly, and light filled the hall. The white light welling up drove away the twilight, swathing the exhausted-looking faces of the people, and every inch of their bodies, in a wonderful and serene hue.

"This is the potential of the new humanity."

Her whole body glittering beautifully, Lina quietly looked at D, then gazed at the shining people.

"The *people* who uncovered this potential, the *beings* who guided the human race to a higher level—were they really so cursed?"

The girl suddenly pressed a hand to her chest. The time had come. If nothing else, her voice was proud.

"I believe I'd like to learn about the history of the Nobility."

†

A s soon as she finished saying the words, Lina collapsed. "Don't come near me! Don't watch! D!"

The people stopped where they were, and the beautiful shadow knelt by Lina's side.

"Just hide my face . . . "

A black scarf fell across the face of the girl.

"Thank you . . . D . . . Stay by my side, won't you? I'm so scared . . . "

"I'll always be here."

"Back at the shack . . . " Lina wrung a voice from her pain. "At the shack . . . the white flower I found in the morning . . . that . . . was your doing, wasn't it? If someone had left it, there's no way . . . you wouldn't have noticed them . . . "

"That's right."

"I was so glad . . . so very . . . glad . . . There were two people who cared about me . . . I wish I could've met the other one . . . "

"Don't talk."

Lina's hand came up. Just before it started to melt and dissolve, D took hold of it gently. It was the first time he'd done so. It would never happen again.

"Goodbye . . . D. Oh, the potential we had . . . "

The weight in D's hand dwindled rapidly, along with her voice. No one moved.

The dazzling light threw long, long shadows across the floor.

When one skinny boy raised his damp eyes at the sound of a door opening and closing, the beautiful Vampire Hunter had disappeared.

†

A few days later, a horse and its gorgeous rider were following the narrow road where the crusted remains of snow conspired with the shoots of young grass.

Though the night was over, a thick cover of leaden clouds shrouded the eastern sky. The rays of the morning sun didn't reach the ground.

An almost imperceptible breeze fluttered the hem of the rider's black coat as he crossed the sea of grass stretching far into the distance.

Behind the rider, there was the moan of the morning's first electric bus approaching.

About fifteen feet ahead of him was a small bench. Humble though it was, this was a stop on a bus line connecting the Frontier and the Capital.

Noticing the horse and rider, the skinny boy seated on the bench looked up in surprise. The next moment, his expression became bashful and he looked down again. His gloveless hands were thoroughly chapped.

The small traveling bag by his side bore the address of his destination as well as his name—Marco.

The horse and rider passed by.

Shortly thereafter, there was the sound of the bus stopping. It drew closer, then passed.

Suddenly, a window opened and the boy stuck his head out. Wildly waving his thin hand, he shouted something.

The piercing groan of the engine and wheels scribbled out his voice. But D could hear him. And this is what the boy had said: "I'm headed to the Capital. Gonna do the history of the Nobility."

A gust of wind blew, as if to chase after the bus.

D remembered.

The face of a boy listening to the final words of a girl. A look of boundless pride in his eyes. The face of the someone who loved.

And D knew.

The messenger who left the white flowers, and let a girl dream.

At some point the clouds broke, and, as he watched the little bus disappear into the sun-showered distance, a faint smile started to rise on D's lips.

If that boy could have seen it, he would have told people for the rest of his days how he'd been the one to bring it out. It was just such a smile.

VAMPIRE HUNTER D

OMNIBUS BOOK ONE

VAMPIRE HUNTER D

VOLUME 3
DEMON DEATHCHASE

Written by

HIDEYUKI KIKUCHI

Illustrations by

YOSHITAKA AMANO

English translation by

KEVIN LEAHY

Dark Horse Books

Milwaukie

VAMPIRE HUNTER D

Village of the Dead

I

The tiny village obstinately refused the blessings the sunlight poured down so generously upon it.

Though a Frontier village like this might see its share of years, as a rule the size of the community didn't fluctuate greatly. The village's eighty or so homes wavered in the warming light. Every last bit of the lingering snow had been consumed by the black soil. Spring was near.

And yet, the village was dead.

Doors of reinforced plastic and treated lumber hung open, swinging with the feeble breeze. In the communal cookery, which should have been roiling with the lively voices of wives and children as evening approached, now dust danced alone.

Something was missing. People.

The majority of the homes remained in perfect order, with no signs of any struggle by the occupants, but in one or two there were overturned chairs in the living room. In one house, the bed covers were disheveled, as if someone just settling down to sleep had gotten out of bed to attend to some trifling matter.

Had gotten out—and had never come back.

Small black stains could be found on the floors of that house. A number of spots no bigger than the tip of your little finger, they might be mistaken for a bit of fur off a pet dog or cat. The spots wouldn't catch anyone's eye. Even if they would, there were no people around with eyes to be caught.

Evening grew near, the white sunlight took on a dim bluish tint, the wind blowing down the deserted streets grew more insistent, and an eerie atmosphere pervaded the village at dusk—like ebon silhouettes were coalescing in the shadows and training their bloodshot gaze on any travelers that might pass through the wide-open gates.

More time passed. Just when the dim shadows were beginning to linger in the streets, the sound of iron-shod hooves pounding the earth, and the crunch of tires in well-worn ruts, came drifting in through the entrance to the village.

A bus and three people on horseback came to a halt in front of one of the watch towers just inside the gates.

The atomic-powered bus was the sort used for communications across the Frontier, but its body had been modified, so that now iron bars were set into the windows and a trenchant plow was affixed to the front of the vehicle. Not exactly the sort of vehicle upstanding folks had much call for.

Every inch of the vehicle was jet black—a perfect complement to the foreboding air of the trio looming before it.

"What the hell's going on here?" asked the man on the right. He wore a black shirt and black leather pants. Conspicuous for his fierce expression and frightfully long torso, this man would stand out anywhere.

"Don't look like our client's here to meet us," said the man on the far left. Though his face wore a wry smile, his thread-thin eyes brimmed with a terrible light as they scoured his surroundings. A hexagonal staff strapped to his well-defined back made his shadow appear impaled.

As if on cue, the two turned their heads toward the even more muscular giant standing between them. From neck to wrist, his body was covered by a protector of thin metal on leather, but the mountain of muscles beneath it was still sharply defined. His face was like a chunk of granite that had sprouted whiskers, and he brimmed with an intensity that would make a bear backpedal if it ran across him in the dark. Twining around him, the wind seemed to carry the stench of a beast as it blew off again.

"Looks like they've had it," he muttered in a stony tone. "The whole damn village gone in one night—looks like we lost the goose that laid the golden egg. Just to be sure, let's check out a few houses. Carefully."

"I ain't too crazy about that idea," the man in black said. "How 'bout we send Grove? For him it'd—" His voice died out halfway through the sentence. The giant had shot a glance at him. It was like being scrutinized by a stone. "I . . . er . . . I was just kidding, bro."

It wasn't merely the difference in their builds that made the man in black grow pale—it appeared that the man truly feared the giant. Quickly dismounting—the man with the hexagonal staff did likewise—they then entered the village with a gliding gait.

There was the sound of the bus door opening. The face of a girl with blonde hair peered out at the giant from the driver's seat. "Borgoff, what's up?" she asked. At twenty-two or -three years old, her visage was as lovely as a blossom, but there was something about how overly alluring it was that called to mind a carnivorous insect—beautiful but deadly.

"Odds are the village's been wasted. Be ready to move on a moment's notice." Saying that in a subdued tone, the world seemed to go topsy-turvy as his voice suddenly became gentle. "How's Grove?" he inquired.

"He's okay for the moment. Not likely to have another seizure for a while."

It was unclear whether or not the giant heard the girl's response, as he didn't so much as nod but kept gazing at the silent, lonely rows of houses. He flicked his eyes up toward the sky and the dingy, ivory hue that lingered there. The round moon was already showing its pearly white figure.

"Wish we had a little more cloud cover."

Just as he'd muttered those words, two figures came speeding down the street as if riding the very wind.

"It's just like we thought. Not a single freaking person," the man in black said.

The man with the hexagonal staff turned to the sky and said, "Sun'll be setting soon. The safest bet would be to blow this place as soon as possible, big guy." Saying that, he jabbed out his forefinger.

Apparently, the giant easily pierced the hazy darkness to glimpse the tiny black spot on the tip of that finger.

"Make for the graveyard," he said.

In a flash, a tense hue shot through the faces of the other men, but soon enough they, too, grinned, climbed effortlessly back on their horses, and boldly started their mounts down village streets that'd fallen into the stillness of death.

†

So what had transpired in the village? Having the entire populace of a place disappear in one fell swoop wasn't such a bizarre occurrence on the Frontier. For example, the carnivorous balloon-like creatures known as flying jellyfish seemed to produce an extremely large specimen at a rate of one every twenty years or so. The beast was often a mile and a quarter in diameter, and it could cover an entire village, selectively dissolving every living creature before sucking them all up into its maw.

And then there was the basilisk. A magical creature said to inhabit only deep mountain ravines and haunted valleys, it had merely to wait at the entrance to a village and stare fixedly at a given spot within. Its single, gigantic eye would glow a reddish tint before finally releasing a crimson beam, and villagers would come, first one, then another, right into its fearsome waiting jaws. But the sole weakness of the basilisk was that occasionally one of the hypnotized humans would bid farewell to their family, and when they did so it was always in exactly the same words. Hearing those words, the remaining folk would go out and hunt the basilisk en masse.

However, the most likely cause of every last person vanishing from an entire village was both the most familiar of threats and the most terrifying.

When news of such an eerie happening was passed along by even a single traveler lucky enough to have slipped through such a community unharmed, people could practically hear the footfalls of their dark lords, supposedly long since extinct, lingering in that area. The masters of the darkness—the vampires.

†

Having arrived at the graveyard on the edge of town, the trio of riders and the lone vehicle came to an abrupt halt. In a spot not five hundred yards from the forest, moss-encrusted gravestones formed serpentine rows, and there was an open space where, little by little, the blue-black darkness rose from the ground.

The fearsome trio strode forward, keeping their eyes on everything, coming to a halt in the depths of a forest that threatened to overrun the tombstones. From that spot alone, an area where something had turned over a large expanse of ground to reveal the red clay and left it looking like a subterranean demon had run amuck, there blew a weird miasma. It was a presence so ghastly it froze the leading pair atop their horses and made the giant swallow so hard his Adam's apple thumped in his throat.

What lay concealed by this ravaged earth?

Moving only their eyes, the men scanned the area in search of the source of the miasma.

It was then that they heard a dull sound.

No, it wasn't a sound, but rather a voice. A long, low groan—tormented and unabashed, like a patient having a seizure—began to snake through the uncanny tableau.

The men didn't move.

Partly it was the ghastly miasma, twisting tight around their bones, that prevented them from moving. But more than anything, they were still because that voice, those moans, seemed to issue from within the bus. When the giant had asked, hadn't the girl said he wouldn't have a seizure? It must've been the bizarre atmosphere billowing through this place that made a liar of her. Or perhaps his cries were because, no matter what illness afflicted them, there was something humans found horribly unsettling and inescapable about their mortal condition.

A few seconds later, a figure appeared from behind one of the massive tree trunks, as if to offer some answer to the riddle.

A veritable ghost, it stepped its way across the red clay in a precarious gait, coming to a standstill at a spot about thirty feet ahead of them.

The figure that loomed before the glimmering silver moon was that of an older man of fifty or so. With a dignified countenance and silver hair that seemed to give off a whitish glow of its own, anyone would've taken him for a village elder. Actually, however, this old man was doing two things that, when witnessed by those who knew about such matters, were as disturbing as anything could possibly be.

He was using his left hand to pin his jacket, with its upturned collar, to his chest, while his open right hand covered his mouth. As if to conceal his teeth.

"Thank you for coming," the old man said. His voice seemed pained, like something he'd just managed to vomit up. "Thank you for coming . . . but you're too late . . . Every last soul in the village *is done for*, myself included, but . . . "

Surely the fearsome men must've noticed that, as he spoke, the old man didn't turn his eyes on them.

There was nothing before his pupils, stagnant and muddied like those of a dead fish. Only a long line of trees continuing on into the abruptly growing darkness.

"Hurry, go after him. He—he made off with my daughter. Please, hurry after them and get her back . . . Or if she's already one of them . . . please make her end a quick one . . . "

Appealing, entreating, the old man went on in his reed-thin voice. Not so much as glancing at the men before him, he faced an empty spot between the trees. With the darkness so dear to demons steadily creeping in around them, it was an unsettling sight.

"He'd been after my daughter for a while. Time after time he tried to take her, and each and every time I fought him off. But last night, he finally showed his fangs . . . Once he got one of us, the rest fell like dominoes . . . I'm begging you, save my daughter from that accursed fate. Last night, he . . . took off to the north. With your speed, there might still be time . . . If you manage to save my daughter, go to the town of Galiusha. My younger sister's there. If you explain the situation, she'll give you the ten million dalas I promised . . . I beg of you . . . "

At this point in the old man's speech, the heap of dirt behind him underwent a change.

A small mound bulged up suddenly, and then a pale hand burst through the dirt. Resembling the dead man's hand flowers that bloomed only by night, this was in fact a real hand.

A deep grumbling filled the forest. Sheer malice, or a curse, the grumbling bore a thirst. An unquenchable thirst for blood, lasting for all eternity.

The figures pushing through the dirt and rising one after another were the villagers, transformed into vampires in the span of a single night.

Appearing just as they had in life, only now with complexions as sickly pale as paraffin, when the moonlight struck them they glowed with an eerie, pale, blue light.

There were burly men. There were dainty women. There were girls in dresses. There were boys in short pants. Nearly five hundred strong, their bloodshot eyes gleaming and their mouths set, words like unearthly or ghastly couldn't capture the way they stared intently at the men. They didn't even bother to knock off the dirt that clung to their heads and shoulders.

"Oh, it's too late now. Kill us somehow and get out of here . . . Once it's really night . . . I'll be . . . " The old man's left hand dropped. The pair of wounds that remained on the nape of his neck also showed on those of the other villagers.

It's hard to say which happened first—the old man lowering his right hand, or the men's jaws dropping. For between his lips thrown perilously wide, a pair of fangs jutted from the upper gums.

"Yeah, now it's getting interesting," the man in black said in an understandably tense tone, reaching for the crescent blades at his waist.

Perhaps the eldritch spell that held them had been broken, for the hands of the man with the hexagonal staff were gliding to his weapon.

The old man zipped effortlessly forward. Along with the mob at his back.

"Giddyup!" As if this was just what he'd been waiting for, the man in black spurred his horse into action. The man with the hexagonal staff followed after him, but the giant waited behind.

A number of the villagers had their heads staved in under the hooves, falling backward only to have their sternums and abdomens trampled as well.

"What are you waiting for, freaks? Come and get it!" As the man in black shouted, the heads of nearly half of the fang-baring villagers closing in on him from all sides went sailing into the air, sliced cleanly like so many watermelons.

An instant later, silver light limned another corona, and the heads flew from the next rank. Even novice vampires like these knew they mustn't lose their heads or brains, but they dropped to the ground leaking gray matter or spouting bloody geysers as if they were fountainheads.

What had severed the heads of the vampire victims so cleanly was one of the blades that'd hung at the man's waist. The blades were about a foot in diameter and shaped like a half-moon. Honed to a razor-fine arc, the weapon was known among the warriors of the Frontier as the crescent blade. A wire or cord was usually affixed to one end, and the wielder could set up a sort of safety zone around himself, keeping his enemies at bay by spinning the blade as widely or tightly as he wished. Due to the intense training necessary to handle it, there were few who could use one effectively.

But now, the weapons swished from both hands of the man in black to paint gorgeous silver arcs, slashing through villagers like magic—to the right and the left, above him and below, never missing the slightest change in their position. In fact, each and every one of the villagers had clearly been cut from a different angle. His lightning-speed attacks came from phantasmal angles. It didn't seem possible that anything he set his sights on would be spared.

Another particularly weird sound, entirely different from the slice of the crescent blade, came from his companion's favorite weapon—the hexagonal staff that was always on his back. Both ends had sharp protrusions, veritable stakes, but normally this weapon would be spun and used to bludgeon opponents. Its owner was using the hexagonal staff in this manner. However, the way that he swung the staff was unique. Spinning it around his waist like a water wheel set on its side, he smashed in the head of a foe to his right, spun it clear around his back, and took out an opponent to his left. The movement took less than a tenth of a second.

In a snap, four shadowy figures hung in the air to the left and the right of the man with the hexagonal staff, and before and behind him as well. This leaping assault capitalized on the superhuman strength unique to vampires.

The man with the hexagonal staff struck the first blow. His movements were sheer magic.

An instant after he staved in the hoary head of the old man to his right, the old woman before him went sailing through the air with her bottom jaw knocked clear off. With almost no delay, the two to his left and behind him were both speared through the heart by the tips of his staff.

What kind of strength did this ungodly display demand? Actually, the man with the hexagonal staff had his right arm stock still up around the shoulder. To all appearances, his right hand from the wrist down didn't quiver or move, and the staff seemed to spin of its own accord, giving the impression of smashing the villagers all by itself.

It wasn't humanly possible.

Still, the villagers numbered five hundred. Even with the skills this pair had, they couldn't keep the vampires from attacking the bus. In fact, the other vampires ignored the two of them and pounded across the ground in a dash for the vehicle.

And every time the wind howled, a number of them screamed and dropped in unison. The wind roared, and villagers fell like beads from a string, only to be skewered together again by arrows from the giant's bow.

The bow itself wasn't the kind of finished good you'd find for sale in city shops. It was a savage thing, just a handy low-hanging branch that'd been snapped off and strung with the gut of some beast. Even the contents of the quivers strapped to both of the giant's flanks and his back were no more than simple iron rods filed to a point.

But in the hands of this giant, they became missiles of unrivaled accuracy.

The giant didn't use them one at a time. Drawing back five at once, he released the arrows simultaneously. The acts of both getting the arrows out and then nocking them off seemed to be simplicity itself. Judging from his speed, he seemed to just be shooting wildly, without taking aim.

And yet, not a single arrow missed the mark. Not only did they not miss, but each arrow pierced the hearts of at least three villagers. This was only the natural way to attack, given that vampires wouldn't die by being run through the stomach, but the question was, how could the giant choose a target and move his bow in less time than it took to blink?

This remained a mystery even as the villagers left corpse upon corpse heaped before the bus.

It was then that a small shriek arose from behind the mounted men. They heard a woman's voice coming from inside the bus.

"That ain't good. Fall back!"

Before the giant had shouted the words, the men were whipping around toward the bus behind them.

With a bestial snarl, the villagers started to run. When the rapidly dwindling distance shrunk to a mere fifteen feet, the ground-pounding feet of the fiends came to an unexpected halt.

A lone youth suddenly stood between them and the bus, blocking them.

But it was not that alone that stopped the rush of these bloodthirsty creatures. For starters, there was the question of where this youth had appeared from.

With the gentle wave in the forelock touching his brow, the youth's face was strong and had a healthy tone, and, from the center of it his innocent eyes gazed at the hell-spawn without a hint of fear.

The villagers, who'd hesitated due to the way the youth unexpectedly appeared, must have deemed him the most desirable of prey. An instant later they were pressing forward toward him, as a single tide.

And then something happened.

Into the darkness were born a number of streaks of light.

Like silvery fish that burst flying through the waves, the lights looked as chaotic as cloth whipped by a high wind, but their accuracy was truly peerless, for each individual flash lanced through the hearts of countless villagers. Five hundred vampires hit in an instant . . . Flames spouting from their chests, the villagers fell. Writhing, then stiffening, the peaceful faces that came with death were surely the ones they'd had until dusk of the day before, returning to them now as serene masks.

From the cover of the bus, the man with the hexagonal staff slowly showed his face. Seeing the corpses lying in heaps, he said, "Wow, pretty damn intense," then gave an appreciative whistle. Once he'd whistled, he looked up at one of the windows on the bus and asked, "Is good ol' Grove doing all right?" His expression showed concern.

He didn't even glance at the young man who'd done all this. That man had already vanished. Every bit as mysteriously as he'd appeared.

"It couldn't be helped, and what's done is done," the man in black said, coming around from the other side. "We've got bigger fish to fry. The geezer said the Noble that grabbed his daughter took off to the north, right? If we go now, we could definitely catch up to 'em, bro. We could track 'em, run 'em down. Ten million if we bring her back safe. Sure he's probably already had his way with her, but what the hell, we'd be dealing with a woman on the other end. We could threaten her, tell her we chopped the girl's head off along with the vampire's, and turned her back into a human. She'd keep her trap shut and pay up."

Behind him, the giant muttered, "That'd all be well and good, if he'd been talking to us."

"What do you mean?"

The man in black looked at the giant's face, then followed the giant's line of sight toward the thicket ahead of them and off to the right. Earlier, that was the same spot the old man had addressed when he spoke.

"Come on out!"

As the giant said this, a crescent blade in the man in black's right hand gleamed in the moonlight, and the hexagonal staff ripped through the wind.

They, too, had known that this unearthly miasma hadn't belonged to the old man. The one responsible for it was in the woods. Their hands went to their weapons. The aura coming from the thicket gave them the same chill that radiated from the Nobility. They grasped their weapons fiercely, wanting to conceal their humiliation at not having uncovered the source of those emanations.

"If you don't come out, we're coming in, but from the way that old man was talking to you, I'm guessing we've gotta be in the same line of work. Hell, it seems you're even more dependable than we are. If that's the case, we don't wanna do nothing stupid. What do you say we talk this ten million deal out all friendly-like?" The giant waited a while after finishing his proposal. There was no answer, nor any movement. His thick, caterpillar-like eyebrows hoisted up quickly.

"Bro, this way's a lot quicker."

The crescent blade flew from the hand of the man in black. While it wasn't clear what it was constructed of, it wove through the trees, speeding to the spot at which the giant glowered. It was an assault devoid of ceremony, but steeped in murderous intent.

There was a beautiful sound. A silver flash of light coursed back out between the trees.

Behind the two men who yelped and jumped out of the way there was the sound of steel cleaving darkness.

What the giant now grasped in his right hand was the same crescent blade the man in black had just unleashed. A red band was slowly running down its finely honed surface. Fresh blood poured from the giant's hand. The emotional hue welling up on that rock-like face was one of fury, and also one of fright.

"Not bad," said the man with the hexagonal staff, giving a kick to his horse's flanks.

The horse didn't move.

Once again he kicked. His boots had spurs on the heels. The hide on the flanks broke, and blood trickled out. And yet still the horse didn't move.

When he noticed it was thoroughly cowed, the man with the hexagonal staff finally stopped giving the horse his spurs.

The door of the bus opened. A girl stuck her head out and asked, "What's going on, guys?" Acutely sensitive to the presence there, her beautiful face turned automatically to the depths of the woods. Imitating her older brothers.

In the depths of the darkness, the presence stirred. The clop of hooves drew steadily closer.

Suddenly the youth was before them, bathed in moonlight. It was as if the darkness itself had crystallized and taken human form.

II

Mysterious as the sparkle of the blue pendant shining from the breast of his black coat was, it ranked a distant second to the gorgeous visage that showed below the traveler's hat.

Astride his horse with the reins in his fist, the beautiful youth seemed as calm as any traveler passing through by happenstance, but one look at him and it was clear he was far from being a mere traveler.

"What the hell are you supposed to be?" the man in black asked in a thick, lethargic tone. The traveler's good looks were enough to send chills down his spine. That, combined with the knowledge that this guy had just batted back his lethal attack, made him speak in this strange voice.

The shadowy figure didn't answer. He moved forward, seemingly intent on casually breezing past them.

"Hold up," the man with the hexagonal staff shouted in an attempt to stop him. "Look, buddy, you might be one of the Hunters that geezer called, but so are we. Sure, we might've been in the wrong flying off and taking a poke at you like that, but there's no harm in us all introducing ourselves. We're the Marcus clan—I'm Nolt, the second oldest of the boys."

The shadowy figure halted his advance.

"This here's Kyle, the youngest brother," Nolt continued.

Eyes gleaming with animosity, the man in black made no attempt at a greeting.

"The great big fella is our older brother Borgoff."

Just as his brother finished introducing him, a sharp sound came from around the giant's thigh. The crescent blade, now in two pieces, fell to the ground with a shower of glittering silver flecks. The unusual break in it was not from folding. It was from squeezing. The giant wiped his bloody palm on his horse's ear. Blood stuck to the creature's coat, forcing the hair to fall in a mat.

"We've got another brother, but he's sick and doesn't get out of our ride. And finally, there's Leila, our baby sister."

"Nice to meet you, Mr. Tight-lips." Behind that oh-so-amiable voice, Leila's bright feline eye burned with flames of hostility. However, when the face of the traveler made a rapid turn in her direction, those flames suddenly wavered.

"The Marcus clan—I've heard of you," the traveler said, speaking for the first time. Without inflection, his voice was like iron, devoid of all possible emotion. The voice didn't match his incredibly good looks, but then again, no other voice would have been more appropriate.

However, the fact that he spoke in such a tone even after learning the names of these men . . .

The Marcus clan was the most skillful vampire hunting group on the Frontier. Consisting of five members, the family from oldest to youngest was Borgoff, Nolt, Groveck, Kyle, and Leila. The number of Nobles they'd taken care of reached triple digits, and word of how, miraculously, none of the clan had been lost in the process circulated far and wide among the people of the Frontier.

At the same time, so did tales of the clan's cruelty and callousness.

Nowhere did it say only one Vampire Hunter or group of Hunters could be hired for a given case. Considering the vengeance the Nobility would wreak in the event of failure, it was perfectly normal for the person concerned to employ a number of individuals, or even several groups.

The Marcus clan always lasted until the very end. They alone. No individual or group that had worked with them, or against them for that matter, had ever survived.

Due to the fact that none of the other Hunters' corpses had ever been recovered, there was no choice but to believe the Marcuses' claims that the Hunters were slain by the Nobility, but rumors spread like wildfire, and now an ominous storm of suspicion swirled over the clan members' heads.

Be that as it may, no one doubted their abilities as Hunters. After all, the number of Nobility their group had single-handedly destroyed was staggering.

Still, when other Hunters heard the Marcuses' name, the abhorrence felt was always coupled with a sense of awe over the threat the other killers felt from the clan's clearly demonstrated ability, and their willingness to use their skills for harm.

In all likelihood, this was probably the first time the clan had ever heard a man say their name so calmly.

"Look, jerk—" Unexpectedly, the giant—Borgoff—made a strange face. "—er, pal . . . I've heard about someone with your looks and a blue pendant. Ten years back, this one village elder told us there was only one Hunter in all the Frontier that was a match for us. That alone he was probably tougher than all of us put together or some such thing . . . But you couldn't be . . . "

Giving no answer, the young man turned away, as if completely unconcerned by the bunch of fearsome villains in front of him.

"Uh, hey, wait up," the man with the hexagonal staff called out. "We're going after the Noble that grabbed the geezer's daughter. If you're not with us, that makes you an enemy, too. Is that the way you want it?"

There was no response, and the horse and rider's silhouette was swallowed by the darkness.

"We're not gonna let him go, are we?" Leila asked indignantly, but Borgoff didn't seem to be listening,

"A dhampir . . . is that what he is then . . . ?" he muttered with an imbecilic look on his face. This was the first time the younger siblings had heard the man speak in such a tone.

Or say a certain, mysterious name.

"I've finally met a man I actually fear . . . D."

†

The spot was thirty miles north of the village of Vishnu, where wholesale slaughter followed tragedy in just two short days.

A lone black carriage rushed along the narrow road through the forest. The six horses that pulled it were ebon, too, and the driver in the coachman's perch was garbed in black. The whole vehicle seemed born of the darkness.

Showering the horses with merciless lashes, the driver occasionally looked to the heavens.

The sky was so full of stars it seemed to be falling. Their light seemed to flicker on the face gazing up at them. The graceful visage of the driver clouded suddenly.

"The stars moved. Those giving chase . . . to me . . . Six of them." There in the darkness, his eyes began to give off a blazing light. "And no mere pursuers at that . . . Each possessed of extraordinary skill . . . One of them in particular . . . "

As if unable to contain his agitation, he stood upright in the coachman's perch, shaking the jet-black vehicle beneath his feet.

"I won't let them have her. I won't let anyone take her away." Light coursed from the eyes he opened wide. Blood light.

There was a sudden discordance in the monotonous drone of the carriage wheels.

When turbulence had raced into that graceful face, one of the right wheels slipped off the axle with a crash. The wind groaned and the carriage lurched wildly to the right, kicking up a thick cloud of dust as the carriage rolled over.

What was truly unbelievable was the acrobatics of the driver. Releasing the reins of his own accord, sailing through the air, and skillfully twisting his body, he regained his balance, landing like a length of black cloth a few yards from the carriage.

Anxiety and despair filled his face as he dashed to the vehicle.

Throwing the door open like a man possessed, he peered inside. His anxiety was replaced by relief.

Letting out a deep sigh, he approached the special metal-alloy wagon-wheel that lay some thirty feet away.

"So, misfortune has decided to put in an unfashionably early appearance," he muttered glumly, lifting the wheel and walking back to the carriage. He looked to the sky once again. In a low voice, he said, "Soon the day will be breaking. Seems I shall be walking to the Shelter, and repairing this when it's night again. That's more than enough time for those dogs to catch up to us."

†

A round the time the mountain ridges were rising faintly from the darkness like the edges of so many jigsaw pieces, the pair halted their horses. They were atop a fair-sized hill.

"Ol' Borgoff's got us doing some crazy shit—riding hard in the middle of the night like this. I tell you, he's all worked up over nothing," the man in black said, giving a light wave of his right hand. The green grass below him was shaken by a dye deeper than the darkness.

In the pale, panting darkness of daybreak, this man alone seemed blackly clad in the remnants of night. In a black shirt and pants, it was Kyle—the youngest of the Marcus boys. The ebon flecks that remained like stains not just on his right hand but on his chest and shoulder as well were splashes of blood from all the nocturnal beasts they'd cut down during their ride.

"I thought he told you to stow that talk. That punk—he's no garden-variety Hunter. You must've heard about him, too," the man said in an attempt to settle his wild younger brother, a black staff looming on his back. The man speaking was Nolt, the second oldest.

"Ha! You mean how he's a dhampir?" Kyle spat the words. "A lousy *half-breed*, part Nobility and part human. Oh, sure, everyone says they make the best Vampire Hunters, don't they? But let's not forget something. We slaughter real, full-blooded Nobles!"

"Hey, you've got a point there."

"If he's a half-breed, he's more like us than the Nobility. Nothing to be afraid of. Not to mention, we even rode all night just so he wouldn't lose us, but if you ask me our big brother's lost his nerve. Who besides us would race through a Frontier forest in the middle of the night on horseback?"

Out on the Frontier, the forests were thick with monsters by night.

Though it was true the beasts' numbers had decreased with the decline of the Nobility, to move through the woods before dawn you still either had to be a complete idiot, or someone endowed with nerves of steel and considerable skill. As the brothers were.

It was for this reason Kyle was repulsed by the oldest of the boys, who'd ordered their charge by night so that the youth they'd met earlier wouldn't get a lead on them. Even he would be set upon by numerous creatures before he made it to this hill. The only reason they'd somehow managed to get there before daybreak was because they'd passed through the area before and knew a shortcut through the woods.

"Well, I don't know about that," Nolt said wryly, being more philosophical than the youngest boy. "We're talking about a guy that fended off your crescent blade, after all."

While Kyle glared at the second oldest, Nolt's eyes glimmered. "A horse—I wouldn't have thought it possible."

Kyle was at a loss for words. Sure enough, the sound of iron-shod hoofs came from the depths of the same forest from which the two brothers had just emerged. "It was no problem for us because we knew a shortcut. But that son of a bitch . . . "

Just as the two were exchanging glances, a horse and rider appeared from part of the forest below them, knifing through the darkness. Making a smooth break for the road, the figure struck them as being darker than the blackness.

"It's him all right," said Nolt.

"He ain't getting away," Kyle shot back.

There was a loud smack at the flanks of the pair's mounts, and hoofs were soon kicking up the sod.

With intense energy, they pursued the black-clad silhouette. The way he raced, he seemed a demon of the night, almost impossible to catch.

"We got orders from Borgoff. Don't try nothing funny." Nolt's voice flew at Kyle's back, about a horse-length ahead of him.

They couldn't have D getting ahead of them, but, even if it looked like that might happen, they weren't to do anything rash. Borgoff had ordered them not to attack in the sternest tone they'd ever heard from him.

But for all that, the flames of malice burned out of control in Kyle's breast. It wasn't simply that he had the wildest and most atrocious nature of all his siblings. His lethal crescent blade attack had been warded off by D. For a young man with faith in strength alone, that humiliation was intolerable. What he felt toward D surpassed hatred, becoming nothing less than pure, murderous intent.

Kyle's right hand went for the crescent blade at his waist.

However . . . the two of them couldn't believe their eyes. They just couldn't catch up.

They should have been closing the gap on the horse and rider who didn't seem to be going any faster than they were, but weren't they in fact rapidly falling farther and farther behind?

"Sonuvabitch!" Kyle screamed. Even as he put more power behind the kicks to his horse, his foe still dashed away, the tail of his black coat fluttering in the breeze he left. In no time at all, he shrunk to the size of a pea and vanished from their field of view.

"Dammit. Goddamn freak!"

Giving up and bringing his horse to a halt, Kyle trained his flaming pupils on the point in the road that had swallowed the shadowy figure.

"We ride all night, only to have this happen in the end . . ." Nolt said bitterly. "From the looks of it, we're never gonna catch up to him by normal means. Let's wait here for Borgoff to show up."

III

A round him, the wind swirled.

His hair streamed out, and the wide brim of the traveler's hat seemed to flow like ink. The silver flecks crumbling dreamlike against his refined brow and graceful nose were moonlight. Though the air already wore a tinge of blue, the moonlight reflected in his gaze shone as brightly as in the blackest of nights. While it was possible for a specially modified cyborg horse to gallop at an average speed of about sixty miles per hour, the speed of this horse put that to shame.

What could you say about a rider who could work such magic on the kind of standard steed you might find anywhere?

The road dwindled into the distant flatness of the plain.

Without warning, the rider pulled back on the reins. The horse's forequarters twisted hard to the right, while the sudden stop by the forelegs kicked up gravel and dirt. This rather intense method of braking was not so much mesmerizing as it was mildly unsettling. Once again, the moonlight fell desolately on the rider's shoulders and back.

Without a sound, the black-clad figure dismounted. Bending down, he patiently scrutinized lines in the dirt and gravel, but he soon stood upright and turned his face toward the nearby stand of trees. This person, possessed of such intense beauty as to make the moonlight bashful to be around him, was none other than D.

"So, this is where they left the usual route then. What's he up to?" Muttering this in a way that didn't seem a question at all, he mounted his horse again and galloped toward the tree line.

All that remained after he vanished through the trees was the moonlight starkly illuminating the narrow road, and the distant echo of fading hoofbeats.

The moon alone knew that some six hours earlier a driver in black coming down the road had changed the direction of his carriage in that very spot. Had D discerned the tracks of the carriage he sought, picking them out from all the ruts left by the number of electric buses and other vehicles that passed this way by day?

Shortly thereafter, the moon fused with the pale sky, and, in its place, the sun rose.

Before the sun got to the middle of the sky, D and his steed, who'd been galloping all the while, broke out of another in an endless progression of forests and halted once again.

The ground before him had been wildly disturbed. This was the spot where the carriage had lost a wheel and rolled.

Starting out a full twenty-four hours late, D had caught up in half a day. Of course, it was the fate of the Nobility to sleep while the sun was high, and the Marcus clan was still far behind. The speed and precision of the pursuit by the team of mount and rider was frightening.

But where had the carriage gone?

Without getting off his horse, D glanced at the overturned soil, then gave a light kick to his mount's flanks.

They headed for the hill before them at a gradual pace, quite a change from the way they'd been galloping up to this point.

It was a mound of dirt that really couldn't be called a hill, but, standing atop it looking down, D's eyes were greeted by the sudden appearance of a structure that seemed quite out of place.

It looked like a huge steel box. With a width of more than ten feet and a length of easily thirty, its height was also in excess of ten feet. In the brilliant sunlight that poured down, the black surface threw off blinding flames.

This was the Shelter the Noble in black had mentioned.

Immortal though the vampires might be, they still had to sleep by day. While their scientific prowess had spawned various antidotes for sunlight, they never succeeded in conquering the hellish pain that came when their bodies were exposed to it. The agony of cells blazing one by one, flesh and blood putrefying, every bodily system dissolving—even the masters of the earth were still forced to submit to the legends of antiquity.

Though the vampires had reached the point where their bodies wouldn't be destroyed, many of the test subjects exposed to more than ten minutes of direct sunlight were driven insane by the pain; those exposed for even five minutes were left crippled, their regenerative abilities destroyed. And, no matter what treatment they later received, they never recovered.

But in the Nobility's age of prosperity, that had mattered little.

Superspeed highways wound to every distant corner of the Frontier, linear motor-cars and the like formed a transportation grid that boasted completely accident-free operation, and the massive energy-production facilities erected in and around the Capital provided buses and freight cars with an infinite store of energy.

And then the decline began.

At the hands of the surging tide of humanity, all that the Nobility had constructed was destroyed piece by piece, reducing their civilization to ruins hardly worthy of the name. Even the power plants with their perfect defense systems collapsed, a casualty of mankind's tenacious, millennia-spanning assault.

While the situation wasn't so dire in metropolitan areas, Nobility in the Frontier sectors were stripped of all means of transportation. Though there were many in the Nobility who'd expected this day would come and had established transportation networks in the sectors they controlled, they inevitably lost the enthusiasm and desire to maintain the networks themselves.

Even now, silver rails ran through prairies damp with the mists of dawn, and somewhere in colossal subterranean tunnels lay the skeletons of automated, ultra-fast hovercrafts.

Before carriages became the sole means of transportation, accidents caused by the failure of radar control and power outages occurred frequently.

To the humans, who'd learned how to use the scientific weapons of the Nobility or could penetrate the vehicular defenses with armaments they'd devised on their own, Nobles in transit and immobilized by day were the ideal prey.

Due to the intense demand from the Frontier, the Noble's government in the Capital—where the remaining power was concentrated—constructed special defensive structures at strategic locations along their transportation network.

These were the Shelters.

Though built from a steel-like plating only a fraction of an inch thick, the Shelters could withstand a direct hit from a small nuclear device, and there were a vast array of defensive mechanisms armed and ready to dispose of any insects who might be buzzing around with stakes and hammers in hand.

But what made these Shelters perfect, more than anything else, was one simple fact—

"There's no entrance?" D muttered from atop his horse.

Exactly. The jet-black walls that reflected the white radiance of the sun didn't have so much as a hair-sized crack.

Looking up at the heavens, D started silently down the hill.

The pleasant vernal temperature aside, the sunlight that ruthlessly scorched him was unparalleled agony for a dhampir like D. Dhampirs alone could battle with the Nobility on equal terms by night, but to earn the title of Vampire Hunter, they needed the strength to remain impassive in the blistering hell of the day.

As D drew closer, it seemed the surrounding air bore an almost imperceptible groaning, but that soon scattered in the sunlight.

At D's breast, his pendant glowed ever bluer. It was a mysterious hue that rendered all of the Nobility's electronic armaments inoperable.

Dismounting in front of the sheer, black wall, D put his left hand to the steel. A chilling sensation spread through him. The temperature was probably unique to this special steel. Perhaps it was because, to render the exterior of this structure impervious to all forms of heat or electronic waves, molecules served as atoms in it.

D's hand glided slowly across the smooth surface.

Finishing the front wall, he moved to the right side. It took thirty minutes to run his hand over that side.

"Sheesh," said a bored voice coming from the space between the steel and the palm of his hand. The voice let a sigh escape as D moved to the back wall. If there'd been anyone there to hear it, this bizarre little scene would've undoubtedly made the eyes bug out of their head, but D continued his work in silence.

"Yep, this metal sure is tough stuff. The situation inside is kind of hazy. Still, I'm getting a picture of the general setup. The superatomic furnace inside is sending energy into the metal itself. You can't break through the walls without destroying the atomic furnace, but in order to do that you'd have to bust through the walls first. So, which came first, the chicken or the egg?"

"How many are inside?" D asked, still brushing his hand along the wall.

"Two," came the quick reply. "A man and a woman. But even I can't tell whether they're Nobility or human."

Without so much as a nod, D finished scanning the third wall. Only the left side remained.

But what in the world was he doing? Judging from what the voice said, he seemed to be searching the interior of the Shelter, but, if the outer walls couldn't be breached, that was pointless. On the other hand, the voice explained that destroying the outer walls would be impossible.

About halfway down the steel wall, the left hand halted.

"Got it," the voice said disinterestedly.

D wasted no time going into action. Without taking his left hand away, he stepped back, reaching with his right for his sword. The blade seemed to drink up the sunlight.

Drawing his sword-wielding right arm far back, D focused his eyes on a single point on the wall. A spot right between the thumb and forefinger of his left hand.

But what had they got there? The instant an awesome white bloodlust coalesced between the naked sword tip and the steel—

A pale light pierced the black wall.

It was D's sword that streamed forth. Regardless of how trenchant that thrust might be, there was no way it could penetrate the special steel of the outer walls. Be that as it may, the graceful arc sank halfway into the unyielding metal wall.

That's where the entrance was. D's blade was wedged in the boundary between door and wall, though that line was imperceptible to the naked eye. With the mysterious power of his left hand D had located it, then thrust into it. Granted that there was a space there, how could the tip of his sword slip into an infinitesimal gap?

"Wow!" The voice that said this came not from the interior, but rather from D's left hand. "Now here's a surprise. One of them's human."

D's expression shifted faintly. "Do they have Time-Bewitching Incense?" he asked. That was a kind of incense the Nobility had devised to give day the illusion it was night.

"I don't know, but the other one's not moving. A dead man, at least by day."

"The girl's okay then?" D muttered. Most likely she'd been bitten at least once, but if that were the case, destroying the one responsible would restore her humanity. Why then did a dark shadow skim for an instant across D's features?

The muscles of the hand he wrapped around the hilt bulged slowly. It's unclear what kind of exquisite skill was at work, but the slightest twist of the horizontal blade sent a sharp, thin line racing across the steel surface.

Blue light oozed out.

D immediately ceased all activity. Silently, he turned his face to the rear. His cold pupils were devoid of any hue of emotion.

"Earlier than I expected," the voice said, as if it were mere banter. "And not who I expected at all."

Presently, the faint growl of an engine came from the forest, and then a crimson figure leapt over the crest of the hill.

Raising a cacophony, a single-seat battle car stopped right at the bottom of the slope.

The vehicle was an oblong iron plate set on four grotesquely oversized, puncture-proof tires. The vehicle was crammed with a high-capacity atomic engine and some controls. The product of humans who'd got their hands on some of the Nobility's machinery, its outward appearance was a far cry from what the average person might call aesthetically pleasing. An energy pipe with conspicuous welding marks twisted like a snake from the rear-mounted engine to a core furnace shielded by studded iron-plate, and the simple bar-like steering yoke jutted artlessly from the floor. Churning in the air like the legs of a praying mantis, the pistons connected to the tires—and all the other parts, for that matter—were covered with a black grime, probably some harmless radioactive waste.

Perhaps what warranted more attention than the appearance of the vehicle were its armaments and its driver. Looming large from the right flank of the rear-mounted engine was the barrel of a 70 mm recoilless bazooka, staring blackly at D, while on the other side, the left, a circular, 20 mm missile pod glowered at empty space. Naturally, the missiles were equipped with body-heat seekers, and naught save certain death awaited the missiles' prey. And finally, ominously mounted atop the core furnace and exhibiting a muzzle that looked like it had a blue jewel set in the middle of it, was the penetrator—a cannon with grave piercing power.

Yet, despite the fact that it had a lot of heavy equipment not found on the average battle car, judging from the size of the core furnace and engine, this vehicle could easily be pressed for speeds of seventy-five miles per hour. It would run safely on ninety-nine percent of all terrain, and, thanks to its three-quarter-inch thick wire suspension, it could be driven on even the worst of roads. It raced across the ground, a miniature behemoth.

A figure in crimson rose from the driver's seat and jerked a pair of sturdy goggles off. Blue eyes that seemed ablaze took in D. Blonde hair lent its golden hue to the wind. It was Leila, the younger sister of the Marcus clan.

"So, we meet again," said the girl.

Perhaps it was the animosity radiating from every inch of her that made her vermilion coverall seem to blaze in the daylight. Her body, jolting to the incessant groaning of the engine, seemed to twitch with loathing for D.

"You might've thought you beat my older brothers just fine, but as long as I'm around you can't steal a march on the Marcus clan. Seems I ran into you at just the right spot. Is my prey in there?" This girl referred to the Nobility as her prey. She spat the words with a self-confidence and hostility that was beyond the pale.

D continued to stand as still as a sculpture, sword in hand.

"Out of my way," Leila said, in a tone she used for giving orders. "It was unfortunate for my prey that they had nothing but this broken Shelter, and fortunate for you, but now I'll be taking that good fortune, thank you. If you value your life, you'd best turn tail now."

"And if I don't value it, what'll you do?"

D's soft voice caused a reddish hue every bit as vivid as her raiment to shoot into her face.

"How's that? You seriously want to tangle with Leila Marcus and her battle car?"

"I have two lives. Take whichever one you like. That is, if you can."

The serene voice, unchanged since the first time she heard it, made Leila fall silent. The tomboy hesitated.

She hadn't realized yet that the blade piercing the wall of the Shelter was there due to D's secret skill alone. From the very start, it never crossed her mind that anything alive could perform such a feat. Still unaware of D's true power, Leila's hesitation was born of movements in her heart to which she was as yet oblivious.

The man in black standing before her left her feeling shockingly numbed. Like a mysterious drug, his presence worked like an anesthetic that violated her to the very marrow of her bones. As if to strip the movement from her heart, Leila roughly jerked her goggles back down.

"That's too bad. This is the way we Marcuses do it!" Just as the crimson coverall settled back in the driver's seat, the engine howled. She'd purposely cut the muffler to antagonize her opponents. The instant her hands took the controls, the massive tires flattened the grass. Not so much coming down the hill, the battle car was closer to flying, and her wheels kicked up the earth even as it touched back down. In less than a tenth of a second it'd taken off again. Its speed didn't seem possible from a mechanical construct.

It made a mad rush straight for D.

D didn't move.

A terrible sound shook the air, now mixing with a fishy stench. The smell was accompanied by smoke. White smoke billowing from the burnt tires, the vehicle stopped just inches short of D.

"You're gonna feel this to the bone. Here I come!" Leila's hysterical shouts were just another attempt to conceal the uneasiness of her own heart. The foot that had floored the gas to run down D had hit the brake a hair's breadth from crushing him. But why hadn't D moved? It was as if he'd read the ripples spreading through her chest.

Without saying a word, he pulled back on his stuck sword. It came free all too quickly. Sheathing it without a sound in a single fluid movement, D turned.

"I thought you'd see it my way. You should've done that from the get-go. Could've saved us both some trouble by not trying to act so damn tough." Leila kept her eyes on D until he'd climbed the hill and disappeared over the summit. An instant later, tension drew her feline eyes tight.

With a low groan, the earth shook violently. Though it weighed over a ton, the battle car was tossed effortlessly into the air, smashed into the ground, and was tossed up again.

Now that D had gone, the Shelter's defense systems sprang into action.

Though it looked impossible to steady, Leila stood impassively in her car. She had one hand on the yoke, but that was all. She remained perpendicular to the car throughout its crazed dance, as if the soles of her feet were glued to the floorboards.

In midair, Leila took her seat.

The engine made a deafening roar. Blue atomic flames licked from the rear nozzles, and smoke from the spent radioactive fuel flew from exhaust pipes off the engine's sides. The battle car took off in midair.

As it touched down, the penetrator over the engine swiveled to point at the Shelter. Unhindered by the wildly rocking earth, bounding with each shock, still the car never lost its bearing.

The air was stained blue.

The ceiling of the Shelter opened, and a laser cannon reminiscent of a radar dish appeared and spurted out a stream of fire. It skimmed the airborne body of the car and reduced a patch of earth to molten lava.

If this weapon was radar-controlled, then there was certainly cause to be alarmed. The second and third blasts of fire, usually vaunted for their unmatched precision, flew in vain, as their target slipped in front or behind, to the left or right of where they fell.

Leila's skill behind the wheel surpassed these electronic devices.

As far back as she could remember, the clan's father had always impressed upon her how important it was for her to refine her skills at manipulating anything and everything mechanical. Her father may have even known some basic genetic enhancement techniques.

Ironically, Leila's talents only seemed to shine when it came to modes of transportation. Whether it was a car, or even something with a life of its own like a cyborg horse, under her skillful touch mechanical vehicles were given a new lease on life. "Give her an engine and some wheels and she'll whip up a car," her father had said with admiration. Her skill at operating vehicles surpassed that of all her brothers, with only the oldest boy Borgoff even coming close.

And how Leila loved her battle car. It had been crafted from parts gathered in junkyards during their travels. Some parts even came from the ruins of the Nobility, when the opportunity to take them presented itself. She'd quite literally forgotten to eat or sleep while she worked on it. Early one winter morning, the battle car was completed by the feeble, watery light of dawn. Two years had passed since then. Loving that car like a baby that'd kicked in her own belly, Leila learned to drive it with a miraculous level of skill.

The very epitome of that skill was being displayed out on this hill-hemmed patch of ground. Avoiding every attack by the electronic devices, the vehicle changed direction in midair, and, just as the laser's fraction-of-a-second targeting delay was ending, the penetrator discharged a silvery beam.

It was a form of liquid metal. Expelled at speeds in excess of Mach 1, the molecular structure of the metal altered, changing to a five-yard-long spear that shot right through the workings of the laser cannon. Sending electromagnetic waves out in all directions like tentacles, the laser was silenced. As she brought the penetrator's muzzle to bear on one wall of the Shelter, a bloody smile rose on Leila's lips.

Suddenly, her target blurred. Or more accurately, the car sank. As if the land surrounding the Shelter had become a bog, the car sunk nose first into the ground.

Leila's tense demeanor collapsed, deteriorating into devil-may-care laughter.

The rear nozzles pivoted with a screech, disgorging fire. Flames ran along the sides of the vehicle, blowing away the rocky soil swallowing its muzzle. The tires spun at full speed. Whipping up a trail of dust, the battle car took to the air tail first. It spun to face the hill even before it touched back down, and the penetrator's turret swiveled to the back, hurling a blast of silver light against the Shelter wall.

The blast broke in two, and, in the same instant, was reduced to countless particles of light that flew in all directions. Even Leila's driving skills couldn't get her through this web of shrapnel.

However . . .

Landing back on solid ground, the battle car kept going straight for the storm of metallic particles, its body at a wild tilt as it pulled a wheelie. The darkness-shredding bullets sank into the belly of the car.

Giving the engine full throttle, Leila pushed her vehicle to the top of the hill in one mad dash.

Fugitives

CHAPTER 2

I

As Leila hit the brakes, a gorgeous figure in black greeted her. "Very nicely done," D said in his serene tone.

Weathering a sensation that was neither fever nor chills racing down her spine, Leila replied with bald-faced hostility. "You still kicking around? If you don't make tracks and fast, I'm gonna have to run you down and kill you," she warned.

Without acknowledging her threat, D said softly, "Someone should take a look at your wound."

"And you'd best . . . mind your own business!" Pain spread through the last words Leila spat. Pressing a hand to her right breast, she toppled forward in the driver's seat. She'd taken a hit in the chest from a hunk of shrapnel that'd punched through the battle car's floorboards.

Walking over swiftly, D lifted Leila with ease and set her down in the shade of a nearby tree. Throwing a quick glance at the sky and the Shelter, D listened in the direction from which Leila had come.

"They're not coming," the palm of his left hand could be heard to say. "Her people are still a long way off. What are you planning on doing?"

"Can't leave her like this."

"You can play nursemaid to the mortally wounded later. Our target's in that steel box right now, completely immobilized. I say finish him off as soon as possible, and deliver the girl. After all, even if she's been bitten already, if we slay the Noble she'll be back to normal. That should please her no end."

Shrouded as always in an eerie aura, D's beautiful visage clouded for an instant. "She'd be pleased? Because she was human again? Or because he was—"

"Don't start harping on that again. Has this fine spring day knocked a few of your screws loose? We're so close, and if you just go do it now you could kill him without working up a sweat. The sun'll be setting soon, you know. I say let the competition rot." As if to corroborate the voice's growing impatience, the sky began to don a darker shade of blue. At this time of year, sunset came around five Night, which gave D fewer than two hours to finish his work.

Despite that, D pulled open the front of Leila's coverall without a word. Evident even through her clothing, the pale fullness of her bosom was now laid bare. The flesh above her left breast burst outwards in a number of spots. Already the bloodied wounds had swollen black and blue. They were like so many eerie sarcomata growing from her white skin.

D stood up, lifted the emergency kit from his saddlebags, and returned. When he opened the lid of the kit, agitation surged into his eyes.

"Heh heh heh," the voice cackled mockingly. "I was just trying to remember when you bought that set. You've been hauling it around all this time and never used it once. Well, the stuff inside became useless a long, long time ago. That's the trouble with *people who can't die*."

"Too true," D muttered in his usual monotone, doing a check of Leila's battle car and pulling out a first-aid kit. Just to be safe, he set it on the floorboards to open it, then closed it again quickly.

"What is it?"

"There's nothing in there. She's pretty much out of everything."

"So, didn't restock it, eh? Never heard of such a cavalier Hunter."

Wounds, you could say, were an occupational hazard for Hunters, and replacing medical supplies was every bit as important as procuring weapons. On arriving in a town or village, it was second nature for a Hunter to race to the arms merchant and pharmacy first, then hit the general store or saloon later.

But Leila had no medical supplies. And yet she was the youngest sister of the Marcus clan, whose five members ranked up there with a handful of veteran Hunters.

Once again D squatted by the girl's side.

Her breathing was rather shallow. Though it seemed the fragments within her hadn't damaged any internal organs, there was some danger of toxins from the shrapnel causing tetanus if the chunks of metal were left where they were. In fact, the entry and exit wounds were already swelling a deep, dirty red.

"What are you gonna do? You know I only work on you. Can't do a thing for humans."

"I know. There's no choice but to deal with humans the human way."

From the combat belt at his waist, D drew a caltrop. He brought one of the points to his left hand.

"What do you think you're doing?"

"If the girl dies, you and I are through."

"Shit. Are you threatening me?" But before the voice had finished speaking, pale blue flames enveloped the tip of the caltrop.

The sharp point heated quickly and turned crimson. D brought his left hand closer to Leila's brow. Her sizable eyes opened.

"What are you doing?" she asked.

"Cauterizing the wound. I'll do it so it doesn't hurt."

"How kind of you," she shot back sarcastically. "Don't expect me to thank you."

"Don't talk."

Leila jerked her face away from the approaching hand. "I don't know what kind of hocus-pocus you can pull, but I'll be damned if I'm gonna let you play around with my body while I'm out. I'm gonna be awake to see this from start to finish. Try anything funny, and believe me, you'll pay."

Undeterred, D set his left hand on her.

"Don't—" Leila's words became a scream. "Stop, I'm begging you. Do it while I'm still awake. Please," she pleaded.

Something glistening welled in her eyes as they gazed at D. It spoke of horrific memories.

Silently taking his hand away, D tore the sleeve of his coat and put a strip of cloth from it between Leila's lips. They had no anesthesia. The cloth was to keep her from biting her tongue. This time she cooperated quietly. The little nod she made must've been an expression of gratitude.

D lowered the hot metal to her skin. Shortly thereafter, a pungent scent and a series of low moans began to permeate the darkening bower.

†

D usk seemed to coalesce around him. He opened his eyes. Nothing could replace this feeling, that the spell that imprisoned him to the very last cell was drawing away like the tide. This was his favorite time.

His eyes hastened to his side. Not far from him, a girl sat quietly on the edge of the bed. She gave the impression of not having moved a muscle since she'd sat down. Her pretty white blossom of a face turned to him.

"What's wrong?" he asked, still lying flat on a bed littered with silk cushions. He'd glimpsed the trail of a teardrop on the girl's cheek.

"There's someone outside."

"Oh. Here already?" In the recesses of his tense voice lay unshakable self-confidence. Now matter how skilled the Vampire Hunter, nothing could match a Noble rising in darkness.

Stepping down lightly onto the steel floor, he glanced at the door and his eyes fairly shot out. Was that a threadlike silver line falling across the floor? Realizing that it was moonlight sneaking in through a crack carved above the door, he turned back to the girl.

"During the day, someone opened it with a sword," she said. "Hunters hired by Father, no doubt . . . "

Discerning a certain something on the blue dress that covered her down to the knees, he knit his brow. It was an elegant silver dirk. He'd been wearing it at his waist. What had she intended to use it for? For a brief while he focused on the weapon, then he made his way over to the video monitors on the wall to check on the situation outside.

†

By the time D had burned then carved away each wound, and had sterilized the damaged skin with a freshly heated caltrop, Leila finally passed out.

"For the most part her worries are over," the voice said. "But bacteria have already set up shop in her body. She'll be getting hit by some pretty intense chills soon. If she can get past that, she'll be able to rest easy. You've gone this far, might as well do the next step. Keep treating her through the home stretch."

With no sign of listening to the somewhat disgusted voice, D kept looking back and forth between the Shelter and the sky of ever-deepening blue. When the caltrop stuck in the ground had cooled he returned it to his belt and stood up, saying, "He should be coming out any minute now."

"You're so cold," the voice said with resentment. "You mean to tell me when he does, you'll just stop treating her? Don't run off like some back-alley quack." But then the voice stopped unexpectedly.

D took a step forward. Like stagnated blue light, the door to the Shelter retracted without a sound. Looking back, he saw Leila. The eyes that swiftly turned forward again held a lurid light. There he stood, the greatest Vampire Hunter of all. The hem of his coat fluttering in the night breeze, D came down the hill.

It wasn't long before the six obsidian horses appeared one after another—followed, of course, by the black lacquered carriage. Machinery within the Shelter had successfully completed the necessary repairs to it during the day.

A young man clad in black peered silently down at D from the coachman's perch. "Out of our way," he said. His voice was strangely soft. "Scum though you are for the way you place a price on people's lives, I still have no wish to engage in a pointless and lethal exchange."

An odd hue of emotion flowed into D's eyes, then swiftly vanished. "I'll take the girl," D said perfunctorily, his demeanor free from violence or exuberance.

The man's eyes were gradually being dyed red. "I took her because I want her," he said. "You should try to do the same. If you're up to battling a Noble at night, that is."

The darkness solidified. Though both the color and light remained the same there, the space between the two of them seemed to have suddenly frozen.

The crack of whipped flesh broke the stillness. Without even a whinny, two-dozen hooves began beating the earth. Whether their intent was to trample the insignificant Hunter or to make him get out of the way, those six madly charging horses unexpectedly came to a dead stop a few yards shy of D.

There was a startled cry of "Mayerling!"

The instant D realized the voice flew from a woman inside the carriage, his body soared into the air like a mystic bird. Still distracted by her plaintive cry, there was a split-second delay before D brought his silvery flash down at the youth's head.

Sparks spilled into the darkness like scattered jewels, trailing a beautiful metallic *ching* behind them. The youth—Mayerling—had stopped D's deadly stroke with the back of his left hand. That part of his hand was bound in steel armor.

Twisting his body out of the way of the three flashes of light roaring through the air toward his chest, D came silently back down to earth on the opposite side of the vehicle.

From the roof of the carriage down to D, the miasma flowed. And from D back up to the roof. At this intense exchange of unearthly auras, the horses whinnied, and the carriage rocked wildly.

Long claws grew from the fingers of the Noble's right hand. But no, they were not simply nails—glittering blackly, they clearly had the lustrous sheen of steel. When danger was near, the vampire's normal fingernails became murderous steel implements.

"Such a refined face, and such skill—I've heard your name before. The name that can make any Noble grow pale. So, you're D—" Mayerling said, his voice a blend of admiration and fear.

"I've heard of you, too," D responded softly. "I've heard there was a young lord praised for his virtue by his subjects, perhaps the only one among all the Nobility. His name was Mayerling, I'm quite certain."

"I always wanted to meet you. One way or another."

"Well, now you have," the Hunter replied. "I'm right here."

"Will you not let us go? I've done nothing to the humans."

"Tell that to the father you made like yourself before you carried off his daughter."

Distress filled Mayerling's countenance.

The tension abruptly drained from D's body.

With a shout of "Hyah!" from Mayerling, the horses pummeled the earth. Speeding by D's side, they started to gallop up the earthen slope.

D raced like the wind.

The carriage was every bit a match for D's speed.

At the summit of the hill, D came alongside the carriage. His right hand reached for the door handle. And then the golden handle just started pulling away. As he watched, the carriage dwindled in size, and D turned himself around and headed over to a stand of trees. That was where Leila lay.

"Heard a strange voice, didn't you?" the usual strange voice said. "Kinda makes you think being hard of hearing might not be so bad. We might be wrapping up this job right about now otherwise."

D squatted down and put a hand to Leila's brow. She was as hot as fire. Her sweat-drenched face was twisted with pain. Both fever and pain were due to her infection. Relentless chills would soon follow.

Without a moment's hesitation, D stripped off Leila's clothes. When her beautiful naked body was stretched out on the green grass, a surprised "Wow!" came from his left hand. "By the looks of it, I'd say this little girl's had a pretty hard life."

From her round, firm breasts down to her thighs, and across her whole back, Leila's skin was covered with the scars of numerous gashes and the stitches that had closed them. This was a girl who lived in the carnage that was the Frontier.

Without seeming to be harboring any strong emotion, D covered Leila with himself.

Crying out a little, Leila clung to his powerful chest. Her fever-swollen lips trembled, letting a mumbled word escape over and over again. A single word, but it was what had stayed D's hand at the carriage door.

†

When Kyle Marcus's mount crested the hill an hour later, there was no sign of anyone or anything in the vicinity, aside from his sister, who was wrapped in a blanket and resting peacefully in her seat in the battle car.

Another thirty minutes after that, the bus driven by Borgoff appeared, along with Nolt, who was riding point.

Kyle carried Leila into the vehicle in a great hurry. They must've been very close, because his expression had changed markedly. "She—she's gonna be okay, won't she, bro?" he stammered. "Give her something, I don't care what."

As Borgoff watched him struggle on the brink of tears, he wore a rancorous expression, but he took Leila's pulse nonetheless, checked her fever, and before long gave a satisfied nod. "She's all right. I'll check out her internal organs and circulation with a CAT scan anyway, but there's no need to worry." Staring down at Kyle where he'd slumped to the floor in apparent relief, he added, "This kinda shit is what happens when you go behind my back and send Leila out alone."

"I know. You can take the strap to me later for all I care. But which one of them you figure roughed Leila up so bad?"

Kyle's face had reclaimed its original viciousness. Eyes staring firmly into space, he was so angry he didn't notice the froth running from the corners of his mouth. His body shook.

"Well, probably not the one who treated her. Which means maybe it was neither of them. You wouldn't think anyone as soft as all that could survive this long out here on the Frontier."

"It don't matter," Kyle said, almost ranting deliriously. "It don't matter which of 'em did it. I'll find 'em both and cut 'em to pieces. Take their arms and legs off and put 'em back on where they don't belong. Stuff their mouths with their own steaming guts."

"Knock yourself out," his older brother said. "Anyway, you're sure there wasn't anyone around Leila? From the look of her wounds, she got them three, maybe four hours ago."

The door opened and Nolt stuck his head in. "We've got some tracks from a carriage passing this way. Still fresh. Maybe from an hour before we got here, tops. There's something else, too—some prints from horseshoes."

"If that's the case, then the two of them must've gone at it here, too. And it looks like it didn't get settled yet . . . "

Nodding gravely at his own words, Borgoff ordered Nolt to take care of Leila and Groveck. He went to his room in the back, returning to the driver's seat clutching a cloth-wrapped package of apparent significance.

"If I've seen D's face, I can spot him," he muttered, pulling from the cloth a silver disk about a foot and a half in diameter. Setting it up on a little stand almost in the center of the dashboard, Borgoff turned his heavily whiskered face to gaze out the window and up at the moon rising in the heavens. The moon was round and nearly full, but, thanks to the clouds obscuring part of it, it looked like it'd been nibbled here and there by bugs.

When he set his huge form down, the driver's seat creaked and groaned. Then Borgoff crossed his hands in front of his chest, and began to stare fixedly at the propped-up silver platter with eyes that looked like they could bore right through it. A minute passed, then two.

Kyle wouldn't leave Leila's side as she lay in bed. As Nolt peered in through the door next to the driver's seat sweat beaded his face just as profusely as Borgoff's.

And then, as the silvery surface of the platter grew smoky, almost like clouds covered it, the figure of a young man in black astride a horse suddenly formed on its surface.

It was D. Turning their way and saying something, he pulled on the reins in his hands and disappeared into a thicket.

It was a replay of D from the previous night, talking with them after the battle with the vampiric villagers. If people or things looked a little different, it was probably because these images were taken from Borgoff's memories. Here was a man who could project his own memories onto a silver platter. Yet, despite this admirable display of what some would call sorcery, Borgoff glared mercilessly at the moon in the sky with bloodshot eyes. No, not at the moon, but at a big mass of clouds under it. The moonlight shining on the clouds edged them in blue.

There was no change in either the moon or the cloud mass, or so it appeared for an instant. Then, even though the moon remained unchanged, the heart of the cloud mass seemed to begin to glow ever so faintly. In the space of a breath, a figure shaped like a man started wriggling there, and, with a second breath, it became a clear picture. Someone was riding a horse down a pitch-black road.

Based on his past memory of D, Borgoff was using the silver platter and moon as projectors to make the *present* D appear in the cloud mass.

The receding figure that seemed to be looking down on them from the distant heavens was a remarkable likeness of D as he raced down the road a few score miles ahead.

II

They'd run full tilt for a good two hours after leaving D in their dust, and, when Mayerling saw that the road continued on in a straight line for the next dozen or so miles, he left the coachman's perch of the racing carriage and skillfully slipped inside.

When he'd closed the door, not a hint of sound from the outside world intruded into the carriage. The girl sat there in a leather-bound chair like a night-blossoming moonbeam flower.

Carpet spread across the floor, and an exceedingly fine silk padding covered the walls and ceiling. In days of old, bottles of the best and rarest potables had sat on the collapsible golden table that seemed to grow from the wall, and this dozen miles of starlit road had run to great masquerades by the Nobility. However, the carpet was now somewhat dingy, there were tears in the silk, and there wasn't a single silver glass on the table. Even the table drooped for lack of a screw.

This model of carriage was said to be the last equipped with magnetic stabilizing circuits, which would hold the passengers safely in position even if the vehicle were to flip over.

Mayerling's right hand moved, and the interior was filled with light. "Why don't you turn on the lights?" he asked. "By rights this dilapidated old buggy should have been scrapped long ago, but that much at least is still operational."

Encouraged by a smile that bared teeth of limitless white, the girl showed Mayerling a smile in return. Yet her smile was thin, like a mirage.

He tried to recall the last time he'd seen this girl's brightly smiling face, but had little luck. Perhaps he'd only dreamt it, and was dreaming this as well.

"I don't mind," she replied. "If you live in the darkness, then I want to, too."

"I'm sure the sunlight suits you wonderfully. Though I have yet to see you in it," he added, heading over to the chair across from her to sit down.

"Do you think we'll make it all the way?" the girl asked hesitantly.

"You think we won't?"

"No." The girl shook her head. It was the first vehement action he'd seen from her since he'd taken her out of the village. "I'll be fine anywhere. So long as I'm with you, I could make my home in a cave in the craggy mountains or in some subterranean world where I'd never see the light of day again."

"No matter where we might be, the Hunters would come," he said, allowing resignation to drift into his jewel-like beauty. "Your fellow humans won't be happy until they've destroyed everything. You're nothing like them, of course."

She said nothing.

"There's nowhere on earth we can relax now. A long trip out into the depths of space . . . " He caught himself. "Perhaps it has become too much for you?"

"No."

"It's all right. Perhaps you weren't cut out for this from the very beginning. A graceful hothouse flower can't endure the ravages of the wild. You were kind enough to indulge my willfulness. We shall take a different course if you so desire."

The girl's white hand pressed down on his pale hand, and her slender face shook gently from left to right. "I want to try and see if we make it. To go to the stars."

Oh, who could have known the journey these two had undertaken was not a fiendish abduction, but rather a flight by a couple madly in love? A young vampire Nobleman and a human lass—linked not by fear and contempt, but by a bond of mutual love all the stronger for its hopelessness. Were that not the case, there was no chance this girl taken from a village where everyone had been turned into vampires would still be untainted, her skin still unbroken.

For the Nobility, drawing a human into their company was part of how they fed, colored as it was by their aesthetic appreciation of sucking the life from someone beautiful. But at the same time, the act was also filled with the pleasure of violating the unwilling, as well as the twisted sense of superiority that came from raising one of the lowly commoners to their own level.

Mayerling had done nothing of the sort. He did no more than lead the girl from her home, taking her by the hand as he let her into his carriage and nothing more. He had not used freedom-stealing sorceries, nor veiled threats of violence against her family to force her compliance. The girl had quietly slipped out of the house of her own accord.

From time to time, such things did happen. Bonds formed between the worlds of the humans and of the supernatural. However, they didn't necessarily become a lasting bridge between the two worlds, and typically the couple concerned would be chased by a stone-wielding mob. As was the case with these two.

The Nobility flickered in the light of extinction, and the girl had lost any world she might return to, so where could the two of them go? Out among the stars.

Mayerling raised his face.

"What is it?"

"Nothing," he replied. "It seems the dawn will be early today. If we're to gain a little more ground, I shall have to see to the horses." Kissing the girl on the cheek, he returned to the coachman's perch like a shadow.

Whip in hand, it was not to the fore that he first turned his gaze, but rather to the darkness behind them. In a place cut off from all the rest of the outside world, he heard the clomp of iron-shod hoofs approaching from far off. "So soon," he muttered to himself. "That would be D, wouldn't it?"

A crack sounded at the horses' hind as his whip fell. The scenery on either side flew by as bits and pieces. However, the ear of the Noble caught the certain fact that the hoofbeats were gradually growing closer.

"Just a little further to the river," Mayerling muttered. "Hear me, O road that lies between him and me. Just give me another ten minutes, I beseech thee."

†

"Oh. He's finally catching up," Nolt said. In the cloud that held his gaze, a small luminous point began winking ahead of D. Light spilling from the windows of the carriage, no doubt. "Give him another five minutes. No matter which one buys it, it's all sweet for us. So, what kind of vision you gonna show us next, bro?"

He didn't get to ask Borgoff anything, as his words died down to muttering when he saw how the oldest of the clan was completely focused on the mirror, to the exclusion of all else.

Perhaps it was due to this unprecedented sorcery, a magic that could choose one scene at will from the moon's gaze—which was privy to all things on earth—and then use cloudbanks as a screen for projecting that scene, but, for whatever reason, every scrap of flesh on Borgoff's colossal frame seemed to have been chiseled off. He looked half-shriveled, almost like a mummy.

When Nolt turned his eyes once again to the screen in the mass of clouds, he muttered a cry of surprise. At some point, the scenery rushing by D on either side had become desolate rocky peaks. "Well then, big bro, you thinking of maybe starting a landslide or something to bury the bastards?"

†

At last, Mayerling's darkness-piercing vision caught the black rider. The tail of his coat sliced through the wind, billowing out like ominous wings.

Could he face and beat this foe on equal terms? While he was fairly self-confident, anxiety was beginning to rear its ugly, black head in Mayerling's bosom. Though they'd only met for a split second, the force and keenness of the blade that'd assailed him from overhead lingered all too vividly in his left hand even now. The numbness was finally beginning to fade. But more than that, the distinct horror of learning the steely hand-armor that could repel laser beams had been cut halfway through rankled him, and caused him concern.

Vampire Hunter D could not be underestimated.

Mayerling's eyes glowed a brilliant crimson, and the curving black claws creaked as they grew from his right hand, which still clenched the whip.

Perhaps anticipating the new death match about to be joined, even the wind snarled. Up ahead, a wooden bridge was visible. The sound of running water could be heard. The current sounded rather strong.

Mayerling's gaze was drawn up. Quickly bending over, he pulled a pair of black cylinders from a box beside the driver's seat. They were molecular vibro-bombs, complete with timers. The molecular particles within them were subjected to powerful ultra-high speed vibrations, and they could destroy cohesive energy to reduce any substance to a fine dust.

Raising a tremendous racket, the carriage started across the bridge. The span was about sixty feet in length. Some thirty feet below, a white sash raced by. Rapids.

He halted the carriage as soon as it was across, then turned. Grabbing the molecular vibro-bomb's switch with his teeth, he gave it a twist. They weren't exactly a weapon befitting the Nobility.

D was on the bridge roughly five seconds later. He rushed ahead without a moment's hesitation.

He didn't think he was being foolish. This Hunter must've had the self-confidence and skill to deal with any situation. There was no choice, then, but for Mayerling to exert every lethal effort in return. "I had hoped to settle this like men, one on one," he muttered as he listened to the thunder of the iron-shod hoofs. "See how you like this, D—"

But the instant he jerked his arm back to prepare for the throw, lightning flashed before his eyes. It'd flashed down without warning from a black mass of clouds clogging the sky, aiming to strike the top of the bridge—and the road right in front of D.

Sparks flying without a sound dead ahead, how could the Hunter avoid the gaping ten-foot-wide hole that suddenly yawned before him? The legs of his horse clawed vainly at air, and D, keeping his graceful equestrian pose, plummeted headfirst toward the fierce, earth-shaking rapids below.

III

Just as Nolt shouted, "You did it!" Borgoff's greatly withered frame suddenly slumped forward.

On hearing the commotion, Kyle sluggishly stuck his head out, too. "What happened?" He looked out the window and up at the sky, but the screen-like properties of the clouds had been lost along with Borgoff's consciousness. "Oh, man, bro—you went and used it again, didn't you? And you're the one who's always going on about how it takes three years off your life every time you do."

Feeling the derisive jibe, the oldest brother said in a halting voice like that of the dead, "He fell into the river. Dhampirs ain't swimmers . . . Nolt, find him and finish him off."

A few minutes later, after he'd watched the second oldest depart in a cloud of dust, Borgoff gave Kyle the order to drive. He headed for the bedroom in the rear to rest his weary bones. There was one set of bunk beds on either side for his siblings. His alone was especially large, and located the furthest in the back.

As he was making his way down the aisle, trying to keep his footsteps as quiet as possible, his meatless but still sizable arm was grasped by something eerily cold. Borgoff turned around.

A white hand that could easily be mistaken for that of a genuine mummy stuck out from the bottom right bunk.

"Hey, I didn't know you were up. I'm sorry if that idiot Nolt disturbed you with all his hollering." Where the eldest Marcus normally kept this gentle tone of voice was a complete mystery.

The person in the bunk turned over, though it was clearly painful to do so. He was a pitifully small lump beneath the blankets. "I'm sorry, bro . . .about not carrying my own weight . . . "

In response to the frail voice, Borgoff shook his head without a word. His bull neck creaked and looked like it might pop. "Don't talk nonsense. The four of us are more than enough to take anyone on. You ought to keep quiet and get your rest." After he stroked it lightly, the slender hand finally pulled back into the blankets. "So," Borgoff added, "it doesn't look like you'll be having any seizures for a while then, eh?"

At this entirely sympathetic question, the other man let the covers he'd pulled up over his head slip back down smoothly. "I'll be okay," he said. "I think I'll be able to keep it under control on my own." His face was smiling as he answered feebly. His brother knew he had to be smiling, but the expression turned out to resemble nothing so much as a rictus. His cheeks were hollowed, his terribly cloudy eyes were sunken in cavernous sockets, and the breath that leaked out with his voice from lips the color of earth was as thin as that of a patient at death's door. The feeble body belonged to Grove, the infirm younger brother Nolt mentioned when the clan first met D.

However, if he were to catch a glimpse of these corpse-like features, even D himself would have been surprised. Grove's face, which held a childlike innocence, was etched with exactly the same features as the vital young man who'd slaughtered the army of attacking vampires that day in one blow, and then left.

†

Mayerling watched almost absentmindedly as his fearsome pursuer was sucked into the dirty torrent below the bridge and was lost from view in a matter of seconds. Mayerling didn't notice that the girl had opened the light-impermeable curtains and poked her head out the window.

"What happened?"

Turning around at the sound of her anxious voice, he replied, "It's nothing. Just one less thing to bother us."

Seeing the bridge behind the carriage, where flames and black smoke were still rising, the girl's face clouded quickly. "What on earth—" she gasped. "Did you make that hole?"

Mayerling wouldn't answer. He could feel in his bones that this was the work of another foe.

It wasn't lightning that'd bored a hole through the bridge, but a destructive energy-beam of another sort. Even now, a swarm of over two thousand satellites loaded with beam weaponry continued their long slumber in geostationary orbit some 22,500 miles above the Earth. Many of them had been launched by the government to help keep the human rebellion down, but there were also numerous privately owned satellites. Each of them was equipped with a means of generating beams that were decidedly man-made. What they fired was quite unlike the natural energy generated by storms. Judging from the beam's accuracy, and how it seemed to be only aiming at D, it'd been fired by a human, and one who undoubtedly felt some animosity toward D. That much was evident; any who would've wished to help Mayerling had long since perished.

It was probably another Hunter. A foe who should be feared for different reasons than D. But was it just one?

Training his boundlessly cold and dark pupils on the silver serpent of current, Mayerling presently turned to face the girl again. "Be assured . . . with the passing of but two more nights, we shall be at the gateway to the stars. Sleep well. Relax, and trust everything to me."

When the girl nodded and pulled back inside, Mayerling looked up at the moon hanging in the heavens and muttered, "Two more days . . . but daylight will come shortly. I wonder if I'll encounter this new foe before those days have passed?"

†

E ven a torrent that flowed with enough force to split rocks lost its ferocity when it had come so far, and when it hit the shore here it no longer bared its fangs. The river widened, and here and there the glimmer of silvery scales from fish leaping out to seek the light of the moon rippled along the surface of the water. Occasionally, the water ran translucent all the way down to the riverbed, and the way colossal snakelike shapes swam upstream on a zigzagging path was rather unsettling.

On the trail that ran just a little way above the riverbank, a rider muttered, "Well, this should put me right in the neighborhood now." The rider, Nolt Marcus, the oldest of the clan, halted his mount. In accordance with Borgoff's orders, Nolt had set off to find and destroy D after D had been swallowed by the muddied current. This is how far Nolt had gone.

The spot was about two miles downstream of the bridge. Along the spine of the eastern mountains, a foreshadowing of the thin blue light of dawn had come calling, but the darkness swathing the world was still thick and black.

Scanning his surroundings, Nolt reached for his hexagonal staff with his right hand. "I don't think I'll find him any farther downstream. So, did the bastard make it out without drowning then?" the Marcus brother wondered aloud. "Then again, I don't see how a dhampir could manage a stunt like that . . . "

The tinge of displeasure in Nolt's voice was due to the fact the species known as dhampir had many of the characteristics of supernatural creatures. As a blood mix between the Nobility— the vampires—and humans, dhampirs inherited some of the physical strengths and weaknesses of both. From the Nobility, dhampirs inherited the ability to recover from injuries that would be considered lethal to a human being. On the other hand, dhampirs lost up to seventy percent of their strength in daylight, they felt an unbridled lust for the blood of the living when they were hungry, and, perhaps strangest of all, not one of them could stay afloat in water.

At the beginning of the era of mankind's Great Rebellion, the vampires' utter lack of buoyancy was prized as one of the few possible ways to dispose of them. However, when it became clear that drowning itself had markedly milder results when compared to stakes or sunlight, a much dimmer view of immersion's value as a countermeasure was adopted. Drowning caused the heart to stop functioning and the body to cease all regeneration, but these effects were easily undone with the coming of night and an infusion of fresh blood.

But so long as a vampire was denied either blood or the onset of night, it would be impossible for him to recover from drowning. In other words, after an immersion, it was possible to put the comatose Nobility to the torch or to seal him away in the earth forever. Because vampires were so vulnerable after drowning, running water still served mankind in reasonably good stead.

That's what Borgoff was talking about when he told Nolt to "Finish him off."

"I'm glad you could make it."

The low voice made Nolt's whole body stiffen. Just for an instant, though. His hexagonal staff ripped through the air behind him— in the direction of the voice. It was as if his right hand had become a flash of brown. The strange thing was, the arc his weapon painted with the speed of light was a full circle. Surely enough, the hexagonal staff had grown to nearly twice its former length, stretching toward the spot from which the voice had issued.

However, when Nolt spun around dumbstruck by the lack of contact, the pole in his hands was no longer than normal.

"That's quite an unusual skill you have, sir," the youth of hair-raising beauty said in a voice of steel from atop a cyclopean block of stone that loomed by the side of the road.

No reply was given, but a flash of brown shot out. The spot it touched blasted apart, and in the midst of the scattered chips of stone D flew through the air like a mystic bird. Had his gelid gaze caught the mark the pole left on the rocky surface?

In Nolt's hands, the staff that plowed through almost diamond-hard stone like it was clay changed direction easily and raced for the airborne D.

There was a glimmer in D's right hand. The arc of brown was countered by a flash of silver, and there was a dull thud. Not giving Nolt time for a second attack, as soon as he landed right in front of the Marcus brother, D swung his blade down.

Tasting the blood-freezing fear of that blade all the while, Nolt leapt backward. The attack he unleashed as he leapt was not a swing but rather a jab, and his staff seemed to grow without end as it struck for D's face. Though he didn't seem to move a muscle, the pole missed D by a fraction of an inch as he launched himself into the air.

A flashing sideways slash. The blade that would've put a diagonal split down the middle of Nolt's face bit instead into the pole that shot up, and the two figures broke to opposite sides.

The end of his staff still aimed at D's chest, Nolt was breathing hard. Tidings of his fear. A thread-thin line of vermilion ran down the middle of his face from his forehead, and it widened at his jaw. That was the work of the blade D brought down as soon as he'd landed.

However, the blood trickling down his face wasn't Nolt's only concern. His hexagonal staff wasn't a mere piece of wood, but rather its center was packed with a steel core that, despite its thinness, could still deflect a high-intensity laser beam. Yet the pole was missing about a foot off one end. Realizing that it'd been chopped off while he was in midair, Nolt lost much of the fever in his blood.

"You son of a bitch," he growled, finally managing to say something. "So I guess you ain't no plain old dhampir, are you?"

"I'm a dhampir," D answered, still holding the same pose in his opponent's blue eyes.

Nolt's mouth twisted up in a smile. "Is that a fact? Then how do you like these apples?" With these words, his staff spun in a circle and struck the ground next to him.

With a gut-wrenching rumble, a chunk of ground a yard in diameter collapsed in on itself. This was no ordinary hollow. Maintaining a depth of about a foot, it became a ditch running all the way to the river.

About to pounce once again, D turned his eyes to this subsidence. Madness gripped the once calmly flowing water. As it coursed down the ditch from the shore, the water gathered intense speed, and, slapping up against the banks, it rose like a living creature. In great rolls, the water gushed into the space between the two of them. First the ankles and then the boots of both D and Nolt sank below the surface.

"How about it, dhampir? Can you move?" Nolt asked with a smile. It was the smirk of a victor. "You know, I've thrown down with your kind before. And this is what I did then. When a part of a dhampir gets wet, it kinda gets all stiff, don't it?"

D didn't move. Perhaps he couldn't move?

"Die, you bastard!" Nolt screamed as he charged forward. Getting a solid grip on the bottom part of the staff, he brandished it like he was going to bring it straight down and smash D's head open. The water splashed from his feet, and he kicked off the ground.

Black lightning raced up from below. Higher and faster than the staff, it danced up over his head. The last thing Nolt saw was the thick water stretching up from the ground like a tenacious predator clinging to D's black boots.

Split by D's blade from forehead to chin, by the time Nolt had fallen back to earth he wasn't breathing anymore. A bloody mist reeled out from his remains.

Without so much as a glance at Nolt as he collapsed in a heap, D walked back behind the rocks where he'd first appeared. His horse was waiting there. Coat billowing as he straddled his mount, the Hunter's eyes were eternally cold as he set them upstream, but they held a hint of sadness as well.

"Run if you like," D murmured. "But I'll still catch you."

While his words hung in the air, his horse clambered down to the shore. Without pausing, it stepped into the water. It wasn't shallow. The river would be about waist-deep on D while mounted.

If anyone was watching, they would've thought the horse was leaping across the surface of the water. Making a massive bound, the horse sank only hoof-deep before continuing to take one effortless leap after another, kicking up a little white spray as it carried D across the wide river.

There couldn't be all that many stones submerged just an inch or so below the water's surface. But clearly it was within D's power to find them in a split second and maneuver his horse onto them.

A Village of Freaks

CHAPTER 3

I

Elsewhere, another confrontation was about to unfold.

The Marcus clan's bus was approaching a section of reddish brown valley, some thirty miles from the bridge.

The reason Kyle hadn't been sent along ahead was that Borgoff had calculated the speed of the carriage and the time left until daybreak, deciding that the bus itself would be sufficient to catch up with their foe. Added to that was the fact that, if Kyle left, he would have had to look after Leila and Groveck himself. Plus, he had reservations about letting Kyle tackle the situation on his own.

He was also worried about Nolt, whom he'd sent to dispatch D. Though considering his brother's special skills with that staff, the task of finishing off a Hunter who'd almost certainly drowned should be easier than busting a baby's arm. Once they'd wrapped up their work here, they could always just shoot off a flare and call him back.

"Hold on. That's a flare," said Kyle, squinting to see it while he kept his grip on the wheel.

"What's that?" Borgoff asked, poking his rough face out of the bedroom. A single streak of light rose into a sky already bright with the radiance of dawn. The streak quickly grew several times more brilliant. "A flare way out here, smack dab in the middle of nowhere? I'd say that couldn't be nothing but the Nobility."

"*Bingo!* Roughly three miles from here. We'll be on them in five minutes. The bastard ain't gonna be able to move a muscle." Laughing confidently, Kyle added, "One good jab'll do it!" As he licked his lips, Kyle stroked the tip of one of the stakes secured to the wall.

"Still, there's something I don't like about this," Borgoff said, folding his arms. "What does he hope to gain by firing off a flare way out here? Even if he wanted help, there ain't no one who'd come . . . " After some consideration, Borgoff suddenly raised his bearded countenance again. "No fucking way!" he gasped. "We'd better make some speed, Kyle. If my hunch is right, that bastard might've called in some serious trouble."

Kyle's face grew tense at his brother's grave tone. "Here we go!" he shouted.

With a sharp change in gear and a stomp on the accelerator, the bus raced forward. The scene outside the windows started to course by at an intense speed. The scenery of the stony mountain crags grew more and more desolate. White smoke gushed from the earth in odd spots and crept heavily along the ground, evidence of nearby volcanic activity. The area around the vents was caked with yellow lumps of sulfur. Even the rocks formed extraordinary shapes—some menacing the heavens like spears, others looking so impossibly fragile that they'd crumble at a touch.

The mere passing of the vehicle caused cracks to form here and there in the depressed earth, and, when something watery but not quite the shade of blood squirted up from below, the tiny insects that flew slowly through this world were seized by spasms and dropped to the ground.

A number of times the bus plowed over bleached bones—mountains of them, contributed by everything from huge fang-baring beasts down to the smallest of vermin. The atmosphere was permeated not only by sulfur, but by strong toxins as well.

Before long, the road narrowed and the rocky surface to either side grew higher, giving the dramatic effect of an avalanche about to sweep over the bus. Neither Kyle nor Borgoff could conceal their concern.

They continued down the menacing road through the valley for about twenty minutes. Then, without warning, Kyle slowed down. "There it is!" he shouted.

Ahead of them, the blurred form of the carriage was visible in the depths of the swirling white smoke.

"What should we do, bro? Just keep going and ram 'em?" The bus had plates of armored steel bolted to the front, after all.

"Nope," the older brother replied. "Gotta keep in mind the girl might still be alive. Anyway you slice it, the Noble can't move by daylight. We'll get out and take care of 'em. Put on a gas mask."

When the two brothers had turned themselves around, the door to the bedroom opened and Leila looked out. Not surprisingly, her complexion was still pale, but her eyes blazed with the will to fight. "Picked a hell of a place to stop," she said. "Did you find them?"

"You get some rest now. And look after Grove," Borgoff said as he slipped on his gas mask.

"No way! Let me go with you!" Leila caught the oldest of the clan by the arm. The muscles felt like stone. "This is a Noble we're dealing with. Even if he can't move during the day, that still doesn't mean he'll be defenseless. You can use all the backup you can get."

"A gimp would just get in the way," Borgoff replied.

"But—"

"Leila, why don't you give it a rest?" Kyle interjected, a javelin tight in his grip. On his right hip, there hung another gas mask he intended to use for the abducted girl. "Look, you heard what Borgoff said. He told you to just leave this to the two of us. I mean, look how high the sun still is. There ain't nothing to worry about."

His voice was coaxing, but had a touch of carnal desire in it, and Leila turned away. She nodded, apparently giving in.

"Now don't you go out there!"

With that final admonishment, Borgoff and Kyle stood on the steps by the door. When Kyle pressed the switch by his side, a semitransparent veil descended from overhead, sealing the two of them off from the rest of the vehicle. This wasn't the first time they had to stalk their quarry in a poison-shrouded environ.

Opening the door manually, the two stepped down to the ground. They wore no other protection besides the gas masks. Artificial antibodies in their blood could handle the rest of the poisonous vapors and radiation.

Their feet didn't make the slightest sound as they hustled over the ground.

The Noble's carriage was motionless, just branding the earth with its faint and lonely shadow. Even the six black steeds hung their heads, appearing either to sleep or to be absorbed in contemplation.

Contrary to what one might expect, this picture of defenselessness sowed seeds of tension and anxiety in the hearts of the pair. Kyle adjusted his grip on the javelin.

Ten feet to the carriage. White smoke robbed the pair of their vision, then cleared.

Without a sound, the pair leapt to either side. Between them and the carriage there suddenly stood a black silhouette. The elongated figure garbed in a black hooded robe seemed to be an illusion, something conjured up by the poisonous vapors.

"Who the hell are you?" Kyle asked in a low voice. The filters on their masks doubled as voice amplifiers.

Giving no answer, the shadow raised its right hand. Flying with a dull growl, a steel arrow pierced it through the wrist. The shadow shook.

There hadn't been just one arrow. Thanks to Borgoff's masterful skill, arrows also stuck in the shadow's head and the left side of its chest. While it was true they were dealing with an unknown element here, three arrows may have been overdoing it a bit. But then, that was the Marcus way of doing things.

The shadow turned its face up. The brothers' eyes opened wide. The hood was empty.

When the plain robe fell flatly to the ground with three arrows still stuck in it, Borgoff forgot to launch a second attack. Something had occurred to him, and, with no warning, he turned and loosed an arrow at the carriage. As he watched it punch nicely through the polished iron plating to the rear, the vehicle's window lost its contours, the wheels twisted limply, and the entire carriage became a single sheet of black cloth trailing along the ground.

A silver flash raced off burning through the white smoke. It etched a graceful arc and ran through the horses' necks. It was the flash of a crescent blade. Their heads drooped, thick necks hacked nearly in half.

No blood came out. There was no flesh or cross section of vertebrae to be seen in the fresh wounds. The inside was hollow. The pair watched in a daze as every last one of the half-dozen horses became black cloth and settled softly on the ground.

Eerie laughter rose like smoke around them. High and low, the weird but beautiful voice that seemed to escape from the bowels of the earth was that of a woman.

About thirty feet ahead of the pair, a slender feminine figure came into focus. Laughing haughtily, she said, "Followed a Noble all this way, have we? I came out here to see the extent of your abilities, but, as I expected, they really don't amount to much. As such, naught awaits you on this road but the boiling fires of hell. You'd do well to scamper off now with your tails between your legs."

Sensing an inordinate evil in the chiming golden bell that was her voice, Kyle shouted, "You the one who pulled that hocus-pocus just now?!" The javelin was in his left hand, and his right held one of his deadly crescent blades at the ready.

"Unfortunately, no," the woman said. "Although, you're actually quite fortunate it wasn't me. Otherwise you wouldn't have gotten off with a mere prank. If you value your boring little lives, you'd best turn back posthaste."

"Where's the Noble?" inquired Borgoff. The strange thing was, he had both eyes shut tight.

"In our village," the woman replied. "He came to retain the finest guards as insurance against maggots like you following him." Laughing snidely, she added, "Perhaps you boys should hire a few of us, too, to serve as Hunters and go after him?"

Beneath his gasmask, Kyle's face grew black with rage. His left hand went into action. When the javelin flew through the air and passed vainly through the figure of the woman only to be embedded in the wall of rock behind her, indistinct shapes appeared all around them, hovering in the air. All of the shapes looked like the woman.

"Bitch," Kyle spat after the flash of crescent blade he swept around passed through the specters without meeting any resistance. He looked to his older brother. "So that's what you were up to, Borgoff?"

Eyes still shut, the giant nodded, and the sneering yet mellifluous laughter stole into their ears again.

"You still don't understand, do you, little fools? May you wander this poison smoke for all eternity." A split second later, her words became a scream.

One of the shimmering figures behind them had been pierced by Borgoff's arrow. When and how the giant fired was a mystery. Kyle hadn't seen his brother's hands move. What's more, his bow and the arrow cocked in it had been pointed straight ahead from the start.

Blood's own aroma mixed with the stench of poisonous smoke.

"You . . . you bastard!" she screeched, the shadowy figures fading as quickly as her cry.

"Bro, you did it!"

"Yep." Borgoff gave a nod, and perhaps it was the knowledge that the woman was gone for good that made his tiger-like eyes shine so strangely. Immediately, the brothers headed back toward the bus.

The door closed, and, once the poisonous gas had been evacuated through the exhaust vents, they entered the main cabin. There, for the first time, Borgoff struck the wall of the vehicle with his boulder of a fist. The ceiling rattled.

"What do you wanna do now, bro?"

"This is a huge fucking mess now. That bastard Noble's gone and holed up in the village of the Barbarois."

Kyle wasn't the only one who grew tense at his brother's words. Leila, who'd been waiting for them, reacted the same way. For the first time, something resembling paling fear flowed through the faces of the siblings. But even that was transient.

"Sounds like fun," Leila muttered, and it even seemed a vermilion flush of excitement was rising in her pale face. "The village of the Barbarois—monsters and freaks have been interbreeding there for five thousand years, honing their sorceries and skills in the darkness. I always hoped to try my hand against them someday."

"Damn straight." Kyle bared his teeth. "If he's holed up in their village, there's a pretty damned good chance he'll— well, actually, the woman already told us what he was gonna do. Said he'd come to hire her and others. There ain't no two ways about it, he's definitely got himself some freaky guards now." Kyle snickered. "I'm just itching for a piece of them. We've all heard rumors about the supernatural powers of the Barbarois. The question is, whose skills would come out on top, ours or theirs? I mean, wouldn't it be great to throw down with them just once?"

"Of course it would," the oldest Marcus replied. "I don't care if it's the Barbarois or the Nobility's Sacred Ancestor himself, we'd dye our hands in their blood. Just one thing, though. Our first order of business is that bastard Noble and the ten million dalas. I don't wanna do any fighting unless we're getting paid for it. For the time being, we'll keep a watch on this nest of freaks and wait for Nolt to get back. Me and Kyle will go. Leila, you send up a flare as soon as you're clear of this corner of hell and then wait there for Nolt."

The brutal siblings looked at each other and let out a lurid, blood-curdling laugh. What then was this village of the Barbarois that even they found so difficult to dismiss? Who resided there? And what were their darkness-spawned powers?

II

Down the road three miles from the spot where the Marcus brothers encountered the strange woman, a particularly high and rocky mountain loomed off the left-hand side of the road.

To the eye of the uninformed traveler, the heap of countless rocks, large and small, was merely a product of nature. But, upon closer inspection, the pieces of stone that at a glance had seemed to be stacked haphazardly were, in fact, arranged systematically by someone or something with an understanding of dynamics. And, as the arrangement of the rocks became clear, so too did the eerie aura surrounding them. A chill was carried down like a ghost from the icy heights of the mountain, rising up the backs of the most courageous and the most fearful travelers alike.

Though the mountain looked like it might be easily scaled, no matter how tough the human that challenged it was, partway up its scaly surface the rocks were laid out in such an intricate way that they'd cave in a second. Even if by some slim chance a climber got through that part, there were places on the route where every rock was rigged to bury the climber in an avalanche of stone.

Still, if fortune smiled on them and, by some miracle, the climber made it into the bowels of the mountain, their eyes would be greeted by a single cavern. While passing through it they'd be blasted by damp winds that seemed to blow from the very netherhells, and then they'd soon come to a fortress constructed from cyclopean stones and colossal trees. Despite the fact that the very human sounds of laughter, shouting, and crying could be heard constantly, and the smoke from cook fires never ceased, there was something in the atmosphere that separated this place from the world of humanity, an eldritch aura which hung in the air. This was the nest of demons that made the Marcus clan shudder—the village of the Barbarois.

It was a mystery just how on earth the carriage and the six-horse team drawing it had got into the village, but enter they did as the light of dawn was finally beginning to swell with the vitality of day.

There were houses in the village, and plenty of men and women. Stopping where they worked or poking their heads out of doorways, they formed a ring around the carriage the instant it came to a halt. Perhaps they were already cognizant of the true nature of their strange visitor, for not one of them tried to open the door.

Pushing his way through the ring which was now several bodies deep, an old man with a hoary mane came into view. His white beard was long enough to sweep the ground, and his back was so stooped that his chest was parallel to the earth. Untold centuries old, his face was obscured by countless wrinkles, and yet every inch of him brimmed with an ineffable vigor.

He approached the door on the left-hand side of the carriage and rapped lightly on the steel surface with his cane. Following that, he nodded to himself, and, after turning around to give a wink to the masses behind him, he put his withered, clay-like ear to the door.

The wind died out immediately.

The deathly silence persisted for what seemed like hours, but in due time the old man started to nod with the kindly countenance of a codger doting on his grandchildren.

"I see, I see. I'm glad you came. It's guards you desire then, to protect your lady love? Very well, very well. So, how many do you need? Three? Hmm, did you have anyone particular in mind?"

The eyelids he had shut like a thin line flew open. A fearsome light spilled from them, but, after a moment, he closed his eyes once more.

"Bengé, Caroline, Mashira . . . Oh, those are the very best, the cream of our village. Fine. When your flare informed us that you were being followed, Caroline headed out to toy with those wandering mongrels, but they'll be back presently. They are entirely at your disposal."

Could one of the Nobility, who should be comatose by day, be holding a conversation with this old man? Not one of those assembled seemed to find this the least bit suspect as the old man's eyes suddenly opened again.

"Oh, so you say you have one more favor to ask," the old man muttered. "What's that? There's another who follows you solo, you say? Hmm . . . a dhampir."

The air stirred violently. None of the villagers moved an inch, as if a ghastly white aura had enveloped them. Moans of shock came from the villagers' lips as the following words slipped from the old man: "His name is—D."

In a while, when silence once again ruled the scene, the mutterings of the old man were adorned with a tremble of unbridled delight. "Ah, the greatest Vampire Hunter on the Frontier—I believe we're up to the challenge. If we lure him into our stronghold and attack, slowly wearing him down, that is. That service, however, shall cost you quite dearly."

†

An hour after his brothers had gone, Groveck's condition took a strange turn. His breathing became rapid and shallow, and sweat gushed from his lean face. His state was more serious than usual, which panicked Leila. His pulse was racing, too.

"A seizure," she mumbled to herself. "But not like any we've ever seen before. What in the name of hell is this . . . "

She put as much ibuprofen as she could into the bottle on his IV, and she was headed toward the kitchen to cool down the cloth for mopping the sweat from his brow when the bus rocked violently.

Metal eating-utensils fell one after another to the floor, and though the sound-dampening carpet tried to preserve the silence, the vehicle was filled by a cacophony. Every wound in the girl's body pulsed sheer agony.

Hastily securing the IV bottle with electrical tape, Leila raced around the vehicle looking out all of the windows, checking in every direction. There was no one out there. They were parked in the middle of a circular clearing about a hundred yards in diameter that wasn't far off the road. With a click of her tongue, Leila dove into the garage to the vehicle's rear.

Ignoring the five cyborg horses stored there with their limbs retracted, she leapt into the driver's seat of her battle car. As Leila turned the key in the ignition, a comforting vibration swept through her. Without looking at the digital gauges beside the steering yoke, Leila grasped the condition of the car like it was something she could hold in her two hands.

"Atomic fuel at ninety-eight percent of capacity . . . Engine, check . . . Stabilizers, check . . . Puncture damage, negligible. Propulsion voltage good to go up to ninety-seven percent. Weapon controls, okay . . . Here we go!"

The rear doors of the bus opened, and, without waiting for the ramp to slide into place, the battle car flew out. She gave it full throttle just as it touched down and took it for a loop around the bus.

The bus was the only thing shaking, and there really was no one out there after all.

Leila parked the battle car broadside to seal off the entrance to the clearing, then stood up in her seat like a vengeful god. "Who's there? C'mon out. I'm Leila Marcus, of the Marcus clan. You won't catch me running and hiding," she declared, trying to keep the pain that knifed through her body from showing on her face. Then, as suddenly as it began, the shaking of the bus stopped.

A cheerful voice came in response. "My, missy, aren't you the high-spirited one."

Leila spun around in amazement. The perplexed expression she'd donned just before turning her head was because she didn't know where the distinct voice was issuing from.

There was no one behind her. Nor to her left, nor to right.

"Where are you?" she asked. "Where the hell are you?! C'mon out, you lousy coward!"

"There's nowhere to come out from," the voice jeered. "I'm right beside you. If you can't see me, the fault is with your eyes."

Her blood nearly curdled. Once again, she scanned her surroundings. She realized the voice spoke the truth. Whoever it was, they had to be somewhere. Right under her very nose, no less.

Leila harnessed every fiber of her being to search in all directions. Like her brothers, she'd honed her five senses to a razor-sharp level. Now her hearing and her sense of touch told her there wasn't another living creature in the clearing. Yet, despite that, she could hear the voice.

Leila was seized by a fear unlike any she'd felt before. It sprang from a loss of self-confidence and wounds that hadn't fully healed.

With the sliver gun from her side now in hand, Leila jumped out of the car. Her bloodshot eyes darted around her. She hadn't given up the fight yet.

A stabbing pain shot up her back.

Catching a hail of fire from the sliver gun she unleashed as soon as she whipped around, one of the chunks of rock hemming the clearing was reduced to dust. Fired by highly pressured oxygen, the half million, one-micron-long, .001-micron-wide needles in the gun could leave the walls of a Noble's castle as friable as unglazed pottery. But that didn't count for much against an unseen opponent.

Leila reached one hand around to her back. The stickiness she felt was blood. Clearly she'd been cut by some sort of blade, but she was powerless to do anything about it. Agony assailed her for a second time, and Leila fell to her knees. Her strength was dwindling rapidly.

The voice returned. "What's wrong, missy? Compared to the wound my colleague suffered, this is nothing. Nothing at all. It'll take a lot more than that to drive you mad, won't it?"

"Who the hell are you? Where are you?!"

"I already told you, didn't I? I'm right beside you. If you look hard enough, you should see me. *You don't see me because you think you can't.* Here, maybe this will help you understand?"

The Marcus girl gave an agonized cry. Fresh blood spilling from the back of her shredded shirt, Leila crouched down on the ground.

What kind of cold-blooded torture was this, slashing the flesh of a defenseless girl with deep cuts and shallow? Perhaps in some sick way her attacker was aroused by the sight of Leila in agony, because the voice had a ring akin to lust when it asked, "Well, how do you like that? Taste more pain, more suffering. Your brothers will be getting a taste of very same treatment from me before too long. Ha ha ha ha!"

The sneering laughter ended sharply. Leila could feel someone shaking intensely right beside her. An unearthly aura was gusting their way, coming from the entrance to the clearing.

Must be Nolt, she thought. *No, it's not.* Another disappointment lodging in her breast, Leila twisted her face around in desperation.

It was unclear how he'd gotten by the battle car, but a black-garbed youth stood casually in the center of the clearing, not making a sound. Forgetting her pain at the beauty of the one who now gazed at her, Leila swooned in glorious intoxication. The unsettling presence vanished in an instant.

Waiting for a while on horseback while he seemed to size up the situation, D quietly guided his horse to Leila's side. "Your opponent's not here any more," he said. "Can you stand?"

Torpidly, Leila pulled herself up. "No problem at all, as you can see. What in blazes brings you here?" Her bluster carried no animosity. Borgoff had told her that someone had taken care of her when she was hurt, and no one but this gorgeous young man could've fit that bill.

"I saw your flare and came. Where's the rest of your clan?"

"In the bus. Try anything funny and they'll come flying out here," Leila lied.

"So they're just sitting back watching their little sister do battle, eh? The Marcus clan has hit a new low."

At D's tone, which merely conveyed the truth without sarcasm, Leila became enraged. She staggered. The substantial blood loss she'd suffered had caught up with her. Her other wounds hadn't healed yet, either. Glancing once more at the cold beauty of the youth staring down at her from horseback, Leila passed out.

†

The next thing she knew, she was lying on a bed. Before she had time to notice her bare skin was wrapped in bandages, Leila flipped herself over and looked toward the door. A black figure was just leaving. Without a sound.

"Wait. Please, just wait a sec!" Leila herself didn't know why she called out to him so frantically.

The shadowy figure stopped.

Leila got up. She jerked the tube out of her right arm. The attached bottle of plasma rocked wildly. It was plain to see who'd gone to the trouble of setting up her transfusion.

"Go back to sleep," he told her. "You're liable to open your wounds and wake your brother."

"Never mind him," she replied. Yet, despite what she said, she peeked in on Groveck across the aisle. Confirming that his condition was stable, Leila felt relieved.

Suddenly the piercing pain returned to her body, and she let out a groan. "Don't go," she cried. "If you go, I'll die."

The young man headed for the door.

"Hold on. Don't you even care what happens to me?" Leila didn't know why she sounded so miserable as she said this. Could it be that she simply wanted him by her side? No, that thought didn't occur to her.

She was going to follow him, but her foot caught on something and she tumbled to the floor. The scream that escaped her was no fabrication.

The youth walked over calmly and picked her up.

"My back—it's killing me." That was a lie. "Carry me as far as the bed."

The young Hunter turned his back to her again.

"Wait! What was that thing? If you leave, it might come back. Please, stay with me."

The youth turned around. "I'm the competition, you know."

"You're my savior. Mine and Grove's. And if my brothers come back, I won't let them lay a finger on you."

"There's something I should tell you first," the young man continued without concern. "I cut down your brother Nolt."

Leila's eyes shot up to him. A wild rage spread through her body. It looked like she might leap at D, but instead she let her shoulders drop. "I see," she muttered numbly. "So my brother got killed . . . I think I understand why. I mean, he went up against you, right? Wait, don't go. I want you here by my side, even if it's just for a little bit longer."

Something besides her anguished cries must have stayed the stride of the icy youth. He returned to the bedroom. Leila lay down on the bed, and the young man put his back against the wall, looking down at her.

"Why did you save me, not once but twice now?" she asked.

"I had some time on my hands."

"You're not after the Noble then?"

"I've figured out where he's headed."

"Oh, you wouldn't be kind enough to share that, would you? My brothers would be overjoyed."

"Is that your sick brother in the bed over there?" the youth inquired softly. He made no attempt to look at Groveck.

"Yep. Fact is, he hasn't even been able to walk or anything since the day he was born."

"But it seems he can do something else instead."

A look of astonishment raced across Leila face. Soon, her sober expression returned, and she said, "You're a strange one, aren't you? Saving the competition twice and all. Even though you had no qualms about killing one of my brothers. What, are you afraid taking down a woman would bring shame on your sword?"

"If you come at me, I'll cut you down."

At D's impassive words, Leila grew pale. She knew he was serious. Here was a young man with the keenness of a mystic blade concealed behind his beauty. And yet, while their eyes were locked, she wouldn't mind being slashed so long as it was D who did it. The thought that she'd even want him to kill her welled up in her breast like an enchanted fog, turning the contents of her heart and mind into slush. That must've been the power of a dhampir—the power of one descended from the Nobility.

"You're a strange guy," Leila said again. "You aren't even gonna ask me where my brothers went? If I hadn't woken up, you'd have left, wouldn't you? Like a shadow. Like the wind. Are all dhampirs like that?"

"How long have you been a Hunter?"

Her own question unexpectedly brushed aside, Leila became a bit disoriented. "How long? For as long as I can remember. Besides, I can't live any other way."

"This isn't a job for women. When it gets to the point you enjoy stalking your prey, that's proof that you're not a woman anymore."

"How tactful of you to say so. Keep your opinions to yourself," Leila said, turning away. Any other man would've had the palm of her hand or a knife headed their way. But because the youth spoke in that unconcerned tone of his—neither reproachful nor teasing—there was something in his words that shook Leila. "I can't very well change my way of life at this stage of the game," she continued. "I've got too much blood on my hands."

"It comes off if you wash them."

"Why would you say something like that? You trying to put me out of work?"

The young man made his way to the door. "The next time you see me," he said, "you'd better forget the small talk and just start shooting. I won't hold back either."

"That's just fine by me," she replied. There was a grieving hue in Leila's eyes.

"Your brothers wouldn't make much of a stink over losing one little sister," the shadowy figure said as it faded into the sunlight. "Any girl who cries out for her mother as she lays dying isn't cut out for Hunting."

And then the youth was gone. Like a shadow melting in the sun.

After he left, his words continued to ring in Leila's ears.

The girl's eyes bored into the closed door, and something in them blurred softly. Just as she was going for the door, a thin hand caught hold of her sleeve.

"Grove?!"

"Leila . . . you're not gonna listen . . . to what that guy said, are you?" The voice from under the blankets sounded furtive and twitching. "You wouldn't listen to that guy . . .go off and leave me and the others . . . now would you, Leila? Don't you forget about . . . *you-know-what* . . . "

"Quit it!"

The scrawny hand Leila tried to shake off held her entirely too tenaciously.

"Don't you ever forget that, Leila," Groveck rasped. "You belong to all of us . . . "

III

T he shadowy figures of Kyle and Borgoff clung like geckos to the rocky face overlooking the village of the Barbarois. The mountain, which was insurmountable to the average traveler, hadn't served as much of a deterrent against this pair.

Sprawled on a flat rock and inspecting the village through electronic binoculars, Kyle raised his head and said to Borgoff, "Damn it, the carriage and whatever's in it went into the forest, but they ain't come out. You think maybe they've already slipped back out the same way they got in?"

"Don't know." Borgoff shook his head. "And it's not like we can just waltz up and ask them, now can we?"

Kyle fell into silence. Somehow they'd managed to climb partway up the mountain without being detected, but even this pair of crafty devils were hesitant to sneak into the village. In fact, their Hunter instincts told them it'd be dangerous to get any closer in broad daylight.

Even though Barbarois seemed like a run-of-the-mill hidden village, with no sign of watchtowers or lookouts, the fact was that in the nondescript shade of the rocks and groves there lurked those with sight as keen as swords.

Conversing only with their eyes, the brothers decided to sneak in by night, when the watch would slacken.

The Marcus brothers knew that the Noble who owned the carriage had called on this village hoping to retain some guards. If possible, the brothers wanted to finish him before he could do so, but, now that it'd gone this far, that was no longer an option. The two brothers weren't at all confident they could slip into this mob of freaks—who were their equals or perhaps even their superiors in battle—and accomplish their aims.

Under the circumstances, there was no choice but to wait for the carriage to come out, but they had misgivings about that, too. They couldn't imagine how the carriage had possibly been brought into the village, and the prospects of it slipping out unseen were extremely good. They wouldn't know it had left until it was gone.

If only they knew the Noble's destination they could at least head him off, but they didn't even know their prey's name. *At the rate things are going, we'll never land that bounty*—the Marcus brothers grew impatient at that thought. And as they fumed, more of their precious time slipped by.

When they'd first got up to their lookout, the carriage was being moved from the square into a stand of trees. Even after they watched the people disperse from the area, it seemed there'd been some sort of a discussion. Common sense dictated that the Nobility slept by day, but then common sense didn't seem to have much say about matters in this village.

So what had they discussed? Well, the Marcus brothers actually had a pretty good idea what'd been covered. They could guess how many guards the Noble had employed and what kind they would be, and maybe where they were headed, too.

The sun was nearing noon. The rocky surface went from warm to searing, and yet the brothers still lacked a good plan. A hue of impatience was just beginning to show on Borgoff's face when he heard a sudden cry.

"Bro, is that who I think it is?!"

Checking Kyle's surprised outburst with his firm, silent gaze, Borgoff felt the same shock as his brother. Off to their left, a figure had just leisurely slipped into the black cavern leading to the village—and it looked like it was D!

"That bastard should've drowned! What, ain't he a dhampir?"

Borgoff didn't answer Kyle's question. He was having enough trouble believing it himself. "Then, I reckon that means . . . Nolt's had it."

Turning to his older brother for only a second, Kyle's face was instantly colored by hatred. "That bastard . . . Killing off Nolt . . . He's not getting out of this alive," he growled. "Ain't that right, bro?"

Though he nodded, Borgoff kept his silence. Difficult as it might be to accept, Borgoff knew that Nolt had to be dead and that D must have killed him. But killing a Noble with an escort of Barbarois would entail risking their lives. This young dhampir possessed an unearthly intensity even they couldn't match, and making an enemy of him as well would be utter madness.

"I bet that bastard's here to scope out the village, same as us. This is our chance. I'll take him down from here with my crescent blades."

As the younger brother was about to stand, Borgoff's hand took a firm grip on his elbow. "Hold your horses, okay? Look, he's headed straight for the gate. He ain't staking it out. He plans on parleying with them directly."

"You're kidding me! Dammit, ain't that even worse? If this keeps up, he's gonna beat us to the punch!"

The words of the wild youngest brother held some truth.

As Borgoff glared fixedly into space, his face grew more and more sad, and sweat started to blur his brow. When his eyes opened, there was a ghastly hue to them. "We got no choice then. I didn't wanna do this, but we'll have to call on Grove," he said.

"Wait just a minute there . . . " Kyle said, his voice rigid. This was the same brother who'd earned a glare from Borgoff for suggesting they send Groveck to scout around the village of the dead they had entered two days earlier.

What kind of power lay in that shriveled mummy of a youth that could offer a solution to their problems?

"I'll keep watch here, Kyle. Once you've given Grove a seizure, you come right back," the older Marcus said.

"Good enough."

Why was it that a lewd smile arose on Kyle's face as he answered? Whatever the reason, it only lasted an instant. Flipping himself over atop the rock, his leather garments sparkled blackly in the gleaming sunlight and he came down the mountain with the light gait of a supernatural beast. Down he went, over extremely dangerous rocks—not one of which could be tread upon without setting off an avalanche.

†

Coming within fifteen feet of the eerie gates, which looked to be wood and stone wired together and strung with hides, D halted his steed. As he looked up at the towering palisade ahead, his expression was redolent of a dashing young poet or philosopher.

The air swished to life.

Where on earth they'd been hiding was a mystery. No one could be seen or even sensed a moment earlier, but all of a sudden a number of people appeared among the rocks and trees. They surrounded D. The face of each was darkly intrepid, but some among them were pale to the point of transparency, or armored in ghastly scales. They were a band that would no doubt cow any traveler encountering them for the first time, yet, for some reason, with D they kept their distance. Once they had him surrounded, they made no move to approach him. On realizing that it was fear and wonder that arose on their inhuman faces, the Prince of Hell himself might've doubted his own eyes.

With a sharp glance from D, they staggered backward.

"I'm the Vampire Hunter D. I have business here. Kindly open the gates."

At his bidding, the mysterious gates swung silently inward. Without another glance at the guards to his fore and rear, his left and his right, D rode leisurely in on his horse.

As soon as they were inside, a terrible aura enveloped D and his steed. Triggered by the eerie emanations D himself radiated, all the eldritch energies in the air seemed to shoot toward them as one. D's expression didn't change in the least, and his horse never altered its stride.

When they had gone a few steps, the strange roiling energies disappeared. The men, who remained positioned around D, exchanged startled looks. The Hunter's unearthly aura had just beaten down their own disturbing emanations.

The village and its inhabitants flowed past D as he rode. The village had been established in a vast wooded region that'd sprung up in the middle of the mountains, and the homes were fashioned from timbers and stone. Most of the residents were self-sufficient as far as food and weapons went, and a building that looked to be a factory could be spied tucked silently among the trees.

While they were rather antiquated, there were high-caliber laser-cannons and ultrasonic wave-cannons visible within the palisade, indicating that the Barbarois were perfectly prepared to deal with their enemies in the outside world.

But what was truly astonishing was the appearance of the inhabitants of the village. Their clothing was the ordinary farm wear or work clothes found in any hamlet, but very few of the arms and legs and heads that protruded from said raiment had the form of anything human. A glimpse of red tongue could be seen flickering from what must've been lips on a face scaled like a serpent's, while another visage was mantled in thick fur like a veritable wolf. Way in the back, an innocent young boy splashed water up from his pool. From the neck down he had the body of a crocodile, and the limbs to match.

There existed things in this world that weren't entirely natural, the offspring of couplings between fiendish beasts and human beings. All who dwelled in the village of the Barbarois were the fruit of those abominable relations.

Most humans from the world below would've fainted dead away at the sight of these demons, but D rode past them silently, arriving at what seemed to be a central square. At the center stood the black carriage, along with a hoary-maned old man.

Halting his horse at the entrance to the square, D stepped to the ground.

"Oh," the old man exclaimed, stroking that ground-sweeping white beard of his. "You dismount? I see you know enough to show respect for your elders. But you have me sorely puzzled. How did you ever manage to climb our mountain on horseback?"

Whether the words that seemed to slither along the ground reached him or not, D took hold of the reins and started walking towards the old man. He stopped six feet shy of him and gestured to the black carriage with his right hand. "I'd like you to hand over the two passengers in that carriage," he said.

The old man smiled broadly—or rather, all the wrinkles on his face twisted up into a smile—but in the laughter that followed there was a hint of scorn. "Young man, you've come into our village in a way no one else has ever managed. I wish I could tell you the passengers in that carriage were yours, but it's too late, too late. We've already sided with the carriage, you see. The contract is drawn, and we've been paid in gold. Paid with the fabled ten thousand-dala coins—ten of them. Could you afford that much?"

"If I could, would you sell out your clients?"

At D's reply, soft as ever, the smile instantly vanished from the old man's face. His wrathful mien was a sight to behold, and it looked like he might even take a swing at the Hunter with his cane. But he unexpectedly threw his head back in a way that almost seemed to straighten his spine, and he gave a hearty laugh. "Ho ho ho. Knowing as you do that this is the village of the Barbarois, that took nerve to say. Oh, what a treat, what a great treat! Why, the last time anyone spoke to me like that was precisely three hundred and twenty years ago . . . "

A strange expression skimmed across the old man's face. As if groping in the misty depths of forgotten memory with fingers that'd lost their sense of touch, he narrowed his eyes impatiently. When he threw them open again, a hue of astonishment spilled from his pupils.

"That face," he murmured. "Could it be that you're . . . "

"I'm a Vampire Hunter," D said quietly. "At the request of the father of an abducted girl, I'm in pursuit of the culprit. I've come here as a result of that, and nothing more. But I understand your position. All I ask it that you put him back outside and let me pursue him in peace."

"Oh. Better yet, a man of principle." The old man seemed beside himself with joy, striking his cane against the earth. "Out of respect for that, I'll share a little something with you. What his requests were. One was that we provide him with an escort to protect him from you and other Hunters. The other was to dispose of a young man named D who was certain to come here."

The square was buried in an avalanche of killing lust. While the two were conversing, countless villagers had encircled them. Not a single one of them had a weapon in hand. Nonetheless, each and every one of them had a fearsome air that made it clear they'd have no problem slaying a few humans at a time.

"What will you do now, D? It was remarkable how you made it all the way in here, but getting back out looks to be somewhat more difficult, doesn't it? Every man and woman assembled here's been trained in the most astounding of abilities. No matter how great of a Hunter you may be, you can't possibly kill them all."

And what was D doing as the old man spoke the indisputable truth? He was looking up at the sky. Gazing at the perfectly clear blue and the clouds cavorting there.

His expression was so intent the villagers stopped closing on him and exchanged looks with each other.

"So, is that where he wants to go then?"

Perhaps mistaking the Hunter's muttering as a plea for his life, one of the Barbarois leapt into the air with a cry like a savage roc. When he straightened up, his body was round overall, yet his stomach was flat as a board, a shape that was reminiscent of a tortoise. The beast stretched his arms toward D's face. The fingertips fused with the nails and became like the horns of a bull. If they but touched him, they'd gouge away a chunk of flesh and bone.

The two figures passed each other—one in the air and one on the ground—and the rotund man landed lightly as he came back to earth.

Maybe it was the stirring of the villagers that called forth the bloody mist. A number of them had caught the silvery flash that shot out faster than the eye could follow in the instant the man had passed D. But, no—they'd certainly seen the man's head pull into his clothing just as D's blade was about to strike. Like a tortoise, the man's body was covered by a carapace that was impervious to even bullets, and his hands and feet could stretch like springs.

But his carapace cracked down the middle just as he landed. The face of the man that appeared from the bottom, the serpentine neck, the tangle of intestines—all of them had been split in two right down to the crotch, and the man sent up a spray of blood as he toppled.

For the first time, the others saw the blade shining in D's right hand. There was no one foolish enough among them to press the Hunter a second time, despite the gut-deep rage they felt at the death of their comrade and friend. The realization that this youth possessed an unholy prowess with the sword seeped into the marrow of their bones.

In an attitude and pose no different from the one that'd greeted his attacker, D turned to the old man and said softly, "You can kill me if you like, but many of your villagers will die, too. Why don't you stand back and let me stay here until night? When the carriage leaves, I'll go right out after it. That's it. As the lot of you have entered a contract to help the fugitive, I'll ask nothing else."

If the decree of certain death the old man had pronounced on D was valid, what D said was equally true.

"So, it's just as I thought then . . . " The old man nodded, his face showing understanding. "Such abilities, such dignity," he muttered. "Yes, I was right all along . . . " Then, waving his right hand so the villagers backed off, he said something unexpected in a weary tone. "If you should ask that all in the village drown in a lake of blood, I could not deny you. I implore you, take the shriveled head of this old fool for our rudeness and grant us your forgiveness."

"What are you talking about?!" someone shouted. This one angry outburst parted the wall of villagers.

A woman in a dress an unsettlingly deep shade of indigo stepped from the mob to stand between the old man and D. The spot of pink on her exposed right shoulder was strangely conspicuous against her white skin. Her voice was a venom-dripping howl as she said, "Why the fainthearted drivel? Elder, have you forgotten the law of our village? Once we have a contract with one who's come seeking our aid—regardless of who they may be— we must uphold the wishes of our employer or die trying. And I, Caroline, intend to do so, with the aid of Mashira and Bengé."

"Absolutely," an impudent voice added in agreement. Pushing his way through the ring of people, a middle-aged man of average height and medium build tossed the hem of his gray coat and took his place alongside the woman. "By failing to honor a contract we've already agreed to, you'd be doing more than just breaking the law of the village. It would mean the ruin of the village itself. Elder, leave this young pup to the three of us."

"My sentiments exactly."

The third speaker drew a dramatic reaction. The voice came from behind the middle-aged man, and it must've caught him off guard, because he flinched momentarily and took a step back.

Framed by the other two but standing behind them was a strangely elongated man, as thin as a preying mantis. His hands and face were as black as if they'd been dipped in ink, and his coat was the color of midnight. Though this was the same color as the leather Kyle garbed himself in, there was something peculiar about it that gave it an entirely different feel.

"I believe we met earlier," the tenebrous man said, winking at D. The man was so thin it seemed plausible no one would be able to see him hiding behind a fair-sized pole. But there hadn't even been a single tree nearby to conceal him. "Allow me to do the introductions. The lovely lady you see here is Caroline, while this is Mashira. And I am Bengé," he said, turning with a smile to the elder. "Since he's already here there's not much we can do. Elder, you may relent, but we're going through with this. You can strip us of our right to reside here if you so desire."

"Friends of his marred my skin," Caroline said in a quivering voice as she pressed her left hand to the pink spot. "I won't forget that. I'll never forget the pain. Even pounding an iron wedge through this rascal's chest won't make it go away!"

"There must be others besides us who feel the same way. Step forward!"

But when the middle-aged man—Mashira—had made this call, the old man shouted "Idiots!" so loudly that the rebellious trio and a number of villagers coming forward to join them flinched. That wizened feline form of the old man had caused the group of malcontents three times his size to tremble.

"Do you fools know I've looked like this since the village was founded? Have you any idea how your ancestors suffered and sweated to build this mountain village after they were chased from their homes for carnal relations with demons? I'll have you know, all their hard work was poised for destruction at one time."

Even the young ones—those for whom the past did not yet exist—were riveted in place by the purposefulness of the old man's voice. It was the sort of voice that would steal into their ears even if they had their hands clamped over them. Perhaps the only one who could ignore it was D, standing solitary and forlorn.

The bloody screams of the old man continued. "On that day—the first day of our ten-thousand-year history—a horrible toxic gas gushed from the earth and onto our land. Half the villagers died, and the other half could do naught but wait for death as their flesh festered. If a certain personage hadn't appeared, the village would've become the domain of the Grim Reaper, and none of you would've ever been born. Listen well, for that person traveled with a certain grand purpose in mind. He'd heard rumors of us, and was the first to rush here. And this is what he said. 'Let five of your strongest, bravest men accompany me on my journey. If you do, I will take away this calamity that has befallen your village, and fortune shall instantly smile upon you.'"

This was the first time more than half of the villagers had heard these facts. Engrossed by this sudden tale of days gone by, the villagers failed to notice two things that were happening. The first was that, perhaps due to something in the old man's story, D's eyes had begun to give off a piercing light. And the other was that a young man was walking down the road from the supposedly locked main gate, making his way through the deserted village as he headed towards the square.

"This entire square," the Elder continued, "and the whole village, for that matter, was filled with rotting, dying souls. But the instant that person's proposition reached their ears, they forgot all about the excruciating pain. And then, one villager came from behind a pile of rubble over there, and another came from back beyond the withered trees. The people went to him as if they'd been summoned by name—exactly five of them. What's more, they were the toughest we had, and everyone knew it."

The young man approached the entrance to the square. Taking a quick peek around, a charming smile nudged his ruddy cheeks as he headed in.

"And then, the village of the Barbarois came back to life." The old man's voice was boundlessly deep. "As soon as that personage had left with the five, why, the ground the village sits on rose toward the sky and came to be where you see it now. In the space of three breaths, new growth budded on the trees, and the flowers bore fruit. It wasn't until later we discovered the toxic subterranean gases had been diluted to harmless levels, too. All we could do at the time was chant out his name and press our faces to the ground. Heed my words!" the old man said, his voice that of the Elder that commanded all. "I'll tell you a law that you youngsters don't know about. When that person or any of his bloodline should appear, then and only then must all in the village bend any subsequent laws and comply with his wishes."

His awe-inspiring tone was an order. Even the rebellious trio was speechless.

The old man bowed deeply to the beautiful Hunter, whose black hair was swaying in the breeze. "Long have we awaited you. All that your highness desires shall be granted. If you wish that carriage ripped apart, or burnt to the ground where it stands, we are yours to command."

As they watched him with eyes full of an awe that surpassed fear, D's reply came to the villagers' ears.

"I appreciate the offer, but you have the wrong person. Let those three go and guard the carriage, as they wish. I'll be right behind them."

"What are you trying to say?" the old man asked in astonishment.

"What an honest fellow," black Bengé laughed shrilly. "Well, since he says so himself, this law you've brought up doesn't apply, Elder. But in light of his frankness, we won't let anyone else touch him. The three of us alone will take him on."

"I have one juicy tidbit for you to take to your grave," Caroline laughed, her crimson lips curling back. "This carriage is bound for the Claybourne States."

"Let's go, whippersnapper!" Mashira cried out as he crouched down. A heavy ax glittered in his right hand.

It looked like even the old man lacked the means to forestall the vicious attack by the trio. Just then, a harsh query of "Who the hell are you?!" could be heard from the rear of the crowd, but the question soon became a drawn-out scream.

The rows of people kicked up sand as they parted, and, at the far end of the straight path they opened, a rosy-cheeked young man smiled brightly. It was an angelic smile, the kind anyone would return without thinking twice. However, the fetid stench billowing up before him was part of the smoke rising from the chest of a fallen villager. Though it was unclear just what sort of energy had struck the villager, flames were still licking the carbonized and perfectly circular wounds on his chest and back.

D became a black shooting star flying through the air. The ray beam that shot through the space he'd occupied an instant earlier continued past him. With nothing to strike, it scored a direct hit to the carriage parked to one side of the square.

"That's not good!" someone cried out. Startled by the flying sparks and energy discharge, the team of horses whinnied especially loudly and bolted for the exit on the far side of the square.

"Close the back gate!"

A few villagers ran off in response to the old man's shouts, but an instant later a beam intercepted them, and they fell forward with their heads blown off. Nobody could tell where the beams were coming from. The square had become a place where bolts of light flitted madly, and, as fleeing villagers vanished in the flashes, the origin of the murderous beams still seemed impossible to determine.

However, the one clear image that greeted anyone who looked back was the enraptured expression of the angelic young man as he stood by the entrance to the square watching the mad dance of the lights. It was inspiring how his face brimmed with joie de vivre as he gleefully toyed with the deadly rays.

All at once, the square reclaimed its original hue. Perhaps it was an aftereffect of the powerful white flashes, but the green trees and brown houses burned themselves into the scene in almost painfully deep tones before gradually returning to their natural colors.

Villagers creeping to the edge of the square—or in some cases crouched on the ground watching where this supernatural phenomenon was headed—saw a pair of figures square off with some thirty feet between them. One was a young man wearing an angelic smile, the other was a Hunter as beautiful as the moon's corona.

Which would prove faster, the racing figure in black or the coursing stream of white light?

Everyone gasped as D fended off one white-hot attack but had two more streaks pierce his body as he dashed forward. But what did the villagers really see and gasp about?

D had held his left hand out in front on his chest. The two bolts of light changed direction right before him, became a single flash, and were sucked into the palm of his hand.

The young man didn't move. His smile still brimmed with pleasure.

D's flashing blade flowed from the tip of his foe's head down to his lower jaw. There was no resistance. Still holding the pose from his downward stroke, D stood a little closer to the edge of the square.

The young man had suddenly disappeared. Dim shadows that played across D's face testified this wasn't the result of anything he'd done.

The old man ran over to him. "D—Are you injured, milord?"

Without answering, D looked back across the square. There was no sign of the carriage. "Can I get down the back side of the mountain?" he asked.

The old man nodded. "There's a passage known only to the villagers. Damn!" the old man shouted, looking around desperately.

D knew why the Elder cursed. The three toughs Mayerling had retained were nowhere to be seen.

†

Kyle pulled his hot lips away from the woman's body now that resistance had given way to moaning, as it always did. From a bunk that until now had been deathly silent, there trickled the sound of shallow but urgent breathing.

"Dammit—he's back pretty damn fast this time," Kyle spat irritably and stood up. "Hey, hurry up and get that IV ready," he ordered Leila, who was still stark naked.

Glaring sharply at her older brother, the tracks of tears still fresh on her face, Leila gathered her discarded clothing.

Glancing at the bruises on her skin and the purple teeth-marks from where he'd just bitten her, Kyle clucked his tongue remonstratively. "You should've just behaved like usual and done what I told you. I don't know what got into you today, but that's what you get for being dumb and putting up a fight." Chuckling, he added, "Of course, I suppose it just made it that much easier to get ol' Grove worked up."

"Quit it!" Leila slapped away the hand reaching for her ample bosom. "Lately, the gap between his normal attacks has gotten pretty slim, you know. If you keep forcing Grove to have more on top of those, even though you know it's shortening his life, what do you think is gonna happen? If his energy goes wild, no one has any idea how bad the destruction would be."

"Shit, you think we can read that far ahead? We've got problems right now. We'll know how things went just as soon as Borgoff gets back. Nah, on second thought I think I'll try asking Grove first. Outta my way."

Cruelly pushing Leila aside, Kyle went to the pillow of the third Marcus brother.

"Hey, bro, it's me—Kyle. Tell me what you saw while you were . . . *in there*. Remember what I asked you to look into before you went?"

For quite a while the rasping sounds that escape from a patient at death's door continued, then ceased.

A sudden gasp. It hadn't come from the man beneath the blankets. A pale thin hand was wrapped around Kyle's windpipe.

"Want to know, Kyle? You want to know?" Groveck wheezed. "You're here having all the fun with Leila . . . while you put me through the tortures of hell . . . And you want to know?"

"Er . . . yeah. Sure, I wanna know." It was all the younger Marcus brother could do to answer, with the hand at his throat.

The hand quickly fell away. Groveck's delicate voice practically sobbed, "Our prey is heading for . . . the Claybourne States . . . "

The Killing Game

CHAPTER 4

I

Twilight had begun to swaddle the woods at a fork in the gently snaking road.

Gently, the girl switched off an electric light patterned after an old-fashioned candelabra. Blue darkness flooded the interior. The day that was hers alone was ending, and the world that was both of theirs was beginning.

The girl liked the sound of the lid opening on the black coffin that lay in one corner of the vehicle. Before long, his hand appeared and pushed the lid away. He stood up and stretched once, as was his habit. And then, pulling a small chair over, he seated himself in front of the girl.

Thank you. That's what he said. In appreciation of the fact she'd switched off the lights. He would never think of telling her she should've kept them on. *Thank you.* That was all.

The couple's romance had begun in the woods in spring. The traveler's carriage had struck the girl when she dashed out suddenly in pursuit of a bird, and the lone occupant had tended her wounds—hardly a unique story, but because the principal characters were a human and a Noble, it could only end in misery.

Sometimes, however, there were exceptions. The girl knew she was dealing with a Noble. And the Noble knew he was dealing with a human. Yet there was neither fear nor scorn between them. They simply fascinated each other.

Their walk through the woods was sweet. For once in her life, the girl didn't fear the darkness. He'd been good enough to teach her. He'd shown her that the night, too, teemed with life.

The girl heard the flowing of a river. She saw the moonbeam fish leaping against the lunar disc. She smelled the perfume of night-blooming jasmine. She heard the poetry the wind recited, and a chorus of tiny, unseen frogs. The night was full of light, too—and he was unfailingly by her side.

He felt as she did. A heretic among the Nobility, he was one who didn't consider humanity inferior. A baron who loved the day as well, but awaited his kind's demise without ever having seen the light of the sun. Finally, he'd seen a goal, an end to his aimless wandering. The girl had given him that.

His travels had left a bitter taste in his mouth. Fleeing from villagers and Hunters hell-bent on killing Nobles, he'd crossed a brutally cold glacier. He'd raced through mountain trails whipped by howling, mad winds. All of which would've been fine if his journey had been for some purpose. Though on the road to extinction, his own destruction still lay a long way off.

And then he'd met the girl. A young lady flitting about a forest filled with living things, soaking up the light of midday. What did rank matter? So what if they were different species? They both knew who was important to them. That was all there was to it.

This chance meeting of day and night began with a gentle gaze and the bashful, tender joining of hands. The girl had just turned seventeen. He understood the hopes and fears in her heart. That being the case, couldn't a Noble and a human possibly stay together? No, not in this world.

It was then he'd broached the subject. *Would you go away with me?*

The girl nodded. *I'll go anywhere. As long as I'm with you.*

And then the two exchanged their first kiss. Devoid of lust for blood or the fear of being fed upon, it was a feverish kiss, but also a demure one.

Tragedy struck the following night. He burst into her home, unable to watch the beating the girl's father gave her when he learned his daughter was going to run away. For the first time, this Noble, propelled by hatred, sucked a human's blood. However, he failed to notice the father had a rare sort of constitution that reacted strangely to vampire attacks.

Whether a bitten human became a bloodthirsty creature like the Nobility or was left a mere mummy depended on the intent of the Noble that drained his or her blood. Though exceedingly rare, there were also some cases where what happened to the victim ran counter to the wishes of the vampire. A drained individual might be left as a human incredibly low on blood, refusing to change. And an emaciated man left to die of blood loss could come back as a vampire.

Everyone the girl's father fed on had become the same sort of fiend with a single bite. Those he attacked sought new victims, and, in the course of a single night, the whole village was transformed into pseudo-Nobility. But the girl had been rendered unconscious by the intense beating she'd received. She had seen none of this.

When she awoke, her love's gaze greeted her. And that's how their journey began. Their journey to the Claybourne States.

†

"I accomplished what I wanted to in the village, but it seems they couldn't dispose of him," the Noble muttered as he reviewed the events of the day from recordings made by the electronic eyes. "Most likely this other man with the strange powers has also learned our destination. Given the speed of this carriage, it's entirely conceivable they'll be lying in wait for us. We shall have to take the initiative."

As the girl turned her questioning eyes on him, he informed her they'd be at their destination before long. He left the vehicle. The pair of escorts riding alongside the carriage bowed to him. One was on horseback, and the other—a woman—was in a small, single-passenger buggy.

"Greetings," the first guard said. "I'm Mashira."

"And I am Caroline. I've looked forward to your appearance, Sire."

"We seem to be one short," Mayerling noted, his tone and bearing in keeping with his Noble rank.

Mashira nodded. "Yes. He's lying in wait for the enemy in the woods up ahead."

"For the enemy?" the Nobleman asked. "Alone?"

"That's correct, sir."

"There's no need to fear," Caroline said in a mysterious tone. Though Mayerling knew nothing of it, the shoulder left bare by her indigo dress no longer showed even a trace of a wound. Her gaze clinging to him as she climbed over to the coachman's perch of the carriage, she looked up at her employer and said, "He won't do anything. He's simply gone to get a peek at the other Hunters you mentioned to the Elder."

"The other Hunters?" Mayerling's beautiful countenance became a grimace, and he stated, "I'm well aware of the abilities of any other Vampire Hunters besides *him*. No, strike that—is the young man who ran amuck in your village one of them, too?"

"Most likely," Mashira replied.

Caroline added, "That woman in the car you mentioned is one as well, sire. And there may well be others. So to Bengé goes the honor of the first encounter . . . "

Mayerling was silent. From his recordings, he'd learned about the girl who'd attacked them while they were resting at the Shelter and her battle with the automated defenses. He was quite sure she'd been gravely wounded back at the Shelter, but if she was still alive then she'd prove a troublesome adversary. Even more so if she were in league with that young man from the village square . . .

556 | HIDEYUKI KIKUCHI

"Well," the Nobleman said to the pair, "while he may be one of your fellow Barbarois, I know only his reputation, not what powers he possesses. No matter how great his abilities, it'll be no mean feat to dispose of all the enemies on my tail. Especially all alone . . . "

His two bodyguards looked at each other. Mayerling may not have realized they were smiling.

"Well, we'll be arriving in the village of Barnabas shortly," said Caroline. "Once he's returned there, perhaps you'd care to ask him about it yourself. But this alone I can tell you. If someone's already encountered him—or worse yet, is pursuing him—without a doubt they shall die before this night is through." Her words were backed with such confidence that even Mayerling, Noble that he was, was perplexed for a moment. "But all that aside, will you not do us the honor of introducing the guest you have inside? Come what may, it could prove somewhat troublesome if we don't know what she looks like."

"Absolutely," Mashira said, nodding his agreement.

After a bit of consideration, Mayerling bent over and rapped lightly on the door. "Kindly show yourself," he said.

While it was unclear how she'd heard him inside over the roar of the speeding carriage, the blue windowpane opened and a gorgeous countenance emerged. Her face was tinged with trepidation from the darkness.

"Oh, my," Mashira blurted out, and his words were not altogether empty flattery.

"Such a beauty," Caroline added, but her burning gaze was concentrated on the person in the driver's seat.

"Thank you, my love," Mayerling said, and the window closed.

At that moment, in a tiny voice even his Noble senses couldn't detect, someone tittered, mumbling, "Nice and pretty, just how I like 'em. Think I'll make her mine . . . " It was clearly the voice of a fourth person, someone who could not be accounted for.

†

T he clear weather of that afternoon had broken, and leaden clouds pervaded the night sky.

A figure garbed in black sped down the street the carriage and its escorts had taken a scant hour earlier. There was no moon, but the black-garbed figure was so beautiful he virtually gave off a light of his own. With the speed with which he galloped, he could gobble up that one hour lead in less than twenty minutes if all went smoothly. Just as he was hitting the heart of the forest, however, he stopped sharply.

Though there were clouds, the darkness wasn't complete. In D's eyes, it was just like midday. About thirty feet ahead of where D halted his horse, a gigantic tree branch hung over the road, and one part of it in particular protruded sharply. Beneath that protrusion hung a long, thin shadow. D alone saw it for what it truly was. One of the trio of escorts—Bengé.

According to what Mashira had told Mayerling a short while earlier, their compatriot had come here to meet D. And, given the work each had undertaken, an encounter with the Hunter would mean a battle to the death. Bengé had already seen D in action, from the skirmish in the village of the Barbarois and the way D protected Leila in the clearing, and he must've been aware of how powerful D really was. The fact that Bengé appeared to confront D despite all that he knew indicated that he had the utmost confidence in his fighting abilities.

"Hello there," Bengé called out, his slim hand raised in a cheerful greeting, but his eyes weren't laughing. "I regret to inform you that you can't pass this way. Oh, but this is the only road to take. Then it looks like one of us will just have to wait by the side of the road—as a corpse!"

Bengé probably figured his conceited tone would draw some sort of reaction. But he let out a shout of fright as he caught sight of D flying off his horse and up over his head with lightning speed.

Indeed, talk was futile. D's sword, which never returned to its sheath without first tasting the blood of its foes, split Bengé's skull in two before he could flee. The reason D promptly spun himself around upon landing back on the ground was because of the lack of resistance his blade had conveyed. There was no sign of the clearly bisected Bengé, only a sheet of black cloth that fell about the Hunter's feet. Cloth that Bengé had been wearing.

A weird, stifled laugh struck the nape of D's neck. "You surprise me, you fearsome man. Were I anyone else, you'd have sliced me in two."

D didn't move. Even with his ultra-keen senses, he couldn't tell where Bengé was. As the saying went, Bengé's voice came out of thin air.

"Well, then," Bengé said, "I guess it's my turn now."

D's right hand moved ever so slightly. Two flashes of light gleamed, and sparks flew from the base of D's neck with the most beautiful sound. Bengé had stabbed down at D with a dagger after he suddenly materialized behind the Hunter, and the sparks resulted from that dagger being parried by the sword that flew back with just a simple movement of the Hunter's hand.

The tip of D's sword swept horizontally as he spun about, but there was no sign of Bengé. D kicked off the ground. Leaping five yards, as soon as he touched down he leapt again. Unable to detect anyone, he touched back down from his second leap. And then he heard it.

"Heh heh heh . . . It's no use, no use at all," Bengé's voice laughed. "As long as *the other you* is here, I'll be here, too."

In the forest ahead of him, a shadow rose silently. D's left hand raced into action, becoming white lightning blazing through the air. But the wooden needle he'd launched only nailed a length of thin black cloth to a nearby tree trunk. Beyond the tree, another shadow arose.

Is that an invitation? the Hunter thought. *Fine.* D sprinted into the woods. An invitation to follow him from the road to the woods—just what did Bengé have in mind?

The hot, humid atmosphere pressed him mercilessly from all sides. A sharp sound ripped through the wind. The silvery streaks that flew in rapid succession from either side of D were batted aside, one and all, by his blade.

"Oh, my. Not bad at all." Bengé's voice had a ring of admiration that wasn't in the least bit exaggerated.

"You said as long as I was here, you'd be here, didn't you?" D said without concern. There was no gloating over how he'd just thwarted the vicious attacks. "I see now. I know what your power is—"

"What?!" Bengé shouted. His daggers flew, as if to cover his shock and indignation. One came from straight ahead, the other from a thicket far to the rear of D—and they were nearly simultaneous. Did the Hunter face multiple opponents?

Deflecting the attacks with ease, D bent down. The instant a flash of white whizzed over his head, he swung his left hand back behind him. He could feel the rough wooden needle it held bite into flesh.

There was a cry of pain.

Taking an easy step forward, D then did something strange. As he turned back to whatever he'd just stabbed, he jabbed another needle into the ground at his feet at the same time. "What's wrong?" he said. "Until that needle gets pulled out, you can't get into my shadow, can you?"

It sounded like someone was grinding their teeth, and then something fell to the ground. A wooden needle stained with blood. It'd been tossed *up* from a patch of ground where there was nothing at all. Thrown out of the shadow of a tree barely cast on the ground by twilight.

As long as you're here, I'm here, he told D. *If you concentrate, you can see me. You don't see me because you think you can't*—that was the secret he'd imparted to Leila.

Bengé lurked in the shadows. But that wasn't all. His skill was such that even D couldn't detect his presence when he'd slipped into the Hunter's shadow. What's more, the way his attacks came from utterly impossible angles suggested he required no time at all to migrate from one patch of shade to the next. The slight delay between attacks was actually just the time it'd take to aim and throw a dagger. Once he'd slipped into his foe's shadow, he became an invincible assassin. So long as that foe wasn't D.

"Stanched the bleeding, have you? Too bad the fog is moving in," said D. Before he'd finished speaking, a dense white flow rolled in from the depths of the woods and boiled up at his feet. The twilit region lost its light.

Without light, no shadows can form.

D alone saw it. He saw the figure on the ground some ten feet ahead, clinging to the earth like a veritable sheet of black cloth. Their duel was as good as decided.

But at that instant the shadow tossed up a tiny ball of light. A blinding brilliance filled the milky white world, and the trees threw shadows across the ground.

"This time you have me beat. But we'll meet again," Bengé shouted, his pained parting words ringing from deep in the forest.

D slipped out of the woods and got on his horse. Within a few hours, he'd be within range of his target.

II

"Hmph. Bengé isn't as great as he makes himself out to be. Looks like he got whipped," Mashira spat after he'd taken his ear from the ground and raised his head.

"As I expected, it was too much for him to handle, was it not?" It was Mayerling who said this. He, Mashira, and Caroline had camped out for the night in the middle of the forest, deciding that it would best to await Bengé's return.

Drifting around them was the savory aroma of birds cooking over the camp fire, skewered on sticks. Mashira reached out for one and offered it to Mayerling. "Would you care for some?"

"No."

"Suit yourself. The Nobility have no need for meat, right?" The Barbarois bodyguard said this as if he'd known that all along, but that was a lie. Somewhere in his tone there was malice. Mashira tore into the golden brown flesh, stuffing his cheeks. His yellowed teeth continued shredding the meat with a vulgar sound.

Not giving her compatriot so much as a glance, Caroline gazed at Mayerling's profile. Perhaps she'd eaten something already, for she ignored Mashira's roasting fowl. Not exactly the eyes of one in love, hers were feverish and clouded with passion.

"If he failed, the enemy will be after us. They'll catch us if we stay around here waiting. We'd best set off at once." Perhaps angered by Mashira's rude behavior, Mayerling's tone was enough to chill the blood. He turned abruptly from the fire.

"Please put your mind at ease," Caroline told him. "Our enemy won't be here any time soon. Not if he's pursuing a different carriage."

"A different carriage?" Mayerling asked as he turned to face them again.

"Correct," she replied. "A shadow carriage, if you will. It's one of Bengé's skills. Once someone begins chasing it, they'll never catch it a million years."

"I'm sorry to say I have no faith in the skills of one already bested in battle," said the Noble. "It occurs to me now that perhaps retaining the three of you was a mistake."

"What are you trying to say?" Caroline asked in an agitated manner. "I'll thank you kindly not to judge the abilities of the two of us unsatisfactory merely because the likes of Bengé proved a failure. Oh, that Bengé is an idiot. We would've been better served to let that damned Hunter go on pursuing us." Beneath her vermilion lips, her white teeth ground together.

"You'll see our true power, and I don't just mean someday. Perhaps as early as tomorrow. I believe there's another pack of bloodhounds on your heels."

"Yes, Mashira's right," said Caroline. "Tomorrow, I shall join forces with Bengé and slay every last one of those dogs, mark my words."

"I leave it to you then," Mayerling told her. "But tonight, we move out. Our destination is close at hand. We should be there the evening after next. A good time for our departure. I'm going on ahead. You two follow behind. By day I shall be sleeping in the forest."

Before long, the shrill sound of the wagon faded away, and the pair who had bowed as they'd seen the carriage off raised their heads.

Smiling faintly, Mashira said, "What right does a Noble doomed to extinction have to order around the famed Mashira, when my skill is known throughout the village of the Barbarois?"

"That can't be helped. He's our employer. We simply have to do our job." As Caroline spoke, she watched the departing carriage with a feverish gaze.

With a more lascivious smile, Mashira asked her, "Are you in love? With him?"

"Whatever do you mean by—"

"You don't have to hide it. He's the real thing. You're a *fake*. It's not like I can't see why that would attract you."

"Hold your tongue!" Caroline bared her teeth. Were those sharp canines she had peeking out between her lips? No—she couldn't be one of *those*.

"So, we've established that then. I have a proposal." Mashira smiled without a trace of fear, putting his best face on for the beautiful woman watching him with flame-like eyes.

"What would that be?"

"We've disobeyed the Elder," said Mashira. "Might we not be better off if we now discarded the standards those in the village live by?" For an instant it looked like she might turn on him for this unexpected overture, but then an excited expression arose on Caroline's face. "Oh, so I see the same thing had occurred to you," he continued. "If we stick to the rules of the village, then he's our employer, as you said. We mustn't disobey him, or turn on him. Lusting after him would be absolutely unthinkable. However, if we were to ignore the rules . . . "

Mashira's gaze was probing her face as he spoke, and at his words Caroline's eyes glittered piercingly. They were the eyes of an apostate who'd set her heart on discord.

"I thought you'd see it my way," the Barbarois man continued. "The only reason he won't so much as look at a gorgeous woman like you is because he's got a girl he loves, and who loves him, too. To tell the truth, I fancy the girl. I want to make her mine. Under the circumstances, wouldn't you say our interests coincide?"

She said nothing.

"During the day, he'll be sleeping. Maybe the girl will, too. If I were to take her and run off while he slept, he'd have no one left to rely on by day but you. Why, she's no more than a slip of a human girl. Could one of the Nobility seriously give his heart to that? He's already beginning to have a change of heart. Do you really think he'd go looking for her? Even supposing he does, once I've shown him proof I've had her myself, I guarantee you he'd be over their so-called eternal love," Mashira snickered.

"You have a point there." The flames painted grotesque shadows on Caroline's pale countenance. "But if I am to take him, body and soul, every last one of the lowly Hunters pursuing him must be slain. Even if the baron was mine, I could never sleep at ease if even one remained. If I agree to cooperate with what you propose, we shall have to leave both our charges alone and do our duty until we can take care of all the others. How does that strike you?"

"Fine by me," Mashira said with a nod.

"What of Bengé? Does he live?" asked Caroline.

"Well, I can't really say. He was certainly alive up till the point he used his shadow skills . . . You plan on letting him in on this?"

"That should go without saying! Once day breaks, I'll go off on a preemptive strike against the scum chasing us, and I'll try to locate our Bengé at the same time."

†

A nd where was D while these two ne'er-do-wells were plotting treachery against their charge? He was galloping down the road, through the fog, on a straight line from the spot where he'd encountered Bengé. In the haze to either side he could see shadowy images of the forest.

From up ahead, the wind carried something back. The creaking of a carriage. The range was about a mile and a quarter. On a night that could only be described as silent, could D's ears catch sounds from such a great distance?

His horse's hoofs beat the earth with increased impetus. The fog became a wall blocking him, then eddied away. Before long, a black carriage became visible ahead. There was no sign of the escorts.

D made a break forward. Even if the escorts had been there, he would have ridden forward without fear. On the far side of the carriage roof he could see only the driver's head. He was lashing away with a whip. D's right hand went to the sword on his back.

The distance continued to diminish. Perhaps the Hunter's approach had been noticed, for the whip danced wildly now. The gap between them widened slightly, and then rapidly grew. This would've been out of the question at the vehicle's usual speed. It seemed impossible that the most renowned steed, even with a legendary rider, would be able to keep on their tail now.

The carriage changed direction. Leaving in its wake a tortured squeal like its bolts were ready to pop free, it went into the woods to the right. It already had a lead of half a mile. And still the gap continued to grow.

D's heels pounded the flanks of his horse. Gradually, the dhampir's eyes began to give off a phosphorescent glow. He shredded the fog, and the gap shrank.

D came up alongside the carriage. Easily standing atop his saddle, he leapt for the carriage roof. It was as if all movement had been reduced to slow motion as D landed feet first on the roof of the vehicle. Crouching down, he advanced on the driver's seat. Ripples of suspicion crossed his face. The driver made no attempt to look his way, but worked the whip mechanically through the air. D's hand seized the supple lash. Even after it'd been taken away, the driver tried to crack the whip.

D set his right hand on the driver's hair. The instant he tugged back, the Hunter was tossed into the air by a violent shock. Incredibly, the hair in his hand, the carriage, and the horses all became a sheet of black cloth that fell to the ground, and D alone, completely ensnared by the inertia of their forward momentum, was thrown through the air.

Just as he was about to slam against the earth, the hem of his coat spread like a gigantic pair of wings, and D turned an easy somersault before landing feet first on the ground.

He gazed at the black cloth he held in his right hand. It cascaded across the ground, stretching another six feet. If spread out, there was enough to cover the floor of a small room. It must've taken a piece at least that large in order to make a carriage and driver, plus a half-dozen horses.

Discarding the cloth, D turned his face to the sky. He'd heard a voice from nowhere in particular cursing. Bengé's voice. D gazed at the sky in silence. In the east, beyond a range of mountain, a faint and watery light was beginning to shine. Surely the phantom carriage had been leading him in the wrong direction to buy Mayerling some time to escape. In terms of distance, it'd bought them perhaps an extra three-quarters of a mile. Racing at full speed, it'd take D less than two minutes to make that up.

Not bothering to search for the source of the disembodied voice, D straddled his horse without a word and galloped off. He was headed west, to where the sun sinks.

†

For the last ten or twenty minutes, the man had sat on a chair in the center of the dilapidated shop, his eyes shut tight. Dressed in black, the man was as thin as a half-starved crane. The sweat coating not only his brow but his whole body was not due solely to the stream of blood spilling from his flank—it also seemed connected to an extended period of concentrated mental effort.

When a faint blueness streamed into the dust-and-grit-covered shop, which was apparently a saloon, the man's whole body quaked, and his eyes bulged open. A scream of "Damn!" spilled from his mouth. Letting the tension drain from his body, the man slumped back in the chair in disappointment.

"Seems I underestimated him—the damn freak. Can't believe he caught up to my shadow carriage," he muttered. "Well, since I've blown it, I'd better let Mashira and the others know as soon as possible . . . " Wearily getting to his feet, Bengé trod across the dusty floor and left the shop.

On either side of a street only the wind ever crossed, ruined houses stood in rows. The hotel, the drugstore, the cobbler, the saloon he'd just come out of—every single shop had broken window panes with gaping black maws, and the signs above the doors swung idly. It was a ghost town.

Here in this town, less than a mile and a quarter from where he'd fought D, Bengé had done his very best to see to his wounds and to manipulate his shadow carriage. Coming to the center of the street, Bengé took a long, thin tube from the breast of his black robe, pulled the ring at one end, and thrust it up over his head. An orange ball of light shot from it, rising with a long tail behind it, and presently it could be seen no more. Shortly thereafter, a dazzling ring of light blazed in the heavens, maintaining that brilliance for a few seconds before it faded away.

"I sure hope they notice that and come for me," he muttered anxiously. When he started toward the horse tethered in front of the saloon, he heard the sound of hoofbeats and a car engine coming from one end of the long, central street.

Without even time to hide his horse, Bengé leapt across the street into the shadow of what looked to be a cyborg horse repair center. He had to wait but a few seconds for the body of a bus he'd seen before to appear from the other end of the street. The drivers must've installed some sort of non-reflective glass in it, because he couldn't see through the windshield.

The wheels ground to a halt right in front of the saloon, the door opened, and a pair of men stepped out. It was the guys he'd toyed with on the road through the mountains a day earlier. Hunters after Mayerling.

A killing-lust welled up, filling Bengé's entire being. The shadows of the buildings fell across the street. Between them and the men's shadows lay open ground. "Come on. Closer. Come to Bengé," he muttered to himself. If even part of one of their shadows touched that of the building where he concealed himself, he could slip into theirs in an instant. He'd become Death, invisible and inescapable.

The giant who called to mind a rock drew closer, with bow and arrows in hand. For an instant his shadow touched that from the tip of the roof of a building. Bengé's form faded away. The younger Hunter set his eyes on the other side of the street, and, when the giant changed direction and the shadow spun to his rear, the shade-like figure in black that silently rose behind the bigger man had the base of its neck covered with what looked like fine silvery feathers.

Faster than the giant's arrows in their indiscriminate flight, a swish of white knifed through the Barbarois' body as it first reeled back with an anguished cry, then went quickly into a face-first drop. Sending black blood out in all directions, Bengé's body split in half just above the waist. The two parts of his body quickly thudded to the ground.

"Is this the guy, Leila?" Borgoff called in the direction of the bus as he checked out the back of the enemy's head and its glistening feathers—needles from the sliver gun.

The driver's window slid open, and Leila's face and the leveled sliver gun appeared. "Yep. I got my payback."

Anticipating that they'd run across the foe who'd attacked her earlier, she had the window open a crack from the very beginning and had kept her brothers covered. And, while Bengé had by no means forgotten about Leila, his scorn for a girl he'd abused once already and his overwhelming confidence in his own abilities had dug his grave.

"No doubt about it—this is one of the threesome Grove mentioned. What the high hell was he doing out here?" Kyle said, spitting on the corpse.

"Dammit, how am I supposed to get any sleep now," Borgoff muttered. "Well, we've killed one of them, at any rate. Where I see he's got a horse tied up there and all, I'd say he's the only one here. But just to be sure, check out the area. Once we know it's clear, we'll take a little break, then head out again."

"Hold on, Borgoff. Can we afford to take it easy? We gotta gain all the ground we can while the sun shines," Leila called out from the window, but Borgoff swept her words away with one hand.

"See, he's got two drivers now that daylight don't bother. Besides, we've heard that it's the Claybourne States he's headed for. Well, if that's the case, I know a couple of routes we can take to head them off, so there's no need to get all flustered. To the contrary, I wouldn't mind letting D go on ahead to see if that Noble and him can't kill each other. I say it's a lucky thing we hit this town looking to bed down under a roof for a change."

Naturally, the oldest brother didn't catch the shade of emotion that rushed into Leila's face at the mention of D's name.

"Still, bro," Kyle began, as he used a finger to wipe the gore from his crescent blade, "you know, a long time ago, that the Claybourne States used to be a space port. There ain't nothing there but rows and rows of trashed rockets. What the hell could they—No, you don't think they could be planning to go to another planet, do you? Maybe for their honeymoon?!"

Even as she heard Kyle explode in laughter, Leila shut the window.

✝

T he road was constantly bombarded by the chirping of little birds from the woods to either side.

In the spring sunlight, D raced on. Compared to when he'd chased the shadow carriage, his speed had decreased somewhat, but that was unavoidable. D's rein handling forced the cyborg horse to gallop at speeds far exceeding its abilities. The knee joints, metabolizers, and other parts already exhibited signs of severe stress. There was some question as to whether the horse would last another twelve hours, even if D eased back to his usual pace.

He had no choice but to wait for a nearby village or motorized mobile shop, but that was a faint hope.

The time was eight Morning. Could he catch up to Mayerling's carriage now that it could run by day as well? The prospects looked bleak. Still, he had to go on. It is the destiny of the huntsman to chase his prey.

How would his opponent react? Surely the Noble was aware that D and the Marcus clan were in pursuit. There was no way the Noble would just keep running. He'd definitely strike back at them. But when, and how?

Aside from the obvious psychological edge, those giving chase weren't necessarily always at an advantage when both parties were on the move. If the pursuers ran into an ambush, the tables could be turned. And there was nothing fiercer than cornered prey baring its fangs in its own defense.

The features of the young Noble skimmed across D's heart. The Noble wasn't lying when he said he wouldn't do anything to the human. D could almost picture the face of the girl in the carriage, and the look she'd have in her eyes.

The scenery before him suddenly changed. Gone was the constant greenery, replaced by a rough desert plain. In various places, the land was fused into a glassy state, and eye-catching machines and vehicles of titanic proportions jutted from the ground. There were heaps of pitiful, mechanical corpses left on the field, each and every one red and crumbling with rust. They seemed to stretch on to the ends of the earth, and the disturbing, ghastly air they had about them didn't seem in the least bit like that of anything mechanical. When night came, would the bitter voices of single-minded machines echo pathetically across the plain?

This was one of the ancient battlefields where, long ago, machines that'd evolved into sentience fought each other out of hatred. Even now, a number of them still hadn't ceased functioning, their bodies squirming around on a pale and feeble current, wandering night after night in search of their enemies.

The ambush could come any time now. That was the feeling D had. As day broke, he'd seen the flash of what seemed to be a Hunter's signal flare in the dawn sky to the rear. Undoubtedly it was the signal from Bengé, reporting his mission had failed and that D was still in pursuit. Of course, the remaining pair of guards would see it and take the necessary countermeasures. The question was, would some of the party keep moving? Both of the Barbarois probably wouldn't come after him, but one of them might attack.

Then there was the other group to consider. No doubt the Marcus clan had noticed the flare, too. They had much more detailed knowledge of this area. There was every reason to worry about them taking some little-known shortcut to head off the carriage. And, in the world of day, swimming with the song of life, even D couldn't possibly hear their footfalls. Would they let him go on ahead? Or would he fall prey to one of their ambushes?

D's face clouded ever so slightly. Perhaps he'd been thinking about the youngest, the little sister. About the girl with the big, round eyes who said she couldn't live any other way but as a Hunter. If she let her hair down instead of pulling it back she'd probably look a good two years younger. With a touch of rouge to her cheeks and some lipstick, she could pass for a regular girl from any old town. She wouldn't have to cry out for her mother, tortured by fever.

D's countenance lost its shade of humanity. Far ahead of him, he'd sighted a toppled column of mammoth proportions. Running in a straight line across the fifteen-foot-wide road was a gigantic, rusted forearm.

†

Just before D had intruded on the ancient battlefield, there'd been a woman by the side of the road in what was just about the center of this vast expanse of land. She was combing her hair in the morning breeze. The dress she wore was bluer than the bluest sky, and the voice spilling from her lips in song was as beautiful as any jewel. If only she didn't have those spiteful red lips. However, a black shadow fell clearly across the cylindrical generator against which the woman was leaning. The demons of the night weren't supposed to have shadows.

It was unclear how long she'd been there, but the woman seemed to be absorbed in toying with the golden thread that was her hair. Suddenly, she looked up. Her gaze went in the direction from which D's hoofbeats echoed.

"Ah, someone's coming," the woman—Caroline—laughed, but her rose-like beauty soon grew tense. "Those hoofbeats don't sound like any human's horse. It's D. Now there's a man to be feared . . . "

Even now, the image of D's swordplay in the village of the Barbarois was burned into Caroline's retinas. But, an instant later, her blue eyes blazed with a lust for blood and battle. A smile warped her ruby lips.

"It seems it was worthwhile waiting here to get some rest and lay an ambush. I will make this your grave . . . "

And, with that muttered declaration of war, Caroline scanned the surrounding machinery, nodded once, then approached one of the devices. Rust coated its surface, and a number of jumbled pipes ran out of it. Caroline laid her hands on one of those closest and nestled it lovingly to her cheek, but, before long, her expression grew terribly lurid. Her mouth opened. Inside, her mouth was the same bloody red as her lips. Two of her canines were exposed, and, when they came in contact with the rusty pipe, the tips sank effortlessly into the metal.

Slowly, twin streams slid down Caroline's luscious throat, leaving a damp trail as they coursed to her ample bosom. The beauty's throat pulsated, and she drank as if ravenous. Over and over, gulp after gulp.

Before long, Caroline pulled back, and the fluid leaking from the holes mysteriously stopped. The Barbarois woman stepped away from the machine like a petal drifting off in the breeze. Showered with sunlight, her red tongue played along her lips. "Ah, that's what I like," she purred. "Now listen well to what I have to say."

The machine moved. Painfully slow. Its five fingers clawed at the sand. Each digit at least a yard long. Measuring thirty feet overall, the device she'd chosen was a robotic forearm that'd been broken off at the elbow.

†

D halted his steed. The arm was sixty feet away. It was like an exquisite piece of sculpture; even the shapes of the muscles and the lines of blood vessels remained discernible through the rust.

While the great machine battles had primarily been contests of combat ability, a sort of conflict between bizarre aesthetic sensibilities had also existed. In response to the geometrical orderliness of their rivals—epitomized by designs that were conglomerations of planes and spheres simplified to the extreme— some uncouth machines had taken the imitation of the human form to a level of beauty and perfection surpassing even the classic artistry of antiquity. Whether or not true "artists" existed among the machines, they not only accurately reproduced human hair on their androids, but every last pore as well.

Unofficial historical accounts kept by the Nobility reserved a special place for the earth-shaking contest between Apollo, with a thirty-foot sword in hand, and Hercules, armed with three hundred feet of spear. The surpassing destructive power unleashed in their clash changed the shape of mountains, wiped away valleys, and stopped the course of rivers. Had the limb now blocking D's path belonged to one of those famed combatants, or was it a remnant of some nameless Goliath?

A figure in blue frolicked on top of the wrist. The morning breeze rustled her golden hair and bore the aroma of her sweet perfume. Only D could detect something else. The foul stench of blood that drifted with it. "I am Caroline of the Barbarois," she said. "And I can let you go no further."

In D's pupils, which reflected only a void, the woman's image laughed coldly. Her body swayed wildly. The arm beneath her feet jolted as it changed direction, pointing toward D. Power coursed into the fingers, and they dug into the soil. Once they were embedded, the arm used them as a fulcrum and started to slide forward like an inchworm. It moved roughly, but with surprising speed.

D was motionless. Perhaps the surreal phenomenon of this rusted arm coming to life had robbed him of his nerve.

When the arm had come within fifteen feet of him, spread its fingers wide, and slammed against the earth, D charged on his horse. The colossal arm hung in midair. It'd sprung into the air from the force of the fingers striking the ground. D might've discerned the time and location of impact from its position, because, as the titanic arm's ten-foot-wide palm made the earth tremble, he slipped out from under it by a hair's breadth.

The fingers slammed shut, tearing up soil. Turning toward D, it lifted just its wrist until it was perpendicular to the ground. The fingers were still clenched. When it flopped forward, it opened them at last. A brown mass flew straight for D and his horse, more than sixty feet away. That distance rapidly diminished.

Perhaps feeling the air pressure to their rear, D tugged the reins to the right. As his horse went a few lengths in that direction, the mass dropped at its feet. It was the soil itself, the same soil that'd been gouged out by the fingers—a fitting projectile for a colossal arm.

Catching the shock wave on its flank, the horse lurched to one side. D danced through the air. Like a veritable mystic bird he flew, landing in a spot some five yards away. His horse regained its balance and dashed back to him.

The colossal arm set its sights on D. It came after him with terrific speed, making the earth tremble. A black fingertip passed right before D's eyes as the Hunter leapt backward. His stone-cold face remained impassive as a cloud of sand struck it.

"What's the matter, Hunter?" Caroline laughed charmingly from atop the arm. "Can't do a thing, can you? You see, this arm has joined the ranks of the undead."

Hard as it was to believe, the arm did have a power plant in the wrist, and it ran on gasoline. And Caroline had sucked some of the remaining fuel from the pipe. This "vampire" had taken what was akin to the "blood" of the colossal arm. Those bitten by the accursed demons became demons themselves. But it hardly seemed possible that the same abominable rule would extend to a mechanical arm.

The colossal forearm was now one of the living dead, a corpse that moved in accordance to Caroline's will. It didn't seem possible that even D could repel these attacks forever, when one followed another with such blistering speed.

In accordance with instructions from Caroline, the arm had chased D right over to the horizontal wreckage of a gigantic torso. Though the body was toppled, the side was still easily thirty feet high, a distance even D couldn't possibly jump.

"Are you finished, Hunter?" Caroline asked, tittering uncontrollably. "The sword upon your back—is it a mere affectation?"

With his rear blocked off, D appeared unable to do anything, and the wrist rose up over his head. A black brilliance surged up from the ground, slipped between the fingers crushing down now like an avalanche, and settled on top of the mechanical arm.

"What?!" Caroline exclaimed. D's coat flashed elegantly right in front of her as her eyes widened in amazement.

"Now we're even," the Hunter said softly.

Thinking to say something in return, Caroline took a few steps back—toward the elbow—as if she'd been pushed back by some unsettling emanations invisible to the eye. The colossal arm stopped dead in its usual inchworm pose. Beads of sweat rose on Caroline's brow. The beads immediately grew larger, coursing down her paraffin skin. The sunlight made the wet streaks glitter like quicksilver.

Both of D's arms hung naturally by his sides.

Various ideas whirled through Caroline's head. There wasn't enough room to flee. And the first time they'd met, Caroline had realized this youth wasn't the sort who'd spare her because she was a woman.

D took a step forward.

"W . . . wait," Caroline said desperately, humiliated by the way her voice quavered. "Even if you slay me, Mashira still remains. Wouldn't you like to know about his powers?" Cornered now, it was the best plan her brain could conceive. For a warrior, learning the abilities of the next opponent they'd meet in combat was more important than anything else. This offer would sway him without fail.

D advanced another step.

"Wait, just wait." Caroline waved her hands and leapt back a few yards. So, this youth gave no consideration to knowledge that might give him the advantage in battle? *I'm going to die, aren't I?* Caroline thought. *Here, on this man's sword . . .* Caroline gazed absentmindedly at the youth in black raiment approaching her. A strange feeling welled up in her breast. *I want to be slain. I want to feel this gorgeous man stab into my bosom.* The ecstasy of death enveloped Caroline in its rapture.

D's movements ceased. Letting out a low moan, the figure in black fell to one knee.

Not knowing quite what'd happened, Caroline instinctively went into action, seeking life instead of death. The colossal arm flipped over, leaving the two of them to drop through thin air. Still, D managed a spectacular landing before one of his knees buckled again. The colossal arm fell toward him. There wasn't enough time to get out of the way.

D's right hand blurred. It looked like it smoldered. There was a flash of silver that intersected the fingers crushing down on him like an avalanche of digits. With a tremendous crash, the foot-and-a-half-thick middle finger fell behind D, and everything else from the wrist forward twisted back. Black streams of machine oil poured down from the wound-like rent in the metal.

At the same time, Caroline landed on the opposite side of the road. She pressed down on the fingers of her right hand and grew pale. There was a thin vermilion line around the base of them.

D leapt. His cyborg horse was under him.

"I'm not letting you get away, Hunter," Caroline cried out. With streams of black oil trailing from it, the trembling hand went into a deadly pounce.

D was moving at a gallop. Could he escape?

The colossal arm went after the horse and rider. Flames suddenly blossomed from the mechanical wrist, traveling all the way to the elbow. Melting in the heat of a nuclear missile—which could reach a hundred thousand degrees—the abhorred demon arm collapsed to the ground as little more than a burning log of steel.

The smoke trails of five missiles hung in the air. From back down the same road that'd brought D, there reverberated the sounds of a nimble engine. The low-profile vehicle with huge puncture-proof tires was, needless to say, the battle car. And Leila was at the wheel.

After killing that master of the shadows, Bengé, Leila had wrangled herself a scouting mission by saying she couldn't help wondering what their foes were up to. When she left, she said

she'd be right back, but an hour had passed, then three. She'd gone searching for D.

Her brothers said the freaks were probably lying in wait for him. They laughed about how sweet it'd be if they all killed each other. And the more Leila thought about how likely they were to be right, the larger the face of that gorgeous young man so full of the void loomed in her heart. *That's just because he saved my life twice*, she thought. But Leila had never been given to thoughts about repaying debts before. If she collapsed from hunger and someone gave her food, she'd have had no compunctions about pulling a knife on her savior to steal the rest from him. That's simply how Leila—and all of the Marcus clan—did things. The very concept of returning a favor was alien to them. But as Leila held the yoke of the battle car and ripped through the morning air, her heart held the closest thing to it.

The instant she entered the ancient battlefield and saw the colossal arm chasing D, it was a movement of her heart rather than her conscious will that made her press the firing button and launch those miniature nuclear rockets. She didn't know that the colossal arm, writhing in pain from the loss of a finger, couldn't have caught up to D at the speed he galloped.

Stopping alongside the arm, which had ceased moving and spouted lotus-red flames, she scanned the area with her sharp gaze. She was searching for Caroline. But the freak was nowhere to be found. With a disappointed cluck of her tongue, Leila stepped on the gas.

†

Having ridden hard for about two miles, D veered off the road and into the forest. A horrendous torpor was sweeping over him. It was the sunlight syndrome, a condition unique to dhampirs. Inheriting half or more of a vampire's characteristics as they did, dhampirs could move about by day without concern, but that was not without its drawbacks. While they remained oblivious, a tenacious form of fatigue was building in their half-immortal flesh from the merciless rays of the sun. For dhampirs working as Hunters, the most dreaded aspect of this affliction was that the symptoms manifested without warning in the form of a sudden feeling of exhaustion and ever-increasing lassitude. It was painfully clear what would happen if someone were to suffer an attack of this while locked in deadly battle.

D's narrow escape couldn't really be called a retreat or a defeat. In fact, it was only thanks to D's superhuman strength that he was able to get himself in the saddle. But, when he got off his horse deep in the forest, D's gait was somewhat troubled.

The ground here was shrouded by multicolored flora and teeming with insect life. D knelt down and started to scoop at the dirt with a knife he pulled from his combat belt. Earth and moss flew with his intense movements. In less than three minutes, he had hollowed out a depression large enough for a person to lie in. With just the lightest shake of his head, D quietly entered the hole. Once he'd used his hands to pull the dirt around him onto his body, he laid back.

The reason vampires in legends of antiquity carried coffins filled with soil from their homeland was not merely because the grave they should've occupied offered them the most serene sleep. Actually, their kind had discovered in ancient times that Mother Earth would draw out the fatigue that accumulated in their bodies and instill them with new immortalizing energy. And D was following their example.

"Heh, this is a fine mess," D's left hand snorted. "Hell, even I can't tell you when the sunlight syndrome will strike. The fact that you're tougher than the average customer only makes matters worse. What's it been, five years or so?"

The voice from his hand must've been talking about how long it'd been since the last attack. Usually, those dhampirs who'd inherited the greater part of their disposition from the vampires went an interval of about six months between outbreaks of the symptoms. Using the date and time of the last one as a rough base, they'd hide themselves for a month before and after the next expected attack, avoiding all combat during that time. These precautions weren't solely out of fear of reprisals from the prey they chased, but also to avoid attacks from their business competitors. There were always plenty of scheming cowards looking for a larger share of the Hunting business, and they'd keep elaborate records of the dates their rivals had attacks, then try to learn their whereabouts before the next one was due so they could do away with them. Needless to say, in D's case, he'd have to guard against a fierce onslaught by Caroline and her cohorts.

"Well, looks like we're on vacation for a while. Good luck," the voice said. But by the time these carefree comments rose from his left hand, D's eyes were already closed.

Journey's End

CHAPTER 5

I

While D and Caroline's deadly encounter was unfolding on the ancient battlefield, Mayerling's jet-black carriage was parked on the shore of a lake some forty miles away as the crow flies. The sky was clear and blue, the trees by the shore benefited from the abundant water, and rainbows seemed to spring from every leaf and twig. Far off, a blue mountain range capped with white snow stretched into the distance, and golden birds skimmed the peaks. As scenery went, this was a truly beautiful and placid tableau.

As he watered the horses on the lake shore, a serious expression flitted into Mashira's wicked visage, as if he were mulling something over. He'd been that way since a short while earlier—when he'd parted company with Caroline. Now, waiting for the horse to finish drinking, he seemed to be gazing intently at the ugly face reflected in the water. Finally, after some minutes of rapt concentration, he muttered, "Okay," and slapped his hands together. Following that, he stooped to pick a number of the white flowers blooming by the shore. As he started walking toward the carriage parked a little way off, a charitable expression, strangely free from worry, arose on his face.

He tapped on a window with shades tightly drawn, and a voice over an intercom answered with an inquisitive, "Yes?" At this charmingly plaintive voice, he stopped the unconscious licking of his lips, and, in an amiable tone, he replied, "I was wondering if you wouldn't like to open the window and get a breath of fresh air. The sky is blue, the water clear, and the whole place is filled with the sweet scent of flowers. Though milord Mayerling slumbers, I believe you have nothing to fear so long as Mashira is here."

There was no reply. Behind the window, she must have been hesitating.

Perhaps seeing some spark of hope, Mashira said as buoyantly as he could, "Here, look how beautiful the flowers are. The ground's completely covered with them. If you're that worried, just open the shade and drink in their color if you will."

There was silence again, and, just as he was deciding his ploy wasn't going to work, the black shutter shot up smoothly. Seeing her innocent face quietly peering out like a moonflower, Mashira smiled inside.

How can I get her to come out here? That's the question that'd wracked his brain since before they had arrived at the lake. He'd considered a number of options, but, in the end, he decided to exploit the feelings she was bound to have as a young human girl. Even if she was with her boyfriend, even if he'd expressly told her not to go outside, there was no way a maiden of her tender years wouldn't want a breath of fresh air after being cooped up in a carriage for days. After all, the darkness was no place for a human to live. Ever since Mashira had taken Mayerling's place at the reins at dawn, he had schemed of using the girl's humanity to his advantage. Planning ahead, he took the carriage off the road and steered it to this remote locale.

"Say, how do you like these?" Mashira quickly thrust the bunch of flowers he'd concealed behind his back against the windowpane.

The girl's eyes became terribly blurred, and her white hand reached out. It bounced off the windowpane in vain.

"What are you waiting for? What's the harm in merely stepping out for bit of fresh air?" And then Mashira became even more empathic. "The flowers are in bloom, birds are singing, and when this place seeps into your pores and makes you even happier, milord Mayerling is certain to thank me for a job well done. And of course, the purse for our contract might gain a little weight, as well. Think of it, if you will, as your way of helping out one poor bodyguard."

The girl's eyebrows knit with reflection. In less time than it took to draw a breath, her pupils sparkled and the door handle spun. The girl stepped down into the meadow, and the darkness of the interior was scattered by the sunlight.

His beautiful prey had finally played into the trap. Gently taking her by the hand, Mashira led her to the shore.

"It's so beautiful," the pretty young lady exclaimed, proving that she was indeed a resident of the world of daylight. Where the little waves encroached on the shore, the girl knelt and reached out to touch the surface of the lake. Ripples spread, obscuring her gorgeous countenance. Pulling back the hand she'd put wrist-deep in the water, she searched for a handkerchief to wipe her face. The surface of the lake returned to calmness.

Mashira was standing behind her. The front of his gray coat was open. Maybe the girl glimpsed something inside it, because she froze without saying a word. When she finally turned and Mashira's hands grabbed her by both shoulders, something brown and tube-like stretched between their abdomens with unholy speed . . . out of Mashira's gut and toward the girl. The girl squirmed, but Mashira's hands never left her. Her well-formed body was pushed down into the brush without any real effort.

"What are you doing? Let me go!"

"Can't do that," Mashira said, grabbing the hand the girl levered against his jaw and twisting it up. "I'm crazy about you," he continued. "You're gonna be mine. If you just take it you don't have to get hurt. I'll take care of that jerk Mayerling, too."

"What are you talking about? Let go. If you don't let go of me—"

"What'll you do? Out in the middle of the woods like this, you can shout but nobody will come. Now, why don't the two of us get to know each other a lot better . . . "

A mouth burning with desire tried to close on her lips, which trembled with fear and anger. It was then that intense gunfire resounded. As Mashira jerked up his head, there were tremendous explosions of pain in his jaw and crotch.

Grunting as she pushed his body off, the girl got up quickly. Behind the carriage, she spied what looked to be a huntsman with a still-smoking rifle thrown over his shoulder. There'd been someone around after all.

The girl quickly ran for the carriage. The huntsman cut her off. Unsettling shadows clung to his scraggily bearded face. "Missy, what in the blazes are you?" he asked.

"Excuse me?"

"Don't play dumb with me. This here carriage's gotta belong to the Nobility. Why on earth would you be trying to get into it?"

"The truth is . . . "

As the girl hemmed and hawed, the huntsman threw a vulgar laugh her way. Suddenly, he grabbed her chin with one hand. With his substantial strength, the man exposed first one side of the girl's neck, then the other. "No wounds . . . meaning you hooked up with a Noble of your own accord, didn't you? You little traitor. Once I've taken care of that bastard, I'll learn you a thing or two. And when you've known a real man's touch, I'll send you to join your bloodsucker."

An unbelievably fierce gale was blowing in the girl's head. *This man means me harm, too,* she thought. *The moment I set foot outside of the carriage, I meet with one misfortune after another. Oh, if only I'd stayed with my love . . .*

"Get your hands off her," she heard Mashira say in a low but clear voice. Still smarting from the blow to his crotch, he remained somewhat hunched over as he came closer. His look had changed. He was so enraged now, almost nothing remained of his expression. "Get your stinking hands off her," he repeated.

"Ha! If you think you can make me, give it a shot," the huntsman laughed scornfully. "I figure chances are pretty good you're just a drifter who ran across this girl the same as me, but trying to rape her here was piss-poor planning. I'll be sure to nail her once for you, too, though. Now run along to hell." And, saying that, he threw the girl down in the opposite direction from the carriage and took the high-caliber gunpowder-rifle in his left hand.

"Wait just a—" Mashira started to say, but with an explosive bang like a hammer striking steel plate an enormous hole opened right in the middle of his heart. His hunched body was thrown back over six feet. A scream rose from the girl, and the air was clouded by a vermilion mist.

"Okay, now to deal with you," the huntsman chortled. "After I've had my share of fun with you, I'll drag you back to town for everyone to see." And with that the huntsman turned around, and an alarmed expression arose on his face. The girl's face had been flooded by a look of sheer terror. Following the path her eyes had taken, now it was the huntsman who froze.

Mashira was coming toward them. Covered with blood, a gaping hole in his chest where he'd taken the high-caliber shell. There was no need to see how his eyes had lost their light when the bloodless face was that of a corpse. The way he walked was strangely stiff. Almost as if it was something he wasn't accustomed to doing . . .

The huntsman shouted something. His rifle seemed to howl in response.

Mashira's head exploded like a watermelon. It may well have been that his steps became swifter at that point because his load had just been made that much lighter.

The huntsman couldn't move. The nerves that drove his body had withered to nothing when the rifle he placed so much stock in had proved ineffective.

The hands of the headless man reached out and grabbed hold of the huntsman's powerful shoulders. "You know, I was just getting used to this body. Now I'll take yours, you bastard." There wasn't even time to notice how this voice so unlike Mashira's reverberated from his belly before something like a brown tube sank into the huntsman's abdomen, rising from the same spot on the walking corpse.

Several seconds passed. For the girl, it was a nightmarish eternity.

"Heh heh heh—the transfer is complete," the voice said from his new belly. The belly of the huntsman, that is . . .

Without wasting time to watch the headless corpse tumbling to the ground, the girl, who'd long since reached her limit of horror, gave a scream and dashed off into the forest. Though the huntsman followed her with his eyes, for some reason he didn't set out after her. "There's no use in her trying to run," he snickered, "but I only gave her *a little of me*, so we're not quite ready to start either. Guess I might as well have myself a little game of hide-and-seek," he muttered, starting after her at a brisk pace.

†

When the last scrap of canned beef had been safely tucked away in his stomach, Kyle threw the empty can into the street. The cylinder rustled hollowly for several bounces and then, as it hung in the air on another, a silvery flash of light split it in two before zipping back to Kyle's waist.

It was the main street of the ghost town. Kyle was sitting on the edge of the boardwalk that jutted from the front of the saloon. When rain soaked streets like these, the mire could be difficult for pedestrians to negotiate.

Parked in front of the drugstore, the bus opened its door and Borgoff stuck his head out. He seemed on edge.

"What do you wanna do, bro?" Kyle asked, getting to his feet.

Borgoff made a concerned face. "Grove's had another attack," he said, looking up at the heavens. "A real bad one this time. His heart might not be able to take it."

"That ain't good. We still might need him to do his stuff one more time if something comes up." With a snort of laughter, he added,

"Maybe me and Leila went at it a little too hot and heavy for him."

"You moron," Borgoff bellowed, his face severe, but he soon folded his arms and donned a morose expression. "Of course, you probably ain't far wrong. I mean, we knew it wasn't any good for his health to force him to send his other self out like that," he muttered.

"Anyway, let's roll," said Kyle. "We'll lose the daylight if we hang around here waiting for freaking Leila. The Noble's making better time than we figured."

"Yep," Borgoff replied, but his face was dark.

This cruel clan had always managed to take care of not only the prey they stalked, but their competitors as well. But now they'd lost their brother Nolt, Leila hadn't returned, and even bedridden Groveck hovered near death.

Leila's failure to return didn't necessarily mean she'd been slain, but, in light of the strength of their foes, the brothers couldn't be sure. Worse yet, Borgoff harbored another fear about his little sister. That she'd fallen for D.

When they'd picked their sister up after she'd been injured in her first engagement with the Noble, every chunk of shrapnel had already been pulled out of her, and Leila was resting peacefully. They'd asked who'd patched her up, but she said she couldn't remember. It sure as hell wasn't the Noble. Which meant it had to be D. In fact, there were signs two other people had clashed near where they'd found Leila. She hadn't made any mention of that. But, given his sister's temperament, it wasn't inconceivable she'd keep it to herself. D was someone they were going to take out, after all. The fact that he'd saved her life would be nothing but pure humiliation.

However, Leila didn't seem in the least bit mortified. And that was just the start. Her expression was pained even while they strategized together, and she seemed strangely tired. Their clan wasn't so soft they'd make a big deal out of that, but her condition seemed to have nothing to do with physical exhaustion. Considering all the facts, Borgoff realized she'd only exhibited these signs whenever they discussed what to do about D. Putting two and two together, he thought, *Bingo!*

But in his heart of hearts, there was one thought Borgoff couldn't get rid of, peerless Vampire Hunter though he was—the question of whether it was really D that'd saved Leila after all. At that point, D must've known for a fact that the Marcus clan should be considered his enemy. By all accounts, he wasn't the kind of man to go easy on any armed opponent, woman or not. Even if half of what people said about D's abilities, his battles, and the list of foes he'd slain could be discounted as idle talk, the remainder was enough to send icy fingers up the nape of Borgoff's neck. *He of all people had saved Leila?* Borgoff found that hard to believe. And that's why he hadn't tried to stop his sister from going out on reconnaissance that morning.

Borgoff swept away the tangled knot of ideas. "Let's go," he said. "If Leila's okay, she'll send up a flare or get in touch with us one way or another."

The two of them got back on the bus. Kyle took the driver's seat, while Borgoff went into the bedroom. There wasn't a single breath to be heard from Groveck's bunk. Shriveled and dry like a mummy, you could've put your ear to his motionless chest and not even heard a heartbeat. Right now, *this* Groveck was indeed dead.

When Borgoff looked down at the lifeless husk of his youngest brother, a pained and human expression crept into his supremely fierce face, and then the bus shook a little as it began to move.

II

Two women were walking through the forest. One of them— a gorgeous, shapely blonde in a blue dress—headed deep into the forest with her eyes fixed on one spot straight ahead. The other—dressed in a light shirt and slacks—looked like she was just out for a stroll in the woods, but from time to time she stopped and checked the ground or looked at how the brush was broken before walking on a little further. Though her eyes kept scanning the forest, she didn't seem to be in the least bit lost. The eyes of both women sought the same thing. The young Vampire Hunter, defenseless in his makeshift grave.

Leila stopped and wiped the sweat from her brow. After she'd fried the colossal hand Caroline controlled, she'd gone right after D. She had no definite reason for doing so, but, judging by the way he'd run off, it was clear something was wrong with him. It wasn't like the great D to be nearly killed by a woman, no matter what sort of freak she might be. There was only one reason for that she could think of—sunlight syndrome.

He would've taken off for the forest then, seeking Mother Earth. It was easy enough to follow the hoofprints. She'd even found the spot where he'd slipped into the woods. That was where the trouble started. The battle car couldn't get through. Without regret, Leila had left her cherished vehicle behind.

She wasn't sure exactly what Caroline would do, but, judging by how the woman's strength compared to that of Leila's brothers or D, and in light of how much trouble she'd had trying to do away with the dhampir before, there was certainly a very good chance she'd be intent on killing D now. What's more, the Barbarois woman possessed strange powers. She might've already beaten Leila to D. It was so easy to kill a dhampir suffering from sunlight syndrome, it made the super-human abilities they displayed in their chosen profession seem like a distant dream.

With a javelin in her hand and the sliver gun shoved through her belt, Leila entered the forest. The hoofprints were fading fast, filled in by quickly growing moss. All she was left with were the instincts she'd refined in her life as a Hunter. The question was, would that be enough to make her a match for the Barbarois woman? Now that Leila had abandoned her beloved car, she'd be no more than a normal human girl to Caroline.

Bearing right for a few yards, she suddenly came into a clearing. She saw the horse tethered to the branch of a nearby tree. D lay half-buried in the dirt by the horse's feet. Choking back a cry of joy, she kicked up moss as she scrambled over to him.

There was nothing out of the ordinary. His beautiful countenance—which sufficed to give her goosebumps even at this distance—was supremely wise and enduringly stern, and his eyelids were closed as if he was deep in contemplation.

Leila's shoulders fell. Something hot spilled past her eyelids, to her great surprise. The last time she'd cried was a distant memory. She seemed to remember wiping away her tears by the side of a blood-stained old woman whose face she could clearly recall even now. *Who had that been?* she wondered.

Forcefully wiping her tears away, Leila laid herself down gently on top of D's dirt-covered body. It was so cold. The chill she felt wasn't from the soil. It was D's body temperature. When Kyle had come along and found her after she'd been wounded in her battle with the Noble, he told her she would've died out there if someone hadn't kept her warm. Of course there hadn't been a heating unit around. D had kept her warm.

It wasn't as if she'd never had feelings for anyone before. She'd been proposed to a number of times. But all her suitors had left when they found out what her last name was. All but one. Leila drove him off. Because that night, she'd been violated by her brothers.

"We're not letting you go anywhere," said Borgoff. Nolt whispered to her that he'd wanted to have his way with her for a long time. Kyle lost himself in the act without a word. As soon as the other three backed off and Groveck's nearly mummified form mounted her, something in Leila's soul flew away. And ever since, she'd been a colder killer than ever before.

But now that special something had returned.

"You saved me," Leila fairly whispered to the gorgeous, immobilized man. "This time, *I'll* protect *you*. I'll defend you with my life."

A strange presence moved through the woods. Checking that the safety of her sliver gun was off, Leila took the javelin in hand and let the fighting spirit fill her. She rose to her feet.

✝

H e was lying on a hill of pure green. As he rarely got to go outside, each time, short though it was, was absolute bliss. Joy bubbled like a fount in his heart. Gentle gusts of wind, showers of sunlight, the scent of dense tufts of new grass, the blue mountain range stretching toward eternity—all these things made him realize what a pleasure it was to be alive. *Now this is living!* he thought to himself.

It was Groveck, or rather, the "spirit" of Groveck that had escaped from the sickly body left in the Marcus bus. The sound of footsteps rose from the forest behind him. He turned to find a girl running toward him. The fear in her countenance spoiled his mood. Just when he was enjoying himself.

"Help! Please, help me," the girl cried out, circling around behind him.

He was perplexed. His forte was getting people to run away from him, not toward him. But the reason the girl had said what she did was soon apparent. Out of the woods stepped a man armed with a large rifle, apparently a huntsman of some sort.

The huntsman looked around restlessly, but soon spotted him and the girl. The huntsman approached them with powerful strides. Grove heard screams of fear spill out from behind his back. For the first time in his life, he felt something unprecedented stirring in his heart. The other man stopped about a yard away and swung the muzzle of the rifle to bear on him.

Grove was a bit surprised. Every inch of the huntsman's body brimmed with hostility and self-confidence. Though he'd never seen this other man before, it appeared the huntsman knew who he was. "What do you want?" he tried to ask, but the other man didn't seem to hear him, and not a muscle moved in his own face. That's the way it always went. He gave up on ordinary communication.

"Give me the girl," the man ordered. His voice was cold. Any fool could well imagine what would happen whether he complied with the huntsman's command or not.

"If you don't want to, fine," the huntsman added. "I mean, it's not like I'm gonna let you live anyway. Strange meeting you here, though."

Grove tilted his head. He just couldn't recall who this other man was. His opponent, however, was kind enough to provided the answer.

"But then, you wouldn't know me in this shape, now would you?" the huntsman snickered. "I was part of the threesome over next to the carriage when you snuck into the village of the Barbarois."

Learning this, Grove was no less bewildered. He could, indeed, recall the trio in question. However, that middle-aged man, jet-black youth, and shapely beauty were all quite different from the huntsman now before his eyes.

"Oh, that's right—I still haven't shown you my true face. The one you saw before, and this one I have now, are no more than temporary hosts. The real me looks like *this!*" And with that, the huntsman pulled up his shirt with one hand.

Grove let his mouth fall open. But there was nothing on the huntsman's belly. When the girl gasped, it was like the signal for the change. As they watched, a number of deep creases that couldn't really be called wrinkles coursed across the huntsman's abnormally protruding belly, and then what looked like a human face bulged from the surface, showing a little nose, lips like purple scraps of meat, and eyes that blinked wide open. The tips of the yellow teeth spilling over the twisted lips came to fang-like points. It was a tumor . . . a tumor that had a face like a person, and a life of its own. The body of the huntsman was no more than a vessel for it to move around in.

"Surprised, junior?" the tumor asked. "This is the real me. I've been hopping from body to body for five hundred years. It'll take a lot more than your tricks to beat me."

At last Grove grasped the situation. Hostility flooded into his heart. Perhaps it showed.

"Let's get one thing straight," the tumor laughed. "If you let your lightning fly, I'll shoot and the girl behind you will die, too. You got that?"

For a moment, Grove was befuddled.

The abdominal tumor added, "Of course, the girl's not exactly in pristine shape anymore. You ought to have a good look at her stomach."

The weird course of the conversation shifted Grove's attention to his rear. Before the fierce report of the gun could reach him, he was struck in the chest by heat and a forceful impact. Flying backward, he saw the blue sky. It seemed his foe had aimed away from the girl. He'd never had any intention of shooting her.

Without even glancing at the punk toppling backward in a bloody mist, the huntsman—that is to say, the eerie countenanced carbuncle—smiled at the girl. "Okay," he said, "come to me now. If that bastard Mayerling gets out and about, there'll be hell to pay. See, I'm not allowed to do anything to his coffin. So I want to get as far away from here as we can before darkness falls."

A relieved expression arose in the girl. Realizing at this point that she was worried about Mayerling's safety, the expression of the countenanced carbuncle—or Mashira—flooded with rage. "Oh, you're being such a pain!" he shouted, taking a step toward her. But, from the pit of his stomach, or quite literally from the middle of his abdomen, a gasp of astonishment escaped. The young man was getting up, perfectly healthy, devoid of a bullet hole or spattered gore. "You son of a bitch," the countenanced carbuncle said. Now he realized what the young man really was.

The world was bleached white. In the blink of an eye, streaks of light coming from nowhere in particular slammed head-on into the huntsman's abdomen. Flames rose from him, the stench of melting fat filled the air, and the huntsman fell into the brush with a thud.

It was almost as if the nerves that had endured this truly unearthly confrontation finally frayed and snapped—the girl started to fall like a puppet whose strings had been cut. Grove caught her gently.

When the figure that easily scooped up the girl had gone down the hill with her and out of sight, a low voice could be heard around the ankles of the still flaming corpse. "Well, spank my ass!" it said. "That's about what I'd expect from one of the Marcus clan. Now that I've seen his powers firsthand, I can't help wondering what the real *him* is like."

†

Leila had never seen the woman up close before. She didn't think her golden hair and creamy complexion were beautiful. She herself suited D better. But it was certain that behind those glamorous looks, the Barbarois woman possessed powers that staggered the imagination. Leila didn't take her lightly. Realizing in an instant that her javelin would be useless against this opponent, she jabbed it into the ground and drew the sliver gun.

Caroline pursed her lips and smiled. "Do you think you can defeat a woman from the village of the Barbarois with a toy like that?" she laughed. "I'll have you know, even the Nobility have no easy time getting into our village."

Instead of replying, Leila squeezed the sliver gun's trigger. Imperceptible needles pierced the woman's stomach without making a sound.

"Oh," Caroline cried, but soon enough she grinned broadly. "A gun that fires needles? You should've aimed for my heart, little girl."

Not knowing quite what she meant by that remark, Leila stood stock still with amazement. Suddenly, something fell from overhead and struck her right hand. The sliver gun went flying. Something speared down into the moss between the gun and the hand she stretched out to retrieve it, foiling her efforts. On discovering it was a thick tree branch, Leila leapt back, but something else caught hold of her by the shoulder. It was another branch, huge and bristling with countless twigs. Twisting the twigs with a crisp snap, the branch wrapped them around Leila's limbs like fingers.

"When I learned you'd arrived here ahead of me, I drank the sap of all the trees in the area," said Caroline. "Sap is the lifeblood of trees. So now, every one of their branches is mine—I have thousands of hands and feet."

"No, you can't be . . . " Goaded by a fearful foresight, Leila writhed, but she couldn't get free of the branches that were now her bonds.

"Ha ha, regrettably, I am not a Noble." Caroline wore the smile of a victor. "However, I have inherited some of their abilities. My mother, you see, was a wet-nurse for the Nobility overseeing Sector Seven of the Frontier."

Oh, it couldn't be that this gorgeous woman was a dhampir like D. Inhumanly beautiful. Mysteriously refusing to dine. Throwing feverish glances at Mayerling—hadn't all of these things indicated the woman's true nature? Even the way she could move about in daylight without difficulty fit the pattern.

However, her powers proved that she was indeed one of the Barbarois. Whatever felt her fangs—even inorganic things like the mechanical arm, or non-sentient lifeforms like the vegetation that bound Leila—obeyed her in the same way that humans followed the will of the Nobles who bit them. While most dhampirs would drink blood, they didn't convert anyone, so her ability was truly fearsome in comparison.

Looking from D to Leila and back again, Caroline let an evil little grin escape. "From what I saw just now, I'd say you're in love with that dhampir. How interesting. I was going to make short work of you, but I've changed my mind. I want you to watch as I go over there and skewer the heart of the man you love. And after that, I'll let you share his fate."

"Don't," said Leila. "If you're gonna kill anyone, kill me—"

"How courageous," Caroline replied with a laugh. "It seems even human scum who make their livelihood murdering the Nobility are far more tolerant when it comes to someone they adore. Well, just wait. You'll follow after him soon enough . . . " Caroline stated sternly, but as she did so an unbelievably chill breeze stroked her back. This female dhampir, possessing powers comparable to D's, turned around despite herself.

There was no change in the way D lay. What could that gorgeous man be dreaming of? Of the ordinary life that he, as a dhampir, could never know? Of days long passed? No, no, of a future painted in blood and pitch-black, with battles that would know no end—of that there could be no doubt.

"Just my imagination?" Caroline muttered as she raised her right hand. A branch from one of the massive trees around her bent at the trunk and pointed its trenchant tip at the Barbarois woman's chest. Grabbing it in her pale hand, Caroline snapped the branch off a yard back from the tip.

Slowly, she went to the side of the sleeping D and placed her feet so they straddled the depression. With both hands, she took a firm grip of the branch—the gigantic stake she'd improvised—and the instant she was about to swing it down from over her head . . .

Leila's scream of "Stop!" and her own strike were almost simultaneous, and it was in the next instant that Caroline cried out "Mashira?!"

The stake was caught in midair. By D's left hand. By the palm of his left hand, to be precise. And, as might be expected from Caroline's puzzled cry, what stopped the keen point was indeed the tiny mouth that appeared in the palm of his hand. The stake had literally been stopped by the skin of those teeth. Above the mouth, a pair of mischievous eyes laughed. And yet, his jaws were so powerful that even Caroline with her superhuman strength couldn't make them budge in the least. Her beautiful visage distorted by surprise and horror, the female dhampir leapt away.

"I'll thank you not to be calling me by strange names," the face in the palm said, effortlessly spitting the stake out of the depression.

"That Mashira—he's one of your cohorts? He's one of my kind then, I take it?"

Without answering, Caroline made a sweep of her right hand. The forest shook. Several gigantic trees bent and swung their branches straight down at the sleeping dhampir.

The left hand countered with an attack of his own. Grabbing hold of the huge branch it'd just spat out, it hurled the wooden missile at Caroline. The branch went with such speed there was no time to dodge it. And yet, Caroline must've managed at least a lightning-fast twist of her body, because it was her abdomen that the huge branch ultimately pierced.

The instant she fell backward screaming, the movements of the branches came to a dead stop. Even Leila's bonds came undone.

Seeing that she didn't even have time to make a dash for her javelin, Leila ran at Caroline. Latching onto the branch impaling the female dhampir, Leila shoved with all her might. Blood bubbled from Caroline's mouth.

"You little bitch you!" the female dhampir screamed. Her whole body twitching in the throes of death, her pale hands seized Leila's shoulders.

Leila didn't stop pushing, even when the blood-rimmed mouth clamped onto her neck. The only thing in her mind was, *I've gotta save D*, and that thought alone.

The mouth quickly fell away. An intense feeling of relaxation swept over Leila, and she allowed the huge branch to be snatched from her grasp.

Backing away a few steps, Caroline groaned again. The huge branch still pierced her abdomen, and from the waist down she'd been dyed crimson by the blood gushing from her. It was a sight nothing could rival.

"Little girl, we shall meet again. And next time, you will be my slave." Blood mixing with the words she spouted, Caroline turned and left.

Leila went to her knees on the ground. She'd just been bitten. Bitten by a dhampir. She felt no wonder, no fear. Only fatigue and a feeling of satisfaction. She'd kept her promise. The promise she'd made to herself. Still, Leila managed to pick herself up and go over to the sleeping D. Gazing down at his beautiful face for a long time, she said goodbye. "I wanted to kiss you," she said, "but I can't now. I mean, you'd wind up a laughing stock if some reject vampire were to steal a kiss from a Hunter like you. So long. If you can, try to think of me from time to time."

Barely managing to take the sliver gun and javelin in hand, Leila walked away. Her tottering figure was soon swallowed by the forest.

But how long would D continue to sleep? After all, the warrior woman who'd risked her life and soul defending him was wounded, Mayerling's lady love had run off somewhere, and the situation was only growing more confused . . .

III

The scene was the road, about two hours after Caroline and Leila's deadly battle had ended. Knifing its way through the wind at a speed of twenty-five miles per hour, the bus came to a sudden stop when something was spotted up ahead.

"What is it?" Borgoff called out in a gruff voice from where he was prepping his bow and arrows in his bedroom.

"A woman just crossed the road dead ahead of us. A blonde in a blue dress—probably that Caroline character Grove mentioned. I'm gonna go have a little look-see." As he spoke, Kyle got to his feet with the crescent blades in hand.

"Wait up—I'll go with you."

In reply to Borgoff's offer, he said, "Don't sweat it. It's just a woman. Besides, what if someone's trying to lure us both outside so they can take out Grove while we're gone? There's another one of them somewhere, you know."

"You've got a point there," Borgoff conceded. "Be careful."

"Hey, just leave it to me."

Smiling with overwhelming self-confidence, Kyle got off the bus. Although noon had already come and gone, the sunlight was hot and white. With crescent blades in either hand, as he was about to enter the woods in the same spot where the woman had vanished, he said, "Just to be on the safe side," and let the blades fly.

There couldn't have been any stranger ranged weapon than Kyle's crescent blades. Controlled with the fingertips of the hand that held one end of the thin wire, the semicircular blades attached to the other end of each line swept easily between the densely overlapping trees and came back to Kyle's hands. If his foe was lurking anywhere within a hundred-foot radius of the entrance to the forest, fresh blood drawn from her head or throat should've remained on the edge of his crescent blades at the very least. Better yet, she might even be dead already.

"Looks like no contact," Kyle said to himself. He went into the woods. Casually taking a few steps, he shouted, "There you are!"

A silvery flash coursed to the base of a gigantic tree, and, just when it seemed it would strike the trunk, it suddenly turned and shot straight upwards.

Caroline screamed and fell to the ground. Not the slightest trace remained of where she'd been staked with a huge branch two hours earlier, but now she held her exposed and bloody thigh and moaned. The crescent blade had slashed it open.

"What do you wanna do, Barbarois bodyguard?" Kyle snickered cruelly. "Don't be shy. Take your best shot, if you're game." While Kyle snorted that she wasn't all she was cracked up to be and extended both his arms for the *coup de grace*, his eyes were blasted by the woman's orbs. There was an indescribable light in her eyes.

Without time to realize how bad this development was, Kyle went and knelt by the woman's side. Her exposed thigh was burned into his retinas.

"Are you okay?" His consciousness drifting in a dream, Kyle heard himself ask a question that wasn't even in his mind.

"I think I'll be fine," the woman practically moaned. "My leg hurts. I really must stop the bleeding—would you be so kind as to lick it clean?"

The fact that this woman was a Barbarois sorceress no longer concerned Kyle. "Sure . . . no problem," he sort of mumbled, then put his mouth to her bare, white leg. His lips were instantly sullied with blood. Licking the outside clean, when he worked his way to her inner thigh, the woman began panting in earnest and wrapped her other leg around Kyle's waist. Kyle's blood-tinted lips pressed in even further.

When the moans of pleasure and lapping sounds had stopped, the woman gently put her hands on Kyle's cheeks. Her unblemished white face approached the blood-stained visage he raised at her bidding. Kyle had no comprehension how fearful the woman's actions had become.

And yet, while his instincts may have guessed the danger he was in, the fingers that reached with exasperating slowness for the crescent blade at his waist were caught by one of the woman's gentle hands.

"Oh no you don't," she chided. "You can use those to serve me once I'm done kissing you . . . " Her voice alone rang in his head, and, before long, the blackest darkness suffused his mind through her lips.

When Kyle came out of the forest a short time later, he raised his hand up over his head to shield his eyes from the sun. Slowly, he returned to the bus.

Borgoff was in the driver's seat. "How did it go?" he asked.

"She wasn't in there. Looks like she got away, but you can't be too careful."

"Hmm. Trade places with me," said the oldest Marcus. Standing to let Kyle take the driver's seat, Borgoff returned to the bedroom. Kyle was holding the wheel mutely. "Say, Kyle . . . "

Borgoff called out to him. Kyle didn't move. Borgoff called his name again.

"Er—What?" Kyle responded, his tone distant and removed.

"I'll let you in on a little shortcut. Pretty soon, we'll come to a spot where there's a red branch sticking out on our left. Turn in there. Once we're on that road, just follow it straight and we'll come out near the Claybourne States."

"Gotcha," Kyle replied.

The vehicle went a bit, then stopped.

"What happened?" asked Borgoff.

"The engine stalled. Looks like the oil charger is all screwed up. Give me a hand fixing it."

Empty-handed, Borgoff followed Kyle off the bus.

"Hold on a sec. I'll scout around first," said Kyle, moving to the front of the vehicle and out of Borgoff's line of sight. Borgoff scanned their surroundings and gave a light scratch to his head. And, having scratched, he leapt.

A bewitching light zipped out of the gap between the vehicle's undercarriage and the ground. As Borgoff looked askance at the pair of crescent blades sparking together in the spot where he'd stood, his right hand went into action. Grabbing the bow and arrows tucked through the back of his belt, he readied them in midair. There was a sound like the plucking of a zither's strings as he loosed two arrows simultaneously. What was really strange about the shot was how his arrows hit the tangled crescent blades, turned a few times, and slid up along the wires attached to the blades.

A low groan could be heard from the far side of the bus.

Borgoff circled around the vehicle to stand over the fallen Kyle. One steel arrow quivered in his brother's stomach and another was stuck through the top of his head. "I didn't want to have to do this to my own brother, but I didn't really have a choice," he told Kyle. "You went and got turned by a vampire. But at least now I know what she really is. I'll avenge you, so rest easy." Notching a third arrow, Borgoff took aim at his agonized brother's heart. "The next time you're reborn as a vampire, try not to shade your eyes from the sun when it's not all that bright out." And he watched until the bitter end, until the steel shaft had pierced his younger brother's heart.

A Port to the Stars

CHAPTER 6

I

H e was at a bit of a loss. On account of the girl. He wasn't entirely sure what he should do with her. Though the girl was as vibrant as a sunny day, she hadn't said anything about where she lived or why that huntsman with the countenanced carbuncle was chasing her. Of course, in this form Grove couldn't very well ask her, so he had no choice but to wait for her to tell him about it. When the girl had regained consciousness, she'd tried to go into the forest right away. Grove made a move to go with her, but she seemed troubled by that so he decided to stay out of it. But, on further consideration, it would be dangerous for a woman to be in the woods alone.

According to what the girl had said, she was going through the woods in a carriage with someone else when that huntsman attacked them, or something like that. Grove had his doubts that the story was as simple as that, because some parts of the girl's tale just didn't fit together right. He got the impression the fuzzier parts of her story were somehow connected to him and his brothers, but that didn't present a problem for him in his current state.

Seeing the girl off as she thanked him repeatedly and left, he started after her a few minutes after she'd vanished into the woods, but she hadn't gone more than a stone's throw from the entrance—

she was just standing there. Ultimately, he ended up going with her in search of her lover, just as she'd asked him to.

After an hour of walking around looking for the love of her life, the girl was nearly exhausted. She was breathing hard and beads of sweat were strung close together on her brow.

So weak, he thought, confident in his own healthy body. At that thought, he felt a swell of pity. He really wanted to help her find whoever she was looking for. After all, there was no telling when he'd have to go back.

Getting the girl on her feet again, he was helping her continue the search when twilight came calling. The woods were dangerous at night. He tried to lead the girl out of the forest, but it didn't go very well. Now he was lost, too. When the girl saw him with his shrugged shoulders, Grove was afraid she might get scared, but to his great surprise she giggled. Whether she'd been traveling with her lover or not, she must've had guts to take a carriage ride this far off the beaten trail on the Frontier.

Though her brightness seemed to know no end, there was just a hint of melancholy in her smile that whipped up Grove's protective instincts. At this point, the girl said something rather odd—that as soon as it was night, her lover was sure to come looking for her. Dubious of her confidence-filled eyes, he couldn't believe that would be the case. They'd be better off asking his brothers—who should be getting closer by the minute—for help.

Circling around behind the girl so as not to startle her, Grove sent a bolt of lightning into the air. The white-hot streak stretched up into the deepening blue of the evening sky without a sound.

†

Borgoff was in the driver's seat of the bus coming out of a cramped valley, and his narrow eyes sparkled at the sight of the energy bolt. "Wow, if ol' Grove has gone to all the trouble of giving us a signal—Well, he must've found something."

†

Dashing through woods sealed in darkness, Caroline glanced up at the heavens and grinned broadly. "That's the same light I saw back in the village," she said. "Surely it's a signal that boy has found something."

†

Deep in thought as he bent over the corpse of what had been Mashira, Mayerling snapped to attention at the heaven-splitting bolt of light rising from a part of the woods not so far away. "I was wondering who might've slain Mashira," he muttered, "Such raw power . . . Well, I don't care who it is. If they've laid a hand on that young lady, it won't be pretty, by my oath."

†

The girl felt oddly at peace. That was thanks to the youth in front of her. His innocent face and baby-soft complexion gave her an unrivaled sense of security. The young man didn't seem to fit into the forests of Frontier, but seemed like he'd be more suited for a life in the Capital.

The sun would be setting soon. Her love would probably be here in no time. No matter where she might be, she knew he'd find her. The girl was positive of that. As she played her gentle gaze over the youth standing before her in the caress of the evening breeze, the girl thought how sad how it was that he looked so healthy and yet couldn't speak a word.

Suddenly, the girl blinked. The young man turned her way, seeming surprised. A grove of trees was visible through his bright face. The youth was fading away.

His sad eyes gazed at the girl, and his lips formed a word. *Goodbye.*

The girl reached out to him. The youth was growing ever more transparent, like glass disappearing in water. *Goodbye*, the girl said frantically. Regardless of who he really was, she wanted to thank him as he left. *Goodbye, goodbye, thank you and goodbye.*

And then the youth vanished. In a corner of the woods growing darker and duskier, the girl was left alone.

The wind seemed to grow chillier. The eyes of countless blood-crazed beasts peered out at her from the depths of the forest.

I'm scared, the girl thought from the very depths of her soul. *So scared. Hurry and save me, my love.*

There was a rustling of the tree branches. It came from somewhere behind her and off to the right. The girl spun around. Someone was approaching. She couldn't tell if it was a man or a woman, or how they were dressed. Fear wound tight around her throat. It was coming closer. The sound of moss being trampled and twigs snapping. Fifteen or twenty feet ahead of her, the figure stopped moving.

A probing voice asked, "Who's that over there? That you, Grove?"

Even though the girl knew it was a woman's voice, her fears hadn't dissipated. She remembered that the man who'd attacked her earlier had two partners, and one of them was female. As for the name of the other man, she couldn't recall it.

When the figure took a step forward and she could make out the face of a woman she'd never seen before, the girl finally gave a deep sigh and let the tension escape from her shoulders.

"Let me guess—Are you the passenger from the carriage?" Well suited to the black hue of the scarf wound about the base of her neck, the woman was none other than Leila Marcus.

"And you are . . . ?" The girl's face, which had filled with joy when it turned out the new arrival wasn't Caroline, grew tight as soon as she saw how Leila was outfitted. A javelin and a sliver gun—there could be no mistaking the trappings of a Hunter. There was no way a Hunter would just be hanging around a place like this alone. Which could only mean she'd come here after her. First Mashira, now a Hunter—with one terrifying encounter mounting on the next, the girl's shoulders fell despondently.

"I didn't get to see your face back there, but you're the girl that was in the black carriage, aren't you?" Leila said nonchalantly. "I'm Leila Marcus. I'm a Vampire Hunter here to get your boyfriend."

The girl braced a hand against the ground.

"What's wrong?" Leila asked incredulously. "You get to go home now."

Though she listened to the Marcus woman's words with suspicion, the girl wasn't focused enough to catch how Leila's voice seemed a little feeble. "Go. Please," she urged the Hunter. "Just hurry up and get out of here."

"I asked you what's the matter?"

"I'm sure my love will be here soon," the girl said. "The two of you will fight until one of you is dead. And I don't want to make either of you kill on my account."

Leila looked at the blue darkness steadily filling the vicinity. She nodded. "I suppose you're right. The night is the Nobility's world . . . " For an instant, the fierce expression of a warrior steeled for battle arose on her face, but it was soon replaced by one that was strangely filled with half-hearted hatred. And once again, this time in a surprised manner, she asked, "Are you . . . you're still human, aren't you?"

The girl nodded.

"So, the Noble didn't have his way with you and drag you off then. Seriously, you didn't go of your own free will . . . That's what happened, isn't it?!"

"Yes, I did," the girl said with a nod. The pale beauty gazed at Leila. There was a powerful light to her eyes. So long as they had that, a person could endure just about anything.

"So that's what happened . . . " A feeling of envy and sadness softened Leila's tone. "You love him, don't you? In love with a Noble."

The girl didn't answer her. Her silence was her answer. But her eyes were sparkling.

Leila leaned up against the trunk of the gigantic tree. At her core was this hot stickiness. It was spreading through her whole body like a fog borne on the wind. It was fatigue. Twenty years worth of fatigue had finally seeped into her body.

Leila gazed at the girl. This girl had been carried off by a Noble and had given up being human, yet still had infinite confidence and trust. She, on the other hand, was renowned as one of the greatest Vampire Hunters on Earth but was now merely awaiting a horrid fate. Could it be that the pursued was happier than the pursuer?

"Doesn't it bother you?" Leila asked the girl.

"Huh?"

"Doesn't it bother you? Living on the run. He has no place to go back to, no tomorrow."

"Neither do I," the girl replied.

"Yeah, I suppose that would help the two of you get along."

The girl smiled thinly. "Never mind about me. Get out of here while you can. He'll be here soon."

"I don't care," said Leila. "I'm plumb exhausted. I'll wait here for your beloved. So, why don't we continue our little chat."

A low voice from behind them said, "I don't suppose you'd let yours truly listen in as well?"

The girl screamed, and Leila whipped around with ungodly speed. The face that greeted the eyes of both was that of the huntsman.

II

At the entrance to the same woods where he'd seen the streak of light, Borgoff stopped the vehicle. For a while, he didn't move from the driver's seat. A strange expression arose on his face when he got to his feet. An expression stripped of every emotion—almost the face of an imbecile.

Slipping through the sleeping quarters, Borgoff went into the arsenal and pulled a small timer and explosive from a wooden crate, then returned to the bunks. Going over to Groveck's bed, he carefully pulled away the blanket. An emaciated face appeared. He put his rough thumb to the barely colored lips. There was a faint flow of air. Groveck was still alive.

A single tear coursed from Borgoff's eye. When that shining bead snagged in his frightful beard, it hung there forever.

"It looks like it's down to just you and me," Borgoff said to the dearest of his brothers. It was this, the third born, that he loved more than Nolt or Kyle, or even more than Leila. "But this job's just about up to the big finale. I really need your power here. Which is all well and good, but you just got back from an attack and there's no reason you'd be having another one right away."

At this point, Borgoff sobbed. "That's why it's gotta be this way. I hate to say it, but you're gonna have to let me give you one. Looks to me like you ain't gonna stand but one more of these attacks. Once you have the next one, there'll be no saving you. That being the case, I want you to give your life for me."

His words could be taken as both sorrowful and unsettling, but what Borgoff did as he wept was horrific. Turning down the blanket even more, right about where his brother's heart was— over the thin sternum and above the jutting ribs—he taped the time bomb. Though the time bomb was just four inches of plastic tubing, the explosive packed in it would easily blow away the ribs and take out part of Grove's internal organs.

That couldn't possibly be what he planned to do to his brother's chest as Grove lay fighting for breath, could it?

Borgoff said he was sorry. His tears flowed without end.

Give your life for me.

While one strip of tape would've been enough to guard against the bomb slipping off, Borgoff put on a third layer, then a fourth, just in case Groveck tried to peel it off. Once he finished his work and had gently replaced the blanket, Borgoff lightly stroked his brother's forehead. "So long," he said. "I'll make it back for sure." And then, with his deadly bow and quiver of arrows across his back, he headed outside with an easy gait.

Evening was about to change from blue to black.

Borgoff ran. His gut told him from which way Groveck's streak of light had come.

His pace gradually quickened. The muscles in his legs creaked and popped as they swelled, and, perhaps more surprisingly, even the bones grew thicker. His upper body remained as massive as ever, but his lower limbs had been transformed into the legs of a veritable giant. And yet, his feet made almost no noise as they struck the mossy ground. In fact, they barely left a dent in the moss.

Perhaps this was a behest from his parents, who were said to have possessed genetic engineering technology. But why was it that when he walked up a slope, his body remained nearly perpendicular to the terrain?

He entered the woods. At a speed nearly five times that of an ordinary person, he headed deeper into the trees. The way his feet moved, it seemed like they didn't know the meaning of the word stop. Soon, however, they came to a sudden halt. He'd just run into a bizarre area. There he could see what looked like a model of the Capital made entirely out of dirt. A cluster of conical buildings roughly fifteen feet high were connected by transport tubes a foot and a half thick. The Capital seemed to run on forever into the forest.

However, Borgoff's gaze was not trained so much on the structures themselves as on the ground beneath his feet. There were white things scattered about—a skull staring fixedly at him with gaping black sockets, a femur that looked like it would make an improvised ax, ribs, a humerus . . . They were all bones. Most of them were from species Borgoff recognized, the rest were from birds and beasts he wasn't familiar with, but the human bones were certainly easy enough to spot. Despite all the remains, the air here didn't have the slightest stench of decay. It was as if something had stripped them of their flesh and blood.

Leaving only his startled exclamation of "Whoa!" in his old position, Borgoff jumped forward a good six feet. He landed without disturbing the moss. At the spot he'd just leapt away from, there were a number of creatures that looked like black grains of rice scurrying around. "Sorry, I can't afford to be dinner for you guys just yet," he called back to the minute creatures. "So long." There was something horrifying about his voice as he spoke, and then, when he was about to make another bound, a shudder ran down his spine. In that instant, he realized who he was going to be up against. The distance to the foe he sensed was twenty-five feet ahead and a little to the right, with the eerie model of the Capital lying dead in the middle.

All the power drained from Borgoff's body. Preparing for battle, he struck a pose that would let him use his muscles just as he wanted. The tension others might feel when a fight to the death was imminent meant nothing to a Hunter of Borgoff's class. Crouching to escape the fierce, unearthly aura shooting through him, Borgoff let an arrow fly with lightning speed. He already had another arrow cocked and ready.

The unearthly aura died out.

The Hunter didn't know where his arrow had gone or what effect it had. But from the way there was no sound of leaves or twigs swaying, he could well imagine.

The air stirred by his right cheek. He jumped forward for all he was worth. What had just split the air and then stuck itself into the ground was the arrow he'd fired. While the fact that someone had stopped his shot with their bare hands didn't surprise him, the awesome power with which it'd been hurled back gave Borgoff goosebumps. Any stone or branch out there might become a deadly weapon in the hands of his enemy.

Up ahead of him, the Hunter sensed someone moving. Picking himself up and preparing to loose a second arrow, Borgoff stiffened. There against the backdrop of blue darkness, a figure in black suddenly stood. Borgoff's Hunter-sharp eyes caught the pair of fangs poking out from the corners of his foe's proper mouth.

"So you're my prey then? We meet at long last," Borgoff said in a tone brimming with delight as he aligned the neck of his deadly arrow with his foe's heart.

"I have no words of greeting for a stray dog out prowling for human flesh and blood," the figure garbed in black said quietly. "However, I have no desire for needless conflict. If you put your tail between your legs and scamper off, I won't do anything to you."

Borgoff laughed. "That's kind of you to offer." The direction his arrow was aiming was gradually changing. Towards the sky. "But I'm afraid I can't!"

What Borgoff did next was nearly miraculous. At almost exactly the same time as the two arrows he shot vertically left his bowstring, he took two more from his quiver and launched them at his target. The speed of his attack was so great, the Noble—Mayerling—was clearly shaken. Another shaft flew through the air as if to block Mayerling's way after he barely blocked the first two and moved to the right. The Noble had to twist in midair to avoid it. The instant he landed, two more arrows thunked into the ground at his feet in rapid succession.

Mayerling leapt backward. A shout of rage split his lips. How could a mere mortal with no more than a primitive bow and arrow put him in such peril?!

However, one last surprise remained in the trap Borgoff had laid. When Mayerling tried to twist out of the way of the whining menace dropping from above, his eyes caught sight of a black light knifing though the darkness. No matter where he leapt, he'd be under fire! And, when his movements stiffened for an instant, two arrows dropped out of the sky on an almost perfectly vertical path and pierced both of the Noble's shoulders with what seemed like calculated precision.

Groaning in agony, Mayerling went to pull the arrows out, but his hands wouldn't move.

"It's no use," Borgoff chortled. "I don't care if you're a Noble or not, you ain't gonna be able to pull them out. For starters, you can't raise your arms. So, how do you like my chaser arrows bit?"

Borgoff's confidence-choked laughter was certainly fitting praise for his own masterful skill. Taking into account where the first two arrows he fired would drop, he'd driven Mayerling there with his relentless waves of attacks. However, Mayerling had been free to move as he liked. What could possibly rope in someone with several times the speed and strength of a human, and herd him right into the target in the instant the arrows fell? Borgoff's ungodly skill—and the chaser arrows—could.

At that moment, something about the scene changed. The ground at Mayerling's feet suddenly had a blackness to it. Something like an inky stain was surging forward, headed in his direction. When he tried to jump out of the way, callous steel whistled past him on either side.

Shrilly, Borgoff asked, "Well, what's wrong? Aren't you gonna run away? Can't escape now, can you? If you move, I'll put an arrow through your heart. Of course, them mints have caught the smell the blood, and if you stand there you'll be their next meal."

He was right. The wave of black steadily approaching Mayerling's feet was in fact a large swarm of fearsome flesh-eating ants, otherwise known as mints. This spot so reminiscent of the Capital was indeed a metropolis—a cathedral for hundreds of millions of the smallest and fiercest of creatures.

"Well, well, well. You don't have time to think it over," said Borgoff. "What'll it be—one right through the heart, or are you gonna wind up in the belly of them mints with nothing but your bones left behind? Nobility or not, you can't come back from just bones. What'll it be?"

When Borgoff had slowly pulled his bowstring taut, he saw the Noble's hands go into motion.

†

W ho the hell are you?" asked Leila. The man didn't look like someone she'd need anything as heavy as the sliver gun against, and she held her javelin casually as she stood in front of the huntsman. It was only when Leila caught sight of the charring on Mashira's stomach that her face hardened. *I'd swear that's a wound from one of Groveck's power rays,* she thought. *And yet, this guy's still—*

"That's not him," the girl cried out in a quavering voice. "Originally, he was one of our bodyguards. But he transferred himself into a different body. He's got this other face on his stomach that—" Before she could finish, the girl doubled over like a shrimp, as if victim to agonizing stomach pains.

Unsure what was happening, Leila let the javelin fly. Her "shoot first, ask questions later," Hunter habits had come to the fore. The man didn't move. The javelin should've sunk into his stomach, but, when the tip of it was stopped by a sharp clang, Leila leapt back. As she leapt, her right hand grabbed hold of the sliver gun at her hip. The handle of the weapon shooting back out of the man's stomach knocked the gun out of her hand.

"Knock it off already," the man said. Apparently he could manipulate the nerves and vocal cords of a corpse, and this threatening outburst from the mouth of the deceased huntsman coupled with the raised barrel of the high-caliber rifle rooted Leila to the spot. "It's been a good while since I ran across a scrappy little hellcat like you," the huntsman said in the countenanced carbuncle's voice. "That's just perfect. I'll make both of you my women. Come on."

As if beckoned by that evil voice, Leila took a few steps forward. The huntsman's free hand lifted his shirt. Seeing the human face that swelled up on his belly, Leila cried out in surprise. Its lips pursed, and a terrifying brown ligament shot out at Leila's stomach.

A scream arose. It belonged to neither Leila, nor the girl. It'd been loosed by the countenanced carbuncle. There was a single needle of rough wood stuck right through the middle of the brown umbilicus the countenanced carbuncle apparently used to transfer itself. When the pain-wracked huntsman spun around in search of his foe, more needles pierced him through the heart and right between the eyes. Of course, the corpse didn't fall.

Though she didn't know exactly when he'd appeared, Leila launched an impassioned cry of "D!" at the rider and mount pausing in a shower of brilliant moonlight.

Watching as the dashing Vampire Hunter got off his horse, the huntsman didn't move.

"D, that's really . . . "

Nodding faintly at Leila's words, D reached back over his shoulder with his right hand. He hadn't let the countenanced carbuncle get away. The needle sticking through the transfer membrane also prevented it from sinking back into its body.

When the whine of a blade leaving its sheath rose from D's back, the huntsman's stomach suddenly bulged. With a *splat* like a stone thrown into a muddy ditch, a gray mass flew from the huntsman's abdomen. Blood and viscera streamed after it. The mass disappeared into the bushes with alarming speed.

"Oh, now this is a surprise," said a low voice issuing from around D's waist. "I didn't think any of my kind could fly through the air. What fun, what fun!"

Sheathing his naked steel, D didn't say a word as he walked toward Leila and the girl. Recovering from the sunlight syndrome took days, and, usually, the tougher a dhampir was, the longer it took for him to recuperate. But D already seemed to be over it, and the eyes he trained on the two young ladies swam with an impossibly black spirit. Perhaps this youth was no average dhampir after all.

"Oh ho ho. It looks like both of you are safe. You ought to thank me for spotting that light. Pretty boy here was still snoozing at the time." The faint voice from the Hunter's hand didn't reach the ears of Leila or the girl.

Following D's line of sight when she realized it wasn't on herself, Leila saw that the girl was slumped on the ground. She ran over in a panic. "C'mon, snap out of it!" she shouted.

D came over and bent down by the girl's side. Laying his left hand on top of the hands she had pressed against her own solar plexus, he asked, "Is it that *thing* we just saw?"

"Yep." At the answer emitted by his left hand, Leila's eyes went wide. "There's still time to save her if you do it now," the voice added.

D nodded. He lay the girl flat out on her back in the undergrowth, and gently placed her hands back down by her sides. His gorgeous hands went into action, exposing the girl's stomach.

Leila stifled a scream. In the center of that smooth, porcelain stomach, an ugly human face was rising to the surface. Its features were exactly the same as the one that'd been attached to the belly of the huntsman just moments earlier.

"All his little pals look the same," D's left hand stated. "What's more, they've got a collective consciousness. The thoughts of one are immediately transmitted to the others. These things can be a real pain in the ass."

"Why would it infect her?" asked D.

"Out of lechery, pure lechery. These critters have an appreciation for beauty and the finer things. On top of that, the dirty little bastards enjoy sex through the senses of the humans they inhabit. I imagine that's what he wanted to use her body for."

A naked blade glittered in D's right hand.

Perhaps realizing what D intended to do, the startled face was about to magically sink back into the girl. But the blade D thrust at its forehead lanced down into the oral cavity of the countenanced carbuncle with matchless precision. Screaming in anguish, it rolled its eyes back in their sockets. Streams of blood erupted from either side of its mouth before it started to fade back into the girl's body.

"That should do it! Now I guess it'll just be assimilated by her normal organs," said the voice.

Whether the procedure had been painful or not was unclear, but the girl had fainted. D stood up.

"What's the story with your left hand, D?" asked Leila.

D only replied, "You were bitten by that woman, weren't you?"

Leila nodded, her expression gloomy.

"Then that's someone else I have to put down."

"Huh?" Leila said with surprise.

"I repay my debts." D replied succinctly. He knew about the deadly struggle Leila had joined.

†

When the Noble's hand reached not for the corresponding shoulder but for the opposite armpit, Borgoff grew pale. Forgetting to fire his next deadly shot, he watched the impossible happen.

Getting a tight grip on the arrowhead sticking through his armpit, the Noble pulled it right out with one yank. Not up, but down. The other end, of course, was fletched with vanes to make it fly straight. Just like the shafts and heads of all Borgoff's arrows, the vanes were made of steel. Gouging flesh and shaving bone, the vanes went in the one direction that'd give the Noble his freedom again—they were pulled *down*. The Noble's actions and his supernatural strength flew in the face of logic.

Now he'll go for the other arrow . . . But just as Borgoff was thinking that, something whizzed through the air. The arrow the Noble had just removed.

An acute pain seared through Borgoff's abdomen. The arrow his foe had just thrown back at him had been going faster than those Borgoff shot. Borgoff stared dumbfounded at the end of the arrow that went in through his belly and jutted out his back. Blood traveled down the shaft in dribs and drabs. He heard the Noble address him.

"Our duel is over, stray mongrel. It shall be *you* that the mints feast on."

Borgoff opened his eyes wide. "I'm afraid not. This fight is just getting started."

Saying that, the Hunter ran. Right to the mint nest. The nest of the flesh-eating ants was little more than a fragile metropolis of soil hardened by an adhesive the ants themselves secreted. A large bird landing on it would be more than enough to crush it—to say nothing of what the weight of a grown man would do to it.

But Borgoff stood on the ant nest. Or rather, he stuck to it. Both his legs were at a right angle to the wall. What's more, he must've been using some sort of trick, because the fragile tower didn't show a single crack.

In that outré pose—which, not surprisingly, drew a cry of astonishment from Mayerling—Borgoff let his arrows fly. They no longer had the same power they'd had a few moments earlier. Mayerling's right hand went into action, and the murderous steel implements were struck down one after another.

Confusing his foe by moving over to one of the passageways and hanging upside down from it like a monkey, the Hunter dipped once more into his quiver. Suddenly, a strange sensation came from his legs. His profuse bleeding had robbed his legs of the ability to render him weightless, and he fell with the crumbling dirt into the very heart of the flesh-eating ants' nest.

His next sensation was that of countless insects swarming all over his body.

Borgoff screamed. Squeezing every last bit of power from his body, he got up and ran. Each footfall crushed towers, destroyed passageways—he didn't even feel the pain in his belly now. The fear of being eaten alive had his heart in its talons.

Deep into the woods he ran, his screams resounding through the trees.

III

The moonlight limned three faint shadows on the ground. D, Leila, and the girl.

Leila let out a deep sigh. The girl had just finished telling them the circumstances that'd brought her there. Only the wind moved near the trio, and darkness had fallen around them.

"There's just one thing I want to ask you," D said. He was still admiring the moonlight. "Are you aware that the Claybourne States are now . . . "

The girl nodded.

"I see," said D. "Then I guess you may as well go. But what'll you do then?"

"I don't know," the girl replied. "Once we get there, our journey will be over. One way or another."

D fell silent. The wind was singing a sad tune in the treetops.

"But it's something good," Leila muttered. "Love's so great . . . So why does it have to go so wrong?"

For a long time, none of the trio moved.

D made the moonlight sway. "It seems he's come for you," he said. His eyes indicated the depths of the forest.

Tears glistened in the girl's eyes. "Don't do this, I beg of you. Please, just let me go to him. If we keep going at this rate, we'll reach the Claybourne States by tomorrow night. Everything will end there. After that . . . "

D faced the forest.

"Don't move," Leila said. D turned to face her. She had the barrel of the sliver gun aimed at his chest. "Let her go. We can settle things once they reach the Claybourne States."

D didn't move.

"Thank you," said the girl. "Thank you—thank you both."

In the depths of the woods, a tall silhouette hove into view. The girl ran to it. Pausing for an instant, the two silhouettes vanished among the trees as if embraced by the forest. Once they were gone, Leila lowered the sliver gun. "Sorry, D," she said.

"Why the apology? I should thank you again."

Leila said with surprise, "You don't mean you would've—"

"Go to sleep already. Tomorrow morning I'll take you to where to left your car. There we part company. After that, you can tail me, go back to your brothers, or whatever you like. You can count on me to take care of the female dhampir."

"I . . . " Leila swallowed the rest of the words. She was going to say she wanted to go with him. But how would she go about traveling with a shadow?

A blanket was tossed at her feet. D took another one in hand and walked over to the trunk of a nearby tree. Spreading the blanket on the ground, he sat back against the tree trunk and crossed his arms. The sword off his back had been placed by his left side.

After a moment's consideration, Leila sat down next to D. D gazed at her steadily. His pupils seemed deep enough to swallow her. Suppressing a wave of rapture, she asked, "Does this bother you? You know, where I'm a vampire victim and all?"

"Nope."

"Thanks," she said. Pulling the blanket up to her chest, Leila lay down on the ground, using her arm for a pillow.

There was a fragrance to the wind. Night-blooming jasmine, moonlit grass, nocturnal peonies, moonshine . . . Sweet and heart-rending . . . There was life by night. The croaking of frogs, music from the jaws of longhorns, the whispering of great silkworms . . . All small and tough and full of life . . .

For a moment, Leila forgot she was the prey of a female dhampir. It'd never been like this for her. "Funny, isn't it," she said as she scratched the tip of her nose.

D didn't move, but he seemed to be listening.

"The night doesn't frighten me a bit. None of my brothers has ever done this . . . Every single night, we had the feeling there were beasts and evil spirits out to get us . . . Even inside the bus, we were still on edge." And yet, now she seemed perfectly fine. "I wonder why I don't mind the night now?"

After she'd said it, Leila was surprised. Had she actually thought that stern young man would give her an answer? She said it herself, quietly, in her heart. *Because I'm with you* . . .

Even after Leila fell asleep listening to the song of the wind, the young Vampire Hunter still trained his gaze patiently on the darkness of the night, anger and grief far from the void that was his eyes.

†

A t about the same time, in a part of the forest not very far away, a strange and truly disturbing event was unfolding.

Borgoff could feel his internal organs being bored through and devoured. There was no longer any pain. Ants were swarming all over his body. They were inside his face, too. He saw his right eye fall out. The sensation of ants crawling around in his eye socket was strangely tickling. Tens of thousands of them were dining on his flesh. Each and every trifling bite splashed a chill over him. It was cold. So very cold.

A strange thing clawed its way out of the grass and came into view of the corner of his remaining left eye. It was a gooey gray lump. Oddly enough, though it lacked arms and legs, it clearly had eyes and a nose.

"Oh, this is a nice little find I've made," said the lump. "It's a little beat up, but if I knock all the freaking ants off it I should be able to get some use out of it. Yessir, when it comes to traveling, you can't beat a human body." Moving over to Borgoff's mouth, it said to him, "You'll have to excuse me. I'm kind of in a hurry, too."

The gooey limbless lump pried open lips that the man himself lacked the strength to open, and Borgoff felt the thing sliding down his esophagus and into his stomach.

IV

T here wasn't really any place called the Claybourne States any longer. Neighboring sectors had only heard about the Ninety-Eighth Frontier Sector's capital region because the spaceport was there, and the Claybourne States had come to be known by the spaceport's name as well. But that name, too, had long since been forgotten, and people hadn't mentioned either in ages.

With its automated housekeeping-systems destroyed, the interior of the terminal building was left to the rampant dust, and the winds that blew in through shattered panes of reinforced glass traced thin, swirling patterns in the accumulated grit.

A drifter who was calling one of the spaceport rooms his home that particular evening found his meager dinner interrupted by the untimely arrival of guests. A black carriage drawn by a half-dozen horses came in through the central gate. Once it halted at the entrance to the terminal building, two passengers got out. There was a man and a woman. What astonished the drifter was the fact that the couple consisted of a Noble and a human. Both of them went into the building, but the way they held each other's hands only added to his consternation. *A human and a Noble?* he thought to himself. *It couldn't be!* He slipped quietly out of his room and headed out of the spaceport as if he'd just had a nightmare.

†

The pair stood dazed in the blue dusk of the lobby. Or, to be more precise, only Mayerling was dazed. The pity in the girl's expression was directed at her love.

"No . . . This can't be . . . " Mayerling mumbled. His words echoed through the emptiness.

The only ships for sailing to the stars visible in the vast complex were horrible derelicts. A photon-powered spaceship with melted engines, a galaxy ship crushed in the middle, a dimension-warping schooner wrecked beyond repair . . . It was a quiet and cruel death that covered the apron. There was no road out there that might carry them together on a voyage among the stars.

"It can't be . . . " Mayerling stammered. "The rumors said . . . " In his mind, rumors that the spaceport still operated on a small scale must've seemed more and more real with each passing day, taking shape and becoming the absolute truth to him. Knowing his kind was doomed, even declaring as much himself, he remained a Noble after all.

As he stood paralyzed, a hand gently pressed upon his shoulder. He saw the girl's face. Her perfectly placid expression.

"It doesn't matter," she said. "We'll go somewhere else now. So long as I'm with you, I'll go anywhere. Together forever . . . until death do us part . . . "

"But—I can't die," Mayerling replied.

Tears welling in her eyes as they clung to him, the girl said in a determined tone, "In that case, make me just like you . . . "

"I can't do that."

"I don't mind." The girl shook her head. "I don't mind at all. I was prepared for that from the very start . . . "

Blue light tinged the faces of the young couple. Mayerling's face slowly approached the nape of the girl's neck. The girl had her eyes shut. Her long, lovely eyelashes trembled. When she felt the lips of her beloved on the base on her neck, her eyes snapped open.

A scream echoed through the lobby.

Mayerling stared in amazement at his love, who'd pulled free of him with that scream.

The girl's violent emotions quickly passed. A tremendous feeling of remorse showed on her face. Her lips quivered. "I . . . I . . . That was a horrible thing for me to do . . . " she stammered.

Mayerling smiled. It was the smile of a man who'd just lost something. "It's okay," he said gently. "We're fine the way we are. If you should wither and die first, I shall follow after you."

The girl crushed herself against him and hung on for dear life. She said not a word, but he softly stroked her quivering shoulders.

"Shall we go then?" he suggested. "Though the pathway to the stars is barred to us, we may yet journey across the earth."

The girl looked up at him and nodded. Stroking her waist-long hair in sympathy, he let his eyes wander to the lobby's exit. A figure in a black coat suddenly stood there. The blue pendant at his breast and his unsettling beauty burned into the Noble's retinas. Holding his tongue, Mayerling pushed the girl aside.

"Your trip's over," D said. "Give me the girl."

"Take her then. That is, if you survive," Mayerling said gruffly. He made no effort to keep his ladylove by his side and avoid the fight.

"This way, if you don't mind," Leila said to the girl as she came over from one of the other walls, took the girl by the hand, and brought her to the corner of the room.

D walked toward Mayerling. He stopped with ten feet still between them.

"You know, D," Mayerling said, discharging the words like a sigh, "there's no road to the stars after all. But then you knew that all along, didn't you?"

D didn't answer.

Vampire and Vampire Hunter discarded hatred and anger and grief, and readied for battle. Trenchant claws grew from the fingertips of Mayerling's right hand. Neither of the men seemed to move, but the distance between them shrank nonetheless.

A horizontal flash of black shot out, and D took to the air without a sound. The eldritch blade that howled with the Hunter's downward swipe hit Mayerling's left arm with a shower of sparks. Again the black claws swiped out in an attack, and again they met only air as D leapt back six feet.

This lobby, where nothing save ages of decay sat in stagnation, was playing host for this one night alone to a condensed conflict between life and death.

†

While her eyes were riveted to the pair's deadly battle, Leila felt warm breath brushing the nape of her neck. "Come this way," someone said to her. The voice was seductive and female. Oddly enough, the girl didn't seem to notice it at all. "Come this way," it said again.

Even when Leila quietly slipped to the rear, the girl and her soul remained prisoners of the deadly duel before them.

A knife of some sort was placed in Leila's right hand. "Take this and stab the girl," the voice told her. "Kill her!" The speaker must've still believed Mayerling would be hers if only she disposed of the girl.

Leila nodded. Her grip tightened on the handle of the knife. Circling around behind the girl, she stealthily raised the blade.

"Now!" the voice commanded.

Leila did a flip. Caroline's rapture-twisted face was right in front of her own now. Before the Barbarois woman's expression could register her shock, the silver knife was gouging deep into the female dhampir's heart. What's more, out of apparent concern about distracting the pair of combatants from their battle, Leila took the added measure of clamping her left hand down like a lid over Caroline's lips. Blood gushed out between Leila's fingertips.

As Caroline's eyes went from a look of agony and disbelief to a haze of death, Leila stared into them and smirked. "Too bad. You know, I noticed something while you were ordering me around. Seems there's at least one woman you bit who didn't wind up your own personal marionette." Leila, it seemed, possessed an unusual resistance to the demon's call, though she had not known it until now.

When Leila turned her eyes from the falling body of the beautiful woman, the death match seemed about to be decided.

As soon as he'd batted down all of the rough wooden needles D hurled at him during a leap back, Mayerling felt composure coming over his mind. It was the next instant that he saw a thick flash of silvery light. His injured arms hadn't recovered their previous speed yet. D's longsword, thrust with calculated precision at this hole in Mayerling's defenses, slid neatly into the Noble's stomach.

As the Noble thudded to the ground in a bloody mist, the girl ran like the wind to his side. "Please, try not to shake me so much," Mayerling told her. He smiled wryly under his pained breathing.

D came over. Two pairs of eyes met, the huntsman and the prey. Both men's eyes had a mysterious hue of emotion to them.

"You did well to dodge that strike," D said softly. No matter how deep the wound to Mayerling's stomach, it wouldn't be the end of a Noble. Once the sword was pulled out, even a wound from D would eventually heal.

"Why did you miss?" asked Mayerling.

The girl and Leila—who'd also come over once her own deadly little battle was done—looked at D in surprise.

Giving no answer, D bent over and took several strands of the girl's lengthy hair in hand. Pulling out a dagger, he cut off a lock about eight inches long and put it in one of his coat pockets. "So long as I have some of her hair, the sheriff's office will be able to confirm her identity," he said. "Baron Mayerling and his human love are dead. Never show yourselves before mankind again."

An indescribable light welled up in the girl's eyes.

D took hold of the hilt of his longsword and pulled the metal out of Mayerling's body. His blade rasped back into its sheath. "There's the ten million right there. Easy money." Without another word, D walked toward the exit.

"D!" Leila shouted. She was about to go after him, but at that moment a roaring wind caught her ear.

When D whipped around at the sound of flesh being penetrated, he saw the steel arrow that pierced Mayerling's chest. From the angle of it, he gleaned where it'd been fired from, and a flash of silvery white flew from D's right hand. It rebounded off the high ceiling and was barely blocked by a figure who made an easy, spider-like dash sideward.

"Borgoff!" Leila cried out.

D saw her brother, too. But was it really Borgoff? There was a huge, gaping hole in his stomach that did nothing to conceal the deep red scraps of entrails, sinew, and bone within. Half of either thigh was exposed bone, and the right side of his face was just a skull. Such was the fate one met when attacked by flesh-eating mint ants.

Laughing maniacally, he shouted, "You're next, jerk!"

Black bits of lightning streaked at D, but each and every one was struck down. The corpse didn't have quite the same skill it'd possessed in life. Hoping to attack from a different angle, Borgoff ran across the ceiling to the wall. He was confident of his speed. Of the speed he'd had in life.

A second later, his shoulder and the top of his head were pierced by flashes of white that shot vertically from below, where by all rights no one should've been able to get him. If that'd been the extent of the damage, the already dead Borgoff wouldn't have had any problems. Due to D's ungodly skill, however, one of the wooden needles rebounded and shattered his right ankle, which was just denuded bone. His remaining leg couldn't continue to support his weight of nearly two hundred and twenty-five pounds, and Borgoff's massive frame fell head over heels from a height of some thirty feet before smashing against the lobby floor.

"Damn it all!" He spat the words down at his own barely fleshed chest. "But if *his* memory serves me, there's still something I can do." Borgoff's grotesque right hand—bones with chunks of flesh still clinging to it—went into his pants pocket.

At that moment, the drifter who was searching for food in the bus parked right in front of the spaceport jumped as he heard a tiny explosion from one of the beds lined up in the back.

D was cloaked in a ghastly aura as he walked toward Borgoff, but, suddenly, a young man stood between them.

"There you are, Grove," Borgoff's corpse said in Borgoff's voice. "Do your thing! Kill all of these fuckers."

Before he'd finished speaking, D leapt. His longsword sank into the youth's shoulder and went through it like water.

The youth wasn't looking at D. He was gazing at the long-haired girl in a corner of the lobby as she cradled a figure in black and sobbed. A hue of sadness suddenly invaded his flushed face. He shook his head ever so slightly from side to side.

"Gro . . . Grove?!" Borgoff stammered in disbelief.

Before his brother had finished saying his name, the young man became transparent, then quickly faded away.

When agony seemed to force Grove's desiccated form to sit up in bed, the horrified drifter inched ever closer to him, but, the instant the youth appeared before him, the intruder was scared out of his mind. The youth's sad gaze was trained on the convulsing body, and then he put himself against it. The second he did, he started to melt into the feeble form, and a shudder ran through the still upright body. Then it moved no more.

Walking to Borgoff's body, D quickly pressed the palm of his left hand to its chest. There was an anguished cry. From Borgoff's feet.

Something squirming around inside Borgoff's thigh seemed to be gradually rising toward his chest, inch by inch, as if it was being pulled up on a string. Past the stomach it went, slipping through organs left exposed by the gaping wound, and when it reached the spot directly under the palm of D's hand, the crunch of meat and bone reverberated. It gave a scream in its death throes, but that ended soon enough.

D pulled his left hand away. The tiny mouth in the middle of his palm opened. From it, something like a catfish tail wriggled out, but it was soon sucked back in. Once again, there was the crunching sounds of mastication, and then its tongue lolled out to lick its lips before disappearing, lips and all.

Without even a glance at Borgoff, who was now a true corpse, D turned in the girl's direction. She'd fallen by Mayerling's side.

Checking her pulse, Leila looked at D and shook her tear-streaked face from side to side.

One of Mayerling's claws was jabbing into the girl's chest. The girl had taken hold of it and thrust it into her own bosom.

D's gaze was somewhat weary as he looked down at the amazingly serene countenance she wore in death. He heard Leila's voice from somewhere. *Love's so great . . . So why does it have to go so wrong?*

The human and the Noble—each died as they'd lived. The human as a human, the Noble as a Noble . . .

"She said thank you," Leila said absentmindedly.

D took the lock of hair out of his coat pocket. That was all that remained of the girl now.

Some time later, the drifter—who'd received a large sum in gold from the gorgeous young man in black to bury the pair—stepped into the lobby. The wind that slipped in with him blew the strands of hair from where they'd been placed on the girl's shoulder, scattering them randomly across the empty hall.

†

A t the entrance to the spaceport, Leila got down off D's horse. "I'm going to this town up north," she said to the gorgeous countenance trained on her. "It's a little place, and it's always covered with snow, but this young guy who runs the butcher shop there asked me to marry him once. He's the only guy who ever knew my last name and said it didn't matter. By now, he's probably got a wife and kids already, but then he said he'd wait as long as he had to. I'm sorta counting on that."

D nodded. "Godspeed," he said.

"Right back at you."

D urged his horse forward. Leila remained stock still behind him, and about the time the blue darkness was starting to hide her, a faint smile slipped to D's lips. If Leila had caught sight of it, she probably would've reflected with pride on how her parting words had inspired it until the end of her days.

It was just such a smile.

VAMPIRE HUNTER D

CONTINUES

This omnibus collects volumes 1, 2, and 3 of Vampire Hunter D. Here is the full list of Vampire Hunter D volumes published by Dark Horse Books to date:

ABOUT THE AUTHOR

Hideyuki Kikuchi was born in Chiba, Japan in 1949. He attended the prestigious Aoyama University and wrote his first novel, *Demon City Shinjuku*, in 1982. Over the past two decades, Kikuchi has written many novels of weird fiction blending elements of horror, science fiction, and fantasy, working in the tradition of occidental writers like Fritz Leiber, Robert Bloch, H. P. Lovecraft, and Stephen King. Many live-action and anime works in 1980s and 1990s Japan were based on Kikuchi's novels.

ABOUT THE ILLUSTRATOR

Yoshitaka Amano was born in Shizuoka, Japan in 1952. Recruited as a character designer by the legendary anime studio Tatsunoko at age 15, he created the look of many notable anime, including *Gatchaman*, *Genesis Climber Mospeada* (which in the US became the third part of *Robotech*), and *The Angel's Egg*, an experimental film by future *Ghost in the Shell* director Mamoru Oshii. An independent commercial illustrator since the 1980s, Amano became world famous through his design of the first ten *Final Fantasy* games. Having entered the fine arts world in the preceding decade, in 1997 Amano had his first exhibition in New York, bringing him into contact with American comics through collaborations with Neil Gaiman (*The Sandman: The Dream Hunters*) and Greg Rucka (*Elektra and Wolverine: The Redeemer*). Dark Horse has published over 40 books illustrated by Amano, including his first original novel *Deva Zan*, as well as the Eisner-nominated *Yoshitaka Amano: Beyond the Fantasy–The Illustrated Biography* by Florent Gorges.